Scrivener of Rome

A tale of the Ancient Republic

Ken Farmer

ISBN-13: 9781980343882

Other books by Ken Farmer
Outlander of Rome
Founder of Rome
Defender of Rome
Artisan of Rome
Wanderer of Rome

https://theromanrepublicblog.wordpress.com

Publishing eHistory
First 11/06/15
...
Sixth 09/03/17

Dead Tree Publishing History
First 03/02/18

Dedicated to my wife
for all the long work of editing.

Forward

This is a novel of the Early Roman Republic and follows the historical timeline as closely as is possible after about 2500 years of myths, tall tales and re-written history. It is set, very roughly, around 400 BC and over about twenty or so years on either side of that date. As a reference timeline, Rome changed from a monarchy to a republic in 509 BC (traditional date - accuracy unknown) and Julius Caesar began his career in popular history by crossing the Rubicon river in 49 BC.

As a caveat, however, know that our records and history from those earliest times are mostly written by Roman historians hundreds of years later, and their main task was to glorify the founding and growth of Rome. While I attempt to follow what is known about the events of that time, I make no claim to the accuracy of either persons or places in this tale.

****

As many of the notes are spoilers, they have been put at the very end of the book, in the chapter titled, Adnotatiae.

****

Non-Spoiler Notes

Length.

A common Roman unit of length of those days was a stadium (plural, stadia) - equal to about a sixth of a kilometer. So, in this story just divide all references to stadia by ten to get miles and by six to get kilometers.

Astronomy Factoid.

I have had several readers question as to why my seagoing characters, in the age of the Roman Republic, cannot steer by Polaris, the North Star, as sailors have done in the last few hundred years. The answer is that, around 400 BC, there was no pole star. Because of the Precession of the Equinoxes (the fact that the earth wobbles like a top in a 26,000 year cycle) the pointing of the axis of the earth moves in a circle around the northern sky, and in the time of the Republic there was no bright star in the vicinity of the north celestial pole. Even Shakespeare got it wrong when his Julius Caesar said, "I am as constant as the northern star..." His stage-character was speaking of something that did not exist at the time and would not for a thousand and a half years.

The Scribe

Fluvius (The River)

I write these scrolls because the duty given to me by the gods is to record. Or, that is what my old teacher at the Temple of Jupiter would have said. For myself, I have seen much reason to believe in the Beings of Olympus and if I am wrong, then certainly the truth is that I have lived a strange life indeed, if the pleasures and travails of my being have not been directed. I hasten to say that my belief has taken a lifetime to develop. In the time of my youth, I believed the priests in total, as did all young men, and chanted with them over their stinking sacrifices to this god or that, but gave them little thought when the rituals were ended. Certainly, I never feared the gods, even during the infrequent times that I thought of them at all. Nevertheless, with that question unanswerable until one has departed this world, I put down my life in total to these scrolls, without need of impress, or glorification of my deeds, for which there is none. No one will read this until I am dust, or safely on the far side of the river Acheron, or maybe the Styx, should the tales of Hades be true.

Know that my given praenomen was Junius, but of no family of name at the beginning of this story. Later - much later, I will replace it with Lucius, and move the name of Junius to the position of nomen, but, the person of Lucius Junius is many words into the scroll.

As an aside, my reminisces will be written in the vernacular of an educated scribe, not the illiterate wordings of a plebeian youngster, at the time unable to make even the marks of his own name. Should my writings give the impression of a cultured and educated fisher-boy, know that these words were written long after my work in the waters of the Tiber river.

My patér was a fisherman on that river, outside of the walls of Rome, as was his patér and those before him. From the beginning, I was destined to secure the same trade, casting my nets to the water, and giving the contents to the womenfolk of my family to salt and dry and sell. As a young man I was content, knowing nothing of any other trade, nor anything about the world in general. The work was not onerous but I knew of no other life. The idea of idleness while surrounded by grandeur was a lesson for a far later period in my story. At the time that my tale begins, I was too young to fend the net poles, and my main chore was to dive to free our nets from the rocks and sticks of the bottom of the river.

From the time I was of an age to stand weaned from my mater, I was given the lessons of the water. A fish I was not, but few along the banks could compose themselves in and under the water as I. More than once, I won a snippet of copper or a sweetmeat from my young friends in the contest to swim from bank to bank without breaking the surface for air. In truth, I had learned the device of rapidly emptying and filling my breathing sacs to the point that my vision would begin to falter and that in some way allowed my body to store the life-giving breath for the swim. When I asked our resident priest of the matter - the wise man who blessed our boats before the start of day - he gave me dismissal with the explanation that the breathing improvement of my skill was imagined.

Such was my life as planned by the gods, if they exist, until one fateful day when we were encamped beside the Pons Amimia - the bridge leading to the center of the city from the northern bank. The Tiber was in full fury with the rains of the new season feeding the source far up in the mountains. Our boat was secured to the trees on the bank, waiting for the subsidence of the waters so as to allow my patér and my brothers to pole the craft up the river to our usual wharfage. Since there was little chance of spreading the net to capture any fish and much danger of losing our appurtenances in the raging waters, we were idle, sitting and weaving rope and repairing any single strands that were frayed.

The morning well gone, the bridge was in full use, with farmers and such moving into the city for the trade of the day. My elder sister was herding our small flock of geese along the grass at the edge of the river, a task that I would even risk the backhand of my mater to avoid. The fowls seemed to know of my distaste, as they would screech and honk if I even approached their presence. Of course, the mutual dislike was not confined to just myself. The clamor would begin if any male dared to stray into their flock.

My fingers needed no guidance to loop and pull the strands of rope, so my eyes could wander to any cause they wished. Then, suddenly, a shout and a cry came from the bridge, and I looked to see a body fall into the water.

Since even I would not readily test the beneficence of the river in the raging flood at that time, a city man would have little chance of gaining the shore in such a current. I stood and looked for the unfortunate as the waters flowed past, as did all on our boat and on the other craft within range of the shout. There, suddenly, I saw the flash of cloth that had to be the man. For a reason that I did not know, nor to this day have understood, I dove into the waters, head first, and swam furiously for the spot that I reasoned that he would be. By chance, or again, by the will of some deity, my hand suddenly encountered the cloth of a garment, then the firmness under it that indicated my quarry.

But, the mere finding of the man was the trivial part of my task. With myself and my burden being propelled downriver at a pace that no runner could have kept up with, my strength was barely sufficient to keep my head and that of the man above the water. I well knew of the thrashings of a person in distress in the river, who has no experience with it, and that he would seal both our fates should I let his arms grab my body in his panic. I used a hand to grip his garment at the neck, but behind, and began a kick toward the shore, using the other arm as a paddle. I had seen fifteen seasons at that time - not still a youngster, but also not completely in my growth as yet. Nor was I in my man-strength, either. In that swirling water, my efforts were as an ant trying to move a large rock, but I knew that eventually the current would push us close to one bank or the other. And, eventually, it did, but far down river and beyond the sight of our boat or even the city itself.

At a bend in the watercourse, I felt my feet touch the bottom, then straightened my body and pulled my burden with all my strength to the shallows before the current swept us away again. On the shore, I rolled the unfortunate to his belly and pushed on his back with both hands. He retched and vomited the ingested water for a time, then just continued heaving long after his belly and breathing sacs were emptied.

I finally noticed that he was a mere boy, even younger than I by a year or so, it appeared. Still, there was no chance of my carrying the unfortunate back to the city and through the dense riverside brush that encompassed us on all sides. I would have to wait until we were found or until he could travel on his own.

It took a long while, but eventually the boy sat up, his body color the ghastly shade of a dead person. I knew from the experiences of my patér and my elder brothers that the forcible emptying of one's belly was sufficient to render that person... well, less than gladsome in spirit. This was no better than the aftermath of too much wine, and even worse in that the imbiber usually does not inhale the liquid he is drinking.

"It would seem that you have survived the offer to the river god, Tiberinus. He has not accepted either of us as a sacrifice, this day."

The boy nodded, and croaked out a reply. "Aye. And I must thank you for my deliverance from his altar." He choked again, and continued, "I am Lucius, of the House of Camillus."

I had no idea of the social hierarchy of the city of Rome, other than the knowledge that some people had far more wealth than others. Soon, I would discover that his family was of those with far more. I nodded and replied, "I am Junius, but of no house. My patér has a fishing boat that is our domicile, tied this moment to the bank below the bridge."

The boy suddenly turned and looked at the river in alarm. "My patér... Did he fall as well? Is he..."

"Nay. You are the only person that decided to swim in the torrent." I paused, trying to be less than critical. "Did you misstep, or..."

Now, he shook his head. "An accursed animal pulling a cart, reared at the squeal of a fowl and before I could move had almost crushed me on the railing. I tried to climb the boards to prevent my legs from splintering and must have toppled over." He looked at the waters, raging only a body length from where we sat. "You, obviously, have much in the realm of water skills."

For myself, it was just a thing - not something to cause the issuance of pride. A fisher-boy either learned the water or would soon find himself as a sacrifice to the river-god after some misstep. I just nodded and said, "Aye. It is a thing I learned at the paps of my mater. Or, not long after." I stood up and looked around. The walking would be difficult, with thorns and prickle bushes thickly infesting the bank. "We could sit here till the next sunrise before being found in this denseness. Can you walk as yet?"

He stood up, uncertainly, then found his stance and replied, "Aye. If we do not have to make a footrace of it." He was younger than I, but of the same height. Of course, his limbs were thinner than mine from his life of ease. I turned, trying to determine the easiest way to move forward without having our skins torn and bleeding from the bushes.

In my daily activities I was usually as naked as a newborn babe - only a fool would do water-work while clothed. But, this day I had been wearing a tightly wrapped loincloth - my only garment when not in the water. Lucius, was wearing a tunic, of good quality it appeared, although it was now destined for the rag-bin when he returned. Much washing would take place before all the mud was gone from the garment and even then, the many rends would make it less than desirable.

Moving this way and that, stooping to move under this branch and that bush, we gradually moved toward the city and away from the river. Even on this overcast day the direction finding was easy. The roar of the river behind us gave ample notice of which way we were attempting to travel. Finally, after much pausing to remove entangling thorns from our garments and bodies, we reached a trail that led to the main via traversing up and down the river. Shortly after that, we had reached the main road, busy with travelers moving to and from the seaport of Ostia.

By now, Lucius had mostly recovered and was walking normally and without an expression of a meal in his belly gone bad. He had even assumed an air of adventure, asking me of my life and giving me a few tidbits of his. Then, as the southern gate of the city came into view, we were startled to see a band of men rushing down the road and with little consideration of any who did not move aside with haste.

Seeing us, or rather, my companion, the handful ran to us and stopped with much chatter. The leader, an overly-robed and breathless man, ran up and dropped to his knees before us. "Master Lucius!" he exclaimed. "The gods be praised for your return! We were told that the furies of the Tiber had taken you in their clutches."

Grinning at me, the young boy replied, "And you would be correct, Terces. Indeed, it was as the river Acheron in flood, and I would be begging Charon for passage without coin were it not for my friend, here."

The man rose, and said, "We must hasten to your patér, who even now is beside himself with grief at his loss. I will engage a lectica for the Master that he may..."

"Nay to that," retorted the boy. "I have feet, and they will still carry me. I need no carrying chair to return into the city. Where is my patér at this time?"

"As we left, the master Camillus was attempting to hire boats to follow you down the river."

I looked at the man, then at his young master before interjecting, "Nay. No river man would stand out into that raging torrent for even a palmful of gold. He would be spending it inside the gates of Neptune were he to do so."

"Take us to him," ordered Lucius.

With that, the five men surrounded my companion and would have begun the escort back to the city but for his command, "Do not block my friend, Junius. He will walk with me, and all will treat him as my equal." I was surprised at his strength of voice. Apparently, the males of noble families learned the art of command at an early age. Certainly, neither the leader, Terces, nor his men made any protest as Lucius took my arm to walk beside him.

The journey through the city was interesting for me. It was very seldom that I entered the walls of Rome and had never reached this far into the city. We were traversing the street of the Via Cuprius - a wide and straight thoroughfare leading from gate to gate. As we walked, my newly found friend expounded on this and that. "The Via Cuprius, as you may know, was the street in which the daughter of King Tullius is said to have driven over his murdered body." That meant absolutely nothing to me - at the time - but I nodded and continued to swivel my head in my gaze at the city. Further on came another tidbit and, this time, I could understand the meaning. "That is the Via Bellonae - the street of the harlots and brothels." His sly grin seemed to indicate some knowledge of the inhabitants, although I thought it unlikely that a boy of his age would be privy to the use of a woman. Certainly, I had not taken pleasure with one as yet, although not for any lack of trying. Unattached females of the boats were never in the position of being alone with a young man - their families knowing exactly the thoughts of a boy whose pouchstones had dropped. And since I had never had metal of any weight, the purchase of the experience was not even considered.

Eventually, we reached the far gate, beyond which was the bridge, only half the river's width ahead. People were milling around, apparently waiting for news of the tragedy that hit one of the city's noble families. I pointed. "Is that your patér? Standing beside my boat?" I could see that none of the craft had moved, validating my statement that only a man whose reason was seized by the gods would put oar and pole to water in that raging torrent.

Lucius said, grinning, "Aye. He will wonder if it is myself or my shade come to accost him."

He need not have worried about being taken for a returned spirit of the underworld. As we approached, my patér, standing on the bow, suddenly exclaimed and pointed in our direction. The noble man turned and unbelieving, stared for many heartbeats before running to embrace his son. I was concerned that my new companion might be crushed to death in the throes of gladness by his patér.

My own family, while obviously concerned at my actions, had apparently been less in despair at what would seem to be an act of self-destruction of leaping into the current. They well knew my ability in the water and that few others on the river would have the ability to survive it. What they thought about my act of jumping into the raging torrent was another matter. Of course, my mater, like all throughout history, was flowing her eye water after knowing that her third son had not been taken from the family.

Eventually, Lucius was released from the grasp of joy and he gave a short tale of his experience, giving myself the entire recognition for his rejoining the ranks of the living. The senior, a man dressed in the massive robes of the nobility - a toga, I would eventually learn - walked to me and put his hands on my shoulders. Looking over at my patér, he said, "Your son has returned my son to life, and this will not be forgotten by the house of Camillus to the end of my life." Turning to me, he asked, "What is your name, young man?"

"He is..." started Lucius but was cut off by his patér.

"I wish to hear the name from the young man, himself."

"I am known as Junius, Sos." Waving toward our boat, I continued, "...and that is my family."

"And you are a fisherman, I may assume?"

"Aye, Sos. My family and my ancestors far back, as I am told."

He nodded, then turned and spoke to one of his retainers. The man handed him a pouch that was then offered to me. "This is not payment for the life of my son. There is no remuneration that would fit such a deed, but good metal can be a boon to anyone, high or low." Utterly surprised at the offer, I said nothing as he turned to my patér. "With your permission, I would make an offer to your son of a possible future."

My patér bowed and replied, "Certainly, Sos. My son would be honored by any boon from yourself, Sos." My mater just stood, her eyes wide at what was happening to her youngest.

Turning back to me, the noble said, "To be a fisherman is a good and sturdy vocation for a citizen and one that is much appreciated by the city. But a boy - a young man of your ability and courage can aspire to a higher plane than that." Several of the words that he used were beyond my vocabulary of the time, but I got the understanding of his meaning as he continued. "My son, Lucius, will enter the collegium at the Temple of Jupiter on the next Nonae of the month, to begin his education for his manhood. I would consider it an honor to sponsor you as his fellow student. If you work with diligence, you could become a scribe in the city. If you excel in your studies, it is even possible for you to attain the rank of Rhetor with my sponsorship." With a wry smile, he finished, "And you will be an anchor to the whims of my son."

I had no idea of what those professions were, and neither did my patér, although he knew that they were far and away above the status of fisherman. He did not allow me to speak first and possibly mar the grandiose offer from the gods. As I opened my mouth, he said "My son will be honored to accompany your son to... to... the temple for learning. He will bring glory to our family by the act."

More talk accrued before the noble and the large retinue retired into the city and little was spoken by myself. But, it was decided by all that I would indeed attend this... this... place of learning that was spoken of with awe. For myself, I had no idea of what I was to learn - the idea of the written word was not in my consciousness, neither did the words 'scribe' and 'retor'... 'rector'... whatever the noble had said, have any anchor in my knowledge. But, any new adventure that appears to a young man is welcome and I would follow this one to see where it led.

It was agreed that on the proper day, a man from the house of Camillus would appear to escort me to the... wherever I was to attend.

Gaining my presence alone, my mater said quietly, "Your patér is a good man, but such metal would sorely tempt him to spend time in a taburna, rather than at his nets. And you will need it for your new life." That night, I took the contents of the purse that I had been given - many weights of bronze - and hid them underground and in a sparse section of the riverbank.

Praemium (The Reward)

My people had the saying, "A fish out of water," to indicate a man who had no idea of his surroundings. I was such a fish. The Temple could have been another life to a boy whose entire being had been spent on a boat in the river.

On the designated day, a slave from the House of Camillus arrived to take me in hand. With a bronze weight from the pouch that I was given, my mater had bought a length of white cloth and made me a trio of tunics for my departure. With the amount left over from the metal, she purchased a pair of sandals. My feet had never been covered since my birth, and I did not like the idea of leather strapped to them, but as students did not enter the temple school unshod, I had no choice but to wear the strange foot appliances. It took many days before my feet stopped their complaining about the unaccustomed attachments.

The first lesson that was driven into us was that students are not coddled by the priest-teachers. All of the students - besides myself - were either noble born or the sons of well-to-to merchants. That was a given, since the school was not without cost, and far beyond the means of the great mass of citizens. Once inside the grounds of the Temple - by itself, an awesome adventure to a mere fisher-boy - the students, no matter their rank, were almost as newly captured slaves to the teachers. In fact, several of the highborn boys took offense at their treatment, assuming that the mere mention of their family name would infuse respect from the priests. They quickly found out, being on the wrong end of a leather strap, that their proclamations of nobility had no meaning within these walls.

I had little trouble since I would not even dream of showing offense to the instructors. I was as the river-mouse, trying to be unnoticed by all as he lived from day to day. My friend, Lucius, also had the good sense to obey orders, instantly, and not insist that he was in any way an exceptional student.

We were assigned to little cubicles in the outbuildings - four to a room that was barely large enough for our sleeping mats. By standing together, Lucius and I were able to be selected to share a room. That was a welcome chance for both of us since we took comfort in at least knowing one other in the mass of new students. Of our other two room-mates, one was the son of a brick merchant and the other from some minor nobility. Like us, they quickly learned to obey and not speak.

Our first days had little to do with whatever learning we were to have. We did chores from daylight to dark, hauling wood and water from arriving vendor carts, stacking the one and pouring the other into vases in the kitchen area. Then we were given rags and told to wash the slab floors, the statues, even the massive stone image of Jupiter in the main foyer. Then, with a mixture of sand and some liquid, we polished the bronze of the temple - the huge rings on the massive doors, the votive lamps, the decorative strips that outlined the areas of worship, and so on. Even though I was told that the learning of a scribe was to enable him to decipher the marks on wax or clay tablets, or scrolls, I began to wonder if the profession was just that of a cleaning slave to the priests.

Finally, a day came when we were split into double handfuls of boys, then led to rooms in another of the large outbuildings. This one, unlike our quarters, was of stone and permanent. And even somewhat elegant - at least to me, who had never entered a building made of rocks until this adventure started. To be honest, I had never even entered a building at all, besides the flimsy huts on the riverbank, until my arrival at the temple.

Thus began my education. We were each given a board, lapped at the edges with a raised border, and into which, each morning, we would place a double handful of clay, taken from the large butt in the back of the common room. This would be patted flat within the borders of our writing board, then used during the day as our scrivening tablet. Depending on the weather, several times during the day, water would be sprinkled onto the clay then kneaded in to restore the needed property for receiving the marks from our pointed stick.

In the honesty of this narrative, I am given to admit that I was as a city vendor of charcoal, suddenly pointed to the river and a net placed in his hands. He would have little idea of either name or use of the brail. So was I out of my known world, sitting cross-legged and listening to the expounding of the instructor. The teacher would write a mark on a large slate and point, saying, "This is the character 'ha.'" Then we would be required to repeat the sound, and write it many times in our clay. Then another mark, this time 'ke.' Over and beyond, we marked and sounded and all the while I was trying to put some order to what I was both hearing and doing.

My confusion became even worse when the priest began to write many of the symbols in a row, then point and say, "This is the word for wheel." Or cart. Or jug. What did that mean? I knew what those things were in actuality, but what did the marks on the slate, and the copy of them in our clay have to do with them? Had it not been for my friendship with Lucius, I would have been whipped from the temple in disgrace, to be returned to the banks of the Tiber as a fisherman. As it was, many were the strokes from the leather of the priest when I gave an answer that was considered less than accurate. It was a time of despair - the worst in my life, even to this time. Almost.

Lucius was slower of learning, as I realized much later, but he understood the concept of the lessons. At our evetime rest, he took me aside and out of the hearing of the others of our cubicle. I had commiserated with him many times over the last few days, and he knew well of my frustration as to what was being taught.

In the dim oil lamp of the walkway, we sat as he patted the clay in his tablet, kneading in the water that he had sprinkled when we left our room. Quietly he said, "You have a name that you are known by, is that not correct?"

That was an obvious statement even to a dullard such as myself. All men had names. I just nodded.

"And I have a name, as does my patér and yours and all people in the city." I waited, not needing to agree. "When I call out, 'Junius,' what do I mean?"

Looking for the trap, I just hesitantly said, "Me."

"Correct. When I say the word, 'Junius,' I am referring to yourself. But your name is not you. Junius is only a description that you are known by." He pointed to the lamp on the wall and asked, "What is that?"

"A lamp," I replied.

"Excellent." He made some marks on his tablet. "These letters, taken together, form the word for lamp. Lamp is the name for that bowl with the flame. It has a name just as you have." I nodded, still not following his meaning. "I can say the word lamp, and you will know of what I am speaking." I nodded again. "If I show you these marks in a row, taken together, they also mean 'lamp.'" He waited while I thought again. "One can speak of a lamp with one's mouth and tongue, or with one's hand by making this series of marks. The great difference is that the spoken name disappears into the distance and remains only in memory, but the words written on clay, then baked, remain as long as the tablet does."

I was still struggling. "But of what use is such speaking with the hand and stick."

He thought for a moment, then started again. "Imagine that you are at your boat, fishing, and I am at my house, drinking wine. I like you and wish you to share my cup. And with my other friends also. I could then walk to the river and invite you to my repast. Then we could walk to the house of Claudius and invite him. All three of us could travel to the far side of the Capitoline and ask Polonius to join us. But by now, with all the traveling, the day is over and the wine must wait for another time."

That story I could follow, but to what end?

"Now, think of this. I get some clay tablets and on each I write the words, "Come to the house of Lucius for wine" and I give them to servants to take to my three friends. You, on your boat, are handed the tablet and read the words and now you know that you have been invited to partake of wine with your good friend. I have spoken to you with my hand. And thus with the others, and without a single word from my mouth, or myself having to walk further than our librarium for the tablets."

I got little sleep that night, thinking over and over of the words of my young roommate. A lamp was a thing of fire that gave light. And it was called a lamp. "A lamp," I said aloud, then looked to see if I had disturbed my cubical mates in their sleep. But the marks, called letters, in that particular order was also the description of that useful flame holder. But why not just draw a picture of the item, rather than assigning it a row of meaningless scribbles. With such thoughts, I finally slept, my questions still unanswered.

The next day, I dutifully stroked and erased, recited and listened trying to make sense of marks, instead of pictures, being the representation of a thing. But the next day was different...

The teacher held up a flask, then poured the contents into a bowl. "This is the oil for the lamp." In my thoughts, I wondered how to draw a picture of oil. A lamp, a bird or boat was easy, but how would one make a picture word for something that held no shape?

The teacher droned on, making the marks for the liquid. But then, he conjoined the two sets of marks. Suddenly, as if the god of thunder made his brilliant stroke of light to the tree next to our boat, as once had happened, I saw the two words as a whole and together they described something more than a thing and another. I quickly stroked the marks into my tablet, then under them the same words, but reversed. I had marks that described both lamp oil and an oil lamp - two entirely different, but single entities but made from the same scribblings.

My inspiration was reaching for new heights. I made the picture of a fish and next to it scribed the markings for oil. I did not yet know the marks for that creature, but the concept was the same.

Now, using one of the words and one that I did not yet know, I had described a third thing - fish oil, a product that I was very familiar with.

From that moment of inspiration, my life moved from being a fisher-boy to a scribe-to-be. The room had disappeared as I gloried in the concept of talking without speaking. At least, until the leather of the teacher cracked across my forearms. He had noticed my inattention and had assumed that I was dream weaving elsewhere.

No matter, the moment was mine and could not be taken from me.

From that day forward, I plied my writing stick and tablet of clay, searching out words and conjoining them in this way and that. And, I may say without bluster, the future saw me move rapidly ahead of my classmates. Not all of my progress to advance was my skills over my mates. Most of the boys had little interest in tablets and letters stroked in clay - they only desired to learn the basics enough to be able to return home and away from the strictness of the priests.

My progress was not unnoticed by the teacher. In a while, measured in a few months, I was the classroom chanter, giving the words for the class to repeat, then writing the proper form on the big slate. More and more, the priest would leave me to instruct while he slipped away for a cup. At the first, the boys used the absence of authority to play and jape while I recited, but after a time or two when the teacher slipped into the room from the back entrance and began to wield his leather strap with vigor... From then, I was still not in command of the class, but the japes were far more muted.

Finally, came three days of rest, during the feast times of... I do not remember, but this festival or that. We were allowed to return to our homes for the nonce, and I happily walked to find where our boat was tied. I must say that my appearance was satisfactory - both of my parents rejoicing and parading me to our neighbors. Even my brothers seem to put aside the normal sibling rivalry to be gladsome at my fate. But, in truth, by the end of the third day, I was eager to return to the temple.

I had changed, and sitting around the fire on the riverbank in the evening, listening to the tale of this catch, and that vending, of the quality of this pressing of oil, or complaints about the price of salt - my mind receded from the uninteresting tales of the riverbank folk. I made the proper responses, and smiled at the fortunes or jests of our neighbors, but in truth, I was willing for the sun to travel more swiftly and allow for the feast time to end.

On the second night, I retrieved my stash of bronze metal bits and hid it in the folds of my tunic, and the next day, with the sun dropping in the west, I gave my farewells to the family and my tearful mater and set my feet back to the temple.

By now, the class had been reduced by many. Some were, in effect, dunces, unable to comprehend the meaning of words, as I had been in the early times, but without my sudden flash of comprehension. Others were without interest in the word-learning, spending the periods designated for scribe-practice with their interminable game of knucklebones, throwing their handfuls of little carven and spotted cubes and rejoicing or nay in the wager. Some were rebellious at the discipline and were beaten until red and blue, then finally sent home in disgrace. A few just disappeared without leaving any knowledge - to their fellow students - as to the reason.

My friend, Lucius, returned that evening. He was a fair student, not enthusiastic about words and learning, but he did well enough. He would stay for the entire year, then return to... whatever the next task of a boy in a noble house was tasked for him.

From him, on that night of return, I learned about the care of one's wealth. As I lay my two spare tunics on my assigned shelf, the purse fell from the folds with a clink of metal. He recognized it as the one his patér had given me that day of our meeting. Aghast, he looked around for any other ears and eyes - the other two students that had shared our cubical were long departed - then reached for it and pushed it under my mat. "Junius. Why are you carrying your riches with you?" It was something of a jape - my purse contained a nice weight of metal, but it was not 'riches' in any sense of the word.

"Where else would I place it?" I answered.

"Certainly not on your person, and never with the knowledge of another. It will be gone an hour after another learns of it." Thus, I learned the first tribulation of wealth - the worry about thieves. On his advice, and as time went on, I split my small hoard, and hid each portion in a place known only to me, and in a compound the size of the temple, the places were many and varied.

The time passed rapidly, now. The days brought further learning, and now our abbreviated class - down to a handful - would walk the streets behind our teacher-priest. He would stop at this statue, and that monument and command us to read the inscriptions, correcting any mistakes and giving some history of the object. Or, he would suddenly point to a sign over a merchant's shop, demanding the meaning of the painted board from us.

We graduated to wax tablets, allowing much finer markings and more words on the surface. Indeed, it was these that educated merchants across the city used for their tabulations of this trade and that vending. However, unlike a clay tablet that could be baked and made permanent, these were strictly for temporary use.

No longer hapless students under strict discipline, our afternoons were now ours to use as desired. We could come and go at will and many used the time for sojourns around the city rather than spending the time with their families. And it must be said, much of their coin and time went to the brothels and street women.

My friend, Lucius, was insatiable as to women. Of course, unlike me, he had unlimited coin with which to purchase the services of Venus. Still, I was young and full of the desire that comes to a man as he sees manhood approach. One evening, Lucius towed me to the brothel of the Sirens - an upscale establishment on the border of the Capitoline quarter. It was immediately obvious that my friend was not a stranger to the house - the guard at the door bowed with a smile as we entered and inside, a huge woman approached with open arms of welcome.

"Ah. Master Lucius, of the House of Camillus! You honor our house once again with your presence." To myself, this was an unbelievable greeting to a boy of a mere fifteen years or so. Still, by now I well knew of the wealth and power of his patér in the city. She looked at myself with a questioning on her countenance and then back to my friend. "And this young man would be your associate, I assume?"

"My good Delila. I am presenting Junius, my roommate and confident in the temple. He has had a busier life than mine and until now has had little time to learn the delights of the fair sex. Perhaps you could find a proper wench to initiate him into the kingdom of Venus?"

Now the woman stood straight, with her hands clasped together and with a huge grin. "Aye, Master Lucius. You have brought your friend to the proper forum to learn the path of female concupiscence." She turned to look about. I began to notice my surroundings in the large room, dimly lit by oil lamps around the wall. The other patrons - about a double handful - were lying at short tables, reclining with their cups. I did not know if they had just arrived and waiting, or were finishing their night of copulation with the enjoyment of wine. Neither did I care. My attention was at the other end of the room, beyond a barrier of a thick rope to mark off the space in which the girls of the house waited for their custom. The rope was no hindrance in reaching the women, but the large guard with a wicked blade definitely was. He just stood, unmoving, next to the wall with his arms folded and gazed over the room, apparently looking for any unlikely disturbance.

The women were not easily seen in the dim light, but I could tell, at least, that they ranged in ages from youngsters with newly-formed paps to several who were at least in middle age. Not that I cared. Like most young men with no actual knowledge of the female sex, I graded all as... well, sufficiently female.

The brothel mistress finally turned and said to Lucius, "A young man on his first voyage usually desires a newly found craft, but..." My friend just waited as she looked around at the girls again, then continued, "...but a seasoned vessel is more kind to a new sailor." She pointed toward the woman. "Vibiana is an experienced mariner for your maiden voyage."

I had barely heard the woman and certainly had no idea of what she was saying. After looking at me for a long moment, Lucius said, "Your wisdom far exceeds ours for the topic, and my friend will follow your recommendations." I was towed to the rope, and a woman was called and introduced to me, after which she led me to a cubicle illuminated by a single lamp.

The night was a haze of memories - pleasant ones, but I could not have told my friend if the action had taken just moments or an hour by the water clock. Years later, after my experience with females was deep and thorough, I could look back and realize that the woman of that night was kind to a novice and made my first voyage, as it was called, memorable and enjoyable.

My stash of coin was wholly insufficient to visit the brothel as often as a young man would wish - that is, every night - but my friend took me along when he made his visits and paid my fee with his. The additional amount was trivial for his allowance and I did not argue. Over the following year, I had tested the skills of most of the women of the house and imagined myself to be quite the experienced man in the sexual act.

At the end of the year, during the feast of the solstice, the primary class ended, and all students left for their homes and new lives. Except for three, including myself, and all of us of the Plebeian class. We desired to become scribes as our profession, and would stay much longer for further learning. I hugged my friend and we pledged to visit each other when possible, Lucius assuring me that I was welcome at any time in his house. Being much more knowledgeable about the hierarchy of the city now, I doubted that a young man of the Plebeians would be welcomed to arrive without notice and knock his presence on the door, but I smiled and pledged my friendship as he left, his few articles of possession in a bag slung over his shoulder.

By now I was literate, and we three students actually did work in the scroll rooms under the command of this priest and that. Many times, I would sit, cross-legged, wax tablet or scroll across my knees, as I numerated various counts as a priest stacked and counted the value collected from pilgrims and offerings. Or, copied various messages to be sent to this temple or that. Once, even, I penned a missive that would be presented to the Senate on the morrow.

Now, my domicile was my own room, no bigger than the student cubicle that I shared with three others, but with only myself, it was sufficient and far larger than the little cubbyhole that I slept in on my patér's boat. My food was taken in the common kitchen and was no different than given to the priests. In all, I was content.

As the new year began, we three were taken for the first time to the city librarium, a vast stone building with many rooms, each with a purpose for the storage of scrolls. Here, under the auspices of the city Magistrate, were records of land ownership, taxes paid, and money owed - and far more. There were rooms of scrolls from the land of the Hellens, or Greece, as it was sometimes called.

Another small room had sheets of writing and tablets from far across the Great Sea - from the land of the great Pyramidios, Aegyptus. These had strange picture writing, such as I had envisioned when first I came to the Temple. Only a few people in all of the city could decipher the meaning of those scrolls and tablets.

One did not just walk in and begin to peruse the writings in the building. No one but a certified magistrate or assistant could enter the scroll storage - upon pain of death. To view one of the spindles, a person would step to a windowed wall and identify themselves and their need. For a small coin, they might request the needed materials from the voluminous lists that were posted on the walls all around the reception room. A magistrate helper would procure the proper scroll and place it in a small reading room, next to an outside wall and one with a high, but barred window for light. The reader would be escorted to the little cubicle, they would find their desired scroll or scrolls on the table, then they would be left to their reading, or research.

The door to the little room was not locked, but opened, like several others, into a common room where a magistrate assistant kept watch. When finished, one would knock on the door and it would be opened by the assistant who would both count the scrolls and inspect them for tampering. Then the reader could leave. I was told, that in all the history of the library, no scroll had ever been stolen, although a few times in the past, one had been altered by the patron. For such an act, the punishment was not light, and could well find the perpetrator hanging from his heels on the city wall, should the scroll have been of importance.

This day, the four of us were in a reading room with a scroll each. Even the priest had selected one for his use. Mine was a history of some ancient King of the city and his trials and tribulations during his reign. It was fascinating, my first encounter with a written text of history. To my sorrow, long before I was through, the teacher indicated that it was time to leave. As we entered the fading light of the outside, I suddenly realized that we had been in the librarium for half the day.

Still, my name was registered as a person allowed to use the facility at will and as a member of the Temple of Jupiter, I needed not to pay for the privilege. Thus, I spent many hours amongst the scrolls in pleasurable reading.

By my third year, I was a fully grown man, somewhat softer than when I was the net-boy on our boat, but I was active enough during my stay at the temple that my muscles did not atrophy completely. Especially, I spent many evenings at the Bathhouse of Juno, just down the street from the Temple of Jupiter. The pools were large and deep, and many times I astounded the bathers with my ability to swim the length of the tepidarium without breaking the surface, and then again back to my start.

Now, as a scribe, certified by the magistrates of the city as qualified to both produce and record official documents, I began to earn some metal by giving service to citizens come to the temple for assistance. A will for this merchant growing old and needing to protect his son or a bill of vending for a small farm for that heir, were just two of the many tablets and small scrolls that I produced. A few times I was engaged in reading a document in the hall of justice, during a dispute between two parties. Once, I even stood outside the Senate-House in the case of the need to interpret some scroll that had been received for consideration by that august assembly. I have to say, that while the remuneration was good, my services were not called, and I never saw the inside of the building.

When my friend Lucius had left the temple, by necessity my visits to the brothels were severely curtailed. Until I actually began to earn some coin, my hand was my usual companion during the night, but now I could enjoy the use of a woman again - not every night, but enough to service my young yearnings with frequent occasion.

Instead of engaging a domicile in the city, I kept my little cubicle at the Temple, paying for the use by assistance in teaching, or work in the administration rooms. On occasion, I visited my family, but while the meetings were pleasant, I would almost immediately look forward to returning to my scrolls and tablets. Our lives had grown too far apart.

Thusly, I might have spent my life but for an unexpected encounter.

Fateum (Fate)

My visits to the brothels were far fewer than during the year when my friend Lucius was at the school, but still, the pressures within my groin would build over the days, and I would usually give in to them about every quarter-month. I had long settled on a few favorites among the women in two of the establishments and settled into a routine with them. For themselves, the women soon learned of my tastes and little time was wasted in the preliminaries before retiring to their mats. They came to know me as a man of normal desires, who did not tend to violence or oddness during the act and that my coin was always good. Were such a thing admitted, I could have called them my friends.

One day, I was standing at my table running the heated scraper over my used wax tablets, when the reception slave entered with the words, "Amiliana, daughter of the house of Purder, the merchant." I looked up to see a young woman, no older than myself at the most. She was dressed as the dependent female of a prosperous tradesman, but her clothes were not even seen by me. Instead, I stared at her tresses - I had heard of rare individuals with hair the ruddy color of the setting sun through the clouds but had never actually seen the like. For an indefinite time, I just looked until I realized that I was being rude in the extreme.

"My pardon, Femina." I waved a hand to approach. She was carrying a folding tablet, made such that two small wax slabs could be closed to face each other so as to protect the writing. I knew that this was a need for either interpretation or rewriting. "How might I be of service?"

She smiled and replied, handing me the closed ledger. "My patér wishes for a scroll to be made of these transactions, and registered with the magistrates. He instructs me to wait until you have validated the correctness of his writing."

"Aye, Femina. Please comport yourself on my bench and I will read these." I opened it on the top of the table and began to read. One tablet described a purchase of a storage building in the Cispius quarter and the other a lease on a merchant stall. The work was trivial - I selected a length of papyrum, the off-white material that formed the medium that would take the ink of my pen and of sufficient length to hold my writing.

The young woman just sat quietly behind me, saying nothing, as I scribbled. My impulse was to turn and look at this intriguing female but I kept my professional being and concentrated on my work.

Shortly, I was finished with two small sheets, with all the forms to make the transactions legal, then selected two small spindles as their holders. An application of wax from my heated bowl attached one end of the papyrus to the round wood and I quickly wrapped the few turns of material tightly, then put a large drop of wax to hold the wrap, stamping it with the seal of the temple. Finally, I could turn and look at the woman again.

Now, I noticed more than her hair. She was attractive - not stunning as some of the brothel whores could seem - but wholesome and in all, a good treat for the male eyes. Her simple stola, the female robes that the upper classes and merchantry women wore in public, was of good material although lacking the gold trim and lace seen on the women of the high houses. I handed her the two small scrolls and her original tablets, and said, "Please have your patér examine the goodness of my work, and if he wishes, I can publish them in the Magistral archives."

"Thank you, Sos," she replied with a smile. "And your fee?"

"Two modi, Femina." That would be a pair of the small bronze ingots, no bigger than the tip of the little finger.

She nodded, and replied, "Might I pay you with this?" She handed me a small round and flat shape - obviously bronze - and about the weight of two modi. It had obviously been stamped in production, and with the likeness of a man on one side and an animal on the other. This was one of the Greek "coins" that I had learned of and had seen a few times in commerce, but had never handled.

I smiled and nodded, "Certainly, Femina. This will be sufficient." I paused, and said, "And your name is... Amiliana, as I believe the announcer proclaimed?"

"Aye. My patér is the owner of a grain yard... and other properties. Our house is on the street of Mercury in the Viminalis quarter."

"And are you betrothed yet, to a lucky young man... if I may ask?"

She grinned. It was like the sun on a clear day. "Nay. But not for the asking of all and sundry matchmakers." A pause as she looked around, apparently to make sure that no other ears had entered the small room. "My patér, I fear, intends to use my trothment as a bridge to a great family, if possible." She looked intently at me, then continued, "You have my name, Sos, but have not allowed me the boon of hearing yours."

"My pardon, Femina. My upbringing had little time for training in the social graces. I am Junius, scrivener trained in the Temple of Jupiter and certified to practice in all quarters of Rome."

"My. For a simple question of a name, you certainly make the answer in full." Abashed, I just grinned and nodded. She said, before turning to leave, "But, should you happen to be at the reading of the Tale of the Sabines, in the Viminalis Forum, on the day of the Calends, I may see you again, Junius, the scrivener."

A few days later I was wandering in that forum, in the quarter that she had named, looking with little interest at the stalls and tables of the merchants. Rather, I was waiting for the sun to fall on the tops of the western roofs and for the time of the thespian spectacle to appear on the acting boards. And, it must be said, as I wondered amongst the crowds, I was looking for a plume of fiery ringlets, issuing from the stola fold of the head. For all my time in the city, I had never attended any of the performances that occurred all over the city, and especially on feast days. In fact, I had actually spent my life as a scrivener student, mostly between the temple and the archives - and with a sojourn to a taburna on occasion, both for the drink and the women. There was much of the city that I had not seen, or even knew about.

The sun began its fall, and the stage was coming alive with playwrights and carpenters, arranging this prop and that painting around the boards, then finally, I saw my quarry. She was standing in the area reserved for paying folk, inside a roped barrier, and among the stone benches that would be used when the performance began. I walked to the opening in the ropes, then stopped as a brute blocked my path, his hand out for... I reached into my purse and withdrew a small flat piece, of the worth of a half modi. The man took it but did not move. His upraised two fingers gave the notice that I had only half paid the fee.

Finally, I was past the guard and slowly walked toward the girl. Beside her was an elder woman, and with a sinking heart, assumed her to be the mater. But as I approached, now able so see around the milling crowd, I knew that she had to be a body servant or slave. Her garb was far too dull to be for a prosperous merchant's wife.

I had no idea if her invitation, given on the day of her use of my services, was just a polite ruse to abort the conversation or if she actually wished to meet me. Certainly, she was not craning her head looking for my approach, but as I reached her position she turned and saw me. "Welcome, Junius the scrivener, of the Temple of Jupiter." It was a jest, but in good form.

I nodded, smiling - actually, probably grinning like the young fool about to use his first taburna woman - and replied, "Salve, Amiliana, daughter of the respected grain yard merchant." The returned jest was feeble, but she laughed. Now I knew her companion was a servant - the older woman made no change in her face to either of our japes. A mater, with bared claws, would already be between her daughter and this unknown stranger, taking liberties as if he were a close and trusted friend.

She saw my sideways glance at her companion and laughed again. "Concern yourself not. This is Seri, my handmaid, and friend from my earliest days. You only need fear her if she thinks you plan something to bring me to harm."

Our converse went on, about nothing and anything, and in truth, to this day I can remember none of it, being encompassed by the aura of a young woman speaking to me willingly, rather than a patron who has given value for the service. In fact, our interest in each other precluded our noticing the performance had started - until, that is, our fellow watchers communicated their wrath at our interruption of their pleasure. Subdued, we whispered for a few moments, then Amiliana rose and waved for me to follow. Outside the patron area, and past the standing crowds, we came into the center of the forum, now far less crowded, with the sun about to descend behind the western buildings. There, next to a statue of... some fantastical god or another, we found another bench for our use.

But, instead of our trivial converse, she just sat for a moment before asking, "Junius. You can read, can you not?" Throwing her eyes to the heavens, she shook her head and continued, "Of course you can. That was stupid of me. My question should have been, 'May you teach another to read?'"

Wondering at the question, I nodded and answered in the affirmative. "Certainly. Have you a brother or family member needing tutoring on the art of the marks?"

"Aye," Then came the surprise. "Myself."

I knew that few females in the city were educated to the letters, and any that were would be in the noble families. For one thing, they would not be permitted in the temples, beyond the statuary forum, and certainly not as a student. It took little imagination to realize what would come to young men and women, mixed beyond the reach of their parents, and secluded in a temple compound for years. For my use of paid women, all meetings were at a taburna or brothel. Being caught with a female in one's domicile in the sacred grounds would be cause for instant dismissal, if not resulting in the unfortunate and his whore being nailed to the upper boards of the city wall.

"You wish to learn the art of scripting," was my less than brilliant statement, as I furiously thought of what she was asking.

She put her hand on my arm. "Junius. Do you know the life of a woman when she becomes a wife?" I shook my head. My mater was the only wife that I knew of to any extent. They cooked, cleaned, gave birth... and pleasure at night to their man. But what...

"It is a life of which every day is the same. Even now, I rise in the mornings, realizing that I have an entire day of doing nothing - or if anything, the same as yesterday. A woman cannot travel, nor leave home on an adventure as my brothers have done. She cannot start a life on her own, nor purchase anything that she can call her own - unless, she is a sonless widow. Even my attendance at this venue is the result of endless begging." I just waited, having nothing to say - indeed, not even understanding in full what she was saying. "My younger brother learned the art of reading from a tutor before he was taken by the red plague from a cut to his leg. He would let me in his room, at night, and in the light of a lamp, would read to me from this scroll or that. Wonderful stories of brave men who founded the Republic, or those who defended it from the barbarians. I desired with all my being to be able to read those scrolls, and I did learn to recognize this word or that, but he was taken too early for my skills to grow."

"And your patér is less than enthused at your wants?"

She laughed again, but this one was not pleasant. "Aye. His answers are that I should continue my lessons on deportment, and the studying of the proper wearing of the stola and the palla. Or that I should learn to arrange my coif better in the styles of the noble women's hairstyles." She stood and walked a few paces, then back, relieving her frustrations at the memories. "I gave him the knowledge that the Temple of Venus has tutorings for young women and that many young high-born females attend, but he gave me a sharp word and forbade the further speaking of the topic."

She looked at me for a moment. "I could pay you for the lessons. I have an allowance for feminine things that I seldom use, beyond a few items on occasion."

I shook my head. "My time is yours, but the practicality is the concern. Certainly, I cannot come to your household for your lessons."

"Nay. But there is a washerwoman whom I have befriended, having assisted her in..." She stopped, apparently realizing that a confidence was about to be breached. "She has a small room that I have been let, in which I have stored... various items that my patér would immediately seize and destroy, should he know of them. We could meet there, on occasion, for lessons."

In no manner was I going to refuse this young woman, for whatever her desires. I was struck, and fully, by her charms, and even beginning to dream weave of her joining with me. Of course, even then, in my youth, I had the knowledge that a young woman's life was entirely in her patér's keeping, and all the magistrates in the city would give credence to his claims. A man who attempted to overrule that right would be subject to the law, and civil courts would weigh heavily against the interloper.

However, there was no law about a young woman engaging a tutor. Any conflict would be between her and her patér, rather than in the realm of law. Several days later, an urchin came to the temple with a verbal missive for me and shortly I was hurrying to the Viminalis quarter, following the instructions that I had been given, and with a bag over my shoulder. At the doorway of a shabby hut, I was met by an equally shabby woman, whose countenance mirrored a life that was less than goodsome. She knew who I was, and just pointed me to an opening in the far wall of the little room. Inside and waiting was the beautiful Amiliana.

With a smile, she rose from the mat and greeted me with a hug - an unexpected action that left me breathless and filled with a rising desire, even though I had relieved my groin pressures the night before at the local brothel. I looked around. The room was just a small cubicle, even smaller than the student room in which I had spent my first years. It was clean but devoid of anything but a worn mat, and a shelf made of a flattened board sitting on two rocks. The single window let in light and was covered with a cloth with a course weave.

Nodding to her servant, that woman left the room, closing behind her what passed for a door - a woven straw mat with ropes as hinges.

On the shelf were several tattered scrolls and a stack of sheets of papyrus of different sizes and shapes. Obviously, these were the items that she was hiding from her patér. We both sat as I opened my bag and drew out a wax fold-tablet and some blank sheets, a pen and a small vial of ink, made from the residue of the heated black rock. Pointing at the items on the bench, I asked, "That is your library, I presume."

She nodded. "When my brother died, I hurriedly took his small collection of scrolls and hid them in the back of the woodpile, else they would have been destroyed, or thrown away. I also have his pen, but the container of ink has long ago dried to a solid."

I nodded, then turned to sit beside her so that we could both use the same tablet. "To begin, I must know what you have already learned..."

The hours went by pleasantly - very pleasantly, and seemed to be only a short count by a sundial. According to her, the patér had traveled to the port city of Ostia and would not return until the morrow. As her mater had died, years ago, this day we could use the entire afternoon in learning. She knew the letters and, therefore, was ahead of the usual student. In addition, she knew many words by sight, if not the use of them in a sentence. At the end of the session, I pulled a very small wax tablet from my bag and handed it to her. "This is small enough for you to conceal, but will be much safer to practice on than papyrus. There will be no scraps of expensive sheets for you to have to dispose of, or to lay around to be discovered."

This time, she kissed me on the cheek, as we rose to leave. In the other room, her servant was napping and shortly they disappeared in the street crowds as they set foot for home.

Thus, it went. About every handful of days, a message would arrive, and I would hurry to the old woman's home. Some days we had the entire afternoon, on others only an hour by the water clock, depending on the reason she had given for leaving the house, or whether the patér was in residence or no.

For myself, my days had become fixed, dedicated to my work as a scrivener, the mornings being filled with wills, testaments, deeds and records of transactions. The afternoons would find me at the city depository, posting this scroll or that sheet for archiving, according to the wishes of my patrons. The duties usually taking little time, I would usually enter the reading rooms for the balance of the afternoon, relaxing with a scroll from history. I would never become wealthy, but my needs were modest - food and a woman on occasion were all that I needed, my living cubicle being paid for with service to the temple. My stash of metal, or coin, as the merchants said, was becoming significant. I had received an education in the commerce of the world, receiving many different types of tokens of transactions from my patrons - bronze ingots from Rome, Grecian staters, hammered cupric flats from Mesopotamia, small gold rings from Egypt. And others that defied any knowledge of their antecedents.

The Priest Primus of the Temple had asked me many times to take the orders and enter the priesthood, he being apparently satisfied with both my work and my demeanor. I was uncertain, and hesitated in my acceptance, not being prepared to spend my time in the veneration of the god that owned the temple. In fact, I was still not convinced of the existence of such deities, or in anything else that could not be seen or touched by a man. In this, I am fairly sure that several of the lesser priests had the same doubts. Certainly, in private and while in their cups, they boxed the ears of the inhabitants of Olympus with regularity. But, the life of a priest was easy, and good - and could make a man wealthy just from a part of the tithes and gifts that flowed through the temple every day. Still, I hesitated, hoping for a different life should my plans mature.

Unlike many, or most, I had no use for great wealth. At least, I thought, at the time. I was too young to know that wealth equal power. And power is the patér of safe-being and long life.

The inevitable happened. A young man and young woman, meeting in secret will eventually grow together, no matter how innocent the reason for their trysts. It happened one afternoon, our hands touching over the wax tablet more than necessary, the girl seeming to have trouble remembering her lessons, then, before even the gods realized what was happening, we were laying together, her hands frantically trying to raise her stola to allow access for my member. I was experienced, if no Eros, and had learned of the sensitive places of a woman from my dalliances with the brothel women. I think that the pleasure was had on both sides - certainly, she seemed to desire that I not withdraw from her female receptacle. Of course, in the natural aftermath, my body receded from hers, despite any urge to remain coupled.

That was just the beginning. Now, our meetings still certainly had a full measure of learning of the words but also was infused with the sweetmeat of coupling before the tablets were opened. It was a wonderful time, and in our innocence, we planned our future lives together. Maybe we would depart for Antium or even Veii. My talent would find employment anywhere in Latium, and in time, when her patér recognized the reality of the situation, we could return to make our household in Rome.

There is a saying among the priests that I brushed off as a sardonic proverb with no practical aspect. "Those whom the gods would destroy, they first make happy."

On that last day that I ever saw Amiliana, I thanked the gods, existing or no, that we were sitting apart on the mat when the patér burst into the small dwelling with his retinue of men. Utterly surprised, we both jumped to our feet as the woven reed door was almost ripped from its ropes. The man, whom I had never seen before this day, stood in the opening with his face red from the choler of his finding. Without preliminary, he barked an order to his men and the girl was rushed from the room, her feet barely touching the floor between two men carrying her by the arms.

Uncertain as to my fate, I slowly backed up to the wall, only a single step, as the man stepped forward. I had no weapon and no training in the use had one been available. I was fully grown, now, and had learned the art of the boy-tussle with my brothers and friends, but that would be of no use against a handful of his servants, two, at least, carrying staves. I was wondered whether to bluster or wait, when the man turned back to me, his daughter now gone from view. Point to me with a shaking fist, he shouted, "Who are you to cleave a daughter from the will of her patér?"

With three of his men standing behind him, bringing the little room to almost full capacity, I decided that the best path was to wind a trail between the truth and nay. "Until your entry, I was instructing the Femina in the art of reading, properly engaged and remunerated." That caught him aback, his expectations being no doubt of a furious denial of what was plainly happening - to him. Having the slight offensive, I reached into my purse and removed a bronze ingot and offered it in the palm of my hand. "Since the lesson was aborted for reasons unknown to myself, I cannot claim remuneration for the lesson. Please deliver her recompense to the Femina."

Now I could see the uncertainty in the face of the man. Possibly, I was just a scribe innocently engaged in lessons, but... "Why need you to hide in the room of a drudge, rather than an open place to instruct?"

Still keeping my expression neutral, I returned, "I teach where I am engaged. The person offering the recompense is the master, or mistress, of the contract. In any event, you will know that she would not be allowed in the halls of the Temple of Jupiter. I assume that this domicile was chosen as being thrifty and quiet - very conducive to learning. And to my understanding, her skill when learned, would be a present to her patér and future mate."

At the name of the temple, I saw his men look at each other. Obviously, it would be no small thing for a member of that august temple to be assaulted for whatever reason, and should the assignation be as I claimed, they could well be the ones facing the magistrates in the halls of the court.

Finally, the patér made his decision, pointed his finger at my face and saying loudly, "The lessons are discontinued. If my daughter attempts to resume them, you will immediately rebuff her and inform myself of her actions. You may keep your fee." With that, he spun on his heels and the entire group departed.

I would have done so as well, but suddenly my legs were incapable of supporting my body. I slid down the rough wall and sat on the dirt floor, my muscles shaking as one who had the trembling disease. My gorge almost rose to the point of loss, but I managed to quiet it until my palpitations ceased. It was a very unsteady man who stumbled his way back to his cubical, that afternoon.

Days went by, as I realized that my dream of life with the fiery haired girl was over. Even should she be willing, the intention of her patér overrode all. Both custom and the law would not be kind to a man who flaunted the express decrees of a man for his daughter. I did little work in the scriptorium, but spent much time in the taburnae, trying to make sense of my life and what I wanted. Wine did not increase the wisdom of the imbiber but helped push the memories aside to the point that the pain of loss was gone. Far later in life, I realized that my love-sickness is the common lot of the young man, happening to one and all at some time during his sojourn in this world. Like most wounds that are survivable, the pain eventually recedes and is consigned to the depths of the past.

Then, sometimes a man received an injury that might be mortal in time.

Late one afternoon - only a while until darkfall - a full month and most of another after the forcible end of my lessons with Amiliana, a man appeared at my table with a missive - or so he said. Rather than give me the scrap of material, he said, "I was promised that the person receiving would pay for the conveyance."

The man was a servant, of middle years, that was plain. His tunic and sandals were rough and plain, but clean - this was no man of a work-merchantry. I looked at him with some disdain, being accustomed to receiving payment for such missives, not to vend coin to receive them. "And who would this mysterious sender be?"

"A young woman with hair of the color of fire."

Eyes wide and heart pounding, I handed the man eight modi of bronze and dismissed him instantly. I had already extinguished the lamp on my table and was unwilling to spend the time to kindle a flame. In a side hall, with the minor statues of Jupiter in various poses, I stopped under the sacred flame that was never allowed to die. There I read on a scrap of papyrus, in the recognizable strokes of

Amiliana, the words. "Beloved one. Know that my woman's moon has stayed twicely, and today the condition was reported by my new serving maid. My patér is most wroth, to the extent of madness, and has vowed retribution upon you. Even now he is gathering his men. I am without coin and have promised this man your recompense if he delivers properly. I will always..."

The record that I write is much more lucid than the actual note, obviously written in utter haste and by a student not yet in the mastery of the art of writing, but the meaning was plain. So was the ending sentence, stopped without completion, which only the imagination could vision the reason for its sudden termination.

I realized that I was in mortal danger. Not only from the patér, in his rage, but should my case of the defilement of an unwed femina be presented to the Priest Primus of the Temple, I would be whipped from the grounds and barred from practicing my art in the city. Or worse.

I wondered if the rage of the patér would override his sense and actually cause him to accost me inside the sacred grounds of the temple. Quickly, I decided that it would be foolish to wait for the answer. Immediately, I began to move around the compound to retrieve my stash of coin, now greatly diminished by my visits to the taburnae and brothels, in my need to forget. Then, in my room, I gathered my few possessions in my scriptoria work bag and departed the main gate into the street.

Now, like a water clock that had run out of liquid, I stopped, wondering at my next move. The boat of my parents was not an option - it was not my home anymore, and I had no intention of allowing them to learn of my shame - at least not from me. Across the river was a terminus, where merchant caravans were both made and disassembled for the cities to the north. I could join a merchant's column and travel to the city of Veii or Caere. Of course, the caravans did not either assemble nor depart in the end of the day, so I was condemned to spend the night sleeping against a tree, somewhere. I thought of finding a taburna in a lesser quarter of the city, but that would cause me to have to travel the streets during the day, and without any idea of the retribution that might be planned...

The workday over, the streets were mostly filled with male revelers on their way to the wineshops and taburnae - and the brothels. I strode for the walls in a fast walk, knowing that the gates would be shut for the night as the sun disappeared. As I moved, I looked back to see if any were following, but it was impossible to tell. Men were going hither and there, and any could be my shadow. Or none.

I made it to the gates shortly before they closed. People were hurrying in both directions, either to enter the city or to escape before the closure would end the procession for the night.

At the river, I looked for my family's boat, but in the fading light, it was not apparent. Indeed, it could have been anywhere along a handful of stadia in either direction. It was of no matter since I had no intention of announcing my presence. Suddenly, I realized that I had left the city without provisions of any kind - indeed, without even the evening meal. In addition to the uncomfortable night before me, my belly would be complaining mightily before sunrise. I thought about returning to the city, to spend the night in some low-quarter taburna, to leave at first light. That plan was discarded when I saw that the gates were closing.

Now in no haste, I started up the rise of the bridge, reaching the center of the shallow arch, then to stop and just gaze over the waters that had been the center of my childhood. Behind me, a few river men walked the bridge, traveling to their boat or wharf-side fish market on either shore, no doubt thinking on the meals even now being prepared by their mates in their domicile.

Under the thin moonlight, I wondered again at the rapidity that my life had moved from being a respected member of the city to a man fleeing the justice of a wronged patér. And for what? A woman. Still, I had been enamored of Amiliana, and she of me I thought. We could have started a happy family, with roots in the city and a slew of sons to carry my name for...

The shadows that rushed to me were not a surprise, even if startling. Had I time to think on it, I would have realized that the missive from the young woman might have been far behind the events of which she had been warning me. The men probably had the temple under watch for the whole of the afternoon. Now, if the patér of the young woman had engaged a trio of assassins, then I was as a dead man. I had no skill with any blade or spear, even had I possessed either.

Their actions were practiced - no doubt discussed before their rush. One grabbed me from behind, his arms under mine with his hands linked at my neck. Another took a blade to cut my life from my body as I struggled. The pugio, the short-bladed dagger, came down toward my body... But, it did not take my life. Instead, it slit my tunic from the belt to the hem. The third man stepped up - a bearded individual, not at all looking like a citizen, most of whom were following the custom of cutting the hair from their faces. These had to be hires from the labor district, the sprawling slums outside of the walls next to the Oppius quarter. That area was a vast and lawless collection of people from every part of the world, come to make their mark in the Republic. It was also the greatest collection of cutthroats and villains in all of Latium. I had never visited the district, but knew that one could hire any action from the inhabitants, no matter the reason.

And my fleeting thought was confirmed as the man, grinning evilly in the dim light, said in an atrocious accent, "I have greetings from Paramus, who wishes to repay a man for his actions upon his daughter." He held the pugio before his face, rotating it to let the light glint from the blade. "And in payment return, he has requested your pouchstones to decorate his atrium as a warning to others who might feel the same needs." His second man, reached down to part my slit tunic, exposing the requested payment, hanging and waiting for the transaction.

For a man, this was worse than the idea of death. By instinct, I recoiled by pushing at the boards of the bridge with my feet. Even though I was not a soldier, nor even a brawler, I was of a goodly size since my ascension to manhood and had strength to match. The desperate spasm with my leg muscles propelled both myself and my grappler, behind me, to the low railing of the bridge, his buttocks meeting the upper board of the rail - the same board that my friend Lucius had climbed to escape the flailing ass that had threatened to crush him. I gave another push with my legs, and in a heartbeat, we toppled over the rail and made the drop to the water.

The Slave

Descendo

I sat on a box, watching the port city of Ostia recede into the distance, the sail of the boat full and drawing well. My thoughts were bitter, dwelling on the ease with which a man can destroy his own life, and without even the knowledge of the act as it is being performed. The thought kept returning that, in a few months, a child would be born of my seed, and that I had little chance of knowing either of the fact or of the little person. Had I been the champion in any of the numerous tales told in the Forum and on the streets by the wandering bards, I should have returned to the household of my love, confronted the patér - slaying any of his men who attempted interference - then, whisked my dearest away - probably over the wall with the aid of a knotted rope - and sailed into the sunset to our new life of love and passion.

I did not believe that I lacked courage, but the idea of a man - trained as a scribe and unfamiliar with weapons and strife beyond the numerous boy-brawls of my childhood - assaulting a household of the city to steal a woman from the clutches of her legitimate patér...

All that would accomplish would be my dangling from a cross tree, nailed up by my hands and feet.

It had been two days since the fall from the bridge.

In his panic of the fall, the assailant released his grip on myself to flail the air while we fell the short distance. I doubted that he could swim, as few not connected with a water-life had the skill or even the reason to accrue it. Unlike the last time that I had inadvertently swum the waters of the Tiber, in this season the river was placid and well within its banks. I could hear the man splashing and choking away from me, but in the dim light of the moon, I could not see him. Nor was I concerned. He could make his own pact with the river god. I was grateful for being swept away from the assailants at the bridge and down the river at a pace that would make any pursuit impossible. My bag was still on the bridge and lost forever, but my purse was still attached to my belt - a weight that was making itself felt. Even with my water skills, it was difficult to stay afloat without considerable effort with the metal pulling me down.

Untying the strings while floating down the current was impossible, and besides, I did not wish to abandon all that I now owned in the world. Instead, I kicked until I could feel the bottom rise toward the bank. Then, with my feet touching the soft mud, I let myself be pulled along with the current, but without the need to support myself afloat. Hours later, I pulled myself ashore at the wharf of a small river-hamlet, wrinkled like an ancient crone. Not even bothering to drag myself above the bank, I just lay in the soft mud under the platform and slept the sleep of the dead.

On the morn, I rose to the light of the sun and moved into the water to wash myself and my ripped tunic of the mud. The men preparing their boats were mildly surprised to see a man, dressed as I was, suddenly appear from under their feet, but the hard life of a boatman did not engender a desire for asking questions that did not apply to his profession. From a fish-wife, I purchased the end of a loaf of bread with a snippet of copper. As I could exhibit a knowledge of the river, I procured a spot on a boat as a pole man, moving downriver toward the sea. The distance was not far and by the midday sun, we were in Ostia, the seaport of Rome.

This was my first visit to the city, and in fact, the first to any city other than Rome. I first found a food-stall and purchased a tub of cheese and a long loaf of bread to ease my stomach. Then a few more bits were spent on a new tunic - the one I was wearing now good for the rag bin and not much else. Since the port city was under the rule of Rome, I could not tarry here. I had no idea how far the reach of the merchant might be, nor even of the depth of his insistence that I pay for my crime to his daughter, but prudence dictated that I find some other locale to anchor myself.

My original plan had been to travel north, to Veii, maybe, but now a southward move might be more productive. The cities of Latium were in the control of Rome, if not actually conquered by them, but distance should make a good measure of safety for myself. Besides, I needed to stay in the realm of my birth-city if my skills were to be of use. I would make a poor scribe in a city in which I did not speak the language.

The port being a very busy one - indeed, the main entry and exit of products to and from Rome - I had no problem engaging a fare on a boat to the south. The only question being of the style in which to travel. That was an easy choice - my purse, not deep to begin with, due to my indulgences when trying to console myself after the loss of Amiliana, would not sustain an upscale berth on a fast coaster, so I paid a few modi for a spot in the hull of a filthy trudge. The leaky boat made the craft of my family seem as a festive river barge in comparison, but nevertheless, it sailed with the morning wind on the second day and now I was safely away from any pursuers - and any remnants of my old life.

The boat had a crew of three, with a single pole and sail, the latter more rags than the old tunic that I had in my new bag, and our progress was barely faster than my patér and brothers could pole our craft upstream. It had no deck, just the hull, now full of clay pots, boxes, and bundles of materials - no doubt trading fodder for the stops down the coast. But, the weather was good, the sun mild even in this late season, and I just relaxed and watched the land in the distance slowly move past. We stood into cities without leaving a mark in my memory except for a few names - Laveinium, Castorium, Aphrodeitium. The boat stopped for the master to bargain with the traders on the docks, then leaving for the next port, many times without a trade.

The lazy days had a soporific effect on myself. I just sat in the shade of the sail, watching the small crew work, or most of the time, their squatting to play the game of bones in the forepeak of the boat. My thoughts wandered slowly and without course. Day by day it went, till finally we reached the major port city of Tarracina.

I walked ashore for a while, the master claiming that the stop would be for at least a day. This city, while not of the size and grandeur of Rome, was large and prosperous. It was under the hegemony of Rome, but not as a subject city. The day was mine, and I needed to refresh my bag of provisions with the least expensive dried sausage, bread, and cheese that I could find. I walked to the Forum, a pale shadow of that in Rome - indeed, in my city even the minor forums of the individual quarters were greater - and strolled amongst the tables and stalls.

I stopped at a vendor of blades, looking at the pugios and daggers. I wished to acquire one, except that the metal left in my purse was sufficient only to purchase poor food for a month and in no way adequate to the vending. My skills with any weapon were nonexistent, beyond sharpening my writing tools, or gutting a fish for the fire, but maybe the appearance of a blade in my belt might give pause to toughs and others wishing to accost me. I turned away, the purchase being only a daytime weaving of dreams at present.

At the benches, now devoid of any slaves being vended, I stopped to read the cryer's board. The leather-lunged individual that usually stood on the platform in the center of any forum, shouting out the news of the day, interspersed between offers from merchants and occasionally a reward for this escaped slave or that stolen ox, was gone to his meal. In his absence, the tidings were written in chalk on a large slate mounted on the platform. But, and more interesting, beside it was the board that contained individual notices for offers of engagement for purpose, written on scraps of material and pinned to the soft wood. Reading the scrawl of one particular note, I pulled it from the board and walked away.

Back at the port, I walked to the magistrate's post and waited for the official to finish his converse with a boat master, then said, "Salve, Sos." He gave back the same greeting, and I asked, "Might I enquire as to the street of the Pallacineae, and particularly the abode of Zethus, the trader?"

The man pointed and explained for a few heartbeats, and, thanking him, I set my foot in the direction he indicated. It did not take long to see that Zethus was not of the prosperous class, at least if the street on which he had his domicile was any indication. It took me several stops at the stalls, inquiring my way before I came to the house of the merchant almost at the end of the street. A wooden fence surrounded a compound with many smaller buildings in a courtyard that was cluttered with... everything that I could imagine. Jugs crates filled with charcoal, baulks of timber, bundles of hides...

Inside, the door to the main building was only an opening with a hide cover that was pulled aside as I approached. A raggedly garbed man - a slave he had to be - stepped out to confront me. "You wish to trade, Sos?"

I shook my head. "Nay. I wish to see a man, Zethus, by his written invitation." I waved the scrap of material at the man.

With a nod, he turned, and I followed him into the building. The room was large, but dirt floored and, as the courtyard, filled with uncountable items in piles, stacks, and containers. As I entered, a man appeared from beyond another opening, this one having a hanging bead curtain that had seen years of use. Zethus was an old man, gray-bearded and with either a shaved head or one in which the follicles of his youth had fallen away. He stopped, looking at me with squinting eyes, then asked, "Who are you boy, and what is your purpose?"

I handed him the scrap of writing medium and replied, "This says that you desire a man of words for hire."

The man had to be a Greek, or at least of Hellenistic extraction. Short-bearded, he was wearing ragged robes - clean, but not in the Roman manner. Also, his words had an accent that showed his antecedents were not of Latium. I decided that he was not as old as he appeared - it was just the garb that made him seem so. "You are a scribe, young man?"

"Aye. Trained and authorized by the Temple of Jupiter in Rome."

He stopped in front of me, looking up and down. "And a man with that background is applying for a position on a dirt street in Tarracina." It was a statement, not a question. "Then boy, you are either escaping a woman or the magistrates."

Older and dusty he might be, but the sharpness of his wit had not dulled with age. He had come close to the mark with that stroke. "Aye. It is true that I feel uncomfortable in my home city. But my problems do not diminish my skill with the pen and stylus."

He looked at me doubtfully, then said, "Come." The next room was his workplace. Stacks of tablets, literally piles of them were all around the walls, and the huge table was filled with more, almost to the limit of its strength. In addition, sheets of papyrus and scrolls, empty spindles, and scraps filled every shelf on every wall. He scrabbled around the surface of the table, then picked up a sheet of writing material and handed it to me. "Read this aloud, boy."

I took the sheet, scanned it for a heartbeat, then began. It was a routine invoice for cattle hides from... I assumed the name was Siracusa, badly written. I began, "From Harmon, of Siracusa, is this rending of the trading. For the consideration..." I read for a time, then stopped as the man reached to take the sheet from my hands.

"You can indeed read, boy. And can you number?"

"Better than the scribe of the honorable Harmon, Sos," I replied. "In addition to his atrocious wording, I can see at least a double misconstrual of his figures. The twice of four and ten might well be four and twenty in his city, but not in Rome. We could call the sum eight and twenty."

The old man looked at me for a sharp moment, then asked, "Do you have a name that I can use besides boy?"

"Aye, Sos. I am known as Junius."

"Then, welcome, Junius of Rome. I will test you for a moon or so, to see if I like you - and you me. If so, we can make the arrangement more permanent."

Thus is was, that I came into the employ of one Zethus, in the port city of Tarracina. In the next several months, I learned more of my employer. He was indeed a Greek, escaped from the many battles between the cities of that land. He was a merchant, of course, trading in anything and everything that moved up and down the coast of Latium. And, indeed, some boats came from far beyond, even the city of Athens and others around the Great Sea. And to be sure, on occasion a ship from the far southern lands of Egypt would pull into the harbor, crewed by the brown skinned natives of that desert land.

Zethus could speak accented Latium well, but dropped back into his native tongue when he berated the gods or his slaves. I began to pick up a knowledge of that language, more from the pleasure of learning than the need to know it. I even began to learn the rudiments of the Greek numbering system, as many of the tablets and scrolls were enumerated with that script.

My first task was to bring some order to the scripting room. The lazy scribe slave, who could barely connect three letters in correct order, merely dumped the old clay tablets and papyrus into piles once they were of no further use. I had those hauled to the rock pile and began to place the current accounts into some semblance of order. Many of the scrolls on the shelves had dates that preceded even my entering the temple, and were useless for anything except scribbling on the blank reverse. I cut them into arm length sheets and stacked them for my use when I needed a medium on which to figure. In a quarter-month or so, the room was orderly, with the baking stove no longer hidden by broken clay fragments, and empty trays ready for fresh clay and marking. The roll of fresh scroll material was placed on a high spindle and the appropriate length could easily be drawn out and cut off.

The old man still had his gruffness, but as I proved to his satisfaction that I was indeed educated in the marks and figures, he became more genial toward myself. My pay was small, but included a small room in the building and my repast. For now, I was fairly content, the memories of why I was in a southern city finally beginning to lose their greenness. I had nothing to do with the trading that took place in the courtyard or the front room on days of inclemency, my occupation being entirely with the accounts and figures of the commerce. That does not mean that I was not amusedly privy to many of the negotiations, as the shouts and protestations of both parties came clearly through the hide door, each claiming that the other was no better than a thieving she-goat, or submitting loudly to the gods that he himself was being condemned to a life of usury and poverty at that quoted price. It took only a few days for me to realize that the old man enjoyed the barter, as did most of his customers. Still, for a while, it was a startlement, as I had worried that blades might flash in the extremes of the arguments.

Once I had proved my place - indeed, my absolute superiority over the semi-literate scribes from the local school - I began to accompany the old man on trading trips up and down the land, sometimes by boat, others in a caravan down the coastal roads. Twice, I made the journey to the island of Sicillia, and once to the far off island of Sardegna. He would examine the merchandise, throwing me figures that I would add and subtract on my wax tablet, then he would make the offer, and if my column showed a good number, coins would pass, and we would move to the next platform. Eventually, I gained his trust for my competency, and began to make the voyages in his stead, his old bones not relishing either the confinement in a hull nor the sometimes cold and violent weather that would inevitably be encountered on occasion.

Again, after my settlement in Tarracina, my needs came to the fore, and I began to visit the local brothels for relief. The act was now just for the alleviation of my urges - the pleasure of the company was missing, and the joinings were short. Still, I might have lived my life out in the role of accountant for merchants, but for my enjoyment of the prospect of seeing new lands and places. For a boy from the Tiber, it was something never imagined in those young days.

I was returning from Sicillia, having received from a merchant a measure of merchandise that had been contracted the voyage before. Besides the cargo, several passengers were berthed, all traders of age, although one had his mate with him. The ship was of a quality quite above that in which I had first ventured onto the ocean. This one was decked, with a tall pole for the sail, and speedy of gait. Unfortunately, before the wrath of Neptune, all vessels of man are mere cockleshells.

The master was standing on the forepeak, staring into the distance. A friendly man, he did not stand aloof above mere passengers as did many under which I had sailed. Indeed, we spent many hours in his after cabin, in talk and remittances about ourselves. His tales of a lifetime at sea were fascinating, and many may have well been the truth. Today, he was not in a joyful temper. Seeing me approach beside himself, he turned and said, "One hopes that your belly is hardened to the sea."

I nodded and replied, "Aye, Captain. It grew from childhood on the water, but what is your meaning?"

He pointed to the haze on the water, far off. "That bodes ill for any in the straits. I fear that we will be encountering waters of less than pleasantness before the morn." His knowledge of the sea was not defective - by first light, the wind had shifted to the quarter of the sunset and with a force to rip the foam from the top of the waves. Before the noon meal, had there been one, the sail had been reduced to a mere tunic sized patch in the wind and by darkfall had been completely removed from the bare poles. The strength of the wind would almost rip the garb from a man's body - any exposed sailcloth would have been rags between breaths. There was nothing now for the crew but bail the water from the hull, and little enough of that, the openings to the hull being closed and nailed down with their wooden covers.

Each of the double handful of men - and the woman - in the forward berth of passengers, had decided that the grasp of Neptune, or his sirens, would be welcome. All were laying on the curve of the hull, in the salty water in the bottom, trying to empty bellies that were long plundered of food.

In the after cabin, and above the roar of the wind and rain, the Captain shouted to me, "It is well that we stood into port an extra day, else we would be through the strait and with no sea room in which to run." Not understanding, I just waited for him to draw breath. "By now, we would be nothing but kindling on the rocks of the lee shore of Latium. Here, we have many leagues of room to wait out the storm."

And wait we did. There was nothing else to do, other than thanking the gods that I was in a well found ship. Had this been the decrepit coaster of my flight from Rome, I would already be knocking on the gates of Neptune, my bloated corpse mere food for the fish. Days went by, with the storm in full fury, before the winds began to subside. Our crew was reduced by one, who disappeared without even a shout that the furies had taken him. Between the evening meal of dried sausage, and the morning break of our fast, he was gone.

Finally, the storm was reduced to a mere gale that once I would have considered a major storm from the wrath of the gods but now welcomed as a blessed relief of almost calm weather. The skies were still totally covered with scudding clouds, giving the master no method of selecting a course. For now, with a partial plan of sail set, we just attempted to stay our position against the wind and without being blown ever further along.

A morning dawned, with the welcome vision of the sun, although still behind the clouds. At least, the Captain could now draw a course to the west, to regain the untold number of leagues that we had lost from our original voyage. I stood by the master as he looked over the featureless sea, not bothering his thoughts of our course. Finally, he muttered, "We must be a hundred leagues to the east of Locri." He shook his head, "Possibly closer to the Grecian mainland than Latium, even. The new moon may come before we spot the coast of land again."

For days, we meandered in the light airs, barely making the distance in a day that we had lost in an hour in the storm. I was not troubled by the time, but the passengers were in constant agitation over the endless voyage, and demanded the exact hour of their return several times a day. Finally, the Captain muttered to me, "I will feed the fish with the next man who demands the measure of our port of call." He waved me to his cabin with the orders to his men that none of the travelers were to be allowed past midships, on pain of a double watch for all.

A half-month after the storm, we were in another gale - nothing like the one that had driven us across the domain of Neptune, but still a blow to cause concern. We had taken a course to the north of west, to intercept the land as soon as possible. As the master explained, there was some possibility of us being too far south to encounter the Latium continent and might sail west for hundreds of leagues before realizing it. It was in the half light of the scudding clouds that the other ship was first seen. I heard the call from the forepeak, as the hand shouted the discovery, and I climbed the ladder to the deck.

The Captain was looking across the waters at what was only a black spot to myself. Finally, I asked, "A unit from a Greek city, maybe?"

He shook his head. "Nay, it is not a galley nor is it likely to be a rowed ship this far out to sea." A pause, then, "A ship with oars swallows food and water like a house full of unwanted relatives. They would be dry and empty long before the reaches could be crossed. Like, it is a merchant as ourselves, beating back to the wanted course."

The ship seemly not closing on us, the sight became without interest in a while, and I retired to be out of the wind and blowing fretment of rain. Night fell, and sleep came. By now, all on board were with hardened bellies to the heaving of the ship and did not interrupt my rest with sounds of moaning and regret of life.

My waking was not from the belly heaves of passengers. Morning it was - I could tell that from the slivers of light that barely showed between the deck boards, but the passengers and time of day were not my concern - it was the grinding noise that pounded the hull that took my attention and all in the hold. Without doubt, we had been cast upon the rocks of some shore and in this gale were probably doomed to a watery death in mere heartbeats.

Now the shouts and cries of the merchants began to cover the noise of the hull which was diminishing as I listened. Even in my agitated purpose, I wondered at the lack of water that should be flooding the ship through broken planks, but from my vantage, the hull was still intact. Before my comfort that we might not be doomed could grow farther it was broken by a bellow from above - a sheik that seemed to come from the gates of Hades. Instantly, the chatter in the hull was stopped, as the passengers listened, wide-eyed, to pounding from the deck - obviously, men running in haste from here to there - interspersed with unintelligible curses and cries of either rage or pain.

I donned my sandals and threw my cloak over my shoulders and stood at the bottom of the ladder, in preparation of climbing and throwing open the hatch to discover our plight. My effort was not needed - the hatch was suddenly thrown back with a force that must have tested its leather hinges. An unfamiliar and bearded face looked down the opening at me. His shout to another on deck was in Greek, which I could now understand, but not enough to place his origin on that in that vast land.

However, the menace of the wicked blade that he was holding in one hand needed no translation. With a sinking heart, I realized that we had been boarded by pirates that infested the waters between those lands and those of Latium. The bearded face yelled a command that I interpreted as an order for the passengers to climb to the deck.

Above, the rain had stopped, and the wind moderated somewhat, but that is not what took my attention - indeed, the elements were not even noticed. Rather, the bodies of the crew of my ship were sprawled on the deck, and not in repose. Some were missing whole arms and one even his head. The captain I did not see, but the Mate was poised, lifeless against the railing, his entrails spilling out between his knees. Even as we watched, the corpses were being dragged and tipped over the side into the water.

The passengers and myself were pushed and shoved, with innumerable curses into a line against the low railing, then knives slashed and our garments were laying at our feet. An individual, wearing only a loincloth but who was undeniably the captain of the reavers, walked down the line of shaking passengers, looking each one up and down, then barking an order to the man following him. His face was scarred - indeed, his whole body gave evidence to the life that he had probably lived since his pouchstones had dropped. The white of scars and disfigurements covering his skin were almost innumerable and many intersected another.

The first man-passenger was examined, an oldster barely able to stand in the swaying of the ship and the fear that was engendered by the evil face of the pirate. A sharp word and a spear were thrust into the chest. As he fell backward, another reaver stooped in front of the screaming man and tipped him over the rail by his ankles. The same fate met the second man and the third. Indeed, of the eleven men-passengers, only three were spared the spear. Obviously, these reavers had no use for graybeards as slaves - we three were the youngest of the lot. Indeed, I was the only one that was well on the low side of middle age.

The only woman, not a beauty and of her middle years, was spared the spear for the moment but dragged to the after part of the ship for the enjoyment of the pirates. Her screams finally died away as her strength waned during the long morning. For whatever reason, the other two men were herded back into the hold, but I was shoved over the side into the smaller ship.

Dregs

The journey to the pirate camp in some unknown place along the coast of the Greek archipelago is not a voyage of which I remember with pleasure. The captain of the pirates had assumed command of the captured merchant and the mate took over the running of the reaver ship. The second of the pirates was a huge man, not old and not young, but of an evil disposition and took pleasure in causing pain and hurt to another. Even his men took care to avoid his wrath, but to myself, he was as the rod of Hades, itself. I was used for every task on the ship, from interminable bailing of the bilge with a pail to emptying the pisspots and waste containers upon command. In addition, I was summoned at all hours to pull this rope and that as the sail was trimmed or moved at the command of the steersman. All of the tasks were accompanied by the lash of a rope across my naked body, and in many cases for the pleasure of the wielder, rather than any need to encourage my toil.

The acting captain of my vessel was cruelty distilled. Called Ypoploíarchos by the crew, I assumed that was his name until I eventually learned that the word is Greek for the first mate of a ship. Many times, I would suddenly feel the bite of his lash across my back, then look around to see him grinning with his evil face. The stroke was not for any reason of stimulus, but only for his lust of causing pain in another. Even the crew, I noticed, stood well clear of him unless their duties took them close.

Days went by. On occasion, when emptying a pail over the side, I could see the captured merchant ship on the horizon, following us to some destination unknown to myself. That we were on a course to the north was all that I could determine, and that from the rising and setting of the sun, but as I had no idea of our starting point, the end of the voyage was beyond my calculation. In the first days, I would have gladly lain down to perish, my body in pain and not only from the lashes but from the work that was beyond anything to which I was accustomed - indeed, beyond that of which I could have imagined that a man could survive. My life as a scribe had done little to strengthen my sinews, and back in the streets of Rome, I would find myself gasping for breath just from a hurried walk to this place from that.

Since then, my life of sitting at ease on the deck of a ship, watching the water and days go by did nothing to enhance the worthiness of my body. Now, on the third day, I had reached the nadir of my despair, in which I was contemplating throwing myself over the side of the ship, to rest finally in the depths of Neptune's realm. But the next day was no worse, and the following began to find my strength growing again, and my limbs tired during my sleep time, but not still quivering with pain. By the end of the passage of the whole moon cycle, I was able to work the day without falling to my knees, there to receive lashes until I rose again. The pain of the lash was still sharp, but my body was lean, with the folds of fat at my belly having changed into firm ridges of skin-waves. I could even contemplate my surroundings as I followed my tasks by rote.

The ship had four in the crew, not old, not young, but men in the prime of life. Their numbers seemed far too few for a roving band of raiders until I remembered that at least half or more would be on the captured merchant. All were born to a life of banditry with little knowledge of more than the sea over which they had spent their lives, and the use of weapons to take what they did not own. The mate, and by reasoning, the captain in the other ship, must have had some knowledge of the art of finding one's way over the trackless waves, but I saw no indication of such.

A day dawned, with the shoreline close and the men all in a mood of waiting. Before the midday sun, we were standing into an indention of the land - a cove, I heard it called - and other men appeared on the shoreline, all seemingly waving to their long departed friends. Shortly, we were grounded on the sands, the men folding the sail then leaping overboard to run up the sand into raucous greetings of their mates.

The celebrations did not include me. I stood for a while, until another man approached the side of the ship. He was a huge, almost naked - or so it appeared - man of indeterminate age. The normal sized loincloth gave the impression of being just a woman's wrap around his body. Like the captain, this man had seen much strife in his years - the white scars gave hints of adversaries from his past. In a few heartbeats, two other men - slaves, from their ragged loincloths - hurried up with a ladder that was placed against the hull, after which the man climbed on board. The merchant ship had grounded not far from ours, and from it, the other two unfortunates from my voyage were called to stand in front of the man - like myself, they were as bare of clothes as the day they had dropped from their dam.

The man just stared at us for several heartbeats, and not with any expression that he was gratified by what he saw. Then he spoke. "I am Herakleides. You will call me Kurios if you speak to me at all, and if I wish to hear your lips flap, I will ask. I am the overseer of the slaves on Sifnos. You will notice that I do not carry a whip. I am a slave just as yourselves, and I have earned my position on this island.

Should you decide to cause me vexation of any kind or to act in a way to threaten that position, I will not need leather to make you wish that your miter had never spread her legs for your patera."

I now had a moderate command of the Greek language, if not sufficient to point to a man's antecedents, but the huge brute sounded as if he had received a modicum of schooling. Certainly, his sentences were not just curses separated by the occasional common word, as had been usual on the ship. However, the interesting part of his speaking was not his diction, but the information that we were on an island.

"You are slaves, and as slaves you will work until you are sold. If you perform to my satisfaction, you will not find me a bad master, but if any of you buckos test me in any way, you will wish for the mercy of Hades. Now, pick up that cargo and follow your fellows." The other slaves, three in number and all young, or at least not having reached thirty seasons, had shouldered a load each and had started up the hill in a single file. The three of us newly come picked up a box, or barrel, and stepped in line behind them.

At the top, among rocks that even the giants could not have moved, was the encampment. There were many huts and several longhouses, one of which was ringing with the shouts and jestings of men newly come from a long voyage. Across the small and flat hilltop was an area of crude shelters - the places of storage for such supplies as we were hauling. Back and forth we went, the sun almost on the surface of the sea when the two ships were empty. It was then that I was introduced to my new domicile.

The hut was fairly large but crudely built, like the storage shelters. Inside was... nothing. Just a dirt floor with some bundles of hay and rags of cloth for blankets. It was obvious which of the three belonged to the slaves before us. The several other sleeping spots had not been used in a while, and there were many more than just what would accommodate the three new men. Apparently, the count of slaves rose and fell, depending on the luck of the pirates and the need of the slave factors of the cities.

Herakleides pointed. "Take a place for your own. On the morrow, you may get some fresh straw - if I feel you have earned it. At darkfall, you will be in this hut, and will not leave other than to visit the privy, there." He pointed to a side of the hut, beyond which I assumed would be a hole for our needs. "Should you be caught beyond those limits by a man of the island, you will probably not live beyond the time they take to draw steel. Should I myself find you wandering away, then you will pray to your gods to allow your life to end even more quickly."

At that moment, yet another slave entered. He, I would learn, was the slave for the cocua, and slept in the cookhouse. He had an iron pot, a jug and three bowls, the latter of which he gave to the overseer, who immediately tossed them to myself. I handed one each to my two new comrades, and waited, assuming that we were to eat. By now, my belly was complaining mightily about its emptiness. The three men of the hut dipped their bowls, then Herakleides pointed to us, then to the pot. I filled my vessel with some kind of... bulligo, I guessed. Just a broth with various vegetables and a few small chunks of meat. As a meal during my life in Rome, I would have thrown it into the gutters in disgust, but after the voyage on the ship as a captive, and receiving a bit of soggy bread and a crumb of cheese for my daily sustenance, this was, at least, palatable.

Herakleides watched for a heartbeat, then said, "Remember this. Any fighting among you will earn a match with myself." With that, he left for the night.

We three from the merchant ship sat and gulped our meal, looking warily at our mates across the floor. I assumed the jug contained wine, but with no cups for its decanting, we would have to finish our stew before partaking of the drink. The meal was in silence as we followed the example of our mates across the dirt floor. Finally, as the meal was finished, and the dregs of the pot dipped out by one of the others, a man rose and took the jug, pouring his bowl full of liquid. He did the same with his two comrades, then turned to hand the jug to myself, with no more conversation than a short "Uhhh."

I was surprised at the weight. There was far more than six portions in the jug. I poured my bowl, then handed it to my nearest mate. A taste gave the proof that it was indeed wine, but sour and watered - little more than the dregs of an amphora, bulked out with water. Still, my body needed liquid, and I managed to empty my bowl by trying to swallow without taste. Now, the other three filled their vessels again, but left them on the ground, apparently to prevent their new comrades from swilling the rest of the wine.

By now it was almost full darkfall. Suddenly, the tent flap was opened, and the kitchen slave entered again, picking up the iron pot and the wine jug and leaving without a sound. I realized, now, the reason for the refilling of the bowls with wine. We had lost our portion by leaving it in the jug and would have nothing else to drink until morning.

So far, not a word had passed in the hut. My assumption was that the three men had been conditioned to keep their thoughts to themselves, as I had learned on the voyage to this camp. Any speaking on my part without responding to a crew member would get me the lash instantly. Then again, maybe it was just the fact that three more strangers were now sharing their quarters that caused the silence.

No matter. My need for rest and sleep was far more than any need to examine my new fellows. On the bare straw, and with only the ragged cloth to cover me, I immediately fell to my rest.

The sun was just a hint of light over the horizon when Herakleides entered and rapped on a house post with a stick. With him was the cook slave, and with the same iron pot and jug as the night before. Quickly we rose and dipped our bowls in the mush that served to break our fast. Seeing the three men across the hut eating with speed, I quickly swallowed my portion, then washed it down with the diluted wine. As I had suspected, the time for our meal was short, catching my other two comrades with half full bowls. Herakleides had returned and threw a wad of cloth to the floor. Loincloths. Just long pieces of rags to cover our man parts. Still, it was better than nothing. Before the unfortunate encounter with the pirates, I had not realized the feeling of helplessness that being totally unclothed would give when around men who were garbed.

Quickly, he told off three men - two of my comrades from the ship and one of the other slaves. They hurried to the path leading to the cove, apparently to help with tasks on the two ships. Another was sent to the kitchen, and the other elsewhere. For myself, he ordered, "You will assist the quartermaster, Rahotep, with his tasks, whatever they might be. In that hut - there - you will find the quartermaster."

In front of the indicated structure, I stopped behind a man - thin of frame and dark of complexion. As he turned around, I saw that he was fairly old - too old to accompany the pirates on any voyage where the matching of metal might occur. But, the striking vision was that he was as shorn of facial hair as myself - indeed, even his head seemed to have been shaved. This was, without doubt, a man from the hot lands of Egypt. He was holding a wax tablet and muttering to himself in a tongue that I recognized as certainly being from that land far to the south, although I had no skill in the language. He looked at me and I said, "I was ordered to report to you, Kurios."

Looking me up and down for a moment, he pointed to the hut behind him, "Empty that hut of all that is inside! Stack it here!" He spoke passable Greek, but with a heavy accent that also confirmed his origins. Hurrying inside the crude structure, I began to haul boxes and sacks, barrels and bundles outside to be set in the dirt of the open. As it was fairly full, I spent most of the morning carrying my burdens the short distance, while the old man just walked around and made marks on his tablet. It was finally emptied by midday, and I was sent to the back of the cookhouse with my bowls, there to receive the meal - again, nothing that I could recognize, but hot and filling for all that. At least, the slaves on the island were not starved of rations.

The afternoon brought the same work, except that I now began to fill the empty hut with the stacks of items on the ground, but only after the old man made the mark on his tablet and pointed for the item to be stored. Some of the cargo I was now carrying into the hut was from the merchant ship, taken in the piracy.

Many times, in the Temple of Jupiter, I had heard the old adage about a boulder being deflected from its course by a pebble, or a trivial decision that leads a man to take one road at a fork, rather than the other, changing his life forever. Such a deflection of my life happened that day, merely because of a marking in chalk, on the side of a barrel. The writing was in Latium script. The quartermaster was standing before the container, moving his finger along the markings and muttering, "Pig...men...tee...em. Pigmen..."

Without thinking, I blurted out, "Pigmentium rutlius." Suddenly aghast at my speaking without askance, I stammered out, "Red dye, Kurios." He straightened and looked at me, then just nodded, and made a mark on his tablet. Waving at the container, then to the hut, I picked it up and stored it. My legs were weak from the realization of what I had risked by speaking. Has he been one of the other pirates on the island, I would, even now, probably be writhing on the ground under the lash.

Finally, the hut was inventoried, and filled, and I was dismissed to return to my hut, with even part of the day left. But before I had made more than a few steps, the old man called, "You. Stop a moment." I turned and waited. He walked up to me and asked, "What is your name?"

"Junius, Sos. I mean, Kurios."

"You are from Latium, it seems."

"Aye, Kurios. Rome."

"And you can construe the Latium script."

"Aye, Kurios. I was trained as a scribe in the Temple of Jupiter."

His eyes opened wider. This was apparently a surprise that a common slave from a ship was educated in the written language. "Can you also read Greek?"

I shook my head. "Aye, So... Kurios. At least to a good extent. I would not be mistaken for one from those lands, but I am in understanding of the language."

"Do your many skills include fluency in the picture language of Aegyptos?"

I shook my head. "Nay, Kurios. But I would learn, if needed."

He thought for a moment then waved me away. "Go to your quarters." I turned and hurried away, wondering what I had initiated this day.

While waiting for the others to return from their labors, and for the meal to be brought, or orders to procure it from the kitchen, I found out why our hut-mates seemed not to wish to speak to we newcomers. As the man stood beside me, also waiting, I asked him for his name and land, giving mine in the same sentence. I got an answer, I think, but it was in a tongue that did not allow me to even discern the individual words, much less the meaning. I had heard the language of Egypt a few times in my life at the temple, but this did not resemble that at all, and the man did not have the dark skin of one from the sun countries. This one could have been from the eastern lands of the great sea, maybe the far and mysterious Babylon, or even the Achaemenid empire. Or, maybe just a barbarian from the far northern climes - his light skin seemed to give a hint of that direction. In any case, only pointing and grunting would do for communications between the man and myself, and, I assumed, his fellows.

As fate called the throw of the bones, I had no chance to figure out the mystery. On the morrow, Herakleides pointed to me and said, "Report to Rahotep after you break your fast." Apparently, the quartermaster saw value in a person... a slave that could construe Latium script. The gods were apparently tossing a crumb of mercy in my direction. Maybe my time of punishment for my sins with the young woman was being shriven. From that day forward, I was under the bidding of the old Egyptian, helping with his duties as the factor of the loot brought in by the pirates. In a double moon or so, as my competency in the written Greek script was proven, I would make the marks on the tablets as the old man examined and weighed and measured the stacks and piles that waxed and waned between voyages.

My quarters and meals did not improve at first - I was now bedding down in one of the huts used for the cargo and still sleeping on straw and eating the same slops, but during the day I was freed from the heavy labor given to my previous hut-mates. Ofttimes they would take the small skiff out of the cove with one of the old gray-haired crew, and trawl their nets for fish. Then, after a successful catch, return not to rest, but to begin flaying the fish they had caught and smoking them over fires. Worse than that were the many voyages to some remote shore to cut firewood, then hauling and stacking it on board to be carried back to the island of Sifnos.

Sometimes, after a day of paying the boiling pitch and caulk into the seams of the ship, or hauling rocks to buttress the wharf, or suchlike, they would arrive at darkfall and collapse onto their straw, the evening meal sitting uneaten in the pot. The next day, on blistered feet and with like hands, they would trudge back to their labors, each just trying to survive another day.

My life, by comparison to my mates, was as the pampered siren of the King's seraglio. Rahotep was unconcerned that I was a slave - indeed, he seemed satisfied to have a man of learning to converse with, rather than his comrades among the pirates, who were fluent only in the curses about the gods - or so it seemed. Many were the stories that he mentioned of his youth, and at times, asked me of my younger life. To spend the idle time when there was nothing to be accounted, or weighed, or carried, I would puzzle out the picture writing of his land, using the many tablets that were marked in that language. For my learning, it made no difference if they were a description of a cargo, or a counting of the weights of green hides. He would correct myself while giving my hand the correct mark, then usually fall back into some musing from his past. Many times, I could believe that I was in a temple learning room, and he was the priest giving the lessons and corrections - until I heard one of the pirates bellow from across the island.

I had soon puzzled out the Egyptian system of numbering. The Greek system I was familiar with - indeed, I considered it to be superior to what I had learned in the temple, it being only necessary to add the figure amounts to arrive at a total. With the Roman method and the concept that a mark could have different values depending on the letters on either side, it was fairly easy to misconstrue a value and arrive at an incorrect result. With the Greek and Egyptian numbers, the order made no difference - one only had to add the values to arrive at the total.

Many were the weights and containers did I move and stack, giving even more condition to my sinews, but in the main, I bedded down each day with unstrained limbs and an unmarked back. Now, I almost never crossed paths with the reavers, as they seldom traveled to the side of the compound where the supplies were stored. In this, I made no complaints, as it was now possible for myself to pass whole months without feeling the lash on my back.

The seasons waxed and waned. The island would be teaming with the reavers for a while, then almost deserted as they departed on another raid. All that would remain, besides Rahotep and myself and any slaves that might be in holding at the time, were two or three of the older men, having far too many seasons behind themselves to match metal with a fleeing and desperate merchant. The ship of my voyage was apparently thought to be superior to the much smaller vessel that captured it. It became the ship of the pirates, the other apparently being vended away along with much of the captured loot on the island. In addition, one afternoon, my five hut-mates did not appear, and on the next day, I was informed by Rahotep that they were on their voyage to the slave markets of Athens. Even the slavemaster, Herakleides, was never seen again, due to some malfeasance on his part, according to my Egyptian master.

One consequence of my having somewhat more freedom of the island, moving here and there at the bidding of the old quartermaster, was that I discovered that the remote compound had a complement of women. Young women. They were the playthings of the pirates, and as such were slaves, but I had no idea of their origin. Desirable young females were not usually to be found on traveling merchant ships to be taken as booty, so I assumed that these were either stolen in the port cities or bought from one of the many slave factors to be found wherever sailors put into dock. Of course, none was available for my use, and in fact, I seldom even laid eyes on one close enough to see her likeness. No, my forays into the sexual act were strictly with my hand and memories.

A day arrived when the ship had returned - not from a roving voyage, but after traveling to a port city to vend the booty captured in the last months. As usual, the coin chest was taken to Rahotep to enumerate and mark in his tablet of accounting. After the count had been made, I hauled the chest to the hut that was - in jest - called the strongroom. As a vault for coin, it was a travesty, being just another hut with a straw roof, and not secured in any way. The reason for the unconcern for thieves was obvious. On an island, and one far enough from another land that the sea stretched unbroken to the horizon on all sides, there was no danger to the coin, even from a traitorous comrade, should he come to an idea to depart in the night with the spoils. The pirates could take their share when wanted, by asking Rahotep for the dispersal, but seldom did, other than minor coin used in their constant games of bones.

The next morning, I rose and walked to the back of the cookhouse to have my bowl filled with the mornings mush, or ragout - whatever would be made for the morning meal - and my cup filled with wine. One change that came with my assistance to Rahotep, was that the cook seldom bothered with walking to find the watered drink for the slaves, and just filled my cup from the pirate jugs. Maybe he was acting on the orders of my master. I had no way of knowing.

As nothing had been brought to the island for at least a month, I knew that we would have no chores of accounting and enumerating this day. I would probably just sit in the shade with a wax tablet and practice my scripting of Greek or Egyptian, as there was little else for myself to be occupied with. Or read a scroll that Rahotep graciously allowed me to unroll. Over time, I learned something of his past - mostly from casual comments and musings by the old man. Like myself, he had departed his city between darkfall and daylight, but not for the reason of a woman. Apparently, there was some discrepancy in the accounts of the trading establishment for which he was the head scribe. Again, like myself, he decided that a berth on a ship leaving immediately would be more comfortable than his mat in his city. Time passed, and he became acquainted with the pirates, although I had not yet received that story.

It had been two years since I had come to the island. Now, more and more, Rahotep would just sit in the sun watching me count and stack and move, resting on his Roman style lounge under a canopy and out of the wind. His arms and legs had been aching as of late, and his appetite failing with some malady that he attributed to the constant winds across the top of the island.

I sat with a scroll of some bard laid across the makeshift table - an unlikely tale of battle written long in the past, and vowed to be truth, in which the gods themselves appeared on the field and threw bolts of lighting and thunder at the enemy. With nothing to do, I was as contented as a slave could be, sitting out of sight and mind of the reavers of the island, and...

Suddenly, I realized that I had been reading for a considerable time - long past the time for the quartermaster to appear, either to order or relax in his lounge. Standing, I was at a loss as what to do. I certainly did not want to stroll into the area of the reavers sleep huts, to peer into each trying to find my master. The Ypoploíarchos was not impressed with my elevation to assistant of Rahotep, and would use his whip as if we were on the boat again, should my back - or any of those belonging to a male slave - come within range. I did not wish to be found by him while walking in the forbidden areas. It was best that I remained out of sight, but with a view of the main compound, so as to rise and appear to be doing work, should any come to my area.

I had not long to wait. In a short while, I could see a crowd standing at the longhouse that constituted the quarters of the captain.

Then, a long litter with... a man. It was now obvious that the old Egyptian had succumbed to his ailments during the night. I watched over the bundles of the hut, wondering what this would mean for my future. I had not long to wait.

Suddenly, I could see a man stride toward my area, and I immediately ducked and entered the hut, pulling several bundles of furs to the floor, and grabbing my wax tablet and stylus. With my back to the door, I counted aloud, this fur and that, giving my idea of the goodness of each, then making a useless mark in the wax. I sensed the person in the doorway, but kept my to my performance, waiting...

"You! Slave!"

I spun around as if surprised, looking at the crewman standing in the doorway. "Go to the hut of the Kapetanios, immediately!"

Dropping the tablet, I sprinted out the door and across the compound to the indicated structure. At the entrance, I stopped and said, "Aye, Kapetanios, at your command."

The captain was seated on a stool, apparently examining a small map. Waiting for his response, I looked around at the inside of the single room hut. Obviously, the leader was a man without need for impressment of his fellows with rich properties. Except that the small house was far sturdier than my hut, and with a floor of planks, it was almost as empty of anything besides the raised sleeping mat, a stool, and small table. On the wall were some weapons, obviously extra, since his usual blade was laid on the mat. Some pegs held a cloak and a spare tunic along with another pair of sandals.

Without preamble, he said, "Know you that Rahotep is dead?" My eyes widened in mock surprise, but before I could respond he continued. "He has reported your talent for numbering and scrolling." That last word was not used appropriately, but I knew his meaning. "Can you do his tasks without guidance?"

This gave me hope. Of what, I wasn't sure, but... "Aye, Kapetanios. I have been engaging in the accounting while he was in his malady. I can certainly continue his work of keeping the stores and numbering the worth."

He thought for a moment, then said, "Then you will take his place. Know that you are still a slave, but if your duties are satisfactory, then improvements may be made in your life."

I bowed and replied, "My thanks, Kapetanios. I will certainly fulfill the tasks at hand."

And indeed, it was true. I was still a slave and received my meals at the back of the cookhouse, but I was fed on the same fare as the crew, and drank the same unadulterated wine. The crew ignored me, although the Ypoploíarchos was still his evil self. His tongue never failed to strike in my direction should he see me but, at least, his whip was becoming a stranger to my back.

I might have lived the life of a pirate on the island, using my skills to merge gradually with the crew as a member. I was sure that my worth would gain me a spot eventually. But an act by the mate - a despicable, cowardly stroke by the Ypoploíarchos turned me against all on the island - indeed into a man dedicated to revenge and nothing else, should it even take my life.

Vindicta

I had made two voyages on the big merchant ship - not raiding journeys but trips to the ports of Prasaie or Ismthmia for trading the spoils of their plundering. I bargained with the traders on the docks, both as vending the cargo for coin, and purchasing supplies for the island. At the first knowledge that I would actually touch on land beyond the island, my hopes were high that I might just disappear into the crowds of the wharves and end my slavery. But it was not to be. When a port hove into sight, a large and heavy iron collar was bolted around my neck, and with only a loincloth as my garb, it was obvious to any that I was a slave, not to be seen on the streets of any Greek city without escort. Had I run, my freedom would have lasted only until seen by the first of the many magistrates of the city. Besides, running was not a choice - at all times, at least, two of the crewmen escorted myself to and from the ship.

But, as soon as the port disappeared over the horizon, the collar was removed and not seen until the next harboring. I swallowed my disappointment and went about my duties, gladsome that my life was considerably more improved since the death of old Rahotep.

Upon return to the island, I would monitor the placing of the supplies in the appropriate huts, then log them into the tablets for accounting. As there had been no more slaves brought to the island since the death of the old man, the crew themselves had to haul the barrels and boxes from the ship to the storage area, accompanied by much grumbling - at least, when neither the pirate officers were in hearing. Still, I did my work well and seemed to make myself satisfactory in the eyes of the captain.

I was sure of it after the return from my second voyage. The next afternoon, as I was counting this and that, the Kapetanios strode up to myself with tidings that almost rendered myself speechless. "You, Scribe!" I bowed and waited. "I am not unsatisfied with your accounting and for your reward, tonight you may use one of the women until morning." Wide-eyed and unbelieving, I just bowed again as he walked off. The rest of the day went slowly, my thoughts on the use of a woman - the first in the two years and more that I had been on this island. And for the entire night. Needless to say, the sun slowed its progress until it seemed to have stopped its course in the sky.

Still, I maintained my work, counting this and making a list of that which might need to be procured on the next trip. I was squatting, trying to retie the rope on a barrel of grain flour, my back to the door when suddenly, all the demons of pain in Hades enveloped my body. I fell over to the dirt, writhing as my mind tried to understand what had happened. It was only a heartbeat before the center of the pain was known, radiating out from my pouchstones with an intensity that I had no idea that a body could sustain.

I do not know how long I groveled in the dirt, wanting to hold my injured man pouch, but unable to even touch it without almost falling into darkness from the feel of my fingers. The excruciating torment caused me to heave the contents of my belly onto the dirt, and again. In a while - I know not how long - I realized that a man was standing in the doorway, barely seen through my red haze of agony. Eventually, I realized that it was the Ypoploíarchos, grinning as he watched me writhe in the dirt.

As my thoughts began to assemble and my eyes regained their clarity, I could see the staff that the first mate was holding. Apparently, he had placed the end of the wood on the ground under my pouchstones, then viciously and with all his strength, raised it to impact on my man parts, But why? I couldn't speak to ask, even had I wanted. It made no matter, as he gave the reason for his assault.

"I heard the Kapetanios offer you a woman for the night. I was troubled that she might be wasted on a eunuch and took it upon myself to find the truth. And, in fact, you are a man of a kind, it appears." Still grinning, he gestured, and a woman was pushed into the hut. "Here is your bedwarmer for the night. Use her well." With that, he left, japing with another as they passed out of hearing.

Still in agony, I looked up at the woman, but without any interest in what I was seeing. In the now half light, I could not even see her features, but her beauty or lack thereof did not even enter my thoughts. I was still retching from the pain, and barely able to even breath, but I could see the female suddenly leave through the open doorway, in disgust at the man that she had been given to, I assumed.

I was wrong. In a short while, she had returned, with... something bulky. Then I saw that it was the mat from my sleeping hut, which she placed beside me on the dirt, but first pushing this bundle and that barrel out of the way. Arranging it to lay flat, she carefully helped me to roll onto the soft bedding - very slowly - and settled me onto my back. By now, the heavings had stopped, but not the nausea, which was slowly decreasing.

Carefully, she untied the knot of my loincloth, and - rolling me from side to side gently - completely removed it, rolling it into a ball and then placing it under my head and neck. Then, just as carefully, she lifted my knees and spread my legs to allow my throbbing man-pouch to hang freely and without restriction. I could not see them from my prone position and, truth be known, was almost afraid to look. My fear that my manhood was broken forever was as terrifying as the pain.

The woman left again, to return shortly with a jug and a bowl which she filled. Lifting my head, she tilted the bowl so that I could drink - nay, gulp down the liquid. That and another full bowl did I drink, which helped the throbbing in my lower parts to subside - or at least, conditioned my mind to the hurt. Finally, I shook my head as she offered more. By now it was full dark, and I still had no idea of her looks.

"What is your name?" I croaked.

She was motionless, just sitting on her knees and legs, waiting for... Not to be used, that was certain. But I was appreciative of her tenderness and care, wanting to know the name of my caregiver. "I be Alitiae."

"Alicia?"

"Alitiae. I be way from Craytos. Magnus gave that me will service counting-man this night." Her accent was thick, obviously not a Greek female and certainly not from Latium or Egypt. "Counting-man not able to use Alitiae this night." She looked out the doorway, then said quietly, "Id shill bastarte." I did not need to translate that. Just the hatred dripping from her words gave me notice that the cruelty of the Ypoploíarchos was not restricted to myself.

The wine was taking effect, and I just lay in the enveloping haze, then realized that the woman had lain down beside me. No matter, this night I would not be taking her, but it was the future that was causing terror in my being. It may be that I might never again...

I woke, alone - Alit... Aliea... the girl had already returned to her quarters, as per her orders. My the pain from my abused pouch was not gone - far from it - but the feeling was different. Instead of radiating all through my body, the hurt was now confined to the two stones, themselves. I hesitated for a moment, the rose on my elbows - very slowly - and looked at the damage that I had received. To my relief, both were apparently still intact, but the sight almost made my gorge rise again. My sac was twice - nay, thrice and more of its normal size, and colored an ugly purpureus shade. Again, I wondered at their usage ever again.

I carefully turned my body to my knees, then almost collapsed from the pain as my sac adjusted itself to the different position. I could rise to my feet, but slowly, making sure to keep my knees apart and apply no pressure to the injured organs. Slowly, one foot at a time, I walked to the door and looked out at the rising sun, deciding to not break my fast this morning. The many strides to the cookhouse and back were too much to contemplate, but I suddenly noticed the jug beside my mat. The girl had left it there. Now I wondered where she had procured the good wine - did she steal it for the benefit of an unknown man?

No matter. It was still half full, and I downed another bowl, giving me much satisfaction as the spirit entered my empty belly. Now, I wrapped my loincloth around my body and made for my own hut, slowly walking to not give any sway to my parts. There, I knew was a barrel with some dried bread and old cheese that would make my morning meal.

Midday brought some relief, and I slowly walked to the cookery for my meal.

There are times in a man's life when a single happening will change his future, and that happened this day and time. As I was returning with my bread and cheese and haunch of lamb, I heard a laughing voice behind me. "Yo, Slave. How was the night? Did you send the girl back to her mat with an aching muni? Is she ruined for our further use?" I turned, knowing that I would see the Ypoploíarchos standing and making jape. And he was. I just looked, but he turned and walked away with his fellow, myself already forgotten.

At that moment, the hatred of the depths of Hades entered my being. Had I been able, I would have walked to the weapons hut, procured a pugio to hide in my loincloth, then walked to the mate and plunged it into his heart, regardless of my fate thereafter. I swore to Jupiter - and to Mars, Apollo and any other gods that came to mind that I would have revenge on the man before I met my final fate. Indeed, from that day on, I had no interest in being accepted to their band, only in finding the way to my vengeance.

As a month went by my pouchstones receded to their normal size and color, and my hand tested their usage. To my great relief, both my manhood and the pleasure of the use was still in evidence. Outwardly, I made no change - indeed, I doubt that the greater part of the band of reavers even knew of what the Ypoploíarchos had done in his jest. But, inside, I was testing all paths into the future. This plan and that scheme was hatched and discarded as insufficient - in actuality, most were ludicrous. But still, as I lay waiting for sleep at night, my thoughts roamed over the future.

Of the four or five girls on the island at the moment, I still did not know which one gave me succor. I could see them from a distance, but had no way of telling one from another. And there was certainly no one of whom I could ask such a question.

Another trading voyage was made, and the girls sold and changed for more. Now, I would never have the opportunity to repay the girl who helped myself, as unlikely as the chance would have been. Then a day came when the ship returned from seafaring, but not with booty and slave girls. This one had blood running from the scuppers. From the snatches of conversation that I could overhear, the merchant that was chosen for looting was not as helpless as it appeared, giving as good as it received. From my count, it appeared that three of the pirates were missing with several more nursing wounds of this seriousness or that.

I stood outside of the longhouse with my evening meal, relaxing in the warm breeze, as the voices spoke of the aborted reaving and wafted through the woven reeds covering the window-openings. From the tales, it appeared that only the skill of the captain allowed the ship to disengage and return at all, and, as I heard, with even a serious blade wound to himself. It was interesting, if having nothing to do with myself, and I walked back to my hut in he gathering darkness. Then I stopped as though the Gorgon had appeared, thinking on a matter that had been brought forward by the ship's carpenter.

More thought as I lay on my mat. The ship had sprung a few minor planks in the grappling with the merchant. And would have to be recaulked. As I looked at the... opportunity from all directions...

Much later, with the half moon above, I rose and looked out the door of my hut and across the compound - there were none to be seen, as I would expect. At most, a crewman might step outside to make his water, but his eyes would still be full of sleep. Besides, none would come to this side of the island in the darkness of night. I moved to a storage hut and counted some barrels - called kegs in the Greek vernacular - in the dim light of the moon. There were five. I picked up one and carried it to a far hut - one that contained old hides and non-vendable supplies that had never been disposed of. There I set it in the far back of the hut, and in a while, its other mates were brought to rest beside it. Finally, I covered the containers with the hides and bundles of old reeds. Now, none of the barrels would be seen unless the ragged storehouse was almost emptied - something that the crew members themselves would not do without the direct order of the captain, and then only with grumbling. The hut and the useless contents would rot away before any on the island would make any inspection of the structure.

Two days went by before the expected query came to me. A crewman arrived to order me to the longhouse. There the captain was waiting - his arm and upper body wrapped in bloody cloth. Apparently, he was one of the more severely wounded crew in the fateful battle. Still, he was ambulatory and lucid as he required from me the amount of pitch that was available on the island.

"Aye, Kapetanios. That material was purchased before my time on the island. I will need to obtain the tablet with the count of that item." He nodded, and I ran back to my hut to obtain the required record. I knew exactly where it was in the voluminous stack of wax tablets, the more so since I had opened it two days before and made certain changes to an amount. Back at the longhouse, I gave the account. "We have none on the list, Kapetanios." I turned the tablet around to face the captain. "There were five at one time, but the marks show that all were taken for use."

The news was surprising. The Ypoploíarchos blurted out, "Taken? When and for what?" Turning to the older man who was the ship's carpenter, he demanded, "When did you use such an amount of the caulking fluid?"

The man spread his hands and shook his head. "Nay. I have a short keg on the dock that I tap on occasion, but we have not used any large amount since the careening of the old ship after that rock that holed us in the Necromillus straits."

The captain frowned and looked back at me. "And none have requested pitch from you? For any other use?"

Now I shook my head. "Nay, Kapetanios. In truth, I do not know what the material is, nor what it is used for." That was a total falsehood. In my youth, I had boiled pitch, thinned it, ladled the black liquid from the cureen, and dipped the cotton banting in it many times in the repair of the boat of my family. Or in the assistance to another fisherman, in return for a snippet of copper for the work.

The captain spoke to me, grimacing suddenly as a sharp pain suddenly reminded him of his last battle. "Inspect all the supply huts. They have to be misplaced somewhere." I nodded and bowed, and left to do the ordered inspection. Of course, I found nothing of the missing kegs.

A half moon later, we were on the ship, voyaging for the port of Prasaie. The number of men on board was diminished somewhat by the deaths of the men slain on the day of the aborted piracy, and another who had joined his ancestors a few days later. In addition, two others were still in their wounds and stayed behind on the island, along with the two older men. That left the ship somewhat shorthanded for a raid, but with sufficient hands for a stop in a port city.

We hove into the port city of Prasaie without incident, and I procured five small barrels of pitch from the port vender. With my two escorts standing outside, I turned to the merchant and said, "I would also purchase an empty barrel, but of good quality and of proof in the water." He just nodded and selected a small cask, the same size as the pitch barrels and wrapped with the same ropes that held the top cover tightly in place. I gave him the agreed coin, and the hired wharf slaves lifted the burdens and carried them back to the ship. More supplies were purchased and boarded before the nightfall. We would leave the next morning.

On the return voyage, I could think of nothing but my plan. If it went wrong, I would die in any one of many ways - some more horrible than others, especially if my scheme was stopped or suspected by the pirates. Over and over I went through the steps, knowing that many things could abort it at any time. A major storm would ruin my plans, as would massive rain. Or even the lack of hot food at the crucial moment. The days went by as we coasted along in the gentle breeze, none noticing my constant prayers to the gods for the calmness to remain. I had little to do, and spent much of it in the hold with the cargo, just to be away from the crew. This was nothing to bring attention as being unusual - a slave always attempted to remain out of sight of free men.

The captain was succumbing to his wounds. The red demons had entered his cuts and were causing the swelling and corruption that ofttimes followed any letting of blood. On the voyage out, he was active and moved around, apparently on the mend, but on the return, he suddenly fell to his mat with a weakness that would not let him rise. As he now moaned and thrashed on his mat, I wondered how long it would be before the mate put a blade in his heart - as much to gain the captaincy of the band as to relieve the suffering of a doomed man.

One task I set myself to on the return voyage was to make sure that the cover of the empty barrel was well tarred, and the ropes were tightly and firmly wrapped round the container. The purpose of the ropes was to strengthen the staves and hold the cover in place to prevent spillage, but in this case, it had another reason. I had little else to do, other than assisting the cook until we approached the island.

Again, apparently my past sins were somewhat atoned for, as the gods maintained the desired calmness of the wind and water. In fact, when the island was sighted, the wind was such as to give barely steerage way. At our distance and rate of travel, it would be morning on the morrow before we hove into the island. It would be a moonless night, and as darkness fell, I took bearings on the island and the stars before our destination was obscured by the night. After the evening meal, I filled the waterbag hanging from the mast, making sure that the plug was firmly inserted into the drinking horn, then cleaned up the fire pit in the stern cook cabin. Here the small cook-fire would be built on a large clay dish, filled with sand, with either a pot suspended over it or a spit with meat to be roasted. After the viands were pronounced done by the cook, and taken on deck to be eaten by the crew, I would toss the embers overboard and clean up the area before retiring back to my space in the hold.

But, on this night, I carried a small leather cup in the palm of my hand, unnoticed in the dark by a crew who was unconcerned by the movements of a mere slave. In the darkness of the hold, and by feel rather than sight, I poured the embers from the leather cup onto a clay dish, blowing on them occasionally to keep them alive. Now I waited. By now, I could tell that the wind had died to a complete calm. Even the usual waves in the water were muted. I wondered if the calmness was a jape of the gods, just waiting to laugh at the pitiful slave making his grandiose plans.

The night was long and quiet, with not even enough movement to make the rigging creak. I realized that my desire for a calm sea would require much carefulness about creating noise when I began my labors. I casually climbed the ladder to the deck, lifting the hatch cover and listening. There was still no sound, not even from the single man still awake - the steersman sitting by his useless tiller - barely a shadow at the far end of the ship. I walked to the railing to make my water, noticing that my guide had just risen from the horizon - Saturn, that star belonging to the Roman god of plantings and husbandry. It was time to decide on my course - either stay a slave or risk all to become a free man again. It was one thing, I began to realize, to make grandiose plans while laying in safety on one's sleeping mat - and entirely another to look out over the vast sea and contemplate what I was plotting to do. Indeed, my carefully laid designs now seemed almost ludicrous as I stared at the horizon far away.

It was at that moment that I heard the captain cry out in his delirious pain. That fixed my mind to action. When the captain passed to his ancestors, the hated Ypoploíarchos would become the new leader, and suddenly the idea of entering the realm of Hades became less than frightful. And, in reality, if the mate died, then I could accept my own death with some equanimity.

I took another look at the deck, seeing nothing else, then climbed back into the hold. I took the empty cask - the one I had purchased with the barrels of pitch - up the ladder and over to the railing. Then I walked to the mast, slowly so as not to be noticed by the steersman, and took down the hanging waterbag, pushing and twisting to make sure the stopper was firmly in the drinking horn. It was laid next to the cask. Now, with one more look around, I climbed back down the ladder.

Walking over to the clay dish - just a dim spark in the absolute blackness - I blew on it to cause the coals to revive. Now, I placed a small piece of old papyrus on the coal and blew again. Quickly, a small flame arose giving just enough light to make out my surroundings. The barrels of pitch I had carefully placed after we got underway, practicing the finding of them, at night, in the darkness. From behind a bundle of cloth, I took the small pugio that I had stolen from the weapons hut. It was pitted and rusted and without a handle on the tang but had a fine edge that I had honed with a rock. The dagger was far more than sufficient for my needs tonight.

Quickly, and by feel alone, I cut the ropes on all of the pitch casks, then pried the wooden covers from their sticky seal of black tar. The pitch was a partial liquid, used to caulk planks in a ship or boat by the use of flayed cloth, dipped in the black sludge and then pounded into cracks and seams in the wood with a hammer and wedge. It was a common material to be found anywhere that ships existed. Even on the Tiber, we used the same method to build and repair our river craft.

With the covers off, I picked up a barrel and carried it the length of the passageway between the stores. On this trip we were hauling light, so the hold was little more than a large empty room. Tipping the container, I poured the sticky liquid around me, trying to spread it as far as possible. The pitch was too thick to splash, but still, I could tell that in any light, even now, I would look like a black man from the reaches far to the south of the Great Sea. No matter. Now I was committed.

For the next while, I emptied the barrels all around the hold, leaving only a clear space around the ladder. By now, my heart was pounding in my chest, not helped at all by the choking miasma of smells from the black sludge. What I was about to do was no small thing, but... Putting a much larger piece of the writing material on the coals, I blew on it, to cause a flame that I enhanced by holding the tender in such a way as to allow the blaze to climb up the papyrus. It was at this time that my plan almost foundered on the shoals of my ignorance.

I well knew that pitch would burn with a bright yellow and smoky flame. Many times, when a boy on the Tiber, our pitch pot would catch fire as we warmed it over the flames to thin it in cold weather. But, it was just a matter of covering the pot with a flat board and the flames would die out. Sometimes, when the cover would be removed too quickly, a large ball of fire would erupt from the pot - just for a heartbeat - before the flame would recede to its normal intensity. Something like that happened now.

By the light of the flaming papyrus, I could see the results of my emptying the barrels. The black sludge was all over the boards of the hull and dripping from the few stacks of cargo. I assumed that, as in my youth, the flame would slowly spread along the black liquid, building up intensity over a while, and giving me time to escape up the ladder. Instead, as I approached the closest splatter of pitch on the deck, the entire hold lit up with a burst of light and a loud "whump" of sound. I found later, that the flame had stripped every hair from my naked body, even to the fine filaments of my eyelids. Had not the threads on my head been cut to their usual shortness, I would likely have become a living torch. Also, the cover to the hatch was blown open with a loud report as it flipped back on its hinges to impact on the deck.

Utterly stunned at the sudden inferno, I just stood for a heartbeat before realizing that I would be baked like a fish on the coals if I did not escape instantly. Turning, I rushed up the ladder and over to the railing. My plan of stealthy firing the ship and slipping into the water was now ash, and almost literally. Already the crew would be scrambling awake at the shouts of the steersman - the cry of fire is the most terrifying call of any that can be heard by a man of the sea. Now, I stooped to take the empty cask in one hand and the waterbag in the other and leapt over the rail.

With one hand in the rope of the cask, I put the strap of the waterbag over my head, and began a gentle stroke away from the ship. Even now, the flames were rising from the open hatch as if it were the over-stoked cookstove of a fisherman's woman. I was fire blind still, and all that could be seen by me were the flames and a few shadows moving across them in a run. I knew they were doomed. The blaze was beyond anything that I had planned, or hoped, and was far beyond any capability of the crew to extinguish. Already, the empty and flapping sail was ignited and for a few heartbeats made a gigantic tower of flame as it became a seaborne torch. The ship would burn to the waterline, leaving nothing but charred wood just above the waves.

I knew that it was unlikely that any of the crew could swim. Aye, as absurd as that seems to a landsman, it was a major factor in my plans from the beginning. Being from the river, where all young men learned the art of water work and movement - or they became food for the fish - I had always assumed that any man living could find his way through the water. After my escape from Rome and forced education on and about the great waters, I had learned that very few sailors of the salty domains can hold to themselves in the sea. As to why that would be true, I have no knowledge. The very concept is as a soldier who knows not the blade, or the fisherman who cannot tell catch from bait. But, the fact was to my advantage. The pirates on the ship would have a choice between fire and water - they would burn or drown. My hope was that the Ypoploíarchos himself burned.

As my eyes became less dazzled, I turned to find the light of Saturn, then adjusted my course to a double handspan southward. In the dark, now lit only by the burning ship, and the stars, the island of Sifnos was not visible. Holding the barrel to my chest with both hands, I kicked a slow movement backward, watching the fire recede both in intensity and distance. I wondered if any of the crew would save themselves with some floating beam, or spar. It was doubtful - with the fear of the water, any who found themselves buoyed by some fortunate floating item would probably thrash themselves into exhaustion, then sink into the depths. Even if they were to have the discipline, the salt water that found its way into their mouths would soon condemn them to an even greater punishment.

Exhaustion was foremost in my mind. I had long to go, and if the wind came up and from the wrong direction, then I too would be soon joining the crew as they rowed into the realm of Neptune. A slow, steady crawl was in order - anything more would just find me without strength to do anything but hold on to the ropes of the barrel. Fortunately, I had the waterbag to rinse the salt from my mouth and give me liquid during my voyage on the barrel.

As I predicted, the ship burned to the waterline and long before daylight, had disappeared from my sight. In my hatred of the Ypoploíarchos, I had killed many other men. But...

I put the idea from my mind and just let myself be carried along by the slow kicking of my feet. At the first light of the new day, I turned on occasion to see if my destination was in view. And, with the brightness of the early dawn, I was relieved to see the island across the waters. It would still be many hours before I would arrive on its shores but at least, it was there. There were still four pirates left in the camp who would have many questions about a slave who arrived without the ship, so it was in my interest to arrive on a deserted shore of the island. The men could easily have seen the fire on the horizon, should any of them have woken to make water and glance in that direction, although it was doubtful that they would fear that it was their own vessel.

The wind came up somewhat, but it was mostly in my favor and by late afternoon, my feet touched the sand of the beach on the far side of the cove. Standing up, or trying to, I realized that I was far gone in exhaustion - my legs, in particular, gave way immediately, and I fell to my hands on the sands. No matter - I had survived, and if I made no ill-timed moves, my life would be my own. I drank the last of the water, then crawled into the brush to rest. In mere heartbeats, I was asleep.

I woke in the darkness, listening to nothing but the low waves on the shore. I stood up and looked around at the dark sky, trying to determine the time of the night. Seeing the group of stars known as the Swan, I realized that it was about the second watch of the night - the mid of night. This was in my favor - the few men would surely be in their sleeping mats. I stepped off toward the camp, then almost fell to my face again. My legs had regained their strength, but the soreness of the misuse was extreme. It was a stiff legged man who quietly slipped into camp.

My first destination was the hut of the captain, in which I had been ordered a few times to receive commands. Inside, it was total darkness, but I slowly slid my feet across the floor to the far wall. Feeling around, I could not find what I was seeking - the spare blade of the Kapetanios. I had no instruction in the use of the sword, and in all probability, little skill, but I could swing one as swiftly as the next man. Still, with no use of sight at all, I could not lay hands on the weapon. It had been long since my entrance into the hut of the captain, and he had no doubt disposed of it or moved it to another place. Finally, as I was about to abandon my search, my hands touched a long object and heavy, hopefully, what I was seeking or another like it. I also grabbed an armful of cloth hanging from the wall. With any luck at all, a tunic would be in the bundle, although in the dark I could not tell if the cloth was work rags or decent garments.

My next destination was my hut, where I picked up the bag that I had stored in accordance with my plan. From there, I went to the smokehouse and filled the bag with an entire ham and a haunch of goat meat. Then from the kitchen itself, a square of cheese and some other staples. My waterbag, I refilled at the large barrel, also taking along the other two that hung at the door of the longhouse. Now I made my way to the cove and stashed my stolen items in the only craft moored there - the little skiff that was used for fishing.

Finally, there was one more item that I needed to procure. In the treasure hut was a wooden box containing only the best coppers and small Greek coins of silver. In the guise of accounting, I myself had sorted through the stolen treasure and ill-gotten gains from the vending of the pirated merchandise, weeding out the shaved rounds, the plated slugs, and the debased metals. I could not steal all of the pirate's metal - there was far too much by weight, and most was just low-value bronzes, but the contents of this box would, at least, allow myself to eat, should I actually escape. There had been no gold and large silver, those coins being handed out to the men as soon as taken. Carefully, trying not to allow the coins to clink together, I filled a leather pouch with the contents of the box.

Thus far, I had not heard a sound from the sleeping men. Now the box was empty and shortly the bag of coins was sitting beside the food and water. For the last time, I cast off from the rock wharf, pushing myself from the cove with the paddle. Outside, on the open sea, I raised the small sail and pointed the craft to the north. I was finally free of the slavery of Sifnos.

Salvus (Saved)

My first order of business, after standing into the unnamed port was to procure a decent garment and to cast off the old tunic of the Kapetanios, stolen from his hut. On the direction of the port magistrate, I found a clothing shop serving the merchant trade and shortly was sporting a new and clean tunic. Actually, I am using the Roman word for the garb. The Greeks called it a chiton, but with either word, the piece of clothing was the same, in both form and use.

I had found that the city was called Lavrion and that it was only somewhat over a hundred stadia from Athens, itself. In Greek measurement, it was about four leagues in distance. I was in no hurry, this being my first foray as a free man in almost three years. I wanted a soft and clean bed, a good meal and a woman, and I set about to procure the three.

With the worth of the bag of coin from the pirate island, I could not stop at the port city for years, but by carefully hoarding my coins and not engaging any but a small cubical on the docks for my inn, I could, at least, eat well enough for a considerable time. At any rate, there was no reason to tarry in a small port with no need for my scribing skill.

I now knew life was fragile, and could be changed in course by any wind of fate. And that it could be very short if one had a misstep. I would move on with my plan of entering the city of Athens, there to establish my new life and fortune. At least, that was the plan I envisioned since I had made landfall three days before.

Fleeing from the island, with my course having been purposely directed northward, the small boat was inevitably bound to intersect land. And it did on the sixth day. Once again, the gods were overseeing my fate, as any storm of size would have swamped the small craft without effort. I had a good wind, both day and night and only passed under a cloud of rain once, which allowed me to refill my waterbags.

On the first morning, as the light came, I found that I had indeed stolen a pair of tunics, but of such ill use as to make myself look as a seaborne beggar. Still, either were more than a simple loincloth, and the change could be made when I stopped in a city, somewhere. The scabbard that I had taken held a blade that was neither a sword nor a dagger, but a long knife, tapering to a wicked point. In that, little difference was made, since I could not use any weapon as a method of defense, other than just swinging wildly at my foe.

The land that I had touched was almost sheer cliffs and rocks, with no sign of habitation on or around the upper plateau. Remembering the maps from the past, I had turned east to follow the coast, spending the nights on the shore when I could find a gentle sand beach on which to heave the boat. On the third day, I had seen a pair of watercraft - obviously fishermen - and knew that I must be approaching a port of some measure. And indeed, around the next promontory was the city in which I now found myself.

I came ashore at the city wharf, with the magistrate looking askance at a man in a ragged tunic, and a cockleshell boat tying up to his dock. Still, he answered my questions civilly and shortly I was striding into the city. After my purchase of the tunic, and the engagement of the tiny cubicle to sleep the night, I searched for a kiosk or taverna for a meal. Finally, back at the dock, I found a factor to which to vend my little boat and gained a few more coins in my purse.

Then, in the afternoon, I counted my coin and determined that at least once I could satisfy my desire for a woman - the last being more than three years before. Interestingly enough, the brothels had comely wenches in quantity, but few men using the service. I would not find the reason until later, but for now, I was soon engaged with a handsome young girl. Indeed, I spent the rest of the day making the determination that the rod of the bastard Ypoploíarchos had caused no lasting damage to my man parts as pertains to the use of a woman. I left only because the day was growing short, and I did not wish to walk the streets of a strange city in the dark. Indeed, I could detect a restlessness among the citizens, many of who looked at my cleanly shaven face and missing hair - burned off in the fire - with askance. Still, it was a port city, and like all, filled with men from every corner of the great sea. I, certainly, was not the only man from far lands walking the streets.

For two days, I just lived aimlessly, glorying in my freedom after the almost three years of slavery on that accursed island. For now, the plentiful - if plain and common - wine and food satisfied my needs as I gave thought to my future.

Across the way from the brothel, was a taburna - taverna in the Greek vernacular - for dock workers. It was not a higher class establishment for the members of the mercantile sector, but it neither was it a filthy hovel that served sour wine to the slaves and working masses. They even served a bitter liquid, called cervisia - made from fermented grain I was told - for the pleasure of the many Egyptian sailors that hove into the port on a regular basis.

This day, I was sated of walking aimlessly and had seen all that there was to view in the small city. Unlike Rome, there was no forum, with stages for acting and farces, or platforms for the sophistic discussion. There was not even a Crier to give the news and orders from the Magistrates. No librarium existed, where one might sit and read scrolls and tablets of the sages and tales of the land. As to what the citizens of the port did for leisure, I had no idea.

That there must be leisure among the well-to-do and the nobility, I had no doubt. Unlike Rome, the population of slaves must have almost equaled the count of the citizens. They were in evidence everywhere, even in houses and merchantries that one would have thought unable to feed even themselves, far less to purchase a bondman. All of those bound servants must have been doing the daily work, leaving the owners free for other activities.

I shrugged off the self-query. Far more important to myself was the need for a determination of my future. However, like my time as a temple scribe, then an accountant, and finally a slave of pirates, my future came to me without my effort. And in the guise of a tumult at the next table.

"Enough! You will have my customers believing that I collect the wrapped and deceased bodies of the hot lands to the south. Certainly, you have held down the stool with the ability of a dead man."

The woman - obviously the wife of the taverna owner - was apparently having issues with the patron who had settled at the table next to mine. Indeed, he had been there since my arrival - two of my own cups in length of time, at least. I certainly would not have the woman aim her ire in my direction. I was now a large man with his full growth, but she would have made two of me. Her girth barely allowed passage between tables and I wondered at the strength of her back, to hold up a pair of mammaries, each of which almost exceeded the size of the barrel that had floated me back to the island of the pirates. The sudden thought of her in the water with her own casks to keep her afloat made me grin, but the expression was misconstrued by the man at the table.

"You take pleasure in the discomfort of others, Roman." It wasn't a question. "I too was once in coin and welcomed wherever I went. Know that you also, may find your needs more than your purse, in time."

I immediately dropped the smile from my face and replied, "Nay, good Sos... Kurios. I was not making jest of your discomfort, merely thinking on a happening in my past." I looked up at the serving woman. "Bring a bowl of whatever this good man desires, and another cup for myself." I dropped another thin coin on the wooden table. Now, her mood lightened, she turned to retrieve my requests.

To the man, I said, "My name is Junius. Please... Sit at my table. I am new in the city and have no one to fill my questions." An offer of spirits, in any land, was usually enough to start a trust and, this time, was no different. The man rose and sat on the opposite stool as I asked, "Might I inquire of your name, Kurios."

Gruffly, and looking over his shoulder at the serving woman, he replied, "Korax, I am, late of the Artemis Third Hekatontarchia in which I was a full Dimoirites."

He might as well have spoken in the language of the Gaulian barbarians as to my comprehension of his statement. I assumed that he had been a soldier of significant rank and in some Greek army sometime in the past. But, at least, I knew his name.

"How did you know that I was from Rome?"

He waited until the huge woman filled his bowl, then took a swallow before replying. "It would be a blind man not to know that you are either from Rome or Aegyptus." Another swallow. "Only in those regions do men shave the hair from their bodies. But, the men of the hot lands are thin and small and dark, and you are none of those. And as another indication, you are armed with a Roman longknife. It was no sage thought on my part to determine your antecedents."

I looked down at the scabbard at my belt, then back to the man. "Why do you call this a blade of Rome?"

Looking at me in askance, he finally replied. "The length is far too short for a Greek sword and it is not curved, therefore it is not from the eastern lands. Thusly, it has to be a blade that your people call a 'breve gladius.'" He emptied the bowl and wiped his mouth on his bare forearm. "One can have length or speed in their choice of blades, but not both. We Greeks want length. Romans seem to prefer speed. I have wondered just which would fare the best in a match between our lands."

I shook my head. "That is unlikely ever to happen. By the time the armies of Rome reached the shores of Greece, or yours trod the beaches of Latium, it would be their grandchildren who would do the fighting. The distance is great and the voyage would be long."

He nodded. "What you say is true, and I am only making chin noise to pay for my bowl. In any case, armies fight with spears and not blades."

I nodded and motioned to the serving woman, pointing to his empty vessel. "You are... out of fortune, as you said?"

"Aye. I work the docks on occasion, earning a copper or so a day. It is enough to keep me in viands and a room, but not to slake my thirst to the extent that I desire. Someday I will return to Athens, but as of yet I have not collected the necessary desire for the journey."

"You were a soldier, as you mentioned?"

He nodded as his bowl was filled again. "Aye. In my youth, I fought with Pericles, and many a southern man did we send to the service of Hades." Drinking and smacking for a few moments, he continued, "But the gods were kind to myself. In the great plague that took the General and the third part of our forces, I only displayed a weak mottling and was back on my feet in a half moon. Then, in the battle of Segesta, I took a point through my leg from a Spartan javelin and ended my service."

I had no knowledge of the history of these lands, and his relating of the events told me little, except that, aye, he was... had been a soldier. I just nodded as though understanding.

He continued with a question. "You are purchasing the wine and have the right of question, but would you allow a query from myself?"

"Aye. Ask what you will."

"What is your reason for stopping in a city of no importance? You have the body and weapon of a soldier, but you are not." He hesitated, then, "You are a wealthy son, perhaps, come to see the world before resuming your duties at home." Another hesitation. "I mean no offense at these inquiries."

I just sat and mused for a while, behind my cup. I felt no need to build myself in stature to an unknown veteran, and certainly no desire to explain the reason for my being far from my home city. Finally, I said, "You have a good eye, and indeed I am none of those you have mentioned. Suffice it to say that I am in this country because of the jesting whim of some god, somewhere, and not because of my desires. But... My youth was troubled, and I would feel uncomfortable were I to return to Rome."

The man knew exactly how to interpret that admission, and just smiled over his cup. We sat for a while, in our own thoughts, until he spoke again. "You have been kind to an old soldier. Might I give my advice to a stranger in our land?" I nodded. "You will probably know that Athens is at war with Sparta these many years?" Not waiting for my reply, he continued, "As such, you are in some moderate danger while you reside in Lavrion." He waved as I opened my mouth to speak. "Not for being an ally or enemy to either, you understand, but as a young man with a good physique. You will have noticed that there are no men of moderate years on the streets?"

Now that he mentioned the fact, I had noticed that most of the males of the town were either grizzled graybeards or urchins of the street. In fact, I had been wondering why the brothels were so... uncrowded. In Rome - or Terracina, even - at the last hours of the day, the women would lay at their backside work until the late hours of the night. Here, they seemed to spend their time just displaying their wares. Indeed, I could not remember any wait for their services since my coming to the city.

"The reason you have not been accosted yet is that no ship of the Athenian or Spartan navy has pulled into port. I will wager enough wine to fill a cask the size of yon server woman's paps, that you have already been marked for the taking." He inclined his head. "Notice the two toughs at the corner table." I looked over his shoulder to see two young men, bearded and lean and, at least, one with a wicked looking and curved dagger in his belt.

I nodded, and he continued. "Crimpers. They sell young men as sailors to the fleets. A pinch of powder in your cup, and you will find yourself at an oar the next morning. As a slave if the vessel is Spartan, or as a freeman read into the service of the ship, if Athenian. And subject to all of the discipline of the captain." He held up his bowl, then took a gulp. "Not a life for a person who wishes to see his beard turn gray." Again the head tilt to the two young men. "I wager that you are already marked on their tablet for vending to the next galley that appears. Your blade may make them cautious, not knowing of your ability in combat, but still..."

I had no reason to think the old soldier was making jape with me, and he had me fairly alarmed. I was in a strange land and knew nothing of the customs and rules. Caution was of the essence. Rising, I said, "My thanks to you, Kurios, for your kind warnings. Be assured that I will take them to heart." Waving at the fat women again, I tossed a tiny coin to the table. "Serve my friend what he desires." With that, I bowed to the old soldier and left the taverna.

Back in my cubicle, I took my blade from the scabbard and inspected it. A fine weapon - plain and practical, it was the tool of a soldier, not the bejeweled and gilded toys that one saw in the parades or festivities in the Circus Maximus. I held it out and thrust toward the opening in the wall, then made a swing at an imaginary foe. This one was probably a secondary arm for the soldier, something to be used if his primary weapon shivered. Finally, I resheathed it, feeling sure that any real warrior would assume that I was a performer in a military farce for the acting platforms. It would be a poor assailant that fell to my strokes.

I knew that I needed a decision and that night I lay long on my mat thinking of my need for direction. I also knew that it would not be in the city of Lavrion - there was little work here for a scribe and any that might appear would pay almost nothing. My purse was still heavy with copper and small silver, but it would eventually be empty unless I found employment. Besides, I was becoming thoroughly weary of the sameness of this little port.

On morning time, I went in search of my casual soldier friend. He was not at the docks, nor at the tavern, but a question to the serving woman in the taverna gained the information of the whereabouts of his hutch. Shortly, I was being led by the ancient crone, who managed the lodging house, down a hallway to a small cubical - one of dozens in the dilapidated building. There was no door, only a straw mat across the opening, which she pulled aside without even a notice.

"Korax! You have a visitor." Beyond her I could see the old soldier laying on a straw mat, and waking to the shrill call of the woman. Obviously, my coin had stretched to include considerably more bowls of wine the night before - beyond those that I had purchased while with him. He rose to a sitting position to bend over, holding his head with both hands. The woman looked at me, then said before leaving, "There - you have him, but what use he will be is not even known by the gods."

I could tell that the night had been interrupted with his belly insisting on emptying itself. The stench was unmistakable, and while his aim with a spear might be sufficient for his claim to be a soldier, it was obvious that his pointing skills at the spew-bucket were deficient. However, my life to date certainly did not give me the moral superiority to look down upon another man. I waited for him to drop his hands, then said, "My good Korax. You need a modicum of food on your belly, with a cup of good wine to make you whole. Allow me to gift you with such in payment for more conversation."

He just looked up at me for a moment, then nodded and slowly got to his feet, with some help from my hand. We left the odorous establishment, and I noticed that his old wound definitely gave the man a hobbled walk, but in no way was it disabling. He could make a good step without pain, it appeared.

I led the soldier to a dockside taverna, that catered to the overseers and captains of the various piers and boats. It served plain, but filling food and wine that was tolerable. It had taken a bowl before his head pain receded to the point that he could listen to my questions, but after hot meats and bread were brought he began to assume his good sorts.

Finally, I began to speak. "My friend. I have no reason to stay in this city. My copper will not last forever, and there is no use for my skill here. But, in the city of Athens, which even a Roman has heard of, there might be a place for one such as I." There was no reply, and I continued, "It would seem that journeying there by sea might be less than wise - at least that is the talk around the boards of the port." Another pause. "I would need to travel there by shank's mare, it would seem."

I waited, watching the man with his face in the bone, holding it with both hands. Finally, he looked up and said, "I did not hear a question in that discourse, but I assume that one was intended. And in that case, I would agree - unless you can berth on a fast ship, you might find yourself between the rock of an Athenian trireme and the shore of a Spartan galley." Another bite, chewed and swallowed, then, "The distance by foot is not great, but you would need to travel under the auspices of a secured caravan. The roads are infested with Athenian deserters, freebooters, and scum, all waiting for a hapless traveler such as yourself." He waved the bone at the weapon in my belt. "You have said that you have little skill with a blade."

I nodded. "And to that matter, I would pay your way for your companionship on the road. Food and drink, at the least. And I would have tutoring in the customs of this land." His eyes opened wider with the words. "As of now, I am as a grain merchant trying to trade on the fish docks and not even recognizing my gaffs." Before he could reply, I said, "You yourself, mentioned the desire to return to your city."

"Aye. And there is a reason I have not. Athens is swollen with slaves and more. I have no accounting, but my belief is that they outnumber the freemen, considerably. As such, there is little work for a man. Who would pay for work, when for a few drachmas, one can purchase a bondman and after, have only the cost of feeding as an expense?"

"Then, am I in error for wishing to travel to that city? Should I decamp for Egypt, perhaps? Or for the lands to the east?"

He tossed the cleaned bone to the floor. "What is your skill, if you have one?"

"I was trained as a scribe. And I have learned to script and parse in Greek."

"You might find work. Then again, you may not. You will need to adjust your appearance as a Roman." Before I could ask his meaning, he pointed to my face. "Ceasing your constant blading of your beard would make you less of an outsider."

In that, he was wrong about the blade. Like most Romans now - except for the elderly - I kept a smooth face. In fact, the idea of a covering of facial fur, to itch and garner sweat and dirt and insects, was an idea of some distaste. I had not had access to an edge sharp enough to scrape hair from my face since my capture by the pirates, and even before then, I seldom used one. Since my youth, I would pluck out the individual hairs when they grew long enough to grasp, and long ago it became an effort that required no conscious thought, but something that I did daily without thinking. The effect made by plucking lasted for almost an entire month, unlike the efforts with a blade that had to be repeated almost daily.

But I nodded. In this land, all men who were not of an age to be entering their infirmity, sported short beards, at the least. The soldier was giving good advice. I would cease my plucking and allow at least a short covering to help hide my foreign looks. I waited for him to empty his bowl, then asked, "What say you to my offer? Should you find Athens to be still unsuitable, I will copper you to return here if you wish."

The Greek

Mercator (Merchant)

As a Roman, I had known from my youth that Rome was the greatest and most magnificent city in the world and compared to all that I had seen since leaving the Tiber, I had found that the superiority was even greater than the common belief of the citizens. However...

At the first sight of Athens, my hauteur was considerably dampened. This was no city to be despised, and if anything, had a grandeur that was even greater than Rome in many respects. The first sight that is presented to the traveler to the city is a hill that is called the Acropolis. Hill, did I say? It was a massive outcropping that made the Tarpeian Rock in Rome appear to be a pebble on the street. On the top were several massive buildings, surrounded by equally gigantic pillars of fluted stone. One structure, the temple of the goddess Athena, after whom the city was named, by itself would have risen to half the height of the famous cliff in Rome. The great Temple of Jupiter in my city would have fit comfortably inside the Greek building. The structure was called the Parthenon.

Leading to the top of the hill was a huge gateway, called the Propylaea, and that served no other purpose than to give the entire hilltop even more grandeur. Behind it were other magnificent buildings - the Erechtheion, and the temple of Athena, Nike, and others. Unfortunately, during my sojourn in the city, I was never able to visit the hilltop and gaze upon the sights at close hand. To enter, a person had to be ritually purified, a process not available to slaves, wretches, foreigners and - I have to say - unclean Romans. All but pure Athenians were denied entry.

Nonetheless, the rest of the city was not to be despised. The land was abundant in that beautiful building material which the Romans called marmot, and the Greeks, marble. Also used, was the white material called calx - limestone - and in the midday sun, parts of the city could be painful to the eyes, blinding one for a considerable time when the person entered the shade of a building.

Just like Rome, the city had a Forum, and it encompassed the same uses, only in this land it was called the Agora. Here the performers, merchants, and sophists could be found. Indeed, except for the buildings not being of brick and the men all with facial hair, this could be the meeting place of my city.

My companion, Korax, pointed to this and that as we walked. I could even detect pride in his voice as he explained the various sights and features of his city. "That is the Areopagus," he said, pointed to a large rock, easily the size of the largest temple. "You will not wish to find yourself on its height." I waited for the explanation, which came immediately. "It is the judgment rock on which the High Court makes its determination of guilt or innocence." I agreed and made a promise to myself to stay far away from the mound.

Another point of his arm. "The Pnyx." Another huge rock, but lower and with a flatter top and a large grassy area at the base of the low cliff. "That is where the debates of the city are carried out. Any citizen can speak his mind to the politicians although I have doubts that it happens often. One can be prosecuted for speaking out if it is found that his speech is detrimental to the city."

The day was warm, and we stopped at an open-air taverna to patch our thirst with a cup or two. It was here that I got a lesson in the differences in our cultures. To those readers who are not my fellow citizens, let me state that Rome is... the word is puritani - and is difficult to translate into words for other societies. I had not even known of the concept until I left the land of Latium and saw the contrast with other cultures.

To put it simply, Romans deny the very thing that men and women crave above all else. That is, the act of copulation between males and females. Without doubt, the act happens in Rome as often as elsewhere, but not in the open, nor is it spoken of in society. Indeed, any display of copulation in public will get one dragged before the magistrates for offending the public sensibilities. Brothels certainly exist in Rome - a fact of which I was personally aware - and possibly in more density than other cities, but the whores are confined inside and out of view of any but the patrons. An obscene scrawl on a wall is considered an offense and is immediately scrubbed from sight by the servants of the building.

But in Athens...

The serving-girl brought our wine - good wine and clear - setting our large cups before us and taking my copper in return. As we drank and talked, a man rose from another table and pulled the girl to the wall. Barely noticing the pair, I drank and looked down the wide street at another eye wonderment - a large flat area, of stone, but with tiers of benches arranged in a semicircle around it. My guide was explaining that it was the Theatre of Dionysus, a place for performances of many kinds. I assumed it to be somewhat comparable to our Circus Maximus and was about to make the comment, when...

The man and serving-girl had been talking, and in my view, but I had not marked the converse other than just seeing it with my eyes. Suddenly, she held out a hand, and a coin of some value was placed in it. Then, backing to the wall and lifting one leg and foot to a stool, she raised her stola - actually called a chiton in this land - exposing her woman's Venus area to view. The man, also raising his tunic, stepped forward to insert his tool and began the sexual act. And in plain view of the patrons!

Wide-eyed, I watched for a moment, then looked around for the inevitable magistrate that would come storming up to cite the pair. What I saw, instead of enraged patrons, was... nothing. Not a single man at the tables was looking at the incredible sight, even those for whom the couple was directly in view. It was as if nothing was happening or that the pair was still just engaging in conversation. Even Korax, when I pointed, merely glanced for a moment, then turned back to continue his discourse on the city. It was the beginning of the realization that, for the rest of the world, the act of sexual joining is as natural as breathing. Still, for the moment, it was startling, at the least.

I left it to Korax to decide where to find lodging that would fit my purse. As we rose from the table and walked into the heart of the city and around the huge mound of the Acropolis, he still pointed out this sight and that monument as we walked. "We will find the least expensive mat-rooms in the Deme of Scanbonidas." That was obviously a section of the city, but the words made no sense to me. He explained for a moment, then I realized that had we been in Rome he would have been talking about a section of the city called a quarter. Crossing a small stream, called the Eridanus, we entered the part of the city he was seeking.

The grandioseness of the city had been left behind. This area had the same aspects as Sucusa quarter in Rome. One needed to walk with one's hand on his weapon and not alone in the narrower alleys in darkness. Still, in the daylight, it was a bustling quarter with all the aspects of one in Rome. Except for the somewhat different garb and beards, it could have been any street of my youth as a scribe.

In a while, he stopped before a building front - made of wood in this part of the city - and then walked to the open door. Inside, he was accosted by the capo, or whatever the Greeks call an innkeeper, and began to bargain. Finally, turning to me he said, "The fee will be four chalkoi per week for the room." Seeing my puzzlement, he explained, "Four of the small coppers, or a half obol. Another chalkoi each for the mats, if we want."

I had no knowledge of the city to say yea or nay, so I just nodded and pulled my small traveling purse from my pocket, handing over a few coppers into the hand of the capo. He turned and led us down a hall to a cubicle - dirt floored and with an opening for light that could be closed in inclement weather. A shout to a slave brought two woven mats for our reclining at night. With that, our search for lodging was accomplished.

During the next few days, I walked the streets of the city, just as a visitor from afar, while Korax searched for old comrades in the barracks and tavernas. I found that the city was much more interesting than the blandness of Rome, or maybe just the difference was stimulating my fascination. Athens had a librarium - indeed, several - but not for my use. The bybliothecae, as they were called, did not allow for any foreigner to just casually enter and begin to peruse the scrolls and tablets. In that, they were just like the magisterial archives of Rome. I would have to raise my social position considerably before I would be allowed entry.

This quarter - this deme - of the city was filled with men without work, as was very apparent. Just as obvious, were the men just watching my passage, no doubt measuring the chances of cutting both my throat and purse before the city guards could intervene. In the afternoons, waiting for Korax to appear so as to walk to our meal, I would practice with my blade. At least, that is what I told myself, having little knowledge of the use of iron in length. The knife - as long as my forearm - was strange looking as compared to a regular sword. It had no curves - just a body that tapered to a point - and a wicked point it was. I had no doubt that the tip could be pushed through the body of a man with little effort.

I would cut and swing at imaginary enemies, pulling it from the ragged leather scabbard hung at my waist. This night, I was still fanning the air when the old soldier entered the cubicle, then backed up with a start so as to be out of the range of my wild swings. "By the stinking crotch of Zeus, what are you about? Is this is some Roman ritual that needs be played in secret?"

Abashed, I mentioned my noticement of the measure of men in this quarter and my possible need to resist any effort against myself. He shook his head, then said, "Aye, a good skill to desire, but swinging like a farmer cutting firewood is unlikely to instill fear in an opponent. Unless he offers his neck as he doubles over from laughter at your method." He waved. "Come, let us eat and discuss this."

At the table in our usual taverna, we began our meal of meat and cheese and bread, and Korax returned to the subject of my lack of blade skills. "I was never a swordsman - only the nobility and wealthy can purchase a blade of sufficient quality to stand the rigors of combat, and my coin was never within distance of the possibility. The metal in the scabbards of these throat-slitters" - he tilted his head to a table of ruffians against the wall - "might do for cutting purses or frighting some merchant into yielding his coin, but against a Persian snake blade they would be holding a shivered hilt at the first stroke. Should you wish tutoring in sword-work then a full blade you will have to have, and one of good quality is measured in silver pieces."

I shook my head. My purse was still heavy, but not with silver or gold.

"But, you are not joining the Athenian army, so there is little need for you to learn the skills of a soldier. The blade you possess is certainly sufficient to protect yourself at risk, but I have little idea of the use of it. The length is too short for sword-work but too long to be wielded in the manner of a dagger."

I knew what he was saying. I had seen the usual Greek blades on the soldiers that patrolled the street, and they were long - very long. Far longer than the soldiers of Rome carried. There was obviously a reason for the different lengths, but I was not familiar with the art of war to any extent and certainly not enough to catalog the different weapons and their uses.

He drained his cup and finished the conversation with, "I will ask in the barracks of my old comrades - maybe one can be found with the skills for your..." He shrugged. "...long dagger and agreeable to instruct you for the payment of a cup or two."

During my strolls in the city, I found the section of moneylenders, and needing to convert some of my large coppers into something of a smaller coin, I entered among the tables and made the exchange. The transaction was trivial but not the method that the man used to figure the amounts. He had a large wooden frame, strung with wires on which were colored beads. His fingers moved the little wooden markers up and down, of this column and that, then announced the totals to me. I figured the same amounts in my mind and agreed with his figurings. But, where he had calculated in mere heartbeats, my total took far longer to arrive. Roman merchants used counting boards, with colored pebbles that were moved up and down columns carved in the board, but each pebble had to be picked up and placed to a new location, with its mates moved up or down to make or take room. This... whatever it was called, with beads on wires on which an entire column could be moved with just the flick of the thumb or finger, was vastly faster. The concept was breathtaking.

My purse now refilled, I just stood for a moment, looking at the strange bead holder, then asked, "Might I ask, Kurios, what that... apparatus might be?"

The lender looked at me in some surprise, then answered, "This? This is an avacus. Some call it an abex." Looking me up and down, he said, "Some in Latium would call it an abacus."

Nodding my thanks, I strolled among the tables, apparently looking for a transaction partner but, in reality, watching the number scribes use this almost magical device. The Greek system of numbering had been much like that used by Romans. Indeed, it is my belief that ours was taken from the much older culture, although that statement would garner a stiff rebuke from my teachers in the Temple, none allowing that any goodness existed that was not learned by Romans. However, the Greeks had begun to modify it considerably, using system of different characters for each digit up to nine, then one for each number of ten, and more for each counting of hundreds. I had to admit that the method was considerably superior to the numbering system that I had been taught in the temple, with Roman letters having different values depending on their placement.

I watched scribes at various tables and in a while I thought I had the rudiments of the operation of the wired board. Then I began to wonder where one might be procured. And the cost of such.

My desires had risen in my groin, but I refrained from entering any of the bordellos in the need to make my purse stretch as far as possible. I knew that I was easily capable of spending the bulk on women by the end of the hot season. And my resolve would often waver, since the women of the houses would fully display their wares to the passing public. My release had to be confined to my own hand and mat at night.

My attempts to find employment as a scribe were completely futile to date. To begin with, I was not a member of the scrivener's guild of Athens and as a foreigner, I had no chance of joining that organization. As such, no merchant would test the wrath of the members of that body and hire a mere Roman, no matter how skilled in numbering. My daily attempts always ended with my sitting in the usual taverna with Korax and commiserating with him on our woes and sharing out tales of the day. The novelty of a shaven Roman had worn off and I was treated as just another patron by both the owner and the men sitting at the tables. Until one evening...

A group of men were at the next table, all complaining about one dock steward, of particularly bad temper, it seemed. In fact, the denunciations grew ever louder as the wine flowed into the cups and to such an extent as to require our own conversation to be conducted in more than a taverna whisper. My friend was regaling me with a tale of the day. "...And Thaxes was too far into his cups to realize that the whore that he had commissioned was actually a barracks boy from the river fort. His efforts to negotiate the usual path were unsuccessful and when he reached down to help steer the course he found that he had grown another member..." Korax guffawed, and I had to laugh at the tale as he continued. "Then, just to pour salt in the wound, he discovered that his..."

A bowl, and not one that was empty, flew past, barely missing my head. The contents did not entirely follow the container. As I attempted to blink my eyes clear of the purple liquid, I heard a shout of, "You jape at a man when he is down, Roman! No garlic eater from that pestilential whore-land makes a gull of me." I stood up, my actions causing the bench to fall backward, as the sweeping arm crossed over my chest, the blade of the dagger missing by a double handspan. The other four men - as well as Korax - had jumped to their feet as their fellow braced himself to follow up the stroke. Had the man not been far gone in his cups I would already be dead with the dagger in my chest, but as it was, his swing had carried him further around, and he stumbled to keep his feet. I frantically backed up to the wall, wiping my eyes clear of the wine.

Now he shouted something about liver cutting and presenting my head as sacrifice to Pluto, or some such, as he approached to further exercise his weapon hand. His actions had caught his fellows by surprise, obviously, as they stood open-mouthed before the drunken fury of the man. Even Korax, a one-time soldier, was wide-eyed at the sudden furor. I assume that my amateur practicing with my long blade was the manipulator of my next actions. Almost without thinking, I pulled the knife from its sheath - an action that I was very practiced with, even with no training on the use of the metal once it was drawn. But, the next play was a jest of the gods...

Our table had been near one of the walls of the taverna. This building had been made of felled trees, the limbs sheered from the trunks, then stacked horizontally and spiked together, with the cracks between them caulked with mud. As such, it was not the smooth stone of the temples and noble houses, nor of the planed lumber of the better structures in a city. Many were the protrusions showing where the limbs had been hacked away.

I had brought the knife to the horizontal position, between myself and my attacker and pointing directly at his chest, now only a handspan away. That was just the reflex action of a man to the sudden appearance of danger. But as my arm came back, my elbow contacted the stub of one of the sheared limbs of a wall log, and the result was startling to all. The small dimple of the elbow, made when the arm is folded at an angle, is known to the medicos as the jocosa ossis - the prickle of Gelos, the god of laughter. As most people have experienced, even a light blow on this depression will cause an immediate reaction of the arm - an involuntary extension that is sudden and if the blow is severe, almost paralyzing for several heartbeats. That last was the case when my elbow contacted the stob of the log. As my reactions in jerking my blade from the scabbard were frantic and with all the speed that I could muster, the impact was hard.

My arm immediately went numb, but more importantly, it jerked forward for the doubled length of my hand. My assailant stopped, a puzzled look on his face, then just fell to the floor, limply as a bundle of rags. Several heartbeats passed before I realized that the end of my long-knife had entered the chest over his heart - to no more than a two or three fingers depth, but far more than enough to draw the life from the drunkard.

As the feeling returned to my arm, I now realized that I was still facing the four friends of the man I had slain - and even a practiced soldier is at a fatal disadvantage with such odds. I could only die in place, swinging my blade as they approached...

But now Korax stood forth, facing the men and holding up his hands. "Kurios! Kurios! It is obvious that your friend misconstrued the laughter at our table as being a jape of his woes. Know that we were engaged in our own jesting at tales and had no cognizance of your troubles. Indeed, we were not even aware that you were commiserating over your cups." The men, I have to say, were not threatening. Stunned, aye. Even surprised at the sudden fury and result to their friend, but none had reached for their daggers as Korax continued. "My friend is late of the army of Rome, and well versed in battle, even to the extent of serving as the training Hastilarius of his Legion. I would dislike for you to fall under his blade for the misconstrual of our laughter." He lowered his hands slowly. "Let us extend our regrets at the unfortunate misunderstanding and grieve with you over your fallen friend."

The four men looked at each other for several heartbeats, then over at me. I lowered my blade, then stepped aside to allow them to recover the remains of their fellow. As they carried the body out the entrance, I finally became aware of the inside of the taverna. All patrons were on their feet, looking over at us and without a word being spoken. After the men had disappeared through the entrance with their burden, the patrons slowly returned to their tables and began the ritual of drink, but now with a new topic for their evening conversation.

Realizing that if I did not sit down, then I would fall as my legs gave way, I also resumed my place at the table. Korax sat again, looking across at me with an expression of utter... surprise is not the word. It was more as if...

He leaned over and whispered, if a low shout can be called a whisper. "By Zeus and his foul jism! Have you played me for a gulled simpleton all of these days?!" He turned and violently gestured for our cups to be filled, then continued. "You have assigned yourself as a novice with weapons, yet in the throes of sudden ambush you cut a man down with a lightning stroke that does not even leave blood on the floor!"

I had to clamp my jaws to keep my teeth from chattering on the rim of the cup, such was the aftermath of my sudden combat. "Korax, my friend." I returned. "What happened was by the chance of the moment. I cannot even say how I did such a stroke. Some god was guiding my hand and metal, perhaps." I shrugged, taking a huge swallow of wine. "That is as good of an account as I can give."

He just shook his head, still in the shock of the previous happenings, apparently - as I was. "Your god has a sense of humor, that I can say."

"And what was that trumpery about my being a training officer in a Roman legion?"

Now he grinned. "I was just salting the ground in case the four were in a mood to avenge their friend. It does no harm to allow a group of rabble to think they are about to accost an accomplished bladesman." He took a swallow. "And at the moment, I thought there might be a grain of truth in the tale."

For the balance of the evening, we sat and casually drank. I reflected on the wisdom of keeping one's laughter to himself while in a taverna. This was the second time that a patron at the next table had taken offense to my innocent jesting.

For the next quarter month, the night remained a wonder in my thoughts and quiet times.

Athens had public baths, but not in the numbers of the facilities of Rome. Still, I found a pleasant retreat at the edge of the quarter that would allow one to bathe for only a partial obol. In Athens, bathing seemed to be confined mostly to the upper classes, since I seldom saw laborers or merchants in the waters. Of course, slaves were completely forbidden to enter.

Still, despite my distance from Rome in both stadia and time, washing of the body was still a desirable function that I enjoyed. After the day's walk around the city, I would enter the bathhouse in the afternoon and just relax for an hour, at least, thinking of what I had seen and wondering about my future. Thus far, I had no vision of any work here. The temples and administrative offices were not accessible by one not a citizen, and a scribe that could not interact with the magistrates of the city, was... well, as a fisherman with no bait.

I had about reached the conclusion, after many afternoons and nights of thought, that I would have to take ship for Latium. Back to Tarracina, perhaps. At least there I could support myself with my skills...

"You are a stranger here, Roman."

I woke out of my reverie, sitting in the warm pool of the bathhouse. The voice came from my side - a man of indeterminate age - not young but not an oldster. He nodded and continued, "Your pardon. I have seen you this last quarter month, but not before. It is not often that we get a patron from such a distance to enjoy our waters."

The man could have been a lowly laborer or the richest merchant in the city. Indeed, he could have even been the king of Athens, had that rank existed here. A naked man sleds all evidence of his being along with his clothes. But, his diction was such that I could believe that he was considerably above the rank of a mere worker. "Aye, Kurios. From Rome, but not of late. My course has taken me considerably off the direct course between the two cities. Junius is the name."

Now he nodded. "My greetings, Junius of Rome. I am Dionysos of Megara, of the Scanbonidas Deme." The same quarter that I was living in, I told myself. He waved off the serving slave, offering a cup on a tray. "Might I inquire as to your reason for the long journey? I ask only for the boon of conversation."

"I came ashore at a city to the south, called Lavrion..." He nodded, obviously knowing of the port city. "...But there was no use for my skills there, so Athens was the next destination."

"And your profession is...?"

"I am a scribe, trained in the Temple of Jupiter, and also conversant with the accounting of both Greece and Egypt." I stopped as the man furrowed his brow and just looked at myself for a moment. "Your pardon," I continued, "Have I said aught to disturb you?"

He shook his head. "Nay. Nay. It is just that... I have hired many scribes in my business, and well know of the profession and, if I may say, you do not fit the description of a scrivener. In my experience, they are white of skin, soft of flesh, and mostly rotund from their inactivity from day to day. You, Kurios, are brown from the sun, thin of midriff, and have sinews in your arms and legs that have done more than push a stick through wax."

Now I smiled. "My profession is easily proven, Kurios. One may pretend to be a merchant, or a soldier, or even a noble in disguise, and not be unmasked without considerable effort, but to determine the worth of a scribe is a task with little effort. A wax tablet or scrap of papyrus is all that is needed."

He smiled in return. "It is true as you say. But, still, you do not have the countenance of that profession."

Now I smiled again, but only in my mind. If I should give him the actual tale he would be more than just wondering - nay, he would adjudge me as a wandering bard with a story for any gullible ears. "It is true that in my last assignment the work was mostly in the sun, and I myself helped move much of the merchandise that I was reckoning, in addition to my marking of the accounts."

He pointed to a waiting slave and held up two fingers. "And the reason that you departed the position...? Again, pardon my inquisitiveness - it is just for my own edification."

"There is no offense in gladsome conversation in the Roman baths, Kurios, and I assume that the same custom rules here. However, to your question, in my last occupation the principle left to meet his ancestors and had no son to take over. Thusly, I was given my due, and secured a berth to this land. And I must confess, I was curious about the ways of more of the world than I had seen." As a story, it had a modicum of truth, without leaving any loose threads to trip me up in the future, should the same tale be asked of again.

Now a slave entered the water, holding up a tray with two cups. The man - Dionysos - took one and nodded to myself. "Take a cup at my pleasure, Kurios. We will drink to the friendship between Rome and Athens."

"My thanks, Kurios."

For a while, we just enjoyed the sweet wine, which I had to admit was the equal of any that I had enjoyed in Rome. Finally, he said, "You have mentioned the reason - or at least your primary motive for being in our city is to gain work. I may have a spot for a man such as yourself should you satisfy my testing of your abilities. You can number in the barbarian picture language of Aegyptos, you have said?"

The offer - and question - out of the aether and without preamble, left me stunned. I held my cup to my face to help cover my expression of utter surprise. After days of looking for work in my profession and not finding even a crier's board with offers... "Aye. I am conversant with the picture numbering."

He seemed not to see my confusion. "The Temple of Jupiter. Then your skill must be somewhat above the usual scrivener, trained in a municipal school." He drained the cup and held it out for the slave to fill again. "My senior scribe is always harping on the lack of ability of his lackeys for the picture writing. If you are amenable, and he is satisfied, then you might find a place in this city."

I thanked him profusely, then he asked, "Know you of the Drakon Guild edifice? Hard by the Dipylon gate."

"Nay, Kurios," I replied. "I have not strode in that area, but I can find my way. On the morrow, if you wish."

"Excellent. Ask for Cleades at the door - he is my senior scribe." Now he rose to standing in the water and said, "Until the morrow, then, I will say, antio."

"Farewell," I returned, as he climbed out of the bath and walked to the drying room to rerobe.

That evening, I was not the only one to experience astonishment. When I mentioned the name of my potential patron to Korax, he choked in his cup of wine, and leaned over coughing, trying to remove the liquid from his breathing sacs. "Dionysos of Megara?" I just shrugged. "The factor of the Dragons?"

Again I shrugged and replied. "I do not... wait, he mentioned a guild... Drakon, he said. By the Dipylon gate."

Korax just set his cup down - hard, and looked at me in amazement. "Do you know who you have been accosted by?" Obviously I did not, as he well knew. "Dionysos is the chief of the gang that controls this quarter, and the most of the grain merchantry in the lower sections. His word is law, even if not legal. You are moving into a precarious world, my friend."

Now, confused, I just said, "He wanted to test me as a scribe. How would that be of any..."

Now my soldier friend finished his wine in one great gulp. "A mouse can live in the den of the bear, feasting on the leavings of the powerful. But he may also become a morsel to the great animal, at will." He shook his head. "You may find great wealth and power in such a position, but you may just as easily become a meal should the man tire of your services in any way. Be cautious, my friend."

With those words still in my ears, I set out for the western wall of the city the next morning.

As I approached the area of the Dipilon gate, I asked a citizen directions, then another. All knew of my destination, and shortly I was standing in the wide street in front of my goal.

I was not sure what I was expecting, but the rambling wooden structure was not at all my idea of the lair of one of the most powerful men of the Plebeians, or whatever the lower classes of Athenians were called. It was different in that it was more than one level - the upper row of windows gave that information. The street was crowded, with tradesmen and citizens going here and there, and a group of men was standing at the covered portico at the front of the building - and not a group that I would wish to meet in bad faith. All were young, or at least well on that side of life, with various scars showing that theirs had not been lives of ease and wealth.

One of the men noticed my approach, calling to his fellows and pointing in my direction. Some jape passed between them and all laughed. As I walked up and stopped before them, one called, "You are far from the stithi of your miter, Roman."

Another immediately followed with, "Nay, Nicias. All know that men of that land suckle from the paps of wolves. Yon Romakos would stare at the nips of your doxie in wonderment at their use." Of course, all could still tell my antecedents, my beard not even having begun its growth. Indeed, the progress had been set back by my plucking of the hairs without thinking of my need.

More laughing and japes and another demanded, "And what would be your purpose for this unexpected blessing of your presence?"

I had long learned, as a boy on the banks of the Tiber and later as a young student in the Temple, that a meek answer to a jab was an invitation for a life of misery as the butt of any and all. Holding my hand on the hilt of the longknife in my belt, I answered, "It is not for the benefit of such noble patrons as I see before me. I am responding to a request from Dionysos of Megara to call upon a man this day, one Cleades by name."

The words were as a command of a general to a troop of tyros. All suddenly ceased their japing and looked at each other. One, of a higher rank than the others, I assumed, said, "Then come with me, Roman." I followed into the wide doorway and down a short hall that entered a large room, illuminated by flaring torches against the wall - needed even in the middle of the day, since there were no openings to the outside in the walls or above. Later, I would find that this room was buried in the large structure that not only had an overhead area but was flanked by warehouses on the back and sides.

This room was a taverna, filled with tables and serving maids. It was very large - the largest I had seen, anywhere - able to hold a hundred men or so, and today was close to that capacity. The noise was considerable, with shouts and groans from the several games of knucklebones. One group was tossing daggers at a carving on the wall, coins changing hands with every throw.

Following the man, we passed a set of steps - again, a new vision for myself. I had never entered a structure with a floor above another. It was quite a startling concept in how to double the available space. Idly, I wondered at the possibility of making an even taller building with three floors, or even four. I shook my head in self-amusement - the idea of a building with such a multitude of levels was not only impractical but probably impossible to build.

Through the men and around the tables I was led, to a door that entered a large room - apparently the supply area for the taverna that we had just exited. The amphorae that were stacked on the floor would have supplied an army. Down the rows of clay jugs was another door, and passing through we had apparently come to the back of the building, as the room was lightened by a windows in the far wall. At a long table, filled with scrolls and tablets was a... scribe, obviously. He turned as we entered.

"Cleades," my guide announced. "This Roman says he has the instructions to report to you." With that, he spun on a heel and left.

The older man just looked at me, obviously wondering about my sudden appearance. Finally, he asked, "Who are you and why would the master send me a man from such distance?"

I replied, spreading my hands in the disbelief that this was happening to me, also. "I was at the baths with Dionysos and he engaged me for his service. As to the reason for my assignment to yourself, he did not speak of it. Might I ask, Kurios, as to your position in this... enterprise?" I knew from the conversation the last night that he was the senior in the scribes of this... organization, but I wished to allow the man to give his own makings.

The man was middle aged, a typical Greek with flowing robes and the graying beard and lengthy hair flowing from his head. Rather than answering the question immediately, he asked, "Dionysos himself, you say? Might I assume that you are within friendship with the master?"

I shook my head. "Nay. It was a meeting of chance only. He seemed to wish for the employ of a scribe who can work with the Egyptian pictures."

"Ah. That is so. I can find any number of scribblers who think they can parse the numbers of this land, but few who can read in that barbarian tongue." On a shelf were several cups, and a jug. He handed a cup to me, and asked, "Are you conversant with the fact that merchants in this land use either of two different methods of numbering?"

Accepting the vessel, I held it out as he filled it - and his - from the jug, I nodded and said. "Aye, Kurios. As I understand, the new is gradually gaining acceptance among the scribes and moneylenders of the city - and maybe the whole land, for all I know."

He pointed to the blade at my side. "You are experienced with the use of iron, I see?" I translated the statement to be a question as to why a scribe would carry such a weapon.

I just smiled. "My travels have been in parts that were... less than friendly, shall we say."

He shrugged. "It is your choice to work with such an encumbrance, but know that you have little need of defense in the employ of Dionysos. No man would be unwise enough, even in his cups, to accost a scribe under his auspices."

For the balance of the day, Cleades gave me the methods of his work and the requirements that were expected by Dionysos. He was the senior scribe for the organization, at the top of the pyramid of the network of scriveners that numbered and accounted both the inbound shipments of grain, and the distribution of such. For myself, I was set to converting the tally of the Egyptian dock scribes into something that could be read and enumerated by Cleades - or at least by the apprentices that he had available in various parts of the warehouses.

Leaving the guild-hall early in the evening, I hurried back to the street of the moneylenders, finding the shop in which I had examined the abaci being vended, I soon selected a fairly large and sturdy one, with fifteen wires of beads. It cost a double tetraobol - enough to enjoy wine and women for a quarter month. Nonetheless, I needed the device. I was not as conversant in the two systems of Greek numbering as I had assured the guild leader, but I would spend the afternoon and evening practicing my counting.

Korax returned and found me still accustoming my fingers to the beads. I was far slower than even the younger scribes of the tables, some of which could add numbers at a speed that would be unbelievable to one who did not know how it was accomplished. I would accrue speed in time, but for now, accuracy was the need.

"You have a new plaything, I see. I assume that it is in conjunction with your newly made friendship with the man of the guild."

Needing to rest both my eyes and my fingers, I set the abacus aside and stood up, stretching. "Come. Let us find our evening meal and I will tell you of my adventures. Even your hollow leg will not hold wine for the length of this tale."

Numerator

The reach of the guild was far-flung, and had its tentacles in all aspects of Athens - at least for the Plebeians, as I called the lower classes. Most of the grain entering the city was under the auspice of Dionysos and his lieutenants. There were other smaller guilds in the city, but they were as mice to the lion in size and power. What I found to be interesting, and would not have believed without seeing, was that grain was often actually purchased before it was grown. It was a concept that took considerable thought for myself to realize the ramifications of such a trade.

Grain was a perishable commodity. It could not be stored for a lengthy time without the incursions of mice and rats spoiling a considerable amount in the warehouses. To prevent such loss, or to alleviate at least some of the spoilage, the warehouses were home to many catti, those diminutive relatives of the lion, imported from Egypt and protected by law from harm. But, even with rodents under some control any grain kept for a time would begin to grow insects and to harbor grubs that would devastate the kernels of a bag. Even if the grain were milled, and stored as flour, the insects would find the feast, growing fat within the ground powder.

Thus, unlike other commodities, grain could not be stored and released at a rate to maintain a uniform price over the entire year. As a result, in a year of bountiful harvests the price would be lowered and in times of troubles in the grain fields, the cost of grain - and bread - could become dear. A man who could find a way to store either grain or flour for a time, without spoilage, would become as rich as King Croesus.

Unlike the lands of Latium, and that around Rome, the soil of Greece was not conducive to the husbandry of grain - certainly not in the amounts that are necessary to feed a city the size of Athens. Thusly, most was traded for and brought from far lands around the great sea. A continual stream of grain ships would make the voyages between the fields and the wharfs of the city.

The guild's reaches were so far and wide that innumerable scribes and numerators were in its service. Some were in lands far away, where the grain was sowed and harvested. Others on the docks where the ships left for Athens, and certainly many waited in the port for those ships to arrive. Then, the bags were counted by the warehouse scribes, giving their numbers to the copyists who made the records in wax or on a scroll. Finally, two master scriveners would total the bounty and give the numbers to the senior scribe, Cleades.

My work began with the comparison of the tablets and scrolls from the hot lands of Egypt. I was not as conversant with either the picture language nor like numberings as I had managed to convey to either the master or Cleades, but here was little chance of my falsity being exposed. The scribe could puzzle out the numbers but had no knowledge of the language. I hurriedly concentrated on building on my ability in the language and as the days passed I greatly increased my fluency.

In a pair of months, I had come to several conclusions, not the least of which was that the guild was a hotbed of graft and corruption. The tallies that were made as the ships were loaded had no correlation to the counting as the bags of grain were carried onto the docks at the end of the voyage. I had no way of knowing if the cause was illiteracy on the part of the counting scribes, or bald theft by one and all, or a combination of both. But, it was a fact that at least one bag in eight either was stolen or did not exist at all.

In a room beyond the main taverna, a comfortable and private space was available for the senior members of the guild - that included myself and any that were employed under the command of Cleades. In addition, a table across the room and near the window was reserved for the lieutenants that reported to Dionysos himself. The lesser scribes and workers either congregated in the guild taverna or at various spots around the huge complex of warehouses.

I could not hide my antecedents as a Roman and I did not try. My beard plucking was so ingrained that I gave up the idea of letting it grow out. The men would either accept my foreignness as it was, or... not. But, my work was of sufficient quality that Cleades was satisfied and with that approval, I needed no other.

Korax and I settled into an inn not far from the guild headquarters. This one was far superior to the hovel that had been our domicile for the since our arrival in Athens. My friend still had not found meaningful employment, but I was satisfied to keep him with me and with sufficient coin to eat and drink. After all, he was the only friend that I had in this land, and as such, might be worth more than the silver in the bag that I had been given.

In my position of enumerating the various profit centers for the trade routes, I was required to visit the port for examination of incoming vessels. For the next two months I roamed the wharves and the warehouses, looking and tabulating, then with Cleades I would discuss my findings and ask questions about this and that. I was careful to hold back any of the knowledge that I might discover about the leakage within the guild. And much of that did I find. One official, Pertronius, the guild Designator for the port, was instrumental in pilfering almost a quarter of any cargo inbound to his planks. Interestingly, he seemed not to care overly if his dissimulation was discovered. Certainly, I had no need of major effort to see his theft of grain bags in the glaring light of day. My assumption was, since his golden nest had been feathered for so long, that he had become careless of the thievery - a common failing among those who steal. For myself, I could not understand such carelessness. The tales that I had heard, even in my short time in the employ of Dionysos, did not describe a guild leader for whom tolerance was a virtue.

I was compiling a list of thieves and pilferers in the long chain of trade leading from the warehouses of the guild to the fields of the grain - in secret of course. I agreed with Korax - any hint such activity becoming known would have sudden and fatal consequences for myself. Most were obvious - scribe chiefs and wharf masters in every port were taking their cup of grain from the bags. Some was also theft that was not of grain - rather, it was the coin that they were paid to do tasks of a scribe. It was obvious that some had vastly overrated their skills and not a few who were completely illiterate, their scrolls being nothing but random marks conveying no information of any kind.

The visits to the port were pleasant, and I enjoyed the chance to visit this brothel or that taverna on the route, but most of my time was spent in the scribery of Cleades, trying to make sense of tablets and scrolls that sometimes seemed to have no relation to each other. In fact, some were no more real than the tales of mythical deeds and monsters in the scrolls of the scriptoriae in Rome. Indeed, the one-eyed Cyclops of the street bards had a greater chance of existence than some of the accountings that were received from the far off ports. I was engaged in trying to balance the actual count of bags in a newly arrived ship when...

"So it is true. A Roman has indeed found his way to this city of dross."

Surprised, I looked around to see a woman standing inside the doorway. The astonishment was for her speech, not the girl. She had spoken in a fair accent of Latium.

She had seen sixteen - maybe seventeen - summers, perhaps, and displayed the figure of a mature female. Indeed, she was the very apparition of a siren, with full mammaries over a narrow waist and wide hips. But her most striking feature was her hair - it was as golden as... well, spun gold and trailed down below her woman's protrusions. I had heard of such people from the north with such sun-colored tresses, but she was the first and only person in my actual knowledge.

Actually, this was not my first sighting of the girl. I had seen her on occasion - sometimes passing through the warehouse taverna, or standing at the balcony overlooking the patrons. And twice in the presence of the master of the guild, Dionysos. When she appeared, the room or crowds went silent, just watching the human goddess as she came or went to her business. Unlike the usual trollop, walking across the floor and gathering hands from all sides to feel of what they could as she passed, the path opened before this golden haired girl as if she were the high priestess of the Temple.

This was Ravana. I knew nothing about her other than the taverna gossip, but to my purpose, I would treat her as a poisonous serpent - something to be avoided at any effort. My past history with women of emblazoned hair was not an encouragement to begin with another. But, for this youngster, the tales had her as a daughter of a northern king, captured in a raid. Or as merchandise paid for with a trunk of gold. Even as a waif that floated ashore one bright morning. Any given story about the reason for her existence in Athens could be heard over the cups in the taverna of the warehouses.

What was known to be a truth was that she was the trophy of Dionysos and forbidden to any other. Supposedly, as the pet and bed warmer of the leader, she had free reign of the huge warehouse compound, but was forbidden to leave. Men looked at her in wonder in passing, but all knew that even the touch of a hand would get them nailed to the cross tree of the loading docks. The strong-arm men of the guild were ruthless and without conscience. Well treated and made loyal with much coin, they would kill their own mitéras on the casual order of their master.

But, for now, my concern was why this girl was in the scribery and addressing me. I stood, looking at her over the table. "Aye, Korê. I am from the city of Rome, but that was years ago when I last trod the streets."

She slowly walked to the table and stood, aimlessly running a hand over a baked tablet. "And you have left your city to abide in a foreign land." Her speech had an accent, but was good Latium. "Willingly?"

I nodded. "Aye." I suddenly realized that she had blue in her eyes. I had never heard of such. She seemed as the average young girl, not the imperious shrew that would be expected of a woman with the backing of a powerful man. Still... "Mostly," I added. "My leaving was hastened by an unfortunate conjunction with a young woman with fiery hair."

Now she smiled. "Ah. Then you departed by night because of her rejection of you as a lover. Or, maybe because her patér did not approve."

A mat-pet she might be, but this girl was no toy with only a female figure to her presence. She had intelligence to match her being. Still, I wanted no part of her - the property of a man who did not forgive transgressions. "Is there something that you wish, Korê?"

She just slowly walked along the opposite edge of the table, absently running a finger around the tablets. "Only to see the Roman that Dionysos has spoken of." She stopped. "You are really from Rome?"

I nodded. "Aye. I was born on a riverboat in the Tiber, then resided within the Temple of Jupiter until I took my leave."

"Do you intend to return, someday?"

I shrugged. The answer was even unknown to myself. "Who knows where the feet of a man may take him in his life. But I will say that I do not have a berth reserved on a ship, as yet."

"Tell me of your city."

I was growing even more cautious. "Nay, Korê. The master does not pay me good coin for story telling of the past. In fact, I fear that he would take it most amiss should he find you here, unescorted."

She assumed a haughty look. "I need no escort among these loathsome Greeks. I may travel to any part of the property that I wish, even to the private abodes of the workers."

That was also my understanding, but... "That may be, Korê, but would you not take pity on a stranger to these shores and allow me to resume my work?"

She laughed. "Very well, Junius of Rome. But we will speak again." With that, she turned and walked back the way she had come.

Relieved, I went back to my scrolls and tablets, but upon the next day I spoke to the master of the incident. "...and, Kurios, I was most uncomfortable with the master's... the young Korê entering the scribery without escort."

He laughed as he replied. "Be at ease, scrivener. She has the roam of the guild buildings, but not without escort as she thinks. I was informed of the encounter even as it happened. She also is from your land, or at least resided in that far place for a while. It is natural that she wish to converse with a man of Latium."

He pushed a cup toward me, then pointed. The slave - a man at this time - hurriedly filled it. "Your responses were correct and I have no suspect of you. I know of your desires and that they be for ripe women, not barely pubescent nymphs such as she. In that, I am with you, but the girl with the golden hair is a powerful arrow in my quiver for the battles I have planned for future commerce with the southern lands." His description of the woman as an innocent girl was off the mark - she had already seen more of the world than many captains of trading vessels.

In my tallies, I roamed the myriad of rooms and warehouses of the guild complex - and, it must be said, when my eyes needed relief from the scribbles of almost illiterate scribes across the world. The area that was the guild property was even larger than I had thought in the beginning. Apparently it had grown over the years, subsuming buildings and domiciles on all sides. As of now, it encompassed the entire area between the main avenue - the Porta Rosa - leading from the Acharnian gate through the Deme of Scanbonidas - and the Avenue of Demeter, and bounded on the north and south by the Agora and the Cross Street of the money lenders.

The original structures still stood in most cases, but now joined together to make one gigantic maze of buildings. Stored inside were not only grain and wine, but materials of cloth, leather and sundry items of mercantile. At the present, a goodly part of the grain storage was empty, it being between the growing season and the winter for the eastern countries. One could walk for a goodly part of the morning, through the maze of buildings and hallways and connecting corridors without ever retracing one's steps.

It was in one of the dusty and empty warehouses that I hid my growing stash of coin under a floorboard in a corner. With no permanent domicile, I had no other recourse, unless I wished to walk outside the gates and bury it in the ground of the hills. Leaving loose coin in a public inn, no matter how prosperous, was not a wise choice - the slightest hint of such a stash could get my throat cut in sleep before the next sunrise.

During meals and periods of rest, I began to get the measure of the others in the organization. Over cups in the private taverna, I met the second of the guild, one Teukros - the lieutenant of Dionysos. A well found Greek, tall and with strong sinews, he was cordial enough to the upper members gathered around the table, but such a man did not gather his position by guile and gratitude. There was no doubt that he could - and would - use the long and naked kopis in his belt to emphasize his rank if need be.

The talk was of the current strife with Sparta. Teukros was saying, "Lysander has landed in Attica. That will not give good results if our fleet cannot dislodge him."

Another, "That would not affect our shipping from Piraeus. He cannot sail over the peninsula unless the gods give him wings."

Piraeus was the port of Athens, an easy walk to the southwest. Attica was a section of the mainland, but my knowledge of its whereabouts was defective, other than knowing it to be on the opposite side of Athens from the port.

"Aye, but from there he can lay astride the routes to Anatolia, and much grain is funneled thought the Aegean waters."

Now, I spoke. "My pardon, Kurios. This Lysander is the Spartan admiral?"

"Correct, Roman." The lieutenant looked at me. "And, despite the speakings of the pitchmen of the Agora, he is a good one." He quaffed a long swallow to empty his cup, then rose. "There will be much blood on the waters before the matter between the cities is settled."

I was not unwelcome at the table - no man with the auspices of the leader of the grain trade would be shunned, and eventually I became just another guild member, to talk and jape with the men. And to many questions did I give reply, to this man and that in curiosity of the land to the west from which I came. But, these men, in the main, were the toughs and peace-keepers of the guild, unlikely to be engaged in the pilfering of the stream of grain.

On occasion, and again, Ravana would appear when Cleades was elsewhere, to sit on a bench and converse with myself. I had no authority to make her leave, but in self-protection, I would pull back the fabric that normally covered the doorway that any in the other room could see that nothing unseemingly was being performed. I knew that the visitations would be reported to Dionysos and had no wish to give even the shadow of impropriety to his... his bedwarmer.

Over the months, I found her story. She was from some barbarian land to the far north, in the cold lands, apparently taken in a raid before her memories began to form. Her first rememberings were of being traded between Gaulean tribes as a... a young female offspring of the sun-god, her pure white skin and golden hair being as unique in the Gaulish territories as any other land. From there she was purchased by a far-trader from Rome and became a temple-priestess in the shrine of Sol, the Latium sun-god.

"It was there that I became a woman. The fee for my use in the night was much gold, and I was well vended." Now her expression became less than womanish, which is to say, bitter. "Especially by the fat Over-Priest of the temple, may his pouchstones shrivel to dried fruit. His tastes would offend even the pot-men of the latrines."

She continued. "But, there, with the kind friendship of an under priest with normal interests in women, I passed the monotony of the days by trading the learning the written word of Latium for the relief of his needs. And I gathered some of the histories of the - your - people. And other learnings of interest."

Then, one night, she was suddenly pulled from her bed-mat and stuffed into a carrying sack, taken to some ship in the harbor. And not with the auspices of the temple priests, apparently, from the sound of audible protests that could be heard by the girl in the sack - cries that ended on an increasing note - and suddenly.

Eventually, she arrived in Athens, to be vended in an exclusive offering attended only by the men of the city who could carry much coin to the slave-house. Thusly, did she come to be the golden-haired siren of the master of the Guild.

She was an undimmed woman, with a curiosity about the world and obviously seeking someone who could converse with some astuteness. "...besides the men in the taverna who can talk only of their svans and past conquests of its usage." Again, over the time, she also found my story. For whatever reason, I felt no need to gull her with some tale that would cover the truth of my less than savory past, but answered honestly and even with smiles as she gently laughed at the futile dreams of a young man for a fiery-haired femina.

As I stacked tablets for later perusal by Cleades, I asked, "And your name. It is obviously not the one given by your people, as you have no recollection of them."

She shook her head. "Nay. It was given at the cursed temple. I have no issue with it and one is good as another." She paused, then added, "I can remember a time, almost as a dream, when I was called something other, but that was before my memories began to harden."

I began to realize that there was more to her visits than just empty talk. More than once, and with subtlety, she would enquire as to my future plans, and predictions on the length of my residence in Athens. This gave me much food for thought.

With the need to maintain a watch for my safety now gone, I hid my longknife under the same boards as my coin, replacing it with a simple pugio - dagger, or kopis, in the Greek vernacular. Nobody would accost a person of the guild - not knowingly, and while the weapon that I acquired from the slaver's island might be much shorter than a Greek sword, it was still a major inconvenience while hanging on a belt from day to day.

More news came about the Spartan fleet. Growing bolder by the day, units were even seen standing off the port of Piraeus. It was obvious that the foray was no more than a boy pushing a stick into a hive of bees to see the reaction, but still, the feeling that some action was, if not imminent, the on the horizon.

My concern was not with Sparta, but much closer to my being. A summons came to attend on the master. This was worrisome - did he find objection with the numerous visits by his woman to my scribery? I immediately rose without finishing my meal and hurried to the far reaches of the complex. This area was far more luxurious than the warehouse area, having woven rugs on the floors and hanging furnishing covering the boards of the wall. Knocking at the door, I received a hail to enter and found Dionysos sitting at a table on which were two cups.

The room was opulent, and that was the least of the description. Besides the floor and wall covering, even the overhead was patterned with a shimmering cloth that gave the appearance of a blue sky. Pedestals around the walls held glittering glass sculptures and marble images of... Athenian gods and goddesses, I assumed. Few temples were furnished with such wealth that I saw in only a single glance.

The overly large room was not only his work area but apparently his sleeping quarters, also. In the corner, beside a large window covered with gauze, was a huge... not a mat, but a pile of cushions covered with thick blankets. As a love nest, it would be as a dormitory of a siren.

I had heard of the tastes of the master for beautiful women at all hours, and in more than single quantities, but this day he was alone and apparently waiting for myself. As I entered he called, "Ah, my Roman friend from the baths. Welcome. Sit and share a cup with me."

I walked to the table - a high one in the Greek tradition, rather than the low mensas that were usual in Rome. As I sat - again, on a chair to match the height of the table rather than reclining on a mat - he pushed a cup toward me. It was already filled and I gave thanks to my host and took a sip.

"Have you found the work with Cleades to your satisfaction?"

I swallowed and nodded, then spoke. "Aye, Kurios. It suits me very well... and you have my thanks for the position." I attempted to display a normal demeanor, although I felt as a man walking a path between serpents. Wealthy men of power didn't share either wine or casual conversation with a Plebeian nonentity in Rome and I doubt that the custom was common here either. In fact, I knew that it was not. I had little doubt that this man had no care or worries about either my satisfaction nor my needs, but I just matched his trivial questions with like answers until he revealed the reason for my summons. And after a few more pleasantries, he did.

"You have had many months to explore the means of my empire. What is your opinion of the guild operations from the view of the warehouses?"

I hesitated for a moment, then decided to give him the full truth as I knew it - I had no doubt of the danger to cozen this man. "Kurios... I would say that your trade is as a female trying to fetch water from the well and using a cracked jug. By the time she returns to her kitchen, most has trickled out along the way. And I have to say that such is the course with your grain." He gave no indication of alarm, or dismay, or even concern as I continued. "There is a possibility that the losses are not real - that they are just mis-figurings by various illiterate scribes along the path of trade..."

He nodded and replied, "But... you do not believe that."

It was a statement - not a question. I shook my head. "Nay. The differences are too regular. Should the cause be a scribe - or scribes - who are misrepresenting their skills to be above the actual, then the errors would be far more irregular. As I can see, the losses are always one part in twenty at this port, and one in fifteen on that dock, and such. I know little of the grain trade but I doubt that rats always eat the same four and ten bags from each loading on the wharf at Alexandria, or that salt water always spoils one bag out of eight on the leg of the voyage from Syria."

"Should not my senior scribe, Cleades, have seen this long ago? It would appear that he, being at the apex of the trade, would be the key instigator."

I doubted that Dionysos actually suspected the scribe of such thievery, else the old man would have been separated from his head long ago. He just wanted more of my thoughts on the subject. "Nay, Kurios. He would know of the losses were he able to read the Egyptian picture language, but he cannot. When finally the sheets and tablets of lading are presented to him, they match the totals that actually arrive at the dock."

"And your recommendations as to alleviate this problem?" That was a stunning question. Even now, after months in his employ, I had only a bare slice of knowledge about the guild and its workings.

I did not even recognize the names of many of the ports and grain fields that were the source of the bags that arrived on the ships. He saw my hesitation and said. "When I first met you at the baths, I will admit that I was not totally honest in my conversation of that evening. In truth, I had been looking for one from foreign parts and who was literate in the counting skills. Before that evening in the waters, I knew your name and that you were seeking employ as a scribe."

"But..."

"You were lately a Roman soldier, high in the ranks of a legion, and a skilled bladesman. You were newly arrived and unknown to any in the city and, as such, you could have no knowledge of, nor familiarity with any associate of any who might be enriching themselves at the expense of the guild." He leaned to refill my cup, then his. "I must say, the conjunction of soldier and scribe is unusual, even for one of Rome, to my knowledge. In any event, I had no wish to hire a scribe who in all possibility might already be a factor in the scheme." Another pause. "I have done so in the past and have received no value for my coin. Either fear or the weight of coin pulls them into the waters of the corruption. Graft and pilferage are as ingrained in the trade as the need for locusts to eat in the fields. But, although one cannot entirely end the thievery, any who become too greedy will pay the price."

I kept my expression under control at the statement of my putative past as a veteran of war. It took little thought to know from whence that misinformation had come, although it was interesting to ponder on how the leader of the guild could find the time to listen to taverna gossip. "And you have the opinion that Romans are in some way more trustworthy than Greeks?"

He shook his head with a thin smile. "Nay. I know that all lands produce scoundrels in quantity, but one must eventually place his wager on the throw of the bones or remain an onlooker." He pointed at my chest. "You will be my Trojan horse and penetrate the bastions of this corruption." As I opened my mouth to protest, he continued, "And your feeage will be in line with the mission, starting now." He tossed a small bag onto the table in front of me. I knew from the sound of the impact that it was filled with coin.

Thus, I became the Roman scribe who had come to learn the Athens grain trade, to hopefully open a new trade route to Rome and its environs - an area that produced copious amounts of good grain sufficient to feed both Latium and the Grecian peninsula.

Sitting that night, in our usual taverna and table, we conversed in low tones about the turn of fate. Korax was dubious of my mission, and warned of it in low tones. "I have no idea how things are handled in Rome, but here, any man who seems to be an obstacle in the pursuit of coin is usually found floating in the river one morning." He looked around to make sure we were unheard. "The dock stewards and grain factors of the trade are unlikely to look well upon a foreigner who interferes with their cushion."

I just took a swallow of the wine and shrugged. "I have not said that I would interfere with anything or anyone. I am now being paid to measure the profit between Egyptian and Roman grain, and determine the ratio of each in the most profitable routes." Shrugging, I continued. "If someone is fleecing the guild, that is the problem of my employer, not mine."

Korax just nodded. "Aye. A good story. If it is believed, then I will not have to find another benefactor to supply my wine and viands."

Accusator (Informer)

It was an interesting discovery, after first coming to this land, that the coinage of the street was mostly argyros, the metal that Romans call argentium. I found the reason to be that the land had huge deposits of the silvery metal in the mountains and had been mined since antiquity. Of course, for the lower classes, there were small coins of chalkos, the red metal that I knew as cuprum. My fee was paid in drachmas, the numerator of a series of coins starting as small as a fingernail and called a Hemitartemorion to a massive piece known as a Dekadrachm, bigger than the circle made with the forefinger and thumb and thick. However, most of the pieces in circulation were the ordinary drachma, made of the silvery metal and about the size of a thumb.

Interestingly also, coins of the golden metal, aurum, coveted to the point of thievery and murder in Rome, were seldom seen in Athens.

Despite my desire to spend my coin, and to the last drachma, in the many brothels along the streets of the Scanbonidas Deme - rather, the quarter in which I resided and labored - I forcibly made myself put aside one-half of what I was paid. As the leather purse hidden in the old warehouse began to become heavy, I took most of the contents and made a foray outside the gate. Along the road to the port, I turned aside onto an empty and rock filled watercourse to find a proper place to hide my wealth. Out of sight of the road, and beside a large rock with a memorable shape, I buried the small jar.

I knew that my sojourn in Athens - indeed, in this whole land - would not be forever. Also, knowing that the regard of the gods for myself was not favorable, based on the experiences of my life to this time, and that my departure would probably be with haste and in the dark of night. This would, at least, give me the chance of recovering enough of my coin to procure a berth on a ship and to flee, once again, across the world.

The days passed without incident as I continued my duties as assistance to the chief scribe, and the more secretive assignment to gain an understanding of the holes in the guild through which grain would pour to a loss at each shipload. Eventually, I delivered a scroll to the Master, full with listed names of those that were overly greedy in their graft. In the ensuing months, several men - even of high stature within the Guild - were found to have become careless in their cups in the evening, apparently having stumbled into the water of the harbor and with their cries of distress unheard by passersby.

Then, one evening, upon my return to the inn, I found Korax with another - this man an elderly graybeard with a missing hand and walking with a crutch. The blade in his belt seemed to be a superfluous weapon for such an oldster.

"Ah, my Roman friend. I have found an instructor who has agreed to tutor you in the use of your strange fruit peeler." He waved at the stranger. "This be Leodes, late of the Artemis Third Hekatontarchia, and the Lokhagos of the Lokhos in which I served." Again, I wondered at my friend's insistence in giving of the structure of the Athenian army to a Roman, who could not possibly have knowledge of either its structure or history.

I looked the old man up and down, unbelieving, then said with more disdain than I intended, "This... patriarch is... he is to instruct me...?" I frowned at the oldster. "My apologies for the efforts of my friend that has taken you from your deserved rest, old man, but I would need more instruction than making water with only one hand."

That was an affront to the man, without doubt. He goggled at me for a moment, then began to fumble in his belt for his blade - a weapon that looked to be as old and frail as himself. Disbelieving, I backed up a pace and reached for my own pugio... my kopis. Surely, he did not intend to fight with me over such words... I had no wish to harm the old fool, so I just stood and waited for his fumbling to end, and probably with his dropping his blade in the dirt of the floor.

Had I bothered to listen, I might have heard the gods chuckling faintly, over their cups and jests.

Suddenly, the fumbling stopped, and the long crutch came up with lightning speed, to impact under my forearm. Instantly, the entire appendage went numb, then another stroke - downward this time, connected with my hand and knocked the kopis from my fingers. Before the pain had even registered in total, my head was gently rocked back as the end of the walking staff was firmly planted between my eyes and given a light shove.

"I will give your first lesson without fee, Roman." The assumed wrath was gone, replaced by amusement and I realized that I had played myself for the fool. "And that is never to denigrate your foe until he is laying at your feet. You saw what you wanted to see - an old man with weak water and sinews to match." He gently pushed the stick again, then lowered it. "Always... And by that I mean at every meeting of a man, assume that he is student of Ares himself, and far beyond your capability in weaponry. Only with that mind, will you have a chance of living to the next sunrise."

Swallowing my pride, and cursing myself for my idiocy, I nodded. "Aye, Kurios. You have the better of me in this instance, and I give my sorrow for my words. They were spoken in haste and were those of a fool."

The old man grinned at Korax. "At least, your friend has the truth of his being." Now, with more seriousness, he asked, "Do you wish for my instruction, Roman? Or, nay?"

Now, I forced a grin. "Aye, Kurios. But, let us retire to yon taverna and allow me to make mitigation for my rudeness. We can best talk over cups to make the transaction. Besides, my blade is at the warehouse of Dionysos and I will have to retrieve it before any lessons."

We settled into a table, and were presented with three cups by the handsome daughter of the Caupo, then I raised mine and said, "Again, Kurios, my acknowledgment of the foolish greeting to the friend of a friend into our dwelling. It was the mark of a simpleton, and not of a man who wishes to be thought of as wise."

The old man just grinned, as he raised his cup. To Korax, he said, "Your man knows when he has misstepped." To me, he said, "The beginning of wisdom is the knowledge of one's own mistake. I have already forgotten it."

The talk went on until the old soldier asked about the peculiar blade of which he had heard from my friend. I emptied my cup and excused myself, intending to hurry to the warehouses and retrieve it from the floorboards. The distance was only a long rock throw, and I dropped another coin on the table so as to allow their cups to be filled until I returned.

This time of day, the building was deserted - the storage area, that is. The internal and private taverna rang with shouts and talk and laughter, as it did on all evenings. As the sun had almost set, the shadows were deep within, but I well knew the way. And, I did not wish to call attention to myself by walking through the structure with a torch or lamp.

Far in the back of the empty warehouse, I moved the small pile of rotten and empty bags, then pulled the loose board up far enough to grip my longknife. In a moment, it was attached to my belt, and I hastened to return to the taverna. The building being very old, the planks of the wall were warped and ill-fitting, letting even the very slight and fading sunlight above to filter to the floor. But it also allowed for any from the adjacent rooms to enter. And now, I could see the flicker of light through the cracks.

Fire is the main horror of city life, exceeded only by that far less common curse of the gods - the plague. And, in these rambling wooden buildings, the danger was not assumed lightly. The common rule was that no fires would be left unattended, on pain of banishment from job and quarter. All lamps and the few torches could only be lit when actually used. And, in fact, there were no torch holders on the walls, except in the areas of assembly, such as the taverna. Thus, any flame would be carried by a person, not left unattended to smolder and drip without notice.

Thus, the light that I could see filtering through the walls had to come from a flame, and as this area of the huge warehouse compound was vacant at this time of the evening, then the flickering had to be from a torch left burning, or an actual fire that had started. I hurried out the doorway and down the hall to the entrance of the adjacent storage area - this one also empty, as the one I had left, and even larger. I could see no glimmer of light of a flame, so I continued down the hallway to the next.

It was in this one that I found the source of the light. A torch had been rammed into the topmost bag of a stack of grain and was still flaring. As such it was of little danger, but why was it burning in an almost abandoned storehouse? All of these back storage rooms had been empty since my arrival at the guild - I well knew of the amount of grain and corn that was stored in all areas. It was my task to enumerate the coming and going of the material on a daily basis. This ancient and dusty room should have had nothing but air.

But, halfway down the floor, was a stack of bags - possibly an eighth of a small shipload in number. Still, the problem would wait till the morrow. For now, the torch needed to be extinguished and for myself to return to the inn.

But... Those plans were destroyed as I approached the pile of bags, and began to view the floor beyond.

I stopped, frozen in place, my skin suddenly prickling with... with... On the floor, were more bags, or so I thought for a fleeting heartbeat. But these were men, and so freshly dead that their lifeblood, dark red in the torchlight, was still spreading on the floor. Now, I frantically looked around for their slayers, but in the mostly empty storeroom, there was nobody - and no place for any to conceal themselves. My longknife was in my hand, but that was just a reflexive action rather than any hope of defending myself from the manslayers that had cut the life from four men.

Still looking from side to side, I yanked the torch from its stabbing in the grain, then quickly backed up to the door, turning to run down the long hallway through the exit that led to an open area between buildings. There, I saw one of the many slaves that were owned by the Guild, walking with a pot and a torch - no doubt to the cesspool for emptying.

"You! Slave! Come here! Quickly!"

The man ran to me, kneeling, and said, "Aye, Master?"

I pointed uselessly in the general direction of the main building, and barked, "Know you of Teukros, the second of Dionysos?"

"Aye, Master."

"Go to the taverna and tell him that the Roman requires his presence here, with haste, and to bring men with arms."

The man looked up at me in distress. "Master. I may not enter the Guild rooms upon any..."

"Do what I say! I will intercede with the second for your trespass." I took the torch from his hand, then shouted, "And run with speed!"

The man turned and disappeared into the dark doorway and I returned to the hallway of the old storerooms. Listening for many heartbeats, I could hear nothing, so I began to walk down the corridor, looking carefully as I passed this door and that. There was nothing, and I had expected that. The entire set of storerooms were empty - or were supposed to be. Except for the one room with the results of... what?

It was not a long wait. I could hear the commotion of men in the distance, then down the long corridor appeared several torches and men, all running and with blades in hand. They could easily see my flame, and took that as their destination.

In moments, Teukros was standing in front of me, somewhat breathless, and demanded, "What is the call, Roman? And the need for blades?"

I just waved for him to follow and entered the room with the bodies. With a curse, Teukros stopped and looked around, seeing nothing else but grain and blood. Turning, he gave a command. "Search the area. You... and you. Phylos! Find the watchman of the north wall and bring him here. Diomenes! Take two men and walk the wall from the Plieny post to the far corner. Abaser! Send word to the Master that strange happenings have occurred and escort him here if he wishes to see."

"Teukros! Here!" This from the men searching the huge store room. In the back wall, and near a corner was a hole, where two planks had been carefully removed to allow access from the alley behind. But, even exiting the building, the thieves would still be within the compound walls - thick, of stone, and unlikely to be breached - thusly, somewhere would be a ladder or even an unsecured gate.

I doubted that this was the first attempt on direct pilferage by the gang of thieves. The planks were not smashed, or torn, but taken loose without damage, to be replaced to leave no indication of the theft. And no doubt used again on another night with no moon.

In a while came the news that the watchman of that sector was not to be found, but that the gate was secured, and no other access was evident.

In any event, this was not a matter to concern myself. I merely stood aside as a living torch holder and let the men examine what they would. Teukros and his Master could discuss the problem and decide on an alleviation. Or so was my thought.

I saw another set of torches enter the doorway - Dionysos and two men. Teukros saluted, and pointed to the bodies. "A nighttime thievery, Kurios. And well planned, I might say."

The man looked around for a moment, then asked, "How much was taken?"

"That is unknown, Kurios. I have no idea where these bags came from, nor how many there were."

"This is strange." I suddenly realized that one of the men who accompanied the Guild leader was Cleades, the head scribe. "Nothing has been stored in these leaky shacks for many seasons."

Dionysos just nodded, then asked of his second, "And these? Slain by your men?"

Teukros shook his head. "Nay, Kurios. It was the Roman that did the deed." My eyes widened in astonishment - fortunately, unseen in the flickering shadows of the torches.

Dionysos turned to look at me, frozen as a statue in the Agora. Another man made a forced jape, "And without a mark on him. His little toy-blade is good for other than peeling fruit, it would seem."

Still speechless, I turned to look at the man, barely comprehending his words in the realization of what was happening. But, my countenance did not reflect my confusion, it appeared. The man who had spoken raised his hands in haste and stammered out an amendment. "Nay, Roman. I spoke in jest, meaning no disrespect for your weapon or skills."

Now, Teukros looked at me in turn. "You strike down four toughs, despite their long blades, and without a mark nor a blemish on your garb? You have strange abilities for a scribe, Roman."

"Little do you know of our friend from afar, Teukros," interjected Dionysos. "He was once an accomplished training officer in the army of his land before he set sail for our shores. I would hesitate in kindling his anger, despite his comradely manner." Looking around again, he finished with, "There is little to do here tonight. Set a new watchman on the wall. Have these taken to the pits on the morn." Pointing at me, he said, "Come."

A while later in his quarters, I was sitting at the table and holding a cup. He filled his own, then sat opposite me. "An interesting happenstance, your being in the unused warehouses this time of night, would you not say?"

This man was far from a fool, and to attempt a blatant falsehood would be dangerous indeed. I needed to deliver the truth if not all of it. "Aye, Kurios. And in fact, I was retrieving a handful of silver for my use."

"From the warehouses?" His puzzlement was plain in his inflection.

"Aye. As you know, I reside in a public inn, and such is not a place to either keep nor hide coin. Thusly, I have put my small stash in a hiding place within the Guild proper, where none would look. Tonight, I was refreshing my purse with it." I shrugged, then said, "As to my arrival when the thieves had decided to make their move... well, it is for the gods to answer that coincidence."

He reflected on the explanation for a moment, then, apparently satisfied, said, "I would have your measure of the issue at hand, and before I give my thoughts."

I nodded, thinking on the night. "My first idea is that these were just thieves, and not connected with the pilferage along the trade routes. But why risk with open thievery what you can just load onto a cart in daylight and safety?"

He nodded. "I would agree. Continue."

"However, all of the far storerooms are empty and have been so since my arrival. I know this from my measuring of available storage space in the compound, and by my wanderings to just explore for my own interest. So..." I paused, then continued, "Some person - or several - within your organization are carrying bags of grain from the forward storage to where they are stacked in waiting for men to haul away at night. And probably a few at a time, so as not to garner any questions by any casual onlookers. After all, a man with a burden of a grain-bag on these premises is not a sight to which anyone would look in askance. Unless, there was a steady march of them during the day."

"Continue," he said over his cup.

"As to your missing guard, I suspect that he was suborned by the thieves and is part of that pack and decided to leave after the scheme was exposed. To stay, would have him trying to explain his lack of watchfulness. The other thought that he was killed as a watchman is not consistent with the idea of the effort. They would have to dispose of the new watcher on every foray, and that would become obvious to the Guild immediately."

I paused at that, hoping that it was satisfactory. For myself, the answers did not come so easily. Since I knew that the men were not slain by myself, then why were they killed? A disagreement about portions while in the act of the theft would seem to be foolish. Normally, that would come after the stolen grain had been vended. More likely, another group of thieves had decided to share in the loot, so to speak, and the attempted association was looked on with disfavor by the original robbers.

He nodded, then rose, as did I. "On the morrow we will attempt to find the close end of this thievery." I wished him a good sleep and departed the Guild building, walking slowly back to my inn. By now, I knew that Korax and... what was the name of the graybeard... Aye, Leodes. They would be long gone from the taverna, no doubt wondering at my disappearance.

I was still disbelieving the events of this day, both evening and night. I had killed men in my life - the pirates, in my desperation to escape slavery, and a man in a taverna by an act that even a street bard would not repeat for fear of being ridiculed, and this day I was being attributed as a bladesman with skills far beyond the norm.

Now I knew, beyond any doubt, that the gods existed. On the slopes of Olympus, in the marbled halls was a large playing board, and on it was an image of a man - in wax, or wood, or even stone - and with the close likeness of myself. Those immortal beings would gather in the evenings for play, cast their bones and then laugh and jest as the little image was danced here, and there, on strings like a puppet of the acting-boards of the Forum. And far below, the flesh that resembled the image would dance in common with the moves of his little double.

Nothing else would explain the events in my life from the time that I saw the young boy fall from the bridge into the Tiber.

In the days to follow, I received an education in the use of blades from the old man. Frail he was, but even so, I would have lasted only heartbeats in any actual confrontation with him, despite the range in years between us. In his younger time, he must have been a man of exceedingly dangerous skill to a foe.

His stick could beat a drum rhythm on my body as I wielded my own wood in my practice thrusts and swings. A swordsman I did not become - only years of exhaustive training and actual use can build such, and certainly not a month of nights of swinging a short stick in the afteryard of an inn. But I learned the basics of such usage. He cured me of the faults of the beginner, who will frantically wave his weapon, as if a matron trying to swat a rodent from her pantry. Or make vastly wide or high traverses which invite his opponent to thrust a point into the chest before the novice even reaches the high point of his swing.

Korax would sit and drink from a jug, watching and making jests and useless comments. He had had a huge laugh, the day after my adventure in the abandoned warehouse when I gave him the story. He shook his head in mirth at the fact that I was now considered a most dangerous man by the members of the Guild - in no small part stemming from that one falsehood that he had uttered in the taverna, months ago - about my being the training Hastilarius of my legion in Rome.

For myself, I maintained my composure with the men of the Guild, sitting with drink and food in the private taverna, speaking little or nothing about either the robbery or my prowess with weapons. I must say, that my stature rose considerably after that night. I prayed to the gods that I might never need to demonstrate my putative skill with a blade.

As the fates would have it - or the gods in their jesting - I had no further use for my blade for my remaining sojourn in the city of Athens...

Induction

As any prideful Athenian would tell, the ships of the city are manned by free men, all in concert to defend the common cause. The service is considered to be far too essential to trust to slaves, most of which would welcome the demise of their masters. However, from the view through the thole ports of the three-tiered ships, the concept was not as pure as stated by those speaking without knowledge of the subject.

No slaves were aboard my ship - that was a given. However, a few were serving with the same willingness as myself - they woke with their heads reeling from the ataraxic that had been slipped into their wine. Then, as they staggered to their feet in the hull of the scow that had brought them downriver, a ship's officer complemented them on their patriotism. This was Piraeus, the port serving the city of Athens, a destination that I had traveled to many times, although not as a passenger laying in the muddy bottom of a river scow.

My current plight was the result of my forgetting the advice of Korax as to where I took my cups.

Only a few days after the strange encounter in the old warehouse, I was back at the grain docks, counting and recording the unloading of a ship from the far land of Egypt. A large vessel, it was, and the sun was almost gone before the last plank in the bottom was uncovered. The long day finished, I began the walk back to the city by following the Long Wall that stretched between the port and Athens. Of course, the entire road was littered with tavernas and brothels for the returning dock workers, allowing the separation of the men from their daily coin.

My day had been long, and my feet were weary and I had stopped at a wineshop to rest my legs for the few stadia that remained between me and my sleeping mat. Many unwise choices have I made in my imperfect life, but this decision to hasten my evening wine was among the worst. I sat at the table, taking my wine quietly and with no desire to enter any of the japing and jawing from the surrounding tables. What I wanted was to lay my head and soon. In fact, I was suddenly consumed by the need to rest, even to the point of considering the engaging of a mat in any inn that might be along the way. I wondered at the sudden exhaustion of my sinews - it had been a busy day, but I had had many of those as a matter of course...

The sun was high when I woke in the trough of the scow, my head feeling twice its size and with hammers beating both on and within. It was a while, but slowly I raised myself to look over the low gunwales of the boat. It took some more moments, but I finally recognized the shoreline only a stadium away. We were being poled along and toward the huge port at the end of the spit of land the Greeks called a peninsula.

Now, past the familiar wharves and docks that I had frequented, past even the shipyards filled with men and the skeletons of ships yet to be launched, we floated. I had never been this far into the port, and the activity that I could see on shore was tremendous. I estimated that at least seventy triremes, those immense ships of war, were in various stages of completion. And it was apparent that the urgency was great - the shipwrights and builders covered the hulls like ants over a sweetmeat. Still, the numbers were dwarfed by the next group of naval vessels that appeared as we sailed around the curve of the shore.

Even the taverna drunkards gasped at the sight of the Athenian fleet drawn up on the shore. Stunned, I just gazed at the innumerable ships as we coasted along as if in a parade. Finally, I began a quick count, trying to estimate how many we had already passed. My total reached an unbelievable number - probably a hundred and a half more. Including the ships in the building yards, this had to be the largest fleet in the world - probably in all of history. Compared to this armada, the few penteconterae that Rome used to chase pirates were as minnows to the leviathan.

A boatman I was, but as a seaman I had much to learn. These ships were completely drawn up onto the sand and out of the water. How it was accomplished, I could not imagine. Each trireme was about a hundred foot-lengths from stem to stern, and although very narrow, the vessel had to weigh as much as a large taverna building. All of the fishermen along the shore of the Tiber could not have pulled such a weight onto the shore.

I need not have bothered in my wonderment - soon, I would be intimately familiar with the procedure of beaching and launching such vessels.

About halfway down the line of ships, was a large gap in the sands, and on the shore, we could see tents erected as far as the eye could see over the bend of the shoreline. It was into this gap that we headed, beaching shortly onto the soft sand. At the shouts of one of the officers, all onboard - to the extent of fifty or more - climbed over the side of the hull and dropped into the shallow water, to follow the officer up the beach. Not far along, we came to an open area of beaten down grass where several more officers were waiting. At the order, the newly arrived crewmen - willing or no - were ordered to form a single line, after which we were counted off in groups of ten and assigned to one of the waiting officers. Mine was a bearded man - of course - of large stature and a blue cloak that indicated his rank, although I did not know that as yet. If he was impressed with his new sailors, he managed to conceal his pleasure well.

"By Posedion and his pox ridden dalkies! Did the tavernas of the city sweep the leavings onto the streets? I need rowmen, not wine-bellied sotheads that will keel over before the oar is through the thole port!" I would gladly have relieved him of his disappointment by offering to find my own way back to Athens, but I doubted that he wanted to hear such a proposal. Indeed, I strongly suspected that he wanted to hear absolutely nothing from his new enlistment. "I am Protensus, the Kybernetes of the Sea Swan. For you lubbers, that means that I am the helmsman and in charge of the ship under orders of the Kapetanios. It also means that I have to turn you wine-swilling scum into oarsmen before our next foray with the Spartans." He waved and finished with, "Come."

Following him through the maze of tents, most empty with the men at work on the ships, we found ourselves in the far corner of the peninsula and in front of yet another man - this one with a different blue cloak. Again, the helmsman spoke to the ten new sailors in his stentorious voice. "This be Anakletos, the Proreus of the Sea Swan. He will give your duties and activities in the manner needed by the ship." He paused a moment, then ended with, "The Kapetanios of the Swan is a good man, and well founded in sea-fare. Do your duties as commanded and you will find him a fair master. But..." Another pause for emphasis. "...He looks with much disfavor on any who mar the performance of his vessel."

With that, he turned and strode away leaving us to the tender mercies of one Anakletos, the Proreus. Later, as I discerned the hierarchy of the navy, I realized that, had we been in a unit of the Roman army, his rank would have been that of Optio or Centurion - that is, the sub-officer standing between the high officers and the ranks.

In any case, he was our immediate master and not one to be precluded in any way. Not if a man wanted to keep the skin on his back. Still, as he spoke, he seemed to be of a milder disposition than his superior. "Follow me," was all he said. Not far behind us was a large tent - tents, actually, that seemed to house the quartermasters of the fleet. From a man at the entrance of one, we received - each - a clean loincloth, a cup, a bowl and a wool blanket. Carrying our only possessions, besides the various clothing that each wore, we were presented to an anonymous tent in the vast array across the peninsula. "This will be your dwelling while in the shipyard and until we set sail. Notice the number pole and don't forget it." He pointed to a short mast, made of a small tree trunk, at the top of which were several pennants - two blue, a red and a yellow. Now I noticed that all of the tents had their identity pole, but with a different arrangement of flags at the peak. Obviously, the purpose was to allow the occupants to find their tent in the gigantic maze of like shelters. "Find an open spot and lay your blanket. Take off those city clothes and toss them in the rag pile. We only wear loincloths in the service - they are much easier to clean and cooler when the body water begins to flow." This was done, and I laid out my blanket in an empty spot in the far end. Looking up and down, I estimated that the tent was quarters for at least half a hundred men - or more. None were in evidence, of course, being at work or training somewhere. Just where, we were soon to find out.

Now, we ten almost naked men followed the Proreus toward the sea and finally to one of the many ships hove up onto the sands. Looking up and down, I could see at least forty triremes in a row on this side of the peninsula, all swarming with men doing... anything and everything. Many were shaving long poles into oars, others scraping the sides and bottoms of the vessels, with even more on ropes pulling this ship or that to one side or the other to allow for cleaning or inspection of the bottoms. Much was the buzz of conversation among the workers, but their talk did not hinder their hands. All were at work with much jesting and calling. It was obvious that these were willing sailors and oarsmen, unlike the handful of unfortunates that had arrived with me on the scow from the city.

Without preamble, we were given bronze scrapers and put to cleaning the short green growths from the hull of a trireme with a picture of a large cygnus each side of the on the forepeak hull - a swan. In addition, there was a large wooden bird decorating the forepeak - apparently in the image of that water bird after which the ship was named.

Interestingly, I was no longer the visible Roman in a sea of Greeks. Many of the workers were cleanly shorn of facial hair, also. Not baby smooth as I was, from depilation, but by the use of sharpened blades to scrape the hairs from the skin, a process that left considerable stubble. I would find later that the reason was comfort. In the strenuous work and heat, a beard was an attractor for the innumerable sea-lice that were found on the shore and come to find a home in the fur that was both salty and warm from the body water that flowed freely under the sun. Some even removed the hair from their privates for the same reason. Thus did I, also, within a day of arriving and scratching my skin raw as I attempted to give my groin relief from the itching vermin.

Knowing absolutely no man in the crew, I just concentrated on my work with the scraper, letting the jests and callings flow over and around me. The task required little ability and my thoughts roamed, examining my sudden change of life from all sides. Again, I thought, it was obvious that I was the plaything of the gods. Or of at least one, who relieved the boredom of eternity by playing me as if I were a doll in the hands of my little sister. Unfortunately, I had no idea of just which deity was honoring me with his attention by allowing me to reach a plateau of satisfaction with my life, then casting me into the roaring waters of fate. This was the third time that I had fallen from a good berth, to begin again at the bottom of society.

Finally, my attention was gathered as a voice behind me said, "You! The new man. Heard ye not the gong for the evening meal?" I turned to see a fellow worker, dressed as I was in only a loincloth, gesturing for me to follow. I set the scraper on the plank from which I had procured it and walked to join my hailer. "My greetings," he said. "You are new to the ship."

It was not a question. I nodded. "Aye. I arrived here at midday."

He nodded in return. "You have been blessed by the gods to be assigned to the Sea Swan. No better ship ever floated in the salt water of Poseidon." I would have been satisfied with fewer god-blessings, but said nothing about my forced entry into the comradeship of the vessel as he continued. "I am called Tros, from the Deme of Collytus." I had entered that quarter a few times, looking around the city in my curiosity. It was a sector of small merchants.

He waited for a few heartbeats, to see if I would respond. As my silence continued, he said, "I was a fuller, engaged with the trade from my patér since my beginning." Again the pause. "But... The plague took my good mate and my two sons and with them went my interest in my trade."

The man was obviously making an effort at friendship, and my continuance of silence in my melancholy state was unseemly. Finally, I rose to the occasion with a gesture. "I am called Junius, from Rome."

That widened his eyes. "I could hear a bending of your words that gave the order of your foreignness, but how does a man from that far land come to seek service with the navy of Athens?"

Now I laughed and managed to keep the bitterness out of the response. "The tale is long. So long that yon ship would be wormwood before I finished my story. I will just say that the path of my feet was guided by some god with a notion of humor."

Now he just nodded soberly. "Aye. In that, I have much experience with the temper of the gods. Else I would not be here even now. But... I could not stay in the house that gave such joy with my family. This work is good, and gives me purpose to my life again."

Suddenly we arrived at the very tent that I had left at midday. Inside, we procured our cups and bowls, and again I followed the man - this time to the mess tents. There, under a huge open air canopy - actually, several side by side - huge vats and tubs of food were steaming. Beside the cover, in the open, were fire pits over which much meat was roasting. Following my newly found comrade, I got into a line that quickly shuffled inside and to a serving table where a slave heaped my bowl with meat and cheese and bread, and a stew of some unknown mixture. The next table filled our cup with wine and we hurried back to our tent to enjoy the repast.

The food was plain but good and there was much of it. This was not wharf rations, and certainly not bound labor food. I doubted that the ordinary family in the city had access to the quality and quantity of what was filling my bowl. Whatever my new fate was to be, at least, it would come on a full belly.

For a time, we just ate, but eventually my hunger was subdued and my interest in my future began to return. Only a handful of men had returned from the cooks with their repast, apparently most wishing to eat elsewhere. "What is your position on the ship?" I asked.

Waving a hunk of bread at me, he replied, "The same as you, of course. We will be oarsmen for the Swan, guiding our ram into the lumber of the cursed Spartans. All in this tent and the next are pullers of the wood. Seventy and a hundred all to each ship." Again the gesture with the bread, but this time in another direction. "Yon area beyond the latrines is for the hoplites, of which we carry twenty. And with several archers and five officers, well... many villages surrounding the city have a count of fewer men than we muster in our single hull."

I was astounded by the numbers. If his speaking was true, then the ship would board almost two hundred men. And that number, added to the complement of each of the ships that I had seen on arrival...

Now the stunning realization hit me as I tried to manipulate numbers of a size that I had never used before. Neither the Roman numbering nor the Egyptian counting had a numeral of such size. In the Greek numbering, there was a symbol for the amount of ten counts of a thousand, given the name of myriad and designated by the symbol M, but it was seldom used and not considered an accepted numeral by most scribes. After all, few, if any, transactions would have need to enumerate such an amount. Still, for my purposes it would suffice.

I scratched in the dirt of the floor with a stick in one hand while eating with the other. Ten counts of kilos - thousands - or XXXXXXXXXX would be equivalent of one Myriad - M. With the number of ships in the Athenian navy, by my estimation, and with almost two hundred men for each, then the total manpower would be... I scratched and then erased with my foot, then scratched again. Finally, shaking my head, I looked at the number in the dirt - MMMXXXX. Three myriads and four kilos to make the number. It was inconceivable. How was such a count of men fed on a daily basis? Where did the wood come from to make such a monstrous fleet?

And my burning question. With such power, why did not Athens rule the entire world?

As the evening fell, the tent occupants returned in groups for their rest. Again, it was easily apparent that these were not pressed men, but citizens of the city who were proud to be a part of the fleet, soon to take the war to the enemy. The banter and jesting was of men satisfied with their lot, not the grumbling of a host who was ordered from above. I realized that my tale of being forcibly taken for use in the fleet must remain my own secret. These men were very unlikely to welcome a man who did not wish to be a part of their ranks.

So. I would do my part, all the while watching for an opportunity to, once again, flee across the world as a man with no domicile.

Morning brought trumpets and another meal sufficient for the work of the first half of the day. Once again, I was put on the scraper and the job of cleaning the hull, but in this case on the other side after ropes pulled the hull to lean in the opposite direction. I saw Tros a few times, apparently engaged in spreading huge swaths of cloth in the sun to dry. These, I assumed were the sails that would decorate the two masts that I could see raised on several of the triremes up and down the sands.

Eventually, my work took me from the stem to the stern of the trireme. In the aft section, in place of the normal rudder or steering plank, were a pair of oars - one on either side. Why a ship would need more than one, I had no idea, but I had no knowledge of warships. The stern of the ship was deeply cut back into the hull, with both men at the oars actually standing over the water.

At the forepeak, besides the large wooden bird on the pole that served as an emblem of the vessel, a large protrusion extended from the lower hull, almost even with the keelson - the bottom-most beam of the hull. This was the ram, of course. As I scraped on the wood of the bow, I examined the weapon with interest. It appeared to be made of bronze, but that assumption was ludicrous. Not only would such a mass of metal cost more than a fleet of ships, it would effectively anchor the trireme on the beach from its weight. No, it must be plating over wood to give the weapon more strength.

The next day was far more busy, at least for me, and much more interesting than standing in the sand and mindlessly moving a scraper back and forth. This morning I cleaved to Tros, and the sub officers did not seem to notice that I had not been assigned the position. Shortly after the break of our fast, the activity was immense - with men lining up on both sides of the hull and grasping thick ropes for pulling. Many others placed themselves at the fore of the hull to push and with the sound of the trumpet we began the pulling and pushing.

I was surprised at the ease of which the ship was moved off the sand and into the water. It took little more than an easy pull for the ship to slide down the beach slope and into the water. Immediately, we formed a line from the vessel to the shore and began to pass bag after bag containing water to the ship. Up and over the side they went, into great water tubs, I assumed, since shortly they were thrown back down to be refilled. Finally, bags of rations were sent aboard, although not in the quantity of the water. Then, at a shout of orders, the men began to hurriedly climb aboard.

Once aboard, I just stood, not knowing what would be my placement in the crew. As I have described, the ship was long and narrow and loosely decked. That is, the hull was not covered for a few paces at both ends, and there were many open ways along the deck. I stood next to... what I would have called a hatchway in the ships with which I was familiar, but in this case, the opening had no cover. Inside and under the deck, I could see different levels of platforms, three to each side, and benches for the rowers. That explained to me how so many oarsmen could be accommodated in the length of the hull. Had they been arranged in a single row, the men would have been belly to backside and with no room for any wood pulling, but in this arrangement, every next rower was offset to the inside and above or below his mate, immediately fore and aft. Still, as the men climbed down to their posts, the inside of the trireme was indeed full. Several of us - I recognized them as the men who accompanied me down the river - were standing and waiting for orders. They were not long in coming.

The oar master - the Proreus - soon had us in hand and led us down the ladder at the front of the ship. Walking along the narrow center aisle, he pointed to this spot and that, telling a man that this was his position and to remember the number painted above the thole port. Mine was seven and fifty - close to the center of the ship.

The long oars were already in place, having been loaded the day before when the ship had been righted from the work of scraping. With their length being more than the width of the ship, it would be impossible to pull them completely inboard - at least to my estimation. At the moment, they were held high out of the water with rope slings, looped over the handle, so as to not interfere with the launching and to prevent damage to the pole by dragging the blade in the sand. The men were chattering - again demonstrating that this was a willing crew - but I just sat and waited. I certainly knew of oars and their uses, but in this massive array of propelling wood was far beyond my experience.

Sitting and looking out the small gap in the thole port, through which my oar exited the ship, I could see nothing but the side of the next vessel for a while. Then I felt, and saw, the movement that indicated that we were moving away from the beach - obviously being poled by sailors on the upper deck. In a few heartbeats, my vision, which had been blocked by the next ship, receded and I could see down the shore to more triremes, all in various stages of movement off the sands. We gradually turned until I could see nothing but the open sea.

Now came the command from the Proreus, standing at the back of the rowers aisle, "Check oars down!" The men pushed down on the handles of the poles and let the capture loops of rope fall away, freeing the paddles for work. Next came, "Level oars!" and the handles were brought to knee level.

"Standby the stroke!" Now a man sitting on a platform at the far stern of the boat began to beat a two mallets on a... it appeared to be a section of log, knee high that served as a drum. It must have been hollow and with a thick metal plate on top - the sound of the mallets striking were far too loud for it to have been wood. He began the beat, no faster than a slow heartbeat, but still the rowers held their positions. I realized that this preamble was just to let the crew find the rhythm of the stroke.

There was some shouting back and forth between the Proreus and some officer on the upper deck, probably the Kapetanios. The

Trierarch, I corrected myself. The captain of the ship he might be, but under way he was referred to with the particular Greek term for his rank and the vessel.

Now came the actual commands to move the ship. "Oars ahead!" I watched, following the actions of my mates ahead as best I could. The handles were pushed forward to the extent of our arms, then at the command of "Stroke!" the blades were dropped into the water and pulled to our chests. Thus began the voyage of the trireme.

I was clumsy for a short while, but it took only a few strokes before I caught the rhythm and my work became as my mates. At this time, the way-making was easy, propelling us through the water at a slow walk, had we been on land. We voyaged for a while, then at a command, the piper at the drum - the Auletes - was given another beat, then the Proreus shouted, "Change the stroke!" The mallets hit with greater frequency and we matched the beat with our pulls.

Thus it went for the morning. I had little chance to look out my small vision hole, and saw little when I did. I assumed that we were maneuvering back and forth in mock warfare as the captains practiced their trade above. At frequent occasions, the command of "Up Oars" and "Check Oars" would come, and we would push the handles down to loop the holding ropes to allow the blades to hold in the air as the Trireme coasted to a stop. These periods of rest were times that we could stand and flex our limbs, garnering strength for the next way.

There was a break in mid-morn, as two young boys moved down the center aisle with buckets of cool water, allowing the rowers to drink their fill. Along with them came two others, also with buckets to allow the rowers to relieve themselves of any water their bodies did not need. Little of that was necessary, as most of the liquid was retained by the body for work.

Again we began the stroke until the midday hour for the rations. They were plain and cold, but filling, and the men could move around to flex their limbs - even to climbing to the deck to gaze around for a short while. Thus far, the work had not been exhausting, but my arms and legs were beginning to complain about the unaccustomed effort. By the evening, though, I was very tired - more than I had been since my sojourn on the island with the pirates. Still, the ship had to be made safe for the night, and in a reversal of the morning launch, the ropes were attached, and other men - this time at the stern of the trireme - pushed and pulled the vessel onto the sands. Only then were we allowed to take our evening repast and retire to our tent.

For the first time since the launching, I saw Tros. He was in good spirits and munching on a meat-bone as he walked back to the tents. Waving the haunch at me, he called, "So, good Junius. How were your nuptials with the Sea Swan this first day?"

With a wry smile, I shook my head. "I survived the joining, but the tale that my limbs will tell on the morrow is something that I do not anticipate enjoying."

Grinning back at me, he said, "This day was easy. The captains were measuring their crews and ships. The Swan is among the fortunate - most on board are veterans and well know their trade. To be on a newly found ship with a green crew is something to make even the gods laugh. The clashing of poles can scarcely be heard above the cursing of the officers."

We settled onto our blankets for the night in talk, Tros not even enjoying his nightly sojourn under the cool night sky, in deference to my sore legs. Up and down the tent, small groups were chattering, in the manner of men in military units from the beginning of time. I began to realize, and was astounded by the fact that the crews - the oarsmen of the triremes - were not recruited exclusively from the lower classes of the city. Several were pointed out to me as being the scions of important houses of Athens - well-to-do and even wealthy young men who aspired to protect their homes and families rather than relax in the luxury of their status. Even more were sons of merchants and magistrates. Of course, there were many young men with no future other than lowly work in the docks, or tanneries and such, but even they seemed to think of themselves as the shield between Athens and the foe.

To the casual eye, no man was there against his will. I knew that not to be true, myself being one such, and knowing that a double handful of others were impressed by the crimpers of the city - and that was just from the one boat that had brought us from the city. Still, none stated their position of unwillingness - a wise decision in such a gathering. To denigrate the service of the fleet in front of these men would put one in grave danger and at the least would find that man broken and bleeding on the next morn - cast from his tent as if a blasphemer.

And I saw the punishment handed out to deserters. During the day of maintenance, a beat of drums down the beach brought us to the surfside to wonder at the clamor. We were several ships away, but the surf was low, and we could hear the proclamation of an officer standing on the stern of the vessel. The veterans of the crew knew what was in store, but it took a while for the newcomers to realize the seriousness of what we had thought to be a celebration. Accusations of desertion from the fleet were read, and the names of three men were pronounced. There was some activity at the surf line, and we realized with horror that the men were being buried up to their necks in the sand, and below the tide mark. Thus, I realized that any plans on my part to leave the service of Athens without sanction would have to be done with caution - extreme caution and planning. Of all the ways that a man might die, being left to drown in the rising water was not attractive to my thoughts.

Thus it went for the next half month. As I suspected, I woke that next morning sore and stiff, but a day of more oar pulling worked out the cramps and within a handful of days, my body had reclaimed the quality of sinews that had been developed on the island of Sifnos. I could now row with any and better than most, being younger than the average and larger overall.

Each seventh day was a day of rest. The men were given their pay, a few obols of silver, and allowed their desires for the day. Since we were at the far end of the peninsula, across the neck of which was a stockade, travel to Athens was forbidden. Still, the vices of the city came to the fleet. In fact, little was to be found in the city that was not made available to us. Drink, gambling, and women were plentiful.

I soon realized that my consideration that the Greek number of myriad was far too large for commerce was possibly lacking in correctness. It could be applied to the number of whores that plied their trade in the tents along the river. I jest, of course - there were certainly far fewer women than that number, but still, the population of women in the temporary brothels was massive. And for a single obol, a man could have any at will.

By the nightfall, the men were empty of both purse and seed, having spent every coin on either women or the throw of the bones - or both - and with a headful of strong wine to celebrate his spending. And, I have to say, the men waking with sore heads - and groins - the next morning, included myself.

Two months went by. We launched and rowed almost every day except for the sixth, which was used for maintaining the ships. And, of course, the seventh for our day of rest. By this time I had the measure of my shipmates, and now called several by name. Many nights, after the evening meal, we dissected the world and the prospects of ourselves in the future of it.

One man, named Aganothon, was more educated than most and somewhat of a historian. Certainly he knew far more of the history of Greece than myself. We were grouped in a circle outside our tent, after a day of repairs and mending. A seaman had inquired about the news of the new Spartan commander. "...Lysander, his name is," replied Aganothon. "A man of talents and the only Navarch to succeed in repelling our fleet in open battle. No other admiral has managed that task."

"He gave us a defeat? That was not told in the Agora." This was a younger man, barely with his full growth.

"Aye. And I was there. With the help of that spawn of Hades, Cyrus of Persia, they struck on a day when the Athenian Navarch had taken his absence, leaving his helmsman in command. The admiral was said to have been seeking supplies in the city of Ephesus." The older man shook his head and spat onto the ground. "High officers do not usually fill the quartermaster role, and certainly not the leader of the fleet. I suspect that he was in the city and searching between the legs of a bawd for his wants."

I had heard of the Spartan admiral, Lysander, in the warehouses of Dionysos but had no knowledge of any past battles in detail. On the last year I had gathered word of a setback of the fleet on some shore, but it made little impression me, and apparently little on the citizens. Certainly, the crier of the Agora did not call out the portent of doom at any time that I had noticed. And the grain ships continued to dock.

I spoke up. "What happened to the Admiral?"

"He was immediately cashiered and left for exile to some remote shore. That is the tale, but I suspect that he took ship between dawn and daylight to miss his appointment with the executioner."

Troy asked, "And this Lysander is now our foe again?"

Aganothon finished his cup first, then replied. "Aye, but the Spartans have some strange law that a military leader can not lead again after a battle." At the looks of disbelief, he nodded and continued. "Strange it may seem, but true. He stepped down and some other noble took command. That unfortunate babe was whipped by us like a cur in the street in the battle off the shores of Arginusae. And do not ask me where that land is to be found. I just voyage to the wars under the deck, like you."

"But he is back, even though the law says no?"

"Parse and his whore-maidens take you, Telemes. Am I a magisterial scrivener of Spartan law? I only can give you what I have learned from the many tales that flow by. For all I know, the Oracle of Delphi insisted that he be reassigned. Or maybe, the assent was given by the throw of the bones." He stood up and prepared to retire to his sleeping mat. "Perchance you may ask him yourself in the near future."

More days went by, then as we beached one evening, a man of our ship, who had been taken off row-duty because of a tussis of the throat, came running to meet us as we began our walk to the mess tent. "There is word in camp of a Spartan move! The command tents are as a hive of bees, overturned!" In the jabbering that immediately followed, none could be heard over his own demands for news. The man was surrounded and prodded for intimate information from the map tent of Lysander, himself.

Tros and Aganothon were beside me as I looked at them and said, "There is little need to listen to this tribunal. Were we to put him on the torture-boards, he could say no more than he has."

The older man nodded. "Aye. News will come soon enough if these tidings are not mere wisps of the Siren's songs." Hurrying up the alley between the tents, we took advantage of the delay of our fellows to enter the mess tent firstly, and procured the best cuts off the bone and the freshest cheeses from the pile.

By darkfall, the entire camp was buzzing with tales and stories, each more unlikely than the last. The Spartan fleet had been seen off the shores of Marathon. Spearmen were assaulting the gates of Athens. The southern prong of the Athenian fleet had was even now in flames. How a thinking man could spew a falsehood like the latter was a wonderment to me when any who wished to view the disaster could walk to the beach and see the supposedly aflame hulls sitting calmly on the sands. Still, the absence of any officers of rank indicated that news of some interest had arrived to our leaders.

The Fugitive

Hellespontos

The piper was beating a slow stroke, one that we had maintained for three days. The fleet, even to a Roman was majestic and almost innumerable. From my vantage point, it actually was uncountable, as the eye could not see the whole even from the upper deck. The numbers of the Triremes alone was almost to the count of a double hundred, with the following merchant hulls another third part of that whole. We were moving up the coast of the peninsula with leisure, but not from any lack of desire to engage the Spartans. Rather, we were bound to the speed of the merchant ships with our supplies, those all lacking rowers and at the mercy of the winds. Thus far, Notas, the local god of the southern winds, was fickle, giving little assistance in our voyage.

Each evening, we would beach and pull the hulls partially upon the sand, make our encampment, then rest for the night without tents or other cover. The men with whom I had friended, Tros and Aganothon, preferred to lay with myself in the rower's nest for our rest. The curve of the hull at the turn of the bilge made a fair mat, although hard, but without the myriad of sand fleas infesting the beaches. On the morning, many of the rowers would look as if they had gathered the pox, so mottled was their skin with the bites of the water insects.

"Word from the Proreus says that tomorrow we reach across the Aegean to the far shores of the land of Persia," said Aganothon. He was finishing his bit of bread and cheese which had been our staple since leaving port. The noon meal would have a cut of lamb, but no meat was served in the evening. With the supply ships always late or delayed, only that food that could be transported in casks or barrels was available. He pointed with the bone that he had saved from earlier. "Lysander has taken the cursed Spartans into the Hellespontos to try to cut our trade with the far lands around the Sea of Darkness." Another pointing, then, "At least that is what the Proreus has said."

Our destination could have been far up the Nilos river in Egypt for all that I knew of it. And I said so.

"You know of the sea of Aegea to the east, do you not? It is the one on which we sail, now." I nodded. "To the east toward the sunrise is the dwelling-place of the Persians, and to the north of that land is a large sea, inland and bordered by... in fact, I do not know. But, it is large - very large, and in my voyaging as a merchant trudge, I never saw the far side. But, on the southern shores, are the cities of Chalcedou and Petra - the main loading ports for the grain from Persia."

"He... This Lysander will not attack those cities, will he? And start a conflict with those people?"

Now Tros spoke. "You can not know what a scum of a Spartan will do. I believe they would invade the realm of Hades, could they find the entrance, and just for the jubilance of engaging in battle."

"He might," replied Aganothon to my query, "but I suspect that his aims are closer and more immediate. Know this. Between the two seas - this one and the Dark Sea - is a narrow body of water that is known as the Hellespontos - the sea of Helles. It is named for some goddess, but the story has long fallen from my memories. But, the waterway between the two seas is narrow and to break the trade between them is as easy as placing a stopple in a jug. According to the Proreus, Lysander intends to be that plug."

The words from the sub-officer Proreus were defective as to our immediate movements. On the morrow, we did not set to oar, but instead waited on the sand for our merchant fleet to arrive on the fickle winds. And it did not until the next day and then only far toward sunset. We began to unload the merchant ships, placing the cargo of barrels and jugs and suchlike on the sands, each ship getting the proper share. That took most of the next day, then on the following, the fighting ships were floated and the supplies loaded aboard.

A Trireme is not a cargo vessel. In fact, with the population of a large village in a narrow hull, each had room for the men and little else. On the lower deck, the only open space was the narrow walkway down the center of the ship, and now it was filled from keel to overhead with containers of water and viands. Also, the decks were piled with more containers and lashed with ropes. It was obvious to me that our supply merchants were not to follow us into battle - probably a wise decision, as they would be like small children underfoot in a brawl between men in the taverna.

Shortly after the noon meal, the fleet stood out to sea, pointing away from the land for the first time, and rowed at a gentle pace across the calm sea. The sail pole was raised, but the cloth itself laid on the deck. In the light airs, it was more of a hindrance than help, with gentle breezes sometimes working against the men on the oars. Night brought the fleet to a stop, with torches on the fore of each hull to give indication to its mates across the waters. A few men would be designated on the oars to hold position until first light when we broke our fast and began the stroke again.

On the morning of the third day, the call of land was heard from above, and in a while, we changed course to where the shore could be seen in the distance through the thole ports of one side. Of course, I had not the remotest conception of our location and even with the musings of Aganothon during our rests, we could have been past the pillars of Hercules for all of my knowledge. That evening we once again drew up onto the sands and the ships emptied for rest. This shore seemed not to have the water insects, and myself and my mates also spent the night resting on the soft and cool sand of the beach.

The next day was only a short stroke to our landing place - this time at the wide beach of a small river issuing from land. Immediately, the supplies on board were removed and set to the beach, and the men ordered to rest for the bulk of the day. Aganothon took the opportunity to wander toward the tents of the officers, carrying a small barrel to give the visage of one who was working under orders. This allowed him to pass by any number of councils, gathering a sentence here and an opinion here. Back at our ship, he gave what he had learned.

"...and this water from inland is called the Aegospotami, apparently." The oldster looked at myself, then said with a grin, "For the edification of our Roman friend, it is a word in the ancient language meaning, 'river of goats.'" He waved down my retort. "Nay, ask me not why. I have seen no animals of any kind since our landing." He continued, "Lysander is indeed in command of the Spartans. It appears that he is in Lampsacus, but ask me not where that city might be. It is foreign to my knowledge of this area. Long ago, as a boy in a merchant, I might have passed such, but no memory of it remains."

Now the babble began, all asking questions that could have no answer from any present, and then giving opinions on the same lack of knowledge. For myself, I wandered to the bank of the river, a double handful of stadia away and beyond almost half the fleet drawn up onto the sand. There, I doffed my loincloth and enjoyed a sojourn in the water, just as I had done as a boy on the shores of the Tiber. Then, laying on a patch of fronds to dry, I relaxed and thought about my life to this day.

I suspected that few men had been tossed hither and yon, as I had been, in the games and amusement of the gods. No doubt the next round of knucklebones on the Olympian gameboard would be played when I least expected it, but as I had no control over my fate in the gaming and no second sight to watch it approach, there was little need to speculate on such. When this war was finished, I would return to Athens and collect my concealed stash of coin and move on... To where I had no idea, but it was very evident that I would always be the stranger in that Greek city.

"You have little interest in the musings of our fate, it appears." I looked up to see Tros approaching, holding a hank of bread and a slice of cheese. Stooping, then falling to his buttocks beside me, he offered the viands and a small waterbag. "And indeed, it appears that our Roman is consumed with deep thoughts."

Nodding my gratitude at the food, I just grinned and replied, "Nay. My thoughts were just roaming here and there. But, unless another has come from the officer's tents, I doubt that I missed any news of import."

He leaned forward, holding his bent knees with his arms. "Nay. Only that we stand out tomorrow for the test of these Spartans. This Lysander will yet rue the night on which his patéras and mitéra lay together to spawn himself."

I made no comment, other than a grunt. One should not jubilate a victory before it is won - that is a mark the gods will never let pass. Still, with the force that I had seen at the command of the leaders of Athens, I had little doubt that the morrow would be a massive victory. At it turned out, my predictions were no closer to the mark than my comrade, Tros.

Morning time found us hauling our ships off the sand even before the first rays of light appeared in the eastern sky. Dry rations were our lot and to be eaten at times of rest. Long before the blazing disk of the sun appeared in the clear sky, we were in a moderate stroke on the calm sea. Even before midday, we were standing off some harbor of unknown name. As the land was on the opposite side of the hull from my oar, I could only listen to descriptions from the men who could get a small vision through their equally small thole ports. For myself, I could see a vast number of Athenian ships scattered along the sea, and many flags being raised and waved, but little else.

The day lengthened, and no battle came. Finally, the Auletes began his stroke on the drum, and we began to pull away from the harbor. Before fall of night, we were back on the beach beside the... what did Aganothon call it? ...Aye, the river of goats, the Aegospotami. The talk this night was about the day - and the lack of any foe to vanquish.

"...Lysander and his fleet are in the port of Lampsacus, but the babling did not care for what he saw out to sea."

"Aye, he knows well what is his fate when he meets us in battle."

"...and his men must know that their leader refused to test us, despite our offer to his face. The grumbling must be great among the Spartans. Even an Egyptian cares not for being thought a coward..."

I lay back on my bed of collected fronds and shut my ears to the babble. I doubted that Lysander was a coward - certainly, his history indicated that he was not, what little I had heard of it. Since he had not accepted battle this day, then either he thought that it would be to his disadvantage, or... or, he had some other stratagem in mind.

What it might be was an unknown to myself, and indeed, over the next several days it appeared that the self-serving statements of Tros were correct. Day after day, we appeared in the morning at the entrance to the harbor of Lampsacus to wait in vain for the Spartans to accept our challenge. Before darkfall, we would row back to our beaching area for the night. Now, our supplies were running low with the merchant hulls emptied and sent back to Athens for more. When they would return was a mystery that only the gods of the winds could tell, and if the airs were contrary, the time might be in months.

To alleviate the lessening shortages, some ships would remain on the beach as their crews began to forage inland for food, and each day, even more would be held back or even sent to other areas along the coast to hunt. That left fewer Triremes to give the challenge each morning until finally only about thirty would row the distance to the harbor of Lampsacus, a duty that was now becoming routine.

The Athenian Admirals or Generals - whoever was in charge - would have had me cast to the sea had they known of the harboring of one who was a play-figure on the gameboards of the gods. Thusly, as the bones were cast on the mountain of Olympus, the laughter that was issued for my cause, enveloped the fleet.

I knew not how the ships were selected for the force of the day, but on this one, the Sea Swan was included. And, indeed, I was not dissatisfied that it was. Pulling an oar at a moderate stroke, then sitting on the bench for the balance of the day japing with the other oarsmen until the time of return, was vastly preferable to thrashing around some wilderness and looking for any animal that might be eaten. Or so I thought.

This day was to be different. As we approached our destination - the harbor of Lampsacus - the ships formed their usual long line, presenting a united front to any Spartans that might issue from the port. But, even as that formation was taken, we could hear much calling and words of consternation from above. Now, with the rising babble of the oarsmen, all commenting on half heard and barely understood shouts from above, the speculations and presumptions ran rampant. Trying to make sense of what I had heard from above, I gathered that the Spartans had decamped in the night - or most of them at least.

For a considerable time, we stayed on our benches, oars raised and suspended by the capture loops of rope. The gabble eventually died down - more from the boredom at each man giving his opinion innumerable times than any sudden realization of what was happening. The sub-officer of the row-deck - the Proreus - came and went several times, but only with the same information that the bulk of the Spartan fleet had flown. I assumed that we would set to stroke, up one coast or the other, to find and follow our foe, but the early morning passed with no orders from above. Through my thole port, I could see the flags rising and falling on the row of ship out my view - the captains obviously giving or receiving orders - or more opinions.

Now the usual game of knucklebones began on innumerable benches of the row-deck, the men having given their all in discussion of something that we knew little about. The games were a vastly more satisfying method of passing the time waiting for either the order to return to our beach camp or some other desire from above.

For myself, I sat with Tros on his bench, only a few oars forward, and talked of this and that - no different than any of the other days that we had been relieved of duty at the poles. I learned some more of his country, and he gained some insights on mine - idle talk of idle men. Then...

The Proreus suddenly descended to his station, but not as usual. He jumped from the upper deck, merely guiding his progress with his hands on the rails to maintain an upright stance. His leather-lunged shout brought all the talk and games to an instant halt. "Rowmen to oars! Move, you piss-sotted bastard-sons of Hades!"

Bone-dice and cups scattered as the men leaped over each other to reach their benches. In only heartbeats, the commands came in quick succession. "Check oars down! Level the oars! Oars ahead." Then to the piper, the man on the drum, "Beat of twenty, Auletes." The rhythm began and, allowing enough pause to give the beat to the rowers, a final command, "Stroke."

This was not a battle thrum from the piper, but still, it was no cruising stroke that we usually used to go from here to there. As the ship gained way, I could feel it began to turn. During a stroke, no chatter was allowed, but each man was furiously wondering at the sudden alarm - I certainly was. As we were turning away from the harbor, toward which we had been pointing, I wondered if the cause was a massive outrush of Spartan ships from the port. That was unlikely, as all the earlier snippets of conversation from above seemed to indicate that there were few in sight. Or, was the foe coming back from their overnight foray, wherever that might have been?

Now the steering oars of the Trireme began to bite, and our turn became sharp, giving me a short glance out my hull opening during the lifting of the pole at the end of the stroke. The other Athenian ships had vanished from my narrow view, to be replaced by the open expanse of the sea. But, suddenly, a shout from forward, despite the prohibition of speaking during the stroke. "Thanatos give us mercy! We are undone!"

"Silence, you cursed whoreson!" bellowed the Proreus. He had a leather whip as a badge of office, which I had never seen used, as this was not a ship of slave rowers, but were citizens serving at their own desire. But... I had no doubt that he would use it to great effect, should discipline began to falter - especially, with any enemy near or approaching.

In a few heartbeats, I had to control my own shout as the turning of the ship began to give me the vision of what had caused the outburst. The horizon was filled with ships - small ships, even tiny. But the size had nothing to do with their construction, but rather that I was only seeing the narrow aspect of each from the front. The Spartan fleet was pointed directly at us and, no doubt, at maximum stroke. The Athenians had fallen into that fatal stance of routine - assuming that this day would be like all the others since our arrival, and to allow the Spartans to capitalize on that assumption. Obviously, noticing the diminished count of Athenian ships each day, as the bulk were foraging for food here and there, the foe had decamped with their entire fleet, disappearing over the horizon for the night and early morning, but now to trap us between the shore and superior numbers.

With my furtive glances - both short and limited - I had no count of the foe, but I could see at least that it vastly outnumbered our mere thirty or so hulls. Over the beat of the drum and the noise of sixty and a hundred oars being pulled, I could hear the footfalls overhead as the soldiers - the Hoplites and in the numbers of about two double handfuls - moved to form their ranks for battle.

Now the opposing fleet moved out of my vision as we completed the turn, to be replaced by many ships of the Athenians - now visible in glances out my porthole and in a line with us. I assumed that a view out the opposing side of the ship would show the same. All had the white bow wave, as no doubt did we, indicating a strong stroke across the water.

I have read that all battles are confusing to the soldier in the ranks. It may well be so, but a Hoplite facing a foe from behind shield and spear on some grassy field had a view of his conflict as the gods looking down from Olympus compared to the knowledge of an oar puller in the lower deck of a Trireme. I have no concept of the battle, even after considered thought long after. Noise, shouts - aye, screams and curses. Over it was the clash of wood on wood, even loud and long series of sharp sounds that I later determined to be oars of this ship or that splintering as a foe closed the side.

"Beat of forty, Auletes!" This was a major increase that took considerable strength to pull. I had no time nor breath to examine the narrow view out my thole port, as the ship leapt forward in response to the drum. As oarsmen face the stern of their vessel, the next happening was directly in my vision. For a few moments, we rowed, then as if by the strike of a hammer of the gods several men at the far end of the opposite line of men were propelled into the air, to fall on their fellows, broken and bleeding. My mind was still trying to understand what my eyes had seen when the loud splintering of the poles of those unfortunate rowers was suddenly submerged in a monstrous sound of wood striking wood. The Sea Swan heeled to the opposite side, then straightened to continue on its course. I saw no failure of the hull in that section, now bereft of oarsmen but we had obviously been rammed by another ship, and apparently with a less than decisive blow.

Our stroke was somewhat defective until the broken bodies of the dead or dying men were moved from where they had fallen - usually on another rower or his oar - but in a few heartbeats, and with much cursing by the designators of the Proreus, we were again in full stroke - almost.

"Fifty, Auletes!" This shout brought us to maximum effort. This beat could only be maintained by a crew for a hundred heartbeats. Even a prime ship of rowers, and I could say that the description could be used for the men of the Sea Swan, would begin to falter should it be attempted for a further length of time. Continued overlong, a man here or there would eventually miss a stroke, fouling his mates and causing chaos to the beat all down the side of the ship. I assumed that we were attempting - and succeeding, I hoped - in avoiding the ram of another Spartan vessel. I did not dare try to look out the thole port for oncoming threats - a missed stroke at this beat would be...

This time, the grinding crash was forward, behind me and suddenly. So suddenly as to propel any man without sufficient grip on his pole backward into his mate behind him. I looked around to see the inevitable river of water entering the hull at the point of impact, but there was... Nothing. Except for men gathering themselves back to their benches, there was nothing to be seen.

"Beat twenty, Auletes! Oars all back! Down! Stroke."

The backward stroke was awkward, being unnatural and made without proper stance by the oarsmen, and was usually less than the perfect rhythm of the forward pull, but we began the work to make the ship retreat from whatever it had hit. And now, of course, I realized that we had intentionally collided with another, the long projecting ram no doubt embedding itself deeply into a Spartan hull.

"Beat of thirty! Forward the oars!" Apparently, now free of our victim, we began the normal stroke again. With the pace of the stroke now close to our usually cruising speed, I could give attention to my surroundings. From above came noises as this man and that group apparently ran here and yon - probably the archers attempting to gain better prospective of their targets. And shouts rang out, not understandable by me since I had no context as to their referral, but it was evident that all above were as engaged as we.

"Fifty, Auletes!" The shout rang out after another command was issued from above. Back to maximum stroke we went, and I could feel the ship heel as we turned sharply to center our ram on another foe. Or so I assumed. The forward crash came again, but this time with screams and cries of men.

Turning, I saw a... a... It took a heartbeat or so to realize that it was the ram of another vessel that had completely penetrated our hull, crushing and breaking any men at the point of impact. In addition, water was in full flow around the protrusion, even now reaching the feet of the rowers one level down from me. Above, more shouts and screams indicated that a battle was in progress between soldiers of both ships. And our travail had just begun.

The Proreus was giving no orders, obviously not having received any from above - he stood, looking up through the hatchway and waiting. It was obviously to me that we would go nowhere as long as the ram of the Spartan ship had us pinned in place.

Then, in front of my eyes, the entire side of the hull, no more than ten rowers forward, disintegrated into kindling and stovewood. Another huge ram slid into our hull, stopping only as the bulk of the Spartan ship touched our side. Again, men were crushed and thrown into heaps, few of which gained their feet again. With an ear bending noise of screeches and more splintering, the ram began to withdraw, but this gave us no respite. Now the open hole was filled with a river of water, sweeping even uninjured men from their feet. I had no time for idle gazing, but it appeared to me that the first ram was withdrawing, also.

Merchant ships can sink, as can fishing vessels and the like. Ballasted with sand or rocks at their bottom keel, to act as a counterweight to the sail, and with a hold even partially full of cargo, or fish, they will sink without effort if the entering water cannot be contained. A vessel of war - a Trireme and the like - will not founder. Of light construction so as to be handy in the water, and capable of being drawn up to the shore at night, they have no ballast and no cargo. As such, the mass of wood will fill and settle until the deck is almost awash, but will float for days on end, until the gradual incursion of the water into the fibers of the wood itself causes it to finally lose its buoyancy. Thus was the end of the Sea Swan to come - or would have, except for another factor.

I moved to stand under one of the several open hatches. Except for the one at the stern of the ship, over the platform on which the Proreus and the piper stood and sat, none had ladders available. These had been taken down and stored on the center line when we stood into battle, and now were under water and struggling men. No matter. With the speed at which our row-hold was filling with water, I would float up through the opening in a short time. Already, my feet were about to be lifted from the bench on which I was standing. Unfortunately, looking up I could see... billows of smoke. The ship had been fired!

"Junius! Junius!" I looked around to see Tros scrambling to gain his feet in the roaring water and the thrashing bodies. It was the first time that he had called me by name, rather than just using the agnomen of "Roman."

I reached down to pull him up to my level, allowing him to set his feet on the same bench. He was in panic, as were the others in the hold. Once again, had I the time for leisure of thought, I would have marveled at the unfamiliarity of seamen of the very medium that was their world. Few could swim - in fact, none at all, it appeared, from the sight of men hanging onto the projections of the hull, trying to raise themselves as the water rapidly gained its level. In addition, many bodies were floating, face down - already drowned or killed by the impacts of the strikes.

I pulled him by the shoulder to shout in his ear. "We will float up with the water, through the hatch and take our leave of the ship toward the shore!" I had no idea how far away that might be now, but as I had no other choices, it was that or enter the dark door of Hades.

Tros shook his head violently. "I... I cannot hold myself in the water." I had guessed that. He would have been a rare sailor to have acknowledged the ability to swim.

I shouted back, "Stand behind me and hold to my shoulders! And do not grapple my arms or we both sink!"

My feet left the bench in the rising water, and with the added burden of my mate, I had to expend considerable effort to keep above the water, but it was only for a short time. With the twin rivers of water entering the hull, I soon had my hands on the coping of the hatch. If the Spartan soldiers were waiting, then we were dead men anyway, but I doubted that even they would remain on a burning ship.

They had not. As my head exited the opening, I could see the carnage of battle, with men laying on the deck, none moving and all covered with the red that had ended their life. The fire, even now was, being extinguished with the submergence of the hull in water. The stern deck was free of char, so it appeared that the fire had been kindled in the waist and forepeak. Still, this ship would never voyage again under command, but would slowly roam here and there with any sluggish currents of the sea.

Placing the hands of Tros on the coping for the moment, I pulled myself to the deck, then reached to yank him by the arms to fall beside me. Then, again, I reached for struggling men in the hatch opening - those who had managed to thrash and flounder well enough to keep their heads above the rising water. In a short while, seven of us were laid out on the boards, recovering from our experiences of reaching the door of Hades, but being refused entry.

Now, sitting up and looking around, I could see the battle in its entirety. Or, what was left of it. With the ships of our fleet overwhelmed with numbers of five to their one, it was not a surprise. Smoke rose here and there from a hull that had been fired, but few were engulfed in flame. The rammed ships had been reduced to awash hulks too quickly for any major kindling to occur. I could see other ships in the same state as the Sea Swan, and not only Athenian. Many a Spartan hull had been broken in their rush - probably as many as those of our mates.

Still, numbers have no meaning to a leader in battle, only victory, and it was such for the Spartans, and none could speak of it in any other way. Our problem was more immediate and not of speculating about battles. Floating around the Aegea, or the Hellespontos, or whatever this cursed body of water was called, was not conducive to our survival, even if the Spartans allowed us to do so, but the shore was far away. Even with the skill of myself, and with some plank or other floating object to hold me up for rest, there would be little chance of slowly paddling so far. I appeared that we had no other option to sit on the awash deck and watch the ending of the battle.

It soon came.

Fugitivus

A half hundred of Athenian crewmen huddled in the upper waist of the Spartan Trireme, under the leveled spears of soldiers, all obviously hoping for any resistance from the beaten mass. One of these unfortunates was myself. From the awash deck of the Sea Swan, we had the leisure to view the battle as few have done - the last of it, at least. The Athenians fought bravely, and to my thoughts, with more skill than their opponents, but the totally mismatched numbers named the outcome, no matter any help of this god or that. A Trireme of Athens would mark a foe, and with good strokes and rudder skill, usually ram that ship broadside - more times than not. But, even with that enemy out of action, before the attacking ship could be withdrawn and way gained for another foray, Spartan rams would find the wood of the stationary vessel, and on more times than not, two or even three of the foe would charge and thrust their underwater weapon into the hull. I saw one Trireme struck by four of the enemy almost at once, breaking into nothing but floating planks and struggling men on the water.

Usually, the Spartans attempted to fire the foundering hulls, as they had done to the Sea Swan. Fire was the terror of all who moved over the waters, with pitch caulked hulls, sunbaked and tender dry wood, and the huge fabric of the sail for kindling, making a pyre as if at the funeral of a noble Roman. Of course, I knew this well, from my childhood on the Tiber, watching this fishing boat and that, blaze and sink, with all crews and families within distance attempting to stem the flames with buckets of water. And usually, unsuccessfully if the blaze had any start before being noticed. And more recently, with a certain ship of pirates in my knowledge, I saw the results of a pitch soaked hull and flame. But, unlike a merchant vessel, fired in accident by its own cook fire, these warships sank to the waterline with such swiftness that fire had little chance or time to make its damage.

It was only a short time before the action was over, but the Spartan fleet did not tarry to jeer at their floating and struggling foe, but immediately set stroke for the far horizon. All but a few, most with some damage or other, began to come to the succor of their fellows, clinging as we to awash decks on broken hulls. My hope was that they would then leave their enemies to the fates and follow their fellows. I had been studying the currents by aligning certain landmarks in the far distance with each other and had determined that there was a slow drift toward the sunset, or there and a little south. Not much and nothing to carry a swimmer on and on to his doom. I was sure that, with a slow stroke and using a large plank as support, I could reach land by morning - or faster, if I could overcome the fear of water in Tros. I needed his legs to kick while holding onto the board - two men would move faster than one.

But it was not to be. After the rescue of marooned Spartans, the ships began to approach the few Athenian hulls still whole enough to support a part of the crew. Eventually, one grounded next to our hull, and with sharp commands ordered my few fellows to board their craft. And to emphasize the disgrace of our defeat, the soldiers used the butts of spears to express their contempt and to hurry us along to the growing crowd of Athenian crew at the center of the deck. And by stripping us of the single wrap of cloth that we wore around our waists. There we sat in a tight circle, staring at leveled spears and wondering if any would see the rise of the next sun.

There were still men in the water here and there - many of them - holding on to this plank and that board, but the Spartans soon decided that the fish in this sea were too scattered to be profitable and set course across the sea, following the track of their fellows after the battle. The floating men would float ashore or perish, depending on the attention of whatever god they claimed allegiance to.

Since leaving the encampment, I had spent most of my time below decks, beyond the few times that I was allowed on deck to stretch and loosen my limbs during times of oar-puller rests, but I had seldom seen anything but ships on the open sea. I had no idea where the Athenian encampment at Aegospotami lay, or the direction, but I had no doubt that we were pulling for that place - and battle. Or, rather, the bulk of the fleet that had departed earlier in the day was probably even now engaged. I wondered if the Athenians would have better course for this one. Of course, our loss of the morning was because of completely unbalanced forces, but now, however, the Spartans would find an Athens fleet of far greater size when they hove over the horizon - one fully capable of matching what I had seen of the foe that morning.

I should have known the value of my prognostications - and in this case, they were no better than many other guesses that I had made in my chaotic life. By the time our ship entered the fray, the battle that I had expected to view had been over for many hours. With a sinking heart, I could see lines of Triremes pulled up on the sand - stadia long lines of them...

And all burning.

The disbelief was palpable in my mates, sitting around me. Moans of despair and curses to the gods were chanted, over and over.

The Athenian fleet had been caught grounded, but for whatever reason was far beyond my imagining. The battle - and even, possibly the war - was ended.

It was long after midday, and I had little hope of either viands or water being offered by our captors, but I doubted that we were to be left to starve or die of thirst. From my listenings to the talk of Sparta, I assumed that we were all destined to be chained to an oar in the hull of a warship - and there probably to live out our short lives. The sight of groups of prisoners on the shoreside gave credence to that belief - men were being herded together at the waters edge, no doubt waiting for transport to their new tasks.

Our vessel touched the sand, but other than men coming and going over the forepeak - without doubt, messengers - we merely stood off the beach and waited. Far in the distance, I could see a group walking towards us, surrounded by soldiers with raised spears. This had to be the commander and his staff, Lysander.

I would not have recognized the man had he dined with me at the taverna, but as the group grew closer, I knew that my supposition was correct. A man in a gilded and plumed helmet, with shining silver-trimmed armor and equally glorious sandals and greaves, could be no one else. As he passed each ship, the officers stood to attention at the forepeak and saluted, to receive a wave of the baton in return. The bow of the ship shielded him from my view at his closest, but as he passed, I could examine him over either side. A man of authority, without doubt, and of considerable military skill - aye, he had proved that this day. Naturally, we were wondering at his opinion of captured foemen. We were soon to find that out.

As he passed down the line of ships - both burned and triumphant - and out of view, we settled back to our waiting. Naturally, I was sitting next to Tros, and we conversed in low voices.

"...the Spartans are a cruel people. We can expect the silver mines or the slave oar - nothing more."

Next to him, another spat on the deck - a waste of precious body water - and replied quietly. "Aye, but our assurance is that whatever task of Hades we are condemned to, our suffering is not likely to cover an extended time."

These were not the assurances that I was in hopes of gaining. Even on the island of the Pirates, I was not starved or beaten, except by the whip of the cruel second - the Ypoploíarchos - on occasion. In my case, however, I knew that there was a force, a presence far above, that could not be reckoned. I wondered if the gods now were grouped around their gameboard, with a wooden figure of a shaven Roman placed on one of the squares. And what might happen when the hand of the immortal, whose turn had come, threw the bones.

I was amused at my speculation - not at the idea itself, but at my half-belief that the gods existed and were aware, in any minute amount, of my mere existence. Whatever it might be, I would...

"Look. Something is happening."

I followed the pointing finger of the man, to see the grouped prisoners on the shore, now apparently being counted off and escorted to this ship or that. And to ours. We received about a hundred in total, out of my estimation - a very rough estimate - of about three thousand or so. I wondered where the bulk of the Athenian crewmen were. With the ships caught on the beach, they had not been manned when attacked. And there were bodies on the shore, but not in the numbers that would be seen had the entire force of Athenians been killed. Had they fled inland? I could think of no other reason for their absence. It had been my ill fate to have been selected for one of the ships to accost the Spartan fleet this day, else, now I might be free - though fleeing for my life across a strange land.

Now there were a hundred and a half of us, all grouped like fish in a basket on the deck of the Spartan vessel. I wondered at the reason for loading the ship so late in the day. This warship was little different than one of Athens, and had no space for food even for the crew, and certainly not for the captures of a hated enemy. Loaded as we were, and sitting low in the water, there was no chance of our reaching the port of Lampsacus until far after nightfall. I assumed that the Spartans gave as little thought to voyaging over dark waters as the Athenians.

But, I was apparently wrong in that estimate. After a further series of orders, given in the shade of the forepeak, the slaves below began the reverse stroke and we slowly backed away from the sand.

But only for a few hull lengths - about a stadium from the shore, a crewman threw a large stone overboard, attached to a rope tied to the forepost. An anchor? Looking in over both sides, I could see a handful of other ships making the same maneuver. Did the Spartans spend the night crammed in their vessel? Then remembering that the rowers below me were slaves, it could be so. There was plenty of room on the upper deck for the officers and men to recline and take their rest, had it not been full of Athenian prisoners. The sun was still handspans above the far horizon and the reason for the maneuver was puzzling.

For the moment.

Now, the Trierarch of the ship mounted a stand at the fore of the boat, while the soldiers suddenly gave their full attention to the group of prisoners. I did not like what I was seeing. Were we to be speared like a scrum fish, then tossed overboard? Or...

All of the Athenian prisoners stood, somehow knowing that the revelation of the fate was imminent. Now the captain called in a jocular voice, "Honored guests! Ferocious ship-men of Athens! Scourge of the middle sea! I give you the greetings of our commander, the great and noble Lysander, son of Aristocletius." His accent was strange, but it was still the speech of the Grecian mainland. "In his wisdom, he has deigned to consider you as worthy foemen, and not as fodder for our mines and quarries. For yourselves, you must prove yourselves worthy of his trust by demonstrating your quality as men - nay, as Greeks descended from the loins of Zeus, himself."

He turned and pointed down the beach to a small hill, visible from most of the fleet. At the top of the low peak was a staff with a huge red banner. "There is your rally point. You must reach the standard to be considered worthy of our trust." Now, the hair on my shaven neck was stiff as bristles. This was not a man giving friendship or even quarter, but one who was conducting a gigantic jape before his men. To reach that hill, one would have to swim the distance of almost ten ship lengths to reach the shoreline. Few aboard could hold himself in the water for the length of himself, far less for an entire stadium. I could certainly do so, easily, and some aboard had to have the skill also, but for our attempt I assumed that the handful of archers, even now still garbed for battle on the forepeak, would have their merriment in feathering any who seem to be having success in their journey. But, my fears were unjustified...

The reality was far worse.

The first man was pushed forward to the pinnacle of the boat, then his arms were taken, each by one of two huge brutes wearing nothing but dirty loincloths - obviously work-slaves of the ship. The Athenian was stretched between them as they pulled his limbs, as if a rope weaver and his apprentice, braiding the fiber under tension. Then, with suddenness, two men swung their swords, high and down, cleaving the appendages from the unfortunate body almost at the shoulders. Even as the man screamed his pain, the Trierarch shouted, "Show us your strokes, now, for the glory of Athens, and make your way to the banner!" With that, the bleeding man was bodily flung over the side, as the Spartans roared with laughter.

As I was in the center of the ship, I had no view of the doomed man, no doubt even now, sinking to the sandy bottom of the water.

But, looking across the waters to the next ship, only a half stadium away, I could see the same cruel deed being performed even as I watched. And, no doubt, was in progress on all the ships to which the Athenian prisoners had been taken. It was now obvious that the Spartan commander, Lysander, had no intention of sparing any who were taken in battle.

Again, the act was performed, but this time with a struggling man, although the two enormous slaves had no need for extended effort to hold the much smaller crewman between them. Some of the men in my huddled mass had no intention of submitting meekly to the deadly jape of their enemy, and threw themselves onto the guarding soldiers, and even in one instance, forcing the man to fall overboard. But, a man with bare hands has little chance against a spear, and in only heartbeats, a double handful of men were dead on the planks, all with multiple wounds from the weapons of their guards.

On and on went the spectacle, the laughter fading as the sameness of the act was performed. I looked around for any path to escape the inevitable doom, wondering in my mind when - and if - the gods above would throw their bones. At any other time I would have laughed at myself for entertaining such a hope, but when a man sees his doom approaching, he will grasp at any dangling thread for hope.

The remaining men seemed to accept their coming fate, although all struggled as they were dragged to the forepeak. For whatever reason, given by the gods or coming from within, my thoughts began to focus, and I receded from the present to explore this path and that. I began to slowly move to the side of the mass, an easy task as my mates had no objection to retreating from the leveled spears of the surrounding guards and seeking the elusive protection of the mass. My hope now was that the jape of the cruelty would turn to boredom as the prisoners were condemned one after another. To alleviate the sense of sameness, a few men were stretched by their legs and had their feet cut off. This elicited a few gales of laughter but soon the routine of mutilation was continued in silence, beyond the screams of pain from the unfortunate of the moment.

I began to fill my lung-sacs rapidly, and fully, as when I was a lad, diving for hung nets and lost equipment. By now I was at the edge of the mass of prisoners, only the length of an arm from the extended and still leveled spears. Almost half of my mates were gone, now mutilated, drowned and sunk, although I knew that most would be floating by nightfall in the natural buoyancy of a decaying body in the water. As I looked through narrowed eyes, I could see that the crew of the Spartan ship was bored of the spectacle, even muttering to each other about this and other issues, in the manner of idle soldiers in any part of the world. I selected the smallest and least engaged spearman that I could see in the line of my side of the ship, and before me.

Slowly we edged forward, pushed from behind by the rear soldiers as they continued to keep their prisoners in a compact mass. By now my vision was filled with floating spots of light, and I knew that my body was filled with the mysterious aspect of air that maintained life. I slowed my deep breathing slightly, so as not to cause myself to fall into that state of vertiginous clumsiness that I had experienced before by exceeding the need for breath.

This moment was no different than that in the hold of the ship of the pirates. My next moves would mean the slight possibility of life, or a likely immediate and painful death. I kept my eyes downcast, as one who had accepted his fate, glancing up and over for only a heartbeat as I measured my chance. Now, the gradual pushing of the mass of prisoners forward had brought me to stand in front of the smaller man that I had selected. With my eyes still downcast, I moved slightly toward the leveled spear point - slowly, as if I had been pushed by the mob of mates but, certainly not in any threatening manner. No unarmed and naked man would be a threat to an armed and armored soldier...

With the lightning speed of the desperate, I lunged between the spear of the soldier and that of his mate beside him, pulling on the shaft to disturb his balance. The long weapons of the Greeks - both the spear and the sword - have the advantage of keeping a foe at a distance, but also the shortcoming that, if that same enemy manages to get inside the swing or thrust of the weapon, the wielder is at a major disadvantage. My sudden jump took all by surprise - which was natural of men standing bored and waiting for the time they can retire to their cups or rest. As I swept past the soldier, my offhand fist met his jaw under the protection of his leather helmet. I have no way of knowing, but in my desperation and fear strengthened sinews, I doubt that his jawbone was intact after my blow. Now, taking my hand from the shank of his spear, I grabbed his short dagger from his belt as I vaulted past the fellow and over the side.

As the entire action took only the space of a long breath, I knew that there was no chance of being either speared by the soldiers nor feathered by the archers as I fell into the water, but there was no doubt that all were waiting for the cursed scum to appear when he surfaced for breath.

With my long and many intakes of air before the lunge, I knew that I had given myself a time of almost a hundred slow heartbeats before I would have to surface. Instead, I dove deeper to descend beyond any seeing of my shadow from above. Then slowly, I stroked back toward the ship, looking up to see the dark shadow of the hull far above. Then, directly under it, I rose into the dark shape until my hand touched the thick keel plank on the very bottom. I followed it slowly toward the stern of the ship to the point where it began to rise.

I gave thanks to the gods - afterward - for my work on the Sea Swan back at the port of Athens. I knew very well the shape of the hull from underneath and the advantage that I might accrue from that very design. At the stern of a Trireme is a platform, wider than the closure of the hull at that point, that allows for the two steering oars to be more widely separated than would be the case if they were just slung over both sides of the rear of the hull. The wide separation gives easier control than either one oar or two closely spaced steering poles. This, I hoped, might be my salvation.

Now, very slowly following the keel member as it rose at the stern, I stopped just below the surface, then cautiously lifted only my face from the water. Careful not to gasp, I opened my mouth wide and took in deep lungfuls to replenish my ability to dive. With no movement of my head, my eyes roamed here and there. And it was as I had hoped. The overhang of the platform was such that no crewman on the deck could view the point where the keel member left the water, unless he hung over the railing at his waist.

Just under the surface of the water, I thrust the dagger into the saturated wood of the keel member, using a hard jab of my arm, rather than the normal swing of a blade - a movement that would be greatly inhibited by the resistance of the water. This gave me a projection to hold as I waited.

And wait I did. The sun was even now touching the far trees of the shore, and the light would be gone in a while. I would charge my body with vast breaths of air, then pull myself under by my hold on the dagger, until the growing discomfort demanded that I surface again. Time passed, and each time I surfaced I would measure the darkness, hoping not to be seen before the sun was fully gone from the sky.

Then, suddenly, I felt myself being pulled gently. As the stern under the steering platform was in deep shadow, now I brought my head above the water to examine my surroundings. On either side, the other Spartan vessels were only shadows, except for the flaring torches at the stern and foreposts. There was little chance of my being seen now, even if some crewman leaned over the railing far enough to view my hiding spot. I realized that the pull was from the ship being gently rowed forward. Apparently, the executions were over, and the vessel was being grounded for the night.

With a hard pull, I retrieved my stolen dagger and let the ship slowly pull away from me, then began a slow water crawl at an angle toward the shore. Eventually, my feet touched the sand, more than the length of a ship from the shore. The sea bottom here obviously departed the shore at a very shallow angle. This would allow me to propel myself by pushing with my feet - a much less tiring method of travel through water than a full swimming stroke.

I set my destination for toward the sunset, but for no other reason than I had to chose between one way or the other. A slight moon was setting, but gave little light through scudding clouds, and I had little fear of being seen. I passed ship after ship, now outlined in the bonfires on the shore - no doubt the Spartans celebrating their victory in wine and roasted meat. And here and there were the dying coals of an Athenian Trireme, burned to the sand in total.

By now, my thirst had become immediate. I had had no water since the start of the battle in the morning, and certainly none as a captive on the Spartan ship. I had naturally ingested much salt water in my escape, which only added to my growing discomfort. I would have to find a stream or pool on the shore by no later than morning - a need that would be very difficult to fulfill, as the night became darker as I propelled myself along. With the growing overcast, the gloom deepened until it became complete. I could no longer see the shoreline - only the fires and torches.

Time passed. And more time, but eventually the end of the torches and fires were reached, and I moved on past empty shoreline. I hoped. My only indication that the land was near was my being able to touch the bottom with my feet as I propelled myself along. Finally, looking back and seeing that the Spartan encampment was completely out of sight, I began to seek the beach.

I emerged from the water and sat on the soft sand. Now I was almost elated - I had survived a travail to which thousands of my fellows had succumbed. Once again, the gods had thrown the bones and the spots that showed were in my favor. I almost believed it.

Still, I wanted much distance between myself and that murderous strain of Greeks, and before morning. I gained my unsteady legs, then began to stride down the waterline, guiding myself with one foot on the sand and the other in the mild surf. On occasion, I would trip on a log or other object, and several times my feet were bruised by a shell or other projection in the sand, but these injuries were far to be desired than the downward sweep of a Spartan sword.

On and on I strode. Now the thirst was become paramount. Still, I could move quickly over the open sand. Should I cast inland in a search for water, my speed would be as a snail, and my chances of finding a stream or other source almost nil. My search would have to wait for first light.

Still, sometimes the gods will toss a bone to a hungry man.

I suddenly found myself slowed by water to my knees - much cooler water than in the sea that I had been used to since my leap from the ship. Reaching down and cupping a hand, I lifted a palmful to my lips, carefully tasting with my tongue. It might have been brackish, or dark with mud, or even be the outflow from the cesspools of a city, but it had no salt and was drinkable. No wine before or since was has ever been as refreshing as that unseen stream. I stooped down and began to gulp the liquid in vast swallows until my reason returned. I realized that I would bloat myself and regurgitate it if I did not moderate my intake.

It took a while for my body to receive the water and it long insisted that it was not yet sated, but I lay on the sand in contentment and allowed the life-giving liquid to dissipate within my being. In a while, I took another long, but moderate drink and lay back to rest. Now my thoughts were on the day and the horrible happenings that it enclosed. Tros had not been a close friend, but he was - had been a friendly mate, and even now seeking shelter on the far side of the river Styx. Aganothon could barely be considered to be more than an acquaintance to me, but he had been an interesting man to converse with, and he had had no issue with speaking on friendly terms with a Roman. Of course, he was spared the terror of the Spartan foredeck, having been crushed to lifelessness by the first ram to hit the Sea Swan.

Thus did I end the horrible day.

Chaos

I woke from a night of strange imaginings and wondered if Korax had left any wine for the morning. If not, I would stop at the kiosk of old Makerios for a cup and a loaf. And, I might even treat myself to a...

My eyes popped open, and I rolled to my feet in fear. The sun was brightening the sky in the east, the clouds still thickly above. Frantically, looking in both directions up and down the shoreline, I was vastly relieved that I could see no visible sign of Spartans in the dawn gloom - or anyone, for that matter. In my exhaustion, I had fallen into a deathly sleep beside the little stream even without knowing. As my heart resumed its normal beat, I took another long swallow of water, then began to search for some viands.

As a riverman from my boy-time, I would never starve on the shore of a body of water, no matter where or of what size. With the dagger, I grubbed for shellfish and crabs, breaking the shells and eating the flesh raw. It was not food from the cookerie of a taberna, but it was filling and would carry me far, but it was salty and I needed to eat my fill while I had a source of fresh water. I could eat no more during the day unless I found another stream.

With another long look to make sure that the Spartans were not approaching from over the horizon, I set off down the shoreline in a fast pace, and a much more assured step now that I could see my path. I had yet to see a single man, or the sign of men - not a hut or trail or even flotsam from passing ships. But in only an hour by the waterclock, had there been one to consult, that changed. Ahead of me in the surf was a log, rolling up and back with the passing waves, but as I strode ever closer the vision changed. It was a body, not yet fully bloated from death, but beginning the process that would turn it into a disgusting and malodorous sight by fall of night. He appeared to be a crewman from a trireme, most likely an oarsman, as he had his single garment - a loincloth - still wrapped around his waist. I had learned from my experience on the yesterday, that Spartan oar slaves wore nothing, so this man had to be Athenian.

With some distaste at taking from a corpse, I untied and removed the garment from the unfortunate and scrubbed it with water and sand, then wrapped it around myself. Now, at least, I did not look like an escaped slave, and my man-parts would have protection if I had to take to the brush.

Resuming my fast pace, I began to find more bodies as I walked - sacrifices to Poseidon - all as freshly killed as the first. Then, in the distance, I could see a large group of men gathered at the top of the beach. In the water was a drowned ship, sideways to the shore and waiting to be beaten to kindling when the winds brought the higher waves to shore.

I stooped, then scuttled to the treeline, still moving but much slower. I was certain that the group were friends and not Spartans, but I would not risk my life and freedom on mere guesswork. Finally, I was above them, looking out of a thick copse of brush. A motley group of survivors they were, with some apparently uninjured but with others sporting wounds and gashes, and not a few laying on the sand and in the process of closing out their lives.

From their speech and words, I knew they were a part of my own ill-used and unfortunate fleet. Standing, I began to walk slowly towards them, making sure that I did not suddenly appear as a surprise - or a threat.

"Yo! Iphiclus!" A man had seen me and was both warning the others and pointing to me. All that could rose to their feet, some putting hand to weapon if they had such.

I raised my hands, apart and open - my dagger was now in my loincloth - and replied, "I am Junius, of the Sea Swan, captained by the Trierarch, Pentheus." I was giving a name that I had heard from casual talk, without knowing if it indeed was - had been the cognomen of our captain.

The men relaxed their stance, as I had given some assurance that I was of their ilk - and a single man in a loincloth would be little danger to even such a motley group as this. I walked to face the person that seemed to be the leader and stopped, waiting for his response.

"I be Iphiclus, Kybernetes of the Phōsphoros, that now lies yonder with the broken spine. You be one from the encampment of Aegospotami?" Ah, the second in command. Either the Trierarch of yon foundering hull was dead or had already left the group.

I shook my head, "Nay, my ship was detailed off the port of Lampsacus, set upon by tenfold our number." We traded stories for a time, the men gathering to listen to my tale of the battle off the port. But not of the slaughter up the coast - not yet.

For their part, they had been an outsailer, a patrolling vessel that stood down the coast watching for the enemy. Late in the yesterday, apparently long after the assault on the beach that burned our ships, their Trireme had encountered two Spartans, apparently sweeping the coastline for any of their fleeing enemy. In the resulting battle, one of the foe was rammed and left helpless, while the other smashed the stern of the Phōsphorous into stovewood, but hung their ram in the wreckage, unable to withdraw. At that point the battle became as a skirmish on land, with each crew attempting to take the other with spear and sword. As the bulk of the Spartan ship was manned by chained slaves, the Athenians easily outnumbered their foe, and eventually became master of the foundering ship. But, as the end came for their foe, the enemy fired their own ship, the pitch calked wood becoming an inferno that would engulf both vessels. With long wood, and mighty efforts, the crew of the Phōsphorous managed to push the flaming hulk from their own ship, preferring to drown than perish in flames.

The other Spartan, low in the water, had slowly rowed itself over the horizon and had disappeared by next light. The captured ship - burned to the waterline - had actually sunk with the slaves still chained to their benches, apparently supplied with some ballast or cargo that overrode the buoyancy of the wood.

As their vessel slowly washed ashore and grounded itself on the sand, the crew abandoned it as a loss, making a temporary camp at the treeline until first light. The officer pointed back the way I had come. "We will leave a few men here to succor our injured, then stride to the encampment at Aegospotami." Then, suddenly, he asked with some sharpness, "Why be you moving away from our forces? You are lost and have taken a wrongness for your bearing? Or be you running from the foe?"

"Aye, you have it rightly at that. I am running from the Spartans, and quickly. As should you, without delay." I began the story of the day, following our defeat at Lampsacus. It was received with great disbelief and even hostility. For a while, I was in fear of being bladed as a despicable deserter, a man with a foreign accent, casting panic and fear mongering in my flight. But...

Again, the fates intervened between myself and the growing anger of the foundered crew.

"Iphiclus! Look. More wanderers from the trees" A small group of men, six in all, had appeared from the treeline, suddenly seeing more of their fellows and stumbling forward to our group. These men had been at the encampment, or rather, in one of the parties foraging for food across the land. Their tale gave credence to mine, and with even more emphasis, as they had actually seen the fleet in flames and the bulk of the Athenians fleeing into the wilderness.

Thus I learned of the story of the calamity, how the bulk of crewmen had been scattered across the wilderness in search of sorely needed food, leaving their ships on the sand to be burned by the

Spartans. The few men at the ships were no more than ants under the shoe of a fishwife to the armored and disciplined hoplites that dismounted from the ships of the foe and began the kindling of the helpless hulls.

With the tale of these men, mine was now given the aura of truth, and much talk began to circulate among the group. Finally, the decision was made to strike across the land to reach the port of Sestus, there to take ship for Athens and give the warning of the disaster. For myself, I had no intention of following such a plan. I had no doubt that the Spartan commander, Lysander, would be anticipating such a move, knowing that tens of thousands of his enemy were now stranded in a far land with no possibility of walking back to their city. That walk would take years in passing, should any try that route through the wilds of Thracia and other unknown lands. Were I he, I would wait off the coast of that same city - and others all along the far coast - to gather more playthings for their evil pleasure and as easily as a fisherman nets fish swimming upstream for spawn.

Now that my tale had been told, the attention shifted to other, more immediate matters, allowing me to enter the trees to relieve myself - at least, that was the reason that I had casually mentioned. But, once out of sight, I moved rapidly through the trees until I had come far enough to take the sandy shore again and begin my fast pace to the west. By evening time, I had put hundreds of stadia under my feet.

The night was as dark as the last, but I continued on for a considerable time until, again, my feet splashed into a stream. This time, I crawled into the underbrush before taking my rest. The next morning, my feet were in motion, even as the first rays of the sun barely streaked the sky - now free of clouds. The blazing disk had barely risen when I stopped, looking both ahead and behind. The shoreline appeared to be curving toward the north in a considerable bend.

Of course, I had no idea of either my location, other than the fact that it was somewhere in the far northeastern corner of the Aegean sea. I certainly had no conception of what I might ahead of my course. Still, I knew what was behind me, and nothing that I might encounter would be the equal of that blood-soaked experience.

Shortly, I knew that the land was indeed, curving away from the direction of sunset, and sharply. It was only years later that I saw an accurate map of this part of the world, and realized that had I continued my walk along the shoreline, I would have completely retraced my steps. My trail would have led to the far side of a long and narrow peninsula and arriving at the very city that had been mentioned as a destination by the foundered crew. Continuing, I would find myself passing closely by the location of the disastrous battle and finally - many long stadia after - issuing into the mainland of Thracia, far to the northeast.

Around a small cape, sticking out into the waters, I suddenly spotted a vessel, drawn up to the shore but not on it. It was not a warship, but some form of merchant, and empty apparently, given the distance from the waterline to the discolored upper line of deepest loading. Now, the question - was it friend or foe? Or a neutral from some country without ally in this part of the world?

I immediately disappeared into the brush, and carefully crept forward to examine the ship at close quarters, but my circumspection had little use. The men working on the ship had not even a lookout that I could see - and working they were. It was obvious that the vessel had lost its mast and a new one was being scarfed and planed on the sand beside it. They were speaking Greek, I could hear, but that was no comfort - that was the language of the cursed Spartans, also. I had no wish to trade my narrow escape from death for more slavery at the hands of those savage people.

Now, sitting behind a thick bush, I just listened to the work-talk and inevitable japes of the men. By my count, there were about six in all - the normal working crew for a ship of moderate haulage. And none were slaves, by their talk, and all labored - even the captain was engaged in heavy work with some kind of double-handed carver. These were Athenians - that had become apparent from their accent and their stories, so, once again, I approached a strange crew in a slow and as friendly aspect as possible.

Again came the call of a stranger appearing from the trees, and shortly I was speaking to the captain of the merchant, one of those detailed to haul supplies to the Athenian fleet. This one had done so, but on the return, and without even clearing the land of the Hellespont, they had sprung the mast. The man was quite fluent in his cursing of the corrupt shipwrights in the port of Piraeus, selling good wood and delivering worm-eaten poles, to pocket the difference.
"...and take this as my vow! Upon our return, the pole-vender of that merchant will feed the crabs that night. I swear by Zeus that it will be so!"

For myself, I gave the truth - a part of it. I was a castaway from a foundered warship in a battle with the Spartans, and seeking a birth to Athens, there to ostensibly join another ship to return to the strife. To the inevitable questions of the conflict, I gave that the foe had received as much or more as they had delivered - again, the truth if only talking about the battle off the port of Lampsacus. And as a veteran of a battle for Athens, I was given the respect due such a man.

But, I said nothing about the disaster beside the river of the goats.

I signed on as a crewman, unpaid except for my voyage, the captain happy to gain a young man of good build and experience in the sea. By the end of the next day, the new mast - although green and shorter than the original - was stepped and secured, and we set sail for Athens.

None apparently noticed my interest in gazing over the waters, and in the direction of which we had come. My worry was that we would stand out to sea in time to meet the Spartans, pulling for the far side of the peninsula, and looking to trap and seize more of their foe. But, as the day grew long, and the winds fair, I knew that the danger was now minimal. A Trireme can outrun any merchant ship that has ever been built in the short course, but for the long run, a well-trimmed cargo vessel, with any wind at all, can leave the warship gasping for breath and water and far in its wake. The Spartans would never attempt to cross the long waters of the Aegean by oarship. Any attempt to do so would result in ships manned by bird-picked skeletons, empty of food and water and before even a fraction of the distance had been passed.

In a few days, after a run with a good wind and an empty vessel, we hove into Piraeus, the port of Athens.

Consternatio

Athens had made no change in the months of my absence, and I had had no expectation that it would have. But, I knew that the mood of the city would change very shortly, as soon as some merchant hove to port with tales of woe. The streets and open air tavernas had their usual custom, and all were speaking in normal tones of this and that, so the news of calamity had not reached the city, as yet.

At the inn, engaged by myself and Korax before my involuntary service with the Athenian fleet, I was greeted with surprise by the inn-master. "By the gods! Have you returned from Hades itself, Roman?"

My leaving, months before, was such that, to this man - and all that knew me - I had just dropped from the face of the earth, without tale or telling. I had no reason nor intention to give my story to this city-man but gave out that sudden circumstance had found me on a ship to far destinations these many months. As I had not stopped at my hidden jar on the road to the port to obtain some coin, I had not even a single obol with me, thus I could not gain my room, but I wasn't yet ready for such. "Korax, my mate that was residing with me. Is he still in residence?"

"Nay, Kurios. He had no coin for the room after your leaving, and I bade him go."

If he was still in Athens, I would find him eventually, but I had other plans than stopping in this doomed city for long. Now I set my feet to the grain merchantry of Dionysos, wondering at my welcome by a man who must have long considered me to have deserted his employ.

At the doorway, the doorkeeper looked at me in surprise. "By the foul stench of Aphrodite's handmaiden! Junius the Roman?" His mouth open, I just nodded. Then, "Where be you... What..."

I did not wish to appear as a man come to beg for his position again, but as one whose mission would not hold. "Nay, Arcas. I return with important information for the master. Is he within?"

The man shook his head. "Nay, Kurios. He has taken a meeting with the guild of... of... I disremember, but it is with the master of the port slaves. He will return before darkfall, or so I was told."

"Then I will wait for him in the scribery." Without giving time for more questions, I pushed past him and into the building. Rather than appear in the main rooms or the internal taverna in nothing but a loincloth, I moved down narrow and deserted hallways to the backside of the structures. My destination was one particular building, in the crumbling and deserted section of the warehouses, and I made my arrival without passing another.

To my vast relief, under the boards were my stash of coin and longknife, safe and unfound all these months. Now, at least, I had fare to leave this doomed city, and coin to purchase viands for the voyage. Back at the front of the complex, I nodded to the door keeper and said of my return later, but for now, I searched for a clothery to doff my ragged loincloth. Shortly, and garbed as a prosperous man again, I walked to the taverna that had been our drinking establishment since my employment with the guild.

Again, the merchant was surprised to see me. "Roman! We have not seen your presence for... many months. How be you back?" The old and rundown taverna on the street of the inn had not changed any more than the city, nor had the old caupo.

I was now garbed in a clean tunic - or chiton, in this land - and new sandals. The ragged castaway had changed into a well-coined citizen again. "My greetings, Caupo. But I cannot tarry for words for the moment. Have you word of Korax, my drinking mate at times?"

"Aye, I see him at odd times. He has not been in much coin since your leaving. I recall that he sometimes gains metal by loading the carts at the brickworks. Or maybe it is the marble vendor..."

The Caupo was wrong in both instances. By dent of asking here and there as I traversed the lower end of the city, I finally stopped to watch the old soldier moving stovewood from an enormous jumbled pile, and into small stacks of measured size. I wondered at his attitude at seeing my sudden return from the shades, and of my abandonment of a friend to grubbing labor, but...

"In Rome, the goddess, Opis, speaks well of those who labor at honest work." The old soldier turned at the words. The expression of Korax, as he looked at the sudden apparition that had appeared in the yard of the kindling vendor was without equal for these long months.

He seemed to have lost his power of speech as his mouth opened and closed, but without issuing words. Desiring to stem any sudden fury at my apparent abandonment of our friendship, I spoke before he found his tongue. "Nay, do not condemn me for my disappearance without hearing of the reason, of which it was not of my doing."

"Zeus and his pox-ridden whores! The Roman it is, or my eyes have been struck by some putrid sprite. How...?"

I held up my hand, then said, "Collect your wage, and we will retire to a taverna and give each the adventures of these long months."

Since the work-tavernas vended wine little better than the contents of the piss-buckets in the latrine, we walked back into the city to our usual haunt. There, I gave my tale, excepting the battles at the end, and again made my sorrows for leaving him without notice.

He nodded over his cup. "Aye, my thoughts at the time were twofold - that you either were at the bottom of the ship canal with a wide gap in your throat or indeed, you had fallen to crimps on the waterfront."

"You had the measure of that, I can say directly. I neglected to maintain the watch that you warranted while in a strange taverna. And I can say, many were the times that I wished for your advice for my next action."

He drained his cup, the first that he had enjoyed since my departure - or, at least, the first that was above the quality of the swill of the work yards. "And now? You will reenter the employ of the Guild? And make your mark on the scriveners of the city?" He saw the seriousness in my eyes as I hesitated, then said, first looking to make sure we were unheard, "But, methinks you have other to say than greetings to a long-lost comrade."

I also looked around, then bent my head toward him and began to speak softly. "Aye, and the news is as the worst tidings from the Lord of Hades, himself." For a long time, I gave him the full tale of my toil in the fleet of Athens.

Time passed, with me speaking and my comrade listening with widened eyes. Finally, he said with a shake of his head, "I can scarcely give belief to your words. And, did I not think I had your measure, even now I would be reporting you to the magistrates for seditious talk." He looked around again. "But it can not be as bad as you say. Possibly a detachment had been caught with their heads stuck in their buttocks, but not the entire fleet."

I held up my cup, and gazed into the depths of the purple liquid, then replied, "Listen carefully, my friend. I stood for a hour and more by the waterclock, on the deck of an enemy row-ship, watching the slaughter of a hundred and a half of your citizens. And in both directions along the shore, I could see other Spartans playing their games of death with hundreds more." I waved him to silence. "Then, at night I paddled past uncounted stadia of glowing cinders that were the remains of the Athenian Triremes, and I have no estimation at all of the numbers in the other direction. I am a master scrivener, trained in the Temple of Jupiter, and even I had trouble finding the numbers to add up the total of the disaster."

A gulp of wine and I continued, "Those are the facts, straight and true, and if anything, even short of the actual size of the disaster. But now, my question for you... What does it mean for the city of Athens?"

He thought for a moment before replying. "If it is as calamitous as you say, then the city is doomed. All grain - or, at least, most - comes from beyond the Hellespont. Some may come from Assyria and a mite from Egypt, but neither of those can replace that quantity from the north. These rocky lands cannot even feed the hill people, and far less a city of this size."

I knew all of this, and more, but... "I will leave the city as soon as I can find a berth. I have found that the Spartans have little fear of causing harm to a citizen of Rome. Will you accompany myself?"

He thought for a moment, his usual japing manner totally submerged. "This is my city. Where else would I not be nothing more than a fugitive? Unlike my learned comrade, I have no knowledge of other tongues, and not the youth to learn." He leaned forward. "But know this, if the fleet of Athens is entirely destroyed, then you will need to find your outgoing berth in haste. The Spartans have no need to blockade the grain routes when they can just stand off the port of Athens with impunity."

I nodded. "At first light, tomorrow, I will take my leave to the port, to find a ship. Any ship."

"Why wait for the morrow? There are many hours of this day left."

"I need to report to Dionysos of my return."

"By the boils on the crotch of Artemis, why? What can you gain from visiting that nest of vipers again, if you are fleeing the city?"

"Dionysos will know of my return. I had to enter his warehouses to retrieve my coin and blade. Should he think that my disappearance was of an inimical nature, I could easily be slain at any point on the walk to the port." I held up my hand to stop his objection, then reaching into my purse and withdrew some coins. "Procure us a room at the inn for the night. Then, tomorrow we will bid farewell to each other, or set our combined course from this doomed city."

At the entrance of the Guild warehouse, a man watched my arrival, then said, "Report to Dionysos in his quarters, Roman." I nodded and entered the huge facility, walking through the busy taverna toward the suites of the Guild master. As I walked between the tables, I listened closely to the talk. The news of the disaster in the north had still not made it to the city, else the taverna would have been in an uproar.

Knocking on the door frame, I heard the command "Enter." Inside was not only the master but reclining on a thick rug was the golden-haired Korê, Ravana. The man pointed to the table, cups already placed and being filled by a slave. "So, the wandering Roman has returned in whole from the adventure with the Athenian fleet." My shock was obviously evident on my face. How in all the creation of Olympus could he have known... A slight smile, and he continued. "I knew of your abduction to the fleet - or, rather, my agents traced your movements from your last known appearance. Little happens at the port that I cannot hear of or find the reason for." He pushed the cup toward me. "Alas, by the time I had the location of yourself, the fleet had sailed and my orders for your release were left standing on the shore."

I just nodded as he continued. "But, I have no word of the Sea Swan returning, and little belief that a man who deserted would return to the city of his service." That last was a question, even if not formulated as one. Again, I just looked at the man with a steady stare until he nodded and said, "Aye. I can see that your tale is not one of joy, and I suspect gives alarm to the city."

I took a swallow of the wine - the goodness of it totally unnoticed. Then, still looking at his eyes, I said, "The Sea Swan is now in the service of the Lord of Hades, as are all the crew to a man, save me, and that is only because of my facility in the water. And, in fact, they are the standard bearer for the entire Athenian fleet as it rows into the underworld, entire."

Now, by his frozen countenance, I could tell that the great man had been shocked and by a mere scribe of the ranks. He sat for a moment, as a statue, then pushed the wine jug toward me and uttered one word, "Speak!"

Again, for the next hour, I gave the sordid tale of the end of the greatness of Athens. He had no questions of my veracity, and certainly no need to cozen himself with self-hope. Finally, he sat back in thought for a considerable time. I just sat and sipped the wine, glancing at the yellow-haired Korê from time to time. An intelligent girl, she had followed my tale of doom with full understanding and was also obviously in the depth of thought.

"What is your intention, Roman?" The question came suddenly.

I put down the cup and replied, "With your pardon, Kurios, I will leave Athens and with haste. Whatever the fate of the city or any reasoning between the foes, a foreign person such as I may foment much suspicion once the news becomes known. I certainly have no ill-will to Athens, and now an immense hatred of the Spartans, but I have learned that a gathering of rabble has no judgment."

He nodded, obviously thinking of far larger matters than the fate of an anonymous Roman, but said, "Aye. Were I in your instance, my thoughts would be the same." He stood, and I jumped to my feet. "I wish you the auspices of the gods, Roman. You have certainly served me well in your brief sojourn in our city. I will direct Cleades to issue a Bill of Notation for your deliverance to the harbor master. It will assist in your finding a berth on an outgoing ship."

With the tablet from the scribe in my hands, I hurried back to the inn to speak to Korax. He was waiting, and we walked to our usual speaking post - the taverna across the street.

Again, quietly, we talked at a corner table. "There are rumors around the city that the matters with the Spartans are not... proceeding well."

That could only mean that some survivor of the battle had landed. It was far too soon for any news of the disaster to have arrived from overland. But I doubted that a shipload of the remnants had arrived, else the streets would be howling with cries of doom. I nodded, then asked, "And you? Will you decamp with me, or stay and greet the Spartans when they sail into port offering friendship."

He hesitated for a moment, savoring the wine that he had been denied for the long months of my absence. Then, "I will grant to myself that I have assisted you in your attempt to lay pose in Athens, and I have taken my pay in drink and food, and a mat for the night, paid with your coin." I nodded. "But, outside this land, I will be as a temple whore in a moneychangers kiosk - with no understanding of worth as to my purpose. Why would you wish an old soldier as tiresome baggage?"

I set down my cup. "In my land, there is a saying. 'A friend doubles joy and cuts grief in half.' And, that 'four eyes can see both forward and behind, whereas two are blind in at least one direction.'"

His mouth turned down with a wry expression as he replied with a grunt, "It is no false tale that you are from the priesthood. I have heard better blatherings from an obol-sage, squatting in the mud of the workfarm street."

I grinned and said, "Aye, I should have stayed in Rome and made my living by eliciting coppers from the gullible. Still, you are not a doddering graybeard, and you have much time left to enjoy. Why stay in a doomed city and dodge the spears of conquering soldiers? Or starve with the rest." I held up my hand to stop his reply. "I have goodly coin - enough to keep us in wine and food for a season and even more. And, once again, I make the pledge that should your desire to return to your birth city become overwhelming, I will coin your berth for the voyage."

He pursed his lips and nodded with a sigh. "Aye. I have seen the aftermath of a city that has fallen to a foe, and while I am not adverse to running my spear through a few of the cursed Spartans, my old sinews would have little chance of matching some boy-soldier looking for loot or slaves." A long gulp, then, "Very well. To the ships and may Zeus point our feet to a land of wine and honey."

Relieved, I leaned back against the wall, then jumped as the sharp stobs of the unfinished wood tried to run me through. "Aye, friend. We will walk to the port at first light - or before. If news of the coming doom reaches the city before we have engaged our ship, not only will the mobs be storming the port, but the cost of a berth will reach the sky. For now, we will procure carrying bags and find traveling rations."

Morning time was still to come, as we made our way down the road to the port. We were both carrying two large bundles of food and a waterbag each, although the one of my comrade was filled with a purple liquid, rather than water. Halfway, we turned aside to examine a particular formation of rocks and shortly had dug up the jar that I had filled with part of my earnings from my labors in the Guild. By the time we had reached the harbor master station, the sun was just appearing behind us and the port was awake and in full activity.

The tablet from the Guild instantly turned the official from a bored magistrate to a man wishing to assist us in any way. His list showed merchants leaving during the day for various destinations, but only a one in the direction of Latium, my preferred direction, and that only later in the afternoon. Eastern destinations were plentiful, but I had no reason to gain even further distance from my land...

Until I noticed a familiar shape on the horizon, now turning the cape that jutted out southwards from the port. And more than one. Noticing my expression of dismay, Korax looked at me for a moment, then said, "You look like a man that has seen his own shade." Following my pointing finger, he looked for a moment, then said, "Triremes. And not in good shape, it appears. But of Athens, obviously. What is your..." The implication sudden struck him fully, and he finished with, "Hades and his bitch woman!" Looking around, he said in a low, but urgent voice, "When they touch land, we will be engulfed in a nest of hornets."

I nodded. The two ships were beaten and battered, one with a sail tied to the mast rather than the usual cross poles. Survivors, obviously, from the vicinity of Aegospotami - outlying patrol ships that had somehow beaten their way free from marauding Spartans. But still, they were two ships coming with news that would hit Athens as a thunderbolt from the furies.

Immediately, I said, "Come," and we hurried to the waterfront, passing this merchant and that until I found a large vessel in the process of casting off. Stopping at hull side, I called, "Kapetanios, I would engage berths on your ship." As the man looked up in surprise, I continued with, "I offer silver for our transport, and we carry our own provisions."

He looked back with some amusement, apparently. "An offer of interest." A thick accent of unknown origin, but he spoke understandable Greek for all that. His declensions were sometimes strange, as were some of his words, but I will render his speech as normal for this script. "You have not even inquired as to our destination. Methinks that you have need to depart this land with haste."

I nodded back, trying to smile and look at the approaching warships at the same time. "And you would be right, Kapetanios, but not for reason that the magistrates are seeking us, but to avoid certain coming unpleasantness." I looked down the line of ships, "But if you have no room, nor desire, tell me and we will take our silver elsewhere."

He shrugged. "Silver is silver. I will take a double Stater each, and your pledge to help with the ropes should we find ourselves beset by heavy weather. And board, we depart immediately."

Before we could lift a leg to climb onto the ship, I heard from behind, "Junius."

I froze. Few people in Athens used my real cognomen - indeed, very few even knew it. Korax always just called me "Roman." But, I knew the voice, and well. I turned in disbelief to see a young boy, garbed in a long work tunic and with a wool cap pulled low over his head. Korax had turned also, confused as to the call and no doubt wondering if my tastes had changed to boys during my time in the service of the Sea Swan.

The gods were not finished with their puppet-toy far below the clouds, from which they watched their play in the world below. And, in fact, at this moment I had no doubt that the magnificent halls of Olympus were echoing with laughter at their latest jest.

"Take me with you, Junius. And I do not ask for favor, but I can vend my way without taking from your purse. It is yours if you allow me to share your berth." The boy handed me a leather sack that I almost dropped from the weight. It had to have many times the value that was in my own substantial purse, but...

"Who is this?" demanded Korax. "I had no knowledge of your consorting with boys."

I was still speechless, and conflicted with both the danger and the desire, but the captain of the ship settled it. "Board if you are taking ship with us, Greek. We are poling for open water, now."

I just waved at Korax to climb onto the hull, then grabbed the newcomer by the arm, fiercely whispering into his ear. "Keep your stance as a boy - sailors do not care to tempt the Dalkies with the bad luck of a female passenger."

In a moment, we were on the deck, and I called to the captain. "We will be three, rather than two." I pulled six large coins from my purse and set them in his hand, then turned to the 'boy' and said, "Get below and out of the way."

The ship was a decked merchant of a goodly size, single-masted and with a crew of five, it appeared, unless others were below. Not a new ship, but it looked to be well found, and in good condition. Not that it mattered, now as our time of choosing was rapidly ending. I could see the two Triremes grounding on the sand, and men climbing down the side. Thus, it began, I knew. By the midday meal, the city of Athens would be as an ant heap, kicked and stirred by a boy in his play.

Korax and I moved to the forepeak of the ship, to be out of the way of the men poling the ship away from the wharf. I was still almost in a daze at the happenings of the last few moments. The danger of the willing abduction the bedmate of the powerful master of the Dragon Guild was low. Had the man any intimation of her flight - and that she was carrying gold and silver stolen from the household - she would have never made it to this ship. But even Dionysos, for all his power, did not have the all-seeing omniscience of the gods. She would have just disappeared and without a trace.

And besides, like his fellow citizens, his worries would soon extend far beyond the disappearance of a mere bed-mate.

But, just how she managed to disappear without chase or detection, was a question that she would have to answer - later, and far past the point where the captain would return if he found that he was transporting a woman.

As the port slowly receded, I was watching the area around the beached warships. I could see little detail, but I knew that the news of disaster was receding from the ships like the ripples in water from a thrown stone. Suddenly, a thought occurred to me - one that immediately turned into a worry.

I looked back to the captain, measuring if his work of port-leaving was finished, then rose from my squat and walked to face him. Lifting my hand in salute, I said, "Kapetanios. Now that we are underway, I have information of danger that would be in the interest of all for you to hear."

His eyes widened slightly, and he waved me to follow to the side of the deck, away from the men who were now coiling ropes and stowing the poles that had been used to push us away from the wharf. Waving me to sit on a crate, he said, "Speak your news, Greek. You have my attention."

I nodded and started with, "Aye, but I am Roman, not Greek, although that has little meat in this story, but..." His eyes widened as I told the story of the Athenian fleet and its destruction, pointing to the two warships across the harbor, and the furious activity that we could see emanating from them, even at this distance. At the end of the tale, I finished with, "...and I have little knowledge of sea-strategy, but in my conversations with men who have... had familiarity with such, they expected the Spartans to invest this harbor and as soon as their ships can row the distance. If you meet such force rounding the mainland..." I left it at that.

He sat there, just staring over the water, no doubt furiously reviewing the fantastic tale that he had just been told. Then, "Gree... Roman, I have no doubt that you saw a battle, but in sea-warfare, the Athenians have no equal. They could not have been totally destroyed - you must have seen only a portion of..."

I leaned over toward the man, then said with no small emphasis. "Listen to me, Kapetanios. This is not a story from a man who heard it from a teller of tales and he, from yet another mouth. I was an oarsman on a Trireme and saw the battle off Lampsacus, in which we were destroyed in total. As a prisoner, I saw the hot coals of the Athenian fleet at Aegospotami, and at night, while escaping, passed even more pyres of burning ship-wood. Athens may have other fleets, or ships in secret that I know nothing about, but I will testify before the gods that few ships that sailed to the Hellespont will return." I straightened up, then finished with, "Save here and there, as those two that limped to the beach."

Finally, he nodded, then rose and called to a man at the stern tiller-arm, in some jabbering language - this ship had a rudder, rather than a lashed steering oar. Then, to me, he nodded and just said, "Aye, we will keep away from the land, in caution. Any foe coming from a blood feast may not discriminate between their enemy and a man of peace, as I am. Any Spartan craft will follow the shoreline, closely."

Of course, he was right. Triremes did not enter the open sea without preparation and stockage for the long and thirsty pull. The Spartans would hug the mainland on their way to invest the port of Athens, stopping at night to rest on the shore, just as we did on our trip to the north.

Assuming that they were coming at all, that is.

But, what would happen would do so whether I worried or not. For now, my concern was our destination. This ship and crew were from the Achaemenid Empire - a name that gave a total blank to my knowledge. Only later, did I understand that the captain was speaking of Persia, the great lands to the east. Their home port was Sidon, somewhere on the eastern edge of the great central sea and this ship ran the trading route between that city and Athens on occasion, following the shoreline to make commerce in any port along the way that had cargo or merchandise for trade or carriage.

I had no idea of the location of Sidon, but I knew that the distance between Rome and myself was increasing by the day. Still, I had no pressing reason to visit this place or that, now that we had - hopefully - escaped the fire that would soon consume the city of the Greeks. I would relax and let the ship carry me where it may.

In the hold, only about half full of cargo, we claimed an open space of hull, forward, as our cabin, but first carrying several kegs of pitch - leaking and odoriferous - to the other end of the hull. By now, Korax was wanting the tale of Ravana and I can say that he did not listen with total equanimity. "By the putrid member of Dionysus, where did you acquire a female trull? And why? There will be no lack of brothels, wherever we find ourselves."

I waved my hand in the semi-dark, illuminated only by the small breathing hatch above. "Hold your voice to a lesser note. I do not wish her to be known as female until we are well away from Athens."

He snorted, but said more quietly, "No ship will return for a single woman - more like, they would just cast her to the fish if reason was needed. But you have not answered my question."

I sighed, then lay back against a baulk of wool and began the explanation.

At the end of the tale, he just sat and looked her up and down, then back at me before replying. "Fleeing for your life ahead of an oncoming tide of woe, you pause to abscond with the bed wench of the most dangerous man in Athens." Now he just shook his head. "Do all Romans take life as such an adventure, to be tested to the utmost on every sunrise? By your previous tales, it was a like wench that started you wandering across the world."

The girl, quietly, but with fervor spoke for the first time since coming aboard. "I am no wench, Greek. Nor a trull, but an educated woman of my own right."

Korax was not impressed. "You lack the common sense of the street woman, Korê. In the Guild, you had the protection of the most powerful man in the lower quarters, and a warm mat for the night, and food for the taking. Why would a woman forsake that for the chance to be made slave by the first man that abducts her in a strange city?"

"Perhaps a discerning woman does not wish to be the sleeping mat for a filthy Greek... Greek!"

"Cease, both of you." I could tell that the young woman and older man were not destined to be close friends for the voyage, but... "What is done is done. Let us relax and enjoy our effortless voyage while we can. I have been on others that took much more effort. This one is as the pleasure cruise on the barge of a noble."

Days went by, and I discovered that Persian sailors - or Achae... whatever he called his people - did not have the superstition that a female aboard ship was an attractor for ill fate. In fact, she could have been a real boy for all the attention she was given. Still, I ordered her to keep her tresses under the cap and to make her water and ablutions in private so as not to arouse men long from home and wives.

It was a run of many days, with moderate winds, threading between islands on this side and that, before we hove into the port of Rodos, or Rhodes, to use the Greek word for the island city. This was a raw city, only established a year or two before our arrival. I had little time to explore the history of this land, but apparently the cities of the island had agreed to unite under one leader and thus build a new capital so as not to favor any one faction. The newness, in effect, meant that this port was not on the main routes of the sea trades, as yet, and few other ships were in the harbor. That the people were descended from Greece was apparent as their language was purely of that land.

During our run to the city of Rhodes, Ravana gave us her actions that caused our meeting on the wharf. "...but your first appearance at the Guild was not the beginning of my plotting. I had been watching and waiting since my purchase in Athens, taking a coin here and there over the seasons, stashing it in secret locations for that time that I would flee the city. You were the first non-Greek that I had talked to since my vending to the Guild master. And the only one, in truth."

I wondered at her thinking and if it was serious. It would appear so from her actions. For a slave to steal from her master was serious indeed. But... A woman, no matter how well coined, cannot just walk to the harbor and purchase a berth on a ship. She would be robbed and ravished immediately, then sent away after the men of the vessel had tired of their play - always assuming that they did not just keep her as the plaything of the crew. Even a woman of nobility did not travel without a man of her family, and even then with slaves and servants, guards and stewards.

And, if by some magic, she did manage to conceal her gender and travel to a far city, there was little she could do there other than engaging in work at a brothel. A young woman could not hire a room at an inn, or purchase a meal at a diversorium - the magistrates would be called immediately, and she would be exposed as a single female with no man or master, then probably to be given as a servant or slave to whichever man had the most authority.

As my thoughts passed on the subject, I realized that she would have to be my companion until...

We assisted the captain and crew in unloading the bales of wool, then stowing amphorae of wine below decks - and some other cargo of assorted variety and value. I saw worth in keeping the master of the vessel satisfied with his passengers - we were moving into a part of the world that I had only known from tales and stories, and friends cannot be too numerous in such a situation.

Leaving Korax on the ship to guard our possessions, including the sack of gold and silver that Ravana had brought, I purchased more provisions and queried the few ships in the harbor for any that might be moving back toward Latium. I could find none that did not plan to stop at Athens, or even to use that city as an end-point - not a destination that I favored. Thus far, the news of the disastrous battle had not reached to this distance, but it was only a matter of days, at the most - sooner if the captain began to tell of the information that I had given him. I doubted that any ship's master, once that story had reached his ears, would sail into such an unknown situation. The trade routes to the west would probably be closed down until the matter between the two cities was settled. Few merchants would wish to sail into the middle of war.

We would go on into the unknown. There was no choice.

Fortuna

Leaving Rhodes, we were voyaging along the coast to the city of Myra, somewhere on the northern edge of the Great Sea. With the moderate winds, there was little work for the crew, other than the man at the tiller, and most just lounged in the shade of the sail. The captain was friendly - even grateful to have a passenger with which to pass the time in idle talk. He asked me about Latium and Rome - destinations that he had yet to see, and in return, I requested this and that about this end of the world.

I was sitting with him on the raised deck of the stern, enjoying a cup of wine from one of the amphoras that we had taken aboard. I pointed to his crew, asleep in the shade. "Do your men also hight from... Sidon, you said?"

He wolfed down a hunk of fresh bread, brought aboard just as we cast off on the yesterday. Shaking his head, he replied, "Nay. Bataa, there - the man with the gold earring, is of my city, but the rest are just port wanderers, moving from this ship to that as the trade goes. The man we call Parm - the tall one - does not even speak and I suspect that the scar at his throat has a tale of that. But he understands well enough and is a good crewman."

A wave with the loaf, and he continued, "Hadar and Massoud, there, signed on in... I disremember, but it was north of Sidon - probably Gisem or thereabouts. All have been with me for many seasons." He pointed to Korax, sitting in the forepeak and gazing over the waters at the shoreline, far away. "And you? A Roman with a Greek companion?"

I snorted and replied. "This would have to be a long voyage, indeed, Kapetanios, for me to be able to give that tale in its entire. A chance meeting, and of two men who could assist each other, and both fairly rootless." I waved my hand to take in the entire horizon. "For my instance, something - or someone - seems to be drawing me away from my city. No matter my place, nor how secure, the fates will cause my departure from my position, and always further from Rome."

He nodded, then said, "And the girl? She does not seem to be your mate. Your daughter perhaps, or that of your companion?"

Now I shook my head and rolled my eyes to the sky. "Nay, Kapetanios. She is merely another strange happening in a life of many such. Her appearance at the wharf in Athens was unexpected and a total surprise to me. Suffice it to say that she is a female from Latium, and strong willed - intending to return by her own effort, if necessary.

And do not think of her as an unfledged Korê - she is older than she looks in those boy-garments and has seen her share of men."

Naturally, he asked about the battles that I had seen. Any seafarer would have the interest in sea warfare, just in the nature of his life-work. I gave what I knew, admitting that I had little knowledge of the arrangement of power at this end of the world, and none at all as to the reasons or purposes for the current strife between the Spartans and the Athenians. I shrugged my shoulders, "To my way of viewing, both are Greek - as to why they seem to be mortal enemies, I have no knowledge."

The days passed, turning into months as we ported in this city, and that, trading wine for iron, and sheepskins for barrels of wax. Finally, we loaded a full hull of some aromatic wood, called kédros, or cedrus - a red wood that was highly prized by the southern peoples. "The Egyptians will pay much gold for such wood," said the captain. "Their land is devoid of any tree, and these will bring the value of this entire vessel and more."

"Then we sail for Egypt, Kapetanios?" I asked. I had no objection - one place in the world was as good as any other for three wanderers.

He shook his head. "Nay. In Geson, south of my city, we will sell the load to an Egyptian merchant. The gain will be less than if we took the entire route, but the land of the pyramidios is far away, and the trip would be measured in months." The Greek word was close enough to the Latium term, pyramis, that I knew of the gigantic structures of which he was speaking, although I had little belief that their size matched the tales.

In the port of Sidon, we stopped for several days, the captain using the time to spend with his family. We had the run of the city, but compared to Rome or Athens, it was nothing but a collection of mud-brick structures and streets of dirt. The wine in the taverna - pothouse, as it was known here - was drinkable, if nothing to praise, but the usual drink was the ferment of grain, called cervesia. Or, that was what it was known as in a civilized city - I have no idea of the local term. To me, it was just a bitter liquid of evil taste, to be tried once and never again.

The captain gave advice and offered the use of the ship for our nightly quarters, warning us of vermin infested sleeping houses and less than honest innkeepers. Seeing the filth of the city, and the people, we gladly accepted his offer for our stay. With the load of wood, there was little room below, but we had managed to carve out a small area for our use.

My main desire was for a thermae, but bathhouses did not seem to exist in this part of the world. Indeed, even the act of bathing seemed to be unknown here, a fact given emphasis when downwind from any of the local citizenry.

By now we were almost crew members, taking a hand with the ropes and poles when necessary. It was a welcome change to the sameness of the days, and it gratified the captain to have such passengers aboard, willing to lend a hand. Korax, for his part, soon made the acquaintance of the crew, even before our stop in Rhodes. He spent much of his time on the in the shade of the sail, casting the bones, trading a few low-value coppers and bronzes back and forth with the other four. He had no common words with the men from the eastern realm of the world, but that has never held men back from their games.

For my part, I usually just relaxed in the shadow of the stern platform, enjoying a life of ease. When I was not conversing with the captain about this and that, I would finger my abacus, practicing my fingers to move the stones with ever more agility. And, Ravana would sit beside me often, but mute and retiring, apparently enjoying her freedom from a life of man-use slavery. She was alluring, but I made no movement in that direction, preferring to service my needs by myself. Using a brothel when in harbor, of which every port had many, was not to my taste, at least, not since leaving Rhodes. The females of the eastern sea were... of such a state of uncleanliness and rancidness of nose, that even my cravings could not bring me to join with such creatures. The female that was usually sitting beside me was desirable, and even beyond that, but to couple with this woman would probably turn loose the fates that even the gods could not control - or so I told myself.

We stood out of Sidon, moving south toward the city of Geson, or maybe Habi, to vend the supply of cedrus in the hold to an Egyptian vessel, or other that would deliver it to wood vendors up the Nilos river. Again, we followed the coast, always having it in sight, though usually far on the horizon. There was a reason for the distance, as explained by the captain. "The coast from here to far past the great Delta of the Nilos is infested with pirates, but not as those in northern waters. Here, if the sea is calm, a long skiff will be paddled out from this river or that, filled with men of a number to overwhelm even a well-manned merchant. But their craft are made for river waters and are not seaworthy, and they hesitate to stand far out from shore. Their freeboard is so low that swells of any size would swamp them, leaving the men to drown far from land." He turned and ordered the tillerman to give a small change to our course. "In the approaches to the great city of Carthago, the threat recedes. Their sea forces are as great as that of Athens, and patrol the waters with regularity, sweeping pirates out of their domain."

"Have you traveled as far as that?" I asked.

"To Carthago? Nay, but the voyage to Memphis I have made as a lad in the merchant hull of my patéras. And after he lay down with the gods, once more, but not since."

"Memphis? Is that a city in Egypt?"

He looked at me with some surprise. "I am surprised that such a literate as you has no knowledge of the great Memphis. It is on the Nilos river, and just a few leagues south of the pyramidios."

Now I nodded. "Ah, the city of Inbuhedj. Aye, I did not know of it by the Greek name."

He stared at me for a moment. "Speak you the language of Egypt?"

"Aye. I learned from a... a tutor after I left Latium. I was... in the employ of a scribe from that land and picked up some facility of his language." I had no desire to give the tale of my slavery on the island of the pirates.

The winds were contrary, although the sea was serene, and it was the good part of a month before we hove into the port of Geson - also known by the name of Raphia by the locals. The captain was dismayed to find the port empty of shipping from the land of Egypt and wondered whether to proceed or try to vend his wood here.

As the city was also a minor trading outpost for the Greeks, I found myself able to move around the city and converse, rather than performing my usual hand waving and pointing as had been done in the ports along the coast of this end of the sea. At a local merchant kiosk, in what might be called a pitifully small forum, or agora, I made the acquaintance of an old scribe from the vicinity of Athens. We - of the ship - were obviously still riding in front of the wave of woe - that tale of Athens and her inevitable demise - as this man knew nothing of the defeat by the Spartans. But from him, I learned of an uprising against the Persians, by several cities of Egypt. More than that, I learned that the land had been under the control of the King of Persia for over a hundred years.

I sat with the scribe, a man calling himself Asius of Thorikos, a city not far from the one in which I first came ashore in Greece. We were seated in an open air wine kiosk, across from his scribery, drinking with my coin. "...Aye, the entire lands from beyond the Dark Sea to the north, and to the cataracts of the Nileos in the south - and further to the east than I have knowledge - have been under their domain for... oh, at least, half more than a hundred years."

I had no idea what 'cataracts' were, but they were obviously far up the long river of Egypt. "And there is war, now, in those lands?" I asked.

He shook his head. "I doubt that it could be called war. It is more to be expected for the frogs to eject the swine from their puddle than for the people of the Nilos to remove their conquerors. More likely, a few magistrates will be killed in riots after the haranguing by some demagogue stirs the people with tales of their glorious past, then the bodies of several thousand of the rabble will be cast into the river by the rampaging garrison soldiers of Persia."

"My captain says that the harbor, here, is empty of Egyptian hulls. I assume the reason is the violence?"

He nodded. "Aye. When the blood dries, the Persians will lay reparations on the land, and the shipowners have removed their vessels so as not to be seized for the toll. I assume, without knowing, that most have moved along the western coast, beyond the Delta, until the situation is cleared up. Maybe even all the way to Carthago, to lay up for safety." He held up his cup for the passing minion to refill. "Now, Junius the Roman, let me water my own needs. You have come from Athens..." I dipped my head. "Then, tell me the news of my city. There have been few merchants from the Aegean sea these past months."

Carefully, not wishing to sound as the furies of doom, I mentioned the war, and that the fleets had sailed for battle, but that I had been gone long from there these many months, and have no tale of how the domain of that city was faring. That last was at least, truthful, if just not all of it. After all, the Spartans could have been utterly defeated in battle before the gates of Athens. Unlikely, but I did not actually know the answer. Eventually, I gave my farewells and started for the ship.

When the captain returned in the afternoon, I gave him the knowledge that I had gained from Asius, the scribe. He nodded. "Aye. That closely follows what I have learned. But it does not give me direction for our divagation." That was another of his Persian words that had no reference to my mind, but I knew from our quandary that he meant... just that, our quandary. "The selling of our load, now, and here, will be for just mendicant coppers from the local cargo accumulators. They, in turn, will get gold and silver for our wood when the trade resumes, but they can wait - we cannot." He looked out over the harbor. "I am of a mind to touch the port of Pelusium, at the eastern edge of the Delta."

I had never heard of the city or port, but it would have been strange if I had. "The city is Egyptian?"

"Aye, but under the firm control of the satrap of Persia for that area. They are far from the center of the uprising, and it would be most unlikely for any in that city to be fomenting rebellion with their fellows far up the Nilos. And they produce a flax and lininum Pleusiacum - the finest materials for making the weaver-threads in the known world. A shipload of those fibers would bring much silver in Greece, or even upper Persia."

By nightfall, he had made up his mind. We would continue south and then west, following the bottom curve of the great sea. We stood out of port at sunup the next morning.

The days were becoming hot and the nights warm, and we began to lay our bedding on the deck with the crew, although, after the mid of night, I would usually retire back to our little cove in the baulks of wood, to escape the dampness of the early morning. Korax, of course, did not even stir in his loud stentorian breathing, even should whirls of wind-driven spray turn his mat into a soaking sponge. Ravana would always awake at my stirring, and follow me below, afraid for her sleep among the crude men of the sea.

When I had given my farewells to Asius, I had wandered the kiosks - called bazaars in that part of the world - on the way to the harbor and had seen a fat scroll on the table of an old man, among the worthless trinkets and curiosities that he hoped to vend to passersby. After a brief examination, and for a small bronze coin, I purchased it. Now, on the deck of the ship, well stood out to sea, I unrolled my purchase and began to peruse the picture writing. Of course, it was a scroll of Egypt, of unknown origin, but with its length, possibly a history or even a tale of the sages. It gave me a way to pass the days, sitting and improving my knowledge of the written language of the land to which we were now pointing.

Interestingly, Ravana began to ask for the meaning of this picture and that, and my reading became an instruction for a pupil. It was pleasant, to puzzle the images, trying to fill in the referent from the characters on either side, and with a woman - a clean and desirable young female - leaning against me and making her own surmises of the meanings. And more than pleasant. Despite all the vows and oaths that might be given to this oracle or that god, a man in the prime of life will not - cannot - long ignore a fully nubile woman that is closely present day after day. And, certainly, his svans will indicate his interest despite any attempt by his face to conceal it.

It was only the second night out of the port when we lay down in the hold in the late of night. And just like that fateful day, years ago, in my need and alone with a female of fiery hair, no words were spoken. Suddenly we were coupled together, frantically trying to release the buildup of pressures that had been suppressed to this time. As she had said, she was no mere trull, nor a woman with little interest nor ability in the act of coitus. Rather, she was experienced - more than I - and knew the actions to bring both to the maximum plateau of pleasure.

Afterward, we just lay in the darkness, waiting for a sleep that was long in coming. For myself, I was resigned to my fate, in wonder just what japing play of the gods would take this woman from my life.

The moon waxed and we plodded along the far and treeless coast, now moving toward the sunset. The winds were moderate, but even so, the vast weight of our load meant that our hull was cleaving deeply into the water, limiting our forward progress considerably. But, as I had no final destination in mind, I was content to let the days flow by as if the liquid in a waterclock.

And, the greater reason for my languidness was the access to a female - a beautiful and very desirable woman. We did not flaunt our couplings to the crew, but neither did we attempt to conceal the actions, as if we were guilty adulterers, in the upper houses of Rome. For these men, the act was as natural as the sun rising, and if anything, probably wondered why I had taken so long to begin my pleasure.

Ravana was an intelligent woman, and fairly educated, if not as a scribe, but she was inquisitive and always inquiring about this and that. And, it appeared, to have a greater facility of learning a language than myself. Even now, she could slowly speak out the meanings of the scroll that we had been reading together, her eyes following her finger across the papyrus. The days were pleasant, and the nights were a time to anticipate - in truth, in such leisure I would have sailed into the sunset to the end of my time.

Of course, that was reckoning without the gods, watching from above and always ready to call their fellows to the gameboard when a mortal began to savor his existence to excess.

On a morning, I rose as usual, and waited for Ravana to prepare our meal. During the voyage, she had gradually become the cocua of the ship, preparing any hot meals for all that wished. In actuality, to say that she was the cook of our vessel was something of an exaggeration, since her preparations were only to warm the hard meats of our store, as to give them some tenderness and taste. Or, on occasion, to actually bake a fish for the crew, taken from the water barrels in the hold - a store of fresh meat that would last for a month or so.

A fire was only allowed on days with little wind, and that was a rule with which I had no issue. I had seen, more than once, the rapidity at which a floating mass of pitch-caulked wood could be turned into a roaring mass of flames. This day, the winds were gentle, and the cook-trough was carried to the lee side of the deck. This was a large shallow bowl, filled with sand, on which a small - very small - fire would be laid. It would allow for the roasting of meat, usually a fish, held over the flames and coals with green sticks. Afterward, the dying embers would be scraped from the sand and tossed with the wind. The crew had already broken their fast, and Ravana was stooped before the cook-trough warming a long strip of jerked meat for both of us and Korax. Seeing me approach, she pointed to a leaf on which lay the smoking strip of fish. "The Kapetanios has not come for his meat."

I nodded and picked up the small meal, and walked to the stern platform where the captain was standing, gazing over the waters toward the way we had come. "Your pardon, Kapetanios - your morning repast is ready."

He looked at me for a moment, taking the fish, then turned his gaze back to the sea. Without any cognizance of what he was doing, he slowly broke off pieces of the meat, and chewed them without notice of their goodness. I could see nothing, but I had little doubt that this was a man with concern on his mind. Finally, he turned to me and waved in the general direction of our wake. "Yon ship has been in our wake on since first light. "

Now I stared at the horizon, seeing nothing but the blue sky touching the equally blue wa... Aye, there... just at the limits of noticement, was a point, darker than its surroundings. We had seen ships on the sea before, and many - why this one was of interest was not apparent. I just waited for more reasonings and eventually, he turned and called to the tillerman in his language The tiller-pole was turned and our course turned as he called to the crew, sitting on the deck. The men jumped to their feet and began to unlash the outhaul ropes, then pulled the huge sail to a new position, angling across the deck.

Finally, my wonderment made me speak. "Why think you yon vessel to be a threat? We have passed and followed many hulls in our journey from Athens."

He did not take his eyes off the far imperfection of the horizon. "Aye, and that is so. By yon ship was there at sunset, on the yesterday, and the morning before. Their course does not change, despite my several maneuverings for testing their intent. They are always pointing towards us."

Now, I examined the strange ship - or, rather the smudge on the horizon - with more interest. After a few moments of thought, I said, "A ship belonging to reavers would be much faster, would it not? Any sea-raider that can barely pace our laden hull would soon starve and be a threat to no one."

"Aye. But these will wait for a time that is to their advantage. The mist of Poseidon or a dead calm that will give their oars movement while we wallow in helplessness."

I walked back to the cook-trough, where Korax was munching his rock-hard bread and piece of warmed meat, and talking to Ravana. In the distance and time from our first boarding in Athens, he had slowly tempered his feelings toward the woman, and even now could sometimes enjoy a natter with her, both giving and taking the japes of the other. I sat down beside him, watching as she scraped the coals onto the wetted board that she used for a scoop, then flicked them overboard. Finally, she stirred the sand to cover any slightest spark or ember that might be alive. I had explained to her, and with great emphasis, the danger of fire to any vessel - even to giving a somewhat altered version of my escape from the pirate ship, years ago.

To my friend, I said, "Putting an edge on the point of your spear might be wise." He looked at me, his eyes widening. I gestured toward the stern of the ship. "The Kapetanios thinks that we might be gathering looks of desire from a ship - there - following."

Both Ravana and Korax stood for a moment, looking in the direction of my pointing. "It is far away to be a threat, is it not?" said the woman.

Korax shook his head, saying, "My eyes do not have the youth of yours. I can see nothing as yet, but it must be far." To me, he asked, "What is the concern?"

"The Kapetanios says it has been following us from the morning of yesterday."

He snorted. "Any ship of sea rovers that cannot catch this tub, wallowing along with a hold full of trees, is not likely to be a menace even to a temple barge manned by drunken priests."

"I gave the same opinion, but he thinks that they might be waiting their time."

By midday, the Kapetanios had lowered his concern. Pointing, he said, "Their bearing is changing to pass between us and the land. And far away. Mayhap, my worries are only cloud-stuff." He thought a moment, then said, "We will stay at full distance from the land, leaving it just at the horizon. That will allow us to turn at the end of our course and take the northern wind directly into Pelusium, and at speed."

By evening the stranger had passed us and disappeared, and the Kapetanios had taken comfort from the sight of the open sea with no other craft in our vision. Now, he was sitting with us for the evening meal, and the conversation was about the land we were approaching. "...and the city of Memphis is an attractor to a merchant like the sirens of the deep waters to a seaman. Our load of the scented tree-stuff would bring twice or thrice the coin that will be paid in the coastal ports."

"But..." He smiled as I formed the inevitable question.

"Why do we not point for that city?" He took a piece of warmed bread from Ravana, then continued, "It is about thirty-five leagues up the Nilos - not an inconsiderable distance to take a vessel of this size up a winding river, even one of such largeness."

Korax nodded and waved with his tail of fish. "Aye. Loaded as we are, the gods would come down from Olympus and greet us as doddering graybeards before we could pole this load up a flowing river."

"Nay, my Greek friend. The Egyptians have powerful gods, and one blessing from them is that the wind almost always blows toward the source of the river, so a sailing vessel can usually make its way against the current without needing effort by either polemen or oars. But, not during the times of flood, I have to say. And, of course, to come down the river, the cloth just lays on the deck and the waters push the ship along."

"Kapetanios," I replied. "I have considerable remembrance of river work, although that was in my extreme youth, and I know that a boat will merrily point to here and there while moving downstream with the water. Like as not, as a bit of wood in a circling eddy-current."

"Ah. You speak with knowledge, and that utterance is the proof of it. Aye, any vessel that is not oared or poled in the main will cause a rock to be dragged behind the stern, sized to the hull, to keep the alignment of the bow pointed down the river. Wharf merchants at the cities will vend the stones for a few coppers, rounded and with a hole chiseled for attachment of a rope."

He stood and threw his bones over the side. "But this is nothing but jaw noise - we will lay into Pelusium to vend our cargo, leaving Memphis and the Nilos to the freshwater sailors."

Unfortunately for the Kapetanios, and unknown to him, he was carrying a passenger that was the plaything of the gods.

The Sea Captain

Incendium

I woke, wondering at the cause. Looking at the faint light streaming down the open hatch, I could tell that the day had barely started - indeed, it would be a considerable time before the sun had lifted above the sea. Then, the thump of feet on the overhead planks gave notice that all was not well, as did the shouting of the captain in the strange language of the east.

I jumped to my feet, hesitating only to pull my tunic over my head, then moved to the ladder in time to almost be knocked asunder by Korax, coming down with only his hands on the side rails to slow his progress. As the hull was steady, I knew that our problems were not with a storm, but had to be...

"Reavers!" gasped Korax, "Rowing for us from ahead." I looked up at the open hatch, then scrambled to the deck to see the men pulling the sail to a long slant fore to aft. The captain was at the sternpost, watching and calling this order and that. I looked over the leeward side of the hull, and saw the object of the chaos, and to my relief, at least, two or three stadia away as yet. A long hull, and open with no deck, apparently, and with... I counted, at least, ten oars on the close side. So, twenty men at the rowing, and no doubt several more at other tasks. Far more than enough to take our ship, crewed with only a handful of men - and a woman - with ease.

The pirate vessel had a tall mast, but no sail was set - an obvious condition since they were downwind of us and we were now sailing cross-wind to our previous course. I stopped beside the captain, but without speaking, so as not to mar his orders. Little would be gained by a passenger loudly calling questions of the master merely to service his own queries.

At a pause in the commands, as we settled onto a course as close to the wind as the ship would sail, without sacrificing our speed, he turned to me and said, "No doubt, yon ship is the same as followed us from the port of Geson. They have sped on to put themselves between us and the shore. I am a fool for not thinking of that game."

Korax appeared with his spear and carrying my longknife and scabbard. "You will get to use the practice that old Leodes gave you, during your sojourn in Athens."

The captain shook his head. "Nay, first they will lay off under oars and match our course, and our slowness from the heavy load will assist them greatly. Then, they will attempt to feather anyone on the deck, before closing to board." We looked at the rowing hull, now approaching us at a slant, as they matched our new course across the wind. The stroke was moderate, and I knew that it was to keep the oarsmen from exhaustion - they had to have been pulling a good part of the night to appear on our beam by dayrise. Still, they would be up to us in less time that it would take Ravana to make a meal.

As I tied my belt, and scabbard, I looked up and down our deck, then out to the approaching vessel, and back. My life had already experienced the dregs of slavery, and I had no desire to do so again. It would be an unlikely event for me to escape such bondage and with a whole skin a second time. But, in fact, I had no intention of allowing my capture for such, even if the men in yon ship were even desirous of leaving anyone alive. My skills with a blade were not that of a veteran of the ranks, but they were vastly superior to those that I possessed before my tutoring by old Leodes. I would go down, but with a troupe of shades to escort me into Hades. All on this ship had little else to hope.

Except of course, for Ravana. She would be an unexpected - and welcome - surprise for the raiders. Of course, once the deck battle was over, she would be the instant plaything for the men, and then later sold to some rich noble as a golden-haired exotic but, at least, she would live. I looked to see her squatting beside the cook-trough, apparently without understanding of our peril, as she prepared for the mornings meal. She was beginning to stack her small fire, but would not ignite it with the flint and steel until receiving permission from the captain. As I walked back to the waist to give her the lack of need to break our fast this day, the thought came unbidden that it might be more kindly for myself to slip up behind her and plunge my knife into... into...

I stared at the cook-trough, then across the waters. Then back to the stern where Korax and the captain were watching the slow approach of our doom. I had had a sudden vision of the woman overturning a bowl of glowing embers into the waist of the raider as it grappled our side. That would cause consternation for any man floating on a mass of planked wood and caulked by...

I suddenly ran back to the stern and stopped before the captain, both he and the Greek looking at me in surprise. "Kapetanios! I have had some experience with pirates before now, and I have an idea that might give us another day of life."

He didn't hesitate. "Speak it! I will accept any advice."

"Nay. There is little time but keep yon ship away as long as possible. I need to make preparations." Turning to Korax, I gestured frantically, and said, "Come! And quickly!"

Without wait, I ran back to the waist where Ravana was stooping, and shouted, "Come with me!" Below decks I waited for Korax to join me, then said as his feet hit the boards on the floor of the hold. "Those barrels of pitch! Where were they put when these cursed trees were loaded?"

He looked at me blankly. "Pitch?"

I shook my head frantically. "The black caulking fluid that is used in the seams of the ship! We moved it when we took berth in Athens because of the foul stench in our sleeping area."

He thought for a moment, then, "Under the forepeak, I think. With the supplies of the ship."

"Get them. All of them and put them at the foot of the mast."

"Take the casks of that reeking slop to the deck?"

"Aye, and hurry." To Ravana, I said, "Listen woman, and carefully. If we cannot fight off these reavers, all on board will be dead, and soon, and you will be a slave in a far away and primitive land. And forever." She just looked back, apparently concerned but not in sudden terror at my words. "Bring your cook-trough into the hold, here, and kindle a small fire. Go."

Immediately, I climbed the ladder and ran forward to once again descend into the hold by the small forward hatch. The boards of the deck, on either side of the mast, could be removed as necessary - as in loading or unloading large cargo such as we were carrying now - but otherwise, entry was by two hatches, one large one aft and the other and smaller, forward. Korax was here, rummaging for the casks of pitch, but I ignored him, looking for the store of wine that we carried. In the dim light of early morning coming down the small opening, I selected a moderately sized amphora, and one with a flat bottom, then stove in the plug and poured the wine into the bilges.

Back on deck, I set the jug by the mast, then ran to help Ravana at the after hatch. She could drag the sand-filled bowl across the deck, but there was no possibility of her lifting and carrying it down a ladder. Jumping down to a rung that just allowed my body to protrude at deck level, I pulled the heavy bowl to my shoulder and descended into the hold. The trough was heavy - very heavy, and I spilled a half part of the sand before I dropped it to the deck, but I gave that no thought. To Ravana I said, "We need just a small fire - nothing more."

Now Korax was carrying a cask across the deck, cursing as the black sludge covered his hands with sticky and unremovable blackness. Like all that I had seen, this one was made of bulged slats and strengthened with a net of rope tightly laced around it - just like the one that I had used to paddle myself from the burning pirate ship years ago. I nodded as I passed, then descended into the forward hold again, this time looking for the ship's torches. These were never used onboard while at sea, in the caution of fire that is taken by all prudent sea voyagers, but were for late arrivals at port when the failing sun began to cloak the last stadium or so to the wharf. Or, on occasion, to allow cargo to be loaded in the cool of the night. I took all of them - six or so - and dropped them beside growing number of casks by the mast. Now, Korax had two of the crew helping, and shortly there were a handful of black striped barrels sitting on deck.

I pointed to them and said, "Cut the ropes." Looking over the side at the approaching reaver craft, I added, "And with haste!" As the cordage dropped away from the first one, I pulled my longknife, reversed it and pounded on the top of the cask until the round plug of wood split and fell into the container. Removing the two pieces, I looked in to see what I had expected - a syrup of sticky blackness.

Pitch is a material that can have several manifestations. I had never seen it made, but I knew that it was gained from the production of charcoal, dripping from resinous wood as it was heated. There are also tales that it can be found oozing out of the earth here and there across the lands, but I cannot give my name to that story. The material itself, can be more or less liquid or solid, with some casks holding what seems to be black clay and must be heated to be used, and more commonly, others filled with the equivalent of black honey and still others, like thick water. Fortunately, for my plans, the pitch in this cask was fluid.

I dipped the torches in the liquid, turning them to allow the dried reeds to absorb as much as possible, then laid them on the deck. Picking up the open barrel, I began to pour the contents into the empty wine amphora as I ordered to Korax, "Break open the another cask." The pitch did not flow as water, of course, but both casks were emptied in a short while. Or mostly emptied - I did not wait for the dregs of the liquid to slowly flow into the jug as if I were waiting for the last of the honey to appear on my bread. Picking up the amphora, I judged it to have sufficient weight - any more, and I would be unable to deliver it.

Now I took the torches to the open hatch and descended to give instructions to Ravana, who even now was nursing a small fire on her sand. With that, it was a matter of waiting for the proper moment - and for the gods to roll their bones for the play.

The crew were still pulling on the sail, attempting to trim the cloth so that our ship would point as close to the wind as possible, but yet have no appreciable diminution of speed. I walked to the captain, followed by Korax, and said, "We have one chance, Kapetanios, and not one with much hope. But if it fails, then we fight until we die. Here is my plan..."

Watching the reaver ship gain closer to us, I thought about my actions that were needed, over and again, trying to find a defect in the weave. It all depended on the sudden...

I dropped to the deck on my belly, dragging Korax down with me. I did not need the haste as the arrows were meant for the men in the stern - the Kapetanios and the tillerman. Behind the casks, I looked over to see a handful of archers - six, it was - standing in the fore of their vessel, even now placing new shafts on the nock. The deck of our ship had no bulwark, as is common in Roman merchants. That would have allowed us safety, by staying below the short wall at the side of a ship. But, our deck was as flat as the desert, with only the mast and any cargo standing on the planks to give cover.

None of the shafts had connected, as the bowmen were still getting their range, but it was obvious that they wished to remove any chance of our maneuvering the ship to mar their approach. It was a good wind, and it hindered their stroke, requiring more effort for the oarsmen than would have been needed in calm. And it certainly assisted us somewhat, but in truth, even a wind from the lungs of Poseidon himself would have added little to our pace, so loaded were we with our cargo of the sweet-smelling logs.

Another volley came over stern, and this one was not without effect. The tillerman - the one called, Bataa - sank to his knees and fell to his face, breaking off the two shafts that were pinned into his chest and belly. The Kapetanios, knelt behind the tiller bar - a poor shield, indeed - and kept the steering to the proper point of the wind.

But, it was only a respite. In less time than a man could raise a cup to his lips, another volley came aboard and the captain sank to the deck with an arrow through his throat. The ship heeled up into the wind, the sail now flapping aback and acting as a hinder to our pace.

I cursed loudly, with my head barely above the top of the cask, seeing the archers now moving their aim to the men at the sail ropes. I knew that we would soon be dead in the water and easy prey for our assailants, who only had to stand off and feather all on board before leisurely claiming our vessel for their own.

It was Korax who made the deed. Suddenly, he jumped to his feet and ran toward the stern. I opened my mouth to shout - to scream at him to return and not make himself an easy mark, but realized that it would make only the difference of a few dozen heartbeats of life. For him - for all of us.

But, he ignored the tiller for the time, pulling the body of the captain to lay under the tiller bar, then dragging the other dead crewman and rolling him on top of his dead officer. Now, Korax had a short, but sufficient shield from the low aim of the archers. The action had caught the archers by surprise, and he had completed his barrier before they could move their point of aim to the Greek. Now, laying on his back, he untied the loincloth of the dead Bataa and whipped it up and over the wooden rudder pole then he pulled the tiller back to the centerline of the ship, allowing us to fall off and begin to forge through the water again. I realized that the bravery of my friend had given me the slight chance to carry out my plan.

Turning to the foredeck, while the archers continued to feather the two men who could not be made more dead in an attempt to kill the new tillerman, I shouted to the crewmen at the other end of the ship, yelling and waving for them to jump through the forward hatch and gain cover below. It was too late for one, laying motionless on the deck, but the other two disappeared from view in a heartbeat.

I turned my attention back to our foe, trying desperately to decide on my moment.

The reaver ship was not close enough. We had to be almost within touching distance of their oars before I could act. For the moment, they were just standing off our side, at a distance of ten long strides, while they attempted again to bring our ship to a halt. Looking back toward the stern again, I could see only the top of a shock of golden hair protruding from the open hatch, and under it two eyes just looking at me over the deck. Now, I had to act, before the other captain had time to think on his next actions.

I waved at Korax, to get his attention, and he nodded from his prone position behind the bodies. I held both hands up for a moment, then brought them together with a slap, then held up an open hand in the gesture that means wait. He nodded, and I looked back at the reavers, praying to the gods at the gameboard far above, to throw their bones with good effect.

Our ship now had good way on again, and was being paced by the reavers, their archers still trying to destroy the man at the tiller, even shooting their shafts in long looping arcs. We needed to make our move before one found its mark. Drawing a deep breath, I moved my open hand downward in a chopping motion. Korax, still laying on his back behind the wall of now-dead flesh, pulled on the loincloth and the tiller moved sharply to the windward side, causing our vessel to turn the opposite way. In a few moments, we were heading more downwind than across it, and our speed began to increase. But not much, as we crossed the distance between the hulls before the surprise was realized by our foe.

The enemy ship was open-hulled, without a deck and far smaller and lower than our merchant. It was made for speed and not cargo, and the oars were contained by rope ties at top of the hull sides, rather than through thole ports as would be the case of a larger vessel. Thusly, they did not shatter as happened in the battles of the Triremes, but were merely pushed aside as the two hulls met. Already, Korax had abandoned the tiller and was running back to my position, stopping only briefly at the open hatch.

I stood, stepped over the casks and picked up the heavy amphora that had been partly filled with pitch. Speed was of essence now, before the archers realized my meaning and feathered me like a straw mark at a festival. As I approached the side of the hull, and almost at a run, I lifted it over my head, then cast it into the center of the ship, just at point where the mast rose from the keel boards. Of course, the clay pot shattered into fragments, spilling the thick liquid here and yon around the mast. Korax knew what to do with the two torches that he had retrieved from the waiting Ravana. Into the middle of the black splotch of pitch they were thrown, immediately igniting the caulking fluid.

The flames were not instant, as is the case with heavily distilled spirits that are ignited, but still rapidly progressed outwards from the torches in a bright yellow and smokey fire.

Turning, I ran to pick up one of the full casks, now shorn of the strengthening net of ropes, then turned and heaved it into the ship also. It did not shatter like the clay amphora, of course, but still, it ruptured, spilling more of the pitch into the hull. Korax did the same, but his aim was better, or the gods were guiding his old eyes. His barrel hit the solid pole of the mast, breaking into sticks of wood and spraying the contents over several of the stunned crew.

He turned to pick up another, but stopped as I yelled, "Nay! Turn us away before we are roasted in our own cookfire." He ran to the tiller, pushing it to the lee side, allowing us to pull slowly away from the other hull. The reavers, utterly surprised at the turn of events, finally began to react to their plight. A few of the archers, gaining their reason, tried to gain a target on our deck - either myself or Korax, but their blood was rushing too fast for any considerate aim. A few arrows went high and low, but none to even approach either of us. As to the others in the long craft, with shouts and yells, they wielded buckets of water, attempting to slow the passage of the flames. Not a few were concerned less with their ship than their own selves, as the black fluid from the cask that had been thrown by Korax had splattered over them, covering hair, loincloths and bare skin with a flammable liquid - some of which had ignited from the central fire.

As the rowers had abandoned their poles in the collision, they had slowed to a crawl in the water, and we gradually pulled ahead. With relief, I saw that the fire was not being contained, and as they left the shadow of our wind, caused by our movement forward, the flames began to grow. I suddenly realized that their sail, laying on the deck, fore and aft and between the rowers, had kindled and was adding more fuel to the fire.

As our stern passed their forepeak, I called to Korax, "Bear toward the land." Running to the hatchway, I called to the remaining two members of the crew, "Set the sail for our new course." I knew that neither spoke Greek to any extent, and I knew nothing of their tongue, but they were experienced sailors and knew what was needed. They climbed the ladder and immediately began to loosen the ropes to bring our sail to hold the wind, now behind us.

Again, I felt the weakness in the legs that comes after a life-threatening experience but managed to stay on my feet as I stood looking at the doomed ship behind us. With the good wind, and directly on our stern, we were falling away from our enemies at a good pace, despite the dragging load in our hull.

"Junius."

I looked down at Ravana, standing at the foot of the ladder. "Aye, woman. Put out your fire. It has done its work." Walking the few paces to the tiller, I stood with Korax, both of us watching the reaver ship recede. "By the gods," I said. "whether Greek or any others. You would have made your old comrades in your Hekatontarchia proud this day. Even now, were we in a taverna, you would be plied with wine and women to make even a satyr hold his head the following day."

"Aye," he answered in his gravelly voice. "I am surprised at myself, also, but then, death makes any man perform tasks that would normally make him run to the skirts of his mitéra." He moved his gaze from the wallowing vessel to myself, then continued, "And you, my

Roman friend. It must be a strange temple where you learned your scribbling craft, that also tutors the methods to fire a grappling ship of raiders."

I had never given him the actual story of my escape from my first encounter with pirates - no man willingly admits that he was a slave at a time in his life. "As you said, a threat to life gives a man considerable ability that might be lacking during his typical day. But, fiery pitch is not newsome to a boy from the river boats. Many were the times that I hastened to cover the vat of caulk that had flamed as it was being warmed. I knew well, its effect if we could torch it on the other vessel."

Now Ravana appeared, looking not at all like a woman saved from horrendous use by a shipload of men. Rather, she was the most serene of any, but maybe from disunderstanding of the threat that we had avoided. She pointed across the water and asked, "Will their boat burn from under them?"

I shook my head. "Nay. I would wish it, but even now it appears that they have gained ascendance over the flames. Any breach in their hull by would immediately extinguish the flame that made the hole. But, with their sail in ashes, and many of their oarsmen with raging skin, they have no chance of following us."

"Unless the wind falls away," added Korax.

I shook my head. "Nay. According to the... our... departed Kapetanios, the north wind is prevalent in this part of the world and at most times of the day and season." Now, looking forward at the two men who had finished their rope work with the sail, a sudden thought came. More than just a mere thought, it came as a cataclysmic realization as if the words were writ by the gods in fiery letters burned into the wooden deck. I could see that the same thunderbolt had suddenly struck the Greek as he looked down at the prone bodies of our captain and shipmate.

We had been given a ship, gratis, by the actions of the gods.

Sanctuarium

The three men had been given to Poseidon, their shades even now settling into their new lives in his realm. The two crewmen that were left - Parm, the mute, and the one called Massoud - had continued their duties as if the voyage had been one of coasting along the patrolled waters of Latium. Both made some sign to the sky - and their gods, I assumed - as we tipped the bodies of their captain and mates over the side, but gave little other indication of distress.

The three passengers were standing at the stern with Korax holding the tiller bar. Once our relief and exclamations of our fiery escape from death and slavery were expressed, we began to wonder at our future. Again, I marveled - to myself - at the strangeness of my situation, my belief now firm that I was as a puppet on strings, as I had seen on occasions in the Agora of Athens. No other explanation would begin to give reason for my survival time and again. Any sage giving such a story on the street, would be ridiculed for concocting such ludicrous tales.

I had become the de facto captain, but I had far less than the knowledge to do so. Certainly, I was comfortable around sea-going vessels, both as passenger and crew and had gleaned much about the vocation since leaving Rome, but... I could not 'read' the waters, nor the airs as could a true man of the sea. The master of that ill-fated ship that had been taken by the pirates of Sifnos had been born to the water. I had seen him predict the coming and intensity of a storm from merely observing the haze on the water and the heaviness of the air. The equally unfortunate captain of this vessel, could point to a direction, and somehow arrive at his destination, despite seeing nothing for landmarks but a dim mass on the horizon that could have been a coastline anywhere around the Great Sea.

For myself, I could certainly steer a watercraft, and point it to this direction and that, and had even learned the use of the sail to best effect. But I had no... no feel for the waters over which we moved. Those weaknesses had to be taken into account for the plans that we would make.

And of course, Korax was a landman, pure and simple. He could hold a tiller bar as well as any seaman, but he knew little more of watercraft than Ravana.

The dark mass of land, still far away had come measurably closer, but as yet there was no sign of any city or port. Still, if we followed the coast, eventually we would come to... somewhere. Looking around, the sea was empty of other ships - our foe having disappeared under a column of smoke far behind us. Rowing into Hades was my hope of their fate, if not my belief. Still...

"We will follow the coast toward the sunset until we find this city of Pelusium. There we can vend our load and lighten the ship and decide on our futures, but in a taverna on dry land."

"Aye," replied Korax. "And a vessel of this size and quality would bring enough to purchase our own taverna in which to discuss such things."

Ravana was still wearing her boy-garb, as she had no other, but now she let her long yellow tresses loose to the wind. Of we three, she seemed to consider our plight to be an excitement or a beginning to some new life. "Might not you keep the ship, and let that be your new profession?"

I gave both my thoughts of my lack of fitness for such an occupation, and Korax agreed. "Aye, we are as stone carvers attempting to take the direction of a merchantry of cloth dyers."

She was not a woman for which the answer of a man in the negative was considered to be the end of the conversation. "But, could we not hire a captain, knowledgeable in the command of a ship?"

I was amused that 'you' had become 'we.' It was quite an assumption by a woman who was without a land to call her own, and who was dependent on the good graces of two men, and with no future should we tire of her.

Still, she had not hidden in the hold of the ship, cringing with terror as most of her sisters would have done, with slavers and slayers coming hard aboard. And, she had followed my orders to the last instruction, holding the burning torches ready for Korax to grab and throw. Had she lost her reason in panic, and we had had to find and fire the burning brands ourselves, it might given the raiders sufficient time to water the pitch enough to prevent the inferno. Her acts gave a her at least a modicum of privilege to speak her mind.

And, what she had just proposed had enough value to be considered, at least...

"Subahdar! Subahdar!" I looked forward to see Massoud pointing over the bow. I knew he was using the term for captain in his language - I had heard the word applied to the master of the ship many times. The rest of his call was nothing understandable to me, but I assumed that he was calling my attention to something off the bow. I walked forward to stand at the forepeak, following his pointing hand. In a few heartbeats, I called the discovery to Korax, on the tiller bar. "City ahead. Come away from the wind two handspans."

"Is that Pelusium?" Ravana had walked forward to look for herself.

I snorted at her assumption of my seafaring skills. "It could be Rome, for any knowledge that I have of our whereabouts." But, by mid-afternoon, we could see that it was a large port city, matching the description that the captain had given, during our casual talks on the deck. For now, my worry was not where we were, but that this ship had to be wharfed and with a steady wind flowing from the sea to the shore. I had seen it done many times, but I well knew that casual observing does not equate to experience.

So, not wishing to give a measure of my fitness for command by driving the ship ashore, shattering docks and wharfside kiosks in a massive spectacle of incompetence, I shouted for the sail to be lowered to the deck when we were still many stadia away from the wharfs. With this steady wind on just the hull, our entry would be fast enough.

Fortunately, there seemed to be few other ships in the port, then I remembered the words of Asius the scribe, back at the port of Geson. Apparently, the Egyptian-owned ships that had fled were still waiting afar for the resolution of the disturbances before returning.

Now, desperately trying to remember the actions of the previous captains on entering port and dockside, I waved to Parm and Massoud to stand by the forepeak with fending poles. Then, with the wooden pier only about thirty strides away, I ordered the two men to slow our forward movement by poling against the harbor bottom. I watched with relief as the ship slowly closed the distance, the wind pushing us along at a slow walk, passing the wharf on the dexter side, then suddenly slide to a stop as the forward keel hit the sloping sand of the shore.

I almost felt as I had escaped another battle, my legs weak and unsteady. And, despite the steady and refreshing breeze from the sea, my skin water was flowing as if I had just climbed aboard after falling from the deck into the sea. Now, well trained and versed in coming ashore, Parm had climbed to the dock and was tying the ropes that his mate was casting over the hull. That was a task that I had not even remembered to order.

But, as my mater had said, long ago, it is a good day that ends without the necessity to curse the gods.

I could see a man walking towards us, in company of another who was obviously a scribe, as he was burdened with a folding tablet holder. This had to be a port magistrate, come to collect a wharfing tax, or ask of our business. All cities on the sea had such, and I had seen the interaction with them on every docking. Only now, I would be the man to which the questions would be placed.

I climbed onto the dock and waited, holding up my hand in greeting as they approached. The principal also saluted, and gave a salutation in what had to be the language of our deceased Kapetanios. That was a given since I knew that this land was under the control of the Persians. However, that knowledge would stand me of little use here.

I shook my head and replied in Greek. "I regret to admit that I have no command of your language, Kurios." Then in my accented Egyptian, I added, "Or, I can speak with some facility in the tongue of the hot lands." And again, in Latium, "Or with the words of my people."

Of course, any official in charge of entry to his city by sea would speak several languages - that would be a requirement. His command of Greek was heavily accented, but understandable. "Ah... You are a citizen of Yaunas. What was your port of departing? Ahtena? Spartena?"

I had no idea of the reference to Yaunas, but I replied, "Athens," He turned to the scribe and dictated a few sentences which were scribed in the wax of the double tablet.

"And your cargo?"

"Cedrus logs and poles."

The man nodded. "Ah. Those will be welcomed by the temples and nobles of the hot lands." He looked back and forth along the ship, then said, "You have voyaged from Ahtena with yourself and three hands? And a boy? On a ship of this burden?" He shook his head. "You have much confidence in your skill, Subahdar."

"Nay, Kurios. I lost three men in an encounter with sea-raiders. I will need to replace them before voyaging further. One hopes that experienced crewmen can be obtained in your fair city."

"Aye. With the Egyptian merchants having fled the troubles, there is no lack of men in the hiring tavernas." He waved to the ship. "Now, to business. The port levy is five Siglos per night. Or a tetrabol, if you have Greek coinage."

A thought came to mind. This port official was unlike most in that he was not overbearing with his importance, and seemed to be of an amiable nature. I turned to face the ship and called to Korax, standing with Ravana, waiting for the result of the negotiations. "Bring four oboli for our harbor fee. And my purse," I added.

Then I turned back to the official. "I am a stranger to these waters, and would wish to enhance my knowledge of the lands.

Should you be amenable, and with the necessary time, I would engage your service in decreasing my ignorance. Or, perhaps, you could point out a man who would take silver for such a service, possibly in a taverna over good wine."

Even without an empty harbor giving little to fill his time, few men would deny the opportunity to silver themselves by conversation over cups. He nodded and turned to speak to his scribe, who immediately departed. I walked to the ship to accept the four coins from Korax, then said quietly, "I am engaging this man for some talk as to our future. Stay with the ship." Looking around, I pointed to the line of bazaars some distance away. "Get yourself and the men some hot food from yon cookeries." He nodded, and I turned back to the port official. "I bow to your selection of a place of conversation."

Shortly, we were in an empty taverna, but most unlike those of Rome or Athens. This one consisted of a tall pitched roof of canvas, held up by rafters made of huge reeds. The sides were open, although I could see more of the material rolled up and tied - apparently to be dropped to enclose the structure if wanted. Actually, the structure was an overly descriptive term for such an establishment - it was more of a permanent tent than a building. In fact, all of the edifices that I could see around the harbor were just as insubstantial. That was interesting, even if the reason unknown.

Inside, however, were the usual tables and stools, and we had our choice of any, as we were the only patrons at the moment. The caupo greeted us at the entrance, obviously glad to finally obtain patrons with coin. The port official spoke to the man, in Egyptian this time, ordering wine and two bowls. Turning to me, he said, "This is one of the few that serve the drink of the grape. Most men of these lands swill the spirits of grain." He made a face, then grinned. "It is an acquired taste, but I would rather have the drink of the north. My name is Jamshid, of Siraf. Might I know the name of my taverna companion?"

I smiled. "Aye. I am Junius, and not from Greece as you probably assume, but a citizen of Rome who has found his way to this part of the world through a series of mishaps that I would not expect you to believe."

"Rome? Indeed, you have traveled far, my friend." The bowls came, and both of us sipped the purple liquid. It was drinkable, if not equal to even the product of a harbor taverna of the north. "I have seen few ships from your land in my stay as port jobber. Few indeed."

I shrugged. "My reference is only to my birthplace. In fact, I call no land my home, and have resided in many for a while, before my wandering legs call me to another." Not exactly the truth, but it would suffice. "I would ask your advice on vending our cargo in Inbuhedj or another city on the Nilos. My deficiency is that I have no knowledge of your river."

He waved his hand in dismissal. "Nay, that is of no accord. Few sea captains will climb the waters of the Iteru on their own - unless, they are of those cities, themselves. A river pilot can be hired for a gold Daric for the trip, and there is no shortage of them with the depression of sea trade. If you wish it, I can summon several for your perusal." I assumed that Iteru was the local name for the river.

"I would be most appreciative, Kurios." The honorific was Greek, but I had no idea of its equivalent in his language, and did not wish to take the chance of offending by mangling an expression.

He waved to the caupo and spoke a few words, then turned back to me as I asked about the... revolution?

"It is nothing to be concerned with. Every few years, some demagogue springs out of the ground, usually claiming inheiritancy from some ancient king of the Haramed. He stirs the weak minded to burn a few magisterial offices in hopes of fomenting rebellion, then usually finds himself hanging head downwards from the walls with his followers." He waved to the caupo for replenishment, then continued, "I can give you a tablet, certifying you as an independent trader come from afar, to show to the harbor master of Inbuhedj, or whichever city you stop at."

"My thanks, Kurios. Inbuhedj will be a sufficient destination, or Memphis, whichever name is the correct usage. It is not my intention to cruise the Nilos for the mere edification of my knowledge, although I would not look amiss in seeing the Pyramidios that I have heard spoken of all over the world."

"Aye, they are as a sight for the eyes." He grinned, and said, "Like all men, I give no credence that any other land may produce greater than his own, but in truth, I have to admit that it staggers the mind to see what mortal man has built in this land."

I raised my eyebrows. "Hmmm. I have assumed that the tales have grown with distance, and with every mouth. Are they as great as I have heard?"

He chuckled. "I cannot give you any description that you may believe without seeing. If I say that some of the pointed structures would pierce the clouds of my - and your - land, you would consider me a taverna boaster. But, I say that even such description is inadequate for the tale, as is the story that they can be seen even when one is a fast day's march away, gleaming with blinding whiteness on the far horizon."

We spoke for a while, then he looked up as a man entered and moved toward our table. At a wave, the newcomer stopped before us and saluted. "Salam, Kotwal." He was tall and of indefinite age and not an Egyptian - his skin was as pale as mine, although burned from the sun where it could strike.

Jamshid turned to me, gesturing a hand at the newcomer. "This be Ehsan, of some begotten tribe of Gandara. He is not to be trusted with your wife, or oxen, or even your wine jug, but he knows the course of the Iteru as few others, even those of this land. And, he speaks Greek - or so he thinks." His grin robbed the statements of any offense. To the man, he said, "This be Junius, a Roman, who wishes to take his ship to a city in the hot lands."

I stood for a moment, and waved at the bench. "Please sit yourself, Kurios, and have a cup."

Grinning himself, he flopped to the bench on the opposite side of the table and took the bowl that the caupo had brought, even without waiting for the order. "And you, Jamshid? Have you mulched sufficient silver from this hapless voyager, and must needs send him away to clear the docks for another?" His Greek was fractured and not as clean as I have scripted it, but understandable for that. But now I had no doubt that this was a meeting of friends, or at least friendly acquaintances.

"Nay," I said before the magistrate could answer. "Your friend has been most helpful to a stranger."

Over the bowl, the river pilot asked, "And you wish to journey to Memphis? Or Karnac?"

I nodded but Jamshid spoke. "Nay. Karnac is over a hundred parasangs upriver from Memphis." Looking at me, he said, "A journey for river skiffs, not a sea-hull as you have." He pointed in the general direction of the wharfs. "That is his ship, newly come this day."

The man nodded. "Ah." Another gulp, then "If you wish a pilot, I am your man. The feeof is a Daric to the city and one to return." I knew that was a small gold coin, about equivalent to a pair of Dekadrachems - the largest silver coins that were struck in Greece. Thanks to the bag of coin that Ravana had stolen from her master, the fee - though large - was trivial to us.

A thought sprang to mind. "I am short of three men of my normal crew."

He nodded. "I can engage some reliable men if you wish. Their feeof will be a Siglos to the day - each."

Jamshid spoke. "I saw Armshid at the hiring board." To me he said, "A good man on the river."

"What will be the time?" I asked.

"That, my new friend, is entirely dependent on the winds. This is the low season for the waters, and the flow is mild, but still..." He paused to drink.

Jamshid spoke again. "I have known ships to make the distance in five days with a good wind though that is unusual. But, I was once on a merchant that spent the time between one half moon and the next, as we sat becalmed in the stream."

I was in no hurry to arrive - anywhere - so the time of our voyage had no significance, and I said so.

He continued. "Aye. But, the flood time of the river will start in half a season, and during the times of the inundation, nothing will move toward the south."

More talk, and finally, we rose. I pressed a large Stater into the hand of the magistrate, with my effusive thanks for his help, then walked back to the ship.

Nilos

I had expected to follow the coastline for many days before coming to the mouth of the river, but only a few hours after we had cast away from the port, a large tributary appeared and the river pilot gave the order to the tillerman to turn into the gently flowing water. The land immediately changed from the bare and treeless coastline that we had seen for months, to a green and lush plain. There was nothing that one would call a tree, but tall plants and flowering bushes were in abundance.

On occasion, we would pass single huts, or clusters of such, making a village of sorts, and surrounding them would be fields of... of something. That they were crops was a given, as both men and women were engaged in the tending of the fields in great numbers.

I would usually sit at the forepeak with the pilot, by the name of Ehsan, I had learned, and we spoke of his land and mine to pass the time. And Ravana would sometimes join us, after her cooking duties were done, sitting silently and watching the green banks of the river slowly slide by.

On occasion, the pilot would call back a new position for the tiller bar as he noticed a ripple in the water, here, or there, indicating a bank of mud on which we might drag our keel. A few times, even with his watchfulness, all aboard could feel the sudden shifting of our weight, indicating that we had indeed come to a stop with our hull embedded in the soft river bottom. At that time, the men, two on a side, would take their long poles, and on command, begin to walk forward with effort, pushing the ship back and away from the obstruction.

In addition to the pilot, we had added two men for the course. Both were Egyptian, small and thin, and even more smooth of skin than myself - these even to somehow removing the hair from their scalps. But, their size had no measure of their worth at work - both could do their tasks as well as I and with even less tiredness, it appeared.

And to my amusement, they once again proved the universality of the game of bones. Even on the first day, did the two new men kneel beside Korax and the crew for the enjoyment of the contest, with only the man on the tiller bar not joining in the chanting and jesting of the game.

The winds were good, but our progress was at a creeping pace, with both the heaviness of our hull and the slow current of the water adding together to limit our daily gain to no more than two leagues.

And, at each nightfall, we would drop our huge anchor-stone over the forepeak and lay up for the night. Even with the moon, the river could not be read by Ehsan, the ripples of the frequent mud banks invisible in the dark.

By my estimate, the good part of a half month would be required before we arrived at our destination. On occasion the wind would drop away completely, and once it blew hard from the wrong direction. At these times, we would just drop our anchor-stone and wait for the return of the proper airs. But, to even out the days, more than once the wind would blow with some fierceness, adding to our day's count of stadia.

As yet, Ravana was still garbed in rags that would have shamed a port beggar, but I would alleviate that situation when we hove into our destination. Her lower extremities were covered with only a wrapped scrap of sailcloth, held in place with a piece of rope while her shoulders and luscious mammaries were covered with a makeshift shawl that appeared to be the upper piece of a tunic. She kept her hair in woven braids and tied under a headpiece that Korax jestingly called a turban, whatever that might be. But, now, since entering the stream of the river, and having plentiful access to water that was devoid of salt, she would wash her tresses in the early morning before making the meal.

This day, she appeared on deck, enjoying the freshening wind that greatly enhanced the moment of our voyage. And, in the interests of allowing the breeze to quickly dry her wet locks, she had allowed her hair to blow in the wind. Suddenly, I heard a babbling from afterward, and turned to see the two Egyptians on their knees, with their heads pressed to the deck wood and between their outstretched arms. Utterly mystified at their behavior, I just stared for a moment, trying to understand their rushed words. But, as their diction was that of the lower classes, and my understanding of the language was far from perfect, I could make little of their exclamations, except for a word, repeated over and over - Hator, or Hador.

Turning, I saw Ehsan approach, he obviously as bewildered as myself. As to Ravana, she just stood, frozen in shock at seeing men bow to her presence. The pilot listened intently for a moment, then looked at me in amusement. "They think she is Hathor, the goddess of the sun, and daughter of Ra." Then, quietly, he said, "She should keep those golden tresses covered while we are in the land of Egypt. These people take their gods and goddesses with great fervor, and should the priests of the land see her..." I just stared at him, still in wonderment at the events of the last few moments. "Who knows the result. She might be killed out of hand as an interloper, or... even made divine. One can never predict actions of the priests of this land."

Or any other, I thought. But to Ravana, I said, "Go below and don your headdress."

Once she had disappeared from view, the two Egyptians rose, but still looked in awe at the hatch in which she had climbed into the hold. And from then on, when she was on deck, even with every strand of her hair under the cover, they would bow to her as she passed, then speak to each other in hushed tones.

The strangeness of the world increased in direct proportion to my distance from my city, was my last thought as I turned back to my scan of the sea. But, that night I warned her never to show her hair until we were well away from this land.

Several days passed and the sameness of the river banks and the greenery beyond was now something only to be glanced at on occasion. I continued my study of the scroll that I had purchased, and again, many times with Ravana looking over my shoulder, and asking this and that of the pictures as we read. Then, suddenly, I heard her intake of breath, and a small squeal. Turning, I saw her pointing toward the shore, a few handfuls of stride away.

Then I saw what had garnered her attention. It was a... a monster, longer than a man and laying on the sand in the rising sun. The long row of teeth that protruded from the even longer snout of its mouth gave notice that one should not sport or bathe in this water. Long-tailed and bronze in color it was, with streaks of green down the sides. The aspect of the creature was one that came with dreams after an evening of over-seasoned food.

As I looked around to the pilot, he chuckled, and said, "A river dragon. The Iteru is infested with them, and they are as dangerous as they look. Every year, hundreds of people on the riverbank are snapped up in their jaws and dragged to death under the water."

"It seems to be badly equipped for such attacks, with such short legs on a massive body."

"Nay. Do not cozen yourself." Now his expression was serious. "When in movement, they can outpace the fastest skiff, and while clumsy on land, their strike from the water to the shore is between one blink of the eyes and the next." He shook his head. "During your stay in the hot lands, I would recommend that you stay clear of the waters of this river, unless on the deck of a ship with tall sides, as this one. On occasion, they will even lunge into the skiff of a fisherman, dumping all in the boat to the water to be taken to their lair at convenience."

Ravana just shuddered, and sat down closer to me, as we watched the animal slowly disappear in the distance, behind us. It took a while before our minds could become clear of the horror, and begin to parse the picture writing again.

But there was more to see. Birds in excess, and of all colors. One turning of the course brought us into a small lagoon that was filled with huge water fowl, covering the surface from bank to bank. Our progress caused them to squawk and move far aside to let us slowly pass, but other than that they seemed to consider the gigantic winged bird of our ship to be only a distraction.

"Why do not the dragons feast on fowl, here?" I turned to see Korax standing and looking at the innumerable birds sitting on the waters. "It would seem an easy banquet for an animal that strikes from below." Then, and with a spit of mouth water over the side, he cursed, "By the verminous crotch of Zeus's woman, they are an evil sight."

I just shrugged, committing the sight to my memory, but not attempting to understand it.

It was obvious that this part of the world was vastly richer in life than the lands of Latium or even Greece. There, few animals were seen in the course of the day, other than asses and oxen, and of course, the ever-present city birds. But here, every day brought a new spectacle.

In another and wider stretch of the river, we saw huge beasts in the water, with round bodies and fat heads and looking to myself like hornless oxen that had been bloated in death.

"River cows," gave the pilot. "Sacred to the temples of the hot lands. Only the parties of the priests are allowed to hunt such." He pointed to a huge bull, standing half out of the water near the bank. "They are a danger to small craft, especially in the mating season. And I hear that their flesh is delicious, although I cannot say that from actual taste."

We continued to pass groups of the river dragons, almost all laying on the sands in passive rest. For a beast that was given such attributes of danger for river travelers, they seemed to be as inactive as lizards, laying on the rocks in the sun. I said as much to the pilot.

"Nay," replied Ehsan. "You are seeing them at their usual activity, and that is just waiting. But, should you fall from the side of this ship, they will enter the water with haste and you will be torn to a meal between them before you shake the water from your eyes." He pointed forward up the course we were taking. "Once we enter the waters of the river, you will see fewer of them. They like the sluggish currents of the Delta."

Now I was confused. "I thought that this was the Nilos."

"Aye. And you are right, in a way. Did I not see a wax tablet in your possessions, below?" I nodded. "If your woman would retrieve it, I can explain my meaning."

After Ravana had obtained my fold box, I smoothed the long unused surfaces with the scraper and handed it to the pilot. He set on the deck and began to make lines in the soft material. Drawing a long wavy line, he pointed and said, "The river begins somewhere at the end of the world, here and far away to the south, and flows into the Great Sea in the Delta, here." At the horizontal line that represented the coastline, he grew a large three sided figure that is the forth character of the Greek language. In his drawing, the figure had a flat side to the sea, and the apex pointed to the river proper. Now, suddenly, I realized the significance of the name, Delta. I had long heard of the area that was somewhere in Egypt and now knew why it was named so.

Inside of this figure, he drew several lines that began at the apex of the delta and fanned out to reach the line representing the coastline. "Just below Memphis, at the beginning of the Delta, the river splits into multiple streams, all much smaller and with slower currents. The one we are in now, the most eastern flow, is called the Pelusiac, but do not ask me the meaning of the name. There are about seven in all, but this is the one that I have used mostly."

"What is the extent of your venturings on the Nilos?" I asked. "Or the Iteru, as you call it."

He pointed the stick at the wavy line in wax that represented the river. "To here, the city of Karnac, many times, and, long ago as a youth on a skiff, to the city of Kom Ombo, about... here." Another mark. "Further, a boat of any size cannot go. This is the first of the cataracts, and makes an effective barrier on the river."

Korax, sitting and listening, gave the question before I could speak. "Cataracts? What might they be?"

Ehsan stabbed several more marks in the wax. "Sections of the river where the waters flow down a cascade of rocks. There are many such barriers in the river as one continues to follow it south, although that number comes from men whose eyes never beheld the actual sights. In fact, no living man knows the extent of the river nor the beginnings of the waters. Or even the reason for its rapid rise and flooding every season."

The sameness of the stream was such that Korax went back to his bones, and Ravana and I to our scroll, learning the picture writing. Even the frequent masses of the river dragons now only received a glance on occasion. About halfway up the river channel, we came to a small village, and Ehsan steered us to dock as close to the shore as the ship would close. That evening, for a few small coins from my purse, we were treated to a feast by the villagers, with heaping platters of bread and cheese, and fish baked over hot coals. Even the grain spirit was available in clay pots, but, while the Egyptians of the crew took great pleasure from it, neither Korax nor I could abide the taste of this beverage, much preferring the wine in the amphora aboard the ship. Ravana almost heaved the contents of her belly onto the ground after an incautious taste of the local drink.

Morning time brought another feast to break our fast, then we were making our course up the stream again.

In seventeen days, by my count, we began to see the lands turn from lush foliage, to short grasses and low shrubs. Suddenly, we came to a joining of the stream with another, and our course now sailed up a much wider body of water that I assume to be the actual Nilos. It was an assumption made in ignorance.

Again and again, we met a fork where the waters decided, to flow their separate ways across the Delta, and the new flow of water from the south widened each time. Finally, the stream met another, of equal size and we hove into the actual waters of the Nilos.

My sense of astonishment had been quickly overwhelmed as we reached the apex of the Delta and joined the actual river. I realized that the term had more meanings than I had assumed. I had always considered myself a river-man. Born on the banks of the Tiber, and spending my early life to almost full growth in its waters, it was not only a river, but the River. Now, I realized that the stream of my early life was as a runnel in the streets of Rome after a moderate rain, compared to the awesome grandeur of the Nilos.

Standing at the forepeak of our ship, as we slowly moved up the approximate center of the water, the two shores were as the coast of the sea, seen afar from the deck of a merchant on the sea itself. My estimation was that the waters were no less than ten stadia across and probably much more. What could be the source of such a deluge? It would seem that an equal sized opening would drain even the Great Sea itself.

Ehsan was slanting our course toward the western bank, as the city of Memphis was situated on that side of the water, although still, at least, two days further upriver, unless the wind strengthened. As I stood, still contemplating the magnitude of the waters over which we were sailing, he stopped beside me, pointing ahead in the distance. "There, just a finger's span off the water..."

I looked, seeing nothing but flat lands - this not of lushness and greenery through which we had passed for the half month, but the yellow of desert and sand, except for the narrow band along the banks. I was about to shrug and query his pointing, then saw the small pointed bump on the horizon. Looking at the pilot, I asked, "A Pyramidios?"

He nodded. "Aye. That is the Greek term. My people call them the Haramed. To the Egyptians they are the Per-Netera. What you see is the tallest one, but we will see many more as we pass the city of Giza."

"And they are tombs?"

"Aye. So I am told. But I have not yet looked in any of them for the proof of that." I looked at him, questioning, and he laughed. "I jest, of course. The Persian King rules this land, but even he knows that any violation of the ancient places would cause such an uprising as would cost much gold to put down. And for an individual to approach the grounds would result in the priests hanging him by his heels from the walls of the city as food for the crows." He gazed at the point on the horizon before continuing. "And men have done so, attempting to find the vast stores of gold and treasure that each contains. Or, so it is said, but not by the men themselves, unless they told the crows of their finds."

Hmmm. An interesting thought, to protect your wealth by burying it under a large pile of stone. But... Even the largest structure, if built by man, can be destroyed by man, should the rewards be enough. Or so I thought.

Now, according to the pilot, we could continue our voyage at night, the worries of mud and shallow waters no longer an issue. At the rise of the sun, we were much closer to the western shore, and many stadia further along in our course. Far enough to see the array of stone ahead, gleaming whitely in the morning sun. I could see three of the Pyramidios, standing high above the horizon, and apparently several more of a much smaller size scattered across the landscape. Indeed, they were very large - it must have taken a myriad of men a lifetime to stack the blocks to that shape. They were impressive, to be sure, but still not the massive Olympian structures that I had heard of in the tales.

Or so I thought. Again.

The day passed, then the night began to fall, and we had still not reached the point of the river where the Pyramidios would be off our beam. It was as if the current were keeping our forward progress to nothing. But, even though the faster current of the wide river was holding us to a slower pace than in the meandering stream in the Delta, I could see huts, and jutting rocks, and such like objects on the shore slowly moving past and behind us. That we were moving up the river was not to be questioned, but...

Morning again, and I myself had stood a watch on the tiller pole. Since leaving the Delta, the heat of the day had increased greatly, with the men always finding their place of rest in the shade of the sail. But the nights were cool in comparison, and the breeze from behind us and over the water was most refreshing. Under the half moon, the navigation was easy, the bright sand of the shoreline easily seen as a white band with no detail.

Now the great stone structures were on our quarter, not ahead but still not abeam, and larger than before, of course. As the sun struck them, they became as gleaming white arrowheads pointing to the sky, the brightness coming from the outer layer of white calx, or what the Athenians called limestone. During the day, I idled beside Ravana and Korax as we watched the group of structures come ever closer. Then...

A strange object without reference to something of known size will be interpreted by the eyes according to the experience of the beholder. And so it was with myself. I could see that the Pyramidios were huge indeed, and each day grew greater in my mind than the last. Each was surrounded with small rocks in a fairly flat field, the greater area obviously being the sacred burial ground. There were no people near them, of course, since I assumed that none but priests were allowed anywhere near the area and those would be in the temples, and not wandering around the sands. But then... I saw movement at the base of the greater stone structure - a small animal or other creature of... of...

At that instant of time, the scales fell from my eyes in a frozen moment of utter stupefaction. The animal was a man - a tiny creature walking between what I suddenly realized was, not rocks, but ordinary sized buildings - huts or houses, or storerooms, maybe. But both the man and the structures were as grains of sand next to a boulder. The actual size of the Pyramidios suddenly sprang forth in unbelievable majesty.

I shook my head, still trying to believe the vision that my eyes were giving me. It was impossible, I thought. None but the gods could construct something of such magnitude, and even they would hesitate at beginning such a task. Soon, we had come level with the array of stone tombs, three of immense size and others much smaller but even those would dwarf any building in Athens or Rome. I knew that I could not speak of the actuality of my vision if I returned to my land, other than the mere fact of having seen them. Like story tellers before me, any listeners would immediately assume that I was gilding the tale and reduce the images in their own minds to proper size for belief.

On the next morning, we were standing off the docks of Memphis, waiting for the early light to brighten enough to select a wharf into which to tie up. Even here, the gigantic white arrowheads were visible, although now behind us, but it was time to focus my attention on the present, rather than structures from the ancient past. I let the pilot guide the ship to the place, trusting his ability to dock far more than my own, but I certainly watched every move, so as to at least know the proper methods in the future.

In Memphis, the docks were pointed into the river, rather than along the shore, as is the case almost everywhere else. This allowed for craft to approach the bank, on the upriver side of the wharf, then for the gentle current to fetch the vessel to its place, held there without need of ropes and tethers. And again, like any port in the world, we were met by the magistrate with his hand open to accept the berthing fee.

Ehsan spoke to the man, giving him the tablet that was supplied by the port master in Pelusium. It was made plain that our vessel was from afar, and not connected to any local merchants, nor any troubles that might be brewing in the land. All was in order, and on payment of a coin and information on our cargo, we were left to ourselves to gaze on a new city.

The overwhelming color of this land was yellow. As far as the eye could see, the land was flat and without green growth of any kind, save for a strip along the banks of the Nilos. The brightness of the rising sun brought a glare that caused the eyes to squint into thin creases, and already the heat was becoming uncomfortable for any standing in the sun - at least, for people from more northern climes.

The dock area was very large, and the wharfs had a myriad of vessels beside them or drawn up onto the bank. The crowds were thick and uncountable. This apparently was the Egyptian Forum - or Agora - and was filled with merchants and citizens vending everything imaginable.

I was at a loss as to our next move, not having any knowledge whatsoever of the method of selling trees. My past experiences were with more common cargo, such as grain or wine. I put off the problem for a while, by calling together the crew and handing them their fees for the voyage, and a small copper as good measure. Since I could speak to the two Egyptians in my broken dialect, I gave to them that they were welcome to sign on again when we voyaged back downriver. My assumption was that both Parm and Massoud would stay on as crew, rather than leave my employ in a far away land.

That accomplished, I was just about to ask Ehsan for advice when a carrying chair approached and stopped at the end of our wharf. The porters set it down and a man - obviously a merchant - stepped out and bowed and began his spiel. Unfortunately, it was not in any form that I could understand, and I knew that even though this was Egypt, the man was Persian.

The pilot came to my rescue and spoke in his strange Greek, "Ochi, Ser. The good Kaptetanios hails from Rome, but he can speak with you in this tongue."

The man bowed again and nodded vigorously. "Ah... My apologies, Kurios. One gets so few vessels from that land this far up the river. The Quadi..." He pointed to the dock magistrate, now speaking to some boat master on the bank. "...gives the information that you carry the wood of... labini..."

"Cedrus," interjected Ehsan.

"Ah, cedrus." He bowed again, apparently believing that the gesture was a necessary function of trade. "I could possibly make an offer for such if I might inspect the goodness of the merchandise..."

I bowed to him in return. "Aye, Kurios. You may inspect any and all in our hold, to any extent that you desire." Turning, I shouted to Korax. "Open the hatches for inspection by the good merchant." I held out my arm, hand open in invitation for him to board the vessel, but just then another carrying chair arrived, this time at a lope and with breathless porters.

And another.

The garments of men - and women - that we could see across the vast port were unlike those of the in the cities around the Great Sea. The reason had become very obvious as soon as we had left the stream of the Delta and entered the great sandy lands of Egypt. My woolen tunic, thin as it was, had become as an oven during the daylight hours and I had removed it for a still-too-thick loincloth, as had Korax. Of course, the crewmen had always worn nothing but the waist covering and had nothing else. Ravana had doffed her motley collection of habiliments for a short skirt and a shawl, torn from a rag of sailcloth patch.

The men wore only a skirt - called a kilt, I discovered later - usually reaching to the knees, as their only garb. That is, those that were covered at all. Many were as bare as the day they were birthed.

But, for those that were clothed, the only difference was in the quality - the workers along the docks with their dull and dirty plain coverings, and the magistrates and wealthy with pleated kilts of spotless and blinding white linen.

The women usually wore a long tube of linen, called a kalasiris, falling from the breasts to below the knees - sometimes to the ankles. It was held up by two wide straps over the shoulders. As with the men, only the quality was the indication of rank among them, although with both sexes an arm or wrist band of gold or precious stones could give notice of a wealthy person.

The merchants that descended on our vessel were obviously wealthy, with the pleated kilts and arm jewelry - one even had a golden chain around his neck. In a moment of time, all were jabbering their desire to inspect our load of tree-stuff. Bemused, I just waved them aboard and waited for their scrutiny of the cargo. I had paid the pilot, Ehsan, his fee for our upriver voyage, but now whispered to him a desire to remain with me as an advisor until the merchants had... done their merchant work.

Koran and Ravana just stood by me, also amazed at the spectacle of the rotund men attempting to climb up and down ladders to inspect the inside of a ship. My current problem was that I had no idea of the worth of our cargo - that being the one important item of discussion that I had not had with the previous captain. I could easily be gulled by sharp merchants in my ignorance.

The first merchant hurried up to me, after an inspection that could have been little more than just smelling the aromatic wood. "Kurios... Kapetanios. I will offer twenty deben of gold for your cargo." In his atrocious Greek, and haste I could barely understand his words, but the meaning was apparent.

I turned to Ehsan to comment but noticed his sudden startlement at a sight approaching our dock. He made a curse in his milk language, under his breath, then said, in a low voice, "Look at yon chair." It was a huge carrying chair, with ten slaves on each end and an enclosed platform covered with folds of cloth, preventing any view of the occupant. The structure and posts shone in the sun with the tone of gold, but it had to be gilding, I knew. Made of gold, a chair of that size could not have been lifted by a double hundred men.

I said back to him. "A man of wealth, for sure."

He shook his head. "It is a priest of Amun. Come for whatever reason, but I have long learned that they are best avoided when possible."

I shrugged. The ornate chair was obviously coming to our ship, but unless we suddenly poled the vessel into the river in escape, tossing the merchants overboard, there was no avoiding the meeting. Or confrontation.

Turning, Ehsan said quickly, "Follow my actions. We will bow to the knee when he approaches, but do not speak until he asks."

The three merchants had noticed the approaching ornate carrying chair, and had hurried to climb down to the dock, but the captains of their groups of porters made even more haste to move aside as far as room could be found. It was obvious that none wished to have contact with... with, whatever person was being carried.

The chair stopped, then at a barked command, set to its resting posts. A well-dressed steward pulled the cloth aside, and a man stepped out. Interestingly, he did not fit my idea of a priest - at least, not those that I had been familiar with in the Temple of Jupiter. Those were rotund, short of breath, and unlikely to walk further than the dining hall on a given day.

This man, like most Egyptians, was thin and dark of skin, but gave the appearance of a man well in control of his body. He was well fed, no doubt, but his sinews were apparent under the skin, and his belly ridged with the bands of strength that indicated more than a life of leisure. He wore a kilt, but of pure whiteness and with folded pleats, and with a huge neckless of gold links and chains, and two wide bands, of the same metal, on her upper arm. And like most Egyptian men, his head and face were shaved, or plucked, smooth of hair.

The steward - my name for the man, rather than any knowledge of his actual title - stepped forward and thumped his staff on the boards of the dock, beginning a long proclamation. My knowledge of the tongue of this land was still far less than perfect, but I could follow most of his words. "All in presence will bow before Senemut, Second Priest of Great of Amun, Lord of Truth, Father of the Gods, Maker of Men, Creator of all Animals, Lord of things that are, Builder..."

I gave up and just waited for the ending to the spiel. To myself, I admitted that the pompous windbags of the Roman Temples would meet their match in this land, and more. We had bowed to our knees, waiting for the end of the proclamation, and out of the corner of my eyes, I could see that all in my vision had also taken the submissive posture.

Finally, some gesture was given that I missed, but Ehsan rose, and I followed. The steward stepped up to me and asked, "You are the

Captain of this vessel?" I acknowledged the fact. "And your cargo is of the wood of brevifolia?"

The word sounded Greek, but I had no reference to it, whatsoever, but Ehsan spoke in my place. "Aye, the cedrus-wood from the shores of Byblos."

"I would see it." I bowed slightly, and extended my hand toward the ship. The priest just stood, looking at me, the vessel, and nothing. Following the steward, I waited until he had descended into the hold through the large after hatch, and then climbed down to stand beside him. Little could be seen but the ends of logs, but apparently he was satisfied. The sweet aroma could not be falsely produced and he could both see and smell that this cargo was as represented. After bending to look down the smaller forward hatch, he nodded and walked back to climb back down to the dock.

There was a conversation with the Priest, but in a language that had no meaning to myself. Then, a wave and a nod, and the steward turned to me. "Amun offers the sum of fifty deben in gold for the entire tender."

Perplexed, I had no measure of what was being offered, however it was more than twice the first tender from the merchant. Still, I knew it was unwise to thwart a powerful figure in a strange land. For all I knew, the Priest could just seize the cargo and have myself hung out for crows. But, beside me, Eshan apparently sensed my quandary and said in a low voice, "A deben is equivalent to about fifteen gold Staters."

I gulped, stunned. That was a Olympian value for... for mere sweet smelling logs. What could the Egyptians wish with such... such... I realized that I was meditating in front of a Priest of the senior god of the land, and then vigorously nodded, "Aye, Kurios... Quadi. I give thanks for your generosity, and agree to the vending with gladness."

The Priest just looked at me and with a slight smile, although that might have been my imagination, then turned and entered his chair which immediately turned and started off across the flat of the Forum, or whatever this huge trading area was called in this land.

Ehsan turned to me and said, "A handsome profit, my friend."

"Aye," I returned absently, still watching the ornate chair as it moved away. Then I asked, "By the swollen pouchstones of Jupiter, what do they do with such wood, and why is it so sought after?"

He made a wry face, then waved his arm around in a sweep to take in the entire horizon. "Look around. See you trees of any size - anywhere? This is a land totally devoid of wood of any use." He pointed. "Those palms that grow near the waters look useful, but they are little more than overgrown reeds. Even the wood for the fisher-boats comes from afar."

"But..."

"Cedrus wood is prized for its immunity to vermin - no insect will call it home - and in this land it is all but immortal, without any tendency to rot or decay. But, mostly, it is considered sacred to the gods and is used in Temples as structure wood. And in the houses of the wealthy. Yon saddened merchants would have sold each log dearly, measuring each board with gold."

We had not long to wait. Within the hour, the steward was back, and with a huge force of slaves for the hauling. I put my crew to work, knocking out the pegs that held the deck boards to the frame of the ship. In a short while, the cargo was exposed to daylight, and the unloading began in a process that was the reverse of that of months ago, when we had taken on the load. A double handful of slaves would heave each log to their shoulders, then pass it to an equal number standing on the narrow boards of the deck that had not been removed, next to the hull side. These would, in turn, pass the log to the carriers on the dock, then with an order, those would move off across the Egyptian forum to... to their unknown destination.

By midday, the hull was empty and floating high above the dock - so high, in fact, as to require a ladder to climb to the deck, now. As the last log disappeared in the crowds, the steward came to me, bowed, and handed me a square of papyrus. "This is the accounting for our vending. You may present it at the Temple for remuneration when you wish. But, if I may give bit of advice..." He tilted his head, as I immediately nodded. "The gold will be safer - far safer - in the Temple coffers than on your ship, or your person. I suggest that you tarry until your departure before you withdraw your gold - the streets are not friendly to one carrying wealth and without guards."

"Aye, and I thank you for your warnings." Which was excellent, without doubt. There was no lack of thieves, cutthroats and the like in any city in the world. As long as...

He read my thought. "And you will have no issue with your withdrawal of funds. The Temple of Amun has existed since the dawn ages, and before the Pyramidios were raised, and has never failed a citizen that trusted it with their cause. Farewell."

Now, like a waterclock that had run dry, I was standing without any use or need, wondered what our next move would be. Obviously, we would need to purchase cargo for our return trip, but that would take... probably days, at least, and I was in no hurry. This was a new land, come to by strange occurrence, and I wished to see some of it.

Turning to Ehsan, I said, "I would assume that inns exist in this land, that will give us food and shelter for the night. I would that you accompany us until we gain our comfort in this strange city."

He nodded. "Aye. I usually reside in a dormitory the river road." He grinned. "However, were I a fat merchant such as you, and desiring luxury, I would present myself at one of the inns along the Street of Ptah."

I had already determined that Parm and Massoud, while they would undoubtedly visit the brothels and tabernae of the city, would sleep onboard, saving their coin for more physical needs. I had paid off the two Egyptian crewmen, giving them an extra small silver coin for their hard work.

The city was very large, more even than Rome or Athens. The reason, I discovered later, was that the land of Egypt is a huge desert with a single river, and life can only exist in the narrow bands on either side of the water. Thus, the limited area gives forth cities are that are few in number, but large in size.

To a Roman - or a Greek or any man from the north - used to the more varied tones of their lands, this city was bland - totally colored in shades of yellow and brown. Bricks, sand and dirt in the streets, buildings and thatched roofs were all the same colors. Here and there might be a monument, or statue, made of the white calx stone, but the rest of the city, entire, was of mud brick.

But, for all that, it was a magnificent city in its own right.

Ken Farmer

The Egyptian

Asylum

Inbuhedj, as the natives called it, or Memphis, to the world, was large - very large - and almost symmetrical. Unlike Rome, built on and around a multitude of low hills, and Athens, constrained by the mountain of rock at its edge, this city had no need to conform to any natural features, except the river. The land was flat and the city builders, hundreds or thousands of years in the past, laid out a very balanced plan for their work.

Two main avenues, running east and west, the other north and south, were called, respectively, the Avenue of the Gods and the Street of the Heavens. They met in the city center, or would have, had not the vast palace complex been placed there. They were wide - over twenty long strides from side to side, paved with stone, and decorated with statuary and stonework at intervals along the center of the pavement.

At the center of the city was the palace compound, square and, at least, two stadia in either direction. Around the walls of the compound was another thoroughfare that encircled the palace and joined the two avenues. Thusly, standing at any of the four gates, one could look far down that street and see the palace. It was impossible to be lost in Memphis for any length of time, as one only needed to walk to one of the major avenues to know his position.

Of course, a myriad of other thoroughfares ran through the city in a more or less regular pattern, but in the main, the design of the city was thus...

Close to the palace, the streets were wide and paved. Near the main temples, the stones were of white calx, somewhat blinding in the high suntimes of the day. It was in this area that the houses of the nobles were also to be found. Further away, the streets became of mud-brick and narrower and followed past the domiciles of the merchants of wealth and property. Beyond those were the houses of the ordinary tradesmen, still with mud-brick streets but of a poorer quality. Finally, and up to the edges of the inside walls, were the shanties and huts of the common people. They fronted passageways that were both narrow and unpaved.

This description, however, covers only a part of the citizenry, and only those with means of living. Outside the walls, except for the direction to the west and into the desert, were the hovels and shelters of the poor. Excepting for the huge area between the port and the eastern gate of the city that served as the forum and trading venue for the people, the winding alleys and narrow lanes were fronted by shelters of all sizes and kinds, adjoined to one another without spacing. They were no different, except in the insubstantial construction of the buildings, than the areas of the poor in any other city of the world. Crude bricks, made by hand and drying in the sun, were the walls of some, but far more were huts of reeds, woven into walls and roofs. Later, I was told and observed myself, that fire would frequently clear a large area, leaving only the brick walls as indication of what had once been shelters.

Thus did the city appear as we crossed the forum and entered the enormous eastern gate and began to walk up the broad thoroughfare of the Avenue of the Gods. Ehsan accompanied us as our guide to at least allow us to find an inn for the night. Immediately, in the distance, we could see the palace, and as we walked, it was like climbing the strata of society. At first, the houses were just shanties, then we were passing the tidy homes of the workers, then the opulent compounds and residences of the wealthy merchant, and finally the magnificent domiciles of the nobility.

I do not wish to give the impression that the walls contained only housing and the palace. Far from it. As we walked, we passed innumerable temples and shrines, to this god or that and some were of a size to shame the Temple of Jupiter in Rome. One such, we passed on our walk.

Thus far, I knew little of the gods of Egypt, other than an indication that the equivalent of Jupiter in this land was called Amun. Apparently, this temple belonged to that powerful being of the pantheon of this hot land - and that deity was a god that was hugely wealthy. Even the streets around the square were of white stone, cut to fit and with the picture scripting of Egypt here and there in the stones. The lack of dirt and sand gave that the street around the temple was swept daily to maintain cleanliness.

Across from a side entrance of the temple - and on a minor street, but still wide and smooth - was the Inn of the Crocodile - a word that had no meaning for me as yet but I recognized the picture as one of the evil river monsters. It was not the usual sleep-crib that one found in the ports of cities, where one dropped his coin into the hand of the caupo, then selected a stall in which to pass the night. Nay, at this domicile, one did not even enter the walls until inspected by the owner. With an evil looking guard standing by his side, the innkeeper queried us for our quality. Without doubt, our ragged clothes did not give any hint that we were of some foreign nobility, but Ehsan gave a good spiel.

"...Aye. Our voyage has been long, even from the land of the Greeks, and our garments less than pristine, but that will be taken care of on the morrow. For now, my principle has good metal for his stay, and he wishes only to rest and partake of nourishment. And as to your questions of my master, know that he is from the great city of Rome, far to the north of the Great Sea."

An interesting discovery, made almost immediately, was that silver was more to be desired in this land than gold - at least by the merchants. When I opened my purse, showing many drachmae - and even staters of silver - the eyes of the caupo opened just as wide, as did his welcome of us to his house. For a single Tetradrachm, I negotiated a stay of a month, between like phases of the moon. At the time, I had little reason to believe that our sojourn in this land would be longer.

Our rooms, three in number, were light and airy, with a canvas overhead that was kept wet during the day by the slaves of the house. As such, it was considerably cooler than the blinding heat of the open street. But, for the moment, my first desire was to bathe, and shortly I was neck deep in a stone tub of river water, with Ravana sitting in front of me, our legs intertwined as we enjoyed the coolness.

The night passed in comfort on a soft bed, after months of sleeping on the ragged mat of the ship.

On the morning, our first task was to replace the worn and far too thick wool garments that the two of us were wearing. Ehsan, of course, having been to this land innumerable times, had the proper kilt of cool and light material. At a stall of better raiments, I selected two knee length skirts, pleated and of good material, if not of the glistening sheen that had been worn by the priest of Amun. Following my lead, Korax did the same.

Naturally, Ravana attempted to examine every piece of female garb in the stall, finally deciding on a body length kalasiris that fell from her breasts to her ankles, held up by the usual two wide straps across the shoulders. It - and the other pair that she insisted on purchasing - were of good quality, such as the woman of a wealthy merchant might select. The tight fitting, yet thin, fabric followed her female curves as if she were covered with a wash of pigment rather than cloth. Desirable she looked, and was, and my svans made immediate salute to her appearance.

While she was not the wife of such, she was, at least, the consort of such a now-wealthy man. But, in all fairness, I had to admit that she was not a mere woman of opportunity, hoping to use her body to good effect. She herself had brought sufficient coin to support her whims for many years, had the customs of the world allowed a single woman to exist alone.

Or, had stolen, I reminded myself, with a hidden chuckle. I had no condemnation for what a person had to do to elude slavery, remembering well that I had damned several men to the fire in my escape from bondage. Still, I paid for all garments out of my purse, which was still well stocked with Greek coin. The heavy bag that Ravana had brought aboard was still on the ship, under a nailed plank at the keel, along with my longknife. I had little worry of the ship, with crewmen sleeping on board, but I had no wish for a thief to swoop through the hold in search of anything of value during the absence of my two men, while at a taburna or brothel.

One aspect of a desert land is that no matter how hot the day, the nights can be cool, even uncomfortably cold. Why that would be is beyond my ken, but I gave no complaint of my ignorance. This evening was pleasant, and after a long and intense foray with the golden haired woman, I just lay with my hands behind my head, thinking of the future. I was wealthy now - and very much so. So much, that should I return to Rome, I could easily purchase a merchantry, or a farming complex, or even a high-level Priestly appointment in the Temple. Or, become a shipping magnus, with vessels combing the Great Sea for trade, delivering the results in coin back to my coffers. Except...

Still, in the back of my mind, was the belief, or maybe just a vaporous reasoning, that the gods of Olympus had not finished their play with me. After all, the games of an immortal being might last for years, as only a brief moment in their existence.

The next morning we walked to the docks, to find the trading venues and possibly to purchase a cargo for a return trip. It became apparent as we walked, that the citizenry had much to say about our foreignness, pointing and whispering as we passed. It was obvious that we were not of Egyptian stock, with Korax and his short beard, and myself, usually a headspan taller and fifty librae heaver than the local men. When I mentioned my noticements to Ehsan, he chuckled and said, "It is not you, my friend - nor you, good Korax - that the people are watching. Rather it is your woman that they examine. She walks like a princess and is dressed as a wealthy merchant's wife, but strides beside you as if she were a man. They cannot fathom her station." In a quiet aside, he said, "Should they see her head uncovered, the very stones of the buildings might fall to rubble."

I looked around, seeing the people in detail for the first time. I had given the matter no thought, but all Egyptians had black hair - as black as the night. There were none with the lighter shades, as even mine was, that may be seen in Rome quite often, and muchly so in northern tribes, nor any with the rare and fiery red hair of the woman of my youth. And the women always walked behind the elbow of their man. It was food for thought.

The huge area of the Port - a forum, as I considered it - was filled with countless people. Merchant stalls ringed the area and were back to back in groups across the middle, as islands in a sea. Peddlers roamed the area selling sweetmeats and juices from the tray of the slave that followed them. Beggars were everywhere, arms outstretched and begging a copper snippet from all that came within reach of their tongues. Toward the river, and upwards to the south, stalls of cattle, sheep, and goats were lowing and uttering in their manner, waiting for either the butcher or the return to the fields, unsold. We found quickly the reason for the location of the animal stalls, on the edge of the forum and south with the prevailing winds, after some incautious steps took us to the lee of that area. Choking in the miasma of stench, we stumbled back to the main venue, eyes watering and nostrils in revolt against the assault.

Melons, grain - both milled and in the kernel - fresh fish, bread, fruit and more was available in abundance. It was obvious that this was a land of plenty, whoever was in control. And there were remarkably few magistrates on hand to keep the order. At my comment on the lack of security, Ehsan nodded and replied, "Aye, as long as the Sun-God is high in the sky. Come the dark of the day, a man needs walk through here with eyes in the back of his head and his hand ready on his metal. Even the constabulary will patrol this area at night in pairs."

Many were the merchants willing to vend any manner of cargo for carriage. I realized that the matter of filling our hold with fine linen was only a matter of agreeing on a valuation, and then loading the ship. But, I was in no hurry - indeed, I had no plans to depart this city in any haste. I mentioned the fact to Ehsan, and he gave moderations to my thinkings. "You must leave before the season of Akhet, else your ship will set sail without you." At my questioning look, he continued. "The season of the inundation will commence in..." He thought for a moment. "...about five or six of your Greek months. Think you that the Nilos is large now? When the flooding commences, what you view of the waters at this moment will appear as a mere stream of the northlands. All lands in vision, up to the city walls will be under the waters, and any object not swept away will be covered in a handspan of mud when the river recedes in the following months."

I nodded absently, reviewing my previous ideas. "I had heard of the flooding of the Nilos, but it is really as you say?"

"Aye. Your ship would be as a leaf in a rushing stream, should you stay. No anchor stone or rope would halt its demise. Even the docks will be disassembled before the wet season else they also be torn asunder and the pieces flow into the Great Sea. The local fisher-boats are pulled onto high land, but that is not a task that can be accomplished with your vessel, even would it survive sitting on hard ground."

I thought for a moment, then said, "Aye, then you have put a limit on our visit. We will sail ahead of the waters and give ourselves much time to reach the sea."

With no need for purchase or packing for many months, I gave to the two members of the crew that we were staying in Memphis for the nonce. I gave that their pay could continue as though we were at sea - that is, as long as they used the ship as their quarters and gave a hint of some security to the vessel. Ehsan had given location of a taburna that served wine, rather than the far more numerous stalls that supplied the grain-spirit that was the staple drink of Egyptians, and they frequented it often. As did Korax, of course.

For myself, I did not voyage halfway across the world to sit in a taburna. Rather, I walked through the city, looking at this and that, fascinated by the differences from my own - or any in which I had ever resided. Temples and statuary to this god or that were everywhere and not confined to the better sections of the city. In fact, the gigantic sculptures that fronted the gates and temples and Royal Palace dwarfed any that I had seen anywhere. In the forecourt of the Temple of Ptah, facing the road and on either side of the huge gates, were eight stone figures, each many times the height of a man. How such were carved, and even more astonishing, how they were moved into their resting place was an action for which I had not even a glimmer of knowledge.

As Ravana and I moved around the city, we had no trouble with entry into the finest merchantries, given our wealthy appearance and spotless garb. An interesting discovery was that the common people did not use coin in their daily activities. Rather, they measured their vending with tablets on which was inscribed a measure of grain, and the seal of a city granary. While a vendor would certainly take a round of copper in trade, any difference would be returned to me as an inscription on the clay. Metal was reserved for large trades by merchants or the wealthy. As a result, I had to purchase a new purse, much larger, so as to carry all the small tablets that I gathered and passed during my forays.

The picture skills of Ravana were still behind my own, but she could parse out a name or sentence with some study. In fact, our roamings were, in the main, a self-taught set of lessons, as we both stopped before this statue, or that pedestal or some notice board, to read what was chiseled or written. There was no Forum that we could find, unless the huge area of the port complex could be called such, but this was not a city of ignorant savages. Many were the schools that we passed, from simple kiosks with a scribe teaching young men a few marks, to formal educational facilities of the temples, with robed priests walking the street and being followed by tablet bearing acolytes - just as in my younger days in Rome.

On the Street of Kings, we stopped before the gigantic gates leading into the compound of the Royal Quarter. I had learned from Ehsan that the ruler here was a mere satrap of Persia. The last actual king who had been Egyptian, was long removed. "This man calls himself Pharaoh, thinking to equate himself with the glorious past," explained Ehsan, earlier, "but he is just the son of King Darius, come to rule the land."

"Pharaoh?" I had questioned.

"Aye. From the beginning of time, that is the appellation that was given to all Egyptian kings."

Of course, all the magistrates of the city and officers of the army were Persian, or Achaemenids, as they called themselves, leaving only the Temples in the hands of any actual Egyptians of power. Even the guards - or soldiers - standing at the gate were obviously outlanders to the city. Their dense black beards and foreign garments gave that knowledge to even the casual onlooker. How a man could sport such facial fur in this climate was a mystery to me - my skin itched at the thought of it. Even Korax had trimmed his usual Greek follicles much shorter, and Ehsan - by his own admittance - had long ago given up his to the interests of comfort in this land of hot days.

We wanted nothing to do with the ruling elite of the city - nothing good could come from attention in that quarter, but across the wide street from the gate was another compound, inside a massive brick wall, but with an impossibly tall... Well, it was like a finger of stone pointing to the sky. Two wooden and massive gates were opened, and an assortment of people was entering and exiting - not a vast number, but a good many. We walked to stand at the opening and to examine the massively tall finger of stone that we could now see in its entirety. In my estimation, it was, at least, the height of ten men, and on a stone pedestal that I would be unable to reach the top of even by jumping.

Pictures and carvings on the stone were as in the picture language, but I could make no course of them. It was as if a scribe had just randomly carved words without need of coherence. Ravana pointed to the stone finger and said, "It is a Tekhenu, according to Ehsan."

"Tekhenu?"

She nodded. "Korax calls it an obelisk." At my questioning look, she continued. "When you were speaking to the merchants on the docks on the yesterday, we three moved to the shade of a fruit vendor's stall. Behind his stand was a small temple with a monument, like that one, but only about as tall as myself. Ehsan said that they exist in vast numbers and all sizes up and down the cities of the river. Most are dedicated to the gods or this king or that one."

This was another temple complex and of massive size and sweep. Like the Pyramidios, this was another structure that would only bring disbelief in its description given in Rome. The Temple of Jupiter, which I had long thought to be the largest and most ornate in all the world, was as a fruit vendor's kiosk in comparison. My mind could not encompass the number of workers and the time that must have been required to construct such a massive compound.

The statuary followed the normal course that I had seen in this land - they were far larger than life-sized and apparently carved from individual blocks of stone. Actually, the term life-sized was out of order for some of the figures, such as the bodies of men topped with the heads of animals or birds. The living forms of such could not have existed outside of the bad night-dreams of a troubled man.

The two sculptures of lions on either side of the flight of steps leading into the main edifice were, at least, lifelike, although of a size that could have destroyed even the hunting party of Apollo.

In this part of the city, the streets were not crowded to excess, as in the merchant's quarter, but still many citizens came and went on their tasks and chores. Since even the poor seemed to have access to this shrine, I assumed that a pair of foreigners would not be violating any mores with a visit.

Following a woman, carrying a child up the wide steps, we entered the dark recess of the massive portal to find ourselves in a enormous room, the ceiling held up by tall stone pillars and the two side walls guarded by more huge stone images of... of...

At the far wall was an image - again in stone - of the god of this edifice, obviously. He was sitting on a throne of a carved red stone and his size matched the dimensions of the complex, with his head almost touching the overhead. At least, he was in the image of a normal man, looking much like the average male citizen of the street.

Before him, several men and the woman knelt, casting prayers to the god as they prostrated themselves over and over. All had brought some kind of offering, from a basket of fruit and melons to a cage with white birds or a jug that I assumed would contain some spirit, and such gifts. As one finished his supplication and rose to leave, a young priest - or more probably, an acolyte - appeared to take the offering and disappear into a doorway beside the statue.

From the snatches of entreaties that we heard, we now knew that this was the Temple of Amun, a major deity of this land, if not actually the ruling god. Suddenly, I could see a man watching from the shadows, and not a novice priest - this one had both the age and garb of an important of this temple. Out of the corner of my mouth, I said, "We will approach and give our obeisance."

Walking forward, we followed the manner of what we had seen, and dropped to our knees, kneeling forward with our arms outstretched in front, palms up, then bowed to touch our forehead to the floor. In a few moments, I raised my head and spoke, "Great Amun, we are strangers to this land and do not know the forms, and in our ignorance we have neglected to bring an offering. We acknowledge your greatness and beseech you to give guidance to visitors from a far land."

I would have been astonished to hear the statue speak, but my words were not for the stone, but for the priest that was watching from the shadows. Still, I had to admit to myself that the gods of this land were powerful. Just the number of temples and statues that I had seen in my wanderings in only a few days exceeded all that I knew existed in all other lands, together. If their riches were in any way equivalent to those in other cities, then they were wealthy indeed.

But... If the gods of this land were both wealthy and powerful, then why had they allowed the people to be ruled by a foreign satrap?

We stood, hoping that we had not, in some way, given offense, then turned to walk across the floor to the open portal. Our feet did not move after the turn, as we were confronted by two men standing and waiting. One was a younger priest or acolyte, but the other...

Aye, in the dim light, I could see that he was the same man who had ridden the ornate chair to our ship, on the day of our vending of the wood.

I waited, to allow the man the first words, which came immediately, "You are the master of the ship from the land of Cedrus."

I nodded, struggling to think of the proper honorific for an Egyptian priest. As I had no idea, I used the word for an important official, "Aye... Suran. We are from Rome, in the land of Latium."

The young priest spoke up with some asperity, "This is he of Amun, the Second Priest to Amun-Rawab himself, and is to be addressed as Amun-Wab!"

I bowed and said, "Aye, Amun-Wab. Please forgive the manners of a man from a far land, who is even now attempting to find the proper customs."

I could tell that the Priest was not offended, but apparently just interested in the newcomers. "How is it that one of that far city speaks the tongue of a land that he has never visited?"

How many times had I been asked that question? I shook my head and replied, "By strange fate and stranger fortune, Amun-Wab. But in truth, I was employed by a merchant of your land as his scribe and keeper of accounts and gathered the ability from him." It was close to the truth, and without desire to cozen the man.

"You are a scribe, then?"

"Aye. Trained in the Temple of Jupiter as a master scrivener, given my credence by the Priest Primus."

He nodded, obviously thinking over my statements, then said, "And you are waiting for your vessel to gain another cargo?"

"Nay, Amun-Wab." I hesitated then, reversed myself. "That is to say, aye, but I have no need of hurry, and I enjoy the exploration of different lands upon which I find myself."

Now he nodded. "Then you will accept the gift of my cups, and talk."

As before, my scripting of our conversation is much smoother than the actual speaking. My command of the Egyptian tongue was still imperfect and no doubt, filled with inaccuracies that would give mirth to a native. But, as a stranger, I had no wish to deny the wish of a man as immensely powerful as the second Priest of the leading god of this land and, indeed, knew that I would learn much more of this culture from such, rather than the stall merchants of the street.

"You honor me, Sur... Amun-Wab. I will gladly accept your invitation."

He looked at Ravana, standing perfectly still beside me, and with total silence, as befitted a woman - a condition that was most unnatural for herself. "This is your mate?"

"Nay. She is a companion, and an issue of the strange fate that I spoke of earlier."

He turned to his young companion and spoke a quick order, and then said to me, "Come. Your female is not allowed past the third pylon, but we can speak privately in the communing chamber."

Down a long hall, then out a doorway into the side courtyard we walked. Past even more statues, we came to a small round and domed structure, of white stone, and inside were comfortable benches for relaxation. The openings in the wall were covered with thick material, but loosely woven so that light could enter somewhat. And, shadows indicated that a man - or men - passed by on occasion on the outside. Eventually, I realized that he - or they - were wetting the material, through which the breeze was cooled by contact with the water.

Cups were already on the pedestal when we arrived, no doubt quickly placed by his acolyte, and at his invitation, I settled onto a bench to wait his pleasure. He looked at Ravana, then pointed and said, "Sit there, woman, by the window. The breeze will be pleasant."

He pushed a cup to me, then picked up his own for a sip. "I assume that your time at the Temple was during your youth. Did you take priestly orders during your scrivener learning?"

"Aye, Amun-Wab. But I did not become ordained to the Temple. I preferred to remain a scribe, and possibly ascend to the arm of a Quaestor, or even a Rhetor."

"You need not call me by my title in private. The name that my dam gave me is Senemut, although I seldom hear it unless in private with my childhood friends."

I nodded. "Aye. And I am Junius, and started as a fisher-boy on the banks of the Tiber river."

"Ah. I too am from humble beginnings. My sire was a reed merchant, and many were the days that I stood knee deep in water with a cutting blade." He picked up the jug to fill our cups, then continued, "I cannot venture as one like you, at whim and to any destination and for that you are in my envy. Indeed, I can seldom leave this temple without a priest-boy running up to tell of some need of my presence. But, I also delight in learning of other peoples and their cultures, even through other eyes and other tongues. I would take much pleasure in speaking with you of your travels in other lands, and even of your own."

I smiled and accepted the filled cup. "Aye. And it will be a trade. I would wish to learn more of your land from one who is intimately familiar with it and the people. I have thoughts of remaining here for a considerable time."

He grinned. "It is a bargain well made. As you are my guest, I will take your question firstly."

"Very well. I have been learning the picture writing of this land, with some success, as has my consort sitting there. In the front of the Temple is a..." I tried to remember what Ravana had called it. Ah... "...an obelisk with picture script, but while the symbols are familiar, they make no sense in their order."

He smiled. "Let me first ask you of the age of your city - Rome."

I had no idea beyond the myths of the priests and storytellers. "A few hundred years, maybe as many as four hundred." What had this to do with my question?

"Aye. And such modest age is a characteristic of most cities of the world. The most ancient that I have knowledge outside of this land is Babilim, or Babylon as it is sometimes called - far to the east of here beyond the Red Sea. Its age is given in the texts as about a thousand and a half years."

I pursed my lips. "That is old, indeed."

"But, yon stele in the courtyard is older than your homeland and almost as old as that ancient city. The Per-Netera that you undoubtedly saw in your voyage upriver..."

Per-Netera? What... Ah, the Pyramidios. I nodded, and he continued, "They are from an age of over two and a half thousand years ago, and there are other, smaller ones that are even older."

Two thousand and a half? That was inconceivable! If true, then Memphis was to Rome as my patér's patér to the newborn babe on the next fishing boat.

He nodded. "Aye, it is as I say. The writing on the stone in the courtyard is from that age, and unreadable by any scholars who have not studied the old language. I could show you the tablets from that time, but as the courtyard stone inscriptions, they would have no meaning for you, unless you wished to learn the ancient language."

The day went quickly, and as enjoyably as I have ever passed a conversation between friends. Unfortunately, as the day waned, the tasks of the Priest required him to end our friendly meeting, and we parted, with intentions to renew our quests for information on further days.

That evening, in the cool of the darkness, after I had cooled my blood with the use of my consort, and she had passed to her sleep, I just lay in thought. This land was attractive to me, and much here could be learned of interest. There was much to explore, and I had thoughts of walking the few stadia to the north to view the massive tombs of stone more closely - or at least as closely as a foreigner could approach.

And...

This land was under the control of powerful gods, and different than those that ruled my land, or that of Greece where I had sojourned for a time. Here, I would be freed from the gameplay of Olympus and their constant jesting with my life. It was true that at every throw of the immortal knucklebones my life had become better - eventually - and my wealth waxed at every turn, but the danger in my mind was that the inevitable tedium would set in - even for the gods. On that evil day, the board would be cleared of its pieces and returned to the shelf for another time. The mortal game-figures would be disposed of like the stones of the Latrunculi board when the street gamers of Rome ended their contests for the day.

Here, maybe, I could live under the auspices of Amun, or Ptah, or some other Egyptian deity in a normal life, without fear of becoming the puppet of the gods. My wealth would carry me - or us - for our lifetimes, with the gold in the Temple and the huge purse hidden in the ship, stolen from Dionysos. Just the silver in my own purse would allow us to live in luxury for a considerable time. I could sell the ship, bringing in even more gold, or even recruit a captain and crew and become a merchant shipper, possibly even purchasing other hulls with the profits.

With such thoughts, I finally fell into my sleep.

Arbitrium (decision)

I had to make a decision about our ship. The season of inundation was less than two months away, according to Senemut, the second priest of the Temple of Amun. I had decided to stay in this land, and make it my own, for many reasons, not the least of which was that I was shielded, in my mind, from the foibles of the gamesters of Olympus. The gods of this land were amiable to my residence, or, at least, they had no objection to one of foreign extraction settling here. I had purchased a small vessel, one that apparently had been used to haul the glistening stone from the quarries upriver, to test my ability as a shipping merchant.

With the Persian pilot, Ehsan, as captain, and Korax taking the position of factor, I purchased and shipped a load of fine linen to the port city of Pelusium, there to vend it to another vessel that would ply the coastal routes. The small river vessel had far less capacity of my large ship, and the profit gained from the linen would have been far more in the northern ports, but still, in less than a month's time, Ehsan and Korax hove back into Memphis with more than a handful of gold and silver.

I found that the life of a wealthy shipping merchant was to my taste. With the stimulation of conversation with the priest, Senemut, and the nightly companionship of Ravana, I was as satisfied with life as I had ever been. It was true that my feelings for the woman were not as those of a young man, who cannot think of any other life than with some female that has captured his desires to the exclusion of all else. She was a pleasant cohort, with intelligence and desirably, and made few calls on myself with the exception of garments. Of course, that is no different with females of any time and place - all would fill a household with habiliments to the exclusion of all else, were they allowed.

I had engaged a male servant, of intermediate age, as her escort, that she might leave the inn of our staying without need of my accompaniment. Females in this city - indeed, in this land - had much more freedom than any other in the world that I had seen of yet - still, it was unwise for a young and attractive woman just to wander the streets alone.

Another factor in my growing decision to make this land my own was the gradual inclusion of myself into the fabric of the upper strata of merchants of the city. Unlike my city of Rome, where one needed several generations of family growth to become accepted by this clique or that, here only the attribute of success seemed to be of importance. As with Senemut, long hours were spent in conversation with the men of the merchants, in topics of seriousness and, as often, of curiosity.

By my noticement, about half of the leading merchants were native to the land, and the rest being of mostly Persian extraction, although many had been here for several generations and were almost indistinguishable from those men whose ancestors may have stacked the Pyramidios. In our conversations, I was told that many merchants from far lands came to reside here every year, but most were unable to accept the hotness of the land and soon departed for cooler climes, usually at the insistence of a mate, unable to dress in her finest without swooning from the heat. And, it was said, refusing to garb herself in the kalasiris of the women of this land, thin and comfortable but showing the form of the female body almost as completely as to the vision of her man.

Indeed, that attitude was not taken by Ravana. She was a female who knew of her attractiveness and reveled in it. In fact, she garbed herself as did many of the younger females of the wealthy district - that is, with the body of the kalasiris sheath beginning below her large mammaries, those only being covered by the wide straps over the shoulders. Many times did I withhold a grin, observing young men - and some of age - watching my consort and hoping for a movement that might cause the strap to bow away from the body, displaying the sweet female flesh beneath.

I had discussed, with Korax, the idea of vending our vessel. Indeed, I considered it to be his as much as mine as we had both fought together to rescue it from the pirates - and to save ourselves from slavery, or worse. In fact, I also counted that half of our gold in the Temple and that in the hidden sack in the ship to be his. However, the Greek had little interest in commerce, beyond his need for wherewithal to purchase the wares of a wineshop. He was of an age still to be interested in consorting with females, but of course, far less often than myself, my being four handfuls of years younger than he. His infrequent urges were easily assuaged in a brothel.

Recently he had taken a consort in the form of a widow, apparently without children and whose mate had failed to return from a voyage many years before. She was of about the same age as he and was quiet and retiring, apparently very happy to give service to a man in return for a nest in which to light. As with the women of this land, she was thin and small, with mammaries more alike those of a budding girl in Rome, but as Korax was satisfied with her company, it was not my place to remark on her likeness. In all my time of my knowing of the woman, she seldom spoke to me, apparently assuming an importance that I did not have. However, she and Ravana conversed muchly, allowing my consort to practice her language skills on a native speaker. As a result, and with her natural ability, her diction became much purer than mine.

As my friendship developed with Senemut, I confided to him about the far northern genesis of my consort and the fact that her hair was of a color not seen in this land, and of the reaction of the two Egyptian crewmen on my ship. At our next meeting, she accompanied me and in the gloom of the little communing chamber, removed the wrap that covered her hair.

Senemut walked around her, looking with admiration at the never-before-seen sight. Finally, he said, "I have come to know of you as a man of integrity, but still... I have to admit that had you told me of this, and without the woman for inspection, I would have given your tale as being a gull for amusement."

"My concern," I replied, "is the reaction, should she be seen by the citizenry. It is not my wish to have her killed for blasphemy to the goddess... Hathor, is it?" He nodded. "Nor assumed that she is anything but an ordinary woman."

He was still inspecting Ravana, looking closely for indications of dye, I assumed. "Is there a race of such, in the north, that might have the look of her?"

I shook my head. "That I cannot tell you, my friend. I believe that such as she is not unique, nor rare, and have heard of like individuals appearing in my city from time to time, even if I have never seen such as she. I can say that it is thought that men and women tend to have lighter colored skin and hair in relation to their proximity to the cold lands. But certainly, the barbarians that live north of Latium, and in the high mountains of snow do not tend to grow hair of gold - not any that I have seen." I shrugged. "But who knows of what peoples may live at that end of the world."

Stopping in front of her, he asked, "Can she speak?"

I grinned. "Aye. She can assault your ear as the most plain-spoken fisher-wife, should you raise her ire."

He looked again, then said. "Woman. Is your birth-city filled with such as you?"

"Nay. I have no knowledge of my birth-place. And my name is Ravana, not 'Woman.'"

Senemut was without the sin of self-importance, and from common-folk as myself. Still, I hoped that Ravansa would realize that this was a powerful man that should not be offended. Fortunately, he just chuckled at her words, then asked, "She has a considerable ability with our tongue, it appears. That is interesting for one from afar and not engaged in trade." To her he said, "So, you have no remembrance of your genitors... Ravana."

She shook her head. "My first memories are in shadow, and I cannot say with truth where I began. I can give you many tales given by my masters, but they would be no more as the stories by the street bards."

He just stood, pondering the unusual person standing before him, then said, "I can certainly understand why your crewmen gave her as being the earthen-attribute of Hathor. She might even become a priestess in that temple, should her attributes be offered properly."

My eyes widened. This was certainly an unexpected development. I opened my mouth to... to... not protest, but in some way give my objection to such an event. Ravana did not have the capture of my being, as a young woman would have on the feelings of a young man with his newly dropped pouchstones, but I enjoyed her company, both on the mat and in accompaniment during the day. I would not care for her loss, and had much doubt that a Roman would have fleshly access to a priestess of Egypt - rather, he would probably be flayed alive just for attempting to approach her.

Senemut waved at me with a smile, seeing my expression. "Nay, I was not making the suggestion - unless your woman... Ravana wished it. But..." He looked at the woman. "You would have riches and golden garments, and power over the people - you could point and they would come, then wave and they would go. But... And do not doubt me on this... Your life would consist of stultifying monotony from daybreak to dark. On your rise from the mat in the morning, you would have the course of your day planned by others, and it would be the same and unvarying from day to day, until your paps dropped and your hair turned to the color of age and you were consigned to the kitchens as maid-helper."

Ravana bowed, and with all seriousness, said, "My gratitude to you, Priest of Amun, and I will take your advice and refuse the opportunity should it arise. But, even the maids of our inn have seen glimpses of my tresses. I cannot wear a head-wrap forever in complete confidence that it will never fail to conceal."

Senemut turned to me. "Then, if I might give other suggestion." I spread my hands in welcome for any advice. "As you know, many - if not almost all - upper-born and high station women shave their heads, and wear a hairpiece instead. The custom has many advantages, even for one who does not wish to conceal a strange color

- they are more comfortable, since the wigus may be removed in private and for sleep and bathing. You might also..."

He stopped as a young acolyte suddenly appeared in the doorway, bowing deeply and waiting for notice. "Aye, Hemmet. What is it?"

"The Amun-Rawab requires your presence immediately, Amun-Wab."

Senumut looked at me for a moment, then said, "I must wait on the Priest of the Temple, my friend. I bid you farewell for the day."

Since it was the noon mealtime, we walked back to the inn, and in the shade of the wetted canvas, I asked her about the suggestion that she had received, and giving that it was her decision. "I would indeed miss your mass of lovely hair, but I would regret it more should you be dragged off to be an offering-inducement in some stone temple filled with mumbling priests."

She replied around a mouthful. "I would try it. And it is not as leaving a favored place, never to see it again. Hair will alway grow back, in time, if desired."

That evening, I sharpened a fine blade, procured from a weapon's vendor across the merchant quarter, then wetted her tresses and carefully and slowly shaved the long filaments from her head. I managed to finish without major damage to her skin, though not completely, as the small pieces of wetted cloth on the small nicks could testify. As her golden threads might be of use someday, and in any case, long hair was a valuable commodity, whether on the head or not, I enclosed it in a bundle of papyrus and stored it on a shelf.

She was somewhat abashed, as she ran her hand over her scalp, laughing in a self-deprecation of her new look. But, for myself, the sight of the transformed woman triggered a desire in my loins that would not be denied. I was rutting as a young man, newly come from the festival of Liber Pater - his assent into manhood - and about to make the ritual visit to a brothel to celebrate the event. As it was long before nightfall, my svans was giving notice that waiting was out of the question. Without further speaking, I pulled her to the mat and began my satisfaction.

The next morning, I made my usual entry into the tavern frequented by the high vendors, waving at several merchants with which I had made acquaintance of in the past months. Sitting at a table, waiting for the serving slave, I could tell that the room was abuzz with... not the interminable talk of trade, with the accounting of this caravan and that shipload. But of...

"Yo, Junius." I looked over my shoulder to see the son of Menhsat, the brick merchant. Shamshet by name, he was about my age and we had made casual friendship over cups since my arrival. His was a wealthy house, with a monopoly on all brick making in the city, courtesy of the couriers that arrived at the palace on occasion with a bag of gold. Like most of the wealthy merchants in the city, his patér was of the ruling class - that is to say, Persian, Shamshet had not been born in Egypt, but had been brought here at such an early age as to have no memory of his homeland, far to the north. And, unlike most of the foreigners, he dressed in the Egyptian way, rather than the overrobed style of his Persian ilk. Still, he carried the obligatory beard of his kind, although, in deference to the heat of the land, it was cut short as in the style of Korax.

I waved for him to be seated, then again for another cup. He immediately began with, "Have you heard the news?"

"Nay. But it is obvious that something has stirred the old men in here. The caupo is vending little wine this day for mouths that have much to say, it seems." I spread my hands in question, waiting for the breathless release of whatever my friend had come to give.

"King Darius is dead."

The death of the Persian King was obviously of great interest to the assembled men of the tavern, but for myself, my casual friend could have been talking about the street beggar sitting in the dust outside the open front of the building. And as such news could have little effect on my life, I had no reason to ask for further depth on the subject, except for the necessity to not offend the citizens of that far land. "Forgive the ignorance of a Roman, but is that a reason to fear, or a need to celebrate the productive life of a ruler?"

He shook his head. "Nay, it was not a revolt. He merely lived to the end of his life. It appears that Artaxerxes was crowned King, in the city of Pasargadea."

Again, neither city nor man had any reference in my mind, and to myself, absolutely no interest. It could have no effect on my life.

But, in that, I was wrong.

A few days later, as the cuts in the scalp of Ravana had healed sufficiently, I brought her to a merchant that vended wigs to the upper strata of the city. She was fitted with a hairpiece that I was assured was the current fashion of the city, and another as a second. The woman had taken only a day or so to become accustomed to the strange feeling above her head and then began to embrace the lack of tresses with fervor. Several times, and again, she commented on the coolness of her shorn head, and the wonder that anyone held for long hair in this land. The piece was held on with a braided gold band, very thin, around the temples and across the forehead. A woven patch of reed cloth at the closure in the back provided tension for tightness. It could be doffed or donned in just moments, although any woman returning it to her head would stand over the reflecting pool for an endless time, making infinitesimally small adjustments. Mostly, to test the patience of any waiting male, I was sure.

It became obvious why only the wealthy women of the city wore such, made of real hair. The cost, in silver pieces, was jaw-dropping. Indeed, a pair oxen in Rome could have been purchased for the weight of metal that I handed to the merchant. All of the garments that I had purchased in all of my life did not come to the total of her two wigs.

Naturally, she had to parade the streets, to allow for both the men and women of the streets to worship at the altar of her beauty. And in truth, she was a stunning sight, in the gold banded and black hair, with a blinding white and glistening kalasiris fitting her from her ankles to the bottom of her mammaries. I had also bought her two golden armbands, of a kind now of a fashion among the noble-women of the city. And, of course, with the wide straps held out by the full mounds of her female flesh, even the old beggars of the street would gaze in desire at the apparition that suddenly appeared as she walked past.

Certainly, for myself, I could feel my desire rising again, and with some evidence under my kilt. That would be immediately sated upon our return to our quarters, but, first, we turned into the huge entrance of the Temple of Amun. There, the acolytes now well knew of our friendship with the priest and ran to give notice of our presence.

In the usual round edifice, Senemut looked approvingly at the woman. "Yellow hair or nay, she is as desirable a female as I have seen." He looked at me and said, "I will offer forty rings of gold for her. She will be an asset to the temple as an offering to the wealthy donors. Especially those with shrewish wives," he added.

I could see the twinkle in his eye and the lightning of his jaw as he strained mightily to hold in his mirth. I shook my head and replied, "Eighty rings is my minimum acceptance. There is another female that I have my eyes on for purchase."

The eyes of Ravana had opened as widely as her jaw had dropped, as she attempted to believe what she was hearing. I knew that in just a heartbeat, we would see the ultimate in female fury as soon as she had gathered her thoughts. I needed to stop her rage before she could give offense to both of us. But Senemut was ahead of me - he burst out with mirth and caused me to do the same. Our laughter alleviated the sudden fear of the woman, but not her rage. I knew that she would be pouting until the midday meal, at least. Still, she sat on her chair under the wetted cloth of the opening and refrained from any outbursts.

To Senemut, I said, now seriously. "You have no doubt heard of the death of the ruler of the northern lands - and these. Will that have any effect on the satrapy that sits on the throne in this..." I stopped as he held up a hand.

He walked to the entrance and gave an order. Through the doorway, I saw an acolyte and a slave departing, entering the temple proper. Then, in a lowered voice, he said, "Aye, but that is not the news of concern. Do you know of a general Amyrtaeus?" I shook my head. "He is the commander of one of the bands of rebels that have been harassing the Persians in the Delta. His successes have been few in the past, but the word of the death of the Persian king was the stroke that allowed the individual bands to merge, under his command."

"So he now has an army."

Senemut nodded. "Aye, and a successful one. The cities of Merimda and Naukratis of the Delta threw off their Persian magistrates and opened the gates for the General. Word has come that he is now marching on Memphis, as we speak."

I sat motionlessly and thought furiously about what I had been told. Revolutions are never pleasant to behold, by my reading of history, and many people are slain by either side and without determination of allegiance. Finally, I said, "Then my friend. I must ask you for advice. Should we stay or board our vessel and depart at once? In truth, I had the hope of making this land my own."

The priest shook his head. "Nay. You are known by all that know anything of you, to be Roman. That means little to most, but certainly none will connect you with the Persians. And you are clean shaven, and almost shorn of hair on your head. You neither look like a bearded conqueror nor dress like one. Indeed, you could almost pass as a priest of Egypt, except for the size that your gods put on your frame."

"Hmmm." A troubling thought came to mind. What of... "I have a close comrade, of Greek extraction, and he, I am afraid, could be mistaken for one of the enemy, if that is what they will become."

"Then I suggest that he take ship immediately, and not return until this matter is settled."

That evening, after Korax had returned from his dicing and drinking, I asked him to the courtyard for a private conversation, out of the ears of any servants and slaves of the inn. Giving him my news, I suggested that he follow the advice of Senemut.

He nodded, thinking. "So that is what the jabber was about in the taverna." At my questioning look, he continued, "Aye. We thought little of it during our game, but the tables were filled with men speaking of some battles in the swamps. I thought it was of strife far up the river, but..." He nodded. "Then the word, or at least rumors of the news, is reaching the city."

"Aye. And, my friend, you have far too close a semblance to the Persian overlords of this city. I would hate to see you run through with a spear, merely for refusing to remove that facial fur, as I have suggested for years." It was a jape, but I was not jesting.

He waved a hand in dismissal. "But, you are only dream weaving at the moment. It may be that the Persian regiment here will send the interloper running back to the skirts of his mitera."

"Aye, and you may have the truth of it," I replied. "But my friend in the Temple has the ear of the upper ranks of the city, and his belief is that the local ranks are fat and lazy and long out of competence with weapons. And besides, he says that half the garrison is native Egyptians that may turn, the day this general appears before the walls."

We talked for a while, then I said, "This is my idea, and you may take it as you will. We will sign on Ehsan as captain, with you as the master, load the vessel with fine linen and you may depart for... Rhodes, or Tarsus, maybe. The profit will be far more than a transfer vending in Pelusium, at the mouth of the Delta. And the distances are great enough that you will be gone for the half year, at least. Time enough for... well, for whatever happens here, to be settled." Another thought, and I added, "Besides, we have to move the ship out of the Nilos before the inundation season, as we knew."

The next morning, as Korax left to find Ehsan at his domicile, I walked to my usual taburna. Again, I met Shamshet, son of the brick merchant, and he was filled with excitement over some news that had arrived. He took the cup as soon as the slave had filled it and swallowed half in one gulp. "...and this Ameirdisu - or Amyrtaeus, whatever he calls himself, is on the march."

I shook my head, pretending to have no idea of his meaning. "I am sorry, my friend, but I have been in this land for far too short a time to be able to claim any knowledge of the ruling undercurrents. Who is Amyrtaeus?"

Shamshet was obviously impatient that his news was not immediately appreciated as being a direful portent of the future. He took another huge swallow, emptying the cup. "You will wake up some morning in the House of the Dead, my Roman friend, with your indifference to the currents of life around you." Again he leaned forward as if that would push the words into my mind with greater force. "He is a rebel, as I said, claiming the suzerainty of Egypt for himself and the peoples, and has apparently taken control of the other rabble in the Delta. And, this is his destination, I will wager any amount."

"A pretender to the Pharoahship?" I shrugged. "My Persian friend, every land has rebels in the wilderness with visions of grandeur." Now a question in which I was actually interested. "What will you do? Leave the city until the matter is settled?"

"Leave?" Apparently, I had insulted the idea of manhood, with even the suggestion that any man of the mighty Persian empire would flee from a mob of rabble. "Nay, there is no danger to the city. Even now, the garrison of the King is being formed for battle. If this mud-footed waif from the swamps wishes to offer his head for sacrifice, then we will provide the sword."

Hmmm. I had heard such gasconade before, by men who had neglected to defeat their enemy before denigrating them.

That afternoon, Korax had arrived with Ehsan, and we talked of our future plans. The Persian was rootless, with little interest in which copper-plated ass sat on the throne of Memphis, and readily agreed to the captaincy of our vessel - sweetened with a share of any profits. Like myself, he had a desire to wander, to see what was over the next horizon, and little desire to settle with a shrew for a mate, and a mud house ringing with the babble of urchins. His wonder was that I wished to stay.

"Sail with us. Memphis will still be here at the return of our voyage. And you will be spared the fate of men who find themselves between two quarreling factions."

I did not wish to explain my fear - even now, only partly believed - of entering back into the domain of the gods of the northern lands, and their propensity to use myself as a figure on a gameboard. I shook my head. "Nay, I was not born to be a deep water sailor. And if matters begin to become uncomfortable, Ravana and myself might caravan to Carthago and let the battlers settle it without us."

An agreement by all was met, and on the morrow, we began to bid for linen from the merchants in the docks. By comparison to the logs that we had arrived with, this cargo was as feathers in comparison to heaviness, and the ship would be both nimble and fast. But... As a sop to the future, while Ehsan was bargaining, and Korax monitored the transfer of our new cargo, I ordered several... items, the likes of which had proved useful on the voyage across the Great Sea.

When they arrived, I called Korax to the forward hold and showed him the six large clay jugs, sealed and resting firmly in a cushion of reed leaves. As he saw the torches, dry and stowed beside them, he nodded with understanding. "If you have to use them, try your best to be upwind or, at least, beam-on to the weather. I had these jugs filled with the thin liquid that flows to the surface of the pitch in the standing vats, with little of the solids. It will burn like the funeral pyre of Vulcan when torched."

In addition, I had a shipwright make two movable... well, walls, is the best description. Usually just laying on the deck to be out of the way, they could be stood on end to give protection from arrows to the tillerman, and to Korax in the midship area. He could crouch behind the wood, then rise and throw the jugs over it without having to expose himself to archers.

Koran retrieved the heavy bag of gold that Ravana had stolen in her flight from Athens. I insisted that half was his, but again, he gave that all he needed was enough to pay the harbormasters and the wine vendors along the way. Still, I made him take a double handful - more than enough to pay expenses, or even to contract for major repairs to the ship, should they become necessary.

There was still over a month to the inundation, and as yet we had heard nothing more of the army of Amyrtaeus. Still, rebels or no, the ship would leave no later than the next waxing moon. Parm and Massoud were still on board as crew, of course, and having little interest in their destination, and three others were engaged - the two thin locals that had hired on in Pelusium and another. Of course, Korax would take his Egyptian mate, and even Ehsan had found a doxy to accompany him for the long voyage.

Thusly, did our plans form for our futures.

Dilectus (choice)

The city became... restless and filled with anticipation, as one who sees the dark band of clouds approaching in a calm that does not even rustle the leaves. Actually, that statement would be completely meaningless to a citizen of a city where rain is seldom seen between handfuls of years, but all could feel that events were about to disrupt the calm of everyday life.

Since our arrival, I had rarely seen a soldier or guard of any kind, save at the entrance to the huge palace complex, but now, patrols could be seen at frequent intervals all during the day - and heard, at night. Korax and I sat at his favorite taburna watching a double line of men in arms, marching toward the western gate. I was not a soldier, as was my friend, but even so, I could tell that the force available to the satrap king of the city was less than fearsome.

Korax was snorting in his cup, watching with disdain as the men marched past. "Had I appeared in front of the Dimoirites of my Hekatontarchia in such a state, I would have regretted the night my patéras lay with my mitéra to seed my being. I would have been consigned to cesspool digging until my pouchstones had shriveled as an oldster."

I had to agree. In this land, few wore armor - any army attempting to do so would be immobilized by heat in short order - but even the minimal soldier garb of the local forces was... shabby, at best. Helms with broken chin straps, kilts that looked to be from the rag-merchants of the lower harbor shanties, sandals with broken straps... Even the weapons were as from the scrap pile of a smith - corroded green blades and bent shafts of the spears and with shields covered with grime and peeling leather. And even more astounding were the soldiers that marched with empty hands, holding neither weapon nor shield. It had been long, if ever, since these men engaged in any military action.

The ship was almost loaded, waiting on a merchant to deliver a bundle of tinted fabric, and it would stand into the river on the day after tomorrow, at the latest. Korax had been... was a good friend, and I would sorely miss the crusty old Greek during his voyage. But, life moves on and seldom waits for a man's desires...

We both quickly rose to our feet, seeing Ravana and her attendant suddenly appear in our vision. Of course, she did not enter the taverna, but before she could send her man to find us, we hurried into the street. This was probably not news of a gladsome nature.

Before I could query her coming, she said, "I was hoping you would still be here." She looked over our shoulder into the gloom of the winery. "Senemut has sent word to the inn, requesting you to wait on him with haste." I nodded to Korax, and hurried down the market street to the Avenue of the Gods, then turned toward the palace. An acolyte was waiting and bowed with no words, waving for me to follow. This time it was not to the round communing chamber, but around the main building and toward a long columned structure against one far wall.

At the doorway to a chamber, Senemut was waiting. He nodded to me, then said to the young priest-novice, "Allow no one to approach within hearing, until I indicate otherwise." The youngster bowed deeply, then retreated to the front of the portico to maintain a guard. Then I was waved to follow.

Inside, the building was dark and cool, with the usually wetted gauze over the openings in the wall. Thick rugs were on the floor and heavy fabrics covered the walls. At the far end of the polished floor was a raised dias - apparently a large sleeping mat of some...

A man. An old man was laying on the softness of the sleeping mat, his upper body and head cradled back against soft cushions. I knew without asking, who this had to be. And that was confirmed in mere heartbeats of our approaching his presence.

"Amun-Rawab," said Senemut without preamble. "This is the Roman of whom I spoke." To me he said, "This is the High Priest of the Temple of Amun."

I began my descent to prostration, in keeping with the respect to such a massively powerful individual, but had barely bent my knees, when the old man spoke in a surprisingly strong voice, "Nay. We have no time for such trifles. Stand and listen." He looked at me for a heartbeat, then continued, "You were trained in the Temple of Jupiter, I am told by Senemut."

I nodded, then said "Aye, Great One. As a scribe of the first order, but without becoming consecrated to the temple." The man was beyond old - he looked as a scroll of papyrus that has been left in water for a while, wrinkled and folded beyond reason. His reason was with him, and his eyes were clear, but I gazed in wonderment at his frail body, trying to guess at the number of seasons that he had watched pass before him. He might even...

"You have come far, for a scribe. According to Senemut, the tale is of great interest. I have hope that I will have time to hear it someday." He reached for a cup with surprising steady hands, considering that his being was beyond ancient, then said, "But such stories are for times of leisure. For now, I am told that you have a ship of worth, capable of traversing the Great Sea." He looked at Senemut and nodded.

The young priest took up the conversation. "Your plan was for your ship to sail in the next few days, is that not correct?"

"Aye. On the day after tomorrow, we had planned. According to all, the inundation season is almost upon us. My pilot informs me that a ship of that size needs not to be caught in the flooding waters."

Senemut walked to the doorway and shouted an order - apparently to the acolyte that had been guarding against any approach by others. Turning back to me, he said, "The river pilot you speak of is Ehsan of Gandara, is it not so?" I just answered in the affirmative, not having time to wonder at the source of their information. "Late of the Persian fleet, in which he was a Premier Subahdar of a stashion of row-ships?"

I just stood and blinked in my daze. Ehsan, a Capitaneus Primus of a fleet? And now steering boats up and down a muddy river? What gods did he offend to... "I did not know that."

"We have called you to warn of a danger to your plans. Our... ears in the palace tell of an order to seize your ship in the service of the throne. Of course, the real reason is that several high-placed lackeys may flee the approaching danger, to wait out the result in safety far from this city. In any event, it must leave immediately if you wish to retain ownership of your vessel."

The acolyte returned at a run, carrying a rolled parchment that he handed to the young priest, then disappeared again. Now the old priest spoke from the bed. "I have heard from Senemut that you have a liking for our city, and wish to reside here."

"Aye, Great One. I have the hope of establishing a merchantry here, possibly a shipping concern. I have already purchased a river vessel that makes the path between here and Pelusium."

"Such an illustrious man is welcome in our city, but you could cement your claim for such if you would."

I was puzzled at the statement and just waited for further enlightenment. Senemut unrolled the spindleless scroll on the side table, weighting both ends with small tablets. Immediately I recognized the familiar Greek symbol and knew that this was a map of the lower Nilos and Delta. He pointed to a mark on one of the streams that spread out from the southern apex of the wet land. "This is the city of Merimda, on the Canoptic distributary." I nodded, and now in a lowered voice, he said, "We would have your ship portage an agent to here, on your downstream voyage."

I needed no explanation. Obviously, the man would have missives for the rebel general, Amyrt... Whatever his name was. I furiously thought about the offer - or demand, whatever it might be. By such an act, I would be seen as a supporter of the Egyptian lands and known to be by the most powerful men in the city, save only those in the command of the satrap of the palace. But, also, I had no doubt that heal-hanging as crow meat would be rewarded to any that was seen to have helped the rebel cause.

"You are deep in thought, Scribe of Rome," said the High Priest. "Do you wish to remain untouched by our troubles?"

I shook my head. "Nay, Sos... High One. I am thinking of... of... certain... I will not be on the ship, as I am neither a seaman nor qualified to command a deep water vessel. My man Korax is dependable and a staunch friend, but neither is he a man to point a ship into strange and long waters."

"The fact that your pilot is a Persian is your concern," said Senemut.

"Aye. He is, to my knowledge, as rootless as myself and has shown no great fondness for his birth land, but in such circumstances..." I spread my hands, then continued. "I have no affection for Rome, having left under duress between dawn and daylight, but should I find myself in a situation to prevent harm to my city, I believe I would make the effort. For himself, Ehsan might feel less than gladsome to assist in the attack against his people, however much he has lost his attachment to his homeland."

Senemut waved his hand in negation. "That will not be a problem. For his own protection, our man will be traveling as a wealthy merchant in need of inspecting his remote assets in these times of upheaval. And in fact, he is a genuine tradesman with interests in that downriver city. Your crew need not know of anything else."

I nodded, then replied, "Aye. But I will have to give to my crew that he has given a usurious fee for the berth, to give a reasonable explanation for the addition of almost a thousand stadia to their voyage."

"It is agreed then. You will undertake this task?"

"Aye, that is so."

"Then you must hurry to the port, and give the command to push off with haste, and before magistrates arrive with orders of seizure. Your passenger will be there within the hour, and with orders to pose as a merchant fearful for his property in that river city."

As I began to hurry out the doorway, a thought struck me. I turned and said, "I will need that map to show my crew their new course." Senemut rolled it into a scroll, handed it to me, and I hurried down the streets at almost a run. Fortunately, both Korax and Ehsan were on board, overseeing the deck boards being replaced over the hold, and then the holding pegs pounded into place. Their eyes widened as they saw me hurry down the wharf, breathless from my long run from the Temple. I gave the warning about the magistracy and the seizure of the ship, then the notice that a wealthy merchant had purchased a birth to the city of Merimda. Opening the rolled map, I pointed to the city of the discussion.

"Have you traversed that stream in the Delta," I asked of Ehsan.

"Aye. Years ago. But why do we alter our course for one man?"

I was not gladsome about giving falsehoods to both men, but with the shortness of time, I had no other plan that I could think of. "For a large bag of gold," I replied.

He nodded. "Very well. It only adds about thirty leagues to our voyage and little effort." He looked around. "Where is this merchant?"

I shook my head. "He will be here shortly, but have your men on the poles and watch for a troupe of magistrates approaching. If any are seen, stand out immediately and do not wait."

Korax said, "I will get the women on board." With that he jumped over the side and strode to the dockside shanty that served as both shade and taburna for the wharfs. Suddenly, I could see a man hurrying toward us, moving this way and that through the crowds. This had to be the... agent. Or priest, or spy. At least he looked the part of a merchant, if somewhat younger than one would expect. I met him at the start of the planks of the dock, and held my hand for him to stop.

In a quiet voice, I asked, "You are from Senemut?"

Just as quietly, he answered, "You are Junius the Roman, obviously."

I nodded, then said, "My crew knows nothing of your errand and should not suspect that you are other than you seem."

"Aye. Senemut gave me the tale. And he sends that the ship should depart immediately. There are soldiers on the way, even now, to seize all ships of any size."

"Get on board, then." I shouted across the bank of the river. "Korax! Make haste, you must leave now." Turning, I ran back beside our vessel and called to Ehsan. "Cast off and hurry. Soldiers are coming."

Korax ran over, followed by his and the pilot's woman, then almost threw both up and onto the deck. Two of the Egyptians jumped to the dock, then they and Korax began to push the ship away and out towards the river. I hurried to help and in moments, the three jumped back onboard as the bow of the vessel cleared the end of the dock and began to drift with the current. With poles, they straightened the course, then I saw the splash as the retarding stone was dropped over the stern to give steering as they floated down river. A rudder or steering oar is useless when the ship is traveling only as fast as the water, but with the stern held upriver by the dragging stone, the course would be made with poles from the bow, pushing into the river bottom.

As I watched them slowly recede into the distance, I suddenly realized that I had had no chance to ask Ehsan about his previous experience as the commander of a fleet. Now, I would not have the chance to speak to either he nor my friend Korax for the good part of a year. At least.

Across what I considered to be the forum of the city - the flat space of the massive trade area of the port - I could see a commotion which had to be soldiers pushing citizens aside in their march. As I did not wish to be questioned about any missing ship, I walked the long way around the outside of the area, then back into the city. There was no rush now. My fate had been set, whatever it might be. I was now committed to stay in the city, come what may, with no exit other than some caravan to somewhere - a desperate measure if made. My other and smaller vessel had departed for Pelusium days before with a newly hired captain and crew and could not return until the end of the flood season - months from now.

As I retreated from the water's edge, I took a long look up and down the river. Even now, the wooden piers and docks and structures near the water were being dismantled in anticipation of the flood. As the larger ships, that usually called this port home had departed for safer domains when the first intimations of a revolt were in the air, little was left but fishing boats, and most of those were trundled far up onto the banks of the river, to wait out the flood. The soldiers would find little to seize when they reached the waterfront. Any who planned to abandon the city ahead of any unpleasantness would have to use their own legs - or those of their bearers.

Now with far less haste than my arrival at the port, I walked back to the Avenue of the Gods, stopping at an open air wine merchant for a cup and some repast. I made no attempt to listen to the individual conversations within ear reach, but I could tell that the talk was of the uncertainty of the future. I had no idea if the citizen of the street would welcome a new leader, one who was of their own kind, or if they would rather that the days just flow by with little change and excitement. Or, even, if they knew of the import of the rumors beyond a vague fear.

At the temple, I could not speak to Senemut as he was engaged in... priestly things, and was unavailable, but I left word with an acolyte, in a cryptic message, that all had gone well and that his man was on his way downriver. With that, I just strolled back to the inn, my need for any action gone. In fact, I was at a loss as to how to spend my time, with my friend away for a year, at least, and little action to be taken on my tentative plans to began a shipping merchantry - at least, until the end of the flood season. My encounters with Ravana would be pleasant, but a man soon gets a surfeit of pleasure after the coupling has taken his desire for the day. Not even a newly fledged youngster, rutting for the first uses of a female, could spend his entire time and being on the mat with a female. I needed something else to fill my days.

Auxilitator (Aide)

The name that the city was known by in the rest of the world is actually from the Greek phrase, "The Good Place," and for whatever reason, Memphis was also the label used by the Persians overlords. Of course, the natives of the city did not use a foreign word in their own land and called it Ineb-Hedj, or Inbuhedj. I eventually found that the term meant, "The White Walls," though why I do not know and never found the reason - they were made of the same yellow brick as most other structures that they enclosed. The massive ramparts were many stadia in length - so long that a man would take most of a day to walk around them, to return to his starting place with throbbing sinews in his legs.

For size, I knew of no other in the world that even approached the area enclosed by the walls, and that was only a part of the city. Most of the population lived in shanties and mud huts on the outside. As I have written, the area that posed as a forum for the Egyptians - the huge flats around the port - was many times the size of the Forum in Rome or the Agora in Athens. Unlike the avenues and streets of my home city, winding through and around the seven hills of Rome, and the city of Athens, bounded by the massive rock of the Acropolis, Memphis was on absolutely flat ground. The main thoroughfares cut straight through the city, the Avenue of the Gods running from north to south, and the Street of the Heavens from east to west. One could stand at any of the main gates and see many stadia along the thoroughfares - the vision only disrupted by the palace complex at the center of the city. There, the roads intersected with a circular plaza that encompassed the walls of the palace and its compound. Only as one entered the areas of the lesser folk of the city, did the streets and alleys become more irregular.

And, like all cities, the nobles clustered together in their own area, in this city, around the palace. Beyond them were the wealthy merchants, then those that were merely affluent, and so on, down to the ordinary vendors and venturers and shopkeepers that were greatly in the majority of the productive city folk. Finally, and mostly outside the walls, were the dregs and sediment of the people, garnering life from day to day in a most uncertain manner.

Both Rome and Athens had many shrines and temples, but the count of both together was as a single kernel to an ear of corn to the number in the city of Memphis. Again, as I have written, the Temple of Ra was gigantic, with statues in stone of some ruler in the far past, each of which was carved on the scale of the huge tombs to the north.

Many times did I just stand in inspection of the many stone likenesses in the city, wondering if they had been carved in place, or produced at some far quarry and brought her by some unimaginable troupe of laborers. It seemed impossible that enough men could be placed around the images to even shift such massive stones, and far less to move and upright them.

Other temples and shrines were evident on any street and avenue inside the walls. A man could not stand in a street, in any part of the city, where his eyes could not glimpse a building of some god or goddess. Sekhmet, Ra, Hathor, Apis is only a very short list of the names of deities, besides Amun, which were worshiped by the people. I wondered if all Egyptians worshiped the list in total, or did they pick and choose the divinity that mostly garnered their attention.

The city was in a state of... not quite turmoil, but there was an undercurrent of fear that could be felt in the vending areas and taburnae. The talk around the grain-spirit and wine tables was centered on the rumors of the approaching army to the north and little else. Soldiers still appeared in the streets, marching here and there, but with no discernible purpose - until they began to descend on the houses and merchantries of the to seize this man or that, and only those of Egyptian extraction. The actions by the magistrates were not numerous, but it was obvious that any man whose fidelity to the current rulers was being examined. And according to the talk of the tables, some men returned and some did not.

For the nonce, Ravana and I walked the streets as a guest from afar, exploring and discovering this and that. She had actually learned much of the city from her native-born attendant and gave me facts and notices that I would otherwise have missed. Those few days after the departure of the ship were lazy indeed. Until a few days later...

The inundation by the Nilos had begun. We joined the massive crowd at the riverbank to watch the festivities and the incantations of the priests before the monument that abutted into the water itself. I had seen the stone edifice before but gave it no thought until now. In the river, just off the stone abutment, was an obelisk, straight sided and with only carvings on the side facing the city, and these were just horizontal marks with a number underneath. It was obvious that this was a method of determining the rise for fall of the water level.

I had assumed that the annual flooding was just a nuisance that had to be endured by the citizens of the land, but Senemut had corrected that belief with some emphasis. "Without the flood, the land of Egypt dies - and quickly. Even now, when the waters are insufficient, famine can spread through the land, and if they are overabundant, then whole villages and fields may be washed away." Interested, I asked him for more information. "The waters bring new soil from up the river, and when they recede, the fields are covered with fertile earth that brings forth the grain that feeds all the land. At the start of the new moon, the priests will join together on the bank of the river, and cast forth supplications to Isis to bring us the waters, in beneficial abundance and with her blessing."

And today was that joining and supplication. We were far away in the massive crowd of citizenry, and could not hear the incantations and invocations, but I could see the sacred jug pour the sanctified water into the river and the wavings and gesturings of the priests. Little else could be seen of the ceremony, and I had decided to depart for some areas where my feet were not trod on by the citizens, standing shoulder to shoulder. I knew that all taburnae on this side of the city would soon be packed to overflowing with men wanting to assuage their thirst after the observance, so I set our feet toward the wineshop near the Temple of Ptah, far into the city proper. But, we had not even reached the gate to enter...

"Junius, the Roman. You will come with us and with haste. Woman, do not cry out on the life of your mate."

With my blood rushing, I looked to either side to see three men, all Egyptian and young - even youthful. Brigands, or worse, no doubt. None had drawn the weapon in their belts, but all had a hand on the hilt. I would be made less than ragout for the cookpot before I could even begin to draw my longknife, and I did not attempt to do so. There was little else but to follow the leading man. In a fast walk, but as men on an important errand, rather than as fleeing from a crime, we moved along the wall on the outside of the city. In only a short time, I was lost in the maze of crooked streets and pathways in the lower section of the city. Had I not been able to see the massive wall to the west, towering over huts and shanties, I would not even have known the direction that we were traveling.

My puzzlement grew. These were strange bandits, to leave a man with his weapon - and his purse - rather than just take us to the closest shanty and finish the robbery. And to know the name of the random man on the street that they were accosting. Far around the city we walked until we had completed a fourth part of the distance around. Had there been a waterclock to measure the time, we had been walking for at least an hour.

Suddenly, the man stopped before a hut, even more shabby than most, and said, "Enter, Roman. Nay, ask no questions of me." I was about to demand an explanation, but thought better of it, and entered the hut. Inside was... nothing. Some crude woven mats were on the floor, but no table, chair or bench. Once inside, a straw cover was placed across the door - nothing to keep anyone out - or in - but now the inside of the hut was shielded from view for any passersby.

Left alone, we just stood for a few heartbeats, then Ravana asked in a low, but urgent voice, "What is happening? Who are these men?" That was exactly the knowledge that I wanted and had no inkling of.

I shook my head. "I cannot say. They are not common street bandits - I still have my weapon and purse, and you, the gold bands on your arms. Neither are they men of the King, or we would be in the palace jakes even now. And... they know my name." Indeed, I was at a total loss at the actions of the men. If they wanted not our wealth, then...

Finally, we sat on the straw, waiting for... whatever was to come. I loosened my longknife in my belt, but I would have had little chance of success against three men or more. We would just...

The straw door was moved aside and a man - a different one - entered, and bowed. That gave me a feeling of relief - thieving brigands did not give motions of respect to their victims before the robbery. Both of us began to rise but ceased as the man waved us to remain seated. He also sat, cross-legged, in front of us.

"I come from a friend, Roman. One who I cannot name, but who shares your desire for knowledge. At least, that is what I was commissioned to say." Obviously, he was speaking of Senemut. "You were about to be seized by the magistrates - and in fact, they were at your inn of domicile even as we accosted you and your mate at the ceremony."

"Seized for what reason?" My relief that this action was initiated by my friend at the temple was almost palpable.

"That I cannot say, Roman. But, far more men than you have been hauled to the keep cells without known reason. However, if you wish a speculation by one who has little to know, then I suspect that you are just an unknown quantity to the men around the King, and they dislike such uncertainty in this time."

The man was not a hired thug from the street. His diction was too pure to be an uneducated hire. He was either a junior priest or trained in a temple as I was.

"So... What are we to do? One hopes it is not to just sit in this hut for the indefinite future."

The man shook his head. "Nay. At darkfall you will be on a boat to the Delta."

"The Delta? I thought river use was impossible during the inundation."

Now the man actually laughed. "You would not be suspected for a longtime resident of this land, Roman. The flood has not even begun in actuality. What you see now at the riverbanks is only the first piddle of Isis to what is to come." He waved his hand. "It will be a safe boating."

I still had many questions and few answers. "Just myself and my... mate? I am feeling gratified at our implied importance, to have the Am... a powerful man worried about our welfare."

The man looked around the hanging straw curtain, then answered, "As to your importance, Roman, I have no cognizance, but you will have the company of a few others whom the powers consider to be at risk by the accursed mongrel that sits on the purloined throne of Egypt. For now, sit and pass the hours until darkfall." He rose and left.

And we did sit and wait, having no other choice. We might have suddenly run from the hut to escape, but to where? I had no reason to doubt that the man was telling the truth. I had done nothing since my arrival but tour the city, openly, and even that had never taken me near the barracks and soldier areas of the city. Of course, I had hurried the departure of my ship to prevent its seizure by the regime, or whoever desired its use, but it was done in the guise of a normal sailing. None but myself and Senemut knew of the reason for haste - except for the two men on the ship, now far down the distributary of the Nilos. As the sailing before the imminent inundation was normal practice, that could not be the reason for accostment by the magistrates.

It was totally dark before the same man - and with a companion with a torch - came to fetch us. I was handed a heavy scroll with the words, "Take this with you, Roman, and deliver it at your destination. If you are accosted, throw it in the river. Do you understand?"

"Aye. But who do I give it to, and where?"

"You will be met. That is all that I can say because that is all I know. Hamer, here, will guide you to the boat. Now go."

Our guide was not of the educated class, but obviously of the alleys and shanties of the vast destitute area of the city. He could barely connect two words in a row. With a grunt, he ordered us to follow, and we meandered here and there through the maze of mud huts and straw enclosures. For all the gold in the temple of Jupiter, I could not have given our course that night, but eventually, we came to the river where a fishing boat - it appeared to be - was waiting, and with three other men sitting in the bottom.

More grunts and some incomprehensible calls in return, and we felt ourselves being pushed into the open waters, then four men with poles, outlined against the brilliant starry sky, began to push us down the river.

Fortunately, the voyage was short, propelled as we were by both the actions of the men on the poles and the rising river. The sun was barely above the horizon when we grounded in a cove on the western side of the distributary. Several boats were there, most drawn up onto a high mound - apparently made for the purpose of allowing the craft to sit out the coming floods.

We followed our grunting guide through the greenery of the Delta - not trees or bushes, but soft plants with big leaves, and totally unlike any growth that I had seen elsewhere. Men began to appear, here and there, and not farmers, but soldiers with spears and blades of innumerable types. Actually, soldiers was too specific a term for men who were both garbed and armed in ways that had no likeness to their mates. Obviously, these were members of the rebel faction that had been taking over the cities of the Delta.

Finally, we came to a large clearing that contained few men, but innumerable tents, and what looked like to be the huts of a village. At the entrance to a straw shanty were two guards, standing on either side of the opening, with grounded spears. As we approached, a man - an officer, obviously - appeared through the doorway and challenged us as to our business. "A courier from Inbuhedj," replied our guide.

The officer looked at me and I handed him the scroll that had been given to me in the city. He looked at the inscription beside the wax seal, then handed it back. The he motioned for myself to follow into the hut. I waved for Ravana to wait, then followed to find a single individual sitting on a bundle of straw, and reading from one of several clay tablets stacked on the floor. "Your pardon, Ami-re." announced the officer. "A courier from the south, and with a scroll to be delivered to your hands only."

I had not even examined the roll of papyrus since obtaining it, but I glanced at the inscription written next to the wax seal. Now I saw the words, "To be delivered into the hands of Ami-re Amyrtaeus by the Junius the Roman, and without delay." So, this was the rebel of the Delta. And I had learned another word - obviously, Ami-re was coincident to the Latinium word Generalis.

The General nodded, and held out his hand for the papyrus as his officer disappeared. I just stood wondering on my next action. I certainly could not just turn my back and depart his presence without an order to leave. Thus, I just stood, waiting as he read the lengthy missive.

Finally, he looked up at me for a few heartbeats, then motioned for me to sit in front of him. "So. You are Roman."

"Aye... Ami-re," was my reply and fervent hope that the honorific was correct and meant what I thought. "From Rome, itself, but several years have gone by since my leaving."

He pointed to the scroll. "The Amun-Wab speaks well of you, and gives that you have made some assistance in our endeavors." This man was also well educated, and lucid of speech. My earlier thoughts of the insurgent forces being illiterate farmers, and led by such, were shown to be wrong. As to my assistance, he must have been speaking of the carriage of his agent on my ship, leaving just ahead of seizure by the city powers.

"Very minor, Ami-re. It was no courageous tale to be bandied about by the street bards."

He queried about my past, of my education in the Temple and travels around the perimeter of the Great Sea. In my mind was the question of why. A leader of soldiers about to commit to battle should be conversing with his commanders about tactics and such, not with questions about an aimless foreigner.

"You have come from Athens, it is written." I nodded. "Know you of the disputes between the two Greek factions - the two great cities in the north and south of the land?"

"Aye, Ami-re. And in fact, I know a vast amount about the strife. It is the reason that I am in this land." He asked, and I gave him the true story of my military service for Athens, and the aftermath leading to my flight from the land. I could tell that he was fascinated, and continued to ask probing questions throughout my talk.

As I came to the end, he asked, "So... You have a knowledge of that land, as one who has actually lived there." I wasn't sure if it was a question or if he was just musing to himself. "The Amun-Wab writes that you are a scribe of unusual acuteness, fluent in several languages and numberings. He suggests that I might find a use for such."

Once again I had reason to thank the gods for my casual friendship with the priest, Senemut. He had not only pulled me from the jaws of possible death but had tried to assure my future, rather than consigning me to the plight of a fleeing refugee. "Aye, Ami-re. I have the wish to settle in this land, and would assist the peoples in retrieving it from the conqueror. If I may, I would assist in that mission."

Thus it was that I became an aide to the General and more than that, even. The city of Naukratis, on the western distributary of the Nilos, about halfway along the side of the Delta, was an Egyptian city, but there was more to its history than that mere statement. Long ago, some obscure Pharaoh - with the name of Amasis - became friendly with the men of the Grecian lands, and granted them privileges, including the use of a small village on in the Delta that they might use as a trading post. Over the years, the post grew into a considerable city, and became, in effect, a snippet of Greece far to the south. There, temples and sanctuaries were erected to Zeus and the Grecian gods, and it became a large and wealthy gateway between the two lands, enduring even into the conquests by the Persians.

It also became an aggregation point for mercenaries, mostly Greek, but from all corners of the world. Men who were too undisciplined to fight in the army of their lands, or who had little patience with years of garrison duty and inactivity without strife. And, it must be said, that many left their lands between dark and daylight, just ahead of the magistrates - or the executioner. Without loyalty to any land, or any cause, they would fight with best effort for a leader as long as his gold was sufficient.

It was to the leaders and sub-officers of such irregular units that I now composed orders on papyrus, to be sent each morning by runner. Or to decipher the irregular scratches sent to Amyrtaeus from such commanders - scrolls and tablets from scribes who would have been sent reeling with contempt from the halls of the Grecian or Roman scrivener-guilds, had they applied. Indeed, many of their missives took considerable thought by myself to ascertain what they were attempting to report.

My immediate superior, between myself and the General, was a man who always saluted with his off-hand. That was necessary since he was missing the other. The soldier was of his middle years, and with an armband signifying that he was of some considerable rank. That I found on the instant that he walked up to me, saying, "I am Kahma, Imi-het of the first rank." I guessed that the rank of Imi-het was something close to Centurion, or Optio, had he been in the army of Rome, and obviously assigned to staff duties because of his disfigurement. And there was no doubt that he and the General had shared much of their lifetime together - he was never barked at by his commander. Rather, the pair spoke almost as equals, when not in the vicinity of others.

It was too much to expect that we would be given a tent, but eventually, a soldier of some rank guided us to a shabby hut with open sides and a woven cover to give shade during the day. Before the sun set, a man bought us another flat of woven reeds to act as our mat and gave us instructions to find the cookeries of the camp.

My worries of having the only woman in a camp of rowdy men was without need. Many were the females around the area, assisting in the duties as if they were at home on their grain farms or fisheries. Of course, after some thought, I remembered that this was an army of rebels, and as such, did not subscribe to the usual formations of men marching to war. Unpaid, they had to have some reason to stay with the formation other than just the will to cast off the hand of the Persians.

"Why do we stay?" asked Ravana that night, after our meal of a grain slurry, bread and cheese. "What have we to gain by associating with a group of rabble that believes it is an army?"

Our shanty was under some wide leafed trees, if such soft wood can be called that, and away from the other assortment of tents, and crudely fashioned huts. As such, we could speak in private, as long as our voices were kept moderate. "If we depart this land, then our chances of ever finding Korax again are minimal, and I do not wish to lose the only friend I have in the world. Also, we would forfeit the considerable wealth we have in the Temple of Amun and our ship. My purse is heavy, but not with an amount to keep us for our lives."

We watched a motley group of irregulars walk past, then I turned back to Ravana. "And, I wish to stay in this land, as should you. If you have any remembering at all, women do not just roam at will, as if they were street urchins, in Rome, or Athens, as you have done in Memphis."

She nodded, then said, "I will say that my time in the city was good. But I have hopes that we do not end our visit hanging by the heels from the walls."

That was my wish also, but I was abiding the wisdom of Senemut, who had given that the chances of this interloper king were good. We would see. It was either that, or stand out into the unknown world again. "We have cast the bones and the game must be played to the end." Suddenly, I saw Kahma walking towards us at a goodly stride, then rose to wait his pleasure. In a low voice, I said, "And we may see the result of our play, now."

He stopped before us and said, "The commanders are gathering, and our movement will be soon. You have been invited to accompany myself with the center force, as a scrivener, should I need to send missives. Procure a bag of writing materials from the quartermaster."

So... I was to be a soldier. Was it possible that the gods of Egypt had some knowledge of the games that were played on the heights of Olympus, and had determined to continue the play of their northern counterparts? That was a question for night, waiting for sleep to come, but for now, I just nodded, and he continued. "Have your woman prepare a bag with three days rations. We will depart at first light."

"Aye... Might I ask our destination?"

With a glint in his eye, he said one word, "Inbuhedj."

Triumphus

To my questions about Ravana, Kahma assured me that the women were as safe here as they could be anywhere. They would stay in the grove, protected by the elder soldiers and non-combatants until we were victorious, or fleeing for our lives back through the Delta foliage.

The latter seemed to be the most likely outcome, to my way of thinking. The men of the army were... irregular at best, and that is stretching the word out of all proportion. They were... Well, the description of Ravana told it best - rabble, all. Clothed in rags, the loincloths and kilts were ragged and torn, and in many cases, missing altogether. To my comment on that last, Kahma gave to me that many an Egyptian army, from the beginning of time, fought as bare as the day they came into the world, and these men were just following that ancient tradition. Still, it was startling for a man used to seeing Roman and Greek soldiers armored from their shinbones to the top of their head, to watch a unit of men marching past as if they were about to enter the thermae for the evening bathing.

The weapons, also, were of the same finish as the wielders. Blades, spears, axes, knives from the meat shop, gaffs of fishermen... anything that would club, or cut, or stab could be seen and in all stages of condition - bent, rusted, green with corrosion and with some in such a condition that I could not determine if it was actually a weapon.

Then, the army itself as a whole did not give me a feeling of being with a unit seriously considering warfare. I had seen a Roman legion marching, rank after rank, past the city and move and turn as a single organism. Even the Greek Hoplites were impressive in their maneuvers, each man following his mate as if connected with ropes. But these men rambled along, as a mob walking to the taburnae after the day's work. Should one tire, he would step out of the stream of men and settle back for a rest, unbothered by any officer or superior. To my utter dismay, some groups at the wayside had enlivened their rests with a game of bones.

As we walked, I began to plan for the inevitable destruction of this meandering rabble, destined to feed the scavengers in a massive feast. From what I had seen of the garrison troops of the city, the foe that these Egyptians would face was not a hardened army - but still...

When they broke and began their inevitable panicked flight, I would hurriedly retire to the rear, find Ravana, then move north to a city where berths could be obtained to the port city of Pelusium. There we would stay until our ship, with Korax and Ehsan, appeared on the horizon. We might have to wait for most of a season, but that was no matter. There was coin enough in my purse to support us for that time. And hers - I had split my metal, giving her half to hold in the hopes that a loss of a purse by either would at least leave us with enough to take ship away.

Interestingly enough, Kahma did not seem concerned. He was a real soldier, telling me of battles and wars without end. Even allowing for the natural expansiveness of the usual veteran, I had no doubt that he had been in many a battle, from the time of his attaining full growth. I could not understand his lack of concern with this jape of an army. He just smiled at my worries and gave back statements of unconcern. "They have a duty to perform, and they will do it well - have no fear about that."

In our walk, I learned something about my escort. He was naturally expansive - soldiers usually have little else to do when not in action but talk. His age and missing limb naturally precluded his standing in any formation for battle, but apparently his deeds in the past were sufficient for him to be considered a valuable observer, watching and sending reports to superiors for their use. Of course, that was obvious since he reported directly to the Ami-re, which reinforced my suspicion that the old soldier was a comrade to the General from far back in time.

I wondered where the General was - he definitely was not leading this mob, and in fact, I had not seen him since leaving the encampment. If he expected this riffraff to confront the enemy and emerge victorious, then my thought was that he might wish to obtain a berth on the same ship as us. To my question as to the whereabouts of that august individual, my soldier companion said, "He is where he is supposed to be - at the head of his army." Before I could point out that there was no indication of any but junior officers at the lead, he continued, "But, this is not the only army that he commands." Aye, I remembered that he had said that we would accompany the center force, and that statement presumes others on either side.

"Will they assault the walls of the city?" I asked. I had seen no indication of ladders, and it was unlikely that the Persian rulers would leave the gates open, once word of our march had arrived in the city.

Kahma shook his head. "Eventually, maybe, but only after we scatter their force that will be sent to meet us." We were walking in a wide open area, grain fields obviously, but fallow and dry at the moment. To the eastern direction was a distributary of the Nilos, while to the west was uncut Delta foliage. He had said earlier, that this entire area, for a day's march in any direction, would soon be under the flood. It was difficult to believe that such a volume of water could flow down a single river, to cover an area almost the size of the domain-lands of Rome, but I had no reason to think that I was the butt of a jest.

"The Persians will march out to meet us, as there are far too few in the garrison to mount any defense of the walls. Besides, they have much contempt for the fighters of the Delta. As they say, 'One soldier of the Achaemenid empire is worth ten of these dirty Egyptians.'"

By the name, he meant Persian, but the statement, if true, was a mark for the army of the rebels. Any force that denigrates their foe before the battle has already received a stunning blow. That lesson I had well learned.

Kahma continued his lecture, more to pass the time than any desire to educate a foreign observer. "No reinforcements can come up the flooding river for many moons, and the garrison at Karnac will hesitate to strip itself of defenses. The Achaemenide have been occupiers of this land for a hundred years, and they have grown complacent, thinking that the feeble revolts by a few demagogs is an indication of the backbone of Egypt."

The ground was beginning to turn to sand, with the foliage on both sides of the wide clearing becoming thin and short. We were obviously on the southern edge of the Delta, about to enter the desert lands. The men halted by some order, and formed their encampment groups, although none had tents, or sleeping mats, even. Nothing was carried but weapons and a bag containing their rations. Fortunately, water was plentiful here, even if several stadia away to the east.

"We will remain here, waiting for the dross of the satrap to come to attend. Already, spies will have informed the ass-king of our presence."

Nothing happened for the rest of the day. In our rear, men were working on... something - I could see dirt flying in the air, but the reason for their labor was beyond my vision. That night we slept with sand for our mat. The next day was the same, with men coming and going at the circle of the commanders, but the troops doing nothing but resting. Of course, the day had barely started when pieces of sticks were carved into the proper shape, and the inevitable game of knucklebones began at every camp circle.

For myself, it was just a tedious wait under a hot sun. How the commander - whoever he was - knew that we would be noticed, I had no idea, but it must have been from the constant coming and going of runners - no doubt scouts, or messengers for such. I knew that we could only stay here for a handful of days before the ration bags would be empty and the men would have to disperse to find food.

The ration bags did not empty.

On the morning of the third day, we could see a dust cloud approaching - the vanguard of the Persian army - or garrison, to be more accurate. To the front, once the foe came into a reasonable distance, I could see horses, paired and towing wheeled transports with two men. These had to be the war wagons that I had seen carved into the walls of innumerable temples and obelisks. Possibly there were ten or twelve in number. To my pointing, Kahma said, "Aye. Chariots. The satrap garrison has a handful, but few in their ranks with knowledge to use them properly." He waved his hand in a wide sweep. "The tales tell of the armies of old, of this Pharaoh and that, covering the ground with such for the distance of a young man's eye. Those were the days when the armies of Egypt could be heard long before they were seen, from the thunder of many feet and wheels."

It took a Roman hour or more, but eventually, the enemy was lined in front of us, more than two stadia away, with the chariots loping back and forth across out vision - no doubt for the purpose of impressing the rabble of the Delta with the power of the satrap king. Kahma looked around, then said, "Be at the ready. They will charge us soon, hoping to put us to flight." For some inexplicable reason, he grinned. "And they will find it even easier than they hope."

Be ready for what, I wondered? To fight? Myself with a longknife and my aged escort with one hand? Then, with an even more perplexing statement, he said, "Come. We will move back and to the side. When the chariots come, they will naturally move toward the middle of our formation."

We were at the rear of the mass of Egyptians, being, supposedly, observers rather than fighters, so our walk was unhindered by any in our way. At the edge of the fallow fields, we stopped and just stood, watching. I knew nothing of land battles, but this confrontation of two rag-tag armies would be my first. And hopefully, not my last.

"The priests are giving the auguries for the battle." He pointed to a small group of figures, in advance of even the chariots, standing and waving their arms. "They will begin the charge soon. Come, we will wait for them beyond our defenses."

What defenses? The ground was as flat as a temple floor as far as could be seen, north and south. We retraced our steps to the rear, and soon we came to a... a... It took a moment, but I could see that the dirt that I had seen flying in the last two days was actually in the construction of a trench spanning the entire width of the fallow grain fields. Not deep, but I began to realize that it was a sufficient obstruction to a wheeled chariot. Apparently, there was more leadership to this motley army than I had imagined.

We did not stop at the trench. Kahma continued to walk a considerable distance until we approached a group of men standing in the center of the vast clearing and next to a tall pole with a banner waving in the wind. We did not approach, since it was obvious that these were officers, but stopped at the western edge of the field at the beginning of the uncut foliage. I was about to ask about the group, but my escort pointed, and said, "The battle begins."

Far away, I could see the dust rise as the garrison troops of the city began their advance. It was difficult to see any details at that distance, but it appeared that the chariots were trotting at the pace of the following men. I knew nothing of wheeled warfare, but that seemed to be a wise choice, to conserve the strength of the horses until close to contact with the foe. The two sides were about evenly matched in numbers, but the Persians gave by far the more look of a disciplined army. They were advancing in marching ranks while the Egyptians milled around like a mob watching a spirited game of bones in a wine-shop. This could not end well.

"They charge!" Kahma pointed. In only moments, the dust obscured the battle, if that is what it was, at the point of contact and the distance gave only moderate sounds of men in combat. Soon, to my dismay, I could see that my predictions were becoming true, and even more quickly than I had feared. Already, men were leaving the dust cloud, to lope from the fray and towards our position. In a while, other men appeared, but running as if the furies were chasing them. And, of course, such actions are contagious to their fellows, who assume that the worst has happened. As we watched, more and more men ran from the cloud of dust, to flee frantically down the fields towards us. My predictions of disaster were coming true even faster than I had feared.

We would need to flee ourselves, and quickly, as the garrison troops would soon appear through the cloud of dust in pursuit of their prey. I looked at Kahma, then froze in stupefaction at seeing the smile on his face. Far from dismay at the utter defeat that we were viewing, he was standing at ease, as one viewing a tedious foot-race in the Circus. My mind raced with thoughts - that my escort was an agent of our enemy, or that he was one of those fighters who welcomed conflict, no matter the odds and the dangers. Or...

Should I run, to save my own skin? Or try to disappear into the Delta foliage only a half stadium away to the west? Finally, in desperation, I asked, "What do we do? This battle is lost!"

Again the smile. My escort shook his head. "Nay. The battle has not begun as yet."

That statement was utterly without meaning, as I could see the results of the rout of the Egyptians. Men were leaping the ditch, a stadium or so ahead of our position, then continuing their flight across the fields. No man could deny that this day was a disaster for the insurgents of the Delta. That Kahma was claiming that a battle had not taken place was utterly absurd.

The first of the fleeing men had gained the area across from us, in line with the banner that was in the middle of the field. As I watched in puzzlement, they stopped their flight and turned to view the land over which they had just run. More and more men ran to the line and stopped, turning to face the way they had come. This was not the usual manner of defeated men, fleeing for their lives.

Now, through the dust I could see the several chariots in full gallop, with the man at the reins, hunched down behind the wicker-work and controlling with his leathers, and the archer or spearman shooting or throwing as they passed the Egyptians. More than once, I saw a man ridden down by the hoofs of the horses, or the wheels of the chariots. Then, they reached the ditch, finally seeing the barrier and drawing their steeds to a halt before it. The tide of Egyptians began to recede like the waves on the shoreline, as all that were still living gained the new position and waited in line with their fellows.

The garrison foot-soldiers, following the chariots, did not stop at the ditch, but leaped it and continued their headlong pursuit of their panicked foe. Except...

I looked along the line of Egyptians. They gave no aspect of being the terrified men that had broken at the first contact of the battle. Rather, they waited without movement, those with spears leveling them toward the rapidly approaching foe. This was unreal, as if... "What is happening?" I asked my escort, with force.

He just said, simply, "Wait..."

The onrushing soldiers of the city's garrison began to realize that their prey was not still fleeing in panic. The front ranks began to slow, rather than rush headlong individually into what was now a dense line of men and weapons, but after the pause, they charged into the line of Egyptians. This was a battle now, and no mistake. But, unlike before, the line of Delta men stood firm, giving as good as they received and even more. I had my longknife out, as the lines began to lose form in the melee, and some of the garrison soldiers were beginning to approach our position, some distance to the west of the actual line.

Then, the reason for all I had seen became apparent. In the distance, and now behind the Persians, men appeared from both sides of the grain fields, leaving the foliage of the Delta and forming ranks as rapidly as they could move. Then, with some unseen order, or signal, they began a rapid march toward the melee of men fighting in the center of the fallow fields.

With sudden insight, I realized that the Ami-re Amyrtaeus was just that, a General, and not just a man who could rouse men to revolt. He had allowed the garrison of the city to attack what they assumed to be the rebels of the Delta, giving orders to the men break at the first contact as if their manhood had been destroyed by the mere sight of armed Persians. Now, those men of the city, winded from their long charge down the field, and with strokes to and from the line of Egyptians, did not even realize at first, that their doom was approaching from behind.

I could see that the approaching formations were unlike the naked or kilt garbed Egyptians, now fighting in the line across the field. These new troops - or most of them - were accoutered in the Greek fashion, with very long spears and round shields. On their heads were the strange helms of the hoplite. Of course, in the heat of this land, few, if any, had the armor that would be worn by their comrades in cooler climes. Rather than a torso of leather, their chests were bare and fewer, even, had greaves on their shins. The garb of most was a loincloth, or ragged tunic. These were the mercenaries from the city of Naukratis.

But they strode forth with the disciplined march of the veteran.

Even had the garrison soldiers of the city been fresh and well led, they were now outnumbered by three or four to one, and without path of retreat. Firstly, the chariots, surprised, and with their riders dismounted and attempting to find a way past the ditch, were overwhelmed and slaughtered - long spears making short work of rider and archer both. Then the regiment of men began a fast stride to the assistance of their fellows. Now, the Persians began to realize their plight as the cries and shouts of dismay began to rise, but to turn to the new foe was to give their backs to the old. The Egyptians had feigned panic, but that of the garrison soldiers was now real, as they gave in to their actual terror and began to disperse, trying to find a way from between the closing millstones.

The position of the sun had barely moved by the time that the men of the garrison were cut down, almost to a man, by a blade in the back, or a spearpoint in the chest. A few attempted to run to the enclosing foliage on either side of the wide grainfields, but few finished the journey. A handful the youngest and fleetest of foot approached our position in blind panic, most having discarded weapons in their terror. I suddenly realized that the two of us were about to begin our own battle and brought myself to the stance that I had been trained by the old soldier in Athens. Kahma had his own blade pulled from his belt, but said, "Nay. Let them pass without hinder."

That was a welcome order to myself, even if I did not understand the reasoning. My escort was no coward - he would not be in his position of authority had he been - but I had assumed that the old soldier would welcome another chance to blood his weapon, especially against men who were already defeated in their minds.

The running men swept past us and disappeared into the greenery, although their paths could be seen for a considerable time by the sudden movement of fronds and brush that we could see across the low foliage. Kahma resheathed his blade, then said, "It is important that the word of this battle reach the city. Those men will deliver it in the manner most helpful to our cause."

Turning from the view of the fleeing soldiers, now gone from view, I gazed over my first sight of a battlefield on land. There was no method to determine the losses of either side, other than the fact that all of the Persian regiment was dead. I knew that there had been some casualties of the Egyptian forces, but those of their foe far outnumbered them. Before I could comment, Kahma pointed and said, "There is the party of the Ami-re. Let us make our report."

The Noble

Noblis

"Master. Your chair is ready." My steward looked at both of the slaves in the room, no doubt trying to find some fault in either their work or their deportment.

I nodded and started for the door of my sleeping room, asking the man as I passed, "And the mistress?"

He bowed slightly, and replied, "The Amatricis has departed, this hour, for the house of Siamun. She leaves word of her return after the noon meal."

We were speaking Latini, as the man with the name of Aulus was also from my land. And not from my city on the Tiber, but a small hamlet to the southeast - no doubt just a farming village. He had been the servant of a merchant who had actually traded in a three corner route - Rome, to Carthago, Memphis and back. At the demise of his master to the red demons that took him after a deep cut to his leg, made by shifting cargo one stormy night, the servant found himself stranded in a far city and without means to return. Upon hearing the tale of another from the land of Latium in the city, he presented himself at the door of my new domicile as a supplicant for work. On a whim, and the wish to converse with another man from my own land, I took him on as a calator, although I had no need for another footman.

But, he was intelligent and hard-working, and soon I gave him the position of Atriensis - steward of the house. His Egyptian was good, the result of many years of traveling here as the valet of his master.

In the courtyard, the lectica was ready, with three slaves on each end, and already standing between the poles. The factor that owned the rented conveyance bowed low and extended his arm in invitation to enter. I disliked carrying chairs, much preferring to use my legs for transport, but the Chamberlain of the Palace had made heavy hints about the impropriety of a noble arriving out of style. Thusly, I began to use the conveyance on my daily trips to the royal quarter and back.

Ravana, of course, reveled in the use of such, and would ride rather than walk even if the distance was absurdly short. I humored her foibles for such, knowing that she was enjoying the first real freedom in her lifetime - and one that few women in other cities of the world could have, being prohibited from leaving even their front doors without the accompaniment of a male.

Settling into the seat, and under the shade of the reeds, I nodded to Aulus, who immediately gave the order to lift and began the walk. Relaxing for the moment, I thought of my new position in the world.

In the six months since the victory in the Delta, the river had crested its flood, then gradually returned to its usual level, leaving the deposits of rich mud everywhere that the water had lapped. Soon ships would be appearing from the north, in the usual return of trade that was seen after the floods. Of course, it was far too early to expect Korax. By now, he would barely have reached his destination at the top of the Great Sea.

The city had also returned to normal, and with considerable enjoyment by the citizenry in the pride of a native Egyptian returning to the throne.

The Persians were less pleased, having vacated the city in panic, and by foot toward the south - the only route open to them in the flooding season. With the garrison destroyed, and the remaining authority mostly composed of native Egyptians, there was no chance at all to hold the city. Long before the general Amyrtaeus had marched his troops to the western gate, the Persian King and nobles, along with wealthy merchants and known collaborators had departed down the southern road to the city of Karnac, leaving behind their dwellings and properties to be looted.

We marched into the gate to the cheering of throngs of onlookers, myself in the party of the general and at the head. I was amused at my new standing, high in the estimation of the new King. I had done nothing to add to the victory, other than deliver a scroll on occasion, and give my opinion of the contents of one that had been received. But, for whatever reason, Amyrtaeus had confidence in my presence - possibly as seasoning to the vast numbers of natives trying for his trust.

The first order of business was telling off detachments to spread out into the city and quell the unrest, and to bring order to the chaotic celebrations. Soon, after a number of thieves and cutthroats were hung from the walls, the remainder scuttled back to their holes, and the city began the return to normal.

Having the advantage of friendship with the new king, and the temple of Amun, along with my considerable wealth, I was allowed to assume the abode of a wealthy merchant, next to the palace, for my domicile - that unfortunate Persian master no longer being in residence. Of course, the buildings and grounds were greatly disordered, after mobs of looters had entered to remove anything of value, but that was of no matter. As was true in any city of the world, gold can heal all wounds of property.

I engaged a factor that supplied a party of slaves, and the cleanup began. In only a few days the compound was cleaned of trash and broken items, then scrubbed to remove the excretions that the looters had left wherever they had found the need for relief.

The domicile was large - far larger than I needed or even wanted, but there was no harm in being seen as a powerful man who had the friendship of the king, and such men did not reside at an inn. Most of the slaves had departed with their masters - whether willing or no, I had no idea, but I was not enthused with the idea of a household with numerous bound persons, to plot and scheme and steal, as I had seen in many domiciles around the city.

Rather, while the river was still in its flood, I with little to do but wait on the King and converse with Senemut - or with other merchants in the wine-shops - I carefully selected a few servants for the household. Firstly was a cosmeta for Ravana, to assist in her... womanly things and needs. The very young girl was the only slave in the household, but she was cheerful and gladsome to be rescued from the inevitable brothel to which she was destined. Her duties included the concoction of a paste, made from the juices of plants, which she applied to her mistress before the evening, that in some way prevented the seed of a man from finding fertile soil. Ravana had always used suchlike from a small vial, brought even from Athens, but now the sticky paste was of a much sweeter effluence than the old.

An elderly widow, on a recommendation by a merchant acquaintance, became our cocus, to prepare our meals. Two young women, also newly made widows, would be famulae and an older woman as the diaetarius - the instructress to the pair of maids.

I had, as yet, little interest in making the assumed domicile as richly furnished as one of the wealthy of the city. As to the household, only the receiving room - known in Rome as the atrium - was furnished to excess, since this was the only part of the household that guests would see. Even my cubliculum - the sleeping room - was furnished with only a raised platform with a mat. A very soft and comfortable bed, to be sure, but still the only item in the room. As Ravana usually shared it with me, even her designated sleeping room was scarcely furnished.

Were I ever to take a wife, then she could assume the duties of filling a furnished domicile.

At the gates of the Palace, the guard captain saluted and motioned my chair to continue. In the forecourt, the factor of the lectica barked a command, and I was gently lowered to the ground. I passed a ring of copper to the man, then turned and entered the shade of the long columned entryway. Like all public structures in this land, the Palace was enormous. Just the long and straight walk to the throne room was, at least, half a stadium in distance. I had spent a considerable time in various halls and chambers of the building and had yet to see even a small part of the whole.

For this day, I walked past the room where the King - the Pharaoh, in the Egyptian vernacular - held his ceremonies and appearances, to an upper chamber with large openings that looked out over the city to the east. This was his favorite room, with comfortable furnishing on which to sit during the extensive planning sessions, and with a massive wooden table to hold all manner of tables and scrolls.

On one inside wall was the largest map that I had ever seen, by far, made of pasted sheets of thick papyrus. It was, at least, six long strides in length and three men lengths in height. But the size was not what interested me. This was the first representation of the entire world that I had ever seen. Many hours, at intervals over the months, I studied the picture of what I had only seen in my mind to this time.

All inscriptions on the map were in Egyptian, of course, and the names were unfamiliar as such, but I could recognize the Pillars of Hercules at the far western end of the Great Sea. Familiar places that I had actually visited were there - Sicillia, and Sardegna and the great projections of Latium and Greece. It was interesting to see that the city and domain of Sparta were actually on a huge island to itself - something that I had not known.

I could now see the route that my steward had traveled - Latium to Carthago to Egypt - and now it made sense. The voyage that Korax and I had taken to find ourselves in Memphis was a long journey around a vast shoreline. Athens, or Rhodes, or any city on the northern shore could be reached in a much shorter voyage by cutting directly across the sea. Whether that was possible or not, I did not know. The voyage would have to be made without landmarks of any kind, steering by the sun and stars, I assumed. There was much food for thought in both the map and possible voyages across it.

The Pharaoh, Amyrtaeus, was not a man to be impressed by his own importance. In my readings of history, I knew that the fact was unusual in the highest degree. Senemut had told me that the usual coronation of the King - in the past - could last a year or more of celebrations and festivals. Amyrtaeus allowed only seven days for the process, receiving the crown - the hedge - on the first day, then performing the shortened ceremonies during the next six. I was in the audience, to see the high priest of the Temple of Amun babble his chants to his god - and others - assisted in his infirmity by Senemut. The chants and benedictions and blessings went on for the entire day, broken only by the massive midday meal for all in attendance. By evening, my legs were throbbing from inactivity, and my mind was numb with the monotony of the procedures, few of which I understood the meaning of - nor even the words that were used.

He received the veneration of all the Priests on the second day, then the nobles of the city on the third and suchlike. On the seventh day, he made the Circumambulation of the White Walls, as it was called, allowing the peoples to glory in his majesty. I wondered from what the name of the procession had been derived, since as I have said, the walls of the city were of ordinary red mud brick.

Following the seven days, he became involved in restoring the city to the former greatness of Egypt, flushing out the few Persian magistrates still remaining, and revoking all laws given during the occupation of the last hundred years. Tax farmers were brought back under the control of the throne, and the men paid from the treasury, rather than from the proceeds of their work. According to Senemut, this act was one of the most significant that could have been made, as it removed much of the temptation for corruption by the money gatherers.

Ordinary citizens of Persian extraction were allowed to remain, and whole in their properties, as long as they gave feasance to the King. Those that had been evicted and looted during the chaos of the uprising were made whole, and the magistrates informed that any man could be a citizen, whatever his origin or birthplace. Only loyalty to the Pharaoh and the city were to be used for such measurements.

Amyrtaeus had had contacts with Sparta, far to the north, wishing to meld a common front against the Persians. To date, he had had many words of agreement, but little action from the Greeks, but now, with successful actions demonstrating that he was more than just a rebel leader in the Delta, the possibilities of an understanding with allies was greatly enhanced. I was in his group of advisers, most drawn from men who had been with him since his early days as a rebel. These were separate from the usual court hangers-on that apparently swarm around any monarchy in the word, and were trusted men of deed, rather than mere drones. Of course, I was as a new-born babe to the others, having been with the King for less than a season. Still, it was assumed that I had considerable knowledge of the lands to the north and, truthsome or no, I certainly had more familiarity than any in the group of advisors. Some had never even entertained the possibility that the Great Sea had a northern shore!

The formation of a regular Egyptian army had begun, since most of the rebels had returned to their farms and hamlets and cities of the Delta. Of course, the Greek mercenaries had been paid off and sent on their way. In no event, did the King want such a unit of men wandering the streets of Memphis, in their cups, looking for women and attempting to assuage their monotony until the next calling for battle. In the training of the new regiment, his units moved up and down the road to Karnac as security against a foray from that direction. It was doubtful that the satrap ruler of that city would attempt any real military action, as he had even fewer in his garrison than had Memphis, and was now blocked from any real support or trade with the lands of the Great Sea.

As the river fell, the activity around the waters resumed its normalcy. Fishing boats set out, as did the small river traders. Soon the seafaring trade ships would return, and missives were sent overland as far as Carthago, to spread the word that the Egyptian people were once again in charge of their own destiny, and a genuine Pharaoh was again on the throne. The merchant fleet that had scattered with the news of the rebellion should now return with haste.

I had decided that a shipping merchantry was a valid and profitable life for a man newly come to this country and with gold to fund his start, and began to make my plans to that effect. At the moment, I had only the one small river trader moving between Memphis and Pelusium, and the ship of Korax, at some unknown location far to the north. As shipbuilding was almost impossible in this treeless land, most vessels were purchased on the eastern shore of the Great Sea. When my friend returned, I would dispatch him to Tarsus, or Sidon - both ports of shipbuilding merchants - to purchase another hull of seagoing size.

Planting was in full course, with the dark wet land smoking in the morning sun. The flood had been of a goodsome level, and would bring a full and welcome harvest. As to the rising waters itself, I can only say that any man of Rome - or Greece, even - who had not actually seen the inundation would not believe more than a part of the description by a man who actually stood on the walls and saw the waters.

The Nilos river is the largest in the world, and even at low times is greater than all others that I have heard of, even should they combine their waters into one. But when the gods or demons or river sprites bring the flood, the quantity of water reaching for the sea is beyond belief. Where such a quantity of water could originate is beyond any reasoning of mortal man. As I had thought, even before the seeing of the swollen waters, had any river of such size existed that led from the Great Sea, that body would surely be drained to the bottom in a season.

I had asked Senemut of the origin of the inundation, but he shook his head and said, "Nay. Only the gods know. Many are the men who have set out to find the source of the blessing, and any that have returned have only given that the river continues on to the south without end. Some have reported a distance of two hundred and a half of iteru and still the river flows undiminished from the south."

I attempted to translate the Egyptian distance to something that would have meaning in my mind, but the numbers were too large without a tablet. Later, in my domicile, I began the figuring on wax and... The distance my friend spoke of was about... about... I flattened the wax and began again, unbelieving. The distance of MMMMM MMMMM MMMMM stadia was... I smoothed the wax and began even again in the Greek system of numbering. Shortly, I was looking at the still inconceivable number - MXXXXX. A myriad and five khiloi - a myriad plus a half myriad. Of stadia. Could such distance even exist in the world? How large was this playing domain of the gods, and did it continue without end in all directions?

As much as I had learned of the world, the amount that was still unknown was as vast as the waters of the Nilos.

Life was pleasant, and with meaning - at least for a rootless Roman, who had never found a land that he could consider his own. With my position on the council of the King and conspicuous wealth as a merchant, I began to receive invitations to this function and that gathering of the nobles and wealthy merchants of the city. All assumed, naturally, that Ravana was my wife-mate, and I made considerable effort to counter that assumption. My actual feelings for the woman were not as a mate, or even as a favored woman at a brothel. She was... as a close childhood friend that could be confided in, and whose company could be enjoyed just by their presence. The fact that she was also a desirable woman on the mat was just honey for the bread.

I knew that she would need to make a match before her beauty began to fade, else she would eventually live out her life as an old crone, helpless and without male protection in her age. My notices that she was an independent woman were sincere and aimed to find her a mate.

The Pharaoh was attempting to gain allies against the inevitable retaliation by the Persians to the loss of the rich hot lands - or at least, the city that was the gateway to the land. I scribed many scrolls to be delivered to the rulers of Sparta, proposing a combined front against their aggression. At the nonce, we were just waiting for the return of the seagoing ships, so as to engage their services in delivery of the missives.

Again, and often, I studied the gigantic map on the wall, realizing that a ship that took the direct course across the Great Sea would reduce the time of the voyage by two parts in three, at least. My wonder was if any captains had attempted the long reach across the trackless waters. I knew - from the tales of my steward, late of a ship that traded between Rome and Egypt, that many vessels made the jump across the waters of Carthago and Sicillia, but that was just mere step on a journey as compared to the vast distance from the Delta to Sparta.

With no men of the sea available for query, I asked Senemut about the notion of such a voyage and his reply and offer changed the course of my life - once again.

Librarium

The librarium was a treasure trove for such as myself. I could have spent my remaining days within the crypt, below the compound of the Temple. Tablets and scrolls without end - even loose stacks of papyrus - were stacked in shelves that were as a maze. Many were of ancient times and so old that the scrolls had to be handled with the utmost care, as the charts-material was as fragile as the web of an eight legged araneus. Of course, most of the ancient writings were unintelligible to myself, as the language was long forgotten. For instance...

The above script, today, means simply, "This offering for the Gods is pure." After much searching and painstaking comparison, I could reason that, in the language of a thousand years ago, the meaning was totally different, referring rather to the building of a... something, possible a granary. The pictures were the same, but the meaning of each and together totally different.

No matter. The number of writings that I could understand, even leaving out those from long ago, was far beyond the ability of one man to read in his lifetime.

When I had asked the question of the priest, Senemut, about the possibility of a voyage across the open sea, he had said, "You are as one asking a weaver about the making of bricks." He waved for me to follow, "There is one who was fortunate to be as free-footed as yourself."

As I followed, I knew of whom he spoke. The chief priest of Amun, the Amun-Rawab was not a stranger to me. After returning from the battle of the Delta, I had sat beside his raised bed several times before, speaking to the frail and ancient man. His thirst for knowledge of the world was even beyond mine, and apparently in his youth, he had seen much of it before returning to the fold of Amun. He queried myself about Rome, and Latium, Greece and any sights that I had seen along my lifetime. No detail was too insignificant for his desire for knowledge. And, in return, I had learned much from him about this land.

The two priests, old and young, were alike in temper. Both were aloof and hieratic when in public and woe unto the acolyte or citizen who gave insufficient respect to either Amun or his servants. But, in private, they were as educated men, caring nothing about slavish obeisances from others. As I have written, my younger friend even desired that I use his given name when we were alone.

In the room of the Priest Primus, I gave my greetings and hopes for another day of life for the ancient man. I had never seen him outside of his chambers, except on the day of the coronation of the Pharaoh. Indeed, he could scarcely walk, and moved only with pain, even with acolytes on either side as support. His remaining years could not be more than the lesser fingers of one hand.

Still, his mind was active and still sharp as a finely honed blade, and he nodded at my question. "Aye. It can be done by a master who is born to the sea, but pilotage is not a trait given to just any man who thinks himself a Subahdar of the ship. Most masters are competent enough, but their skill is in the handling of their vessel, not in the pointing of it. Their course is always within sight of land, moving from known landmark to the next."

He took a cup from the acolyte standing on the far side of the bed, then continued, "To be a pilot of a ship requires a knowledge of the stars, and the sun cycle, and still one may become lost should a long period of inclemency settle upon the sea." He stopped, apparently resting for the nonce, then, "I strove across the wide in a long dewatowe-ship as a lad, and the master had the sight of direction, but I never discovered the magic of the skill."

I had no idea of the description of the vessel from the strange word but assumed that it could not possibly have been an Egyptian-built river boat, as most of those were made of bundled papyrus reeds and would been as froth on the waves to any slightest blow. He called to an acolyte and received a small holder with a palm-sized tablet in the formers. A few words were scribed, then, accepting a scarab from the boy, he pressed it into the mud to imprint the official seal of the Temple of Amun. He handed it to the novitiate, who disappeared from the room.

"Present that tablet to the keeper of the records in the Temple of Ptah. It will admit you to the archives where you may find your answers."

That had been several months ago, when the tablet, baked to hardness, was given to me as proof of the trust by the Amun-Rawab. With that in hand, I was admitted to the crypts under the temple and to the myriad of scrolls and tablets stored within.

The Temple of Ptah, the Creator, was even larger than that of Amun, covering an area, at least, half the size of the Royal Compound.

Like all impressive Egyptian buildings, it was a forest of thick and tall columns, holding up slabs of stone far overhead. As in the Temple of Amun, Ptah was represented by a gigantic stone likeness in the huge receiving room, accessible from the street by all, including the common people. Behind that huge chamber, the bulk of the complex was forbidden to the uninitiated, of course, but I had access to a building that was far in the rear of the compound. Over the doorway was the inscription...

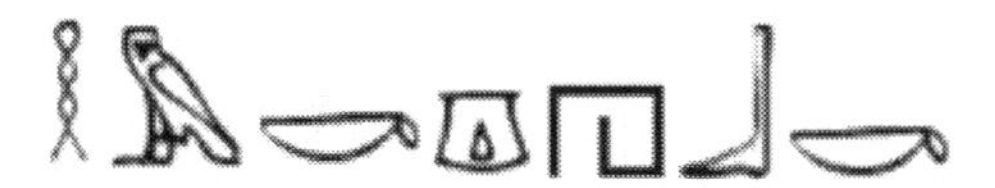

The first time I visited the building, I stopped to examine the writing, but it was totally meaningless, which meant that it was written in an older tongue. It was only after a considerable while - measured in months - that I finally deciphered the writing to mean, "The House of Writings." To a Roman, it would be "The Librarium." The building was older than Rome itself - vastly older.

Down the stone stairs, in the vast maze of rooms that held the scrolls and tablets - and some from a time unbelievably remote - no torches were allowed. The dry papyrus would have burned like pitch and in fact, the shelves were actually cubbyholes made of stone slabs, so as to minimize the spread of any fire that might be started. Many jugs of water were stored at intervals as a measure against such disaster. A small oil lamp was all that was allowed, and even that with the flame encased in a wire mesh of copper, and with only enough oil to last for the part of an hour.

Reading was impossible in such darkness, so any materials that were to be examined were brought up the steps and into the main building, generously supplied with tables and benches for the use of the readers. The wide openings in the walls and slits overhead in the ceiling gave ample illumination for examination of the materials.

Just as in the magisterial librariae in Rome, nothing could be removed from this building upon pain of death, and a young priest was always on watch at the door. But, unlike Rome, I needed no magistrate to retrieve the scroll or tablet - or loose sheet - that I wanted. I could roam the archives as I wished. In any case, unlike the librariae of Rome, this one had no list of materials, no index to the knowledge within, only rooms with items sorted by rough categories.

Actually, that was not completely accurate. The old priest in charge of the building and his apprentice were the index to the underground knowledge. He - and to a lesser extent, his helper - was a walking list to the treasure below, and I would always consult with the oldster before trying to locate any specific materials on my own. Except for the old man in charge of the archive, I was the only one whoever used the building - another difference from my home city. Apparently, Egyptians were forward looking, with little interest in examining their past. I made sure of his friendship, bringing extra food and drink from my home to share with him during the times that I spent in his domain.

For the first weeks, I just roamed here and there, trying to build a... a map in my mind to the literary treasures within. I had discovered, that not all were in the Egyptian picture script - there was a considerable quantity of scrolls and tablets from far countries, even Greece and Latium, and many foreign writings were from the lands to the east, most now under the domain of Persia. As I could not read the language of the latter, those had no interest to me.

I reveled in the history of this land, and others, wondering at the extent of trueness in the writings. One thing I learned, was that the battle in the Delta, just ended a few months ago, was not the massive conflict that I had assumed it to be. In the records were innumerable stories of military actions, any one of which would dwarf our battlefield as the Nilos dwarfs a piddling stream running into the Tiber after a storm. In fact, the numbers of men commanded by a Pharaoh named Ramses were so immense as to strain the belief of the reader, but many scrolls gave the same count, and I had to believe it to be within a close factor, at least. Our little army of the Delta would not even have been the King's guard to such a host that once covered the sands to beyond the reach of the eye.

Many times did I just sit and wonder at the question of how such power was overcome by the Persians, a people from afar and fighting at vast distances from their sources of men and supplies. Possibly the answer was in the maze below the House of Writings.

Just before the festival of Ra, a breathless lad ran into our household with gladsome news. This was a messenger-boy that I employed for various duties, mostly accepting this and that invitation, but also to query the port-master on a twice-daily basis for any inbound ships. His news of the ship of Korax and Ehsan slowing sailing into the port was a moment of joy.

After sending the boy elsewhere with a missive, and not waiting for a chair, I hurried down the long streets toward the eastern gate, then across the forum to the docks. The news was correct. There, only a stadium away, and preparing to turn into the wharfside, was my ship. And Korax standing on the bow, waving at myself. From the waterline of the vessel, I could tell that it was heavy loaded, assumably with trees again. Nothing else would have such weight.

I just stood waiting for the ship to slide up to the bank, helped by the polers on board, who then allowed vessel to drift against the wooden dock. Before it had stopped, I leapt over the side and strode up to Korax, arms open and in greeting. With a huge grin, he returned my embrace and said, "For the first time in my life, I am glad I lost the wager." At my puzzled look, he continued, still grinning like a jape, "I had staked two Tetrabols that your head would be on a pike at the wall, rather than still on your shoulders. I am overjoyed to see that you laid your own wager with the winning side."

Now I was grinning as well. "Aye. It is fortunate that my house is well supplied with good wine, as I have many tales to tell over cups." I looked back over my shoulder, and called, "And you Ehsan. You have indeed found your way over the trackless sea and back. After I had made the discovery that my friend and Kapetanios was not a lowly river pilot, but instead, once a Premier Subahdar of a stashion of row-ships, I was worried that he might feel the need to visit his old occupation out of need for excitement." Before he could reply, I waved him to silence, "Nay. I jest. I will hear of your past over friendly cups, and later." I pointed to the deck. "What is the cargo?"

Ehsan shouted an order, then replied to my question, "Logs and tree planks. And a heavy load, for sure."

"Cedrus?" That would be more wealth, indeed.

Now Korax answered. "Aye, about one part in three. It was all that was available, and even that amount came from two ports - Aradus and Tarsus. The remainder is ship wood - thick and strong." That would bring much gold also - not in the amount brought by the odiferous cedrus, but still muchly wanted in this treeless land by builders and shipwrights.

On the dock, I noticed a man with a servant approaching. I pointed, "That is my agent for the port. Let him handle the transaction for the cargo. Come, we will get you to a place of rest and good food."

It was with wonder that they entered my domicile, hard by the Temple of Amun and not far from the Palace itself. At their questions, I just shook my head and said, "All in its own time. Firstly, the baths and then a feast for both of you. We can talk over the food and wine." The two women of the men were given over to Aulus to be shown the rooms that would be theirs.

In this house, we sat in the Greek manner, on cushions rather than reclining in the Roman fashion and the two men, now clean and relaxed in new garments, filled their bellies with the first good food in a month or more. And talked of their voyage, the ports they had visited, the transactions that took place along the coast of the Great Sea.

Korax turned to rummage in his traveling bag, extracting a leather sack that he heavily tossed to the table in front of me. "The linen and fabric brought much gold in those far cities, even after our purchases of the return cargo."

"Beware a Greek with a gift of gold." We looked up to see that Ravana had finally appeared, come from one of her interminable outings with the young female nobles of the city. She stopped and looked at the long absent men for a moment, then, "I welcome you, Ehsan, and am gladsome to see that you have not succumbed to pirates on your journey." Then to Korax, "It is true what they say. A Greek will always return to plague oneself, and even from the dead."

Korax waved a bone, then replied, "Aye, woman. It is so and I see that you have increased your status from that of a mere bedwarmer for such a Greek." Neither had become close friends during of their acquaintance, but over the voyage here, and before the fall of the city, they had entered a... truce with each other, so to speak.

Still, I did not wish the banter to fall into harsh words, so I interrupted. "Sit if you will, and hear the tales of their voyage." She nodded, leaving the room to change garments, soon returning wearing a loose tunic and a bare head.

After the meal, I gave my stories, and the reason for my appearance as a noble of the city, then began to discuss my thoughts from the past year. Our discussion went on even into the darkness, on the veranda above the atrium. Here the air was cool, and the breeze refreshing.

"...and any ship of size will come from the north side of the Great Sea." Of course, Ehsan knew far more about the subject than Korax - or myself, despite my researches on the matter. "Myra and Tarsus have good shipyards, with access to wood that makes for solid vessels."

"How many do you desire to purchase?" asked Korax.

I shook my head uselessly in the dark, illuminated only by the brilliant starry sky. "Only one large sea-going vessel, for the nonce. This is a new trade, to be learned slowly and carefully. I have already purchased a share of another trader that makes it way to Cyrene and back on a round course. My agent will buy the remainder of the hull when it next lands at that city." Realizing that more explanation was needed, I continued, "The master is aged, and wishes to take ship back to his birth-land, wherever that is." I drained my cup, then said,

"Added to the cargo of the coaster that trips to Pelusium, the profit is good. And of course, your load of wood will bring much gold from the merchants here."

There was silence for the while, then from Ehsan. "Give us your thoughts."

"That you load the hold with fine linen, then depart for a shipyard of your choice, and use the profit to gain us another hull. I wish one with a removable deck, like ours, so as to allow loads of long timber from the tree-lands. Nothing else brings greater profit in this land."

"The new Kapetanios and crew?"

"That I leave to your experience."

Korax spoke. "So... You have decided to make your nest in this land?"

"Aye," I replied. "The land is good to the body, and without the plagues that blow from the swamps around Rome during the wet season, or the breathing disease that strikes with the cold rain and snow from the mountains. And, through little effort on my part, I have risen to a high point in the strata of this city as a friend of Amun and even sit as an advisory to the Pharaoh."

From the silence, I knew that the last statement had caught my friends by surprise. I waited for their questions that soon came. The idea of a low-born Roman becoming the advisor to an Egyptian king... of any foreigner even approaching the presence of any king anywhere was only the stuff of street-bard tales. Still, I assured them that it was true and, indeed, I was scheduled for an appearance at the palace on the morrow.

Scientia (Knowledge)

The other great city of Egypt, that of Karnac to the south, was still in the hands of a Persian satrap but was entirely cut off from any contact with the known world. The usual river trade was, of course, now blocked by the Pharaoh at Memphis, and while a single messenger or small party on the two-humped beasts, called camelae, might make the journey overland through the deserts, little of any significant value could be transported by such means.

The city would not starve, although without the benefit of the fertile Delta that helped feed Memphis, the people of Karnac would not be over-fattening themselves. Still, the traders and merchants of that city would soon find their coffers empty, with no vessels appearing with supplies to buy nor any hulls to load with the products to be shipped.

A few smugglers dared to flout the siege of the river, and set off in the dark of night in small boats, loaded with the items most desperately desired in that southern city. Only the advisors to the Pharaoh knew that those men were not in mortal danger should they be caught, but were instead, recruited to make the night voyages. Profit they made, but their main cargo was gossip, freely given at the port of Karnac, and in the taburnae of the city. Tales of the return of a True Pharaoh of Egypt and the joy of a populace free of the oppressive taxation and statutes of the Persians were spread with coin and drink. And repeated the next day, and the day after, by the common folk to another, wishing for such goodness to descend upon themselves.

With the death of the Persian King, Darius, in the last season, reports that we were beginning to receive indicated that the turmoil over the succession was keeping the eyes of that land away from the revolt of their southern domain. The missives to Sparta, sent after the taking of the Memphis, had not yet had time to circle the full route, but we were in hopes that the Persians would soon have another unfriendly power to their west. And much closer than Egypt to their ruling city.

I spent the days on which I was not at the palace in the crypt of writings under the Temple of Ptah. Much had I learned, in just the short while - most with little practical use, except for the interest of the reader. The realization of the length of time that the bank of the Nilos had been populated, and by a civilized people, was difficult to swallow at my first readings. But with tablets and scrolls in vast numbers giving the tale, and with concurrence in their stories, I finally had to believe in the vast antiquity of this land. The gigantic tombs, the Pyramidios, had been built at a time when Rome was only an empty land between the mountains and the sea. Indeed, the progenitors of my city would not yet be born for thousands of years when the massive blocks were being carved and stacked. The span of time was difficult to accept for a man who had considered the world to have begun a few hundred years ago on the banks of the Tiber.

One of the stone rooms, below, held drawings by past architecti - massive numbers of them. Many of the constructions described were apparently long destroyed, or at least, massively changed, as I could not correlate the sketches with any existing building. But, there were tablets without end, giving directions and numbers for the building of the great tombs - the Pyramidios. I had not, as yet, discovered the instructions for any of the three massive monuments just north of the city, but many others, and not of a diminutive size, were detailed. I found it interesting that the tomb structures were almost solid, rather than a shell of stone covering an open area, as is the case with any other building. Of course, after thinking of the concept of the Pyramidios being, in effect, hollow, I realized that there was no material in the world that would support such slanting walls over an open area. Atlas himself could not have held up such a mass of stone.

The details of the tombs were highly interesting, but of no practical use, and I continued my prowling among the dusty archives. I found many of the tablets and drawings for edifices that I was familiar with in the city, including the early plans for this very temple complex. Most of the scripts were from some far past dynasty and, therefore, unreadable by myself, except for puzzling out of a few phrases, picture by picture, but the numbers had changed little from those times. With the help of the old priest of these archives, I deciphered the age that this temple was first laid out in stone, and was astounded by the age of the complex - almost a thousand years these stones had stood on one another. At the shake of my head, the old priest said, "Aye, during the time of Pharaoh Nakhtnebtepnefer, it is said, Ptah himself came to earth with the command to raise this temple to his glory."

He waved to his apprentice, and said, "Give the tale to our friend."

The young man took a deep breath, then began to recite, "Beautiful was thine awakening, O Ptah, who voyaged from the sky, awakening all men from their mats and all the creeping things in their holes. As the firmament was dark with emptiness, and void of the songs of the sky, you saw upon the land, and the seeing was good, and with goodness and..."

I stood there listening, wondering at the memory of a boy at such an age, and how young he must have been when taken into the temple as a novice. The poem was beautiful but devoid of any real factual information, obviously being a collection of myths about the god and his temple. But a guest, when in the house of another, listens with good humor to any utterances thought important by the host. I would not denigrate a god before his priest - and certainly not while within the confines of his temple. There were other and easier ways to perish, should one desire to end all.

One morning, while I was following the adventures of an ancient Pharaoh, by the name of Sankhkare, and his expedition to some land called Punt, a novice hurried into the crypt with a notice of a messenger waiting above. It was a summons from the palace.

As I walked into the meeting room, high above the roofs of the city and the King's favorite venue for his consultations, I could tell that something of import was being discussed, or had arrived by messenger. The Pharaoh looked up as I entered, saying in a jovial voice, "Ah. Our well-traveled Roman arrives." I bowed, and he waved me to approach. "Here is a missive from Sparta, and we are in some disagreement as to what it is speaking of." He pointed to a flattened roll of written material on the long table. "Read, and give us your thoughts."

With another bow, I leaned over the scroll and began my reading. It was written in well-scripted Greek, and with a fine hand. The actual wording was typical for the scribe of a magistrate, filled with flowery phrases and stuffing, making the missive much longer than was needed to give the meaning. Finally, I looked up and said, "In the main, it states that the Spartans have agreed to your proposal for a united front against the Persians. They will require..." I looked at the figure again, then continued, "...four thousand medimnos of grain per four-month to feed their army."

"So, we are in effect, hiring the Spartans with grain." It was a statement from one of the high-level officers in the room.

Another asked, "How much is four thousand of this Greek... meden... med...?"

I reached for one of the many wax tablets on the table, then a stylus. Scribbling for a moment, I answered, "That would be about three thousand Egyptian khar." More marks in the wax and I said, "About twelve ships of the usual seagoing burden."

Continuing my explaining of what I had read, I pointed to the Greek script. "They will contest the Persians in the area of the city of Abydos..." I stood and walked to the huge map on the wall, taking a long reed as a pointer. "...here on the eastern coast of this embayment of the Great Sea. To my understanding, during my time in Athens, this has long been an outpost of Sparta..." I spoke until I had exhausted the meaning of the missive, then turned to receive the nod of the King.

All looked at the great man, waiting for his opinion, as he obviously mused over what I had said. Finally, still staring out over the city through the great opening in one wall, he said, "The grain is trivial and a bargain, if it gains us time to strengthen our presence before the Persians look our way again." Following that, he began to give orders to the appropriate men to see to the hiring of vessels and dismissed the group.

As I turned to go, he said, "Hold, Roman." I turned and waited until the room was empty of all by myself and the King. He then waved to me to follow him. We moved to the eastern wall, through which we could reach a balcony far above the ground. Spread before us was the half of the city, and far in the distance, the Nilos and the port area. Finally, he said, "You intrigue me, Junius, the Roman." To my surprised look, he smiled, and continued, "Of all the associates and staffers of my following, you seem to be the only one who does not appear to desire something from me."

I was astonished at the statement. What could a son of a river man demand from a King? I searched for an answer, but had not even begin to develop one when he continued, "I know something of your story, from that first day in the Delta when we spoke, but you go deeper than that." A longer pause as he continued to look out over the city, now sweltering in the midday sun. Finally, "Junius, the Roman, do you have any belief in the gods?"

Frozen, I just stood with a blank expression. What answer could I give that was... The Pharaoh was a god himself, according to all beliefs in the land. To deny that would be most unadvisable, even fatal, but... "You may speak with candor and without fear." He was just looking at me with a normal gaze.

Taking a deep breath, I began. "Great One... I..."

He waved at me impatiently, and said, "You may leave off the verbal obeisances in our privacy. I am not so vain as to think that words make me greater than my deeds. 'Ami-Re' will be sufficient." He gave a wry smile. "I am now wishing daily that I was just a general of rebels in the swamps, still. Life was much easier then, and my men straightforward and with no need of a regiment of painted drones in the throne room, all currying favor."

I nodded. "Aye... Ami-Re." I paused for my thoughts, then said, "My life has been as the ridiculous tale of a street bard, moving from one unlikely calamity to another, and each time making a miraculous jump to safety at the last moment. And, it has happened so many times, that I have begun to wonder if my life is not my own, but pointed by some divinity... somewhere." I shrugged, then continued, "Such a notion is ridiculous to a thinking man, of course, but..." I grinned for a moment, then said, in jest, "If my friend, Korax the Greek, while in one of his endless games of knucklebones, were to watch his opponent throw the value of Euripides time and again, he could justly believe that a weighted set of gaming bones was in play. Thus, it is with the events of my life."

I looked out over the city, following his gaze. "As I have said, I was educated in the Temple of Jupiter, to become a Scribe Primus, and only a ceremony away from becoming an ordained priest, had I wished it. Many are the tales that I have heard about a god descending from Olympus to give succor to this man, or punishment to that one, and attested to by upstanding men of the Temple." I paused, then, "But, in honesty, I have never seen such an action, nor have heard the great image of the god speak. Or move. Or act in anyway different than a massive statue of stone."

"And yet, we are here," said the Pharaoh.

"Aye. The world and all men were created by something, but as to what..." I raised my hands in helplessness.

There was a long silence, then he spoke carefully and in a low voice. "I have little belief that the gods of this land - or any other - are any more real than my nighttime dreaming. Certainly, like you, I have never seen a single instance of the hand of a god reaching down to change the affairs of men." He sighed, then finished with, "But, to the people, Pharaoh is a god, and therefore so must I be. I would that godly powers came with the scepter."

Then, in an instant, he moved to a new subject. "Is it true that you have a consort with golden hair?"

The sudden shift caught me by surprise, and I just stood for a moment open-mouthed, before the need to immediately answer the question of a king forced me to speak.

"Aye, Gre... Ami-Ri. She is of some northern land, brought south in her infancy."

"But she is not your mate?"

"Nay. Only a friend. A female friend, but a good one, intelligent and pleasant and with an inquiring mind." I thought about my reply. It was true, Ravana was indeed a friend, no less for being a woman, and with the added benefit of nightly encounters. I thought of something. "But, her golden tresses are in our household, and she wears the black wig of a citizen."

I explained the reason for hiding the fact in some detail, and he nodded, saying, "I will return from the foray up the Karnac road in a handful of days. I would see this golden woman at that time. Bring her to my chambers."

Of course, Ravana was both stunned and elated with the prospect, and on the morrow, I sent her and her attendants to the wig-merchant with certain instructions.

I had spent a considerable time making a series of maps from the huge one on the wall of the meeting room of the palace, and now I called Ehsan and Korax to the Taburna of the Nose Horn for discussion. With a marked stick of wood, I measured the distances from the issuance of the Nilos to various destinations around the Great Sea. Pointing to the figures that I had put in the wax, I asked Ehsan for his opinion - both of the possibility of the direct route and his skill in navigating open waters with no landmarks.

He nodded and said, "Aye. I have heard of it being attempted, but I have never spoken to a man who actually made the voyage. I suspect that most is just seaport talk."

"I have heard the same," I replied. "But..." I had had long discussions with Senemut on the topic, and he had asked for the attendance of several men of his acquaintance - ancient men, of age and in their dotage. But, all were men of the Great Sea, and more importantly, were still alive after a lifetime of voyages. Long hours did I give my ear to the tales of the garrulous captains, but in the stories were nuggets of fact and truth. "...but, in my queries of the old masters, most vessels that were lost had no binding reason to set forth for such a distance, being mere oversized river boats." I waved my hands in emphasis. "Ours is a well-found craft, and with a planked hull and high freeboard." I had learned much of the vernacular of the sea from the captains.

Korax spoke up. "That does not alter the fact that none of us know of guiding by the stars or sun-travel."

"Aye," I replied, nodding. "That is why I have engaged a sea-pilot, recommended by the captains to which I have spoken."

Ehsan just sat in thought for a moment, finally saying, "The direct route, if feasible, has advantages. We would be free of the threat of shore-pirates." More thought, then, "And the rapacious open palms of the port factors along the coast."

"How long would the voyage take?" asked Korax.

I laid the measuring stick on one of the maps. "The distance from the mouth of the Delta to Rhodes is about five thousand stadia. Using the different times between ports on my voyage to here, I can calculate the speed of our ship in a fair wind, and that is about thirty stadia in an hour - a Roman hour. Less, of course, when we were loaded to the deck with heavy logs." A quick dabble in the wax, and I said, "The distance to Rhodes should be covered in fifteen days at the most, if the wind stays."

Korax whistled through his teeth. "That is fast indeed."

"Of course, it is at least another quarter month to Sparta - or Athens - from Rhodes, but compared to the months of sailing around the rim, it would be as if the god Mercury were pushing the ship." I pointed to the map again. "Or, even the more direct route could be taken - to the island of Creteus and then beyond to the Greek mainland."

Ehsan just stared at the papyrus for a while. Then, "This sea-pilot... I would speak with him before deciding."

I grinned and stood up. I waved to a far table, and a man of middle age immediately rose to his feet - rather his foot and crutch, and hobbled to our table. Pointing to the bench in invitation for him to sit, I said to my friends, "This is Ahirom of Damaskos - a city somewhere in the lands of Phoenicia, and a man with extensive knowledge of the Great Sea. This is a claim that I have verified with various men in the captaincies."

My friends were staring at his missing leg with some disbelief, until Ehsan said, "You wish a berth on a ship, even as one who cannot even bouse cargo?"

Ahirom was a man with who had long become reconciled with his missing limb. I had had long talks with him, over cups, at the taburna and my home, and knew that his was a mind of unusual potency. His scripting and reading was far less than mine, but he had a grasp of numbers that equaled myself. Over this map or that, I had had many discussions - arguing this and that and with great pleasure - of the shape of the world and the paths between the cities scattered across the great sea. He had been a master of a coaster, moving between the Delta and the ports of the Great Sea to the north, until that day when a lee shore and a wind from Hades cast himself and the vessel upon the rocks of the Tyre coast.

But, during his captaincy he had pointed his ship to small jumps across the bend of the sea at the port of Gaza, leaving the land below the horizon, then greater distances until he could point his course directly from Pelusium to Sidon, and Aradus, and even to Tarsus at the far northern corner of the Great Sea. His collection of maps was far greater than mine and more importantly, laden with notes about the winds and the waves and the stars of this season and that. That this was no buffoon, talking his way into a berth, I was certain. Certain enough to risk my ship and fortune on his ability.

And he was no man to recoil from notice of his infirmity. He responded to Ehsan with spirit, and without rancor. "Aye. And men to bouse cargo are as wine in a shop - easily obtainable with a hail and a coin. But... A man to point you to a profitable port, and in the least time, without following the shoreline like a plodding camel drover, is not found standing on the planks of the dock."

"And have you made the voyage to... Sparta or Athens? Across the wide?" Ehsan was still doubtful.

Ahirom shook his head. "Nay. But to Heraklion, in the land of Creteus. Thrice. And that is almost three parts in four of the distance to the land of the Greeks."

Korax, the inveterate landman, apparently was growing into the seaman. He asked, "What do you follow in times of intemperate days and the clouds obscure all but the sea?"

"Then one must know the patterns of the wind, and the differences in each of the seasons. And, if one suddenly notices that the waves do not follow the wind, the one can assume that the former has changed." He tapped a map - one showing the entire Great Sea from the coast of Phoenicia, on the eastmost end of the waters, to the alleged pillars of Hercules at the far western reaches. "In any event, even a lost ship will eventually reach land, saving only that they carry sufficient food and water for the voyage. One cannot sail off the end of the world in a body of water that is bounded on all sides by land."

Now I spoke up. "And... There will be no row-ships of reavers to be encountered in the middle reaches, unless they be sun-bleached bones, given as an offering for the sin of rowing out of sight of land."

We talked long into the afternoon, with Ehsan, and Korax on occasion, feeding the pilot with a pointed question. But, by the time of the evening meal, the one legged man had convinced my friends of his competence in pointing a ship. Or, at least, had lessened their fears of his being a braggart looking for a soft berth.

I made sure that the vessel was stocked with twice the usual rations of food and triple that of water, on the unlikely possibility that setting off into the unknown might indeed be considered a foolish goad to Poseidon. Or Neptune. Or whatever gods might rule the sea at this end of the world.

My belief in the deities - any deity - was still formless and changing. In one thought I would chastise myself in the notion of an invisible, untouchable and unknowable entity. Then, the uneasiness would return that what I had seen and experienced could not possibly be a matter of mere chance.

As to which thought was the truth, I had no desire to find the answer, as yet. There was much that I wished to see and do before that ultimate question was answered, as it must eventually be, for every man.

Separatio

Ravana was standing in a glistening and pure white kalasiris and looking like a golden-haired goddess. Her clothiers had somehow dusted her garment with tiny shards of a desert sand crystal that glinted in the light, giving a spectacular vision of Hathor come to earth. The long sheath started below her mammaries and was held up by two narrow straps hiding the points of her nipples but little else. Because of the interest of the Pharaoh in the color of her hair, we had engaged the wig merchant to produce an elegant hairpiece from her shaven locks and once in the relaxing chambers of the King, she exchanged her black hair for gold.

As she stood there in that stance that only a woman can take, one leg forward and bent, and the opposite arm held slightly away from the body, I, myself was stunned by her appearance, even with my intimate knowledge of her in all aspects. There was no doubt that Amyrtaeus was gazing upon the apparition with intense wonder, and not only with the interest of one who had never seen such a color in a woman but also as a man whose desire was rising like smoke from a roaring fire.

Of course, the woman knew full well the effect she was having on the two men but maintained her poise as if standing in a forum, waiting for her order to be filled. I knew that she was enjoying herself, immensely. After all, it is probably very seldom that an escaped bed-wench is allowed to display herself before a king.

Finally, Amyrtaeus spoke. "My apologies for my thoughts of your exaggeration of the woman. She is indeed a vision of the gods." Again, he looked for a while, then asked, "Her name?"

"Ravana is the agnomen she is known by, Ami-Re."

"And she is Roman?"

I shook my head. "She considers herself to be such, as she grew to womanhood in that city, but in actuality, she is from some northern clime that even she cannot remember."

He nodded absently. "Aye. You have said that." More inspection, then, "And she is not your mate?" I shook my head. "That is interesting in itself. How one could resist such a vision of paradise is beyond my understanding. Perhaps, boys are more in your needs." A jape, but one with a questioning tone.

"Nay, Ami-Re. I only claim that she is not my legal mate by Roman law - not that my mat is not warmed by her."

"And you have no attachment to the woman?"

"Not as wife. She is a friend and a good companion but follows her own path. And, she is wealthy to her own accord, needing only a land where a woman can stand to herself until she finds a man worthy of being her mate." I paused, then asked somewhat hesitantly, "Is the Ami-Re considering her as a... consort?" I was hesitating because of the knowledge that a king seldom cares for questions from his menials, and certainly not about his personal desires.

"Aye. But I have not earned the loyalty of my men by usurping their wives and women."

I waved toward the female, still standing as if she were in the clothing merchantry waiting for a fitting. "I would keep her as a friend, if not a mat-mate, Ami-Re, but her course is her own desire. That has been the full part of the agreement in our union since the beginning of our friendship, as we left Athens." I bowed slightly. "If I may, Great One. The buildings of this city intrigue me as does the Palace, and I would explore it for my own edification. May I go and leave the both of you to... talk among yourselves?"

With his eyes sparkling, but looking at the woman, he replied, "Aye. If the Chamberlain gives disapproval of your walks, inform him that I grant you access to any part of the royal compound." Then, he said, "Wait." Walking to the table, he ripped a part of papyrus from the greater roll, then, with the King's scarab dipped in the marking fluid, stamped his seal onto the scrap. "Take this. It will gain you access without challenge."

As I bowed deeply and turned to go, I was... not stunned by the sudden events, but I was surprised, at the least. And in a way, relieved. Ravana was a wonderful woman as a companion for my urges, but I had no desire to make her my mate - she would be far too strong-willed for my daily routine once the coupling of wifehood ended her ranging around the city as a freely traveling woman. Her white skin would be black and blue from the beatings that I would have to give to keep my peace of mind intact.

Like all structures, the Palace - as large at it looked from outside the Royal enclosure - was even larger from inside. The area that I had just left contained the King's chambers, and next to it, those of the Queen - unoccupied at the present. But, I begin my description in the middle of my wanderings.

At the huge gates, facing north along the wide avenue - The Street of the Heavens - and beyond the huge forecourt, a long covered walkway led into the center of the compound. The cover stones were high overhead, more than four man lengths in height, and held up by a double line of stone pillars - not fluted as in the Greek and Roman fashion, but round and smooth and covered with either carved or painted picture script. At the end, the walkway entered the huge throne room, again with the ceiling held even higher by even more massive pillars. Ways led off in all directions to the servants quarters, the kitchens, several temples and courtyards, each with its own obelisk or water pool. Behind the throne was the hall leading to the chambers of the royalty and to the east was the meeting rooms where the officers and priests would meet with the king. Westward were the many sleeping rooms for the permanent inhabitants of the Palace.

As I wandered, I noticed that - for the size of the walled Royal Enclosure, probably a thousand paces in each dimension - the compound was almost empty of persons. The Ami-Re was still more of a General than a Pharaoh, and not enough time had elapsed since his assuming the throne to allow for the aggregation of the myriad of drones and hangers-on that any king would collect like flies to a dollop of honey. A few slaves cleaning and hauling, a servant or two hurrying here and there were all that I saw in the main.

Even the palace guard was far less numerous than one would expect in such a place. Four men and an officer were at the gate, and two men on each of the corner watch posts were all that I saw. I assumed that there was a barracks in the compound, somewhere, with considerably more men that could be called to the ready.

I did not even see the Chamberlain since I never approached the always busy reception area or the throne room, and my scrap of parchment with the royal scarab-mark went unchallenged as I wandered until the sun was beginning to fall behind the wall.

At my home, Ravana had not returned, and I wondered if the King would take her to his mat even this day. On my scrivening table, I sat with a cup and examined the few tablets that my steward had left, giving accounting of the purchases for my moderate household. Seeing nothing wrong with the numbers, I set them on the stack-table for disposal. Calling for a light meal of cheese and bread, I walked to the terrace on the roof and sat to watch the setting sun. There was little for myself to do in the coming days, other than continue my readings in the librarium of the Temple of Ptah - but that was a prospect to which I was looking forward. With the three ships gone, my agent had no reason to send me accountings for cargo vending and there was little need for my service to the King as to the administration of the city. Of course, I enjoyed my evening discourse with the other merchants and lesser nobles in their houses, or the better taburnae of the quarter.

The sun was about to touch the far horizon when my Steward appeared and stopped, waiting. I turned my head and said, "Aye, Aulus?"

"Your pardon, Master. A messenger has arrived from the Palace."

I stood immediately and hurried down the stone steps to the atrium - at least, that is what a Roman would have called the large room used for visitors and relaxation. There, a Palace guard was waiting, in his spotless skirt and with his baton of authority. I recognized the young man as one who was on the staff of the General while in the Delta. As I stopped and nodded, he immediately began his spiel. "From the Pharaoh Amyrtaeus, he who is blessed by Amun himself, Lord of the Upper and Lower Egypt, High Priest of every temple in the Land..." I shut my ears to the stream of useless attributes, wondering once again at the verbosity of the hot lands. To the people of Egypt, a garrulous braggart in a Roman taburna would be as a mute on the acting boards of the Forum.

But, eventually, he had exhausted all possible complements and titles, "...sends this message to his friend and advisor, Junius the Roman. That the woman, Ravana..." The unfamiliar name came out as Raveena to the man, "...desires her cosmeta..." This Roman word was totally butchered, but I understood the meaning, "...and her elixirs and night garments that she may take her sleep in comfort."

I nodded and turned to Aulus. "Gather the servants and the waiting girl of the Mistress. They will deliver certain items to the Palace, and you will accompany them as my representative." He bowed and shortly the young girl-maid of Ravana was waiting, holding the chest of potions and liquids needed for a woman to function. Two of the men-servants carried a much larger wooden box with selected clothing - selected by the young cosmeta, of course - and other women's things of little meaning to a man.

I turned to the messenger and said, formally, "My greetings to the Pharaoh Amyrtaeus, Lord of all the Lands, and give to him, that on the morrow, should it be desired, I will arrange for the properties of the woman, Ravana, entire, to be carried to the Palace." In moments, I was standing alone as the small group hurried out the compound gate on their way.

Almost alone, now, in my large domicile, I poured myself a cup - a full one - and climbed back to the terrace, sitting as the last of the sun disappeared behind the far horizon. My thoughts were... of sadness... and relief, and...

Sadness because of my extreme fondness for the outspoken and vivacious woman that had shared my mat since the voyage to this land. It would be very unlikely for another like her to be found in my lifetime, and I was not speaking of her unique looks, but of the quality of her company. The couplings with her were of little importance - as it is said in Rome, "In the throes of desire, all women are equal." Finding another to share my mat would take little effort, even were I a lowly laborer outside the walls. For a man, still on the green side of middle age, and wealthy beyond most, the problem would be selecting between the innumerable candidates that would now appear.

The relief was, that I knew in the back of my mind, that this day must come. I was no rutting youth, dreaming of a life of bliss with an unflawed woman, our passions lasting from our first union to our death biers. Coupled together in formal marriage, and without the relief of encounters with others, Ravana and I would have been as two dogs in a yard, each finding reason to quarrel on every day. But, it would be selfish in the extreme for myself to enjoy her while in her flowery youth, then turn her out when her bloom began to fade.

Again, I was no passion-beguiled pup, and knew that the sadness would pass, and my life would continue just as it did before when a certain fiery-haired girl had left my life forever.

In the following days, I kept my mind busy in my readings, deliberately not thinking of my absent bed-mate. Even my svans was passive, not requiring any service for the nonce. My ardor would return, and with vigor, I knew, but I was unconcerned of when such would happen.

A formal delegation came from the Palace, with the assistant to the Chamberlain, several menials and with four slaves carrying a chest and guards to follow. The scroll that I was handed said in part, "...for my friend, Junius the Roman, to assuage the loss of that which must be most precious to a man, and in gratitude for the bestowance of his treasure without rancor..." On it went, but it had little meaning compared to the contents of the small coffer. After the delegation had left, I pulled the latch and opened the lid of the chest, aghast at what I could see. The box was filled, literally to the overflowing with golden rings, almost to the weight of myself and more. Later I realized the significance of that thought. The contents of the chest were equivalent to the weight of Ravana herself.

The gratitude of a King, should a man be so fortunate to receive such, can be overwhelming.

As I was perusing the stack of ancient scrolls in the room of the architects, I suddenly noticed a fat roll with the following words in the title script, written on the spindle end...

I had seen that somewhere... but where? The pictures were known, but their order was meaningless, which meant that the scroll was written in some long ago dynasty.

After I had been exposed to the massive depth of years of Egyptian culture, I began to realize that the picture language was not composed of discrete meanings, cataloged by certain years, that changed suddenly for another. That is to say, the first scribes of the hot lands - those that constructed the language - did not suddenly abandon the old writing for a new, and others afterward discard theirs for even a newer. Nay, the language would have... I had no word for the concept, but the language would have changed gradually from generation to generation, probably smoothly from that first written script to what was used in this time. The same pictures were used, of course, over the thousands of years, but when connected together, the meaning would be different.

To put it differently, looking at the language from those earlier times to this day, as if it was a man, a watcher would see a child, then a young man growing into middle age, then to his elderly years and finally an ancient graybeard with creaking bones. Should one be able to compare that child with the old man, they would seem to have no relation to one another, yet they would still be the same person. The language as well, grew from childhood to an older style that had little likeness to each other - and gradually, not in steps from one age to the next.

Suddenly, I remembered where I had seen the words. Copying the pictures to a scrap of papyrus, I left the temple and strolled down the avenue to the gate of the Palace. And there, engraved in the stone arch, above the entry gates, was the same script.

It was late, but the following morning I was back at the librarium with the scroll spread opened on the long table in the reading room. This had to be the original plans for the Palace, and indeed, it was. Over the hundreds of years, certain changes had been made, but in the main, the drawings were a faithful representation of the Royal Enclosure of this day. I had no use for the information, but it was fascinating to see the detail of the huge compound from the aspect of the builders.

Of course, I could not take the scroll from the librarium, but I copied several of the drawings to sheets of papyrus, and then strolled into the compound to compared what was drawn with what was built. I had long had access to the Palace, summons or nay, and the guard captain just saluted as I strolled through the gate. Slowly, I began to learn the symbols of the old language as I studied the labels of the structure that I was examining. The string of pictures for the culina - kitchen - area was much the same, but the script for the stables, far in the back, were totally different. Idly, I wondered that, in a thousand years, would a scribe be able to read what I had written in the script of my home city, or would it have changed completely into a new language?

During my stroll, I saw neither the King nor Ravana - or anyone, besides the infrequent servant. I wondered if both were as two lovers newly joined, with little interest in anything outside the cubiculum. I shook my head. Nay, a King that ignored the outside world for any length of time would find himself on the wrong side of the river Styx, and suddenly. He was probably on one of his frequent examinations of his new and still-green army.

The flood time came again, and I knew that no ship could be expected until the waters began to recede. I wondered at the trip of my friends, across the wideness of the Great Sea, and if the pilot that I had engaged was steering them through the domain of Poseidon even now. I hoped not, but only time would answer that question. Good news came from the spies that traded with the upper city of Karnac. The people were becoming restless and even openly declaring the need for the rejoining of their city with a legitimate Pharaoh of Egypt.

Ravana had become the official consort of the King, appearing at all official ceremonies in the throne room. I wondered if she would eventually be Queen, and if a foreign born woman could even become so. The priest, and my friend, Senemut informed me that it was possible, and indeed common for a Pharaoh to take to wife the daughter of a far kingdom. He spoke of many such joinings.

And, as to Senemut himself... Before the ceremony of the coming flood, the old Priest had gone to his reward in the land beyond the sunset, and my friend had been elevated to the Amun-Rehab - Priest Primus of Amun and all of Egypt, from the cataracts to the Delta and all lands to either side of the Nilos. I was standing in the first rank, in the great throne room, as the Pharaoh himself gave the wand of Amun to Senemut, and began the weeklong ceremonies to celebrate the coming of a new spokesman of the god.

Ravana was there, standing behind the King, now garbed in the finest linen, and with both wrists and upper arms encircled with bands of gold. Her wig now was of the yellow tresses that I had shaved from her head, but I knew that she was letting - or had been ordered to let her hair grow again. She was talked about by the people, and not just the common folk, in words of awe. I doubt that many actually thought of her as the goddess Hathor come to earth, but most had a vague idea that she was in someway connected with that deity.

This day, she saw me standing behind Senemut and winked with a smile. I had to raise my hand to cover my grin, and could tell that she was stifling her own mirth with difficulty.

A young widow was now meeting my own needs, pretty and quite versatile on the mat. Of course, she had none of the world traveling knowledge of Ravana, but that was not what I wanted from her. I had my needs of intellectual intercourse filled by my acquaintances with whom I lifted cups in their own domiciles - or mine - and the taburnae. My friendship with the Pharaoh and the High Priest of Amun lifted my status far above what it would have been as a newly come merchant shipper. In fact, as the educated, wandering Roman, I was quite the novelty for gatherings around the city, and invitations from matrons arrived almost daily - and not only as a guest to the household. Many different mats did I use for sleep - and other activity - during those times.

Thusly did I settle into life as a citizen of Egypt.

Chasma (Underworld)

My faith in the pilot, Ahirom - or my gamble with an unknown - paid off handsomely. The direct route across the Great Sea from the Delta to Myra, or Tarsus, or Aradus cut the time for a voyage by at least half, and usually to a third or quarter of voyaging around the coast. And the pirates that infested the southeastern coast were totally avoided. Not long after the receding of the flooding Nilos, the ship appeared, stacked again to the planked deck with cedrus logs and once again, my coffers grew even fatter with gold. Not that I needed any more and in fact, the excess wealth was becoming burdensome.

I had made a discovery during the time they were away, and one that I kept to myself. Actually, I made two, but I will reveal the other in its own time. As to the first...

Wealth and gold have always been high in the force that drives men to work, or steal, or even kill. Most merchants, if not all, have an inborn drive to collect all that can be pulled into their hands. Nobles, have less of the drive, as they grew from boys without the knowledge of life without coin, but still, none that I have ever known would refuse the opportunity to gather more. I was no different in regards to the desirably of having a sufficient amount, but... In that word - sufficient - there is a world of meaning.

I knew full well that I enjoyed the status of being wealthy - I would have been considered touched by the gods had I not, by myself and all others. But, the realization began to reveal itself in my mind that I actually cared little for the aggregation of coin and gold beyond what I needed to maintain that status. Another way to state the proposition is that enough is enough, and any further more is just excess.

Of course, I kept my feelings to myself, including my partners in merchantry, as they would definitely have assumed that the aforementioned touching by some god was actually happening. Thus, I stored the profits from my ventures in our strong room with little further thought about it.

My household was still almost bare, in comparison to the teeming domiciles of the rich merchantry and nobles of the city. Besides Aulus, my steward, the cocua in the kitchen and her maid, and a few other servants needed for the maintenance of such a large dwelling, there were no swarms of menials filling the rooms and hallways to scheme and plot. Of course, when our ship hove into port, the number swelled with the addition of both Korax and Ehsan and Ahirom - and their women.

As our needs were modest, and our resources rich beyond any belief of our former lives, there was no need for the ship to immediately return to the sea after being unloaded of its cargo. I insisted that my friends linger in the city for a considerable time, to enjoy at least a portion of the riches that they had earned for us. But, soon, the wandering desire would begin to emerge, especially in Ehsan, and the ship would set sail again.

More than once, and over the several years, I made the passage in the place of Korax. Mostly, it was my own wanderlust that made me take the voyages, but the first time was because of the infirmity of my friend after falling from a height into the hold, and garnering a clean break of a leg. Leaving him to watch our household as his limb waited for the time of repair, I decided to accompany the ship on a trading voyage. Thereafter, I would do so about once in the year, and mainly for my own enjoyment. We did not need the wealth that was brought in, but a man must have an occupation, and this was ours.

After the next ceasing of the flood, an event of major importance occurred. The city of Karnac rose in rebellion, evicting the satrap King and telling for the real Pharaoh. Of course, the underlying discontent was seasoned and served by the many agents and spies that Amyrtaeus had planted in the preceding year. I traveled to the city with the Pharaoh as he entered the gates to the cheers of the massive throngs of people, now ecstatic that a true son of Egypt was now on the throne of both the Upper and Lower regions of the land.

I had little interest in the festivities but spent my time of two months exploring the city. Just as Memphis, it was huge and little different in the makeup, having temples and shrines mixed among the myriad of housing and merchantries. Poorer it was since it had been under virtual blockade of the river for most of two years, but now trade would begin flowing up the river and along the roads from both Memphis and the Delta.

Now, as to the second discovery that I have mentioned.

One day, two years after my discovery of the scroll of building for the Palace, I was wandering the grounds of the Royal Enclosure waiting for a meeting to begin. What it was, I disremember, but while waiting, I was examining the script on the side of a wall that was the long entryway to the Royal Quarters. The hallway was dark, with few openings to the outside for light, and I was using a torch and a short ladder to bring my eyes to the level of the upper pictures. As I stood on the upper step, I noticed a hole in the stones, about the size of a man's fist.

My torch showed nothing except that the opening was deep, and I verified with my arm. It was punched or chiseled all the way through the stone. I could feel only air with my hand. As a hole in stone is of little interest, I gave it no more thought that day.

Sometime in the following days, I unrolled the building scroll of the palace again, casually looking at the particular wall that had held the script that I had examined. The walls of that corridor were original, obviously, but interestingly, of different thicknesses, the one with the hole being almost three times as thick as its mate. From the floor of the hallway, no one would notice but an architect, and he only by carefully measuring round the perimeter. To anyone else, the thought not only would not occur but would be immediately discarded as utterly unimportant even had they noticed.

But... I noticed that in the drawing, were lines, made of very short segments and separated by equally short spaces indicating... It was if the thick wall were hollow. Now, I unrolled the scroll far along its length, calling a new novice to assist me so as to not tear the ancient medium. Using an empty spindle, I had the youngster begin to roll up the first of the papyrus as it reached the end of the table, so as not to fall onto the floor in a pile.

On and on I rolled and examined the drawings, looking for that particular hallway of the compound, until I reached a section that seemed to be almost a... I am at a loss for words to describe it. It appeared to be a spectral drawing of the structures, with dotted lines within and running to and fro across the entire area. Further on was another set of drawings that had no relation to the buildings of the Royal Enclosure, except that they were drawn in the same locations of the existing structures. An earlier construction of the Palace, perhaps. If so, then it was ancient indeed, having been replaced a thousand years or more before and built some staggering number of years before that.

Unfortunately, the writing was so ancient that I could understand no more than a picture here and there. Very unfortunate, since the drawing was liberally scribbled and the understanding of the writing would have greatly helped my own understanding of what was being given. The mystery stayed in my mind, and I casually thought over the strangeness on occasion in the following days, then...

With the King and his consort, and indeed, almost all of the Royal party traveled to the city of Karnac, I returned to the hallway with my ladder and torch. But, this time, I had a small pouch of stones.

With my arm inserted as far as it would go, I dropped a rock, then immediately put my ear to the hole. In a longer time - much longer - that I expected, I heard the clunk as it hit bottom. Again, I did so. And again, except for this last time, I began a rapid count as I opened my hand, noting the number that I had reached. Now, holding a stone at the same level of the hole, I released it to fall to the floor, again counting until it hit.

The stone inside the wall had taken almost twice as long in its fall.

This was an intriguing mystery. The long wall of the corridor was not only hollow but apparently the hollowness extended deep under the ground. During the rest of the daylight hours and those of the next day, I examined the scroll minutely, even transferring several drawings to my own sheets of papyrus. Armed with these, I began to examine the structures of the Royal Enclosure closely, even climbing to the top of several.

By now the servants of the palace were used to seeing me standing for hours, in this hallway or up that ladder, examining writings or carvings and they gave me little notice. And besides, no menial is going to question the actions of a friend of Pharaoh. I was not engaged in anything of an inimical nature to the King, or anybody - merely extremely curious as to the structures that some unknown builders had erected over a thousand years ago.

Far in the back of the compound, away from the main gates, was a temple to a minor god by the name of Heket, whose domain I never learned. For my exploration, it was ideal, as it was seldom visited and there being no priesthood for the deity. The remoteness from the daily activities of the palace was far enough that I seldom caught sight of anyone, nor even heard voices.

But, on my drawings, the little structure had the dotted markings within one wall.

I walked around the building, tall but only about thirty paces in each dimension. As all other temples, it was covered with carvings in one of the old languages that meant nothing to me. Holding the map for examination, I walked inside and oriented myself. Except for the statue of the god in the far middle of the floor, there was nothing else except stone benches around the walls and the two rows of stone pillars holding up the ceiling. The layer of sand and dust on every surface gave notice that no ceremonies to this particular god had occurred in many years.

The wall behind the statue, opposite the open portal was my destination. It rose to a height of four men, and without opening to the outside, as had the other walls. But, in two places, equally spaced from their adjoining walls, two niches could be seen at the top, giving a space with a height of about a leg's length under the stone slab ceiling. The shadows of the openings gave notice that the space did not penetrate the wall to the outside.

I had brought my longest ladder, light and strong, made of joints of thick and dried reeds woven together. Very shortly I had it placed and was climbing into the shadow of the ceiling. There, I found what I was expecting. A flat shelf in the top of the wide wall, but with a large square opening in the center. It was a black pit, shear and forbidding. In the dim light, I could see no more than a few hand lengths down, but the stone that I dropped proved that it was very deep.

My excitement was palpable now, with my imagination running wild with what I was beginning to believe. I now knew that the short sentence of pictures on my map meant shaft, or well, or something of the like. And the same sentence was repeated on the drawings many times - innumerable times.

I now had to expand on my plans. The rest of the day was spent in the purchase of several items of need before I went further. That evening, in the taburna frequented by my usual acquaintances, I was of little diversion in the usual discussions of trade, or profit, or just gossip - my mind continually receding to think of the discoveries that I might make on the morrow.

There was no rush for my exploring, but as my ships were voyaging, and the Pharaoh away for the month or so, this was the perfect time to indulge myself in fantasy. I planned and thought, imagined and plotted, hoping that I would find more than just a deep shaft and nothing else. I procured a heavy leather bag and filled it with a meal of hard rations, a waterbag, torches, string and suchlike. As I continued to think on the morrow, I added this item and that. On the following morn, the sun was barely over the eastern wall when I was back at the deserted temple - this time with the leather bag filled with my supplies.

Firstly, I prepared a torch by tying a thin rope to its mid-section, so that it would hang sideways when suspended. At the top of the ladder, I struck the flint and iron to ignite it, then held it as I leaned over the top of the wall to look down the shaft, if that is what it was.

It was. I could now see far down, but not to the bottom, and it was indeed a stone shaft, smooth sided and without handholds or any way to descend or climb. Now, I lowered the torch on the rope, carefully and slowly, watching as the flame sank into the darkness.

Unlike my wilder imaginings during the previous night, it did not continue into an infinite abyss, but finally touched on what appeared to be an ordinary stone floor, far below. That relieved one of my fears - that the shaft might end in a well of water, black and deadly.

Pulling the torch back up, quickly, I climbed down the ladder and stretched the rope across the floor. Now I knew the depth of the shaft - about nine or ten manlengths from top to bottom. Deep, but not impossible.

My next actions had to be done carefully, else I would doom myself to dying of thirst in a shaft with no hope of rescue. I took two long pieces of ironwood from my bag, both thick and strong, and tied a thick knotted rope to the center of each. Placing the logs to straddle the hole, and protruding two foot-lengths on either side of it, I dropped the attached ropes down the shaft. The reason for two was just caution. Should one slip, or break, or fall, I would have the other with which to climb back with.

Now, tying the large bag to the end of one of the ropes, I gently lowered it to the bottom of the shaft. Then, taking a smaller torch in my teeth, I took a deep breath, then a death grip on a rope, and lowered myself into the hole. My descent was rapid - much faster than my return would be, but I was still in the prime of life and climbing a knotted rope was the least of my abilities. I hoped.

My feet touched, and I quickly looked around, to the extent that the small flame allowed. Fears of lurking serpents and hordes of rats were much more vivid than they had been while standing in the sunlight on the yesterday during my planning. I had little expectation of anything living in a barren hole, but I was not so skeptical as to leave my longknife behind.

But there was nothing but stone and...

On the floor, I could see splinters, or shards of... some kind of reed or wood, and tatters of cord, but what it might have been was a mystery. The stones were covered in an inch of dust or fine sand, smooth and untracked. I might have been the first person that had descended into this tunnel in hundreds of years.

Looking up, I could see the faint light of the small square opening far above, and comforting, my twin ropes leading up to the top. Suddenly, I realized that the air was... cool. Even more so than the coolness of the morning air. I wondered at the reason.

I pulled a much larger torch from the bag and lit it with the smaller. Now, I could see a considerable ways along what was a stone corridor running both north and south. Since I knew that the walls of the Royal Enclosure were only a few strides to the south from the temple, I intended to first explore to the north, toward the palace itself.

On the yesterday, I had tasked a servant of my household to cut a long spool of thin flaxen cord to lengths that I marked on the floor, between marks that I had measured to be twenty-five strides in length. These were knotted back together, then rewound onto the spool. This would be my measuring system in a world with no visible landmarks.

Tying the end of the cord to the heavy bag, I began to walk down the corridor, examining both floor and walls carefully as I walked. It was a tunnel, actually, made of cut stone and only wide enough to walk without rubbing one's shoulders on the sides. The ceiling was about two foot-lengths above my head, although I tended to walk in a crouch at first, without noticing. The walls were unadorned. I had yet to see a single figure carved into the rock. Interestingly, except for a few strands of web that I felt on my face, there was no indication of insects or animals of any kind. That was easily understood - in this desiccated and barren burrow, there was absolutely nothing to feed on. It was a far stance from the stories that I had heard of the tunnels under Rome, carrying waste and refuse from the city, and home to rodents and vermin of a size that far exceeded the level of belief of a person who had not seen such.

My sheets of papyrus - copies from the scroll of the builders - were in my pouch, to be consulted if the corridor actually followed the drawings. As I walked, I unrolled the string from the spool, feeling for the knots as I came to them.

I had not yet reached the forth knot when I came to an obstacle - a pile of sand reaching halfway to the ceiling of the tunnel. Apparently a crack in the rocks or a very small hole in the overhead had allowed for dirt and sand to filter slowly down, grain by grain over the years, until it made the pile that was before me.

Carefully, I clamored over it, the pile sliding with every touch of my body. The absolute dryness of the particles was an indication that this corridor was never touched by water. In fact, I needed to move with slowness so as not to raise a choking cloud of dust. Beyond, the corridor continued into the distance, until...

A blackness appeared over my head. Another shaft. I leaned the torch against the wall, then pulled out my sheets of papyrus. In the flickering light, my scribbles were only seen with difficulty, but I measured across the drawing with a finger, then began to compare it to the amount of string that I had rolled out. My best guess was that I was under one of the buildings that was the quarters for the slaves of the compound. And again, on the floor, as under the other shaft that I had descended, were a considerable amount of sticks and slivers of wood, some bound together with slivers of reeds, just as the river boats are built even today.

Suddenly, with a flash of insight, I knew what these pieces of wood had been. Ladders. Ladders to climb the shafts by whoever used these tunnels. That made sense. The depth was far too great for anyone to climb unaided, without rope or ladder.

I looked up at the square in the ceiling, but saw nothing but black. Taking the torch down the tunnel for about twenty paces, so as to remove the glare of the flame, I came back and stopped under the shaft. Closing my eyes for a while, to allow the fire blindness to end, and with my back to the torch, I looked up to still see nothing but blackness. If the top was open, as the one in the temple, then it must enter into an enclosed room with little light. Still, by averting my eyes, I could just imagine that a very slight gleam was there, but when I looked directly at it, the blackness returned.

Regaining the torch, I continued my way, twice finding more piles of sand that had leaked in during the vast time from the building, although not as severe as the first. In addition, I now began to come to other corridors that led off the one that I was following, but for this first foray, I continued only straight along the original. Finally, my string ran out, indicating that I had come almost an entire stadium under the ground. As I had no ink to scribble on my papyrus, I had also brought a wax fold-tablet and made copious notes along the way, noting every intersection and shaft that I had passed. And marks of distances, including the sand pile obstructions and the one side tunnel that was blocked by the collapse of the ceiling onto the floor.

By now, my excitement had taken as much from my sinews as a full days march across the desert. It could not even be midday as yet, and I almost drained of strength. It was time to return. In a short while, I was under the shaft, looking up at the knotted rope and preparing my climb. The bag I left, as it still contained many torches and the jug of fluid with which to charge them. I would use them on another day.

Grabbing a rope, I climbed knot by knot, slowly, until my head rose above the top of the shaft. Then with a final heave, I pulled myself up and over to the ladder. Once on the floor, I sat down against the wall, as weak as a man just coming from a bout with the swamp-disease. The physical effort had been little, but the exhilaration of the adventure had been exhausting.

That night, my consort slept alone as I lay on my mat, sleepless, my mind reeling from what I had discovered. I knew now that the reach of the gods of Rome was sufficient to touch a man across the Great Sea, despite my previous assumption that I was far beyond their power. There was no other explanation as to how a fugitive Roman, come to a strange city in Egypt, could make such a discovery that was unknown even to a single citizen of the city.

The Citizen

tempus Transit (Time Passes)

In the five years since my coming to Egypt, I had prospered, even enjoying life to the fullest. Wealth and women I had, and in abundance. I was high in the friendship of the Pharaoh, probably more for the reason of my disinterest in gaining power or influence at court or in the magistracy, than any use I was to the King's purpose. Many were the evenings that Amyrtaeus and I sat on his high terrace, looking east over the city, and discussing the world - not the problems of the city and the rulership, but of far lands and unknown peoples across the world. I believe that my friendship and the casual conversations were a balm to a ruler after a day of juggling this power faction and that.

And factions did spring up, after the bloom of the return of a native Egyptian Pharaoh had faded. This was no different than any land, and Egypt certainly had no lack of men who would commit any act to climb just one more rung on the ladder of power. One of those was a man with the name of Nepherites of Per-Banebdjedet, a small city located on a middle distributary of the Delta. In the revolt, he was a general of the rebels, and the second in command under the Ami-Re Amyrtaeus. Now, he was the general of the army, reporting only to the Pharaoh.

My concern with the man was that his appetite for conquest far exceeded the power of Egypt. For now, the people considered the land to be again resurrected as a mighty country, taking its place in the world as of old. But, my knowledge of their history, now, was far greater than the citizens and even the educated nobles. In fact, except for a few scholars and priests, such as my friend Senemut, I could claim to be the leading authority of their history, exceeded only by that few, if even them. My researches in the librarium and among the many histories recorded in stone around the city allowed me to know that, compared to the domains of ancient kings of Egypt, this one was as a child among adults. Indeed, the Egypt of the Pharaohs Khufu, Amenhotep, or Ramses, just to name a few - a very few of the ancient kings - would have considered the Egypt of today to be a minor country, unworthy of significant attention or in spending gold and men to conquer.

Yet, General Nepherites continued to solicit both the Pharaoh and the nobles to march an army across the eastern desert and fall upon the fertile lands controlled by the Persians. He failed to understand that the perceived decay of that domain was not from rot of purpose, but only as a result of turmoil among the hopefuls for the crown of that land. I knew that when the Persians settled into a stable society again, with a powerful leader, Egypt would be hard pressed to prevent the march of soldiers into their own cities.

But, I had no slightest control over such policies, and gave them little thought, nor did the King ask for my opinion on such things.

Ravana was in bloom as the favored consort of the King. She stood at his side at every official ceremony and was a favorite among the peoples when she made her appearances in the city. Many were the comments that I overheard about her golden hair, and beauty, and the favor that the gods had bestowed upon the woman. At the Temple of Hathor, during the high holy days, she blessed the women that came to implore the female deity for a fair childbirth, or that the husband would return from his far voyage and suchlike - all the things that women have worried about since the beginning of time. Ravana always gave fair predictions to her supplicants - never turning one away with mean words. I knew that the priests of that temple considered her as a spigot of gold, reveling in the gifts and portions that were brought as offerings in the name of the golden-haired siren.

Of her beliefs in the goddess that she served on occasion, she had not even a modicum of such thought. In fact, over the years I had come to realize that she had no beliefs in any gods whatsoever, taking life as a single entity between birth and death, and without guidance from beyond. From the first time that I had discussed it with her, she ridiculed my notions that the beings of Olympus were steering my life for their amusement. I accepted her skepticism with good nature, being still in a state of wonderment about the topic myself.

She was still my friend, although not of the mat, obviously. With the permission of the King, we sat many times on the high terrace, talking of this and that. She would ask about Korax, who never came to the palace, naturally, and of my current woman - and the ability of that person on the mat. Even with no known ancestry, she had become a noble woman, acting and speaking as if she were indeed descended from the highborn. And she was enjoying her life, tremendously. As to her duties, to support her master, the Pharaoh, she gave no falseness, gladly coupling her life to his. Except for the requirement that an Egyptian queen be descended from actual and recorded royalty of some land, she would have long since donned the distaff crown.

Of course, I still spent much of my time in the librarium, reading and enhancing my knowledge of Egypt and indeed, the ancient world at large. Once, Egypt had ruled even further than the Persians did this day, and much information about those ancient days could be found in the underground vaults.

And, for my own amusement, I continued to explore the hidden underground that only I, in all the land, had knowledge of.

Some of the corridors of the secret passages had been closed, for some reason, with a wall of brick. As our ship was being loaded for another voyage, I gave the factor a list of rock and stone tools to procure for me from one of the northern cities. Iron was very expensive in Egypt, for the reason that, with no suitable trees within thousands of stadia, charcoal for its production was almost impossible to procure in sufficient quantity. Copper tools, used for chiseling rock, would be useless in a very short time. Perchance I would wish to look beyond those later walls, sometime, and the iron would allow me to do so - within reason, of course

I continued my search for knowledge about the secrets that I had found in the city - the network of underground tunnels reaching under almost all buildings in the Royal Enclosure, and even reaching into the city to others. I was far from reading the ancient scripts with facility, but after years, I could pick out the meaning of most sentences, if I could find them in some context with their subject.

It was still a secret - my secret. Many times I wondered about telling the King of the world under his feet, but each time I hesitated. Why? I am not sure of the answer myself. I think, in the main, that I was like a young boy who has discovered a shallow cave on the banks of the river, or an opening into a building that leads to an unnoticed cubbyhole. Such a discovery is a treasure to a boy - it becomes his own domain, hidden from even his friends, and a place to store precious his valuables. Or even just a refuge to hide from a wrothful genitor, when that patér has spent too much time at his cups, or the mater is vexed about undone chores.

In any case, I did not reveal my discovery and only made my explorations when the King was at his palace in Karnac, leaving the compound in Memphis shorn of all but a handful of servants.

My forays into the Royal Compound were frequent enough that the few servants and slaves began to take me for granted - that strange foreigner who spent his days in the perusal of the many carving and painted scripts on every wall and building. Still, a ladder against a wall in an unused temple would be an instant reason for wonderment if and when someone walked in to find it. And if they waited, eventually they would see a man emerge, as from nowhere, to their surprise and his. To guard against such, I permanently attached a thick knotted rope that I could use to climb from the temple floor to the narrow platform of the shaft opening. If I was entering the underground, I would draw the rope up behind me, leaving an empty temple with no unusual additions for wandering eyes. When through for the day and leaving, I would just drop over the side, hanging by my hands for the moment, then letting go to fall the remaining distance. It was a goodly fall, but I was still in my strength and it gave me no trouble. A small and thin cord, colored the same as the stone of the walls, was left hanging above eye level. With a gentle tug, it would pull the climbing rope from its coil at the top, dropping to allow me to begin my explorations anew.

Much did I find during those explorations, including the reason for the hole in the wall that first led me to my discovery. I had contracted a carpenter to build a light ladder - several, in fact - of reeds, that could be broken into sections only as long as I am tall. The reason, of course, is that a full-length ladder could never be maneuvered through the turns of the narrow passageways, far less be dropped down the access hole. In fact, the length of the pieces was just short of what would fit into the shaft, given the closeness of the ceiling above the shaft opening.

Below, one ladder was permanently left in the access shaft for my entry and exit, but the others I could assemble elsewhere. Finding the shaft that was under the first hole that I had found, I climbed to find - just that - a hole in the wall, the shaft ending a double foot-length above. Many - in fact, most of the vertical shafts lead nowhere but a similar hole, almost always far up in a wall and in the shadows. Some even had the wooden plugs still in place, although rotted and fragile from their age. These were - had been - no doubt, to inhibit any sounds from below and to keep out nesting birds.

I realized that there could only be one reason for such shafts and holes. Long ago, someone - the King, priests or palace guards - could climb a ladder just like mine, quietly pull the wooden plug and listen to the conversations - and plotting - of the servants, slaves and guests - anyone within the buildings of the Royal Enclosure. No doubt, many men and women over the years were appalled to find themselves hanging by their heels from the city walls, in utter disbelief that their quietly spoken words had been given to the king by some magical entity.

Many of the corridors were filled with sand, trickling down in some past time through an imperfection of the ceiling. Some were even collapsed - permanently destroyed by the crumbling of the tunnel ceiling or walls. Still, because of the maze-like arrangement of the corridors, most blockages could be bypassed through another path.

Several other shafts, wide enough for access, and far above the ground level were found, including one in a room of the palace - one of many used for visitors and guests and adjacent to the chambers of the King and - nonexistent at this time - Queen. But I knew that a much easier way of entering the maze had to exist. The need to stack a ladder, then climb, all the while leaving the evidence leaning against a wall that something unusual was happening, would not have been feasible, if the tunnels were to remain secret. After all, long ago when they were actually used by whomever, the need would be while the King and all were present, not while they were away for any reason.

On the drawings of the master scroll were access places, I was sure, but several months went by before I found one.

Thus far, I knew that tunnels left the Royal Enclosure in two places - one next to the first shaft that I had used, and other at the front wall with the gate. The first one was blocked only a few strides past the point where I climbed up and down, but the other was long and straight. Again, the depth of dust indicated that none had passed this way in many centuries. With my knotted string, I walked the corridor slowly, examining both walls and ceiling as I passed. There was nothing - not even scribbles from the men who used this hidden walkway long ago.

Then, at a slightly widened area of the tunnel were the first stone steps that I had seen underground. Elated, I climbed the narrow steps, until I came to...

Overhead, at the top of the climb, were slabs of stone making a ceiling, jointed, but still solid. For an hour I examined it minutely, looking for the secret of the access, finally deciding that there was none. Some time in the long past, again indicated by the depth of undisturbed dust, the stairwell had been covered, maybe in some rebuilding, or need to hide the passageways.

I took note of the distance that I had walked along the knotted string and made a sketch of the angle of which the tunnel had left the Royal Enclosure, then ended my searches for the day. On the morrow, or the day after, the King would return, putting an end to my exploration for several months, at least.

The next day, I walked the distance - in the street, of course - stepping off the knots and hopefully walking directly above the hidden tunnel underground. There, I made the discovery that the tunnel entrance was - had been in the Temple of Amun. Actually, it wasn't a discovery as much as a confirmation. The last night, as I looked over my drawings and notes, comparing it with my knowledge of the city, I had thought that might be the case.

Senemut was gone to Karnac with the Royal Party, but all in the temple knew me, and of my friendship with the High Priest. And of my interest in Egyptian carvings all over the city. I could walk the grounds of the temple with no notice besides the infrequent acolyte bowing to me with a polite word of greeting. That day, I strolled all over the compound, and buildings, apparently examining scripts on the walls, and with tablet in hand, but it was just a show. I was actually looking at the floors, trying to determine just where the ancient access place had been.

I was unsuccessful. Obviously, the stone steps had been paved over after the use of the tunnels had ended, and the memory of such a path into the underground, long forgotten now.

I was standing the crowd inside the gates of the palace watching the preamble of the King's retinue on their return. First were the guards, then minor nobles and officials, then the upper magistrates, led by the Chamberlain himself. Then, on a huge chair, carried by fifty or more slaves, came Amyrtaeus looking to neither side but only ahead, as befits a Pharaoh. All bowed as his chair entered the gate, then was lowered to allow him to step off and walk down the long entry corridor. Now came the chairs of the greater nobles - and Ravana. She was looking as resplendent as always, smiling to the crowd and then following the Pharaoh into the palace.

Now that my duty of greeting was finished, and the day only half gone, I had decided to continue my researches at the librarium of Ptah. As I turned to go, a sub-officer of the guard suddenly appeared in my path.

"I have a message from the Pharaoh, my Lord." I nodded, wondering how I had been elevated to the status of high noble by the title. "He wishes to see you on the terrace when he has finished his ablutions."

Nodding again, I just replied with "Aye," then turned and walked into the palace. In a while, I had settled into chair on the high platform, under the wetted canopy and shade. A servant offered a cup and I took it, sipping the wine without much noticement of its excellence. This was an interesting development - why would the King wish to see an itinerant Roman before resting from the long journey from Karnac? And why...

I stopped my musing as a voice behind me asked, "Are you here to see myself, or just to enjoy wine at the Pharoah's expense?"

I rose from the chair and turned to see Ravana standing inside the doorway. Beautiful as always, she now displayed her natural hair - coifed in the fashion of a wig, but nonetheless, her own. And the skintight and paper thin kalasiris did nothing to conceal the lushness of her body. Even the wide straps over her shoulder were of such sheerness as to allow the points of her mammaries to protrude like small berries.

"You are looking superb, Ravana," I grinned. "And the waif from the far north is now a consort of a King. Dionysos would be proud."

She crinkled her nose and replied with, "May his cursed Greek pouchstones shrivel and fall off." She walked to the far bench and sat down. "We have both come far since Athens. And you not least of all. The accountant of the treasury tells me that you have prospered well with your enterprise."

I sat across from her. "Aye. Very well indeed, and far beyond what I need for my life. Or Korax for his, even, despite his bottomless capacity for wine." I looked at her for a moment, then continued, "And I still have your pouch that you brought to the docks in Athens. All you need to do is ask for it."

She smiled and shook her head. "What would I do with gold here? My days of haunting the garment kiosks is long past, although I would enjoy such a trip again. I merely need to speak a word, and clothing merchants are summoned to my chambers before the hour is up." She made a wry face. "The garments are supreme, but the enjoyment of the search is gone."

I nodded. "Aye, the position of consort to a King is indeed difficult." I could not keep my mirth from boiling up for more than a few heartbeats, and we both broke out in laughter.

"Old friends make for good memories." The voice was male and behind us.

Both of us jumped to our feet and bowed to the King as I said, "My apologies, Great One. I failed to hear your approach."

He waved his hand in dismissal of my regret, then said to Ravana. "I would speak to our friend alone." She nodded and bowed, then hurried from the terrace. Turning back to me, he indicated that I might be reseated. "You are well, my Roman friend? And still on your quest for even more knowledge, I would wager."

"Aye... Ami-Re. I have spent many days in the perusal of the history of this land, and have discovered many astounding facts of such." An understatement if any sentence ever was, I thought to myself. "But, how may I help the King so suddenly after his return?"

He walked to the edge of the terrace and looked over the city before replying. Now I knew that this was not a meeting for the discussion of miscellaneous topics, but was indeed of a serious nature. I waited for him to collect his thoughts. Finally, he turned and asked, "Is my information correct that your large ship is in port at this time."

I nodded. "Aye. It arrived from Tarsus in the middle of the last moon. It will stand out again before the inundation." That was about two months hence. This was interesting, but I would wager that he needed a quick voyage to... somewhere. Possibly for message taking.

"Ah. Then I would contract it for a run to Sparta with a courier. Yours is fast and, as I understand, is one of the few that can find the way on the direct route, rather than following the coastline for months."

"Aye, Ami-Re. That is so."

Now he nodded and continued, "I would wish it to remain without cargo, as to allow for its speed to be at the utmost that can be gathered. I will, of course, compense you for the empty voyage of no profit."

I shook my head. "That is unimportant, Ami-Re. I do not crave gold above any important interest that must be met."

Now he shook his own head and with a wry smile. "You are always interesting, Junius, my Roman friend. In all the city, you must be the only man with a contempt of gathering gold."

I smiled. "It is not that I despise wealth, Ami-Re. Indeed, not. But, I have discovered that, when I have enough for my needs, more is just a burden to be hidden and guarded. And, I have far more than my mere needs, with thanks to the fates and your friendship." I paused, then, "Might I enquire as to the need of this hurried message?"

Now his expression lost any humor. "Aye. Nepherites has exceeded my commands - again. His regiments have ventured down the eastern road of the Delta - for training, of course, as he says. But now I have received missives filled with bluster about the glory of Egypt and the chance given by the gods for gain and loot by acting with dispatch for opportunity. He intends to attack and seize the city-port of Pelusium."

"Is that possible?"

"Without doubt. The city has few defenses beyond the city patrols, and it has no wall. Even the two training regiments with Nepherites can easily take control. I doubt that there will even be resistance - that would be futile and risking a slaughter by green and undisciplined troops." He sat down on the bench before me. "Nay.

My concern is that twisting the tail of the Persian lion is unwise at this time. Memphis and Karnac are far away from their capital, Persepolis, and any attempt to gain suzerainty over us again would be a massive undertaking, requiring a long march over wide deserts. But, Pelusium is a major trading outpost of their empire, with links to us even now, and to Carthago and other cities along the southern coast of the Great Sea. I fear that they will react violently to the loss. And despite the boasts in the city about the ancient times returning, Egypt is in no way prepared for a war against such an enemy."

I was gratified to know that the ex-General of the rebels had not swelled with his own importance over the past few years since his victories. I knew - as did he - that his victory was with mercenaries and troops only somewhat better than untrained rabble, and against a regiment of city guards lulled into fatness and sloth by the last hundred years of peace. Against a trained and hardened foe, his old army would be as grain under the millstone. Even the standing regiments, as now constituted, were, in total, only a fraction of the size that could be fielded by Persia, and most were green and unblooded - not a comfortable thought when one is contemplating battle with the largest empire on the earth.

I said, "My ship is yours for the mission. Give the order and it will depart. I will only need the destination to give to the pilot."

"Sparta. I have hope that they will harry the Persian on their northern flank to the extent that they will ignore us. To that end, I have promised ten more shiploads of grain each month to support their army."

Curae (Worry)

I woke each morning with a feeling of... I could not bring it to a vision, but I could feel the tremors that made me fear that the gameboard of the gods was in play again. I was, once again, settled and happy with life, spending my days in learning, my evenings with the leading men of the city over cups, as is done all over the world, and my nights with various women of desirability. I was wealthy, well regarded by the King and many of the powerful of the city... It all had the likeness to the still summer day, when one cannot see the approaching storm, but can feel it all around in the skin tingling fluid that makes the hair rise from one's arm.

Then, after I had broken my fast, the feeling would dissolve with the sunrise, and I would ridicule my notion that I had any importance to any deity, anywhere.

I did not bother Ravana with my apprehensions, knowing that she would pour derision over any idea that a god was controlling my life. But Korax gave some credence to my misgivings, and in a manner that assumed that what would be would be, despite any effort on my part to avoid being a figure on the gameboard again. "If the gods are controlling, then nothing mortal man can do will change a single moment of his life." And he was correct. All I could do was wait for any events that might happen.

Nepherites did, indeed, take the city of Pelusium, although, as the King had said, it was more a matter of the immediate surrender by the leading magistrate, than any victory in battle. Still, to hear the men on their return, one would gather that the campaign was as bitterly fought and as heroically won as any in history. The taburnae of the city rang with the shouts and boasts of the returned soldiers.

The stature of the general rose highly in the opinion of the citizens, all ignorant of anything military, but the crowds always adore a victor, and many were the peans and laudations to his skill over cups and bowls of the Egyptian spirit drink.

At the palace, the praise was muted. The Ami-Re gave much displeasure to his General for the unapproved foray. Still, Nepherites seemed not to consider muchly, the vexation of the King. Certainly, he did not appear as a cur that has been kicked for cause by his master.

As the Pharaoh and his court made the journey to Karnac, for the part of the duration of the low water of the Nilos, I once again began my exploration of the underground maze of the city. Now, it was just for interest, rather than any belief that would find vaults of treasure, or scrolls from ancient times - or anything of value. In the main, it was an adjunct to my learning some of the ancient picture language, having to parse out a meaning, word by word to understand this mark and that figure on the building scrolls.

That the tunnels were built for the purpose of keeping a secret watch on the members of the court and, possibly, the priests, I had no doubt. Some of the vertical shafts that I had found apparently had no listening hole above. Assuming that they had been plugged at some time in the pasts, I ignored those blank shafts for a considerable time. But certain marks on the old papyrus made me examine one with a ladder. What I found cemented my belief that the tunnels and passageways were made for spying.

Moving a ladder to a shaft in the middle of the Palace, underground, I climbed, assuming that I would find just a vertical shaft leading nowhere. But, my climb had just begun when my torch revealed a dark blackness on two of the opposite walls. Man high, these were more passageways, but within the walls of the palace itself. Stunned, I stepped off the ladder into one, following it for a considerable distance - and almost falling down another access shaft in the floor. At intervals were wooden plugs, these of ironwood or maybe cedrus, as they were still intact. Carelessly, I pulled one from its hole to examine the stopple, and with an utterance of more disbelief as to what I had found and was still finding. The exclamation could have totally undone my secret.

This hole in the wall was much smaller than the others at the tops of the tall shafts, being no larger than an infant's wrist and slanting downward from my tunnel into the room to which it was drilled. Through it, I could clearly hear voices - close and loud - and it was only by the graces of the fates that the speakers had not heard my own careless exclamation. I was not quite sure which part of the palace I was in, but it apparently was the hall of servants, because I recognized the voice of the wine steward. He and two servants were conversing in jest about one of the serving girls and her ability to bend her body to unnatural contortions, and the willingness of her do to so with a man - if he had coin.

I paid little attention to the conversation as I peeked through the hole. The stone was thick, of course, almost the width of a foot-length, and the vision through the aperture was very limited, but enough to know that the hole was high up the wall and slanted downward so that the viewer could see the floor. I realized that the height of the opening was deliberate and to prevent both the wonderment of the occupants of a room at a the hole itself and to prevent it from being plugged or covered.

Later, I examined the holes in several of the empty rooms and found that they were indeed high up on the wall, but also always at a joint in the stones, and cleverly disguised as a defect in the joining of the wall material. One would have to climb almost to the tall ceiling to examine it, and still it would look as no more than a small and uninteresting flaw in the wall.

By now, after several years of exploration, I had filled sheets of papyrus with sketches and detailed maps of the underground, and could read the script on the original builders scroll with considerable alacrity. Again, I examined the entire scroll, end to end, but there was no mention nor drawings of the corridors within the walls of the palace. For whatever reason, the builders had not documented that feature - at least not on the master building scroll for the Royal Enclosure. It was obvious that they had been constructed during the building of the palace, as it was impossible for them to have been added later, but possibly they were detailed on a scroll that I had yet not found.

It took several days, but I found all, if not most of the internal passages, and was astounded to see that even the chambers of the King and Queen were not excluded. That was a stunning find. What man would dare spy on the Pharaoh? That fact almost indicated that the secret passages were for the use of some third party, besides the King, but who would that have been? Again, what entity in Egypt - in any land - was powerful enough to monitor his own king?

Over the following months, as I refined my map of the new passages, I overheard the profane arguments in the quarters of the guard, the blasphemous conversations of two young Priests and their thieving plans of pilfering the offerings that were left for the god. Many times, I just grinned as I listened to a pair of servants, in their amorous activities, in the middle of the day, when all good menials should be working, not skulking in an empty room enjoying the pleasures of the flesh.

Before the King returned from his journey to Karnac, I had begun to slow my exploration in the underground. Little else was left to find and what was found was just empty stone passages with no purpose, now. My interest was wearing thin, and I was becoming bored with the maze below. More and more, I confined my researches to the scrolls and tablets elsewhere in the great librarium vault - histories of the land - and lands - and stories of mythical heros and deeds.

But then...

As I approached the gate of the Royal Compound, I saw that the usual guard captain was absent, replace by a man unfamiliar to me. As I lifted my hand in greeting, he stood forth and said, "What is your business here?"

That was a shock. I had free access to the entire enclosure by will of the Pharaoh. This was a strangeness, but I replied, "I am studying the wall carvings in the greater hall, by permission of the King."

He shook his head. "None may enter without reason given to General Nepherites. Do you wish an inquiry for your need?"

I hesitated, then replied, "Nay. My studies are of little urgency. I can wait for the return of the Pharaoh Amyrtaeus." An uncertain feeling in the back of my mind told me to stay away from the attention of the power seeking officer. Besides, the inundation would be ending in a half month, and the King would return.

After the flood had ceased, our ship had returned with missives for the King, in response to his messengers. And despite my insistence that no remittance was needed or expected, he had given me a bag of gold of even more weight that would have been the case had the ship returned with a cargo. I just tossed it into the hidden vault on the grounds of my domicile. I say vault with a sense of jesting. It was just a hole carved into the stone floor and under my heavy mat platform - a bed, as Korax insisted was the proper word. Of course, only he and I knew it was there and besides, it took almost my entire strength to lift the frame and place it on a block at one end so that I could then crawl under it to reach the hole. It was unlikely that any others in the house could do so, even if they dared.

I did not speak to the Pharaoh of the General and his apparent assumption of command in the Palace during the absence of the King. Should I cause the usurper to endure the wrath of his superior, and knowing that I was the cause, then I would feel most uncomfortable when the Royal Party next left for Karnac.

But, the incident caused a humorous thought of mine from a year ago, to rise to some urgency.

As I have said, the tunnel at the place that I first dropped to explore, led both north and south, but the southern corridor was blocked with sand only a few strides beyond the entry shaft. Months ago, curious, I had attacked the sand with a spade and found that it was indeed just a pile, filtered down over time from above. Beyond, the corridor immediately moved from under the Royal Enclosure walls and into the city proper. But, unlike the maze of tunnels in the other direction, this one just continued straight for about a half stadium, then ended in a rock wall, with no other shafts or diverging tunnels along its entire length. I had no idea of its purpose.

On the southern side of the Royal wall, the city was of the domicile of merchants, not noble or wealthy, but of good consideration at that - solid citizens with profitable kiosks, or taburnae, or merchantries of custom. I carefully surveyed my maps of the underground, comparing them with distances, angles and the surface buildings. After considerable walking and stepping off paces, I had a good idea of what edifices that the external tunnel was under. Now, I put some of my unused wealth into service, and purchased the home and compound of an elderly merchant, he gladly taking my gold for his retirement in comfort.

For my next move, I needed a helper that I could trust, and of course, that was Korax. Taking his oath of silence, I told him of the underground discovery that I had been exploring for almost four entire seasons. Naturally, he looked closely at me to determine if I had been at my cups for far too long a time, and was spinning a tale as a street bard.

"By the swollen ballstones of Zeus! What you say is beyond belief." I waved my hand downward, quickly, and he moderated his voice to a quieter tone. "You. A Roman from afar, have discovered a hidden secret that is not only incredible in the tale, but one that no other man of Egypt has knowledge of? And that you have explored this wonder for years and doing it totally unseen by others during that time?"

With a wry grin, I just nodded.

"Then, my Roman friend, I have to say that the choice between your tale being true, and the odds of your being in the taverna for far too long a time, then... Well, I have to say that the second is my choice for the truth of this matter." I just shrugged. "And why do you determine that now is the time to tell me of this marvel?"

Now I became serious. "As has happened to me before, the sunshine is becoming hazy, with the hint of thunder in the air. I feel it in my bones that another happening is due to change the course of my life, just as it did in Rome and Athens. I have been far too long without adventure, and this time, we may not find a convenient ship about to depart from the calamity. Thus, we must make our own plans."

Unlike Ravana, Korax did not so lightly dismiss the gods, and could well believe that one might become a puppet for such deities. He knew of my adventures in the past, save that of being a slave of the pirates, and accepted that they were the gameplay of Olympus. Thus, he gave more credence to my feelings of impending trouble than the existence of an underground system of streets and alleys.

I could not take him into the Palace, then down the shaft to give truth to my tale. I had been within the great enclosure so often that my presence was almost invisible to all in the compound, but a strange and bearded Greek would stand out like a river dragon in one's bath. He would have to take my tales as truth for the nonce.

Shaking his head, and still with some disbelief, he asked, "What is your plan, and the use for myself?"

Tonitus (Thunder)

Word was put out that I was building a merchantry for the cargo that my fleet of ships would be bringing to the city. Of course, few knew that my 'fleet' consisted of exactly one sea-going vessel, a coastal runner and a river trader. No matter, it was a good cover for my purpose.

Korax had taken the river boat to the city of Naukratis, that Greek outpost on the western distributary of the Nilos, and had returned with three slaves that had once been citizens of his country, making sure that none spoke the Egyptian language. Immediately, with sand spades and the iron tools that I had procured years before, they began digging a hole in a storage room of the small compound.

While Korax was on his boat, I had measured and plotted as carefully as possible, even climbing to the top of the temple in the Royal Enclosure and raising a pole with a strip of cloth at the top and over the hidden shaft in the building. From the top of the merchant compound, I could see the flag and used it to determine a direction from the temple. Hopefully, I was within a stride or two of its path, but I knew the exact depth of the tunnel, and if it wasn't intersected by that level, we would dig sideways until it was encountered.

As the ground was hard packed dirt and not rock, the digging went fairly quickly, with the spoil being evenly spread around the compound yard. Any attempt to haul oxen loads in a cart, to the outside of the city, would instantly inform the all that digging was happening within.

My survey was good, and in a depth of only about two man lengths, the edge of a stone slab was encountered. As the rock was flat, I knew that this was one of the ceiling stones of the tunnel. Altering direction of the dig a little, soon we could stand on the stone and in a day or so the dirt shaft was finished. Then, with four poles, made of the river trees on the bank of the Nilos, we cornered the hole, then lined the shaft with woven reed mats. It was not substantial, but would keep dirt from continually falling from the sides of the shaft as we climbed up and down on the reed ladder.

Thus far, the slaves only knew that they had dug a hole, and that would be all they would learn. With a gold piece in hand, they were led to the boat and soon departed for a city of the Delta, now free men...

...As long as they did not return to Memphis. I made sure that they understood that imperative.

Now, with the long iron chisel and mallet, it was up to Korax and myself to penetrate the roof of the tunnel. I was certain that the bash of iron upon iron could be heard as far as the port itself, but as I walked to the street, letting Korax wield the hammer, it was audible, but not overpowering. If we finished quickly, few would bother to notice.

Even before I had returned to the shaft, the hammering had stopped. I looked over the edge to see Korax climbing out. Below was a huge hole in the stone. Vigorously rubbing the dirt and dust from his hair and beard, he said, "The slab was only three fingers thick. When the rod broke though, I just whaled the rock with the hammer and it shattered and fell into the hole." Now, swilling from a jug of water - almost the only time I had seen him drink anything but wine - he shook his head and said, "I take back the words of doubt, my Roman friend. Your tale apparently has more than just dream-dust behind it."

Over the next half month, we transformed the merchantry into... well, a merchantry. At least to all that passed the gate. I accoutered the living spaces with comfort and Korax and his woman moved into it as their dwelling. Over the next few months, bags and barrels and wares sewn up in matting were stacked in the courtyard to give at least a hint of being a working storage for our ships. The hole itself had a wooden cover and on that, empty amphorae. Empty, in case of thieves. Any that happened to sneak into our compound should look in the jugs, then move on to more lucrative loot.

As another precaution, for a fear that even now, I could not define, I brought half of our gold and placed it inside the tunnel, just below our new access. My wish would have been to find a corridor that led even beyond the walls of the city, but I had no slightest indication of any such. In fact, only three even left the Royal Enclosure - ours, the one to the Temple of Amun - permanently closed from above by a stone floor - and another leading east, but blocked by a collapse within a few strides of the wall.

As an escape from the Palace, it might be, but as to leaving the city, it was useless.

The year following the flood was good, and my misgivings were put to ease, somewhat. The overbearing Nepherites had seasoned his ambitions, and the Persians had not reacted to the capture of their remaining southern outpost. The reasons were that their empire was still in a state of flux, with men still vying for the kingship, but mainly in that little had changed as to the purpose of the port of Pelusium. Persian ships - as did all from every land - still called with cargo to be offloaded to river boats and accepted more from the same. Except that the tax farmers had different masters, the merchants of that city had seen little difference in their trade after the usurpation of their city. Commerce has little interest in the squabbles of kings as long as it does not affect the movement of goods from place to place.

Sparta had, of course, accepted the additional grain shipments from Egypt, but as to their agreement to enhance their pressure against the Persian Empire - well, that was still to be seen.

I was still called to the Palace, to attend meetings and give my opinion whenever the talk happened to touch the northern lands. It was an amusement to myself that I was considered a consummate authority on such, even though my actual knowledge was shallow at best, knowing only Rome as a young man and Athens from the view of the street. More pleasurable were the quiet exchanges with the King as a friend, rather than my god-appointed Pharaoh. He used our conversations about this and everything as a balm against the daily rigors of rule, and the difficulty of resurrecting the greatness of Egypt to that of old, and with only a small part of the resources needed for that task.

I doubted that he could do so. I knew from my extensive study that the Egypt of those halcyon days of monument building grew to greatness, in the main, because of their distance from any other power. Centuries of quiet isolation from the rest of the world, enforced by almost trackless deserts and distances and, of course, the Great Sea, allowed the land to grow by putting all of its resources into building, and few into defending from those without. By the time they had touched other lands and empires, they were of a greatness to swallow any in their path or destroy those who would threaten the greatness of their creation.

In addition, the Nilos was a vast source of fertility for the people, seldom failing to bring down a harvest of mud to enrichen the fields of grain and growing foodstuffs. Unlike the people of most lands, Egyptians were spared the periodic famines that occurred when the gods withheld the rains or flooded the fields with roaring waters. Or caused the cold season to arrive before the harvests. Or gave the fruits of husbandry to a plague of locusts...

Now, the world was populated with peoples as numerous as Egypt, and more importantly, far more powerful in the military sense. Every northern power had long since supplied their armies with weapons of iron, whereas the regiments of the Pharaoh were still equipped with spearpoints and blades of bronze. Not in the entirety, of course, but iron weapons were the accouterments of the well-to-do soldier, whereas the humble ranker still used a copper edge that might have been handed down from his male genitor, many generations removed.

I was certainly not a sage of military history, but even in my shallow knowledge of strife between lands, I knew that matching copper with iron on the field of battle was certain doom for the wielders of the ancient metal.

My palace conversations were not limited to the King. Ravana was now in full bloom, a mature woman with a knowledge of the world beyond her jars of unguents and paint. We still enjoyed long conversations, occasionally - in daylight and full view of servants and passersby in the palace, of course - about the past, the future and anything that might have stimulated our interest since our last nattering. I learned that she had repulsed several intimations by Nepherites for a clandestine meeting - in his chambers. Ravana seldom gave oath, but when the name of the General entered a conversation with myself, she was as Korax in his most imprecating mood. I expected the birds overhead to drop from their flight, and the very walls of the Palace to tremble at her words. I soon learned to keep his name from our conversation.

Then came an event of sadness.

I had accompanied the Pharaoh to the City of the Sun, Heliopolis, downriver from the Pyramidos and just past where the various distributaries began at the head of the Delta. My duty was to scribe several missives to the rulers of Sparta, to be delivered on the next grain ships leaving for that far land. On my return, I found Korax waiting as I walked down the footbridge from the King's barge to the Royal Wharf. My jesting greeting was not returned in kind, and I realized that my friend was waiting with news that could not be gladsome.

He took me by the arm and led me away from the stream of men leaving the ship. I waited as he looked around, the said, "Ehsan has gone to his reward, wherever that is for Persians."

Surprised, I exclaimed, "He has passed from this life? How?"

He shook his head. "The medico priest is waiting with knowledge, although I had little success in following his reasoning."

We hurried across the port and into the city, then to the sector of the city in which Ehsan had made his comfortable home.

There, the women of the house - his cocus, maidservant and, of course, his mat widow - were wailing in the small atrium, around the body of my friend, laid out on a bed of reeds. It was indeed, Ehsan, he of some begotten tribe of Gandara, late of the Persian fleet, in which he was a Premier Subahdar of a stashion of row-ships. His count of the seasons was more than mine, but less the that of Korax, therefore the reason that he had reached the end of his thread of life could not be natural.

Waiting was a physician, a priest of the forth or fifth class, as it is noted in Egypt. He bowed to me as I hurried up and asked, "Of what did the captain perish?"

The priest, a man of about thirty years, replied, "He had been given medicaments and cathartics for the condition of bloating this season - and since before the inundation moon. He complained of somatesthesia of the gut, and the intumesce of the belly after his meals. The temple prescribed a purgative and an evacuant for the bowels to rid the body of worms and the foul helminth that cause the condition." He looked at the body, being wailed over by the women before continuing, then, "But in the last moon, his water was running red with his life's fluid, and his droppings were of an evilness that indicated the condition was taking him without pause. Thusly, he went to his god during the night, and with the blessing of the exit of pain."

I had understood much of what the priest had said, if not the particular medicaments that he was given, but knew that my friend was one of those that had succumbed before his time by some evilness of the body. I well knew that, besides the god-given lifetime of a man, to be sixty years and five, that many met their end far sooner, and not at the hand of an enemy. And most had no reason for their sickness but that their stars had been less fortunate than a fellow man. I certainly had not known of the ailments of my friend, but that was, no doubt, his choosing. No man wishes to display the evilness that may extrude from his body in such times.

I had never had the story of his being, that of an important man in the fleets of his land, where he was highly ranked and raised to command above many. And now, I never would.

Now Korax walked to us and looked back at our friend for a heartbeat before saying, much more quietly, "But, we were drinking to the rising moon only a handful of days ago. How could he come to this end so suddenly?"

Now the priest spoke. "Wine was the balm that made his last months bearable. He used it in excess to ease the fire in his belly. It was that, or fall on his own knife, as such an evil condition can be more than a man can dispute without crying out to his friends and womenfolk."

No matter. What had happened could not be undone by mortal man. I looked at the priest and asked, "I will stand his debts for his treatment. What is the accounting?"

The man bowed, and said, "Nay. He has paid the temple fee and leaves this life unhindered. And now, I leave you with your sorrow." Bowing again, he turned and walked off, down the street.

I said, "We must honor our friend, and lay him to rest."

Korax started as if stung by an insect. "We will not give him to the House of the Dead, in the company of those body defilers, to be sliced like a fowl on feast day and dosed with their stinking incenses and reeks!"

"Nay! Nay! He is not Egyptian and needs not their rituals. We will inter him in the Achaemenian fashion and with a sepulchral monument fitting to his worth. There is no lack of Persians in this city, and we can find the proper forms for our friend."

And thusly, it was so. In three days, we followed a man with the knowledge of Persian rituals and placed our friend under a stone of some magnitude. As his wealth, built up since he became our captain, was now ours, it was only fitting that we make his woman comfortable in her grief. Korax ensured that the house was free of debt, and I arranged for a goodly pension at the temple, to be drawn by the woman at the new moon each month.

That evening, sitting on my terrace, looking up at the brilliant stars, my thoughts roamed widely. I had come within a mere finger's breath of death innumerable times, and yet, here I was, whole and wealthy and living a goodly life. And there was a man, of good character and strong, struck down to death merely by living his life. Once again came my self-question, asked innumerable times in the past - were the events affecting the life of a man directly from the will of the gods, or even from their godly play on the gameboard, or did mere fate choose, by happenstance, those who lived and those who died?

Events began to coalesce, bringing my fears of uncertainty to a greater pitch. I made the journey to the port, there to meet with our agent and discuss repairs that were needed to our greater ship. That vessel had been a faithful servant since the time that the gods of war had placed it into our hands, but like a person, any ship aged and became infirm in time. Our current captain had complained before now about the growing weeds on the hull, where the water was always touching. Such growth slowed a ship, and even greatly, should they be allowed to flourish.

A morning with the shipwrights, and with gold passing from my hand to theirs, the preparations were begun to careen the hull onto the sands of the shore, there to allow for the workers to clean the bottom hull of the long filaments of green. I had no actual use in the procedure, but as one who has great interest in the proper outcome, I waded and strove with the workers and slaves on the ropes as the hull was heaved onto the shore, beam wise to the water. Now, it was rocked sideways toward the shore, revealing half of the area to be cleaned. After a work of two days, it would be re-floated, then pulled ashore once again, but with the other side revealed for the work.

By the time the sun was dropping towards the walls of the city, I was tired, muddy and looking less like a wealthy merchant than a port worker coming from his wage of coppers. A binding thirst drove me into a port taburna - one that I would normally be unlikely to visit to drink of their watered and sour wine.

The tables were mere stacks of fired bricks and the seats only of woven reeds, but I was not there to examine the goodness of the taburna but to clear my throat of dust and phlegm. I sat at a small table, next to a patron well gone in his cups, and mumbling to himself in a dialect of which I could barely understand a word. The caupo brought a bowl of his best - he said - and I relaxed and began to partake of it. It was not of the quality of the King's table, but surprisingly, it was refreshing and a decent thirst quencher.

I just sat and sipped, idly giving thought to hiring a chaïr for the long journey to my domicile, rather than use my aching legs. As the day grew longer, the taburna filled with workers coming from their tasks, and pausing before moving to their homes for the evening meal.

At the long table, men caroused and drank and japed, and spent considerable breath in cursing the foremen and merchants which both controlled their work and their recompense. Eventually, the topic was broached about the great General Nepherites and his brilliant victory over the Persian scum that had oppressed the people of Egypt since before living memory. At that statement, I wrinkled my brow in surprise - that officer was merely a single entity in the victory of the Ami-re Amyrtaeus. How could any man give praise to another for the Pharaoh's long effort in freeing the land?

Then, I realized that the "victory" being referred to, was the usurpation of the port city of Pelusium. That was even more absurd, as more men were wounded on both sides by the edge of their own weapon than by that of their foe. In fact, I knew that the occupation of that city by his regiment was a bloodless a victory as has ever been recorded. Yet, it was being discussed here as if it were the equivalent of the ancient and monstrous and blood-soaked battles between the Egyptians of Ramses and those of the Hittites. As I watched and listened, I noticed that one man was the... arbiter of the discussions, giving forth with a demagoguery about the qualities of the General, then allowing another to run with his words. When the topic might change or fall away from his need, another reference to the officer would begin the discussion again. Without actual reference to the Pharaoh, the man seemed to be suggesting the General as being the superior leader between the two.

Now, as I looked more carefully, the man had some familiarity, but I could not, with any intensity of thought, place the face in any specific memory. I continued to listen as the number of cups taken by the men had the effect of both raising the voices of the gabblers and lowering their fear of speaking against the ruling authorities. If a magistrate or member of the city guard should stroll by, and hear such...

I suddenly froze in place, the half-tipped cup in front of my lips. I had suddenly realized where I had seen the man now giving his rebellious words to the carousing workers and stirring the pot of resentment against the Pharaoh. He was a member of the unit of the Palace guards. Now the place and face came to me in full. I had no idea of the rank nor name of the man, of course, but I was certain that he was one that I saw on occasion, in their morning formation or escorting this guest or that.

I leaned back into the shadows, holding my cup in front of my face in the natural manner. There was little chance of the man recognizing me, muddy and disheveled as I was, and in the shadows of the corner, but I wished to take no chances. I knew now that evil was afoot.

And within the month, the evidence of wrongdoing was cascading into a flood.

Tempesta (Storm)

The troubles began with the passing the Feast of Isis and that epigomenal day on which her Son, Horus, reaches his southernmost realm in his sun chariot, before beginning the return to illuminate the land of his people.

The Pharaoh had been away for a month, up the river to the city of Tod, just before the first cataract, and the outpost that guarded the frontiers of Kush. Much trade flowed into this city from the south, and many merchants grew wealthy from the pelts, ivory, gold and copper that came from the vast lands to the south. The General was left in residence in Memphis, taking command in the city in the absence of his leader. I came to the Palace on the odd day to sort through any received missives from the far northern lands and to immediately give start to a river boat to the King with any that were of importance. Thus far, none had been more than accountings of grain delivered.

This evening, I was on the usual terrace that was my usual relaxing place when in the Palace. The view from here of the eastern part of the city and the port was magnificent. And with the setting sun now behind the bulk of the Palace edifice, it was usually cooler than any other place available to me. I was startled to see Ravana approach - I had had no idea that she was in the city of Memphis, rather than in Karnac with the King. Unless he had returned without my noticing... Nay, that was improbable in the extreme. The return of the Pharaoh after an extended absence was cause for ceremony that could be heard from one end of the city to the other - the linen-wrapped departed in the City of the Dead would have heard such a commotion.

I rose to greet her, then stopped, my eyes opening wide to see her expression. She was as a man in the grips of choler, after an insult in the taburna and too many cups. Her usually pale white face was as the setting sun through low and reddening clouds. Even her maid-in-waiting, usually hovering next to her mistress for any need, was standing away in self-preservation. I kept my words and poured a goodly measure of wine in a golden cup, handing it to the seething woman. She swallowed the liquid as if she were a taburna slut in the port, and held it out for another.

This woman from the far north was self-taught to nobility, and could stand with any highborn female in the city, with even her accent smoothed to a pleasant inflection through constant practice. But, this day, her words were in Latium and such that she could have burned the ears of the aforementioned taburna slut. I was no fool, and certainly not a rutting young man willing any risk to speak to a beautiful female, thus I just sat with a carefully neutral expression. Not for gold would I have asked about her vexation.

In a while, she began breathing normally, and her face returned to its normal shade, although she was still obviously brooding about... whatever had happened. Finally, after her third cup, she asked, "When is the King to return?"

I raised my palms in indication of ignorance. "Nay. I do not have the information, but I doubt that it will extend past the half month. Any longer would risk being upriver during the start of the inundation." In fact, the rites to the river god for a good flood would start in two days. Hesitantly, I said, "I am astonished that you are not with him..."

She drank again, then replied with less heat than before, "In the days before the Royal Barge set out for the journey, I came with the flux of the bowels. It was an evil seven-day period that I experienced and that is no deception, be sure of that. And another length of time passed before I gained my strength enough to even leave my chambers." She put the cup down and asked, "Will you return to Karnac before the court leaves that city?"

"Not unless a critical message should arrive, needing my insight. But I doubt it. There is little time left before the flood and I might well meet the court coming down the river." I hesitated, then asked, "Why?" The question I wanted answered was the reason that the female sitting before me was seething, but I would wait for the knowledge to be offered.

We could see two women walking towards us - noble females wanting to ingratiate themselves with the person closest to the Pharaoh. It was the one insect on her honey-bread of life, as she had often told me. She naturally enjoyed the friendship of young women and was often seen in company with such during the day, but the constant attempts of older dowagers to insinuate a like friendship was a burden.

She shook her head, and replied, "Nay. Forget that I ask." Suddenly, she stood and said, "I am evil company this day and for that I give my sorrow. I will retire early and try to rest my thoughts. A pleasant evening, Junius." Then, before she turned to hurry away, she whispered, "Make your rest in the Palace this night and wait." Now she hurried to the steps, followed by her hand-maid.

Now my uneasiness that calumny was in the air was certain. I could think of no reason for Ravana to be in the state of rage, nor who could have brought her to such, nor why she insisted that I bed in the

Palace this night. She had no official powers whatsoever - even I, as a minor noble and with the friendship of the King, had more authority to order this and that from the servants of the Palace. But, in the unofficial realm, she was the most powerful woman in the land. Obviously, one who is the favored mat-woman of a king is one who can have her wishes fulfilled on demand. Only the Pharaoh himself would be immune to her wrath for any vexing action, and he had been absent for an entire moon.

That night, as I lay for my sleep in the cubiculum that had long been assigned to me, but seldom used, I was alone. I had no use for any of the willing females that would have warmed my mat this night, as my thoughts were of such intensity that even the most desirable of them would probably have failed to cause a response in my svans. Thus, I just lay for hours under the coolness flowing in from the open window, exhausting my thoughts without reaching any conclusions.

And I was waiting in anticipation - the plea from Ravana for my presence in the Palace that night could only mean one thing, and would be a matter of...

I froze, almost breathless, as a creak came from the thick wooden door. I moved my hand to my side, feeling for the hilt of my longknife as I listened and watched for the intruder. I knew full well, that should I be seen as an obstacle to any nefarious plans around the Pharaoh, then the removal of my person would be the merest piece of any conspiracy.

The moon was a waning gibbous lamp and gave some light through the window, although she had no direct rays into my room. But it was enough to see the door slowly open and a white face peer around the edge. Without sound, I rose and took my long practiced defensive stance, waiting...

"My Lord?" came a quiet call. I had a sudden realization that flooded into my being, that my long night of questions might be coming to fruition. The voice was from the cosmeta and maid of Ravana, and her presence had to be a direct order from the golden-haired woman herself. I quickly moved to the door, pulled the slight girl into the room, then closed it, looping the holding rope around the catches.

Nighttime assignations, in a palace filling with nefarious plots, were not the usual chores of a menial, and I could feel the trembling of the girl in her arm. I pulled her to the far side of the room into the faint light from the covered window.

"Speak," I whispered. "Your mistress has sent you. Or have you come of your own accord?"

"She wanted me to warn you of danger to your person, My Lord."

Before she could continue, I asked, "What was the vexation of your mistress, today?"

Almost inaudibly, she said, "The soldier-leader Nefertus accosted her in her chambers, with an accusation of betrayal and plotting against the divine Pharaoh." I choked back a massive exclamation before it could emerge, as I was disbelieving what my ears were hearing. She meant General Nepherites, of course, but... "He gave that she was intending a woman's plot, by ending his life with her blade during their coitus, then joining her band of betrayers in flight." Still looking at the slight girl with incredulity, I told myself to keep my silence and not interrupt the flow of words from the frightened maid. She said, in even a lesser voice, "He was standing as close to her as I am to you, My Lord, and fingering his blade between them."

"I am not 'My Lord,'" I said uselessly. "Who is in her band of supposed miscreants?" She just looked at me with a frightened expression, until I suddenly asked, "Me?" She nodded.

Now I was cursing to myself, and not quietly, when the woman leaned forward and said, "His concern was not for the Pharaoh, My Lord. But for the man-swelling in his kilt."

Now my hand went to my own knife. "He... He did not violate the consort!"

"Nay, My Lord. But he stripped her of clothing and left her standing naked as he japed about the need to search for needles and blades."

This was as a night-dream after an evening of carousing in the taburna and devouring an excess of rich foods. "She... Ravana did not submit with..."

Now the young maid shook her head vigorously and spoke with more emphasis, even pride. "Nay, My Lord. My mistress is slight, and the man is large and vigorous, and her sinews were as nothing in combat with his, but she gave no quarter with her issuance of rage." I would have chuckled had the situation been less dire, as I could well imagine the fiery woman scorching the air with her words. "He did not violate her with his man-thing. And, at the end, and after his hands had well searched her body, he left with words of laughter and disdain for a foreign woman come to conquer the land."

That made no sense. To accost the consort of the Pharaoh - even by the most senior officer of the realm - was insane. Amyrtaeus had overlooked many of the overbearing actions of his general, but this... The man would be fortunate to still be wearing his skin when he was hung by his heels from the walls when the King received the tale...

When he received the tale...

I was deep in dark thoughts when the maid interrupted with, "My Lord, I must hurry back to her chambers."

I nodded and just stood in my room as she hastened away. My sojourn in my adopted land had just taken a turn for the worst. That there was malfeasance in the wind was obvious. It was an ominous tale that I had just been told. It was as if the General did not have a concern about the news of his actions reaching his superior.

Now, any chance of sleep was gone. I now realized that the conspiracy against the Pharaoh was real and definite. The man in the taburna, speaking the praises of Nepherites, was not - could not be as a single deed. Probably, agitators all over the city were fomenting evil thoughts against Amyrtaeus and lauding the deeds of his general. Again, it was underlined by the actions of the offense in the chambers of Ravana this day, apparently done with no fear of retribution. That could only mean the usurpation had begun, or would begin shortly. And as I was well known as the friend and consultant of the King, then...

My life was soon to be ended - of that, I had no uncertainty. In fact, the wonder was that even now I was not laying lifeless in the rubbish pits of the city. The reason was, no doubt, that I was of such insignificance to the plotters that I had fallen out of their notice, or my demise was something to be handled at leisure at a future time.

Or, the guards could even now be marching to my cubiculum.

I put my head out of the door, still open from the maid's departure, and looked both ways down the hall. Except for a dying torch far down the way, there was nothing. With my hand on my longknife, I quietly strode away from my room, and toward a side exit of the Palace. Stopping at each turn, to examine my path, then moving to the next turn, I quickly moved to the far back of the compound, the temple of Heket, in which I had first discovered the access shafts to the underground maze.

Quickly, I pulled the line that dropped the knotted rope and in a few heartbeats I had disappeared from the world above - safe, for the moment. Praising the gods of all lands that I had made an external access from the outside, I moved along by feel, not even bothering to ignite a torch. The distance was not long, and soon I felt the ladder leading upward to our false merchantry.

Quietly, and with some effort, I lifted the platform that covered the hole - the jugs above were empty, but still the weight was considerable - and emerged in the little storage hut. Not wishing to surprise Korax in his slumber, and receiving a spearpoint through my body with his reaction, I stood at the door to his bedroom and quietly called his name.

Both he and his widow woke, and with puzzlement. "Junius? That is you?" I would have grinned, had the situation been less dire. Korax never used my name in his waking moments. I was always 'my Roman friend,' in our conversations.

"Aye. And with trouble. Stir yourself."

At their eating table, we sat as his widow lit a small oil lamp and then brought cold cakes left from the evening meal. I gave Korax the tale of Ravana and my experience in the taburna with the agitator. And my thoughts on what was happening. Or was going to happen.

As always, he was unwavering in the face of news that was less than gladsome. Without exclaiming his disbelief or wailing about the fates, he just said, quietly. "Our ship is loading for the next voyage," he said. "We can board and give this land a view of our backsides."

The vessel had been cleaned and refurbished, and our agent had begun to bid on the linens and fabrics to be the next cargo. But... "It may not come to that. If I can warn Amyrtaeus, this rebellion may yet be suppressed."

"Where is the King, now?"

"In Tod, above Karnac. At least, he was. The Royal Barge will return shortly, before the floods start."

Korax swore. "By the putrid wine-breath of Bacchus. He might as well be in Rome." He swallowed a gulp from his cup, then waved away the jug of his widow. "If you are seen boarding a river-boat for the south, the river-dragons will feast on you before the city is lost from sight. I suspect informants on the wharves are watching for such movement even now - by anyone. The General would be a fool to let any from the palace leave Memphis for that direction."

"But..."

"Nay. Let me finish. You need to fall from their vision and hope that none notice. Let me make the preparations. To any of importance, I am nothing. Who in the city would suspect a Greek of conniving?" I nodded. His words were sound. Hidden, I had a chance of escaping this tragedy. Otherwise, I could be executed on a word at any instant.

He said, "What of your priest friend? Senmet or whatever his name is?"

I shook my head. "Senemut. He is in Karnac with the court. And I know of none that I dare trust in the Temple of Amun to get word to him."

Finally, Korax said, "If the Pharaoh and his followers have not the sense to know what is happening under his own roof, then it little matters of a Roman from afar gets word to him. Besides, he is hundreds of leagues away and far beyond your help."

I nodded, if unwilling to agree. The Ami-Re had been good to me and had offered me friendship with no expectation of any useful reason. To just abandon him, and run to save my skin, was not a pleasant thought. But still, Korax had the truth of it - the Pharaoh might as well be at the ends of the earth for any hope of my reaching him before the evildoers struck.

Then, I had a thought. "What of Ravana. We cannot leave her for that scum to use as his bordello-wench."

Now Korax gave a hint of a laugh, although there was no laughter in it. "Once again, you are fleeing for your life, and stopping to abduct the bed-mate of the most powerful man in the land." He held up his hand to stop my protest. "Nay, I jest, and not with good taste. But, how do you plan to obtain her? If you walk back into that Palace by the front gate... I would not wish to view my Roman friend hanging by his heels from the city walls as I cast off to leave."

We settled our talk, then I retired to rest the balance of the night, although there was little enough remaining. When I woke, the sun was an hour up, and Mira, his widow-wife, told me that Korax had left for the port - the first time that the woman had ever given her words to me, I think. I ate a meal without noticing its composition, all the while furiously thinking on our plight. A considerable time was spent in cursing the gods, now once again playing with their gameboard and little carved figures of mortals far below, throwing the bones and laughing at the count.

Then, still not having a purpose, but unwilling to hide in the shadows of the merchantry, I climbed down the ladder to the tunnel and followed the passages back under the palace. At one of the entry shafts leading up to the hidden wall corridors, I climbed and slowly moved along, listening at each hole that I came to. By now, after my extensive exploring, I had a full understanding of the relationships between the spy warren and the rooms that they accessed. Every part of the Palace did not contain a hidden passage in the walls, of course - far from it. There was little reason for the builders to plan for the surveillance of the innumerable rooms and the public areas of the immense edifice, and it would have been unrealistic for them to have tried. Not only would the building be even more massive than it even was, but the use of thick walls everywhere would also have given away the secret long before now.

Still, the gathering places of the servants and slaves were available, as were the meeting rooms that were used by the magistrates and administrators. Even the King's conference forum had a listening hole. But, on this day, I moved to the planning room of the Palace guard.

Carefully removing the ancient wooden plug, I leaned against the cool stone with my ear to the hole. And, indeed, men were present and talking. For an hour on a waterclock I listened but heard nothing but the normal give and take of soldier commands. After some thought, I realized that unless the revolt was imminent, it would be very unlikely for the rank and file - or even the middle ranking officers - to have knowledge of it. The morning went by without any addition to the knowledge of the - my - situation. Finally, I retired back to the compound to attempt to gather some of the sleep that I had lost the night before.

Flumen (Flood)

Korax had come and gone several times during the day but, before the sun had set, he was back with word that our ship was ready to stand out at any time. And that he had seen the General, in the middle of the day, at the training fields adjacent to the port. More interesting, he told me that he had watched the man enter the Palace gate a short time before. With that news, I called him to move the cover of our hidden shaft aside, then replace it as I climbed down to the corridor. With only a small oil lamp for light, I hurried to the shaft under the guard officer room, then climbed into the narrow access between the walls.

For a while, I only heard the casual talk of this officer and that, dictating ordinary orders to a scribe. But, my patience and hopes were fulfilled when I heard the shout of a soldier and clanking as all in the room rose to greet Nepherites. Of course, I did not hear an outline of their rebellion - that would have been far too much to expect of a sudden listening, but I heard much of a subsidiary purpose, and far more than I needed to absolutely confirm that the plans for the usurpation of the throne were real - including the murder of the Pharaoh. Many were the men marked to be destroyed - for the purpose of gaining their wealth, or as men known to be fervent supporters of the Pharaoh. Or both. I did not hear my name put to the fatal list, but I had no doubt that it was there.

And, apparently, he had recalled several regiments of soldiers, supposedly in training at various towns up and down the river, but who were now in some encampment nearby, and ready to be called to action. Then my hair rose on my neck as I recognized a voice - that of the Chamberlain of the King. How he could be here, rather than with Amyrtaeus far up the Nilos, I had no idea, but I knew that the trusted advisor was playing the part of the traitor.

Unless, Amyrtaeus had already returned...

Nay. That was impossible. The procession of the King into the city after a long absence would have been a huge affair, and Korax would have certainly mentioned it as the first news of the day. Even I, hiding in the merchantry, would have heard the clamor of the people. Besides, his return was not scheduled for the quarter month, at least.

Little else was heard that enhanced my knowledge of the plot, and when the General left for his rest, thus did I.

Far into the night, we sat and talked, but without improving our plans. All that remained was the time for our departure, and that would have already come, had I had any idea of how to warn Ravana of the coming tragedy.

"Can you not guide her through the tunnels, then to here?" asked Korax. "We could be on the ship at first light and afloat before the fast was broken in the Palace."

I shook my head. "If it were stairs leading down, I would already have done so, but how to get her over the wall and into the access shaft in the temple? She is young and vital, but a woman cannot climb a rope, even to save her life." We just sat and relaxed in the cool evening air for a while, then I asked, "The ship is ready?"

"Aye. Provisioned and loaded with some cargo. I have stopped the loading on the pretext of searching out new bids. Should we leave here with haste, I would rather that we have a light hull with speed, and not wallow like an overladen coaster."

"Take a large purse of our gold and stow it under the cargo. I would rather not port in a strange land as a destitute castaway."

"Aye. I have thought of it."

The night passed without incident, but the next morning I was back in the tunnels and listening here and there. The morning passed without my learning anything else - of importance to our flight, that is. Much did I hear of the treachery of the evil General, sadly given trust by a man who thought of the traitor as a friend. But nothing approached the japing that I heard as the high officers sat for their midday meal.

The usual profane japes and jests, common to all military men in the world, flew from one end of the table to the other. Then, I heard an officer call to another, "What of the golden-haired minx, Commander? Will the General take her as consort?"

At that statement, I became as motionless as the man-headed stone lion, beside the great Pyramidios, that Egyptians call the Kepera-re, and the Greeks, the Sphinx. Another answered with a laugh. "For the time that it takes to empty his man-pouch of seed, perhaps. The General says that his own consort wishes a hair-piece of the same golden color as the King's woman. He has promised to have one made from the long hair of the wench." Now there was a guffaw. "But, I fear that only her head will be taken to the wigmaker."

Both cold in feeling and hot with rage, I quietly cursed all to the wrath of Hades, which was about all that one man could do against many. Especially with a thick stone wall between myself and the japing scum.

The rest of the day, I listened here and there, but heard nothing that I cared about, nor did I expect to. But a resolve came to me. It was time to put my hesitation to the mat.

Late that night, I gave to Korax that he would wait until the hour before dawn, then if I had not appeared, to go to the boat as soon as the gates leading to the port were opened and leave this land forever. As I sat on the edge of the shaft, about to step onto the ladder, he put his hand on my shoulder and said, "Do not fail to return. Life would be dull without my Roman friend bringing me to a new adventure at every turn of the seasons."

In the tunnels again, I carried only a torch and another rope, besides my longknife. I had almost left the weapon behind, as any impact of it on stone would be as a gong in the still of the night. Now I moved to the shaft under the old temple - the first one that I had discovered. Leaving the torch stuck in the sand of the floor, and newly charged with the liquid from a jug, a few moments were taken to prepare for what I hoped would be a need. Then I quietly let myself down to the temple floor with the thick knotted rope.

I had made this journey more times that I could count and needed no guide of light to make my way. That was fortunate since the moonless night was black and at this late time, few torches were still burning. Around the maze of statuary and pillars, I slowly moved until I came to the side entrance that I usually had used. Now the path was dark indeed. I could not see even my own feet, as I slowly stepped along, my hand on the wall to give direction. One corridor and a turn, then another - a long hallway and then I came to the wide concourse of the Royal chambers. Suddenly, the ease of my travels came to an end.

Peering around the corner at the doorway to the consort chambers, I could see the hallway had a flaring torch in the holder, and... under it, a guard. Was she already confined and if not, what was the necessity for the watchman? It made no sense to me - as the consort of the King, and one easily recognized throughout the city, she could not just walk out the gate of the Palace. Confining her to a room seemed useless. It could not be for her own protection - no man would dare attempt an intrusion on such a woman, despite the uncertainty of which protector was hers at the moment.

Nonetheless, the guard was a blockage to my plans. I was in furious thought about my actions. To wait was to risk her being moved from her luxurious quarters to some unknown place, and under full guard - or worse, being killed before my return.

And indeed, worse it was. As I thought, I heard a tread, and a hail. Looking around the stone corner again, I could see another man had arrived, but not as I hoped, to change the guard, but as a second. From the words, I knew that the man had gone for some sustenance for them both, and just now returned with a jug and a platter.

There comes a time when a man must risk all or retreat before his fears. I was past the age when a young man would dream of his ascension to the ranks of the heroes of history - such as Aeneas and Cincinnatus - with brave deeds and actions. If I turned now, and departed this land on the morrow, then Ravana was probably doomed, and I would have proof beyond need that I was not and would never be such a man as whose name is remembered down the long hall of history.

I was dressed as my normal self - that is, with a short kilt and belt and nothing else but sandals. I looked like what I was - a scribe of some ability and wealth. More importantly, I was known by most of the occupants of the Royal Enclosure. It was my hope that the guards just around the corner would see what their eyes were accustomed to. I moved my scabbard around so that the longknife trailed down my back leg, rather than at my side. In the shadows it might not be seen, although I had worn it many times in the Palace over the years, especially when having just come from some less savory part of the city.

Taking a deep breath, I strode around the corner into the concourse - not hurriedly, but at a normal walk. Too late did the thought come that, had my name been put on an actus list during the day, then both men would suddenly see more than a mere scribe.

I was halfway along the distance before the chatting men noticed my presence. I maintained an unconcerned expression, but I was as a man walking on a narrow and rotting wharf with river dragons below. I was waiting for a sudden shout that would tell me that my welcome in the Palace was ended. The two men were just palace watchmen, engaged for the enviable post by some past passage of gold from one hand to another, and not hardened soldiers, but a short blade is at a disadvantage against two spears, no matter the craft-level of the wielder.

One finally noticed my approach and gave a hail that gave notice of his lack of fear. To his mate, he said, "It is the scribe that haunts the walls and pillars for his learning." Raising his voice, he called, "Yo, Scribe. You are engaged in your readings at a late hour."

I raised a hand in friendly greeting, and replied, "Aye. I am coming from a rendering of a long missive from the Greek lands." I shook my head in mock dismay. "Generals give little heed to the sleep of a mere scribe." Then, stopping before them, and with an expression of bewilderment, I asked, "Why need you guard an empty corridor in the night?"

The other guard replied, "It is not the corridor that we guard, but the golden-haired wench behind this door. She is not to be allowed to leave without orders from General Nepherites."

"But... she is the consort of the Pharaoh. What has the General to do with her?" I wondered if two lowly guards would know of the imminent usurpation.

The first said, "As you said. The General gives his desires and all hurry to obey."

I nodded and looked down the corridor, as if preparing to go. "I wish you a quiet duty. Are you standing the watch this entire night?"

"Aye. Until the forth hour, at least."

Lifting my sinister hand in farewell, my other drew my longknife with all the speed that I could summon. In less than a heartbeat I had driven the point into the throat of one guard, as my free hand suddenly gripped the vertical spear shaft of the other man. That man had barely time to react, and even before he could order his sinews to pull his weapon away, my point went into his chest.

And far too deeply.

Releasing my grasp of his spear, I pushed the palm of my hand over his mouth to stifle the dying scream that began to emerge. With my knife lodged in his ribs, I struggled to keep his silence as he fell to the floor. Then it was over, the man - men dead on the stones. Now, I had to plant a foot on his chest to extract my weapon, all the while cursing quietly as I remembered the lessons of Leodes, in Athens - the old Greek soldier that had tutored me in the use of my blade. "A heart is only two fingers past the skin. Jab and withdraw and move to the next enemy. A deep thrust, as if you were a barbarian of the mountains, will just risk leaving your metal stuck in the ribs of your foe, and you a mark for his mate as you try to withdraw it." He had the truth of it, and I was fortunate that there was no waiting fellow to avenge the death of his partner.

I quickly cleaned the blade on the skirt of the man, then pushed on the door. It moved, then stopped - obviously, the occupants of the room had put the keeper loop of rope over the catches. Quickly looking both ways down the corridor, hoping not to see doom approaching in the form of the captain of the guard, come to check on his men, I knocked lightly, then quietly called through the narrow opening. "Ravana. It is Junius. Open the door."

I heard a stirring, then an eye peered out at me. The door was pushed closed, then swung open. "Junius! Where... What are you doing..." She suddenly noticed the men on the floor and stepped back with wide eyes. Behind her was her cosmeta, Vera, and just as open-eyed.

This was not the time for long explanations. Any moment a guard officer might arrive on his nightly sentry-go. "We must leave and now!"

"But..."

"Now! I will explain later, but the General intends to give your hair to his consort - and your head, also." As an indication of my haste only now did I realize that the woman was a bare as the day of her birth.

Without further talk, I turned to pull one of the bodies into the room, then the other. As an action to hide the fact of my elimination of the guards, it was obvious that it would be totally futile. Under the flaring torch, the life-blood of the men was clearly glistening on the stones - and the dragging of the bodies was easily indicated by the dark smear leading into the room.

Again, Ravana showed herself to be no flighty female, holding her demeanor even with two dead men at her feet. Even her wide-eyed maid was just staring, and holding the usual screams that would have issued from most of her sex. "How do we leave the Palace? The gates will have been long since locked and guarded since darkfall."

"No matter. Come, we leave now."

"Vera. My chiton - the simple one. And yours."

I had not given a thought to her assistant. But... "Nay. The maid is not in danger. She needs not come with us."

Even as the younger girl was pulling the simple tunic over the head of her mistress, Ravana spoke, and with firmness. "Vera has been my recourse in all, and even since my arrival in this city. I will not leave her as a plaything for those scum!"

I knew better than try to argue with the stubborn female. As I pulled the torch from its holder in the corridor, I said to the girl, "It will be dark. Hold the hand of your mistress and do not let go. And neither of you make a sound for any reason." Bending, I crushed the flaming brand of the torch into the stone floor, and absolute darkness fell on us. Then I pulled Ravana by her free hand into the hall, closing the door behind us. "Now, in complete silence, follow."

Slowly, so as not to cause the women to trip as we journeyed back the way I had come, we moved in total silence down the hallways. I had sandals, but the women were unshod, and their feet made no sound whatever. It was my hope that neither trod on a rock or splinter, to make a fatal exclamation that would echo far along the stone corridors.

I did not expect to encounter a man in this remote section of the compound, and at this time of night, and we did not. Shortly, we were in the temple of Heket, standing below the wall that hid the shaft to the underground. A ladder would have greatly alleviated the problems of getting two women over the wall, but I had long ago removed it as a telltale mark of my secrets. And, once again, a woman cannot, even to save her life, climb a knotted rope. I had not planned on escaping with two women, but hopefully, my plan with the second rope would work.

Whispering, I said to Ravana, "I am going to pull you up to the top of the wall. On the other side is a ladder leading downward. Climb down and wait. Do you understand?"

With her quiet acceptance, I wrapped the end of the rope that I had brought under her arms, then across her chest and, after tying the loop closed behind her back, I climbed to the top of the wall. Planting my feet in the low opening, I quickly pulled her from the floor until my hands felt the loop around her body. With one hand I pulled her beside me and removed the loop of the rope from her body. Pointing down the shaft, faintly illuminated by the torch far below, I just said, "Climb down."

Hesitantly, she put a foot, then the other on the ladder and with my help to start, began the descent. Without waiting, I moved down the knotted rope again and shortly the maid was pulled to the top and was also pointed to descend the shaft.

Now, at the bottom, I began to breath easier. We had left the confines of the Palace without being seen - and killed - and safe from detection, now. It wasn't long before I was knocking on the covering board of our access shaft in the merchantry. Korax was waiting, and soon we were in the atrium, and I was enjoying a cup of wine, the more to relieve the pent-up strains in my possession, than any desire for the drink.

Ravana, of course, was filled with questions, but those could wait. My worry was more immediate. To Korax, I said, "Long before sunup, the dead men will be found in her room, and the guards - the whole army - will be scouring the city for us. The city gates will be kept closed until we are found."

My friend shook his head, seemingly unconcerned. "And why would they search the city?"

"Why? Did you not hear what I said? I left two guards spewing their lifeblood onto the floor of the woman they were designated to watch. I doubt that the General will consider it as a minor offense."

He held out his cup to be filled again, before replying. "Aye. The woman has been taken, or escaped. Possibly they will even assume that she slew the guards." Before I could protest, he continued. "But, why would they suspect you? Would a mere scribe, with no skills in battle, be able to slay two armed guards? Nay. They will be looking, not only for the woman but the skilled agent that the King has managed to insert into the Palace staff, itself." A long swallow, then, "And I suspect that his night's rest will be spoiled by the fear that his dastardly plans have been unveiled."

My friend, in his calmness and ease, was making sense of some goodness. Why would the General suspect that the deed was done by a fugitive scribe from the northern lands? I was known as the friend of the woman, but few probably remembered that she had been my own mat-mate, if they had ever known. Still...

He continued, "The hunt will begin for the woman and her abductors, certainly, but it will be the Palace grounds that will take the brunt of the search. With the unassailable walls and the gates closed for the night, they will be certain that the malefactors are still within. The search will not enter the city until every last stone has been turned within the enclosure of the Palace."

I nodded slowly. My friend was thinking well and clearly. Far more than myself, certainly.

Ravana finally spoke. "We will have to warn the King. You owe that to him for his friendship."

I nodded in the dim light of the oil lamp. "Aye, and I have spent sleepless nights in trying to find a way to do just that. But how? Our two coastal vessels are gone on their trading missions, and they would be the only chance to climb the river. The big ship would be so slow, unless the winds are very favorable, that the guards could easily catch us before the day was over and then we would be boarded and fed to the river dragons. The sight of the big vessel moving upriver, rather than down, would be as a written missive to the General of our plan." I frowned in self-deprecation. "And my little trick with the fiery pots would be useless against a horde of poled river craft."

"But..."

"I have a plan. A small one, and have little hope that it will work, but it is all that I can think of."

Korax spoke. "We should leave here just before the early rays of the sun, mixing with the street vendors and merchants as they open for the day. The gates will open at sunup, and we can be aboard the ship and be away before the cry issues from the palace. A lead of only an hour or so will put us ahead of any pursuit, especially if we can enter a distributary before being noticed. They will have little idea of which one we have used."

With that, we finished our preparations for leaving, which only consisted of the other two women dressing Ravana in a garb that would disguise her being, and especially the hair that would be as a trumpet blaring her presence.

Then, we waited for the first light of day.

Asylum Falsus (False Sanctuary)

I stared across the waters at the gigantic points of stone - the Pyramidos on the west bank of the river - and for the last time. I was disappointed that I had never - would never - see the tombs from a close distance, to walk around the massive structures and examine their being, closely. But, a man must have some measures in life that remain unfilled, else he would have no reason for living to the next day.

I looked back up the river in the morning sun. I could see many fishing boats slowly moving here and there, but no evidence to hint that we were being pursued. And if such pursuit did not begin in the next hour, we would be gone from any chance of hindrance.

We had left the merchantry before the sun had marked the eastern sky, moving to the eastern gate and each carrying a large basket as if we were taking our wares to the port for vending. In the streets were many early risers, all merchants and vendors readying for the day, of course. The few small details of street guards were just marching along with their usual speed, and without any indication they were looking for desperate assassins and an escaped noble woman.

We reached the eastern gates just as the slaves were pushing them open, slowly and with a massive creaking sound from the hinges. Korax had had the truth of it - we had moved unhindered to our ship as if the day had been a normal thing, and we about to begin the day by preparing the vessel for its next voyage.

On board were the entire crew, except for the captain, told by Korax the day before to make themselves ready for an instant departure, but of course, not the reason why. The master was not to be found, and we could not risk the wait in hopes that he would appear. The one legged pilot, Ahirom, was vastly more qualified to be a captain than I, even with his infirmity, and I gave him the post immediately. As I had no intention of making our voyage across the open sea, but instead, of following the coast to the west, a pilot was not completely necessary. Still, it was a comfort to have the man present, so as to have at least one experienced seaman on board.

As they prepared the ship, I moved along the wharves, attempting to carry out the only plan that I could think of to warn our friend, the King. Finding a coaster apparently about to depart, I called the master to the wharf for an offer. It was quickly made, as the heavy piece of gold swept aside all questions. The vessel departed, and I searched for another. Shortly it also was standing out into the river and being both sailed and poled up the river.

Both craft carried a scroll, sealed with wax and with my mark, and addressed to Senemut in Karnac. I hesitated to attempt to send the missives to the King himself, fearing that the rivermen would be sent away by his hangers-on as interlopers and the scrolls discarded without being read. But any man in Egypt could approach a priest, no matter the rank of the petitioner. The scrolls, of course, detailed the plans as I knew them for the usurpation and murder of the Pharaoh.

I knew of nothing more that I could do for my friend, the King.

The ship was pushed away, and into the gentle current, and we pointed downstream with the dragging stone to keep the alignment of our course. I watched the wharf recede, and there were no details of guards hurrying to stop the ship from leaving with the malefactors against the General - no cries of an officer for that ship to return. It could have been a normal departure of the trading vessel, just as it had been over the years.

Now we were entering the section of the river that entered the top of the Delta, and by my orders, we took the far western distributary. At the moment, I had only a slight idea of our destination - my thoughts were only that once again, I was a man fleeing for his life and into the unknown. And, not for the last time, I dwelled on that divine gameboard on Olympus, where even now, a carved figure of myself was in play.

As the pilot carefully steered us down the stream, avoiding the shoals and mudbanks of the low water, the three of us sat in the bow, just watching the slow movement of the river banks move past. Even now, nobody onboard knew that we were fleeing, and not merely voyaging. Except for the three of us. Nay, the number was actually five, since both the woman of Korax and the maid of Ravana had some knowledge of the fact that this was not a normal departure.

I looked back up the river where the last glimpse of the massive tombs were disappearing into the distance. "Some new occupant of my home will have a welcome surprise when he discovers the fortune that is hidden under my bed. I doubt that he will tell the vendor of the property of his find." I shrugged, then said, "But, a man who values his gold over his life is a fool."

"You left your gold because of me?" asked Ravana.

I shook my head. "I left it for all of us. But, I had Korax to bring a goodly part of it, that was stored in the merchantry compound, to the ship beforehand. It will be far more than enough to allow us establishment in some other land."

Korax put down his ever-present wine cup. "The man that you have spoken of... The one who will assume your domicile will find nothing but a hole under your mat. While you were waiting out the day hiding in the merchantry, and I was setting the ship for the voyage, my woman and I emptied the stash of every last bronze piece." Lowering his voice, he said, "It took us three trips, but all is below even now, under the stacks of linen."

"Did not the menials in the house wonder at your work?" I asked.

He shook his head. "Nay. I told Aulus, your head lacky, to give a day of rest to the servants, as you would not return for a considerable time."

Ravana asked, "Where will we go?"

That was something that I had contemplated during that long day while waiting for the nighttime. "My thoughts are that we will abide in Carthago for the nonce. It is a city of some magnificence, I am told, and comfortable for one who can pay the innkeepers. We will wait for news of Egypt, and then decide our next course." I shrugged. "Maybe my missives will get through to the King, or even that he will defeat that spawn of Hades without my warnings. We could then return to our lives in Memphis."

"Missives?" asked Korax. I suddenly realized that I had not told them of my last efforts just before we stood out from the wharf. I gave the story and my hope that Senemut would receive one of the scrolls.

The next day we were in the open sea, and with an almost empty ship, were moving rapidly along the bare coast, now far out of danger of being caught by any vessel of the usurper. I had told the rest of the crew the reason for our hurried departure - not the story of Ravana, but that a revolution was in play and that we would stand to the side and watch the matter play out - one way or another.

My plan of stopping at the far away city of Carthago came to naught. About five thousand stadia from the Egyptian Delta, we came to the port city of Cyrene - Kyrēnē in the Greek vernacular - situated on a huge bulge of land projecting into the Great Sea. For us, it was merely a convenient stop for fresh food and water, but upon exploring the city, we found it to be an almost magical spot at the edge of a great desert.

The city was Greek, founded many years before - hundreds, actually - by settlers from Thera, one of the myriads of islands in the middle of the Aegean sea. It straddled a lush valley, the waters of which emerged clear and cool from a spring not far inland. Facing the Great Sea, the days and nights were usually greeted with a cool breeze off the waters - pleasant to sleep at night and work in the day.

The city was clean - far more so than any that I had ever seen. Indeed, the magistrates would descend in their combined wrath upon a man who was so bold as to make his water against the walls of the streets, or a wife who was seen to toss her meal-scraps onto the paving stones. Throughout the city were public latrines, and designated compounds in which to place one's trash and discards, later hauled away by the city slaves to a dump far out of the city.

But, our transient stop for supplies was lengthened when I found that the city also was host to many thermae, and built in the actual Roman style, with three pools of varying temperature for the clients. That evening, after a sumptuous meal, I relaxed in the best bathhouse in the city - indeed, for so long that my skin took on the wrinkled look of an oldster of many years.

Even as the baths, the governing of the city was also as that of Rome. A conclave of men, elected by the people of their districts, made and kept the laws, led by one man chosen from the elected, to serve no longer than one year. Any citizen could apply to his representative for consideration or justice - something unlikely in a city like Memphis or Athens.

We lodged in a fine inn, facing the sea with a room each for all, except that Korax and his woman lived together, of course. The four crewmen did not dwell with us, of course, but cast their mats on the ship. They had little complaint, as I continued their wage even with the stay in port. I ordered that one man would always be on the ship, in a rotation, and the other might enjoy the city as they would. To be paid to loiter and visit the tavernas and bordellos was as paradise to such as they.

Ravana had entered the city with her spirit in abeyance. After the excitement of our escape, the realization finally descended upon her that she had lost her man - a mate in fact, if not in law, for whom she obviously had had deep encompassing feelings. Her feeling of abandoning the King in his time of need was overpowering at times, despite my insistence that there was nothing else to be done. Vera, her maid and cosmeta, tried her best to lift the spirits of her mistress, bringing sweetmeats and dainties from the vendors, with money that I had provided, and encouraging her to visit the garment vendors to look at this pretty chiton and that attractive female stola. I knew that time would heal the wounds and it was best to let the woman alone with her feelings.

And as everywhere she traveled, the people marveled at the color of her hair.

The days passed, and no word from the Nilos - gladsome or no - came on the coaster boats that plied the southern waters of the Great Sea. I soon found that, despite the welcome of the merchants to any guests with heavy purses, this was not a city in which we could establish new roots and begin again. All that I knew was scrivening, and sea-merchanting to some aspect, but both trades were under the firm control of guilds that allowed no foreigners into their ranks. A man could not even write his own words for commerce, but must needs hire a scribe to pin the missive. A ship might visit the port to vend or purchase cargo, but the fees on any hulls that were not of Cyrene were steep indeed. Still, as we were not engaged in commerce, the dockage toll was moderate for our ship.

Both the city and the climate were pleasant, and I saw no reason to move on to any other destination merely to wait for any news of... of what might have happened in the city from which we had fled. As this port was half the distance away from the source as Carthago, then the word would reach her first.

Unfortunately, I had neglected to remember that news moves in both directions.

Two pleasant months had passed, with still no word from the traders coming from the Nilos that anything of importance had happened in that far city - at least none that was made public knowledge in the Agora.

But, eventually news did come.

The three of us were eating the midday meal in the common room - a pleasant terrace looking down the slope of the city toward the harbor. I would have gladly allowed Ahirom and the two other women to dine with us, but this was, in effect, a Grecian city, and in those, sea-pilots, servants and even unattached widows did not sit with their betters. The caupo of the inn would have almost expired, should I even have suggested such impropriety.

Suddenly, the innkeeper appeared with an officer of the city magistrates. "This is the Dikastís of the city magistrate. He has words for you from the council."

The man's rank - Dikastís - was easily determined by the brassard hanging from his neck, and I knew that this was one of the officials that maintained the laws and peace in the city. He stopped and examined a piece of papyrus, then said, "I have an order for the woman, known to have the hair of gold, and her principal to appear before the council."

I did not know the meaning of the summons, but I was greatly fearing what it was. If the news was unwelcome, then it would be from

Nepherites, assuming that he still was in possession of his head. My hope was that it came from Amyrtaeus, wishing to find his consort after the failed usurpation. I had included the knowledge, in my scrolls sent up the river, that Ravana was fleeing for her life.

"Now?"

The man nodded. "Aye. The council awaits."

Korax stood and said, "I will come as well."

It was encouraging that the man had not brought a detail of guards, nor did he seem to assume that we were miscreants. In fact, except for a small dagger, he was not even armed. We had discarded our kilts for tunics and the women, their kalasiris for the female garb of the locals, as to blend in with the populace and might have been ordinary citizens walking the street with the magistrate.

The Chamber of the Council was a high ceiling pillared edifice in the center of the city - elegant and of fine white stone, but with nowhere the dimensions of thus in Athens or Rome. Inside the foyer, a scribal tallyman asked our business, which was given by our escort, and shortly we were standing in a large theater in front of several men, easily identified as leaders by their elaborate chitons. All were bearded in the Greek manner, about half with the white of the oldster and the rest, the black of a younger man.

Immediately, our magistrate guard came to attention and said, "Counselors. I bring the woman and her fellow traveler, as you ordered." Turning to me, he said, "Make yourself available to the Dimarchos of the city."

An elder - the mayor, according to our escort - approached but I only had eyes for a small group of men standing aside and several strides away. Egyptian, certainly - smooth shaven and wearing the garb of that land. Now I knew that this summons was because of a pursuit of Ravana.

"Your name, Kurios," asked the oldster, politely.

"Junius, Dimarchos. A scribe of Rome, educated in the Temple of Jupiter." I waved my hand to the woman. "This is my mate, also of Rome and that man, Korax of Athens."

"Junius of Rome. The reason for your summons is a charge, brought by a delegation from the city of Inbuhedj, that the consort of the Pharaoh of that land was forcibly abducted from the city, against her will, and with the captors did cause violence to her guards in the seizure. How say you to such a charge?"

I was thinking furiously, discarding one falsehood for another. The rulers of this city would almost certainly not care to offend a powerful neighbor on the mere testimony of a stranger, but it was also obvious that they would not just bend to the whim of such, either. Else, we would already be bound and on ship heading back up the Nilos.

I could not long delay my reply, else I appear to be a man developing a falsehood. Desperately hoping that Ravana did not betray my construct, I began my explanation, it being built even as I spoke. "Demarchos, I am a ship merchant, traveling the coastal lands of the Great Sea in my quest for lading, and I swear before the altar of Jupiter that my mate has been with me since I obtained my first vessel. The mere notion that she is a royal consort is... is... the stuff of fantasy."

"I agree," returned the oldster, "that when the delegation gave their deposition, I myself considered it to be... farfetched. But, there must be few women with such a coif of that color in all the world, and it is known that the consort of the Pharaoh has such."

I nodded, still building my construct, hoping that it did not collapse of its own weight. "Aye, Demarchos. And I have seen the woman, on the carrying platform of the Pharaoh during the Festival of Khoiak. But, it is well known that the consort is adorned with a wig of that color. And as can plainly be seen, the tresses of my mate are hers, and natural."

The mayor walked forward to examine the hair of Ravana, then nodded. "Aye, it is as you say. But, you admit that you have been to the city of Inbuhedj itself, and with the woman."

It wasn't a question, but I answered it as one. "Aye, Kurios. Many times. Our trade route is one of great profit, coming from the northern shores of the Great Sea with the wood of cedrus, greatly prized by the people of Egypt. From there, we load with linen, and return around the trading circle."

Now a man from the Egyptian delegation stepped forward and said with some heat. "Let not this charlatan spew his lies, Demarchos. The woman is named Ravana and was ripped from the possession of the Pharaoh by this man - man who killed the guards protecting the consort and fled before the sunrise. And he is no ship merchant, but the once trusted scribe of the Royal Entourage."

The man was giving the events correctly, but it was guesswork on his part - or someone's. There was no one who saw me in or near the palace on the day of the abduction. I kept my demeanor, looking at the man as if he were spinning some bard's tale of difficult belief. "My ship is in the port, giving some proof to my assertion of merchantry. And you are claiming that I, a scribe as you say and that I admit, stormed the palace, killing any guards in hinderance of my errand, and then... what? Did I overpower the night-guardians and single-handedly open the massive gate with my own sinews? Or did I jump over the wall of the Royal Enclosure, of a height exceeding that of five men, to escape? And with the royal consort in my arms? Should such an act have actually happened, then it speaks ill of the worth of the guardians of the palace, to be undone by a mere scribe." I turned to the mayor. "My pardon, Demarchos, but the man who accomplished the abduction that the honorable Egyptian is describing would be as an acolyte of the war god, Ares, himself. Rather, I suspect that the royal consort is in hiding for reasons unknown to the citizenry."

The mayor looked at Ravana, standing still and mute. "And her name is?"

"My name is Kóre, given by my genitors at birth." Not so mute, after all, as she spoke with some emphasis.

"Silence! A woman does not speak on the stones of the Council Chamber!"

"Your pardon, Kurios. May I speak?" We turned to Korax, myself with surprise. He was standing with an amused expression as if this was a play arranged for his own edification.

The mayor nodded. "Aye, speak your words."

"My name is Korax, of Athens, and once a Dimoirites in the regiments of the great Pericles. I wish to swear before Zeus that I have known this man, Junius the Roman, these many years and that I have accompanied him since our first meeting. And that this woman, who calls herself Kóre, has also been his companion for as long as I have known her." He looked at the Egyptian delegation with some distaste that was not feigned, then said, "I know not of any affairs of consorts and women in the city of Memphis, but my friend is indeed a ship owner and merchant and a scribe of some repute, and in that I swear that his words are truth, on my head as a Greek of Athens."

It was good. A council of Greeks would give greater stature to a proclamation from a fellow speaking their tongue without accent. And, so far, none of us had given an absolute falsehood, but much was left out of our stories.

The mayor turned to the Egyptians. "One would think that an abducted consort of the King would use any opportunity to expose her captors, yet this woman that is claimed to be of such rank, seems to be quite content to voyage in a trading vessel. It is disbelievable that a woman of the gilded palace would give up such a position for the life of a trader's mate." Now speaking to his associates, he said, "Nevertheless, a formal complaint has been lodged by the legitimate ruler of a neighboring land, and this must be respected. The Council will take this matter for discussion and decide the need for action." To the Egyptians, he said, "We will take the declarations of your party to further clarify the claim of your accusement."

Turning to me, he said, "You must remain in our city while this matter is discussed and settled. As such, an impoundment will be made to your vessel, but you will remain free, and as guests of our city."

That was a most unwelcome statement, as I had already determined to stand out of the city before the darkness fell on the day, to put as much water as possible between us and the lands of the Nilos - and quickly. Now...

The leader of the Egyptians was even less gladsome at the commands of the old Greek. "Your pardon, Demarchos, but the Pharaoh will take your actions with offense, after our presentation of the horrific crime done against the throne."

The leader of the council might have been an old man, but he was not to be intimidated by the threats of a mere courier. "The Pharaoh of Egypt does not rule here. His desires are respected by the people of Cyrene, but we have our own laws, and they will not be abrogated by his need for haste. We cannot violate the sanctity of our guests over an accusation, even from one of such highness. The accused have come to our city as visitants and have made no offense against our principles. As such, they are given the same rights as a citizen to reasoned discussion of the charges made against them."

"Dikastís, Hebu. See that the delegation from Inbuhedj is made comfortable and is given every courtesy." To myself, he said, "Junius, the Roman, you are still a guest to Cyrene, and with the only proviso that you may not leave the city until this matter is sealed, you may go and await our summons."

Go, we did, but not to enjoy our sojourn in the pleasant city. Rather, we returned to our inn, and gathered in the far end of the upper terrace and began our discussion in earnest.

"You did well, woman. Had you used the name of Ravana, we would even now be in the city jakes and waiting our transport back to Memphis."

She was unconcerned with my praise, asking, "Is this delegation from that bastard usurper? Or from the King himself?"

I shook my head. "We have no knowledge that any rebellion was made in Egypt, successful or no. If Amyrtaeus received either of my scrolls, then he is hopefully still alive and on guard against the General. And he will know that you fled for your life."

Korax asked, "Why would Nepherites trouble himself with a woman that he was going to slay? He must have far more worries than recovering a mere trollop from the northlands." He grinned to rob his words of any offense, and probably to protect his pate from having the wine jug shattered on it.

I shook my head. "The only construct that I can build is that the King did return, and Nepherites is giving reason to him for the absence of Ravana. To say that a trusted associate of his court slew the guards and fled with his consort is believable, especially since the King knew that she was once my own woman. It would only take a short stretch of belief to think that I desired her possession once more."

I took a sip - this was not the time to fuddle my thoughts with quantities of wine. "More importantly, as long as we stay in this city, we are in danger. At any moment, the council may give us to the Egyptians - especially, should any threat of an army appear on the horizon."

Korax shrugged. "Tonight, we can board our ship, toss off any guards and give this city the view of our backside..."

"Your pardon, Kurios. An associate has arrived with words for you." I turned to see the caupo motion to our sea-pilot to approach us.

"My thanks, caupo." I waited for the innkeeper to leave, then said, "Aye, Ahirom. What tale of gloom do you bring?" That he was bringing news that was less than gladsome was clear in his countenance. "And quietly. Our words need not to be heard by the servants below."

"The city guards have boarded the ship and have removed the sail!" He handed me a scrap of writing medium. Interestingly it did not seem to be papyrus, but this was no time for useless knowledge gathering. It was a receipt from the city, with the seal of... some magistrate, stating that our cloth had been impounded by order of the council. There were words that the property was still be regarded as ours and would be handled with the utmost respect, and prevented from coming to harm, under indemnification by the city treasury.

"By Dionysys and his wine-puke," swore Korax. "That is news that puts us in the anus of woe. We certainly cannot stand out under a bare pole!"

My thoughts were racing, testing this and that. Obviously, the three males of our party - and even with the crew in assistance - could scarcely seize our impounded sail, carry it to the ship and re-rig it, all the while fighting with the city guards as we attempted to stand the ship out. Any plans from this point forward almost certainly meant the loss of our vessel. It would be like losing a faithful friend to a sudden stroke.

But, again, a man who cannot abandon his property to save his life is a fool.

Fugae (Flight)

I had been impressed with the city of Cyrene. It was the most... or least... I was unsure of the words in any language to describe it. The citizens were as... unoppressed as any that I had yet seen. The taxes were collected by agents paid by the treasury, and independently of the amount that they collected. Thus, the tendency of a tax farmer to enhance his remuneration by oppressive levies was avoided. Any man could apply to the courts for the rightment of a wrong done to him by another, or even a city agent. Banishment was the punishment for a major wrong, rather than death by the cruelest methods as used by the rest of the world, although the deliberate murder of another could result in the headman's axe being used. A woman could walk the streets without fear of violation, and a man could carry his day's earnings without fear of a cutthroat. Even the tavernas were chary of the deliberate fleecing of their more inebriated patrons.

On the negative side, the city ran by rules and regulations and restrictions without end. To build a new wharf, for instance, would require no bribes, as in other cities, but might take an entire season as the requests slowly moved up the chain of administrators and magistrates, each having to give the project his sanction, before moving to the next decision maker.

In effect, the bureaucracy of the city was the saving of our lives. The city council made a leisure task of the investigation of the accusations against us, requiring ever more details from the Egyptian delegation, then needing to schedule a further meeting to discuss the new information. And while they talked, we plotted.

Bribes were, of course, by no means absent in this city. That would take even a decree from the gods to reduce, but the scale of them were more along the lines of a business transaction, than the rampant piracy as in other lands. And in fact, there was a junior scribe, attached to the council, a young man just starting out in his guild of service. He spent his days making notes as given by the members as they talked. I followed him one evening, to find his ward and haunts after the day's work was over, and made my acquaintance with the young man in a taverna. As his daily pay as a novice scribe was just sufficient to keep him alive and little else, he was quite amenable to accepting a stipend from myself for news of my party, as it happened in the council rooms.

And, as it turned out, it was well that I did.

I had to admit that our ship was lost to us. Under the usual circumstances, we could have swarmed the ship at night, thrown the two guards into the water, and stood out with the offshore wind. But, with our sailcloth stored in some unknown location, it was unlikely in the extreme that we could both locate and seize it for use before the arrival of the alerted city watch.

So be it. But, I had no wish to abandon the stash of gold hidden under the partial load of linen. All of us were carrying heavy purses - upon arrival in Cyrene, I had deliberately parceled out part of our wealth to be carried separately from the ship, in the case of the vessel being seized, or raided or even pirated away from the port. Together, the removed weight would allow us to easily restart our lives elsewhere.

Still, the idea to just leave what was ours, to be taken by others, grated on my being.

The crew had been told off and remunerated for their loyal service over the years. I assumed that they had already signed on to another vessel and had departed, as I never saw any of them again. Ahirom had elected to stay with us - with his missing leg, he was very unlikely to ever find shipboard work again, despite his extreme competence in finding his way across the sea.

On a night with the moon absent, and even the stars obscured by scudding clouds, Korax and I were sitting on an empty pier a half-stadium from where our ship was moored. He was very uneasy at my plans for the night. As we sat on the terrace, a few days before and making our plans, he had said, "The three bags, each, weigh as much as my woman! I know that you have an extreme ability in the water, but such weight will drag you down as if you were a stone statue."

I merely waved his objections aside, with, "I need no Greek to tell me about waterwork - especially one whom I have to watch while in the bathhouse together, so as not to allow my friend to drown in a placid pool no deeper than his chest." My jest did not quell his fears, but I was more worried about our plan to escape the city than the effort to recover our stash.

Again, just like that last night in the Palace underground, I was carrying a thin rope - actually, three in count - for use later. But, in addition, I had a thick and sturdy leather sack for my use. Late it was, when I slipped into the water, as naked as the day that I was brought into the world. As I quietly floated along the shore, far enough out to round the projecting piers, I thought back to another night - one in which I was also skirting the shore in silence, but with a difference.

Now, the purpose was merely for the possession of gold - then it was to save my life from brutal death.

Unlike that night, long ago, this distance was trivial and shortly I was holding on to the poles at the end of the pier, listening. I doubted that the two guards that had been detailed for the guard duty of the ship this night were even still awake, but I would only have this one chance. A misstep and another effort would be impossible.

It would be impossible to scale the high sides of the almost empty ship - at least not without throwing a rope and hook over the side, but, given the need for silence, that option was not even considered. Rather, I climbed the rough poles onto the dock, then just lay motionless, looking and listening. I heard nothing and saw even less. It was truly a black night, with only a dying torch seen here and there on the slope of the city.

As the eye is attracted to motion, I moved with exquisite slowness as I crawled down the dock. The curve of the ship meant that the distance from the wharf to the deck was much too far at the forepeak for myself to board, and I continued my slow crawl until I reached a part of the ship where the side approached the topside of the dock.

Now, even more slowly, I crawled over the side and onto the deck, making sure that my weight did not cause the ship to bobble even slightly. Even now, I could neither see nor hear the guards. My fear was that they might be sleeping below, on the soft linen, and therefore the use of a torch, even in the hold was out of the question. I would have to find the sacks by the description of their location, given to me by Korax.

At the small hold opening, in the forepeak, I lifted the cover and slid it aside only enough to give me access to the ladder. The rungs creaked unavoidably as my weight was put on each, but I paused between each step for many heartbeats before descending to the next. I doubted that it could be heard even if standing above, but I was taking no chances.

Finally at the bottom, I was standing on the bare boards of the hull. I could follow the midsection of the ship by feeling of the keel member and moving along it until I encountered the softness of the linen. Now, I began to feel under the piles by slipping my arm along the hull boards, waiting for the touch of leather. Korax had placed the sacks on the centerline, but I could not feel anything within the reach of my arm.

Now, in the dark, I began to pick up bales of the cloth, setting them gently aside - in effect, making a valley between the cargo until I suddenly heard a clink as I moved the bottom bundle. And there they were. I could feel three separate sacks - the proper number - and I began to unwind the rope around my waist. Carefully - so carefully, I picked up the first sack to place directly under the opening in the deck, then the same with the other two. It was heavy - very heavy - but not much larger than a taburna's amphorae - even a king's ransom of gold takes up little space. My fervent hope was that Korax had not skimped on the quality of the sacks that he had bought. If one parted a seam and spilled coin and gold rings to the deck, the resulting clamor would wake even the sprites of the deep.

With one end of a rope, I tied the first sack closed, using multiple knots and cinching them with my full strength. Then the other two with the remaining ropes. Finally, back up the ladder I went, again one rung, a wait, then another.

The deck was still quiet, although the guards could have been within spitting distance for all that I could see. Now, taking a firm stance, I began to pull on the rope, lifting the first bag from the hull bottom and shortly depositing it onto the deck. Korax was correct - it weighed as much as a grown woman. Fortunately, the thick leather muffled any slight noise that the coins made as they settled into new positions, but it would little matter in a very short time. Carrying the bag to the absolute forepeak of the ship, I let it into the water with the rope, slowly enough that it did not splash. Twice more did I move between the hatch and the forepeak. Then, in a heartbeat, I was over the side and hanging by my hands on the deck edge. With my body straight and rigid, I made little splash as I dropped into the water.

My chest pumped, as I charged my breathing sacs with the air that would allow me to remain underwater for a considerable time. As my head began the dizziness that told me that I was fully aerated, I pulled myself to the sea bottom using the rope attached to the a bag. Immediately, I picked up one sack of gold and began to walk along the bottom - not fast, but easily, the weight firmly planting my feet into the mud of the bottom.

This was the part of my plan that Korax had disbelieved, even to the point of ridicule. The idea of walking on the bottom of the sea was something that could not even be visualized by a man for whom the water in a thermae bath was sometimes considered forbidding. My vow that I had done it many times as a youngster made no impression on the Greek. But I well remembered the use of a large rock to both take me to the bottom of the river and to keep me there as I attempted my work - usually to free our nets from some snag without damage. Or to find a fisher-tool that had been dropped by my brothers.

Eventually, my breath would fail, and I would rise to the surface, holding onto the rope while I floated and breathed deeply again, restoring the lifegiving air to my body. Then, I would tow myself to the bottom with the rope, and the walk would begin again. It was not long before I was at the end of the last pier, and I deposited the sack at the base of one of the poles. Twice more I made the trip, then I was on the shore and telling Korax that we had possession of our wealth again, despite what happened to the ship.

The next days were spent in trying to find a ship on which we could depart. Rather, the search was for the master of a ship that I could trust to keep secret the fact that he was berthing outlaws leaving against the will and orders of the council. Then came the news that gave us little time to act.

Korax came running to the port, where I was walking the piers looking for a vessel from Carthago, or Seracusa, or suchlike. "Junius!" With the use of my name, I knew that the news was dire. "Your infant scribe from the council brings word that we are to be brought before the entire Chamber in the morn. And that Ravana will be given over to the Egyptian bastards."

The seriousness of the news brought forth an idea that I had had, and had rejected, then entertained again. Now I had no choice. "Come, we return to the inn."

In our my room, with the woman of Korax in the doorway to warn of approaching servants, I told of our new danger, and my plans to escape it. "You remember the empty stall beside the pier? The one that hides our gold at the end?" My friend nodded. "That will be our assembly place. We cannot leave here at sundown, carrying our bags and all that is in our rooms - that would be an instant betrayal that we are fleeing. The caupo would, no doubt, inform the magistrates immediately. During the day, take a bag to the stall, then come back for another, while stopping at a kiosk to purchase another to put in its place. Should any look in our rooms, they will assume that we are at the thermae for the evening. You will meet at the pier at sundown, but try to stay out of view of any watchers. The port is busy in the evening, but still, the less we are noticed, the better our cause." Other instructions followed, including the purchase and filling of several waterbags and sacks of hard rations. Then, I left to survey the fisherman's area of the port.

The day slowly waned, all the while with my fear waxing that we might be called to the council even this day, rather than the morrow. If that happened, then an alteration of my plan would be risky in the extreme - involving the violent takeover of a fishing vessel or coaster trudge. Fortunately, that worry did not come to fruition.

The sun was reaching for the horizon, and I was standing on the beach that the innumerable fishing boats used for the night docking. I needed more than just a skiff since we were six in number and had far to go. Finally, I selected a likely craft and met it as it ran onto the sand. The crew was a man of middle age and two much younger in his crew, likely his sons.

Holding up my hand in the universal greeting, I called, "Yo, fisherman. How was the catch?"

Surprised at a tunic clad man, even lacking a beard, standing on the sand and calling out greetings for the day, the master stood from his steering oar and replied, "Fairly well, as it were. More than some days and less than others."

"Excellent. I have a need for fresh fish and have gold. Be you interested in vending your purchase?"

Now, wide eyed, and somewhat suspicious at the unheard of offer, he hesitated, then apparently decided that one man did not constitute a raiding party of pirates. "Aye, where is your cart, or bearers?"

I shook my head. "Nay. I would deliver them to the first pier, yonder, at the receiving port. If you would, pole your ship to follow me along the shore." He turned and ordered his boys to push the vessel back into the water, then, rather than pole the craft along, the youngsters waded the shallows and pulled it along with the forerope.

I was waiting at the pier, hoping that a seagoing vessel would not suddenly appear to use it, but it was at the far end of the line of wharves and only used when the port was full. As they hauled up to the dock, I raised my hand, with five fingers outspread, and waited for the master to climb onto the boards. Looking back, I could see Korax, having taken my signal and ambling along, looking disinterested in the surroundings as a man wishing the day to be ended so the cups could be filled.

The master of the fishing boat straightened and looked at me, saying, "What is your offer for our catch, Kurios?"

Now, with Korax at my side, I drew my longknife and pointed it at his midriff. "I give my sorrow for my deception of you, but it is your boat we need - not your catch. Nay, boys!" This to the two young men whose hands naturally went to their daggers at seeing harm being threatened to their patér. "I am a master of this blade, and my man is a soldier of the Greek army." It was a falsehood as to my own prowess with the knife, but it made little difference against a fisherman and his sons. "Do nothing but stand and this day will prove to be profitable to you." To the man, I asked, "What is the value of your vessel, fisherman."

He was trembling, but not cowering - a natural reaction for any man suddenly with a blade pointed at his belly. "It is my only livelihood. Without it I cannot feed my family."

"I would agree, but that was not my question. Given my experience, I would say that your vessel would bring five and thirty drachmae." I held out my hand. "I will give you three gold Darics for your boat." It was an unheard of price for a clinker-built fisher - the man could purchase his own small fleet of the like with those three coins. A fact that I pointed out immediately. "You can buy a much finer craft for your trade, and pocket the rest as the wages for two entire years of good catch."

I doubt that the poor fisherman had ever seen a gold piece, and silver seldom enough. His eyes were wide as he stared at the gleaming coins, seen even more yellow in the light of the setting sun. Thrusting my hand out at him, I set them into his palm, that he might weigh the metal and feel the genuineness of the coins. I nodded to Korax, and he turned and ran down the dock, returning immediately with our party, all carrying a bag or sacks of supplies and water. With my order, the two young men climbed out and onto the dock as I continued to converse with the fisherman.

"Tell the magistrates about the theft of your vessel - they will hold you blameless for the loss. But do not speak of the gold, less you find yourself with a slitted throat on your journey home. And bade your youngsters to keep their silence also."

My people were now in the boat, and Korax was setting the sail, following the directions of Ahirom. I hoped he knew of the working of this craft. The sail, instead of being tethered at the corners, it was held with a slanted cross pole on the mast. I had no idea of the action of the set of the sail to the wind of this scheme.

There was one more task to complete before we left the environs of Cyrene behind us. "Korax! Hold these men until I return." He climbed back to the dock, as I ran all the way to the end. Without hesitation, I leapt into the water, letting my air escape and my body to sink to the bottom. It was only a heartbeat before I had the ropes, attached to our leather sacks of gold, in hand and was climbing back to the platform of the wharf. With straining sinews, I pulled the sacks off the bottom and struggled with them, one at a time, back along the wharf to our new command. With the help of Korax, we carefully laid them in the center of the boat, midships and next to the pole. Had we stumbled and dropped the massive weight, the sack would have plunged through the wood to the bottom of the harbor again.

I turned to the three fishermen, and said, "I wish you a good catch in your new boat, and you have my gratitude for saving our lives in the bargain." Korax pushed us away from the wharf and Ahirom pulled a rope to set the sail to the thrust of the evening breeze. The water began to ripple around the hull as we pulled away on our course to the west.

By the time the last sliver of sun had disappeared over the waters, we were already far out of hailing distance of any who might be watching from the port area. Korax already had his woman, Mira and the maid, Vera, throwing the fishermen's catch overboard - the lighter the load, the faster we would move through the water, and besides, when the sun rose in the morning, the fish would become an affront to the nose in a short time.

Ahirom was in the stern, on the steering oar and holding the setting ropes. I told him to call me for relief when the star known as Semetu touched the horizon. In these winds, I could certainly steer the boat without much concern. It would be better for him to rest, and be ready for conditions that might overwhelm a fair weather sailor.

Moving forward, I had collapsed in the bottom and against the boards in the forepeak - the reaction of my effrontery of stealing a vessel from an honest fisherman. Well, if not stealing, at least forcibly acquiring.

Ravana came back, now just a shadow against the stars. I moved aside, allowing her room to sit beside me and between the strakes. She was quiet for a moment, the asked, "What is your plan, Junius? Will we stop at Carthage as you originally planned?"

I shook my head, uselessly in the dark. "Nay, I misjudged the intensity of Nepherites and his desire for you - whether for your head or your body - and it almost cost us our lives. I will not make that mistake again. We will put much distance between the southern lands and ourselves. It matters not where we light, as the word will eventually come from Egypt as to the events there."

"To Rome, itself, perhaps?"

"Aye. It is a destination that would serve, and I would see my city again." I wriggled my body, trying to find comfort on the hard boards of the hull. "But, that is far, and we will have much time to decide our next place of nesting."

Just then, Korax, he also just a shadow against the sky, came forward and sat beside us. There was a period of silence, then he said with some measure of drollness, "As a young man, with my pouchstones barely dropped, I craved the heady life of the soldier, to assay the world and make my mark in it and collect gold and women along the way." I just listened, puzzled to hear my usually taciturn friend speak as voluminously as a sage in the Forum. "But, after being a companion to a footloose Roman, I have learned that even a life of battle is as the dullness of the washerwoman's day compared to your escapades across the world." There was even a chuckle in the dark. "I crave to see the next adventure that the gods above will lead you to as they dice over your carven figure on their gameboard."

The Roman

Reverto (Return)

We could not point straight across the Great Sea as if we were still in our now-lost ship of trade. In fact, we dared not even leave the sight of land in this little cockleshell of a boat, in fear of a tempest suddenly arising to send us to Neptune's domain with little effort. In fact, twice, before we stood into the harbor of Carthago, we were compelled to pull onto the sandy shore as the winds rose and lashed the waters into froth.

Our voyage to Carthago took a pair of months, the little fishing boat being built neither for speed nor comfort. Thrice, we stopped in the cities along our route, Charax, Leptis and Thaneae in that order. All were minor ports that supplied fresh water and wine, and food and our stay was only long enough for the replenishment.

At one prominent outcropping, easily recognizable in the future, we hove into the shore and buried our bags of wealth under the rocks. There it would stay forever, or until our need bade us voyage back for it. Our purses were heavy enough to serve for many years, without the need for the massive stash of gold to be carried and hidden and worried over. And we now had no fear of exposure as travelers carrying a king's ransom, to be murdered on the day it was discovered.

Finally, we passed a spit of land and before us was the grandeur of the huge city of the Phoenicians, called Qart-hadašt in their tongue. I wished for the time to explore yet another wonder of the world, but we tarried only long enough to procure berths in a comfortable vessel to Seracusa. Another reason for our haste was that the city had been in this strife and that, with both Rome and Greece for years, and thusly, both myself and Korax felt less than welcome in Carthago.

But, mostly, I wanted more distance between Memphis and ourselves.

Now we could sit on the deck and plan our future in comfort, rather than bailing a fishing boat, and maintaining a constant watch for sudden storms. Muchly did we three talk, with Ravana finally shrugging off her sadness at leaving her royal mate behind, and of not knowing of his living or death. I assured her, that if the news finally came of his surviving the treachery of his General, then we would return to the city, should she desire. But, she was no immature and passion struck femina, and took the loss as one of the calumnies of life.

She had her memories, and few women can claim to have been the consort of a king.

I knew of the island of Sicilia, having voyaged to the port of Seracusa several times when I was a scribe and merchanter for the old Greek, Zethus, in the city of Tarracina. In fact, it was a voyage from that island, years ago, on which the fateful wind blew me far to the east and into slavery. It was a place of pleasure, with the days neither too hot nor too cold, and the major ports of Seracusa and Panormus giving a guest all the amenities of any city in the world. Or at least, any to which I had ever been.

The populace being a seafaring people, I would have considered the island as a place for us to light, and begin again, except for one factor that gave me pause. The city was ruled with an iron hand by Dionysius the Elder, a tyrant and despot of the worst kind. Any man who fell into the dislike of this ruler was one that would cease to draw breath before the next sunset. Unlike Cyrene, or even Memphis or Rome, there was no appeal to any decree by the evil potentiate.

We set ourselves to an inn to await the next comfortable berths to Latium, enjoying the baths and the endless variety foods that were available in kiosks all throughout the city. After the plainness of the fare of the Egyptians - bread, onions, olives and other vegetables, with meat only on occasion, and that usually less than succulent - the wide variety of the islanders was a treat for us. Of course, the cosmeta of Ravana and the woman of Korax had known nothing else than the simple foods of their land since birth and looked in askance on many of the strange viands that were placed on the eating tables of the cookeries.

I had placed a commission with the port factor, to send word when a suitable vessel might hove into port, and spent my first days sitting on the veranda, with a view over the city and all the way down the slope to the harbor. Ravana usually sat with me, but Korax, naturally, sought out the local wine-shops for both drink and camaraderie with others. This was a Greek city - or at least, descended from that land - and the old soldier felt comfortable with the patrons of the tavernas.

On the third day, Korax appeared of mid-morning and in a jocular mood - almost mysterious. He sat and accepted a cup from the inn-servant, then just gazed out over the city and the sea. After years of being his friend, I could easily tell that he was forming his thoughts, and they would come when he had decided that they were in order. Finally, he said, "Your intention is for us to voyage to Rome, is it not?"

"Aye, possibly, although there are many cities along the Latium coast that would be sufficient for our position. I have made no determination as yet." I paused, then said, "But my thoughts are not the ruler of our little threesome. Have you another destination, perhaps?"

Rather than answer, he gave out another question. "I have some claim on a portion of our gold, do I not?"

What was this? Korax had never cared for wealth, as long as his purse was sufficient to drink and dine. I answered with some force, "My friend, you have more than a claim on a portion. A third each is the share for both of you." I waved him to silence. "I would be dead or enslaved on a Spartan ship were it not for you, and the loot that Ravana brought from her Athens servitude was the seed that allowed us to find ourselves in any domain that we wished."

Now his face turned from somber to a look of satisfaction. He stood, then said, "Come with me, my Roman friend. I wish you to make acquaintance with the siblings of an old comrade."

As I stood, Ravana asked, "Is this a man thing, or may I accompany you to the... meeting?"

Almost booming, Korax replied, "Aye. You might enjoy the sight also." He had come far, from that day in the port of Athens, when he had raged that I was inviting a mat-doxie to follow and hamper us in our flight. The pair had become civil in their relations in the long years since.

We sauntered down the winding paths of the walkways into the harbor area, until we came to the long shoreline of the shipwrights. Then, out on a long narrow pier, he led us, until we could see along the shore with no obstruction. My eyes opened wide, and I blinked to look again. There on the water was the ship that we had abandoned in Cyrene, almost three months ago.

But then, nay. It could not be. Not only for the reason that its presence here was impossible, but the wood was too bland, showing that it had not been seasoned by years at sea. But a twin it was - almost. And there was another, unfinished. Korax enjoyed my startlement for a while, then said, "We have found the yard in which our ship was born. Or at least, the people who made suchlike."

Now, as suddenly as a bolt of lightning in a storm, I realized the thinking of Korax. "So... Your idea is to purchase another ship."

He looked at me sheepishly, like a boy caught out by a sudden discovery by his patér. "Aye. I... We... Ahirom and myself would have little use in the city of Rome, where he knows nothing of the tongue, and I only that has been learned from yourself over the years." He looked around at the ships that were the topic of our conversing, then continued, "My return to my own city is not choice that makes me gladsome. As we have heard, it is nothing but a satrapy of Sparta now, and will not be other until I am long become dust."

"Where is Ahirom?" I asked.

Korax point. "He is among the shipwright factors, beginning the search for a possible purchase."

I nodded. "That would be interesting. Let us find him and gain his..."

Now, my friend violently shook his head and said. "Nay! Pardon, my Roman friend, but those greedy factors, seeing a wealthy patron as you are, would only drive the asking price to the height of yon clouds."

I looked at him with a quizzical expression. "But you are as wealthy as myself - I have made that clear."

Now he grinned. "Aye, but I look as a Greek trudge without two coins to rub together in a port taverna. And Ahirom did not garb himself in a noble manner when he set off this morning."

That made sense. And it was true. Both Ravana and I had visited the vendors and purchased suitable habiliments for wealthy travelers, as our garb that we had worn since leaving Cyrene had become less than suitable for presenting oneself at a fine inn. Even Korax had doffed his worn tunic for a new, but even so, he hardly looked like a wealthy noble in his scruffy beard and flopping hair.

But, he was correct - there was no need to give avail to a vendor as yet. "We will meet in our taverna this evening and discuss the matter. I see no..."

"Nay." This from Ravana. "I wish to be a part of this discussion, and I cannot sit in a wine-shop of men."

I nodded. "Aye. Then we will have our cups on the terrace of the inn." I waved to Korax. "Till the evening, then."

Ravana and I, having the entire of the day to ourselves, walked to the Forum - or rather, the Agora, as this was a city of Greeks. There, we found the usual sages and philosophers giving sway to their conceptions and constructs on this speaking board or that. The ruler, Dionysius, was a collector of scholars and mentors of intellectual constructs, it was said, and such were welcomed to the city, and supported in their living.

And it was also said that he was a poet himself, comparing himself with the famous cantors and versificators of the past. What was not spoken, in public or aloud, was that he was a horrible wordsmith and that his interminable sessions of reciting were a trial to those who could not avoid his invitation to hear. In the taverna, the night before, an inebriated patron gave me a tale as a jape but insisted that it was true. To wit, a man of some import was invited to a reading of the words of Dionysius, but at the end was critical of the poetry. In a rage, the ruler sentenced him to the quarries, but his friends persuaded the despot to retrieve the man from the pits. Dionysius did so and allowed the man to, once again, listen to his wording. At the end of the recitation, the ruler asked of the opinion of the reprieved listener, who replied, "I would that I were back in the quarries."

It was a tale, obviously, but a good one.

We stopped before a columned notice board and looked the announcements. Unlike Rome, with a crier's platform in each quarter, on which a leather-lunged Praeco stood, reading announcements at the top of his voice, citizens in Syracusa were expected to be literate and read the news themselves. I noticed a proclamation that Platon, son of Ariston, late of the deme of Collytus in Athens, would be giving a discussion of his work, Meno's paradox, at the Theatre of Anankey. I wondered if this was the philosopher known as Plato, whose name and work I had heard of when in Athens. I had never seen the man nor attended his lectures, but without doubt, he was, or had been before the Spartans, a celebrated sophist of the city. If it was indeed he, then it was obvious that the man had fled the fall of the city as did I.

After a question of a citizen, we found the small theater, carved into a hillside, and in which the lecture had already begun. On payment of a small coin, we were admitted and sat high in the round stone benches. That the man was an articulate sophist, there was no doubt, and his meanings were very abstract, but brilliant.

He posed the problem of doubling the area of a square figure, drawing a large even sided figure in chalk on the huge slab of slate that was used for such demonstrating. The figure stood on one point, rather than flat, but still, it was a square. Then, he challenged the audience to double exactly the area of the figure without measurement and posting a small coin as his wager. Several men rose to the task, and failing were laughed off the platform, their coins now in the purse of the philosopher.

Finally, after no others were forthcoming, he demonstrated the answer, by drawing another square outside the first, but with the corners in the center of the lines of the previous, thusly...

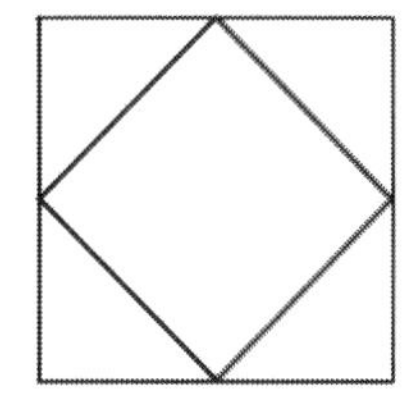

He demonstrated other truths of numbering, all simple but exceedingly elegant. When the lecture was over, all in the audience agreed that the man was an intellect of the ages and a sophisticated addition to the city.

Ravana was merely bored, of course. It is well known that the female has no abstract reasoning abilities, her skill being in the physical and conjugal spheres, but she maintained her silence, and made no fuss as I sat, enthralled.

Upon returning to the inn, to wait on Korax and Ahirom, I called for a wax tablet and demonstrated to myself the truth of his demonstrations. Indeed, the square in the square was exactly half the size of its parent - or double the size in reverse. I spent the bulk of the afternoon pleasurably lost in the fascinating world of sophistry, trying to follow the explanations of the other presentments that I had heard at the theater. When we settled to our next domicile, I would try to find more information on the man from which Plato had received much of his enlightenment, Pythagoras of Samos. I had heard the name in passing, somewhere, but had received no connection to anything that he had proclaimed or done, but I would find out, hopefully.

In the evening, both Korax and Ahirom arrived at the inn. The pilot was domiciled at the harbor, of course, as the capo of the upscale devorsorium in which we were ensconced would have paled at the idea of a mere ship Kapetanios lodging among his betters. As it was, the innkeeper looked in askance as the man joined us on the terrace, but I assured him that I needed conversation with my captain.

After the cups had been filled, I asked, "How was the day? Did your search find a hull that was satisfactory?" I was still not certain that I wanted to reenter the shipping merchantry again, but I had seen in Egypt the advantage of having one's own vessel at instant command.

Koran swung his cup in assent. "Aye. They are built upon order, of course, but there are several slipways empty of construction at the moment. Ahirom has spoken with several shipwrights, and either seem satisfactory. All would be anxious to bid on a hull."

I looked at the pilot and asked, "Would it have the same carriage as our last?"

"Aye, Kurios. If we wished. The ship would not be identical - none ever are, even coming from the same slipway and shipwright - but except for the lightness of the color, the two would seem the same if wharfed together. A yard or two will build vessels that are even larger, perhaps half again, but in my converse with other captains, I am told that they are slow and very tending to gripe in slow wind."

The discussion went on into the darkness as the torches were lit on the deck. Despite her stated desire to partake of the conversation, Ravana soon tired of the talk about wood and sail and spaces and retired to her cubiculum. Eventually, a tentative plan was agreed upon and we bid each other a gladsome night.

Domus (Home)

The port of Ostia looked little different than the day I had left, which of course, was not to be considered odd. For myself, however, the change since was tremendous. That young man, years ago, that entered the port fleeing for his life, would not have recognized the man that he had become. On the voyage, we had ported in Antium for a day and night, and I purchased fine garments for myself and Ravana, that we might look the part of wealthy merchants on our arrival.

And indeed, the ploy was successful, as the port magistrate bowed and scraped before us as we landed from a vessel so new that the sail still had its whiteness. Korax was also sporting new garb, in the Greek fashion, but alas, even with the newness of his habiliments, he still wore them with all the aplomb of stage actor in a farce.

Our new ship was, in essence, the rebirth of the old. With the negotiations and building, it had taken the half part of a year before we trod its decks as owners. There was little difference in its plan - the deck boards could be removed for stowage of large cargo, and it had three hatches instead of two, and a short rail at the sides.

The shipwright did not understand my additions, but gold rules, and he built them to specifications. At the very stern, a short wooden wall could be raised on either side of the tiller bar and latched to stand upright. I had learned, in an action with pirates, that the steering-man needed to be most protected of all on board. And, in the waist, midships and on either side, two other wooden partitions could be raised, these just to chest level - high enough to protect, but not so tall as to inhibit the tossing of items over the side - such as the clay pots, filled with liquid caulking pitch that were stored in a well close at hand.

I had insisted to Korax, that he train the crewmen, just as if he were back in his old regiment, for such an attack as we had experienced. And to run the routine over and over, even to the act of throwing overboard old pots, to make the activity as realistic as possible. As I told both he and Ahirom, one can fight pirates many times during a lifetime of voyages, but one can only lose the battle once.

The port magistrate and the shipwright both, looked in askance at my giving the captaincy to a man with a missing leg, but Ahirom had shown his worth to me many times, and that legs did not make the competency of a man. In the manning of the boat, he demonstrated such. I had made the comment of the necessity of calling a crew-factor to hire the sailors that would soon be needed. It was as if I had jabbed the pilot - now Kapetanios Ahirom - with my longknife.

"Nay!" he blurted. Then, "Your pardon, Kurios, but that would be most unwise, begging your pardon. That will run the risk of hiring a band of knaves bent on taking the ship as soon as out of port." He looked into the distance, obviously exploring a memory from the past. "I have seen it done - a ship returning with the original master nowhere to be seen, and a tale of storms, or pirates, or unseen rocks - even though the vessel shows no sign of weather, battle, or repairs."

I bowed to his knowledge and left the crewing to him. He carefully selected men from different parts of the city, and even those with no common roots. Two Greeks, a man from the far shores of the Great Sea and a Carthaginian. Korax, of course, would be the factor, and determinor of their destinations. In the years since our flight from Athens, my friend had become quite the seafarer, rootless and apparently happy with his lot. Naturally, he would take his woman, Mira, along during the voyage. Our original ship had been his domicile for much of the time, and now this one would replace that lost home.

We stood into Ostia with an empty cargo hold. Ahirom wanted time to acquaint himself with the handling of the ship before loading it down with lading. For our maiden voyage, we had retraced our path back to the promontory where we had hidden our wealth, to retrieve it and now to easily hide it in the bowels of the large vessel. The Kapetanios - or now a Captain by title, as we moved into the domain of Latium - had made several changes to the sail plan, moving the fore ringbolt a stride or so back, and the waist rope, here and there, then watching the waters as they flowed by the hull. Eventually, he gave his satisfaction as to the ship, and we sat on the forepeak, watching the far shore slowly move past as we hauled northward.

Rome was known for its fine iron work, and that would be the cargo for the first short voyage. Of course, iron was not linen, and a full load left almost the entire hold empty - even with the ship squatting to the loading mark on the waterline. Still, the ship could not leave. There was the matter of the heavy bag of coin hidden in the hold. We could not carry it to Rome and stash it in an inn. Such an act would risk exposure and our throats being slit before the sun rose. And there was the problem that I could not carry the bulk without notice by passersby, and even partial bags would stagger the women. Nay, we would have to find a domicile before Korax could depart.

Engaging three berths on an upriver barge, I sat in the waist, watching the familiar banks of the Tiber slide past as we were poled up the river. Rome was no stranger to Ravana, but as a female priest-slave in a temple, she naturally had far less direct knowledge of the streets. Of course, to me, it was home - to her it was just another city.

We debarked at the river wharfs at the Via Aurelia and entered the city directly into the Capitoline quarter. Our noble attire and heavy purse gave us instant attention by the capo at a devorsorium, and we settled into a set of rooms. On the morrow, we would engage a dwelling agent to find us a permanent domicile.

After our evening dining, we relaxed in the courtyard and talked, the maid Vera sitting with us, to the appalled glances of the wife of the caupo. Ravana was musing on my mood. "You are less than excited with the prospect of a new ship and its voyaging," she said. The female had been with me long enough to assign my moods.

I nodded. "Aye. I would not have told Korax, but I have no interest in sea-going trade now. That part of my life is over and done. But, my friend is happy, and I have no doubt that he will bring us even more riches."

"And us?"

I shrugged. "We still have no news of Egypt - if our friend is alive or dead, or the land is in the turmoil of revolt." Now was the time to speak of what had been on my mind for months. "Let us talk of you."

Her eyes widened slightly as she waited. Probably her femaleness knew what I was about to say, but she maintained her silence as she nodded.

"You are a friend, and a close one, but you are not my mate, and I have no hold over you. Nevertheless, Rome is not Memphis - no city in the world, is, to my knowledge. Here, a single female cannot exist without the suzerainty of a man. She can neither own property, nor purchase residence in a devorsorium. Likely, she would be assigned by the magistrates to the Temple of Caelestis or suchlike, as an unattached and unowned female." I was about to make the jape of her unique hair making her the premier attraction at brothel but wisely choked off the jest before it emerged. It might be comical at some later date, but not now.

She nodded and replied. "Aye. I have known it, even though I have refused to bring it to thought."

"My thoughts run to this. You are past the age of becoming a bride to the son of a magistrate or merchant, but it is possible that a widower would find in you a proper mate, just as Korax has done with Mira. You could stay with me as... say, my mater's sister come to find such after some tragedy has struck your family."

She just looked at me, somberly. "I will never forget that you rescued me from the clutches of that swine of Athens, and from an even worse fate in Memphis, even killing men for me when you could have fled in safety. We have seen both excitement and tragedy together, and as to your skills on the mat... I have had worse." This was said with a slight smile. "My respect for you has grown as you have not once attempted to push your needs onto me in my sorrow. Few men of my acquaintance would fail to do so."

Now I grinned. "I am not so ineffable as that. Many evenings in Cyrene and Syracusa did I find relief at this brothel and that. And with my hand, on our voyaging. But to continue my posing... If you do not wish to pose as a relation, I would not take it amiss if you were to become my mate again, in the eyes of the citizens. It would not require you to share my mat, but such an arrangement would have good effect. You would have a place in the city, and as such your freedom to do as you wished with an escort servant, as you had in Memphis."

She smiled. "I am not averse to warming your mat, but I would wait until the green memory of Amyrtaeus has receded. And as you said, there is no word of his demise, and the way may yet be open to my residing in Memphis again. There, even if not the consort of a King, a woman can find her own way." She paused for a long while - so long that I thought the conversation was over. Then, "I cannot offer myself as a wife to a man wishing to continue his family." That made no sense to me, until she said, "I am barren of any possibility of becoming with child."

Wide-eyed, I blurted, "How could you possibly know such? There is no..."

"I lay with you for... how long? From the voyage to Egypt until the King took possession. No seed took root."

"But..."

"You are fertile of seed. The fire-haired girl of this city was proof of that."

I shook my head vigorously. "But, you anointed yourself with the potions and pastes that women use to prevent such. I saw you in the deed - and later as Vera applied such."

"Aye. But, such dosing, even with pessaries, is not absolute. Any woman will eventually nurture a seed that will sprout - no matter her efforts to the rejection of the planting. But, in all that time, none did. Hold..." She held up her hand to stop my objection. "With Amyrtaeus I used no such potions and devices, and still no result came from his takings, even over the many years."

I just sat and thought of the revelations that I had just heard. It made no difference to my desires. When the gods mixed the clay to form myself, they had left out the urges for familyhood. I had little desire to live the part of a gaffer with children and grandchildren roaming around the courtyard. Finally, I said, "Then let us just take our lives day to day. As we ourselves have experienced, no man or woman can see the life that is yet to come. We will attempt to enjoy what we have, and give no worry about what might be. Already, our lives have been far richer than even the noble people of the world, and I see no reason to think that our adventures are over."

With that, we departed the courtyard for our cubliculum to take our rest - on separate mats. I was no longer a man-boy with a pouch of aching stones, turning every activity with hope that I might lay between the legs of a female, but it was gratifying to think that once again, I might enjoy this golden-haired siren on my night-mat. But... There was much more to think about than coitus, and it was time to do so.

The following day was enjoyable, as I made my re-acquaintance with the city of Rome. Our first destination was the Temple of Jupiter. I needed to determine if my name was held in disgrace by my acts with the young woman years ago and if so, then we would need to depart to find another home city.

In the courtyard, I told Ravana to wait as I approached the priest taking the offerings before the statue of the god. Bowing, I said, "Greetings, Sos. I would inquire if Vonones, the Priest Primus is within?"

The man looked at me in surprise, before saying, "It takes no deep thought to know that you have been absent from the city these many years. Vonones has been with the god since the... I remember not, but it was during the governance of Titus Lusius, years ago." Before I could ask, he said, "Fundanus Ivmarus is the Primus now."

Ah. I remembered him, vaguely. A teacher for some of the courses that I had attended. Hopefully, he would remember me. "And might I confer with the honorable Primus?"

"And you are?"

"Junius. Scholaris of the first class, although not ordained to the service of Jupiter. This was my collegium in my youth."

He opened his eyes wider, then turned to call an acolyte. The boy ran off and I waited, watching the priest accept this fruit, and that grain, or a white pigeon - all in the name of Jupiter and his blessings. Very shortly, I saw my old teacher approaching, much more rotund than when my eyes had last beheld him.

"Great one. This is Junius, calling himself a scholaris of this temple."

The man looked at me, then the light of recognition came into his eyes. "I remember, you. Junius. Aye. A goodsome student as I remember."

"And you, Sos. The Priest Primus of the temple. You have greatly accumulated status in your life, also." It was encouraging that he had not yet ordered me whipped from the grounds for the disgracement of my position.

"You have been absent these many years."

"Aye, Sos. By strange happenings and even stranger fortune. But I have returned, having accumulated considerable wealth, to make Rome once again my city, and I would have the Temple recognize my doctrina for my dealings with the magistrates of Rome."

He motioned, and I followed him into the scrivener chambers, it looking no different than when I was a young man marking tablets and papyrus. The students and acolytes moved respectfully aside as the priest entered and walked to the wall holding the records of the temple. He removed a scroll, then put it back and selected another. Unrolling it partly on the table, he read for a while and then looked up at me. "Junius. Arrived in the second year of the governance of Hiberus. Satisfactory as to your terms and offered a priestly ordainment by Vonones himself." A pause, then, "As I remember, you suddenly left without notice."

"Aye, Sos. I was smitten by a woman and rejected, and in a fit of immatureness, decided to try my fortune elsewhere." Not exactly a falsehood, but the statement covered far less than the whole of the tale.

He smiled. "A characteristic of young men everywhere. Even I had my sparkling eyed femina when in my youth, and thought that the world would end if I did not have her." He rolled the papyrus back onto the spindle and deposited the scroll on its shelf. "I will have no problem in giving you credence to the magistrates. You are now back in Rome to stay?"

I nodded. "Aye. Unless even stranger fortune draws me away, but my wandering youth has departed, and I yearn for a permanent domicile."

I asked him to give me a recommendation for a property factor, and after a few more exchanges of experiences in the years that I had been absent, I joined Ravana and we departed. The tradesman in dwellings was only down the street and shortly we were shown into his presence by the doorman. I gave him an idea of what I was wanting, and he began to pull sheets and tables from a table, to place them before me. In a while, I had selected three to examine, and we followed him back into the Capitoline quarter to examine the edifices.

Of the three, two had no effect on my desires, being faceless housing with nothing to excite the buyer. But the third was delightful, and on the western slope of the hill facing the river and the Field of Mars. Unlike the other two hulking compounds, needing handfuls of slaves and servants to both maintain and clean, this one was smaller, with a minimal courtyard and a terrace on the top of the square structure. With only five cubiculare, a cookery, and an atrium - and a heated stone bath, it was perfect for myself and Ravana. And with room for Korax and his woman when they were in the city. In the back were rooms for several servants and storage.

This structure had something that I had never seen - water that flowed into a basin on demand. Questioning the marvel, the factor led me to the roof to see a wooden cistern, to be filled from the fountain in the square and holding enough water for days. Then the negotiations began, my offering half of what the factor said was the minimum amount that the owners would accept. Giving him our address at the inn, I bade him contact me should the price fall to an acceptable level.

And of course, it did. Later, walking to the magistrate's building for that quarter, I found that the necessity for the sale was the death of the owner and the penury of the sons. That was interesting in that the family had to have had wealth at one time, or they could never have resided in the Capitoline. I could have probably had the house for much less, but the cost took only a small sum of coin from my purse. In three days, the proper forms were filled out - by me - and filed with the archives - again by me - and we took possession of the property.

It was only in the following month that I began to discover that my city of Rome was, in actuality, impoverished - with the wellborn and commoners alike suffering from the interminable wars that had started at about the time of my departure as a youth running from an enraged patér.

I left Ravana and her maid to clean the domicile from top to bottom - hiring a factor with slaves to do the work under her orders - and left on the boat to the port of Ostia. For the next two days, Korax and I bartered and bought raw blades and spearpoints, pans and grills and suchlike. They would be taken to Carthago and traded for rugs and woolens and copper ingots. The ship loaded, I brought Korax to Rome that he might see our new house and know its location. And to bring the heavy bags of gold from the ship to a place of greater safety.

For reasons of security, the stash was split into several smaller bags, then put in chests and labeled as household items.

We had much time to talk about our plans, the trip by boat upriver taking the whole day at the low water time. Of course, coming the other way, one could leave at daylight and be in the port before the midday meal. At the house, there was no furniture and no servants, but that was of no matter. Ravana had purchased soft mats so that we did not need to recline on the stone floors. That evening, long after dark, we sat on the terrace and enjoyed the cool breeze and conversation.

The next morning, with smiles and hand grasps, I saw him to the riverboat and watched until it floated out of sight around the bend.

Reddo (Return)

Korax had been gone a third of the year when news came up the river. Late one day, I listened to the cryer, then with a coin bade him let me read the scrawled missive myself. The tidings were of sadness, but not unexpected. I slowly walked back to my... our household, wishing not to be the bearer of the words.

In the door, I said to one of the servants, "Bring a cooled jug and cups to the terrace. And ask the mistress to join me there." She bowed without a word and hurried away. We had hired a cocua and maid for the kitchen and two female domestics to maintain the house. In addition, I had a young boy - a street orphan - whom I allowed to live in a small room at the end of the house and gave him a copper now and then to perform certain chores. Work such that would not be meet for a female maid, such as hauling water to the roof cistern and kindling and firewood for the kitchen and suchlike. As I had told the cocua to allow the youngster as much food as he wanted, I had no problem in retaining the young man in my service. For the first time in his short life, his belly was full from day to day.

This being Rome, the usual tall table and chairs were now a round mensa and mats and pillows. Now, I lay in recline before the low table, sipping from my cup and waiting for the woman. Thus far, she was playing the part of my mate, even though we were not sharing a mat at night. For myself, I was handling my needs at the upscale brothel just beside the Temple of Jupiter - two women there were my favorites, and by now well knew me and my desires.

I heard feet on the stone steps and watched the body of Ravana rise through the opening. She had cast off most of her pensiveness and now could enjoy patronizing the garment shops of the quarter. In fact, this day she was wearing a stunning stola, trimmed in yellow and with a matching palla over her head. I assumed that she had just come from some female gathering.

She doffed the head scarf and reclined across the mensa from myself, taking the already filled cup. Then she asked, "Has Korax returned? You seldom leave the Archives before the light is gone for reading." As in Egypt, I spent much of my time in the reading rooms of the magisterial stacks and librarium.

I shook my head, taking another sip to put off the need to part with my news. Finally, I set the cup down and said, quietly. "I was at the platform of the crier and then I visited the Censor to gather more of what had been said." A pause, then, "There was a great battle on the road between Memphis and Karnac, between the forces of Amyrtaeus and those of the scum Nepherites. The word is that our friend was slain in the battle. At the moment, that is all I know." Actually, that last was a falsehood. According to the missives that had arrived at the office of the Censor, the Pharaoh had been captured when his army was put to flight, then cruelly flayed alive by his foe. That detail she would not hear from me.

Her lips tightened, and the water began to flow from her eyes. I picked up the pestal and struck the little gong on the mensa. Almost instantly, Vera appeared at the top of the steps. Standing, I said to the maid, "Your mistress has received news of an evil nature. Assist her." I immediately descended the steps so as to give the woman privacy in her sorrow. And mine.

To assuage my own grief, I walked to my favorite taburna at the northern foot of the hill. The wife of the caupo, one Socellia by name and a bright and friendly woman of middle age, came to serve me at the table. Knowing of my tastes, she brought my cup already filled, then placed it in front of me. I just nodded and put down my small coin, without comment. Standing there a moment, she said, "You have received news that is not gladsome, Junius."

"Does feyness come with your wine pouring - or do I have spies in my household?" A jape, but not in jest.

She pursed her lips and replied, "When such as you, always the image of the self-satisfied man, appears one day looking as if he were Atlas himself, with his overburden, I need no conjuration to know that he is greatly troubled."

I nodded. "Aye. It is true that I have received unwelcome news." I pointed to the cup. "But, this will ease my thoughts, so keep it flowing for me."

I did not join my fellows at the center tables - rather, I pulled a fragment of papyrus from my belt and pretended to study it. At the moment, I had no desire for the japing and jesting of others. Rather, I just sat in my sadness and thought of life in general.

Depending on my mood at the times of my mentation, I assumed that I was just the plaything of the gods, and on other thoughtful occasions, refused to countenance that they even existed. In my life, I had always leapt from the fire before it became consuming. Always. I had no particular significance to the world - at least none that I knew. So... Why was I the man who escaped time and again to live life elsewhere? And why did a good man like Amyrtaeus die, leaving a cursed bastard like Nepherites to live? Did that mean the gods existed, or that they did not?

Of course, in my increasing befuddleness, I was attempting to answer questions that had been posed by the greatest philosophers of history, and with no greater success than with my thoughts. Finally, deciding that my dispiritedness had been properly liquified, and any more would cause me to lose face by falling on mine, I rose and departed for my house and collapsed on my mat.

Our stash of gold lubricated our entry into the upper reaches of the wealthy merchantry. As we became known as a bright couple - all assuming that Ravana was my mate - invitations to this atrium and that ceremony began to arrive. She made friends of the women quickly, and was always seen in the company of this group or that. I was much more relaxed in my friendship-making, caring little for the company of merchants with their interminable talk of corn prices and shipping rates. I gradually found a few fellows of letters who shared the love of learning with me, and many the nights did we lay around this mensa or that, discussing anything and all that might strike our fancy.

Of course, the upper strata of nobility was closed to us, just as it was in any city. No amount of gold will replace an atrium full of statues of genitors receding into the far past. I came to know several men of noble linage, but only as acquaintances, and without the boon of being considered one of their ilk. It mattered little to me. I had seen life at its worst and best and knew that it had nothing to do with the rank of one's ancestors.

Of course, one of the first journeys that I had made on coming to the city, was to the riverfront to find my family. The trip was unsatisfactory, as my patér and mater had long gone to their rewards, and my sisters married to unknown men up and down the river. My brothers had little remembrance of myself and less interest. The saying was true - a man who has left home can never return to the same. I gave my family no more thought.

And I had wonderment about a certain fiery-haired femina, and what had become of her - and her putative child. I knew, of course, that if still alive, she was far past being an alluring femina, and more likely a rotund matron. But, I gave it only thought and little else. It would do no good - for either of us - to have those few days of bliss remembered in a meeting.

And always, in the back of my mind, was that gameboard in the sky, and the little carved figure that represented me. Many times, lying on my mat at night, the old adage of that great tragedian of Athens, Euripides, would come unbidden to my thoughts. "Those whom the gods would destroy, they first make happy." That elusive gameboard was still in play, as I would realize far later. The cusp that was passed this time was not even noticed.

Easily in view from the terrace of our domicile, and across the wall and was the Campus Martus - the Field of Mars - in which the Roman army made their exercises. Unknown to us when we came to the city, a war had been in progress with the city of Veii, and its two allies, Falerii and Capena. In fact, it had been a strife since before the time that I had settled in Athens, with the advantage ever moving from one side to the other. I had learned that the citizenry of Rome had become distressed with the cost of the interminable strife, in both coin and men. Indeed, within the walls of the city, the female population now outnumbered the males to the point that for every five women, there were only four men or less - and many of those were missing limbs or eyes or suchlike as makes a normal man.

I could see, daily, from my house, the regiments in training moving here and there in mock battle, and I had decided to walk the distance to examine the field and men at a closer advantage. Doffing my far too formal toga for a tunic, I crossed the bridge and turned into the area that was covered by the tents of the quartermasters. I then pointed my feet to a ridge on which I would be able to see across the entire field, but suddenly I passed by what had to be the tents of the commanders and stopped before the large board that held orders and decrees.

On it was the list of regiments in training, and a name caught my eye. I wondered if it were truly he, or merely a coincidence of names. The latter was most likely, as Romans seem to have a limited supply of appellatives, and any one combination of praenomen and nomen could name hundreds of men of the city. As an officer of some unknown rank passed my person, I turned and said, "Excuse me, Sos. Might you point me to the unit of Tribune Spurius Camillus?"

The dusty soldier stopped and looked me up and down for a moment, obviously unimpressed by a clean and unsoiled citizen of military age, but apparently too good for the army and willing to let other men fight for his protection. Still, he answered civilly, "Aye, Sos. Yon be the regiment of Tiros assigned to the noble Tribune." He pointed to a large group at one side of the field. His hand moved and he added, "That be the tent of the Tribune."

"My thanks, soldier." He touched his helmet with a hand and resumed his course as I walked around the field toward the unit that he had indicated. I was obviously not just going to walk into the midst of a unit in training, but still, I could approach the area from the outside of the training area.

I could not tell one man from another, with all looking alike in helms and armor, although the officers had fore and aft red brushes on their helms, and the sub-officers the same, but sideways. Back and forth they went, charging and thrusting, moving this way and that, all in a cloud of choking dust that usually obscured all but the men closest to myself. It wasn't long before the sight became tiring and I retreated to the tented area where some enterprising merchants had erected tents just outside of the area. These were temporary taburnae, and no doubt very popular with men who had been breathing dirt for hours. At the moment, of course, they were empty, and I was served immediately.

Eventually, the sun began to drop and finally, the regiment on the field stopped their incessant runnings here and there, and were called to formation and dismissed. I rose and walked to the tent that the man had pointed to earlier. Eventually, an officer appeared - with others - and I knew that this was, indeed, my friend from the Temple. Years had passed, and his appearance was totally different, of course, but I could still see the outline of that young boy in the man walking towards me. I wondered if I was on a fool's errand. A noble Tribune might not welcome the reacquaintance of a commoner, no matter the friendship of boyhood.

I stood as he approached the tent, and said, "Salve, Tribune."

He looked at me quizzically, then asked, "Do I know you, citizen? You have a familiar aspect, but..." From the tent came a slave who immediately began to untie the leathers from his midriff, after first taking the helmet that the officer had doffed.

"Aye. Indeed, you do. We spent a year together in that tiny cubiculum in the Temple."

He stared, then said, in surprise, "Junius? By Mars and his beguiling doxies! I would never have recognized you with the span that the gods have put in your shoulders. Come into my tent." Shortly, he was ungarbed to nothing but a filthy tunic, caked with dust and it was soon pulled over his head by his slave. Naked, he was a well-built man, without fat or slackness - obviously, a soldier who had used his body intensively over the years. As his man sponged the worst of the dirt off his skin, he continued, "Tell me of yourself, and where you have been these many years. Nay. Let us to the Thermae of Minerva and speak of each other."

My fears of being an interloper to a noble were unrealized and shortly we were striding over the bridge and into the city. At the complex of pools, we made the ritual of cleansing in the apodyterium and then jumped into the tepidarium.

"Now," he said. "Where have you been these years, my friend? I had stopped, one day, in the temple on my way to the brothel of the Sirens to invite you to accompany me and the priest said that you had just disappeared between the dark and dawn."

I nodded, then began my tale, in total except for the slavery with the pirates. I changed the story to be one of a hostage that had escaped, but in the main, my tales were truth. At the end, we were still in the warm pool, wrinkled and puffy, but clean.

He shook his head in reaction. "I envy you, Junius. You have seen the world and more, and I have experienced nothing but a small section of Latium and much blood soaked dirt. Many times I had plans to voyage to Greece for my edification, but every time some disaster has come - either a lost battle or a new enemy." He began to move toward the edge. "But let us finish our bath, then you can hear my dull tales in front of a cup of wine."

My friend had immediately been inducted into the Army upon reaching his growth, and became a Tribune - a common occurrence for the sons of the highest families of the city. And as the war with Veii continued interminably, he garnered much experience in his new position. "...But the city is on a high hill, and has still not fallen. It is as the city of Troy, reborn into our time, but without the mythical horse to give us entry. Our siege is in its seventh year, and even now shows little progress."

I knew of Veii, only about ninety stadia from Rome, and a major city of the Etruscans. In fact, for hundreds of years, that was the ruling city of Latium, with suzerainty over Rome from the earliest days.

"And you are training new levies?" was my question. "I would have thought that a man with your experience would be at the front the line."

He smiled and lifted a leg from the floor. I could see a large gash, closed but not entirely healed. "Aye. And I was, but a cursed arrow from the walls found its way into my flesh. During my period of convalescence, I was consigned to herd Tyros across the field. But, as to the war, the people were becoming restless, and impatient in the taxation and recruitment for a war with no ending, and my patér was given the Consulship and defeated one of the allies of Veii, Capena, even looting the city. Naturally, as a victorious soldier, the Senate relieved him immediately and assumed command of the army."

He waved away the serving slave. "Rome has great fear of a successful general, and few are honored beyond the time that it takes to proclaim victory. He is at our home, now. You will come. He will take much gladness that you have returned from the dead."

I wondered at that statement. I doubted that a man such as Marcus Camillus had given a single iota of thought to a commoner from the river, but after deliberately arranging the meeting with an old friend, I could hardly refuse the invitation.

The house of Camillus was on top of the Capitoline and was magnificent. Stone and brick it was, tall and built more like a temple than any domicile that I had ever seen, even in Memphis. The compound of Dionysos, in Athens, though vastly larger, was a rambling shack compared to this edifice. In the gigantic atrium, a man was lying on a pillow and apparently engrossed in a scroll - one of several on the low mensa. The light was fading, and the torches had already been lit, and I wondered how his much older eyes could read in the growing darkness. Like us, he was garbed in a simple tunic, the day having been very warm and woolen robes being a trial in such heat.

He looked up as we approached and my friend said, "Salve, my Patér. I have brought an old acquaintance that you may remember." The man stood, looking at me, but obviously without recognition. I had not expected him to recollect my aspect - he had only seen me the one day, unlike his son that shared a room with me for an entire year. "You will remember the young man who dragged me from the river, after my fall from the Pons Amimia over the Tiber. This is he - Junius."

Now the face of the man lit with recognition of the event, if not the man. He stepped forward and offered his wrists in the Roman manner, saying, "Indeed I do. Welcome to my abode, Junius. I have not heard of you in... since my son left the temple."

Spurius grinned. "Aye, Sos. He has been far, and with many tales behind his travels."

"Sit. Sit." The senior waved to the mats at the low table. Calling to a slave, he ordered more cups and wine. "You do not have the aspect of a scribe, Junius, but rather that of a soldier with your lean frame and the weapon at your belt."

I nodded as I reclined. "Aye, Sos. A scribe I am, certainly, but in other parts of the world, one must also be as a warrior, or take an early death."

"He has traveled the circumference of the Great Sea in those years," said Spurious. "Athens, Rhodes, Tyre, Memphis... just to list a few."

"A traveler throughout the world... I envy you, Junius. Tell me, have you..." For hours by the water clock - a real one in this house - that actually chimed the hours. I wondered how, but later saw that it was a slave that struck the gong when the vessel emptied. That told of the wealth of a house - to have a slave just to stand and strike the hours.

The senior Camillus was a scholar, himself, with an overwhelming desire for knowledge, even as myself. At my description of the battles in the Hellespontos, he queried my memory for an interminable time, asking detailed questions of this tactic and that maneuver. The darkness of the evening did not halt the questioning - a sumptuous meal was served, and the talk went on around the viands and wine. He was impressed with my ability to both read and write in three languages and in my friendship with an actual King in Egypt. In fact, I was afraid that he would begin to query me on the battles that freed the land from the Persians, and that I would be reclining on the mat for the bulk of the night. Fortunately, he called a halt to our session, and I prepared to make my departure - after assuring the senior that I would gladly return and given more sustenance to my travels.

"You are always welcome in my house, Junius. I would especially hear more of the secrets that you found in the Palace of the King - and soon. That is a story most unbelievable."

I bowed to the older man, then to Spurious. "Salve, and my thanks for the welcome. I shall certainly make a visit again, as you wish."

As I turned to go, Spurious said, "You know the hour that my duty is over. Come tomorrow and we will share the baths again."

Revelationis

Korax had been gone the better part of a year, and my concern was growing about his absence. Of course, I knew full well that every year a certain portion of shipping, the world over, left port to never be seen again. Ravana was insistent that I was building worries on nothing, saying, "That Greek will outlive the pair of us. Even Hades himself would have trouble pulling that scoundrel down."

As to the woman, we were again as man and mate. One night, I was laying in the coolness of the air flowing in the gauzed window, when the squeak of my door was heard. In the dimness of reflected moonlight, I could see a tall white body enter and approach - and had no doubt who it was. In a moment, the naked female dropped to her knees, softly saying, "I would ask if I am welcome on your mat, again, Junius. The days are growing lonely with the recession of my memories of Egypt."

I just moved over and put out my hand to pull her down. We did not suddenly give in to the impulse of passion as if we were newly fledged youngsters with desires that could not be held. Rather, we just lay for a while, beside each other, until she said, "I would avail myself of your offer to be your mate, not only in aspect but in reality."

"Aye. I have been hoping for it since we arrived in Rome."

"I have no future elsewhere. My years will not suffice for a marriage in the normal way, and I would not cozen a man by offering him a barren wife. But my needs are still great, and you are a kind man and skilled in the use of a female." She chuckled, something rarely done since the news from Egypt. "And I know that you still have much need for such, counting the times of the month that you visit the house of Women across from the thermae."

I just lay, with my hands behind my head, not reaching for any touching or beginning moves to stimulate a female. "I had not noticed that you were counting my dalliances with the women of the street," I jested. Thus did it begin again. Not raging desire, but the enjoyment of a man and woman comfortable with each other.

"Master. There is a man bearing a missive at the door."

It was early morning, and I had only just broken my fast, about to decide on my usage for the day as the housemaid came with the message. I nodded and replied, "Show him to the atrium."

I waited and in a few moments, a young man with the red armband of a message runner appeared. These could be found in both Rome and Ostia, usually bearing scrolls or tablets between the cities for the use of merchants. Their fees were set by the magistrates, and I tossed the proper coin to the runner, then said, "My thanks, boy." He departed, and I read the scrap of papyrus, then rose to find Ravana.

She was still in her bath as I burst in, shouting, "Korax has returned! He has sent word for me to come to Ostia for the inspection of cargo."

Surprised, both she and Vera just looked at me for a moment, before I continued. "I depart immediately. Wish you to come?"

Ravana nodded for her maid to continue the bath, then replied in a much more tranquil voice. "Aye. It would be a welcome change from the days, but not immediately. I am a woman and such do not just throw on a robe and depart. I would think that a man of your erudition would know such."

She was jesting, of course, as was I in my reply. "Aye. But try to arrange yourself for travel before the midday meal."

Still, it was not long before the three of us were sitting in a river barge as the crew poled us along with the current. Coming off the wet season, the waters were still fairly rapid, and our journey would only be three hours - four at the most. His message had given the wharf at which our ship had tied up, and in a short while, we could see the vessel ahead. And Korax, standing on the dock watching bundles being unloaded.

Without even a curse to the gods, he hurried to us and we embraced. Even Ravana seemed happy that the old Greek had returned with a whole body. Then I said, "I had resigned myself to thinking that you had settled down on some remote island and were raising a family. Did Ahirom lose his way, and you came by way of the pillars of Hercules?" The old Greek was all grins - almost euphoric with his spirits. For such, I asked, "Either the sirens have bewitched you in the turn of the Messēnē straights, or you have more to tell me."

He nodded vigorously. "Aye, and if you had eyes that had not been dimmed by the grime of Roman city-life, you would see the reason."

Confused, I looked him up and down, then to the ship. Then to the cargo being placed on the stones of the receiving area. Bundles it was - woolens probably, linen perhaps. Much of it and good profit, but nothing to be... Suddenly Ravana grabbed my arm and said, with emphasis, "Look! There!" I followed her pointing finger, two wharfs down and at another ship. And one beside which Ahirom was standing.

I just stared, then looked at the grinning Korax, then stared again before striding down the shoreline to the wharf in question.

Then I just stood on the planks, stunned at the vision in my sight. This ship was a close relative to our new one, but obviously much older and weatherbeaten. It was, in fact, our original vessel, abandoned in Cyrene when we fled for our lives. Now, mouth open, I turned to see Korax walk up and stand beside me. Then I waved to the pilot - nay, the Captain - now standing on the deck, watching the unloading of the hull. He waved back and called, "Greetings, Sos. We are well met again."

"Well met indeed," I shouted. "Touched by the gods, I am, is the more likely tale." To the Greek, I said, "Am I to believe that you stormed the port of Cyrene, stealing the sailcloth, then the ship, standing into open waters with the city watch close on your stern."

He shook his head. "Nay. It is a tale indeed, but nothing involving blades or throat cutting. But the story is long and will wait for our unloading to finish." He turned an hurried back to the other ship, to watch the scribes as they tallied each bundle being discharged. For myself, I walked the plank onto what seemed to be a long lost friend, come home at last. I gave more words to Ahirom, then just walked around to examine the vessel, as the unloading continued.

It was almost evening-dark when the last bundle was assigned to the factors that had purchased it, and Korax received the tally-tablets that we would present on the morrow at the shipping magistrate, to receive our funds. During the afternoon, I had taken Ravana and her maid - and the widow of Korax - to the most exclusive inn that the port of Ostia could provide, telling her to order a goodly meal for three men and two women after the day was finished. I told the caupo that the two men, arriving later, would be my guests, and I wished no ill words for their station when they arrived. With my coin - and my countenance with hand on my longknife - he made no protest.

At darkfall, I arrived at the inn with both men, finding that Ravana had reserved the entire courtyard in the rear of the compound, and torches were already flaring, and the smell of goodly meat and breads was in the air. They set their kit and baggage in the corner and we sat down to the feast.

The meal was sumptuous and extended, so numerous were the questions that I asked. One had to partake between sentences.

Korax began the tale, that started as we had planned. "As to how we came by our old ship again, I can say in all honesty, that Ehsan purchased it for us." That was a statement that bordered on insanity. Ravana and I glanced at each other, wondering at the statement of the Greek. I myself saw the body of our ship captain placed in the Persian tomb, and I had yet to learn of a departed friend purchasing a cup of wine for his comrades, to say nothing of making a gift of a sea-going vessel. But, knowing the tendency of my friend to take many roads before he came to the end of a tale, I kept my silence.

They had voyaged to Carthago with the load of ironwork, bringing good coin. In that city, they had found a load of exquisite white wool that was highly prized in either Mira or Tarsus, and even a hull full of the bundles would leave the ship nimble and lively. That voyage took two months, being at the northeastern end of the Great Sea. There was no cargo of value to be accepted at that port, so they made the short voyage to the island of Cipros, as the Greeks knew it. Romans call it Cyprus.

That inland is rich in copper - a metal that is valued in any land in the world. A partial load was taken, then Korax announced to his captain that he wished to purchase a small boat, storable on the deck and that they would visit the shores of Phoenicia. "Aye," said Ahirom in one of his rare comments. "I thought that the sea dalkies had taken the mind of my shipmate. Those shores are nothing but ship killing rocks and shoals."

Korax continued, "I did not wish to speak of what I sought until I knew that my knowledge was good."

"What knowledge?" I exclaimed.

"Stand to, my Roman friend. All will be revealed. Do not deny an old Greek when he has a rare story to tell. Now, at the coast we..." Below the city of Tyros, on the eastern reaches of the sea, is a jutting promontory. I had passed it several times in my voyages, but my memory had no touch of it.

"The day was raw, and the wind giving us a lee shore, so we put into the small port of Asod to wait out the western wind. The wait did more than we had wished. The had wind laid to with such a small extent that it took us two days to move the short distance back to the promontory."

There, while Ahirom slowly sailed back and forth, Korax and two of the crew launched the small boat and paddled to the shore. He was searching for a white rock in the mass of broken black stone, and indeed, it was there. "In less time that it takes to walk a league, I was back at the ship with a leather bag, taking from under the odd stone. The little voyage was worth the effort."

"Aye," said Ahirom again. "My fear that I myself was in the clutches of the sea sprites myself when he opened the bag to show a full talent of gold." Stunned, I just looked back and forth at the two sailors. A Greek talent was almost two hundred Roman librae - over half the weight of Ravana herself.

Now Korax laughed. "Nay. Hold your expressions of exclaim. All will be told. You have my oath on it." A gulp of wine and he continued, "You have heard that Ehsan was a... Navarch of a Persian fleet."

It was a statement, and aye, I had long known of it. "Navarch is the Greek term," I answered. "He was a Subahdar... a Premier Subahdar of his ships."

"As you say. But more than that, he was a son of King Art-ter-axis, or some such." I was astounded. Artaxerxes had been the ruler of Persia for half a hundred years. And Ehsan was his son?

Korax continued. "When the King died, his brother - Ehsan's, not the King's - took the throne, but he was killed in a few days, and then other pretenders and bastard sons fought one another until some relative of his, called Ochus, managed to capture the throne. He then proceeded to kill any other possible throne-claimers that he could find."

"Ochus?" I muttered. "That name does not meet with my slight knowledge of Persia."

Korax grimaced. "Aye. That is because the self-made king took the name of Darius." Ah. Of course. Darius the Second, whose death caused the emptiness in the Persian empire that gave entry to Amyrtaeus to throw his enemies out of Egypt. "That is as it was. But, as to Ehsan - he escaped during a night, taking his wife and son and miter in a small boat - and his family fortune - southward and all the way to Pelusium. But, on the way, he hove into the rocky shore south of Tyros and stashed his gold and silver under the white rock, taking only what he needed to begin anew elsewhere."

I nodded. "And that elsewhere was Memphis."

"Aye. But, although his miter passed on with natural age, his wife and son were taken by a plague not long after entering the city. Now, saddened with grief, he took the life of a river pilot, more for the reason of not wishing to settle in another land than any other."

I just sat in wonderment. Much did I not know about my previous captain, although... "How know you so much of his life?" Before the question was asked, I knew the answer. And Korax gave it.

"I voyaged with him for years. Much did we talk about old times and places." He assumed a grimmer expression. "At the last, he knew that some evil was hatching in his body. On the final voyage that I took with him, as we passed the rocky outcrop, he gave me the secret and his blessing to recover it if I wished."

Now I just lay back and thought over the words of Korax, and remembering back to the man of the conversation. Of course, every man has a part of his life that he wishes to remain unknown to others - I certainly did. And Ehsan had no obligation to give me the tally of his.

"Ehsan was the son of the King of Persia?" This was from Ravana. "One would never have known it from his demeanor. He was always gracious with me - and not giving barbed words to a woman as is the want of some men." Korax just grinned as she looked at him.

"Aye," I agreed. "He was a good friend, indeed, as well as an excellent captain." Suddenly, I asked, "But what does Ehsan have to do with our old ship?"

"Ah. The tale continues." Korax leisurely filled his cup, enjoying my impatience with the delay. "At Pelusium, we loaded with linen. I thought it unwise to venture up the Nilos to our old..." He stopped suddenly, his face stricken with concern. I was becoming alarmed at the sudden change, but in a few moments, he continued to speak. "I offer my apologies for rambling so and forgetting the news of most importance to... to any here." He took a long gulp of wine, then said, "Your friend... and yours, Ravana, has been killed. In battle, it was said, but I know..."

I broke in before he gave any horrible descriptions about the death of Amyrtaeus - details that I did not wish for Ravana to hear. "Aye, old friend. You are not remiss in your news. We had it ourselves months ago and have waited out our sorrows, and we would not visit the grief again, so continue with your story of the ship."

"Uh... Aye... Well, with the hull full of linen and many bars of copper, we rove along the coast, planning to make the long haul across the sea to Syracusa. But, before we cast out into the void, a massive storm was in the making, and we had to stand into the port of Cyrene for refuge. And not without some measure of fearfulness, I might say. I doubted that a mere Greek would stand firm in the memory of the rulers of that city, but still, I kept my face covered in my rain garb as we wharfed to the dock."

"We spent our night on board, so as to assure ourselves that the mooring was firm and that the ship was not working against the boards. On the morning, as the rain slackened, I looked to see our old ship - still in place as we had left it. Such was my surprise, that I walked the shoreline to that wharf and examined it closely. Nothing had changed. It was just as if it were waiting for its friends to return.

In fact, I was without knowledge of why a valuable vessel had not long been sold off, in revenge of our fleeing, if nothing else."

"I was at a loss as how to find the story, being without the presence of my educated Roman. But, using my mastery of taverna-skills..." This with another grin, "...I discovered the existence of the craft of a... a Dikagoryoas." He meant a Dikigóros - a man skilled in the laws of his land or city. In Rome, he would be an Attornatus. "On the recommendation of a patron or two, and my coin that made the wine flow freely, I found the residence of one such, and commissioned him to find my answers."

"You took a chance at peril," I said. "You might reside in the city for years without recognition, but by connecting yourself with the old ship, a magistrate might find in his memory that man who once stood before the council and gave oath."

Korax nodded but said with a dismissal wave. "Aye, but no names were given and I never approached the magistrates of the city - not those in real power. And my name during the stay was not the one my dam gave me." He gestured toward his captain. "The ship had been turned to point out to sea, and the sail already poised for instant raising. Ahirom was watching for a Greek fleeing for his life ahead of the spears of the city watch, and the cloth would have been raised and the men poling away from the dock even as I jumped the gap to board."

"My man, laden with a palm of gold and the promise of more, found that our old ship had indeed been set for vending, but the process was still in the hands of the magistrates. An old captain in the taverna, long past his time to walk a deck, told me that the ship would be wormwood before the functionaries of the city would finally issue a clearing tablet."

I could have guessed that. My own experience in Cyrene had shown that the administration of the city was as a massive merchantry in itself, with thousands of magistrates, scribes, officers and such, touching every aspect of life, and the speed of decisions was as the progress of an oared boat into a fierce gale. I wondered if the characteristic was common across all domains with a republican form, although the only other city with such a type of governance was Rome itself, and it had not submerged itself in smothering rules and decrees. As yet, anyway.

Korax was ending his tale. "...And with the gold in the bag of Ehsan, we... hastened much of the delay and finally, a tablet was obtained allowing us to purchase the ship and depart. A crew was found, and I captained the ship, following closely behind Ahirom in the other, of course, else I would still be wandering the sea, looking for any land."

I smiled to myself. Aye, gold will always hasten an official - or slacken him, whichever is needed. But... "You did not spend a talent of gold on a single vessel, did you? Even on one that is like a member of the family?"

Korax shook his head. "Nay. The weight taken from the bag is not even discernible. Had the entire been spent, you might have expected a fleet to have arrived. Look yourself." He glanced at the door for any servants that might be within hearing then, "It is in our baggage, there - split between the two of us for easier portage. And the sooner you take it to a place of safety, the easier my throat will sleep at night."

I looked at him in surprise. "Ehsan did not leave his family treasure to me! It is yours."

"And what would I do with such wealth? My woman and I wish only for a warm mat, good viands, and full cups. And Ahirom would not trade the entire amount for his captaincy." He waved his cup. "Speak no more of it - I will not contend with you on the subject. Ravana shared her stash with us, and your riches gained over time you have shared with me. We three are all a family, in that aspect."

I nodded slowly. "Aye, it will be safer in a hidden strongroom than on a ship, but know this - any amount is yours at any time."

Ravana and I stayed in Ostia for five days, as we purchased more cargo for the next voyage. To my question of a captain for the new - our original ship, Korax informed me that he would stand the position. By now the landman had become an accomplished seaman after years of voyaging, although far from having the knowledge and experience of Ahirom. But, the two ships would stand out together, with the one-legged captain pointing the course and Korax following. And, two vessels have a better chance against pirates, just as two men can stand much more firmly against brigands.

As to their plans, I had no issue. My friend was enjoying his vagabond existence on the sea, and it was not my position to dictate to his life. I wished them good voyaging and told Korax to come to Rome when next he touched the port of Ostia.

Incidentia

My house became as an intellectual salon, with men, young and old meeting at any hours to discuss this or that. I cared not for their antecedents - only that they were intelligent and lively in their debate and conversations. Ravana usually appeared as host, her beauty and grace eliciting many comments of admiration for my having captured such a treat. Of course, in my presence, the remarks were held to respectfulness, mostly due to the few times that Korax had come to stay, he being between voyages to every part the Great Sea. His tales of our adventures and battles before the group were, if not greatly embellished, were at least overly complementary of my skill with the blade. I could have been excused for thinking myself a son of Mars after the recitation this story or that, always of desperate fighting, both on the sea and the sands of Egypt. I grinned behind my cup as the row-skiff of the reaver pirates off the port of Pelusium seemed to morph into a trireme of imposing size, manned by skilled sea-troops almost without count.

Often, I would meet Lucius after his day's duty on the training fields, and we would sojourn to the baths, there to talk of this and anything. At least, until his leg gained its strength again and he was posted back to his unit at the siege of Veii. After, I only saw him about every second month, when he returned to Rome for his schedule rests.

Many times, though, a servant would appear at our door with an invitation to visit the senior Camillus. I would then spend most of a day in that elegant atrium, speaking with the noble about my view of the world, here and there. He was muchly interesting in Greece, saying, "It is inevitable that our two lands will come in conflict, someday. Two dogs may not share a neighborhood without striving to determine which is to be the leader."

I was doubtful. "The Grecian mainland is many thousands of stadia by ship, Sos. What land in all the world would have the sustenance to both berth and support an army at such a distance?"

He nodded. "Aye. You have the meat of it, but... It will happen, even if not in our times."

I would not have cared to be either involved in the assault or planning. I had studied the disastrous attempt of the Athenians to land an army on the coast of Sicilia - only half the distance that I had mentioned. A waiting army - and especially, if in the fury of defending their own land - had all the advantages. Their supplies were near, as were any additional regiments. The defenders could withdraw to reassemble for the next battle and maneuver to strike elsewhere. The invaders coming from the sea were months away from any assistance or food. Their options in the case of a failed battle were limited - being only to face the blades of their foe, or to retreat into the sea to drown. In the case of the Athenians, both actions were their fate, finally losing thousands of men and hundreds of ships in a total debacle.

But, the talks with the older man were stimulating, and much did I learn of the base on which Rome was governed. Early on, I realized that my understanding of the underpinning of both Athens and Egypt were far greater than my home city, and my assumptions were far off the mark in many areas.

The time passed, with the war in the north seeming as a black pit into which men and gold were thrown, never to be seen again. The mood on the street among the citizenry was less than supportive of the Senate, although I had yet heard no rumblings of major resistance. Among the young men, however, the desire to escape the city before being called to the training field was growing.

One morning we were on the terrace, with even the staff of the house, and all enjoying the first cool breezes of the coming diurnal season. Unlike the norm of the city - and most others that I had visited - little ceremony was played between the principles of the household - myself and Ravana - and the staff. Indeed, although my golden haired mate had no idea of her genitors, I knew that I was as common as the maids, if not more, and only the actions of the remote gods, or fate itself, now made me more than what I was born.

Suddenly, the bronze ring-knocker sounded on the wood of the front door. The cocua rose from her sitting mat, saying, "It will be the kindling-vendor. He is to bring a cart of stove-wood this morn." She and her maid descended the steps, and we continued our discussion of the coming festival of Diana, in which I had no interest, and the festival in the Forum, in which I had much. Ravana, too, had no desire to attend the ceremonies to listen to priests drone praises to a goddess - and one who had never been seen to give gratitude for the laudations - at least not to my knowledge.

But the festivities in the huge square were different. Many skilled performing troupes would be giving plays on the boards and those I enjoyed, as did Ravana. And it must be said, the more lewd and salacious the acting, the more she enjoyed the performance. "I hope the company from Atium is in attendance this year," she said. "They can show the truth of men that even I could not give with any performance."

I just crinkled my nose at her, and began my reply, then broke off as her eyes widened in a vision behind me. Turning, I saw the cocua had returned to the top of the steps. "Your pardon, Sos. Soldiers are at the door asking for admittance."

Totally surprised at the news, I hurried down the steps and across the atrium to the open door, seeing... In amazement, I saw that it was Tribune Lucius. And another. But my unuttered implication was not for the men, but their condition. Both were ragged and dusty - nay, covered with filth to a degree that even the bright red polish of the armor was hidden. "Jupiter's pouchstones!" I exclaimed. "What in the name of all..."

"My apologies for our sudden intrusion, my friend. But I have need of a scribe that can be trusted."

Still stunned, I just waved the men to enter. "Come, we can talk in the atrium."

It was at this point that Ravana took a hand. "Wait, friend of Junius. Are you in need of haste, as if fleeing from peril?"

The Tribune shook his head. "Nay. It is not so immediate as that, but..."

"Then a slight delay will do no harm." Turning, she spoke in sharp and hurried sentences. To the cook, "Two cups of cooled wine for the men. Our best. And prepare some viands, after. Vera and Papiria, heat water and fill the bath. Varia, find two tunics and have them ready for men when they have bathed." Turning back to the soldiers, "Come with me and let us doff those... garments. One would think you had enlisted with the latrini collectors."

I just shrugged and waved for the men to follow my woman. In a while, Lucius climbed to the terrace to join me, he now wearing nothing but a clean tunic. Led by Ravana, she pointed him to a mat beside the low table, then said, before leaving again, "I will see that your man is fed and rested."

My friend lay back, and took a goodly swallow of the wine, then said, "Would that some of my Centurions had the gift of command as your woman. She would make such a soldier that even Hades would tremble at engaging."

I nodded in agreement. "Aye. A retiring flower she is not. But enough of that - what disaster is happened? Do we expect the army of Veii at our gates at any moment?"

"It is not so dire as that, but not for the lack of our generalship desiring to ease the path for such. I wish you to scribe a missive, but in such a way as cannot be read should it be intercepted on its journey."

Puzzled, I just asked, "How would I write a letter that another cannot read?"

"Are you not literate in the picture-scrabble of the Egyptians? I would have it scribed in such a tongue."

I nodded slowly. "Aye, and I am to assume that the person that receives the script can also read the language?"

"Nay. My patér does not, nor does anyone around him. I have in mind to commission you to carry it to him."

This was ominous. "What is the trouble that you fear, or has it happened?"

"Nay. All will become clear when you write what I have to say."

Calling for my papyrus and pens, I laid out a blank sheet and began to put down his words, changing them from Latium to Egyptian. As he spoke, I realized that the army had suffered a major defeat, just barely stemming a rout by the Legion and the pursuit by the army of Veii and their allies. The scroll was considerable, at least the length of a man's arm and more before I was finished.

"The Senior is at our villa in Tivoli, about sixty stadia up the Via Praenes. I will detail my aide to guide you. He has been there himself."

"Should not you deliver this?" I asked. "He will have many questions that I cannot answer."

"Nay. I cannot desert my men, and must be back at my position before the day ends. This is much to ask a companion, but I will make you well compensated for the effort."

"To Hades with your recompense. I do not take coin in the assistance to a friend. A moderate walk in the country does not require any effort for such a minor favor."

He shook his head. "Not so minor as you may think. The fools that caused and allowed the rout will not reward a man who spreads the word of their incompetence. They will know that I have journeyed to Rome for the day, and will assume that I have come to report to the Senate. I am surprised that I have not been hindered thus far. Travel fast and do not fail to watch behind you."

"But your patér is... has not the Consulship now. He has no more authority than myself. What can he do as such?"

"You are correct, but without the entire story. Our villa in Tivoli is... well... magnificent I have to admit in all honesty, with steaming mineral waters filling the private thermae. Many of the nobles, especially those whose tastes run to an excess of wine and rich foods, attend our company to bathe in the healing waters. The chief Consul and the Praetor are there with him now, along with the Censor Primus and several other high Senators. By telling my patér, you are also informing the leaders of the Senate." He rose as did I, seeing Ravana enter, followed by Vera and another maid carrying the equipment of the Tribune. "Now I must return, and you must be off."

He walked to the top of the steps and shouted, "Adiutor Cimber!" A call of "Aye, Sos!" came from below, then quick steps and he appeared, now re-equipped in his helm and leathers - all cleaned and polished as if just come from the parade ground. And, of course, his gladius in its belt sheath. "You will do as we discussed on our march here. Nothing has changed, but that the scribe Junius must report to my patér as fast as the road can be walked."

"Aye, Sos!" came again.

Quickly, the Tribune garbed with his own equipment, his aide assisting in the tying of the laces, then he turned and said, "This will not be forgotten, Junius. I will see you on your return."

With the scroll in my shoulder bag, the aide and I hurried to the eastern gate and quickly set foot on the Via Praenes, the wide road heading into the morning sun and the road to the small city of Tivoli. For the first hour, we passed stadia of grain fields, on both sides of the way, now with slaves cutting the harvest and oxen carts rolling this way and that with the ripe stalks and heads. The road was busy, but not crowded, and became much less traveled as we left the flatlands and entered the low hills.

Cimber, the aide, was hesitant to speak at first, but after assuring him that I was no noble, to be genuflected to and considered his better, he became more open. As we steadily walked, he began to give me the tale of the strife from which his Tribune and he had come. "...And the two fat Senators with the commission of Consuls of the Army have little use for plans and strategy, preferring to remain in the shade of their canopies and ordering this battle won and that position taken, without regard to either terrain or numbers."

"Why would the Senate put two such in charge of an army, and why more than one Consul?"

The man spit into the dust of the road. "Ah. It has been a common occurrence in the last several years. Many nobles wish to strut before their fellows in Rome, with tales of desperate battles, won only by their own stratagems when in command. Few serve longer than a month or two before their backsides begin to long for the mats of their own atrium, and the water of their baths. In a siege, it seldom matters, as the conduct is pointed by the Tribunes and Centurions. But, when the enemy stages a major foray, as in this last engagement, more is required of the leading generals than pointing a hand holding a wine cup and demanding victory."

The talk passed the time, and the stadia steady moved beneath our feet. We were in the low hills, the road now winding and much more narrow, and now, only a small caravan of asses or an ox cart or two were passed at intervals. We were far from the incessant noise of daytime Rome, now being able to listen to birds and the rustle of small animals. It was now that we heard rapid hoofbeats behind us. Too late did we take alarm, failing to remember that such animals are seldom seen on such rural roads and never ridden by any but soldiers of horse and the rare noble, out for a gambol. Turning we saw three riders appear - uniformed calvary.

I looked to either side of the road - the thin forest would offer no protection to men trying to outdistance riders. We would have to receive them in the open road. Now, seeing their quarry, the horses were stirred to a fast canter, then stopped a handful of strides from us. As the riders slid to the ground, they drew their blades. It was obvious that their orders were not only stop us from reaching our destination but to dispose of us as well.

The three men were accoutered as my escort, with the exception of the leader having a white brush on his helm. All had red polished leathers over the torso, with the usual pedal skirts and greaves to cover their lower bodies. I was the exception, wearing nothing but a white tunic and sandals, tied with my belt and longknife scabbard.

And my appearance was our deliverance.

Cimber had whipped out his gladius to meet the onrushing attackers while I moved aside in apparent fright, natural to any simple citizen in reaction to a sudden onslaught. As the three moved in a spread to take the aide from all sides, they ignored me - what man would fear a mere scribe, standing in fear of manly soldiers moving together? As the closest one passed me, and his attention on Cimber, I drew my longknife with silence and speed. The man did not even realize that he was slain, as my knife entered between the lacings of his fore and aft leathers. And not deeply - that lesson I had learned in the Egyptian palace and a mistake that I would never make again.

His fellow saw the action in the corner of his eye, and shouted a warning, turning to confront me as the blades of the leader met that of the aide. He raised his blade in a sweeping overhand swing that was interrupted as I thrust my point at his chest, directly. The wide stroke stopped as he stumbled backward to avoid my longknife - a thrust that would not have connected even had he not moved.

The leader, now realizing that he had a foeman at his back as well as the one he was confronting, tried to move sideways to remove himself from the fatal position, but the hesitation allowed Cimber to slash the offhand of the soldier, then swing to batter the blade aside. I did not see it, but immediately the edge of the aide's blade almost severed the neck of his adversary.

My opponent, was now swinging with abandon, trying to quickly step backward, but was now entering the brush of the side of the road, giving him fear of losing his balance totally. I waited until the blade had descended once more, cleaving nothing but air, and not even within two hands of myself, then quickly lunged forward and pushed the point of my longknife into his chest. The hardened leather of the Legionary is proof against most slashes, unless delivered with much strength and with both hands, but it has no chance of stopping the needle-sharp point of such as my knife. The man fell at my feet.

I quickly turned to view the plight of my escort, but he was standing over his foe as well. Then it was as if the gods had made the day stand still. I was suddenly infused with a feeling of... it was like the sudden taking of a woman that one has desired for much time but could never have until now. I realized that my lifetime denigration of myself as an unskilled novice of battle was just that - a belittling of myself without warrant. This man... These men were soldiers of the Roman army. Not street toughs, or port brawlers, but supposedly men trained to battle, and I had been... was superior in arms to them, and I knew the self-appellation was true.

Had I any reason to believe that the old Greek soldier, Leodes, late of the Artemis Third Hekatontarchia, was still alive after all these years, I would have sent him gifts and gold to make him the King of the Deme in which he lived. His transfer of blade-skills to me had allowed me to continue my life once again.

"Your pardon, Sos. But... You are..." I could see Cimber trying to choose his words, and I knew exactly what they would be. "...You have skills that one does not expect of a scribe."

I grinned, stupidly. "Aye. And should we be associates for any time, I can relate the long story of how they came to be." I looked up and down the road. "But for now, we must hurry on our journey." Another thought, then, "But first, let us drag this scum into the bushes. I doubt that another unit will be following them, but if so they would be enraged to find their comrades left in the road as food for the crows." Their horses were still in view, having skittered away some distance, but they would do no good for two men who had no equestrian skills. We would leave them as a present for any farmer that passed along.

Shortly, the sight of the ambuscade was behind us and out of sight.

Epicinium (Aftermath)

Much happened after my hurried journey to Tivoli, not the least that I had become high in the magistracy of the city. But the intervening three years between then and now had made me pensive about my homeland. On occasions, when I was alone on my mat at night, Ravana asleep beside me and my slumber would not come, I wondered about Rome and its future. The city was as a young man, just into his growth and realizing his strength and vigor, but also without discipline and self-denial. Within her walls, the people were satisfied and overly proud of the heritage. But, the gladsomeness did not extent to any who were ruled by Rome, being considered almost as barbarians, unworthy of consideration, or even life. It did not bode well for the far future, should the land grow to be as one of the great domains in the world, even as Persia, or as Egypt was in the far past.

For myself, I had no reason to be unsatisfied with my lot. I had still my power and wealth, given to me by the Consul Camillus in his glory, and when he fell it was not taken from me. Men still called me Sos, with respect and many of the intellectually advanced came for my advice - as much for the pleasure of speaking with another of acuteness, as for the service that I could provide. Ravana was the center of the younger women of the Capitoline. Her uniqueness of looks and refusal to accept the passive roll of a woman made her the envy of wives of the quarter - although many of the dowagers had reservations of the brash woman, still on the youthful side of middle age.

The city was being transformed by the flow of wealth from Vii and her allied cities - temples were growing, and beginning to shine with gold leaf, and marble statues. Even the gigantic statue of Juno, in Veii, was laboriously hauled to Rome as booty, to be set up in the new temple on the side of the Capitoline hill. The lectica of the wealthy filled the streets, and even the lower merchantry and magistrati could often be seen being carried through the streets, as they gloried in their newfound opulence.

Rome had increased its domain in the land of Latium by another whole, and its influence reached even further. Conquered land was been given to needy citizens, and soldiers of the campaigns and the influx of grain and foodstuffs was such that even the beggars of the street were belly-filled. Rome had become the dominate power in the region.

Occasionally, and unbidden, my thoughts would suddenly come of happiness and the reaction of the gods to such a state. But, again, my life changed on that day that I strode to the villa with the message scroll.

We had reached the small city of Tivoli and the villa of the Camillus family. Lucius had not exaggerated - it was magnificent in the extreme and more like the palace of a king than the casual retreat of a noble. At the villa walls we were met by the Centurion of the Senate guards and several men - here because of presence of such august members of that body. The officer was unimpressed by the two men who strode up to the gate, both covered with road dust and with a considerable amount of what looked like blood on their garments.

I stopped before the officer and said, "I have an urgent missive for his excellence, Marcus Camillus."

He looked me up and down, with obvious distaste, before replying, "The Senators are at their baths, as is their host. Give me the message and I will deliver it when they have returned from the pools."

"It cannot be read by any but myself, and it is imperative that I give it to him at once. This concerns the Roman army at Veii."

It was evident that the gruff soldier was not used to having his commands questioned. "Ragged scribes do not demand entry to the presence of the Senate..."

I had had enough. Stepping forward and looking him directly in the eyes, I barked, "This ragged scribe will see you assigned to guarding the latrine pits of the Field of Mars if I do not speak to Marcus Camillus before another twenty breaths are taken!"

The Centurion's eyes widened. No mere commoner in a soiled tunic dared to speak to an officer of the Roman army as I did - and certainly not to one assigned to the Senatorial Guard, but... any who did...

He nodded, and said, "Come with me." Turning he strode through the gate, followed by myself and Cimber. Through marbled and columned halls we walked, then a huge open-air atrium, and then more hallways. Far in the back of the compound were the stone pools, steaming with the waters from the hillside, and surrounded by stone benches, topped with reclining mats, and tables of all sizes. Slaves stood against the walls, holding small amphorae of wine at the ready and a continual flow of kitchen maids came and went with platters of viands.

It looked like the entire Senate was here, most laying around the pools and talking, but many floating and relaxing in the waters. Of course, the many men just gave the impression of numbers. Probably no more than two double handfuls of the nobles were in residence. But, these were some of the most powerful men of Rome.

The Centurion changed his course, now striding for the senior Camillus, reclining at a mensa with two others. All were garbed in simple tunics, except those entering or in the water, who were, of course, bare. With no need to display themselves before the inferior plebeians of the city, the overly thick robes of the toga had been discarded.

Camillus glanced toward us, then back to the speaking man, then wide-eyed, back to the apparitions that were approaching. He stood as the Centurion stopped before him, saluted, and said, "A messenger, Sos. With an important missive, he says."

The older man nodded, and said, "Aye. That is all." As the officer saluted and turned to hurry away, the noble exclaimed, "By the gods! Junius..." He stopped as I handed him the scroll.

All conversation in the large terrace had stopped. A man in a bloody tunic, and escorted by a soldier in the same disarray could not be the bringer of gladsome news. In a moment, Camillus looked at me and exclaimed, "This is written in the picture tongue of Egypt!"

"Aye, Sos. That was specified thusly so that I could not be read had it... it not reached your hands. I can dictate it to you."

A man strode up, elderly and one of the few wearing a robe over his tunic. "I can read the writing of the hot lands." Taking it from the elder Camillus, he unrolled it and began to read. It was obvious that he was indeed fluent in the picture writing if he was actually reading as the scroll was being steadily unrolled from the spindle. Finally, he looked at me and asked, "Is the information scribed here accurate?"

I nodded. "It is accurate to the recitation that I received to compose it. I have no cognizance as to the actual facts, but as they came from Tribune Lucius Camillus, they are unlikely to be erroneous."

"My son gave you these words?" exclaimed Camillus. "He is in Rome?"

"Aye, Sos. He was at the time that I departed this morning."

Now there were exclamations from all, demanding a telling of the news within the scroll. The elder Senator rolled the papyrus back onto the spindle, then began to read again, translating as he went. "There has been a disaster at Veii. The army of the city of Fregena has broken the lines in siege. The..." He puzzled out a sentence, then continued, "The Legion has retreated to the..." On he read, detailing the disaster brought about by the two amateur consuls, and only saved by the professionalism of the regular army Tribunes and Centuriae and the lack of willingness of the ranks to be pushed any farther.

More questions were asked of myself. Of course, I had not the answer to most, only being able to pass on what I had received from Lucius. Finally, one of the Senators asked, "Why do you appear to have come from the battle? As does your man?"

With some disbelief by the listeners I briefly recited a description of the ambuscade, with the news of the attackers being regulars of the Roman cavalry causing exclamations by more than one man. "You... and this soldier fought and slew three horsemen of Roman cavalry, and without harm to yourselves?" The Senator with the question was less than believing.

Before I could answer, Camillus spoke. "The friend of my son, this Junius, has more than the ability of a scribe - that I can assure you. But, that is unimportant. This situation must be resolved immediately!"

The bathing was over. The Senatorial guard was called to order, and soon the carrying chairs began to stream out of the villa and down the road toward Rome. It was with exhausted bearers that the procession strode into the gates of the city, just as the watch was beginning their closure. My task finished, I departed without notice to my own domicile.

Days went by, and not without excitement. Of course, the news had entered the city, becoming more dire with each telling, until men were scrabbling in their houses for long forgotten weapons and wives were burying their market coins under this wall and that floor.

The full Senate met in hasty session, and took the statements of the two incompetents that had let the army be surprised. Of course, they gave the failure to this man and that, making sure that all knew that they themselves were blameless, and had their instructions been followed, the siege would have been victorious. As both were highly placed nobles and Senators, there was never any question of punishment for their failure, and the whole situation of command was ignored.

Upon reaching the city, it was discovered that the Tribune Lucius had been detained by the magistrates on the orders of the Consuls. Of course, his plat of release was signed and delivered immediately, before he could be put to the torture or worse. It was only later that we found that the tent-slave of the Tribune, was the source of information that caused the three horsemen to set out on the road to prevent any news from reaching the leading Senators. The obvious reason was to prevent any tales from reaching those in power until the two Consuls could place the blame on others.

The Senate, now fully in session, immediately recalled the senior Camillus to the Consulship, giving him full authority over the conduct of the war and the supporting policies of the city. Immediately, a detail arrived at my household with the command to report to the headquarter of the Consul. Upon arriving, I found myself assigned to the immediate staff of Camillus, to handle all messaging and written orders. "I need a man that I can trust to put my words to the papyrus in good order," he said. "Some of these Adiutorae were not as diligent in their studies as you, and some of their missives could not be construed even by Athena herself."

Thus did I follow the Consul during the bloody battles that followed. In his tent, one evening, he asked again about the hidden tunnels of Memphis, obviously trying to pull his thoughts together rather than any desire for an interesting discussion. Then calls were made, both in his Legion and the city, for any who had a knowledge of the structure of Veii. For months, I interviewed this man and that, traders, merchants, laborers, soldiers and thus, making voluminous notes of their memories of the city.

Rome and Veii could, in a way, be called sister cities. Both were settled by people of the same ilk - that is, of Etruscan derivation, and both were built in similar ways. With a writ from the Consul, I journeyed back to Rome, and consulted with the structae and operarii that built and maintained the services of the city - the water wells and channels, the sewers and waste ditches. Even into the underground catacombs and burrows did I go, with the head of the operarii giving me the details of operation and the problems of the maintaining of such. Unpleasant it was, with unsavory odors and filth, and vermin of any kind imaginable, including rodents that were almost the size of small dogs.

But, at the end, I had begun to fathom a method for reducing the stubborn city of Veii.

And, therefore, I have a measure of responsibility for the butchery that followed. In my life, I have only killed in desperation or defense of my existence - or that of people close to me. But, now... If the gods actually exist, then I will have much to answer for when my shade is brought before the table of justice. In my defense, I can only claim that I would have not been a participant had I known of the result of my researches.

Behind the low hill that hid the putrid pits from both the noses and eyes of the citizens of Veii, slaves were put to digging a tunnel toward a particular wall of the city. As the ground at this point was low, water seepage was a major problem, requiring another large body of slaves to continually remove the inflow with buckets, and at all hours of the day. In addition, the soft ground was not conducive to tunneling, and had to be supported along its entire length with poles at the sides and overhead. Even with that support, many collapses during the digging hindered the work, requiring even more work to replace the damaged sections.

But, in a half-month or so, the diggers had intersected the main sewer drain from the city, breaking through the bricks to enter the stinking channel. Immediately, and before an inadvertent discovery could be made by the defenders, a quick survey was made of the passageways, with the finding that the widest path to be taken actually coursed under the privies of the Temple of Juno. With all haste, the staff of the Consul concocted a brazen plan that sent an elite unit of legionaries into the sewers in the middle of the night. With stealth, and breaking into the compound, the unit fanned out into the compound of the temple, slaying all that they encountered. When the temple complex was secured, slaves began to break out the floor of the privy and set ladders for easy emergence by the troops that would follow.

During the balance of the night, men were fed into the tunnel, to egress in the temple grounds, and with savage warnings by the Centurions and Optios for complete silence. By the break of day, almost five Maniples - a thousand men or more - had been fed through the breach and at sun up, the gates of the temple were opened and the assault began.

As the Maniples began to spread through the city in the growing light, they splintered into ever smaller groups and had no guiding hand from their officers. Wanton and merciless slaying was the order of the dawning day, even of men who were not in arms and those of an age as to be no threat to the invaders. Young and old males alike were slaughtered in the frenzy that only began to die down much later, as the gates were forced and the bulk of the army entered. Even then, it took the blows of the Centurions and Optios and Decanue to bring sense to the rampaging troops. Those who failed to obey were speared and bladed on the spot.

When the sun reached the zenith of the sky, the city of Veii was an abattoir of blood, with both the street stones and the walls splattered and splashed with redness that slowly faded to brown as it dried. On my entry, I immediately assumed that there had been a desperate battle between the invading forces and the defenders, but I began to realize that few bodies of Romans could be seen. What to me had been a proud event of victory to the citizens of my city, now became a disgusting memory of evil. I wished nothing else than to return to Rome and begin the forgetting that I hoped would quickly come.

But, it was not to be. I was placed in charge of the multitude of scribes that began to enumerate the booty that was now to be carried from the depopulated city. That included the women and children of Veii, now mostly without men to feed and protect them. Most were taken as slaves on the pretext that such helpless beings could no longer survive in their ruined city. The count was in the thousands and for days, the road between the two cities was filled with the slow marching of wailing women.

The sum of the gold and silver and treasures removed from the city was vast - even the statues of the temples were ripped from their mountings and eventually hauled to Rome. The Consul Camillus was greatly enamored with my work, both in the planning of the unique assault, and in the honest accounting of the plunder, and awarded me with a vast bounty as my share. And, to my repugnance, with five females slaves.

Back in Rome, the celebrations were joyful and immense, lasting for four days, during which the Consul rode through the city gate on a chariot behind four white horses. As I was marching directly behind the Consul, the roars of the crowds were painful to my ears and the jubilations tiresome, as the day crawled by on leaden feet. Finally, after almost a month, in which a quantity of tablets were scribed and baked that would have weighed more than the immense stone carving of Jupiter in his temple, and a length of papyrus was written that could have stretched between the two cities, I was relieved of my duties with the army and returned to my home. Permanently, I hoped.

Ravana had been surprised when the five women were escorted into the atrium by the two soldiers that had temporarily assigned to me. I explained the reason for their presence and bade her give them duties within the household. I had no use for them - my household did not need more maids, but the alternative was to sell them at the auctioneers, and that I would not do.

My service was not yet over. Camillus was given the Consulship and Dictatorius authority once more, the following year, to end once and for all time, the alliances of the Veii. All that remained of any strength was the city of Falerii. Again, the Legion was put on the road, but before there could be a battle, the city leaders offered capitulation and it was accepted. Shortly afterward, offers came in from the cities of Aequi, Volsci and Capena, and with the conclusion of treaties, Rome had doubled the size of her domain and was supreme in comparison to all others within her reach.

As my reward, and on the recommendation of the Consul himself, and verified by the Senate, I was made the chief archivist of Rome. And it was fortunate that it was done in the celebration of the newly won greatness of the city. Within a year, the Camillus senior was banished from the city, victim of the overweening desires of the nobles and the Senate.

The Inferno

Scintilla (Spark)

With the auspices of the Consul Camillus, I was appointed as chief magistrate - the Archivest Primus - of the city document repositories - a position that I relished, I must admit. I had many duties, such as preparing any missives to other cities not in the Roman domain. And, all incoming correspondence from afar must come through my offices, to be copied and archived. I was one of the few allowed in the Senate Chamber during formal discussions, both to monitor the scribes and testify to the truthful copy and translation of messages being presented. Few offices, available to a Plebeian, were more powerful than mine.

I instituted a policy that no falsehoods would be promulgated by the Office of the Archives. Many times, when an official sent a scroll to our scribes, for copying and issuance, I would send it back with many sentences and statements crossed out, and requesting a rethinking of the missive. More than a few magistrates considered a scroll as his personal cryer board for issuing peans of his own value. Some would even issue self-laudations that were less palatable to a thinking person than the spew in the port taburnae from over-cupped patrons. My office refused to parrot such, and I was proud of the fact that my character was considered honest and above reproach by commoner and noble alike.

And again, in the back of my mind, and on sleepless nights on my mat, my thoughts would return to the amount of time that I had been in Rome and without incident. Figuratively looking over my shoulder at times, I wondered if the gameboard of Olympus was still in play, and if my little carved figure was still among the playing pieces. Then, the day would dawn, bright and fresh, and I would laugh at my thoughts of imaginary beings looking down on man from above.

Korax would arrive, many times bringing Ahirom, after returning from their voyaging. We would feté them as if they were returning royalty. Ravana had long since mellowed toward the Greek, and made both he and his widow welcome on their appearances. As to our one-legged captain, she would gently chastise him for not finding a needsome woman of his own, for those long nights when becalmed in some far sea.

My friendship with the house of Camillus had cooled with the slaughter that I had been made a part of, but I did not deliberately break our fellowship, but only let it wither with the absence of that family in my life. Rather, at least twice during a month I would send a long scroll to their villa in Trivoli, giving the news of the city. And not just news, but also gossip and happenings in the Senate and even the talk of the streets.

The populace had proved to be fickle in its praise of their hero. As the allies of Veii had either surrendered or accepted the suzerainty of Rome, there was no plunder to be received from the short action. The people, expecting more caravans of loot from those cities, were most vexed at the absence of such. Also, Camillus refused to allow the conquered lands to be distributed among the people, and that was a resentment that weighed against his glory. But, the Plebeians were not the reason for his demise. Rather, the Patricians - the nobles of the city were most wroth at being prevented in acquiring vast new properties from the conquered peoples. To my mind, most seemed to think that the reason for the war was to enrich their households and pour more gold into their vaults.

The result was that Camillus was brought before the Senate on the charge of embezzlement of the plunder from those defeated peoples - loot that did not exist since none was taken. Rather than admit his guilt - of which he had none - he accepted exile, and his family left the city to reside in their villa at Tivoli. That city, being independent of Rome, although nominally an ally, was a place of refuge for the family, should the Senate become even more overweening.

Unlike that noble family, now, my household was high in the estimation of the city. My position caused me to interact with Plebeian and Patrician alike, and there was little happening in the city that did not come to my attention. My senior scribes were tested by me, and any that were found wanting were not dismissed but sent to enhance their learning.

Such was not the case for any that I found to wield a crooked stylus. I gave no mercy to scribe that bent the truth or took coin to shift the balance of numbers to another without reason. They were dismissed and banned from further scrivening in the city of Rome.

My gatherings with the intelligencia of the city were naturally constrained with my new duties, I no longer having the entirety of my day to myself and my desires, but I was a frequent visitor to the gatherings that happened in this atrium or that. In fact, it was one evening when I was amusedly listening to a pair of young men attempting to argue each side of one of the paradoxes of Zeno - the one named Achilles and the tortoise. I was in the atrium of a minor Senator, and the give and take was entertaining, and much was the laughter by the listeners, when behind me a voice said quietly, "Your pardon, Magistrate." I turned to the steward of the house standing behind me. He leaned closer and said, "A runner is in the foyer with a missive for you. Of urgency, he says."

I nodded, the rose and followed him to the street-door. There was one of my junior scribes who bowed as I approached, saying, "My apologies, Sos. I bring word from Master Regilus. He would see you at once about an urgent matter." Regilus was my chief scrivener, but what he would consider so important at this time of the day - and almost night - I could not imagine. But, giving my farewell to the host, we set foot to the magisterial offices of the archives.

There, around a table, a furious discussion was happening as we strode into the room. Seeing me, all quieted and Regilus stood and said, "My pardon, Sos, for the late summons, but a missive from Clusium has arrived. One that is most disturbing."

Clusium was a city far to the north of the Roman domain. Nominally they were an ally, but the distance was such that little intercourse happened between the two cities except for the frequent caravans. I took the scroll and read it, then again. The tongue was not Latium, but a combination of the old Etruscan language and that of Rome. Still, I had little trouble parsing the meaning but immediately gave the scroll to a scribe fluent in that northern language to be translated into a new script that could be given to the rulers of the city.

As the translation would take several hours, and the Senate was not in session at this late hour, I decided to deliver it in the morning. Leaving instructions to make four copies, and to have them proofed by at least two others to confirm an accurate translation, I departed for my household. As the sun rose, the next morning, I was waiting in the foyer of the Senate House.

"Your pardon, Sos," I said to Tertius Fabius, the first Senator to arrive and a member of the powerful house of Fabius. "A missive has arrived during the night. It appears to be of some importance." The Senator took one of the scrolls and began to read. His brow furrowed as he measured the significance of the words. Finally, he absently rolled it up, still pondering the meaning. Finally, he pointed, "And those?"

"Copies, Sos."

"Let me have them. I will bring it to the attention of the Senate." He turned to go, but then said, "Inform me if other missives arrive."

That evening, as I arrived at my home, I had the pleasure of seeing that Korax and his woman had arrived. As usual, I called for a feast, and we spoke into the night, under the pleasant sky and the torches. This time was different - he had a concern that was finally spoken after the usual recitation by all of the happenings since the last visit.

"I have a candidate for a Kapetanios for our original ship. He is Greek and well thought of in Athens, although, like me, he fled the Spartan bastards when they took the city. He has been dwelling in Tyre and captaining a coaster between that city and Rhodes."

Ravana spoke. "You wish to abandon the sea? I was of the impression that you had found your life's dream."

Korax nodded, accepting a filled cup from his woman. "Aye, and I have enjoyed it, but... My eyes are failing, and past the dim light of evening, I am without sight. My second is competent, and there has been no difficulty, but..." He shrugged. "There comes a time in the life of any man when his duties must be relinquished to the younger."

My friend was older than I by a double handful of years and more, but not yet a decrepit graybeard. Still, he was entering that phase of life when the body begins to complain about efforts that are nothing as a younger man, but become tiresome far more quickly in age. I just said, "You need not my permission to hire a captain. As I have said many times, the ownership is yours as much as ours. And, we certainly do not need the trade to live out our lives in comfort."

"Where will you settle?" asked Ravana. "Athens?"

Korax shook his head. "I would not live past the first time that a Spartan magistrate spoke to me. My spear would be in his belly before my thoughts knew that it had been cast." A drink, then, "Nay, the city of my birth may arise again, but it will be long after I am dust."

I spoke now. "We can find you a very comfortable household here. You can speak Latium sufficient so as not to feel a stranger." Indeed, over the years, he had picked up enough of the tongue of my birthplace to function in Rome, although he could never pass for a native, even in the quarter of Sucusa, where the lowest of the classes lived. Still, with my place in the hierarchy of the city, he would have a comfortable existence, free from the petty rules that sometimes haunted the powerless.

He spread his hands. "There is yet time and no need for any hurried decisions. I would feel at home in any place as well as another. A rootless man cares not where his mat is located, as long as it is not far from a friendly taverna." He pointed at me with his cup. "And you, my Roman friend. Is this your final place of nesting?" His eyes suddenly widened, apparently reading more in my expression that I had intended to covey. Tilting his head, he said, "Speak of it. Is there some darkness on the horizon that may auger stormy weather?"

I hesitated before replying, then said. "I do not know. I can feel the tendrils of... of... the same feeling I had in Egypt, when I could not touch on the troubles that I could not see."

Ravana looked at me sharply. "What are you meaning. Tell us."

I spread my hands in negation. "It is not anything that I can point to and demonstrate. But, as a young man in Rome, then Athens and Memphis, I was a respected citizen, with wealth and stability in the cities. Then, at the height of my success - in each place - I was driven to the path of wandering again by sudden violent turmoil. Now, again in Rome, I have everything except place in the nobility. I am the highest of the scribal magistrates, my wealth is even greater than some of the noble houses..."

Ravana folded her arms and looked at me severely. "Tell us not that you are still worried about your movement across the gameboards of your mystical beings!"

Korax was not as dismissive of divine intercession as she. "Speak not so flippantly of the gods. They may not affect the daily affairs of man, but their power is not to be so easily discarded."

The golden-haired woman had no patience with such talk. "The gods are a tale to keep order with young children, and grown men who have not the intelligence to see that they are no more than the air. Or for the priests, who grow fat with the offerings of unlearned folk."

Korax held up his hand for peace, or maybe surrender, then said, "Wait. Let us hear of the reason for our Roman scribe's unease." To me, he asked, "What cloud is on the far horizon that you fear may grow into a tempest?"

I hesitated, forming my words, so as to not come across as fearful of my life to the point of fleeing. "Today - or rather, last evening - a missive was received from a far city to the north, one Clusium by name. A large tribe, calling themselves Senones, has sent representatives to that city for the purpose of negotiating the purchase of land for resettlement. They have petitioned Rome to assist them in the dialogue."

Ravana raised her hands in question. "What of it? Rome is always conversing with this land or that, and sometimes with violence occurring. What is it of this message that has triggered your fears?"

"I do not know. The issue is minor and far away. Still, the shadow lingers in the back of my mind."

"Who are the Seno... Senons... Whatever their cursed name is?" asked Korax. "I have never heard the name."

"Senones. According to my senior scribe," I replied, "they come from the far reaches of Gaul - that great and anonymous land that stretches from the Apennino mountains to the north to some far off border beyond the kin of civilization. Most would call them barbarians, although our female friend here is probably from that region, and she is certainly civilized."

"Are you that worried about such a nebulous mist on the horizon of the future?" asked Ravanna.

I nodded and replied, "Aye, and to such an extent that I would ask Korax to have at least one of our ships stay on the short voyages so that it will be available for our use should the nonexistent gods decide to laugh at our expense."

And little did happen that year. The incident did not seem to be the opening of a barbarian invasion of Latium by the northern tribes, and the discourse between that far city and the newcomers was civilized and even friendly. This was all to the good, as Rome had been depleted of many young men of military age from losses in the interminable war with Veii. We would be at a disadvantage should any strife spring up in the next generation of time.

Korax did indeed give up his seagoing, settling down in a comfortable abode in the Latiaris quarter and only a short walk from my domicile. His selection of captain proved satisfactory, and between him and Ahirom our ships were quite satisfactory served - bringing in considerable wealth, in the following year. Wealth, that I had no use for, to be sure, but it gave employment to good friends and the crews of our ships.

Flamma (Flame)

In the spring of the following year, I was engaged to assist in a delegation to Clusium - that city still in negotiations with the migrating Gauls. The chief ambassador was Quintus, the son of the Senator Marcus Fabius. In assistance were his two other brothers, Numerius and Caeso. I was appalled at the choice of ambassadors, although I kept my thoughts to myself, of course. But, a trio of men less suited for negotiation could not have been found by scouring the whole of the city. Self-important, haughty to the extent of refusing to even speak to a Plebeian, far less a slave, they exuded their superiority at every opportunity.

The younger Caeso even fancied himself as a valiant warrior, sporting a bejeweled and gilded gladius in an even more elaborate scabbard. During our march to the north, I would watch him wield his weapon around the fires of the night-camp, giving his wishes that some brigand would attempt to accost the party. It was my astonishment that he did not cut off his own leg - or that of some innocent party - in his braggadocio. His brandishing of his blade to one and all proved to me that he was not even suited to carving meat in the kitchen of his own household - far less to use it against an experienced opponent.

Our party of about fifty, including servants, slaves, scribes and a unit of infantry, along with the principles made the distance without incident, and was received by the rulers of the city with great fanfare. It was obvious that the criticality of the situation was not sufficient to cause any haste in the negotiations. Rather, we were feted for several days, attending this ceremony and that festivity, all the while attending banquets that might have fed a legion. The nobles of our party found lodging in the city while the bulk of the Roman contingent set up tents just outside the gate.

The three brothers of the house of Fabii fed upon the acclaim as those who have won a mighty victory, despite the fact that their only accomplishment to date was the consumption of an inordinate amount of wine and rich foods. I attempted to arrange the meeting with the representatives of the Senones, but although the Gauls were very agreeable, the elder Quintus refused to agree that the auguries were forthcoming in sufficient prediction of success. A half month went by, then the whole, before our party, and that of the city of Clusium set forth on the road to the small hamlet of Asignia - the agreed upon neutral location of our conference.

Making sure that my detail of scribes and assistants were groomed and garbed properly, and equipped with every possible utensil that might be needed in the negotiations, we fell in behind the leaders of the city and the Roman party for the short march to the small hamlet. Weapons were forbidden in the conference - save for small blades and daggers - but beyond the reaches of the conference area, bands of both city guards and men from the Senones encampment patrolled on the slight chance that bandits might take the opportunity to strike. The leading citizens of the city and tribe - unarmed - would be a rich haul of ransom for such brigands.

The Chief of the Senones was one Brennus, a large and vigorous man and in contrast to the Romans and men of Clusium, fully bearded and with long locks of hair - a characteristic of all Gauls, I would come to find. Still, he was no ignorant primitive and his Latium, while accented, was correct and well parsed - too well, in fact, for a man of the wilderness. I wondered at the education that he must have received in the past, to speak in such correct and proper phrases.

The party that he had brought to the conference was of older men, of course, and after the round of priest blessings of both sides, the speakings began. I had three scribes taking down all conversations, and it left me with nothing to do but observe the proceedings.

The crux of the proposal of the Gauls was a desire to settle the empty lands on the far side of the Tiber - the same flow of water that passed beside Rome, although at this distance it was less of a river and more of a stream. And, of course, not navigable by any but small fishing skiffs. As the peoples of the north were herders in the main, rather than farmers, the hilly lands were suited for that husbandry. As Clusium would have no use for the far extent of their lands unless growing beyond all bounds as a city - a very unlikely prospect - their main objection to the proposal was the lack of desire to have a powerful people suddenly appear and settle in their domain. Questions as to the population of the Senones were not answered in completeness - a lack that gave great pause to the party of Clusium. In my opinion, the reason for the lack of specificity was that it was likely that the wandering tribe had no idea of the extent of their people. The bounds of Gaulish kingdoms were indefinite, and any number of men could be claimed by this tribe or that.

Still, the movement of the Senones into the area was a fact, and that had to be accepted unless the city of Clusium desired to drive them away by force. I doubted that it was an option, and hoped that it was not to be considered. As yet, the discussions were gentle and made with deference to each side. Almost.

In all of this, the three ambassadors from Rome were a humiliation to our city and a despicable set of voices in the talks. By the Laws of Nations, the Jus Gentium, accepted by all lands of any importance, any negotiator was assumed to be neutral, with no prejudice with or for either party. All questions and answers and dialog went through the supposedly unaligned spokesmen. In the case of the Roman delegation, it was obvious that such neutrality was absent - at least for the leaders of the party.

The questions of the elder brother, Quintius, were formed as a query to a menial, and answers from him as commands to a servant. I was greatly impressed by the Chief, Brennus, and his senior negotiators for their calm acceptance of the impolite give and take. The veiled insults were ignored and the returned conversation respectable. I was not the only person with a dislike of the three, and it showed on my face without doubt.

On the afternoons, once the conferences were over, many times I would walk along the stream, even wading into it for the coolness of the water from the springs, high up in the hills. It was on one of these outings that I had my encounter.

I was sitting on a large rock with my feet in the stream, idly throwing stones into the water, wishing for the talks to end so that I might return to my home when a voice said, "It is seldom that one of the city cares to savor the cleanliness of the wilds."

I had recognized the person before I turned to see the man, alone, standing in the path. Standing, I said, "Aye, Sos. My childhood was in the waters of this river, and the sight and feel of it are still a small pleasure."

The man was the Chief of the Senones, Brennus by name, standing in a light pullover that was not quite a tunic, but also not a set of robes. Even his weapon was absent, being replaced by a small dagger. "You are the chief scrivener of Rome - the Archivest Primus, as I understand."

It was not a question. "Aye. Since the appointment by the Senate, but a scribe from the beginning of my youth."

The man stepped forward, and sat on the large stone in front of me, waving for myself to be reseated. "My pardon if I am impertinent, but you have not the look of any magistrate that I have ever seen. In my experience, they tend to rotundness and are slack of sinew. And such usually do not carry a blade in a worn scabbard."

I smiled. "I have been told such many times. But, although I have always been a scribe, I have been involved in many other endeavors in my life that required more than sitting with a tablet and stylus."

He looked out over the waters, obviously measuring his words. Then, "As you are from the Romans, and by oath, neutral in these discussions, I would ask a question, should you allow." I nodded. "What think you of the attitude of the men of Clusium toward our peoples and the proximity of our desires?"

I thought for a moment, then replied. "I doubt that they have objection to a productive people on the horizon - such intercourse between city and pasture means wealth and opportunity for both. My understanding is that they have the fear of being... swamped, shall we say, by a fecund and vigorous tribe, no matter the friendship."

Now he nodded. "Aye. I can see the apprehension and understand it. Many of my people have the fear of being... softened by consorting with inferior and soft city folk, as they put it." Now he gave a wry smile. "As if such attributes rub off merely by proximity. Still, I need land for my people, and that overrides all else." Now he picked up a stone and absently tossed it into the stream. "There must be a way to alleviate the fears on both sides that will give us peace and satisfaction." Now he took a different tact. "My thinking is that the Roman negotiators are neither neutral nor admirers of northern folk."

I looked around, more for emphasis, than any fear of wandering ears, then replied, "Sos, if I may beg of you, do not judge Rome by the antics of those three fools. I myself have trouble holding back my shame when they speak their babble."

He nodded. "Aye, I have seen your discomposure."

"I am not noble myself, and had no discussion of their appointment, and in truth, have no slightest idea how they received it, except for the fact that their patér is high in the Senate of Rome. If you wish my advice..." He nodded. "...treat them as the wind in the leaves, of no significance and with no information to convey. Make your treaty with the folk of Clusium and ignore the intercession of the Roman contingent."

He stood and said, "You are a good man and true. You are welcome around my fires at any time while we are here in discussion. Or even later. In fact, I would welcome a man of your erudition, with which to match words, during the slow evenings."

For a month, the talks went on, and in mostly friendly fashion. In my evening wanderings, I availed myself of the invitation from the Chief and strode into the camp of the immigrants, just beyond the waters of the river. As most of the people did not speak Latium, but rather their own guttural language, my visits usually consisted of just observing. It was obvious that this was a people who were not primitive in the sense of being unenlightened forest dwellers, but a vigorous and active tribe. The children were numerous and well fed, the men strong and robust - as were the women in their constant work. Even though the females were not alluring to myself in their lack of cleanliness, there was no doubt that they were a strong part of the family life, giving orders to both children and young men and taking no refusal to their commands.

Had the gods allowed a look back into the mists of time, I believe that the early founders of Rome would have appeared almost identical to the peoples that I was observing.

More than once and, in fact, a double handful of times, I was recognized by the Chief and called to his tent or cookfire. There we engaged in pleasant conversation into the darkness, with myself doing most of the talking. He - and several of his chieftains - were enthralled by my descriptions of the cities around the rim of the Great Sea. I have no idea if they believed my tales of the gigantic tombs of Egypt or the mountain with the magnificent buildings in Athens, but if not, none were so impolite as to express disbelief. It was gratifying to demonstrate before these men that not all Romans were pompous and self-important.

It was during one of these pleasant sittings that I discovered the source of his education in Latium. By the tale, his patér had been defeated in battle by the King of Arretium, a large city on the northern edge of the land of the Etruscans, and Brennus, his son, was taken hostage as assurance of good behavior by the defeated Senones. His youth had been spent in the palace of that city, until his release as a young adult. For myself, I gave the story of my very common genesis as a fisherboy on the banks of the Tiber and the fate that made me a scribe in the Temple.

In the evening, if our casual talks lasted into the night, Brennen would order an escort for myself across the darkness to the Roman encampment just outside the gate of Clusium.

"You! Scribe!" It was on just such an evening that I, returning from my stroll to the river, that I was accosted by a voice behind me. I turned to see, in the fading light, that it was the youngest of the Fabii, Caeso by name, and the man who thought himself a natural born bladesman.

"Aye," I replied, wondering at what evil fate would require me to converse with this despicable braggadocio.

Beside him were his two 'guards', a pair of young nobles cut from the same cloth as their leader, and equally as swaggering. "You spend much time in the camp of the barbarians, Scribe," said Caeso. "One would think that you might be in connivance with our foe."

"My title is Archivest Primus if you please, and my time out of duty is my own."

The man was taken aback. Being rebuked by a Pleb of the commoners was not an occurrence with which he was familiar, but I had learned long ago - even before the night that his genitors had produced this aberration of nature - that a retreat from a bullyboy was an invitation to become his footmat.

His startlement turned to ire at this sudden dissension from his mark, and in front of his followers, for worse. "You are what I say you are, Scribe. And if you wish to hold your position, you will immediately modify your attitude before your betters."

"What do you desire?" The fading light robbed me of my enjoyment of his expressions. "You did not journey to this path to speak to a mere scribe."

"Had you been at your quarters, and concerned with your duty, then I would not have been required to hunt you down to deliver the missive, that you are to report immediately to the council." With no more bandying of words, I hurried to the building used by that group of men for their deliberations. There I was handed a message for the Chief, Brennus, to meet on the morrow.

That missive began the tale of the destruction of Rome.

It had been suddenly realized by the people of Clusium, that the northern encroachers were, in fact, already engaged in the activity about which they were negotiating. That is, their people were settling into the hills, running their flocks and building huts of living and longhouses of meeting. Treachery it was not, but the natural force that drives a people to begin to better their lives, wherever they are set down. It was not the Gauls, but the cursed spawn of the house of Fabii that now worked their infamy.

It was at the meeting by the river that Quintus Fabius gave his pompous declaration. I assume that he had conversed with the elders of Clusium, in a secret meeting of which I was ignorant - as were my scribes - and had decided on a stiffer round of negotiations.

Standing before the group, in the clearing at the side of the river, Quintus gave his pompous oratory to the assembled groups, flanked by his smirking and self-important brothers. "...And as the leaders of the Senones have seen fit to abrogate even the appearance of civility, and in that they are, even now, creating that which has not seen the end of discussion..." On and on he went, with veiled insults toward the Gauls and their people, and speaking of the greatness of the

Latium peoples. And the need to prevent the pollution of such greatness by the acceptance of inferior races from beyond the mountains.

In fact, his insults were not so veiled as all that. As I stood, internally cringing at the words being given by a highborn Roman, my thoughts were on the reason for the deliberate baiting of the Gauls. Was it just the too-common contempt by nobles for men that they considered to be far below their own quality, or, did they actually wish to see strife between the roaming tribe and the cities of Latium? I could not fathom the gain for such conflict - to Clusium, Rome, or even the Fabii clan.

Looking at the Chief of the tribe, I could almost see amusement on his face - certainly he was not writhing inside from the insulting words spewing from the mouth of the Roman speaker. Not so, for his chieftains - many were obviously fuming at the insults, and more than one had his hand on his dagger. Finally, as Quintus wound through his speech, he gave the pith of his talk - nay, it was almost an ultimatum. "...And it is decided that the tribe of your peoples will vacate the lands on which they have settled, moving back across the mountains. Only then, can further discussions be held to the point of the reasons that have been requested."

I held my breath. This was almost a demand to depart or fight, and I doubted that the Senones would just fold their tents and march away. Looking at his chieftains, a few of whom were keeping their tongues from speaking only by the method of the clinched jaw, I knew that they would welcome the chance to match iron with the Roman windbag before them. I had long suspected that only a handful of the party of the Gauls could understand Latium, and now that was confirmed, as most were looking at their fellows and wondering at the fury that was being kindled.

Still even voiced, and apparently not disturbed by what he had heard, Brennus merely said, "I would hear from the delegation of Clusium." Looking at the city leaders, he asked, "Do you concur with the Roman, or does he speak his own desire?"

Sharply, Quintus barked, "Nay. You violate the rules of the assemblage by querying the other concerned party directly."

The Chief nodded. "Ah... I had assumed that such a small infraction would not be taken amiss on the back of your own usurpation of neutrality."

That was unexpected, I could see. "What is your meaning?" In his refusal to see the members of the tribe as men of any substance, any criticism from such was jarring to his noble-born instincts.

"As you wish. Then... By the given laws of the Jus Gentium, the neutral party in negotiations is assumed to be just that, non-aligned and unbiased toward either side. Do you have the belief that the Roman contingent fits that description, even taking the benefit of stretching the words out of all meaning?"

Now, the middle brother, Numerius Flavius, blurted out his mite. "One should not be critical, who is, even now, abrogating the agreements and taking the liberties before the dialog is finished."

Brennus still kept his composure, giving the measure that he was the greater man of the argument. His reply was calm and staid. "And might one ask of the nature of this supposed offense? We have come at call and left each day upon agreement. Has one of my party committed insult to any person here? If so, make his name known to me now."

Quintus took up the speaking. "It is the actions of the people of your tribe who have committed the transgression, by settling upon the land and before any agreement has been reached."

"If by settling, you are meaning that my people have taken measures to feed themselves and their flocks whilst we are in talks, then yes, it is so."

"A stone statue would starve whilst waiting for a Roman to finish the blathering that he considers negotiations." This was from a young man of the immigrants. Brennus waved his hand for the young man to cease his talk, but the effect on the assembly was startling.

In fact, it was almost humorous, had the possible results not been so dire. The three brothers hesitated, obviously listening to the statement in their minds again, and not believing the words. I looked around at the others in the tent. My scribes were desperately trying to keep the derision out of their countenances, knowing the severe punishment that would descend upon any laughter. Even the party of Clusium was more bemused than offended.

However...

Caeso especially was outraged, quickly rising and stepping forward with his hand on his dagger. The party of the Senones leapt to their feet to fend off any act of aggression toward their leader - who was still sitting on his mat as if the reaction to the statement had been only of moderate interest. My sense of amusement instantly disappeared in the real danger that a war would begin now, in this tent, and among an assembly brought together for peaceful discourse.

The Chief of the Senones said, "I give apologies for the words of my man, unbecoming to the dignity of this assembly, and he will immediately give acknowledge of such." That the man was a leader was obvious to me, and to all with any sense of knowledge of leadership. His tranquil temper, even in the teeth of obvious bias, was exemplary.

And it was obvious that none of his party were of a mind to tempt that temper, as the man who had blurted out the jape bowed, and said, "Aye. My speaking was of poor taste and my vexation badly controlled. I give my sorrow for my words."

The level of wrath in the tent subsided, then Brennus continued. "I understand the concern on the part of our hosts, the citizens of Clusium, to a peoples who have come, suddenly, and uninvited. We will move our flocks and kine back to the slopes of the mountains, but our people who remain for the duration of these negotiations must have shelter in which to live, and thusly, our huts must remain. But, you have my oath that nothing of permanence will be built during our talks." He stood and looked over the assembly. "For the nonce, we will retire and let the blood cool from the heated comments made by the parties this day."

With that, the session for that day was over. Unfortunately, the remaining daylight was sufficient to allow time for an evil act that almost destroyed the city of Rome.

Conflagratio (Conflagration)

"Sos! Sos!" I had barely lain back on my mat, unrolling a scroll that I had brought for my pleasure when my senior scribe burst through my tent opening. "There is a contention... a... a... You should come!" I leapt to my feat and was about to follow, then turned to grab my belt and scabbard. From the countenance of my scribe, it might be less than wise to leave my tent without at least a pugio - my dagger.

At a run, I followed my man down the road that led to the hamlet of Asignia, but even before we had left the sight of the walls of Clusium, we came to a group of men... two groups, both obviously standing in rage at the sight of the other. My fears had been realized - the young fire-eaters of the camps had apparently decided to meet to carry on their own negotiations - but with blades rather than words. One group, of course, was the Senones, and the other was of Clusium men - but with young Caeso and his hangers-on standing with them.

As I approached, I was gladsome to see that they were not actually engaged in strife, but were as young bucks, trying to intimidate the other with... Suddenly, as I came around the side of the groups, I could see a man, laying in the road and unmoving. Hoping that both sides would see me as a neutral, I walked up and stooped to examine the prone figure. The long head and facial hair made it obvious that he was a member of the immigrant tribe and only took a heartbeat to determine that he had breathed his last. I suddenly recognized the man who had garnered the wrath of the younger Fabius this day. My sudden noticement that his pugio was still in his belt was disturbing. Why would...

I stood as movement caught my eye, then saw the Chief of the Senones striding up and through the line of tribesmen. His countenance was grim, but he said nothing until he strode up to where I was standing. Looking down at his man, he looked at me as I shook my head and said, "Nay. He has joined his ancestors."

"What was the cause?" he demanded.

I shook my head again. "I have just arrived this moment myself. He was lying there as I came from the tenting place."

Now, one of his own young men began to speak, and hotly. He was using the guttural language of their land, so I had no direct knowledge of his words, but it took little imagination to know what he was saying.

Standing aside, I looked at the Caeso, standing there with a look of grimness himself, no doubt knowing that he had gone too far, and was likely to face a real warrior to test his self-assumed skills with the blade. His two companions were definitely distressed and obviously wishing for a reason to be elsewhere. The rest of the band of Clusium men - boys - were also apprehensive as to the next moves that would be made. Fortunately, following the agreed upon custom, all were only armed with their personal short blades, and would be unlikely to begin a general melee with such...

My eyes rested on the belt of Caeso, and his gladius in scabbard. With a sinking feeling, I realized that the young fool had violated the law of agreement by arming himself with such. Surely, he did not strike down the man with such a...

Now, with a hard stare, Brennus stood forward to stop in front of the young Roman. "It was you that did this deed." The sentence came as both a question and a statement.

The young Roman had discarded his haughtiness - in fact, I would have wagered a good coin that he was clinching his buttocks in his fear of soiling himself. "I have the right to fend off any danger, even in such circumstances."

The Gaul looked at him for a long moment, then replied, "Your understanding of peril is different than ours. You slay a man who has not even drawn his weapon? And one who is armed with a hand-blade, while you are wielding a sword? And in total violation of the covent of Jus Gentium, which says that the neutral power of negotiations shall hold themselves above strife with either party?" Turning, he spoke rapidly to his men, who immediately picked up the body of their comrade and began to carry it along the road.

To me, he said coldly, "Inform your principles and those of the city that our discussions are ended. Our response will be given before darkfall on the morrow."

As the men of the Tribe disappeared around the turn in the road, the arrogance of the young Roman fool returned. "More to the better, I say. Why the men of two great cities should treat with barbarians is beyond my understanding. They should be whipped back to their dens and given the taste of civilized metal."

I was disgusted beyond standing. Immediately, I left, rapidly striding away before my pent up wrath exploded into the open. At the tent of Quintus, I told the guard of my having a missive, and in a moment was facing the noble. Giving him the message from the Chief of the Senones, he naturally asked, with some surprise, the meaning. It was with disbelief that he learned of the slaying, and in moments, a guard was running down the road with a summons for his youngest brother.

Taking the moment to excuse myself, I returned to my tent, wondering on the morrow, and if we would face a hostile band of men marching down the road. As I passed my senior scribe, I waved for him to follow. There, I asked his knowledge of the strife. He was agitated, but said, "Nay, Sos. I only received the news after the fact, as did you. But..." He turned and looked around the tent encampment, finally pointing across the way, "...young Placus, there, apparently saw the whole."

"Summon him here, immediately." In a few heartbeats, the youngster ran up and stopped before me, bowing his respect. The young man was a scribe-apprentice, brought for his own learning and to assist in routine scribal duties. "What did you see on the road?" I asked without preamble.

The youngster swallowed, then began hesitatingly, "Sos... I had... was carrying the chamber pot of our tent to the dumping place at the... the pit of... I was returning and heard the arguing on the road and stopped to listen..."

He looked around, almost fearfully, no doubt wondering just what horrible disaster would now befall himself for the crime of speaking ill of one of the Patrician class. I waved him - and the senior scribe - to follow me to a large grassy area out of hearing of the encampment. "No one can hear us here, and your speaking will be a secret between us. You have no fault in this matter and have no worry about retributions."

He nodded vigorously, then continued, "Through the bushes I could see the men of the city and those of the barbarians standing and giving words of discord to each other."

"They are not barbarians," I interjected, "but men of the north come to find land to live."

"Aye, Sos... Uh... The men of Rome were with the group of the city, also..."

"The younger Fabius and his lackeys, you mean."

"Aye, Sos. And in fact, the man of Rome was fielding the speaking of their side. I did not understand most of the converse, other than it had many curses and insults." He gulped, then said, "Little was happening except the contentious words, until suddenly..."

"Fabius cut the man down, did he not?"

With a pained expression, the youngster nodded. "Aye, Sos. Instantly, and without any challenge. He just drew his long blade and thrust. The barbar... man of the north fell without even a sound."

There was little else to learn, although I asked many questions. The bastard of the Fabii family was a murderer, no less, and a coward with a gladius to challenge a man who is only carrying a short dagger. Again, I wondered if we would be in a war with the men of the north by the morrow...

We were not - at least, not yet. The sun was well up when a messenger arrived at my tent, formally announcing his reason and the missive. It was a request to wait upon the Chief in his camp. And, "...the safety of the person of Junius of Rome is guaranteed by the oath of Brennus to the spirits of his ancestors."

As of the early hours, the principals of both the Roman party and those of the city had not appeared, as I had not expected them to. As the meetings had been abrogated by Brennus himself, there would be no point, and possibly much danger, in appearing at the hamlet again. Thus, I nodded my consent and followed the man down the road. Fording the shallow river, we were soon standing in front of the hut of the Chief, and as my escort called, the man appeared.

Without preamble, he said, "Despite the actions of your city folk, I still believe you to be an honorable man. I would trust you with a message to the leaders of your city..." I nodded. "Not those of the Roman party in your encampment, but the Senate in Rome itself." He stood aside and waved a hand in invitation to enter his hut. "As you are a scribe of that city, I would have you ink the scroll yourself. I wish no misunderstanding to come from ill chosen writing by my own advisers, who might mar the meaning of my words in their translation." Again I nodded and entered to sit on a mat just inside the opening.

Almost instantly, a blank sheet of papyrus was thrust at me by a menial, and a quill and inkpot. Feeling of the material, I realized that it was not the reed medium that I had thought, but some other like material - thicker and of a darker shade... Unfortunately, this was not the time to indulge in my ever-present knowledge seeking, as the Chief sat in front of me and began speaking, slowly and with great enunciation.

It was with increasing incredulity that I penned the words. The folly of that young imbecile, Caeso, was becoming even more apparent as I wrote. The missive was short and straightforward, if alarming in the extreme, but I rolled it onto a stick and tied it with a short piece of leather. I stood as he did, then said my first words, "The leaders of my party cannot learn of this, themselves. I would not live to reach the outskirts of our camp should they do so."

He nodded. "Aye. Your thoughts walk along with mine. This is my plan, should you agree..."

Back at my tent, I scribbled on a scrap of papyrus, then gathered my few belongings, making sure my longknife was hidden within the folds of my spare tunic. I sought out my senior scribe, giving him both the scrap and some short instructions, to be followed when he saw any of the men of the Fabii, or their followers, pass by the camp - something that might not happen for days, since they were ensconced within the city waiting for... what, Jupiter only knew. Maybe for a delegation from the Senones to arrive with apologies, perhaps. I would not doubt that by now they had convinced themselves of the full blame of the immigrants for the dissolution of the talks.

Now, strolling casually, as if I were walking to the river to bathe, or wash my garments, I came to the small path that connected the eastern road with the southern. Now, I strode at speed until I came to the junction. There, waiting for me, was a party of the men of the Chief, armed in full now - my escort to the city of Rome. Their leader handed me the scroll that I had penned only that morning and, in broken Latium, said, "Come. We go at pace."

Unlike our journey north to Clusium, with plodding chairs and burdened asses, we traveled the road at speed. All were young men, and I myself was only of early middle age, and we strode along quickly, stopping for short rests only at the infrequent intervals when a clean stream crossed the road. A quick meal of jerked meat was taken once, and again at darkfall. Nighttime was spent on the mossy ground, without mats or tents or coverings of any kind, and the first light of the sun saw us off again, eating our stiff meat on the road. Before midday, the sight of the temples on the hills of the city came into view, and my escort gave me on my own. Even as I watched, they disappeared back up the road from which we had come.

Within the hour I was in the northern gate and striding the streets to the Senate House. It was adjourned at the moment for the midday meal, but I found the senior Aedile in his kiosk at the entrance. His surprise at seeing me, but no others that had returned from the northern conference, caused many questions, but I gave him that the scroll that I carried could not wait. He was somewhat hesitant of summoning a Senator without a reason, but my hint that war might be on the horizon caused him to hurry out of the building and into the streets.

I just stood in the foyer, idly looking at the statues of elders of the past, my mind thinking on my own actions that might be needed. Once again, I could hear the soft rattle of bones in the cup being shaken before the throw. "The gods have little of importance in their lives," I muttered, "to spend their time with the puppet figure of a lowly scribe." For one who had made mighty efforts to disavow the very existence of the beings of Olympus, my disbelief was once again being challenged.

Suddenly, I turned and straightened as the Princeps Senatus strode into the foyer, followed by two other Senators and the Aedile. The leader of the Senate stopped, exclaiming, "Archivest Junius! We have had no word the return of the delegation."

"Nay, Sos. There is only me." I handed the scroll to the Senator. "This is the reason for my sudden return, and it is not gladsome." He stared at me for a moment, then the small scroll before taking it and pulling the leather cord loose. In a few moments, his eyes widened, and his head bowed to approach the writing as if that would gain him more understanding.

Now, one of the other Senators said, "What is the message, Titus?" With no answer forthcoming, he looked at his fellow, then said, "Come, Titus. It cannot be as serious as that."

Now the leading Senator stared at me again, then turned to order, "Summon the Senate entire, and instantly." To me he asked, "This is truly written?"

I shook my head. "I did not see the action, but I can affirm that the... incident took place, and by the persons named. My arrival was after the fact of the stroke, but man was still pouring out his lifeblood as I approached." I hesitated, then added, "I had the full story from a man who was engaged in his work and in sight of the contention, but not a person of either party involved."

"Hold yourself at the ready. The Senate will wish to take your statements, I have no doubt."

The afternoon was long and contentious. I was asked the same questions over and over as if I would suddenly discover some iota of information that had been lost during my return to Rome. The Priests Primus of the major temples were called for their conference, and opinions of the actions as stated in the scroll and by my testimony. On one subject, the temple leaders were agreed. "Caeso Fabius has put shame upon our city if indeed he has caused such offense as a neutral party. The violation of the Jus Gentium is serious indeed, and will cast doubt upon the veracity of our intercourse with other lands if the action is not repudiated immediately and by the Senate."

The Princeps Senatus called the session to quiet, then waved the small scroll material. "The insistence that Fabius the Younger be handed over to the Senones for justice is one that must be discussed. I will hear all sides of the discussion." For the remainder of the day, the arguments few back and forth. It was apparent that the Fabii family had both bitter enemies and supportive friends, and all had to be heard. As the light began to fade, the Senatorial scribes were instructed as to the words to be given to the criers of the city on the morrow, then adjourned until the morning.

As I walked in the door of my household, the little maid started in fright, then just stared, before suddenly disappearing down the hall with the word that the Master had arrived. Ravana came out, both surprised and pleased, and in moments, we were embracing closely. As we settled into the atrium, she naturally plied me with questions on my journey, but before I could begin she held up a hand and said to the maid, "Tell Socellia to make a meal for the master. And bring wine as we wait."

I gave her the outline of the tale, and my fears that we might once again be involved in a struggle that would affect our lives greatly. Then I asked, "Korax?"

"He was here on the yesterday. He visits on the odd day, just to inquire if any needs have come up. He is a good friend, but do not tell him of my words." She grinned, then pointed to the table as the maids brought in the platters of food.

"In the morning, send a message to stop in the evening. There is much we need to discuss."

As it turned out, there was much more to discuss that even I had supposed. By the end of the next day, the populace of the city entire had made a hero out of the younger Fabius. I was astounded at the reaction, but for whatever reason, the tale seemed to resonate with the common folk - a noble of Rome standing his ground against a barbarian come to take what was not his. The script given to the criers was fairly truthful, but it was somehow perverted by the ears of the mob into a glorious and honorable act by a young man worthy of honors.

In vain did the priesthood insist that Rome was in the wrong, and the young man had grievously violated the Law of Nations. The Senate, while beginning their thoughts that followed mine, began to bend to the public attitude as the realization came that the populace would not condemn the act - nor the Fabii.

Korax put down his cup, waiting for the maid to fill it again. "I was wondered when the gods would lay out their gameboard again." He had arrived at my household in the evening, to wait my return from the Senate house. "Once again, as an alleviation of tedium and ennui, you do not disappoint."

I frowned. "This is not a jape, my friend. Once again, we are at the cusp of violence, and likely to be swallowed by it."

Ravana asked, "Do you think that a roaming people from the outlands could threaten even a city like Rome? Surely our count of just street vendors is greater than their whole tribe."

I just lay back in thought. Pursing my lips, I weighed the question that I had been asking myself these several days. "I would have said no, had I not seen the Senones and their people. They are not as the people of the street are thinking - a dirty tribe of naked men, wielding fire-sharpened sticks for weapons. Nay, these are vigorous people, well armed and literate, even if not in the written word."

"What are their numbers?" asked Korax.

"Far too few to defeat Rome, as to the population in the encampment at Clusium, but there is no writ that their extended clan does not reach to the horizon beyond what I have seen."

"Are you considering that we depart the city?" Ravana did not seem to be disturbed at the prospect, or that of staying.

I gave a wry smile. "We are rapidly running out of lands to which to flee unless we take ship beyond the Pillars of Hercules and into the unknown."

"Aye," chimed Korax. "Maybe we will discover the western lands of the Egyptians - filled with pots of gold and jars overflowing with honey."

"My thoughts were of a closer destination. Possibly Terracina to the south. At least, until the gods tire of their gaming, as they will."

Ravana had little use for such god talk, rejecting even the idea of any such in any land. "I will travel wherever you will. Unless we find a land such as Egypt, then a loose woman has no life."

Would that we had, and that very day.

Calamitas

My cell was barely long enough to allow me to lay prone and only high enough to raise myself on my knees. The wooden door was penetrated with a hole at the bottom to allow a platter almost inedible food to be inserted, but that was only once a day. So starved I was for light that I would lay on my belly, looking through the opening, to see the reflected light of the torches that were carried by the guards as they moved up and down the outside corridor. With no method of determining the passage of days, I could only guess at the time of my incarceration - but the length was measured in months at the least.

My fall from the position of Archivest Primus had been rapid and completely unexpected, although I might have guessed such had I seen the signs following the return of the negotiating party from Clusium. The Fabii brothers had been met by their patér at the gate and rode into the city as conquering heroes, come from a mighty victory. In the Circus Maximus they were greeted with roars from the great crowd, few of which could hear the self-congratulating words of Quintus, and his tales of vanquishing the barbarians with the threat of the might of Rome.

In the face of such popularity, the Senate could do little else than support their new found status as leaders of the city, even with the priesthood still claiming evil from the abrogation of the agreements of neutrality. The demands of the Senones to produce the murderer of their fellow tribesman were ignored, with the exception of a satirical reply, delivered to the camp of Brennus. The contents of the missive, given to the criers of the city, produced much laughter on the streets, but a corresponding rage among the injured party.

Shortly thereafter, a missive came to Rome from the Chief of the tribe, and one that was not in any way written to amuse, but gave direct intent. The men from the land of Gaul now considered Rome to be their mortal enemy, and the strife to be to the death.

Thinking that the city would now come to its senses, and reject the folly of their attitude toward the three self-aggrandizing men, I was dismayed to learn that the two elder Fabii brothers were proclaimed Consuls, to lead the army in the coming war. And, to round out the absurdity, the younger Fabius, Caeso, was elected Tribune of the Army. My failure was not to flee the city at that moment - and in utter haste.

The next day, the archives were entered by a Decanus of the army and his eight soldiers, pushing aside any in their way. As I looked up, the officer stopped and announced, "By order of the Consul

Fabius, Junius the Archivest is removed from his office and given into the office of the Magistrate Judex on the charge of high treason." Turning, he made a quick motion with his hand. "Seize him." Before I could even recover from my surprise, two soldiers had thrown me to the floor and tied my hands behind me. Another rope was placed on my neck and I was pulled out of the building and down the street toward the Mamertine prison on the eastern slope of the Capitoline hill.

There I stayed, each day longer than the last, hearing little and seeing nothing other than the gleam of light through the opening at the bottom of the wooden door. I wondered if I was to rot in this cell, forgotten even by the men who decreed that I would be placed here. Then one day, if the word can be applied to the passing of time that cannot be measured...

"Crawl out, dog!" After the months of darkness, the torch in the hand of the guard was as the direct sun into my eyes. Slowly, I turned to my hands and knees and unsteadily crept out of my cell. Now, standing for the first time since being entombed, I was roped by the neck again and pulled along the narrow corridors, then up a flight of stone steps. As I entered the street, I was as no more than a blind man. Even the glare through my closed eyes was painful as I stumbled along behind the soldiers. Finally, looking through slitted eyelids, I could see that we were approaching the Temple of Jupiter.

I knew that the courts were adjudged in concordance with the priesthood and with the charge of the priests, thus was not surprised that I was taken into the grounds of the temple. The courtyard was as crowded as I had seen and it was obvious that I was not the only person being accused this day. At least, a handful of men were brought out in ropes and back through the gates just in the time that I stood waiting.

Finally, an acolyte stood on the stone steps and called formally, "Summoning Junius of Rome! Present the legal body of Junius of Rome!" Pushing me before them, the officer and two men climbed the stone steps and strode into the vast hall of the Temple. Inside were a hundred men, at least, all in the formal robes of the Patrician, including most of the priests of the temple. We stopped in front of the raised dais, facing the Priest Primus and the leaders of the Senate. It was with a sinking feeling that I also saw that the youngest member of the family of Fabius was included on the judging stand.

Calling the crowd for silence, the Jus Civile - the judicial magistrate - read from a scroll. "The man, called by his own praenomen of Junius, is accused of treason before the city, in that he did conspire with the enemy of the people and consorted with such during his official duties in the Delegation of Clusium, recent. Testimony has been heard of his meetings with the chief of the Senones, and without any need for the occurrence of his mission. Finally, he met with, and carried out the orders of the aforenamed enemy, leaving his post at the Delegation and without notice to the leaders of the mission..." There was more and fairly true except for the constant iteration of my betraying my people by colluding with an enemy.

As a Roman citizen, I was entitled to be judged by the Duodecimo Tabulae - the twelve tables - that codified the law as to the accused and the accusing. It was obvious that in my case, the judgment had already been rendered, and my presence was only for hearing my punishment. I had no doubt that the power of the Fabii was instrumental in this travesty, but why a nonentity as myself would garner such attention from that powerful family was a mystery. Apparently the chance of the smallest revenge for any slight was of importance to a man with an overwhelming sense of self-importance. My mission from the Chief of the Senones had been taken as an attempt to cast ill-repute upon that clan. But, my thoughts were of little use to my plight.

At least, I knew that my fate was not to be thrown from the Tarpeian Rock - that was a punishment for noble sinners, only.

Finally, the Jus Civile stood forth and proclaimed my fate. "As decided by the presiding priests, and in accordance with the laws and with the testimony of witnesses to the crime of treason, the citizen, Junius, will be crucified for his crimes upon the wall of the Circus Maximus, three days hence. For his past services in the honorable manner, attested to by the Priest Primus, as alleviation, he will be granted the boon of totalitas in his person, and given his body, intact."

The Priest of the Temple had apparently interceded to modify the punishment in a way that I would not suffer the indignity - and pain - of having my bones broken by an iron bar while on the crossbeam. That was the grant of totalitas given - the wholeness of body. In its way, it was merciful, but also cruel. A person with his bones shattered usually died within hours, whereas a healthy person, just suspended by his wrists could suffer for days.

A gong sounded, and again I was taken back to my cell in the prison.

My thoughts in the ensuing days were many and varied. I continued to meditation on that gameboard of Olympia. If indeed, my carved figure was in play even now, then some event, some action by this person or that force would give an opening for my escapement from this decreed death.

After that musing was taken to its exhaustion, I would then chastise myself for putting hope in imaginary and invisible beings that had never once been heard or seen by any person in my knowledge - or of any other of any repute. My life would end, as all do eventually, on the posts in the Circus...

That brought up a welcome diffusion of my evil thoughts. All executions of Rome were done in the Field of Fallow, outside the Esquiline gate. Why would they now be happening in the city, itself? Of course, a man in a cell of the Mamertine has no source of information, and my ruminations were composed of questions without answers.

Then, eventually, my thoughts - and hopes - would return to the gameboard on that mountain, far away, to begin my thinking circle again.

No such event happened, specified with the roll of the bones of the gods, to send me once again on my way, escaping my certain death as a figure in the tale of a street sage. On the third day, I was again told to crawl from my hole, my filthy and ragged tunic was torn from me, and I was led to the street in chains, this time to wait for the other unfortunates that apparently had been condemned with me. In a short while, we - about ten of the condemned and a Contubernium of eight elderly soldiers and an officer - were paraded down the street to the Circus Maximus. Even in my despair - and, I will admit, my abject fear - I noticed my surroundings as we proceeded. I had seen such processions before, although with distaste and with little interest, and at those times, the street would be lined with crowds, japing and throwing rotten fruit and dung at the unfortunates. This day, there were few in evidence and mostly women who just stood aside as we walked past. What that meant, I had no idea, but it was a small boon to the doomed men, to walk to their place of death without ridicule.

At the Circus, I saw that the executions would take place on the backside of the stands where the upper-class plebeians would watch the happenings on feast days. This, in effect, was a long wooden wall and would take the place of the stipes and patibulum - upright poles and crossbeams - of the execution field outside the Esquiline gate.

Now, as I watched, the first of the condemned were lifted, and long spikes were driven into their outspread wrists. And for most, more nails pinned their ankles to the wood. Three times, as the Decanus read from his scroll, other orders were given and a soldier proceeded to lash the legs of that unfortunate with a long and heavy bar, breaking the bones with a sound that could be heard over the screaming of him and the previous victims.

Finally, it was my time. Four soldiers, two on each arm lifted me from the ground as two of their comrades placed the tip of a spike at the small of my wrists, then with a large hammer and sure blows, sunk it through my flesh and into the wood. I would have soiled myself at that moment, had I had any nourishment of any amount in the last three days, but even my pride could not prevent the screams of pain that I bellowed. The pain was worse than any that I had ever experienced. The blow to my pouchstones on the island of the pirates was as a love-caress by comparison.

Barely lucid, I heard the officer give an order. "This man receives the Totalitas Grant." I was cringing, waiting for the spikes through my feet, and indeed there came the sound of hammering, but no pain. In a moment, I realized that a small log - only the length of a man's foot - had been nailed at the point where my feet could reach. With difficulty, I could support my weight now, relieving the horrible strain on my wrists, although the reduction of pain was only of degree.

The hurts that crawled down my arm were overwhelming in the extreme, yet I could still have my thoughts. In utter chastisement of self, I cursed the foolish belief that I had been a favorite plaything of the gods.

Finished, the soldiers departed, leaving two of their fellows to watch the condemned begin the slow ending of their lives. The guards were mandatory, both to prevent any associates or family from releasing the men, and to keep any citizens from abusing the criminals with severity - and, therefore, ending their lives before the maximum punishment was obtained.

As to the latter, there was no need in our case. Not a single citizen of the city appeared for his entertainment at our fate. Had my thoughts not been submerged by my pain, I might have wondered at the absence of any cruel audience.

The day and night went both on leaden feet and with the rapidity of the bird of prey. There was no sense of time passing, but the change from day to night and back seemed to take eternity. My only relief was in the fact that severe pain will remove itself, causing the affected wound to numb and become unfeeling. Thus, even though the area of the spikes was lessened, the rest of my body became as a battered dog, hit by a wagon of the street. Pains began in every part of my body from the unnatural position to which I was confined.

I might have slept. Or not. My thoughts that came were of hate - for the family of Fabius in general, but mostly for the person of the youngest member. I would have made any pact with the demons of Hades for the boon of being in the presence of the man who was the instigator of my death. But, even in my state of unreality and pain, I realized that the wish was without hope of fulfillment. I was reduced to the realization that he would eventually cross the river to the land of the dead, and there I would have my chance at vengeance.

The morn brought not only light but now an overwhelming thirst as sauce to the pains that were now just a covering blanket for my body. I had little sense of thought, but through glazed eyes I could see that the condemned man beside me had perished during the night.

My envy of his release from the torture was deep and bitter.

The relieving watch used a long iron tool to remove the spikes and drop the body to the ground. Slaves dumped the remains into a cart, no doubt destined to be pulled to the putrid pits - the final destination for executed prisoners. And again, the two relieving guards sat in their shaded canopy with easy duty, conversing and passing the hours as soldiers do anywhere they are on watch.

Mercifully, I fell into that state wherein a man enters before his final exit from this world. With my awareness of being gone, my pains receded also. Now it was a matter of waiting for my body to give up its life spark and for my being to entered the blessed state of death. It was most cruel, for the living men of the world to interrupt that state of bliss, to again make me aware of my fate...

"Take heed! Do not crush his hands under the iron."

My eyes were fogged, as if becalmed off the shores of Atria, and little of notice could be seen. It was darkfall now, or my vision had departed. I could see little and perceive even less. But, I could feel my arms moving - mainly from the difference in pain that now indicated some happening.

"Now. Carefully... Carefully. Support his head... Now, the blanket..."

Ah... Now I understood. It was the Dalkies of Hades, come to collect their newest associate. Now I would be given succor by the release of my being from my broken body, to be made whole again in the service of the dark underlord...

Then came the dissolution and emptiness of death...

Miraculum

My entry into Hades was not as I expected. My body was not given succor and newness. Rather, I woke in severe pain, covering my entire body, with even my eyes failing to discern any notice of the underworld. Except... A numen was hovering over me - a woman, apparently, but not as any spectral shape that I could discern. Little did I care, as I fell back into darkness.

Again and again, I opened my eyes to see... nothing but the fantastical shape of the hovering spirit. Or spirits - they seemed to change shape at will. A time went by. Days. Months. Lifetimes. I moved between brief periods of dazed vision and interminable lengths of darkness, never approaching any state of awareness of my new domain. Until...

I realized that my eyes were open and were seeing... what, I did not quite discern. A hut, apparently - I could see the straw of the roof and the woven sides made of reeds. My pains were still with me, but no longer as a blanket covering me from head to feet. Rather, the sharpness of my sensations radiating from my wrists was apparent - and severe - but no other.

There was a woman, sitting beside me and smiling. Familiar, she was, but I could not quite place...

Suddenly the veil fell from my vision. Mira? The sense of disbelief was paramount. The woman of Korax was with me in the domain of Hades? Of course not, I chastised myself. This was still the cruel world that I had apparently not departed as yet. And that fact was proved as she called, "Korax. He has returned from his darkness."

Later, I would realize that she had spoken almost as many words as I had ever heard from her, but her call was forgotten as the bearded face of my Greek friend appeared in my vision. And others - Ahirom and Vera, the maid of Ravana.

Korax was grinning. "I have hopes that my land is never engaged in strife with the Romans. They are inordinately hard to kill."

My voice was little more than a croak. "Since I see my Greek comrade here, then I can assume that this is not the golden slopes of Olympus. It is obvious that I have crossed the bridge to Hades." I looked aside with only my eyes - the only part that I could move without even more pain. "And you, Ahirom? Is there no longer a deck to trod." Now my eyes swiveled, and I gave a single word as a question, "Ravana?"

"Nay," the Greek replied. "The time for questions is later. For now, you must just lay and rest." I just barely moved my head in a nod and the vision of the people dissolved as I entered my slumber again.

On the next awakening, the hovering spirit was Vera. She was engaged in... something out of my vision. "What are you doing, woman?"

She looked at me in surprise, then said with a smile, "The bindings on your wrists are receiving fresh moss of the tree, Master." I just stared, then she continued, "It is a poultice to ward off the red demons of the flesh." Again, just that amount of speaking effort was exhausting, and I once more dropped off to slumber.

In the days that followed, I was always with pain, but each day it alleviated to some small degree. I began to gain some small strength from the thin broths that I was given, to the amount that I could hold. And finally, I could converse for a time without falling into an exhausted slumber.

"...and the city is emptied of men - even those of advanced age," Korax was explaining. "All have set foot on the road to glory against the barbarians who are even now forming for battle." That explained the age of the guards that had taken me to the wall in the Circus and the lack of crowds on the journey.

As to my questions of Ravana, he just shook his head grimly. "Nay. I have not seen her since that evil day that you were taken into custody. The magistrates fell upon your household, although for no reason that I can understand, since they well knew where you were on that day." He nodded toward the maid. "Vera, by the goodness of the gods, had gone to market and was not present. She came to our house with the evil news, and we hid her, just in an abundance of caution."

"The members of the household?" I asked.

"None were taken, but all fled when the magistrates left with Ravana."

"Where was she taken?"

"Nay. I have been unable to find even a hint of her location, other than the testimony of Equitia. I saw the maid of the cook in the market square and took her aside for my questions. Hers is all the knowledge that I have of our golden-haired woman, and that only of her seizure and removal."

I could wonder at the reason for her being seized, but without any information whatsoever, the exercise was just one of uselessness. Was she taken to the Mamertine? And if so, why? A Plebeian woman had no power in Rome, and certainly no political value in her removal or... or execution.

I wanted my thoughts on some other wonderment. "How did Ahirom come to be in Rome?"

Korax poured a little wine into a cup, then diluted it with water and handed it to Mira. The woman carefully held it to my lips to allow me to sip. "I sent word to our agent in Ostia on the day you were taken from the scribery. A month later, his ship hove into the docks, and he hurried up the river. I needed more than just myself to storm that cursed prison to free you."

"Storm the prison?" I asked with disbelief.

"Nay. I jest, but we did not know the manner of the charges against you nor the severity. Our hope was that you would only be fined, and thus we could arrive with the payoff. We had much trouble believing the criers when they gave that you had been condemned to the crossbeam..."

He stopped speaking to look around as Ahirom came into the room. "What is the news?," asked Korax.

The one-legged seaman looked at me with a grin. "Ah, it does this old heart good to see you coming back to life."

I moved the side of my mouth in a wry expression as I replied. "Aye, but it is a matter of degree only. If I only twitch my hand, it is easy to imagine that I am still on the wall."

The pilot sat beside Korax, accepting a cup. "The word is that the army is moving to some locale by the name of... Aliea... or Allia perhaps?"

"The stream that flows into the Tiber?" I asked.

He spread his hands. "I know nothing of this land, and only have the name. But the criers are already speaking of the great victory to come."

I tried to shake my head, then thought better of it. "Once again, an army speaks of that which has not happened - a sure prediction of defeat. But... you were speaking of your actions after my seizure."

Korax nodded. "Aye. We had learned of your sentence from the Cryer, as I said, and saw you being led to the Circus. Our plans and our cart were positioned on the assumption that the executions would take place in the usual area, outside the Esquiline gate. The change to the Circus was a major blow, and meant that we could not act until the evening of the morrow."

"On that subject, why did they change the location?"

"Ah... I only found that a few days later in the taverna. Because of the bulk of the army, and more, is with the Consuls Fabii in the field, the guard positions for the magistrates are now held by oldsters, long retired from service and few in number. As we are at war, the gates are opened late and closed early, and the access to the field is hindered from within the city." He smirked. "And the talk of the real reason is that the guards refused to be locked out of the city during the night with such evil as barbarians tromping down from the north."

I just gently nodded as he continued. "At darkfall, we watched the guards being changed, then approached the wall of execution, arm in arm, holding cups - empty - and japing loudly in the walk. The two guards merely laughed to themselves to see us approach. After all, what soldier has fear of such men as we - a Greek with his beard turning gray, and a man struggling with a pole in place of his missing leg?"

Now Ahirom spoke. "And they never learned the fear. At the signal word from Korax, we both plunged our daggers into their hearts as one. They did no more than make the death rattle as they fell."

"I held you as Ahirom wielded the extraction bar to free your hands from the wood, then we put you in the cart, covered with straw, and pulled you to here."

I carefully looked around. "Is this your home," I asked Korax.

He shook his head. "Nay. I had too much fear that I might have been associated with you, although I doubted that any in the city had ever noticed a wandering Greek in their city. When he arrived, months ago, we purchased Ahirom a small domicile in the Sucusa quarter. And that is where you are at this moment."

I lay back, exhausted by the tale. Still, my thoughts took no effort, and one was at the forefront. That a man who has such friends as myself, has riches beyond all the gold and silver and treasures in all the world. Only the uncertainty of the plight of our woman friend spoiled the realization of our being.

Day by day, my strength improved, gaining ever faster as I began to eat properly. I could now sit up, if not walk far, and the pain in my wrists was receding to a dull ache. I had been fortunate in that the two spikes had entered my flesh in such a position that was between the two bones of the wrist, and I had no internal damage to other than my ligaments. And that the red inflammation that often struck deep wounds did not appear, or was alleviated by the moss that the two women placed over the holes in my flesh, then bound with strips of linen.

Although I was a considerable distance in time from wielding a weapon, Korax had purchased a replacement for the one that had been lost when the magistrates had entered my house on that evil day. Since then, the empty dwelling had been visited by many looters and little remained but empty rooms and stone tables. I had no fear of my wealth, it having been split into multiple locations and buried far below the ground and with great effort to erase the fact of its presence.

And I had little interest in the coin. In the scroll of one's being, life is at the head of the list, as are friends and the ability to learn. Gold is far down the roll - so far as to be unseen by the reader until he almost tires of the reading - at least for me, now.

I could not leave the house, of course, and seldom even left the small room that had been used as storage. The men had told me of the statements issued from the platforms of the criers of the city, given rewards for the treasonable citizen who had escaped his ordained punishment and the dastardly criminals that had killed the two guards on that evening. Should my face be seen by anyone, utter destruction could be brought upon all in this household.

In fact, that was the crux of the problem that confronted us. Many were the nights that we schemed on the method of removing my presence from the city. Once I was healed and fully ambulatory, then it would be possible to attempt the flight. All made many suggestions, and some with good possibility - a rope over the wall or being hidden under the contents of an ox-cart, and suchlike. The goal, of course, was to reach one of our ships, docked in the port at Ostia. Once onboard, I would be a free man again, and we could sail off to any destination around the great sea.

We might even have tried the cart idea now, with the bulk of the males in the city off to war and the guards of the magistrates mostly old and almost infirm, but... I had to know the fate of Ravana. Such as she could not have just disappeared from all eyes, unless killed and disposed of, but such a misfortune would be unlikely - women who are taken by force are not destroyed, but enslaved at the least.

How I was to find her fate had so far eluded me, as I could not show my face out of this domicile? Both Korax and Ahirom had visited many taburna in the city, giving leading questions as to her location, but had received nothing but musing and imaginings. Possibly, as before, she had been sold to a traveling slave trader and even now was a mat slave in some far city.

The wily Greek was even more astute than myself, although I will say in my own defense, that continual pain is not conducive to deep thought. He had engaged a young man of the street, of less than the years needed to be considered an adult in this city, but still of enough as to be able to move freely about without the danger of being grabbed for labor by some kiosk owner. That youngster became the factor of Korax, now engaging many of the very young street urchins and handing out good copper coin for information - either yea or nay. The promise of a handful of gold to the young man and silver to the boy who brought information of a golden-haired woman caused much effort in the under strata of the city.

As Korax was in possession of all the gold that had been earned by the ships in the past year, along with his own considerable stash, there was no need for the coin that was buried around the courtyard of my previous domicile. Still, as it was possible that we could leave at an instant's notice, and with the necessity of goodly bribes, Korax had visited the compound at night, digging up one large stash and bringing it to the house. There it was packed with other necessities - baggage that could be toted at a moments notice, should the chance to escape the city suddenly appear.

Suddenly, the attention of the magistrates was not on the apprehension of an escaped man, but on their own skins. I was walking back and forth in the small domicile, flexing my limbs to build my strength again when Korax strode into the house. I could tell that something of importance had happened, but his appearance gave no hint that it was the doom of discovery.

At my question, he said, "I do not know as yet. The streets are as a hive of bees, overturned, with men running this way and that to no purpose."

"What was the cause?"

"Riders from the army. Messengers that entered the Senate House and have not exited as yet." He took a cup and a half loaf from Mira before continuing. "The people have not the least idea of any reason, but they assume that it is dire."

I sat down and mused on the slight information for a while, then said, "It can only mean a defeat for the Legion, or a setback at least. Any news of victory would have been proclaimed as the men rode through the gate."

He nodded. "I will visit the taverna at the evening hour, and try to find the reason. But... Think of this. The chaos may give us chance to depart this cursed place of fools." He held up his hand, knowing of my protest. "Aye. But gold can purchase agents to pursue her fate from another city, and in much more safety."

In a while, Ahirom entered, giving much the same story. "The Cryer of the Forum has little to say. The crowds at his pedestal are insistent, but he can only give that no scrolls have arrived for his issuance."

The day broke, and with it stories and tales and rumors without end. Wails of doom and destruction came on one wind, then cries of joy and peans to the gods for the great victory that had been won by the Legion of Rome on another. It had taken all of the day and most of the next before the actual truth began to filter out of the Senate - now populated only by ancient men who had been unable to follow the army to garner their measure of glory, as did their younger fellows.

Indeed, the Legion under the command of the Fabii brothers had taken a defeat on the banks of the Allia - a stream flowing into the Tiber about a hundred stadia upriver from Rome. This in itself was not disastrous - the Roman army had been defeated many times in its history, but always regrouped to win the day. The important question was the recovery and reassembly of the army after the battle.

That comforting thought gave way to the reality of the future. Unlike the present, the armies of those past times had competent commanders who could react to both victory and defeat. The list of follies that were being scribed against the names of the Consuls grew with every runner from the north.

Ahirom sat in the growing darkness of the evening, having just come from his favorite taburna. "The Cryer of the Forum is giving notice that the army is split, with each half on either side of the Tiber."

"Aye," I replied. "That is in keeping with the news of Korax, here. Quintus is leading his formations westward - possibly toward Veii." I thought for a moment, then continued, "Though why is a mystery. That city is a desolation of broken stone now, after the victory of Camillus over that people." Any army that attempted to hold up in those ruins would starve, and quickly. "What news of the eastern segment of the army?"

Both shook their heads. "Many tales and rumors, all different that the one before, but nothing of any substance." He stopped for a moment, then said, "We should make our exit soon while the chaos is reigning."

"The gates are closed and blocked, and only the small openings for entry and exit," said Ahirom. "Citizens are not allowed to leave, and certainly not our Roman friend. A rope over the walls is the only possibility."

That was a problem in itself. Both men could easily lower themselves via a rope for that distance, but the women? I doubted it. Vera might, unless she took fright and froze on the rope, or released her grip and fell. And Mira was not a young woman by many years. She was solid of character and unlikely to panic, but still, the result was likely to be two women with broken bones at the base of the wall.

And myself. My strength was returning quickly, but there was no possibility of my wrists and arms yet supporting my weight while hanging from a rope.

Both men had to agree with my statements, with Korax making a jape with a grin. "Aye, we will wait to see what comes about. And I wish to see just what miracle that the gods will produce to deliver their favorite Roman from evil, once again."

Suddenly, I fell silent with my thoughts. The time of pain and my recovery and all that had happened since that evil day had prevented my idle musings as before. But, the jest of Korax brought back the old thoughts - thoughts that I had entertained, half believed, and then firmly rejected time and again.

But... Once again I had escaped certain death, and in a way that would be rejected by the storytellers of the streets as being too unconvincing in the extreme. In the annals of Rome, I doubt that one man in ten thousand, condemned to the crosstree, had lived to speak of it. And yet, here I was, regaining my strength and living another day. Mere fate could not possibly account for my life. Were I in a game of bones, and the count of Euripides was thrown again and again, without fail, then I would know that my opponent had weighted the cubes before the game.

My life, counted as a game, had been unending play in which I had thrown the value of Euripides time and again and without fail. That small figure of my imagination, carved for the gameboards of the gods of Olympus, was no longer a fantasy in my mind. Was I, an unlikely entity from the most common and lowest of antecedents, actually in the favor of the gods?

The Defender

Catastropha

The news, as it trickled into the city in a slow, but steady flow, was not of defeat, but rather, the description of disaster. The Roman Legion had not been thrown back, but almost utterly destroyed. The men fleeing from the battlefield were not soldiers moving to regroup, but rather crazed wretches running for their lives, discarding both weapons and armor in their desire for speed. Many arrived at the gates of the city as naked unfortunates, their very garments having being torn off by the briars and brambles through which they had fled.

Of the many nobles and Patricians that had accompanied the army, few survived, they being in the main, of advanced age and vulnerable in the extreme. As to the Senate, it was now composed of no more than a handful of oldsters, defective of hearing and short of breath. By my count, almost four in five of the men of Rome were either food for the crows or skulking through the brush between the Tiber and the ruined city of Veii. And those that were left in the city proper were either youngsters or graybeards of little use in repelling barbarians.

On the wedge of goodness, and one that was very thin, the hard core of the Legion was still intact, though small in numbers, but well led by veteran commanders. The maniples of the Wolf, the Scorpion and the Ursa had made a fighting withdrawal back to the city, and mostly intact. Unfortunately, their numbers were scarcely more than half a thousand - far too few to defend a city the size of Rome, even should each kill ten of their foe.

It was with some small satisfaction that I watched the fall of the house of Fabii. Numerius, the middle son and co-Consul was killed in the fighting, and the elder, apparently still alive, was now in the ruined city of Veii, with the remnants of most of the army. The patér was among the foolish leaders of the city who had considered a war against barbarians to be a cause for easy glory, sharing in the inevitable victory over the primitives of the northern lands. Their sudden entry into the domain of Hades must have been a great surprise to them all.

As to the younger brother, Caeso, given the position of Senior Tribune by reason of his family's position in the city...

Any tales of woe will increase with each mouth that speaks, and those about the youngest Fabius were dire indeed. But, his ill-deeds were abominable enough, even without the exaggeration of repeated telling. Of all the family, he fell the furthest in the stature of the people. Despite the warnings of his officers, he had led his Maniples of the Legion across the stream, at a point where the narrowness of the far bank funneled the men into a long line that was easily crushed in the flanks by the waiting Gauls.

That tale was dire enough, but history has many stories of incompetent commanders. It was his appearance in Rome that completed his downfall. He had appeared at the gates on his horse - with his two aides and boyhood comrades - their animals frothing and in the last extremity of life, having been whipped and ridden at pace for a hundred stadia. It was not long before the populace realized that he had fled from the fighting, leaving his men to their fate, unshared. The finally tally was when the three Maniples had marched into the gate, in disciplined formation and with their weapons and armor. It was their tales of the leader that gave the last blow to the reputation of the Tribune.

To women and old men who had lost husbands and sons, he was soon considered to be a pariah, fit only to be scorned and, on occasion, receive the contempt of the city by the action of thrown fruit - or stones. Even the doors and walls of the House of Fabius received condemnation in the form of scribbled phrases of contempt for his cowardliness.

In the interim, the search for Ravana had produced nothing. The street urchins of the city had found absolutely no trace of the woman. The search was not assisted in any way by the fact that most of the men who had anything to do with her disappearance - or my condemnation - were now either dead or fugitives across the land of Latium. It was becoming obvious that she had been taken from the city long months ago and was now in some far part of the world, to begin her life anew as...

I hoped that her new master was kind and that she would be able to cozen him into comradeship, using her vast skills of femininity - as she had done to me.

We began our plans to exit the city, to travel to the port of Ostia and our ships. From there we would stand out and voyage to... Carthago maybe. Or Caralis on the island of Sardinia. Even Rhodes was becoming a major port for the tradings in the eastern half of the Great Sea.

In the evenings, before my slumber overtook me, I sometimes thought with drollness on my plans of settling in another land. Given the whole and history of my past, the chosen city that allowed my citizenship was indeed doomed by the games of the gods.

The news, dire enough in the part that was truth to the tale, became even worse. Ahirom came from the Cryer of the Forum with the news that the Senones were on the march to Rome itself and even now were at the city of Fidenae. It that was true, then the enemy was only thirty stadia from the walls of the city.

A Centurion of some repute was now in charge of the army, ignoring the commands of the Senate to protect the property of the members above all else. He knew that with only half a thousand men, any attempt to make a stand on the walls was futile. With such a defense, evenly spaced along the walls, each man would scarcely be within hailing distance of his mates. Rather, he was fortifying the hill of the Capitoline - a natural fortress in itself, although not built as such. But, the steep slopes of the hill and the sturdy stone houses of the nobles were fortifications in themselves. Only the three main roads leading into the quarter needed to be blocked, and day and night, both soldiers and citizens and slaves were hauling stones taken from lesser buildings in the city. Both Korax had need for caution as he moved around the city, else they he impressed for labor by the soldiers. Thus, Ahirom was our eyes and ears in the streets - his missing limb giving him an immunity to impressment.

The citizens began to flee. Some toward the port of Ostia, others to the perceived protection of the army remnants in Veii, and some even toward the mountains to the southwest. I suspected that most would starve, as a city man had little knowledge of finding food in the wilderness. By now, my wounds were healed, in the main, although I would always have some stiffness in my wrists, and some aching when the weather was damp. But my hands and fingers worked and could hold a stylus or gladius with equal skill.

Our plans, of course, were to move to Ostia and we began our final packing of food and the few items to be carried. Then...

Korax called me to the front room where I saw three strangers, and of all ages. An urchin, a young man and a workman of some profession, wearing a leather bib - either a butcher or meat merchandizer, apparently. Seeing me, my friend said, "By the sweat of the crotch of Jupiter himself, this news comes at the cusp of the day!" He pointed to the older man and said, "This is the Master. Give your tale And quickly - there is little time for talk."

Bewildered, I just stood as the man began. "This man said that you have coin for news of a woman with golden-hair..."

My heart began to pound with force enough for my wrists to ache, as I replied with force, "Aye, and much if your news be useful."

"I have never seen such, but... I was the meat jobber for the table of the Tribune and his staff, on the banks of the... the... whatever the cursed stream was called. Before the battle that ended it all."

What was he about to say? That Ravana had been with the evil bastard son of Hades during the battle at Allia? That could not be - a thousand soldiers would have seen such a female carried in the baggage of the officers and I would have long heard of her presence.

I jerked my head to continue. He spread his hands, then said, "But the Tribune japed many times of a trophy that he had taken from some man who had ended his life on a crosstree. And that the woman was tressed as the sun, with long and shiny locks that could almost be seen in the darkness."

I was barely able to hold my tongue with the slow and stumbling words of the butcher, but I refrained from interrupting his labored thoughts. Korax however, was not so patient. "Out with it man. Did he say where she was kept?"

"Aye. In his home on the Capitoline." He hesitated, then finished with, "Waiting for the return of her victorious master, he said."

I just stared into the open doorway, looking at nothing in the narrow lane outside the house. Korax opened his purse and gave several coins to the man, with warnings to keep his news to himself. Then he paid the young factor and his urchin who had found the man - and generously, although in the case of the youngest, a palmful of silver was given rather than gold pieces. Any showing of a gold Darius or Stater by the boy would just get him slain when he tried to vend it.

Now, the four members of the household drew near, waiting for my determination about the startling news just received. It did not take long. "Korax. You will take the party down the road to Ostia, to the ship. Hold it there for my arrival, but if the enemy approaches the city, stand out for the city of Tarracina. Wait there for me in the inn of..." What was the name of that cursed deversorium on the waterfront? "...The Inn of the Tortoise. I can walk the distance in a few days."

"Sos. The enemy is almost at the gates of the city." Ahirom was not enthusiastic about my plan to any degree. "You cannot linger here while the citizens flee for their lives."

Korax had a wry expression on his face. "Nay, that is an indication that you do not know our Roman friend, in his history. This will not be the only time that he has tarried in the face of death, to succor a woman."

I pointed to the back of the house. "Take the bag of gold. I will not need it, and do not want the weight to hinder me in my... actions."

Korax just nodded, turning to say, "Gather our baggage. We leave at once."

I was surprised - actually astounded at his calm acceptance of my decision to stay and search for Ravana. I held out my hands to my Greek friend, he carefully taking them by the fingers, rather than the wrists as is the custom. "We will meet again. Be sure of that."

"Aye." He replied. "As sure as the rising sun on each morning." He stopped for a moment, then finished with, "Remember the words of old Leodes - keep your blade between you and your foe at all times." Turning, he said, "Come, we leave now and with haste."

It was with great sadness that I saw my friend... friends leave my presence, and probably for the last time, I had to admit. Even old Mira, who had spoken no more than a double handful of words to me in all the time of our acquaintance, was a friend of closeness. She had not left my side from the time I was taken from the wall until I could stand to make my own water. And Vera, the cosmeta of Ravana, long since manumitted from slavery to become a companion to her mistress - she had picked the best meat from the bone and the freshest bread from the loaf for my halting meals.

And Ahirom - a mere captain hired for his ability, had himself put his being at risk of being nailed to the same wall from which he had pulled the spikes to release me from death.

And, of course, Korax. I needed no thought of his friendship - one that was as close and more - as a man to his mater. I wished them a long life and an easy death in their far ages.

Now, for the first time since the day of my seizure at the archives, I strode the street of my own accord again. I had little worry about being recognized as the archivest who had been condemned to the cruelest death. Any person of that action was long dead or fled, and who would believe that a man once nailed naked to the Circus wall would be striding down the Via Aurelia as a free man?

I was wearing two woven bracers on my wrists, to cover the telltale evil red spots that would have given question to any who saw, and they protected the still sensitive areas from abrasion. It would be many years before the scars faded to the point of being unnoticed.

At the eastern side of the Capitoline hill, I climbed to the stone wall that even now was being built, stopping before the plumed officer. He turned to look at me in askance, as I spoke. "My name is... Lucius, an educated scribe and citizen of Rome but with skills in battle. I would assist the defense, if I am allowed."

He looked at me in surprise. "A citizen who weighs the fate of the city over his own skin? You are indeed a novelty." He pointed further up the hill. "Report to the Centurion at the Senate House. He will say yea or nay to your offer."

I walked without haste across the top of the hill, by coincidence passing by the massive domicile of the Fabius family, but seeing nothing but the brick walls and closed door. I knew that the household must be fairly deserted, with only the youngest son in residence - and maybe the Domina of the family. At a tent in the small square I found the commander of the remaining units dictating this order and that to men, who came and went as porters onto a boat.

At his query, I gave my spiel again, falsifying only my name once more. He asked, "You are a scribe?"

"Aye, Sos. Trained in the Temple of Jupiter, but my travels have been across the world, and not without strife that required my blade to adjudicate the matter." He looked at my worn scabbard, seeing only the plain hilt of the gladius, but noticing that it was not the gilded toy of the young nobles, used to impress young women rather than destroy a foe. It was not my old and faithful longknife, lost when my household was pillaged, but similar. More rounded than that old blade, it still had a sharp point rather gentle curve of the usual short sword. More importantly, it felt much like my old weapon, and needed little familiarization to use.

"You are welcome, citizen. At the moment we are closing the entry points to the hill and gathering staples for our meals." He turned and shouted, "Optio!" A man turned and saluted. "Assign this man... Lucius, you said?" I nodded. "...with four soldiers for another gathering detail." To myself, he said, "Your task is to bring any foodstuffs to the hill that will not perish. Grain, jerked and smoked meat and fish, and the like. Only supplies that will last. We will have no need for cheeses and lacte, to mold and putrefy before the sun rises again." He looked at me hard, then finished, "Take them with force if necessary."

"Aye, Sos." In a short while I had been introduced to four men, soldiers all and not just armed citizens. They were all uneducated in the extreme as to scripts and numbering, but their weapons - spears - were well polished with use and notched from battle. Down the hill we went, through the one opening that remained for access of foraging parties and into the streets. On a thought, I led us to the area of the fish venders and smokers, well known to myself in my younger days, many times having hauled baskets of fish to this kiosk or that.

The shops were still occupied by merchants - not as many as usual, but not abandoned by any means. Apparently the citizens were hoping for some miracle to save them from the coming foe, or else just refused to give up and abandon their livelihood. Of course, the possibility was that, since the average citizen had never left the environs of the city, they had no slightest idea of a destination for escape.

Many were the wails of woe as we emptied their small storages of smoked fish, calling on the gods and the long departed magistrates for justice. As the purloined man-carts were filled, I discovered that I did not have the pitiless heart of a looter. By my orders, the merchants were left with sufficient foodstuff to last themselves for at least the half month - which by all reports, was far longer than they would be alive.

We seized slaves from the merchants to pull the carts back to the hill, at least, two having to be killed to encourage the rest to remain to their tasks. By the end of the day, we had made our foraging trip twice, assisting the slaves to haul it up the hill into the storage area, then releasing them back to their masters. It was made plain by the Centurion that no useless mouths were needed on the hill.

The following day went much the same, with many loads of foodstuff brought to the hill. But the third day was not used for foraging. On that morning, the front ranks of the Senones appeared on the road that followed the Tiber. And the battle of Rome began.

Oppugnatio (Assault)

With only a few hundred trained soldiers, the possibility of defending the enormous perimeter of the walls was impossible, even with the citizens willing to stand into battle. The day had barely turned to full light before the Senones began their attack. Unlike an army of Latium - or even Greece and Egypt - they stopped for no inspection and planning of their attack. As far as I could see, they had not even broken their fast, although that was unlikely. Like as not, all carried their jerked meat and rations with themselves, rather than have a common kitchen area as do most formally constituted armies.

It was obvious that some scouting had been done - probably by small groups of men unnoticed as they stood in the fields outside the city. A hundred - nay, many times that number of crude ladders were carried by the front ranks. Those were certainly not constructed that morning, but rather over the preceding days.

It was now obvious to myself that both the delegations from the city of Clusium and Rome had been fools - the men of that far city for not scouting out the extent of the peoples come across the mountains to treat for land, and the Romans for assuming that it was some minor tribe on the move. Looking across the grain fields, I could see numbers of men that far exceeded those that had been in the camp on the side of the upper Tiber. Brennus, the Chief, had been wily enough to keep the bulk of his tribe afar, so as to lessen the fears of the owners of the lands on which he had wished to settle.

Had the foe moved to assault on all sides of the city, it would have fallen before the sun had risen halfway to the overhead. There were far too few soldiers and citizens oppose the oncoming horde if the attack was spread around the city entire. Instead, the Gauls concentrated on the eastern wall, apparently because of the easy access across the fallow grain fields.

And, had the battle been on level ground, rather than the ramparts of the city, the men of Rome would have been as a sand flea standing to a heavy tide on the beach.

Still, the men of Rome were not to be brushed aside easily. As the multitude of ladders rose against the walls, they were just as quickly thrown down. And in the instances when the attackers gained the height, he was usually met with a spearpoint, and fell, many times sweeping his fellows below him from the rungs. I was with my small unit of foragers, not from orders but because of familiarity. The comradeship of men whose names have only been known for a day or so gave greater confidence in battle than that of fighting alone with strangers.

We fought our section of wall throughout the day until the sun began to fall behind the hills of Rome. The few bowmen made slaughter far in excess of their numbers, and I now realized the reason for the lament from this officer and that for the reason of their fewness. The army of Rome, I had been told in casual conversation, was once strengthened by a mighty force of archers, capable of filling the sky with wood and striking the foe far into his ranks. But, over the years, the skill had been allowed to decay for the much easier and quicker learning of the spear, and now only a few small units of the weapon remained.

By the time of the fading light, my arm was as wood, and my abused wrist feeling as if dipped in boiling water. I had killed men in my past upon need, but those were as fleas to a leviathan compared to this day. The count of heads that I had lopped, and skulls cleaved by my gladius were beyond the ability of a scribe-novice to number. My tunic was as one from the dyers, made for the Festival of Mars, and splotched with red from the neck to the hem. A small amount of the dye was my own, with a slice on one leg and a small puncture in my side, but most came from the spewing necks of the men who failed to attain the rampart before my metal struck.

I knew, from some small experience, that a spear was a fearful weapon, capable of striking at distance, but should the wielder allow a foe to enter his reach with a short blade, then the spearman was doomed. Several times I batted the long haft aside then jumped to enter that area in which his weapon was useless. Still, I knew that my great advantage was the height of the wall, giving me stance and readiness against a foe clambering from a crude ladder and in disarray for my stroke. Had the battle been on level ground, already I would be nothing but fodder for the crows.

Many Romans fell that day, including one from my small detail, with a spearpoint through his thigh, but the ground under the ladders was stacked with the bodies of the attackers, in the amount that had to be ten or twenty to our one. Still, even should those numbers continue with such unevenness, the city would be shorn of fighters long before the attackers had diminished to a point of defeat.

As the night grew closer, the Senones ceased their attacks, retreating across the fields to their night-camp. Inside the walls, the citizens began to cheer with the perception of victory, to the disgust of the Centurion. In the wide area of the small forum of the Mons Oppius quarter, he had made a temporary headquarters and now called his sub-officers to meet. Having no orders to not attend, I followed along.

"We cannot man the walls on the morrow as today. Our losses are one in five of the soldiers and half of the fighting citizens. Another day will see us without even men to hold the Capitoline." There was more discussion of strategy among his officers, but the range of options for the defense was limited.

One of his Optios said, "If the leader of the barbarians is other than just a brigand with many men, he will now know of our strength and will spread the assault to the other walls on the morrow."

The Centurion nodded. "Aye, possibly. If he is an illiterate of strategy, it is very possible that he will just throw his men against the same wall as today. But, it is difficult to ascertain the mind a foe of which nothing is known."

"His name is Brennen, Chief of the Senones Tribe, down from the lands that we call the lower Gaul." The entire group turned to look at me in surprise. "He has seen about forty seasons, is large and vigorous of body, and sharp of mind. He has no skill in lettering, but he is no fool nor a man who will be deflected from his course."

There was a period of quiet, then a call from several officers. "Who is this man?" "How can you know such?"

In the glaring flames of the torches, the Centurion stepped forward, then nodded. "Ah. The scribe, Lucius. And one who did not hold back from the battle, by the look of his garments." He waved me to step forward. "Say your knowledge, Lucius the scribe."

"Aye, Sos." Carefully, I put my story together. It was very unlikely that these unlearned soldiers knew anything of the... events in the city concerning a certain Archivest, but I did not need to deliberately put my head in the mouth of the lion. "I was on the delegation that traveled to Clusium to treat with the incoming peoples - they call themselves the Senones. The people were friendly and shared their cookeries with any who wished. I, myself, in times of idleness, had conversations with their chief, he having great interest in the sights and peoples and my experiences around the Great Sea. Thus, I can give my belief of his being and his strong character. He is not easily angered and accepts trivial insults rather than replying with heat. But, he will only take deliberate affronts for a limited time before he acts."

I paused for emphasis, then continued, "As I said, this is no bandit leader, knowing nothing but the spear and slaying for loot and pleasure. I agree with your officer, Sos. On the morrow, his reading of our defense will change his mode of attack, now knowing of our deficiency in numbers."

Thus, for the morrow, a double set of orders was given, either to be executed depending on the actions of the attackers. For now, I was as tired as I had been since my swim from the burning pirate ship. I walked to one of the fires being used as cookeries, cut off a slice of pork with my dagger and filled one of the empty bowls with wine, then walked into the shadows to find a deserted house and a mat.

An empty stall - a vendors kiosk of some kind - supplied a bundle of straw that would be welcome. With a sigh of relief, I sat and thought about the day. Or began to...

"It was a hot day on the walls, and no denying," came a familiar voice.

In utter astoundment, I froze, the cup halfway to my mouth. Then, rising on my aching legs, I stood and exclaimed, "Korax? By the stinking breath of Apollo's bitch-woman! Why are you not in Ostia?"

"And miss the next throw of bones on the Olympian gameboard? Nay, you would not deny me the chance to watch the gods in their play to rescue their favorite game-piece?"

"You fool! You will just die on a Gaulish spearpoint with the rest of us. Why did you not go to safety with... Tell me not that the women and Ahirom are here with you!"

He refused to accept my ire, instead, sliding his back down the wall to sit on the ground. In the dim light of the quarter moon I could see that he, also, had visited the cookfires. "Nay. Ease your liver, my Roman friend. Ahirom and the women are safely ensconced on the ship and it is fully crewed and stored. I put them there myself. They are stood out in the harbor and waiting. All that is needed is to pull the anchor and sail away to safety, should any... evil appear on the horizon." He stripped a bite off the bone with his teeth, then mumbled. "The other ship is taking the short trading route between Tarracina and Syracusa and back until told otherwise. And the captain has been ordered not to stand into Ostia until he has seen us again."

"Still, you are an old man and should be watching the sunset with your woman, not matching spearpoints with men that could be your grandsons."

"And you, as a scribe, are trained to stand the wall and lop the heads of barbarians as if they were mushrooms on a rotten log?" He waved his cup at me - only a shadow in the dim light. "And well did you wield your stylus, as I watched you write the scroll of death for each man as he tried to contest your position on the wall. The Tagmatarches of the Artemis Third Hekatontarchia would have made you a Lokhagos on the spot."

Now I was entirely taken aback. "You were on the wall this day?"

"Aye. Watching the next set of ladders to the north of you. The spear of this old Greek, who was once a full Dimoirites, still enters easily even into the bodies of the young grandsons you spoke of."

"By the unwiped backside of Vulcan! Now I have no surprises left in my life to discover!" I munched on the meat for a bit before continuing, then, "But why? This is not your battle, to die for a city that considers you an outsider!"

"Did not you fight for my city?"

I frowned uselessly in the dark. "You know fully that I was not on that cursed Trireme of my own accord." A pause, then, "And you are japing with me on a matter of seriousness."

"Aye. But enough banter. Let us rest for the morrow. As you say, these old bones are not as they were some years ago and need their rest."

Laying back, I was still appalled that my friend had cast himself back into the lion's den, but still...

There is no more comfort in adversity than a proven and steady friend by your side.

At the first light of the morning, the Legion and citizens arose and fed. There were far fewer of the latter this day, with the bodies of those slain still laying on and about the wall and many others obviously deciding during the night to watch the battle from afar. And my - our - prediction came true. We watched as the masses of Gauls moved around the walls to stretch their assault far beyond our ability to man the walls. The Centurion gave his orders and men moved to their positions.

For myself, I knew that the wrist of my weapon-hand would not take the abuse of yesterday. It was not useless, but it would fail long before the day was done should the battle become fierce again. Fortunately, it did not. For a while the ladders were thrown down, and even more heads were cleaved, but as the foe began to overwhelm the top of the wall, the horns were sounded and the Legion began its withdrawal.

The men moved back, fighting with the advantage of now knowing their terrain, and the Senones more times than not, finding themselves in a blocked lane or ally, then attempting to ascertain their position in a forest of buildings. By the midday, the battle had backed up to the Capitoline hill and the soldiers streamed through the single breach in the stone blocks, then to take positions on the top of the wall encircling the hill.

Of course, as the 'wall' was, in reality, the buildings of the quarter, with the few entry roads blocked by new barriers, the men were standing on the rooftops, far out of reach of spear and blade - of either side. The ladders of the foe were far too short for use - for the reasons of both the height of the structures and the steep slope of the hillside. In addition, the roofs had been prepared with a collection of stones and rocks, usually about the size of a man's head, but when flung from the heights onto the faces of the men below...

Properly aimed, the heavy missile usually broke the head of the unfortunate looking up at his doom, then rolled down the slope breaking, or at least severely injuring, this ankle and that leg of his comrades. Still, a serious assault was not mounted upon the contrived fortress - as yet. Rather, the foe roamed the city, slaying any that were encountered in their path.

Among the men of the hill, besides the soldiers, were some citizens, young men and old, who had no intention of passively dying upon the spear of a Gaul, and who had been tested in the flames of battle on the wall. As we had no station in the army, we became as a unit of reserve - with the full agreement of the Centurion - to rush to any sector that was being hard pressed and add our numbers and iron to those defenders.

This day, however, little was done but sit on the roofs of the buildings and watch the city being despoiled. All but myself and Korax, that is. I had another mission in mind, and for the preparation, was scouting out the land.

The vast edifice of the Fabii clan was not one that edged the hill but was in a prominent place in the center. It was almost empty, I had been told, with only the skulking Caeso still in residence. Why he remained, rather than fleeing for safety as was his want, I had no idea, nor did I care. Tonight, I would enter his home and discuss this matter and that with the young noble. Of course, he might consider conversation with a lowly commoner to be far beneath his station, but I hoped to reason with him this night.

We walked to the western edge of the hill, looking down at the steep slope and the Tiber, only part of a stadium beyond the walls. My tentative plan involved using that river as our escape, as I had done once before when also leaving this city in the face of utter danger. Immediately to the south, and part of the fortress walls, was the Temple of Juno. I could hear the quiet honking of the sacred geese that roamed the compound and from our height, could see the slow movement of a solitary man as he moved around the grounds. Few priests were left on the Capitoline - or anywhere - as most had followed the army to the witness it and their own destruction. The temples were virtually deserted, but unsullied by the defenders, of course, except for posting men on the external walls, if that building fronted the hillside.

The inactive day gave my arm and wrist some relief, now usable again but still with soreness and aching. In one of the abandoned houses, I found a store of tunics and an atrium pool. Shortly, Korax and I were reasonably cleaned and garbed, and we climbed back to the roofs to watch and wait. There was little talk, the men realizing that if this hill fell, then the history of their city would pass to the memory of sages and dusty scrolls in some far archive.

The evening fell with little force applied to the hill, except an arrow on the occasion that would loop over the buildings - or fail to even reach the rooftop. We were not under siege, as I would have thought, and no mass of men were stationed at the bottom of the slopes to prevent any foray from the hill.

The evening meal was sufficient for the work of the day but carefully rationed by the quartermaster with an eye on the length of time that we might be residing in the midst of thousands of the enemy. I sat for a while outside the command circle listening to the Centurion and his officers plan this strategy and that defense. The hope of the men was that the supposed army at Veii had been gathered from its flight after the battle of Allia, and would eventually march to give weight to the defenders of the Capitoline. For myself, I thought that unlikely in the extreme, should Quintus Fabius still be the Consul. He had no military ability to any extent - now a proven fact - and I doubted that any man would follow him into a brothel, far less against the Senones for battle. The army could prevail, but only with a proper leader, such as the Centurion at the center of the circle to which I was listening.

Unfortunately, even in the face of a disaster and total dissolution, a commoner - even a veteran and proven man of strategy - would never be given the post of leader of the Roman army, entire.

For now, I was just waiting for the lateness of night for my own reasons...

"Sos! Sos!" A man had just run out of the dark to the circle, stopping to salute then exclaim, "The barbarians are firing the city!" All scrambled to their feet, to climb to the roofs of the buildings on the perimeter of the hill. Korax and I also stood to the ladder and mounted to the heights that I had used to look down on the city during the day.

The scene was terrible, but as yet it was nothing to what it would become. The spark of fires were to be seen all over the city - from the Salaria Gate in the north of the Viminalis quarter to the Caelius hill in the far south. The Capitoline was on the western edge of the city, but from its base to the eastern wall, multitudes of fires were growing.

The structures of the Temples and Magisterial offices, along with the wealthy merchants were mostly brick and stone, but the roof trees and coverings were wooden, as were the internal walls and floors. And those were only as one in a hundred of numbers of the edifices of the city. The rest, the houses and huts and shanties of the plebeians, from the prosperous merchants to the poor laborers - those were of wood and straw and reeds, entire.

No sound was made by all who watched the growing horror. Spots of flame grew and became fires that engulfed the entire building, then they began to join and soon entire blocks of structures were the base of towers of flame. The friendly and warming cracklings of a warming fire were being replaced by a growing roar of the flames. Suddenly, a man cried, "Look. What can that be?"

Another said, "And there!" pointed to a different quarter. Strange and spectral flames of green were rising in the midst of the city-wide inferno. As we watched, the fantastic tinting of the blazes grew even deeper, and rising far above the building being consumed underneath.

"It is the upper faces of the Temples," said a man behind us. I turned to see an officer - an Optio - standing and looking at the grim sights. "The copper sheeting of the roofs is being heated to the point that it too, catches fire, and the flames of that metal are as we see - colored greenly throughout. I have seen such in the smithery of my patér."

I crossed to the northern edge of the roof, looking across the Forum at the magistracy buildings, now buried by leaping flames. It was with a sickened heart that I watched the destruction of the documents of commerce, the treatises of the ancient sages, and, aye, the fascinating tales of men and gods in their heroic endeavors, that had been recited every day by the stories of the bards of the street. And worst of all, the recorded history of Rome that was being destroyed by the leaping flames. Even if the city survived, it would be as a new-founded colony, with no past beyond the memories of its surviving citizens.

Helpless, we stood and watched the destruction of Rome, the hatred growing with each leap of the flames. Then, Korax stood behind me and whispered in my ear, "Methinks that the attention of the garrison is not concerned with the center of this hill."

He was right, of course. The Vestal Virgins, themselves, could be dancing naked in the streets of the Capitoline and be totally unnoticed this night.

Retributio (Vengeance)

Korax rapped the knocker on the door, then again for emphasis. I merely stood and waited, apparently serene in my desire to visit this household, although uninvited as it were. Again the rap, and with a vigor that might itself shiver the door if the fastenings were in any way insecure. Finally, we heard the sound of a release of the bar being lifted, or a ring latch removed. Slowly the heavy door creaked open and the face of an old man - a house slave without doubt - looked out. For a moment, he just looked at us, in the flare of the torch that Korax was carrying, then said, "The Master wishes not to be interrupted for any reason."

I paid no heed to the given desires of the Master as spoken by the slave, stepping forward and pushing the door with such force that the old man fell to his backside. Korax yanked him to his feet and growled, "Take to your quarters and let not your face be seen before daylight unless you wish to taste the point of my spear." The man scuttled away in fear as we strode into the hallway. As I had seen the household of an upper-class noble when in visit to the family of Camillus, I was familiar with what we would see - the innumerable stone heads of past ancestors, woven material covering the walls and floor, the atrium with the massive pool and pots of flowers. And scattered benches and tables for leisure. Tonight, the reclining benches were being used for the purpose of repose.

Two young men were reclining in the Roman fashion, the table before them holding the cups of wine which were obviously the tool being used to forget any perturbations that might be troubling them. One turned his head, but without seeing our approach and called, "Nonus! Who was the whoreson banging on the door at this hour?" With no answer from the slave, he turned to look with sotted eyes - eyes that took an interminable time to finally realize that the two men approaching were not of the staff of the house.

With a curse that brought the head of his companion from its cup, the man rose unsteadily, to face us on wobbling legs. "The army is forbidden to enter this household without sanction by the Master." Obviously, the man assumed that we were Legionaries come for whatever reason - maybe to implore the help of two brave men in repelling the hordes outside the quarter. He was wrong in his assumption.

My gladius entered the heart of the man just gaining his feet as the weapon of Korax speared the life from the one who had spoken. I thought no more of our actions than had they been against vermin caught in my fish-basket on the boat of my patér. Neither of the noble drones of Caeus were more than puny obstacles between myself and my long craved meeting with their master.

We quickly searched the rooms on the bottom floor of the huge house, finding that it was indeed deserted, except for the cringing slave in his miserable quarters and another old woman - probably the cook. Next, we mounted the elaborate steps to the upper part of the house, now carefully looking into each room as we passed. As most of the doors were open and showing nothing but the glare of the Hadesfire of the city through the windows, we were could see that they had no occupants.

"There." Korax was pointing to a door at the end of the hall. Barely, in the gloom, we could see long slivers of light through the cracks of the planks. I nodded as we quietly walked forward, with myself giving a prayer to Jupiter that my quarry might not in his cups this night. At the end of the hallway, we listened but heard nothing, then Korax gently pulled the elaborate loop of rope that would open the door. It barely moved, then he let it close again without sound. He grinned and nodded.

There was the pause of a moment as I thought briefly of the actions that brought me to this house, then jerked my head sharply. Korax pulled the door open, and I strode in as if it were my own cubliculum. Time slowed to a crawl as I looked around the huge sleeping room - one that was larger than the entire houses of most citizens. Oil lamps were around the walls, giving usable light on this night, although should one remove the thick woven coverings over the several windows, the inferno of the dying city might illume the room as if in the light of the sun.

Nothing took my attention but the man in the room, sitting at a table in the Greek manner, a cup before him and a scroll. And...

On the bed, a woman, naked as the day she was birthed, but with the golden tresses that I remembered, although now much longer than her usual style. There was a collar around her neck and a chain leading somewhere, the sight causing another mark to be added to the fanciful scroll of my mind - a mark in a tally of wrongs to be discussed with the man before me.

It was her reactions that began the long-awaited encounter. It started with a look at the men entering the room who were obviously not the two drones belonging to the master of the house, then a sudden recognition that was immediately rejected by her mind. The sudden scream brought the youngest Fabius to his feet, wondering at the cause. It was difficult to determine which was the more stupefied -

the man or the woman. He must have known of the killing of the Circus guards and the removal of myself from the wall or, at least, my body as he probably hoped, but I had no doubt that he had gloatingly told Ravana of my death by crucifixion, but not of the possibility of my having survived the unsurvivable.

I merely stood, my gladius sheathed, and took my eyes from the woman - the time for the joy of reunion would come later. Now was the time of discussion between men, and in such, a woman is of no course.

Caeso slowly stood, still trying to believe the sight that his eyes were displaying, but he recovered soon enough. Sneeringly, he said, "Not content with escaping your just punishment, you return to beg for more." Backing up to a table, he picked up his scabbard, without haste as I was still standing with no move of menace. "This time, I will drive the nails myself, and through more than your limbs." He slowly drew the blade, tossing the scabbard to the floor.

I still just stood, looking at the weapon with contempt. It was a court toy, with a gilded hilt and blade that had been silver-washed, and made thinly to keep the weight to a lesser amount. I would not have depended on such for defense against my enraged sister, far less an opponent with a soldier's weapon.

"Besides being a despicable traitor, you have dared to enter my household as a skulking thief." He looked past me at the open door, then called loudly, "Gallerius! Cominius! Attend me at once!"

Korax was just leaning on his spear, grinning at Ravana in her total dazement, but looked up to say, "They are waiting, pierside at the river Styx, oh Mighty one. But fear not, the boat will not pole for Hades until their master arrives to pay the fee for all."

Still, I waited, the pleasure of the moment almost as the climax with a woman. Caeso, however, had less patience. This was probably the first time in his life that mere commoners had dared to display impertinence to his face, and his training for such an event was nonexistent. I suddenly realized that his incensed outburst was real and not feigned - that he actually harbored the belief that his birth had made him superior to all other men of lesser position - and certainly over that of a mere scribe of the Plebs.

I finally spoke, slowly and with great emphasis. I wished him to have food for thought for his long sojourn in the domain of Hades. "All know of the identity of the actual traitor of Rome - that Domina-bitch of long ago that whelped the first pup that would become the beginning of the family of Fabius and a long line of mongrel dogs. And each litter even more worthless and nondescript than the last, until the line reached the nadir of ineptitude in the man I see before me." My treatise was unrehearsed, merely stated for my own pleasure. For all of my knowledge, the earlier generations of the Fabius family could have been - and probably were - upstanding and honorable Romans.

But to the man before me, reddening in the face even as I watched, the words were as salt in an open wound, especially as coming from a despicable commoner and one who had been condemned to death by crucifixion. He had not the experience to know that a man who can raise the ire of his foe has half the battle won.

His lunge with his blade was as Forum player, japing the soldier that he is portraying. My gladius slid out of the scabbard with ease, hitting the jabbing iron of Caeso with edge to flat. I did not wish to shiver his blade with a hard stroke - the shattered end might continue on its path and sting myself, even with no arm behind it. The touch of my iron merely moved the point aside to pass far from my skin, but with the wielder standing forward in a wide stance and with no balance for the next stroke. I took a long step forward, now well inside of his weapon's bite and brought my foot up with strength - a strength that was fortified with a hate now bubbling to the surface of my being.

His weapon clattered to the floor as the young man fell to his knees, clutching his manhood in a vain attempt to alleviate the massive hurt to his pouchstones - a hurt that I well knew, from the stroke of the Ypoploíarchos on the island of the pirates. I stepped back to allow him room to feel his pain. Suddenly, I felt the need to lecture a man deficient in the art of self-defense.

"Long ago, on an island, I learned the lesson of hate, and to never deliberately debase a man that you do not intend to kill. Hatred is the longest lasting emotion and will stand the passing of years without end. It also engenders a need for vengeance, and even to the death of the wronged, if that is the necessity required to requite the deed." He looked up at me with pain-glazed eyes, and I knew that he was proficient in the art of hating. And becoming even more so by each passing heartbeat.

I walked over to the raised and large bed platform to look at Ravana, still wide-eyed in disbelief at what was happening. I could see that the collar around her neck was held closed by the last link in the chain, but that the link was split. It had been inserted into the collar holes, then through the next circle of chain-metal, being closed with a hammer, most likely. I gestured to Korax, then pointed to the link. Walking over, he examined it, then nodded.

I turned back to my student, preparing my next lesson. Caeso had gripped his sword, and had risen to his feet, although still with his face distorted in pain. I moved to stand between him and the door, waiting for his attention to move from his pouchstones and back to his tormenter. Korax had taken the torch and left the room.

With a sudden lunge, the young noble swung the blade in a sweeping overhand stroke, as if he were chopping stovewood for the cookery, although I doubt that he had ever even entered the place where the lowly menials prepared his food. Again, I pushed the blade aside, the desperate swing continuing until the end of the gladius struck the floor.

As he desperately pulled with both hands on the hilt of his weapon, trying to extract the point from the wood of the floor, I spoke again. "After the island, I learned the folly of assuming the quality of a man by examining his appearance. An old Greek of Athens, by the name of Leodes, gave me the lesson, much as I am now giving you." I paused, then continued, "But, as he was a much more learned instructor than my humble self, the lesson was given with far less pain than with my clumsy efforts."

With a last mighty pull, he staggered back holding his sword. I stepped forward to stare into his face, but out of the reach of his metal. "Aye. I can see that you are learning the lesson of hate, and well." I nodded, satisfied, then continued, "Later in my life, I met a general - a man of some repute, good and true - and he taught me that sometimes the greatest stroke can be aimed at the front, but delivered to the back." I suddenly hit his weapon arm with the flat of my blade, and with considerable force, causing him to turn on his unstable legs. Now, the point of my gladius bit, but in the side of his neck. Watching the gush of redness spurt from his flesh, I knew that the cubiculum slave would have a considerable toil to remove the splotches of life-blood now beginning to soak into the polished wood of the floor - and in ever increasing amounts.

Now he backed against the wall, not lifting his blade, but allowing it just to rest the tip on the floor. His flaming hatred had been extinguished as suddenly as a cook fire that is doused with a bucket of water. I was no grizzled veteran, although recent events were sharpening my martial skills, but this younger man was as a child who beats his fists in enragement against an older brother for the theft of his sweetmeat. And that realization came to him with emphasis.

It was now replaced by fear. He now realized that his pretension of warriorship was sufficient to impress the females of his family, and the slaves and servants and fawning friends, but it was just that - a pretension. He fell back to wield his only remaining weapon.

"I can make you wealthy beyond even the nobles of the hill. And remove the decree of your death. I will speak to the Senators this very night for your quarter." His eyes kept blinking as he attempted to maintain his stance, but I knew that he was already dead. My presence - or nay - would make no change to that fact. I could see the red life emerge from his neck with every pulse of his heart. His imminent demise did not lessen my hatred for the man, who had not only tried to destroy myself, but whose cowardly act at Clusium was even now in the progress of consuming my city and most of the citizens who had called it their home.

"After you nailed me to that wall in the Circus, and I had given my final curses for my fate, succor came in the form of unimagined friendship. I knew from that moment that all the gold of Croesus was as a coin of lead when compared to the value of a friend. And I would not trade that friendship for your noble name and all the gold on the slopes of Olympus."

I doubted that he understood my soliloquy, or even heard it as words. When the blood tunnel of the neck is pierced, however slightly, the life of a man is measured in mere heartbeats. He was swaying as a tree in a wind, held upright only by the three point posture of his legs and the support of the sword.

Hearing a sound behind me, I glanced to see the flickering of torchlight through the doorway, growing brighter until Korax appeared, holding a hammer and a bar. Apparently he had found the quarters of the auturgus - the servant worker that maintained the edifice of the house and the multitude of chairs and carts and conveyances needed for a noble household. Even as he entered, the thump of a body to the wooden floor behind me drew my attention back to my nemesis. As I watched, the light left the eyes of the young man, and in a few drops of the waterclock, my vengeance was complete.

For a moment, Korax and I just looked at each other, unspeaking our thoughts. Then, suddenly as a waking person, we turned to approach Ravana, standing beside the mat platform and with her face attempting to display relief, astoundment, and disbelief all in one form. "Junius," she said, over and over as we approached.

"Lay her down on the floor," said Korax. I pulled her away from the wall, then gently pushed her down until she was laying prone.

The Greek knelt and carefully placed the end of the iron wedge into the split of the chain link - now touching the wooden floor - then with the hammer, hit a sharp blow. The split of the link was easily widened and in moments she was free of both the collar and chain.

Pulling her to her feet, she wrapped her arms around me and with a cataclysmic burst of weeping. Looking over her head at Korax, I said, "Check the other rooms for some garments. She cannot emerge as a naked female among a host of soldiers." He nodded and disappeared again with the torch.

Now she was bubbling with more questions and statements than could be answered in a half month, but as she waited for no reply between them, it was of no matter. "He said you were crucified. I did not believe it, but... How did you find me? Where is..." I just let her talk through her tears.

Finally, as she began to slow her talk for need of air in her bout of singultus - hiccups, as Korax called them - I managed to insert a word or two. "Nay. There will be much time for questions, but as for now, we will wait until you have regained your poise. Much has happened, and is happening that you are probably ignorant of, and your freedom - even our lives - may be in short measure."

Korax returned with an armload of garments. "The rooms are full of female garb. If these do not suffice, there are many more."

I scrabbled through them, saying "Nay, she cannot appear in a stola. The less attention she garners the better for all of us. Remember the aversion of the Centurion for useless mouths on this hill, and I am afraid that the category includes all women."

"She has no chance of hiding those bumps under a tunic," replied the Greek, pointing to her prominent mammaries. "Even a half-blind graybeard will see that she is female."

Ravana had caught her breath. "Is there a strophium in the pile?"

Korax and I looked at each other blankly, having never heard the word before. She just moved to the scattered mound of garments, tossing clothes to either side. Finally, she stood up with a band of cloth, an extended hand in width, then pulled it over her head. As it was far too loose, she removed it, untying the knot. Wrapping it around her mid-section, she measured the length, the retied the cloth into a band. Now, the undergarment, pulled over her projecting mammaries, flattened them considerably - not to the point of being unnoticed by an attentive male, but at least not allowing them to protrude and wobble as waving pennants of her sex.

The best we could do was a thick tunic, stretching to below the knees, and tied with a cloth belt. Now, her hair was the problem. It had grown very long since the time that I had last seen her, and the golden tresses would be instantly noticed even by men watching the fires of Vulcan.

We departed the room of Caeso - I looking at him for the last time - and followed Korax into the rear of the house. There, in the rooms of the slaves and servants, we searched until we found the cap of a workman, woolen and shapeless. Shortly, the golden hair was encased within, and Ravana was no longer immediately recognizable - at least at night.

At the door of the house, we paused while I slowly opened it to determine if any soldiers or citizens might be standing in the street to see us depart the house of Fabius. My eyes, used to nothing but the oil lamps of the house, and the torch of Korax, blinked as the light shone in the door. For a heartbeat, I thought that we had tarried in the dwelling until daylight, but another look gave the knowledge that the illumination was not the warm rays of the sun, but the evil glare of a dying city.

It was fortunate that no person was in sight, as the fires made visibility as good as a sunlit day. I motioned for my friends to follow to another abandoned house - this one on the edge of the slope. Inside, I did not climb the stairs, as the roof would be filled with men and soldiers, watching the inferno. Rather, I moved into a room that would gain a view of the city through a window. There, we stood and watched the burning of Rome.

Of course, Korax and I knew the sight that would appear through the window, although the flames had grown since while we were transacting our business in the house of Fabius, but for Ravana, it was a sudden sight as of Tartarus - the flaming domain of Hades. She gasped and put her hand to her mouth, unbelieving that she was awake, and not squirming in the night-dreams of rich food and drink.

Time passed. On the morrow, our thoughts would be as to our future plans, but this night was just to watch a sight that would be unbelieved in the tales of oldsters to their children's children, on some future evening as they sat before the fire. Even should some priest, or scribe, scribble a description of this night, the readers of future times will assign it to the same fanciful construct as the stories of gorgons and monsters and heroic god-deeds.

Finally, I drew them away from the window, and we walked to the small servants quarters that I had made my house during the siege.

There, Ravana would stay during the hours of daylight, until some scheme was concocted to allow us to escape this sight of Hades.

Suddenly, exhausted, I lay down on the mat for rest. For that night, Ravana shared my mat, but not in the meaning of Eros, but as womanly assurance that I was still there during the dark hours. The fact of her freedom was known by her inner being, but not yet believed, thus, she clung to me as a drowning woman until the morning.

Obsessio (Siege)

By the following evening, the fires had consumed most of the city and were now just banked coals, giving little flame. The sun was blotted out by the thick clouds of smoke that rose from every quarter of the city. And to increase the assault on the eyes and breathing sacs came the sweetly sickening aroma of roasted corpses - the remains of the citizens who had failed to flee the city in time and had been speared down, in the streets.

A few forays were made against the hill, but the contrived fortress of the Capitoline was immune to the reach of the crude ladders of the Gauls. Without a single stroke of a blade or thrust of a spear, the attacks were thrown back with massive losses among the unfortunates who were sliding and stumbling on the steep slopes. The thrown and dropped stones, falling from a height twice that of the city walls, smashed and broke the attackers as if they were clay pots.

Then, arrows with fiery points were shot into and over the hill, in an attempt to emulate the massive burning of the city before. From the first fiery shaft that appeared, men were detailed to watch for any that struck, immediately dousing the shafts with water.

Little happened after that. We could see an encampment below the hill, on each road leading from the quarter, except for the western Via - immediately terminating at the burned bridge. This was obviously to maintain the siege while the rest of their army turned to other duties. From our heights, we could see the bands of the Gauls marching away from the city, no doubt to pillage and loot the nearby hamlets and villages. As the storehouses and granaries had been fired along with the rest of the city, the area inside the walls was even less hospitable than the sandy Egyptian desert.

The view of the city from the roofs of the Capitoline was as of Hades. The major buildings were still standing, shorn of their combustible roofs, and blacked with the fires of the night. Piles of bricks and partial walls marked the lesser areas where the prosperous merchants had lived, but in the far quarters of the poor was as a black desert, with nothing but a cryer's stone block still standing, or a part of a stable that had somehow escaped the flames. With the city empty of most structures, it was easy to estimate the number of Gauls roaming the city, and that number was far in excess of the men on the Capitoline hill.

The Centurion and his officers met daily, attempting to ascertain the proper path forward. For myself, I saw nothing that could be done. Certainly, the fortress of the Capitoline was well stocked with food, and the few wells were deep, although dug for the purpose of supplying clean water for this noble family or that, not designed to water an entire quarter. As the population of the hill was now only a fraction of the previous number of occupants, we could hold out almost indefinitely. But to what end? A few hundred men could not drive away the Gauls, to allow the scattered citizens to return and rebuild. And if the Senones decided that their homeland was the surrounding plains, then Rome - and we - were eventually doomed.

I was making plans to leave - the three of us. That I could see no future here was a given, but also, as Ravana did not exist to the garrison, three people were sharing two rations. As the hidden woman needed much less sustenance than an active man, it was not a pressing problem as yet, but eventually, it would become so. I had hunted around to find a sufficient length of rope to allow us to descend the crude wall at the western end of the hill - two actually, since I could not hope that Ravana would be able to descend hand over hand in the manner of a male. She would need to be lowered, just as I had lifted her in the escape from the Palace in Memphis.

With the utter intoxication of her rescue and my sudden appearance as from the dead beginning to cool, Ravana could tell us of her experiences. As I had thought, the raid on my house was at the instigation of Caeso himself. She had been taken immediately to his household and the chain and collar was attached. There she lived, without release until the appearance of both Korax and myself. She had not been abused physically, other than being required to service the young noble at will, but the torture consisted of being told the fate, as it happened, to myself. "That bastardus of Set gloried in his tales of your imprisonment in the Mamertine and later, the news of your... death. I had no desire for a life chained to a mat, for the use of a man that I hated with all the fiber of my being. My nights were filled with dreams and schemes and plots to destroy that spawn of Hades, by cutting his throat while he mounted me and was in his throes."

She lowered her head for a moment, obviously the memories still green in the extreme. "But... he well knew of my hatred and I was never allowed to possess even the shard of a broken pot."

She was returning to the existential woman of before, but with a subtle change. The realization of the fact that she was a woman - however self-reliant - in a world of men, had been forced upon her being. One evening, as Korax was obtaining our ration, she sat next to me and said, quietly, "You have been more than a mate to me since our first meeting in Athens. And few men would risk all to bring succor to a loose woman as you have, and time and again." A pause, then to my astonishment, she said, "I will be your mate, and only yours, for as long as you will have me. And when my paps begin to fall, I will not complain should you take a younger femina for your needs."

Speechless, I just sat for a moment trying to find words. She smiled in the dim lamplight, and said, "And I well know of the level of your needs, far above the common man." With that she lay back on the mat, pulling me onto her. As I had had no woman for months, and indeed, little time to notice the lack, our joining was short, but as the sudden and violent storm of a summer day. When Korax returned with our scanty meals, he found two people relaxing apart, and in casual conversation.

Little happened on the hill for the next half month. The Gauls maintaining the siege at the base of the hill were still there, and even fewer than ourselves. Officers gave requests to lead a sudden foray against them, confident of our ability to rout and destroy the foe in a sudden attack. The Centurion forbade all such raids. "We cannot lose men except for immediate cause. Our few hundred are all that remain between the Gauls and the ending of Rome itself, and no replacements are forthcoming. Even the utter destruction of the band below the hill would be a drop in a wine jar to their numbers."

For myself, I could not understand how the men at the base of the hill could maintain their siege in the massively thick miasma of the thousands of decaying bodies in the streets of the city. Even on our high hill, we were sickened on occasion, when the winds were from this quarter or that. How any man could sustain an existence deep in the sea of stinks and reeks below was beyond my understanding.

One night, late, I was woken by a touch to my arm. My hand was instantly on the hilt of my gladius until Korax spoke, quietly, "Something is happening. What, I do not know." I rose immediately, pulling on my tunic and sandals, and we exited the servant's building to enter the main via of the quarter. Torches were glaring in front of the Senate House, and we hurried in that direction. We found the Centurion and officers gathered around a man...

I could see that the tunic of the man was wet, as was his hair. It was obvious that he had swum the Tiber and climbed the western slope to the barrier. How he entered the fortress, I did not know, assuming that he had called from below and had satisfied the defenders as to his legitimacy. That he was a messenger from the remnants of the army at Veii was evident and confirmed to me with his statements. And that he was bringing news of great repute was seen in the excited manner of all who were standing around him.

The Centurion was querying the man about the status of the Legion in that deserted city and the man was giving his knowledge. "...and Camillus gave prophesy to the citizens of Ardea and Corea and Antium, telling them that the paths of their lives gave them only two choices - die or fight, and to decide quickly." I knew that the cities of which he spoke were to the south, opposite the direction to Veii. "He gathered the males of those cities and villages, and more, to make a defense at the Polmanian marshes." The messenger looked around, then pointed to a stone bench on the steps of the Senate House. "Your pardon, Sos. If I may sit? My legs have gone far this night and are not as young as they were when I was a young spear-Velite in my old contubernium."

"Aye." The Centurion pointed to a man and ordered, "Bring a cup for the soldier."

"My thanks, Sos," said the soldier. Sitting, he continued. "Then, word came that the barbarians were in their cups and celebrating the looting of the hamlet of Albalonga. In a quick march, Camillus fell upon the sotted and weary scum, utterly destroying all but a few that fled into the trees."

There was a murmur of approval around the circle. And a feeling that the dawn might be about to break from the black night of Rome.

After a goodly swallow of sweet wine, the soldier proceeded with his message. "That army is now under the leadership of his son, Lucius and is fortifying the hills at Ardea. The Senior Camillus has gone to Veii, at the supplication of the surviving Senators there. He was offered a Generalship with the Consul Quintus, but said..." He paused, then said, "The words he uttered may cause offense to the name of Fabius."

"May the excrement piles of Olympus be poured onto the heads of that family and all their putrid kin!" The Centurion literally spat out the curse, and it was underscored by the mutterings in the ranks. "Speak your words without fear of that clan in this encampment!"

Wide-eyed, the man nodded. "Aye... Ah... Camillus said that he would rather lay on the love-mat with the corpses of barbarians, than associate with the family of Fabius." Another gulp of wine, then, "The Senate instantly proclaimed him Dictatorius for the period of a year, and bade the senior Fabius, Quintus, to depart their presence with haste."

"As his first act, and before the dismissed Consul had turned to go, he took a spear from a soldier, and ran it through the body of the senior Fabius. His words were, 'Death to all fools!'" Now the applause in the ranks was palpable, with men grinning and slapping the backs of their mates.

"His message to you is thusly..." Now the man stood, and straightened. "'From the Dictator Camillus, to the Centurion and men of Rome, even now standing as a Roman wall against the barbarians come to destroy our lives and our future... A thousand years will pass and still the bards and sages will speak of the deeds of those brave few that dared to stand against the hordes from the north. You must hold until the Legion can accumulate the force that can march to the relief of the city. Thus, I charge you, men of Rome.'"

The man fell silent, but his words had struck fire into all that listened. The grins and japes of both officers and men were evidence of that.

The Centurion gave an order. "Decanus Marcus! Find this good soldier a mat and a rasher of meat if he desires - he has well accomplished his mission this night."

The month passed, with all watching the horizon for the Legion of Rome to appear, but with the knowledge that a scattered army is not reconstituted in mere days, even by such an august man as Marcus Camillus. I - and Korax - took our turned at watches on the roofs of the houses, as did all within the fortress of the Capitoline - citizens and soldiers alike. Despite my first belief that the hidden Ravana was the only female in the garrison, I found that I was in error. Several women had come forth - a few Dominae of from great houses and others that were servants and slaves of such - all having emerged from their hiding after the first nights of chaos. Of course, none came into the daylight with any knowledge of the burning of Rome, nor the fact that they were now inside a fortress from which there was no departure.

Despite his desire to have none on the hill except men of fighting age, the Centurion could scarcely throw the women over the walls - nor the aged Senators and their wives. Instead, the women became the cocuae of the camp - preparing the food for the men under the hand of the quartermaster. It was soon realized that this arrangement was superior to the previous issue. Now, each man could be assured of equal rations and that none was eating more at the expense of his fellows. Also, the cook-fires were in the center of the square and easily controlled for both the cooking and later, banking until the next meal. Now the many individual fires were prohibited elsewhere around the hill - it would be a disaster for an ignored flame to begin again the work of the Senones.

For Ravana, the emergence of the other women was as a gift from the gods. Rather than sitting, day by day in an empty room, with only her black thoughts and two men for company and that only when we were not required elsewhere, she could move around in the company of other females - at least in the quartermaster area. They were forbidden to wander around the quarter for obvious reasons - their own safety from men long from their women, and the need for the soldiers to watch the foe without the distraction of bouncing female flesh that could be glimpsed under tattered garments.

With the permission of the quartermaster, I would escort Ravana to our small room for the night, delivering her back in time for her duties with the morning meals. The work was a balm to her spirits after the months chained to a mat.

The Gauls had built their encampment in the forum, erecting tents for the men who were not elsewhere in the countryside and pillaging loot and food. Again, my wonder at the establishment of a camp in a city of decaying bodies, although enough time had passed that the miasma had decreased greatly from that first quarter month. Still, the air of the lower city was not that of a flowered atrium.

On the hill, we were ignored - not even arrows were lofted into our quarter. We assumed that the Gauls were merely waiting for our foodstuffs to become exhausted before we either treated for mercy or emerged in a last desperate and self-destructive battle. Neither was true. They were merely waiting for our complacency to wax and our vigilance to wane.

Much later - years, in fact - as I had the leisure to examine the past and the siege of the Capitoline, this night was another wondrous manifestation of my status as a game figure on the board of the gods. Of the hundreds of men inside the walls, how else could it be believed that a commoner of the basest antecedents, even once a mere fisher-boy on the Tiber, was the one man standing in the place of need? Without that throw of the bones or just the whim of that game-playing deity, Rome would have ceased to exist.

As it happened, I was awakened that night by a need to make my water with some urgency. Afterward, the night being cool, and with the western wind fresh and blowing the smells of the city away, I walked the empty via of the Capitoline toward the western wall. Climbing to the top of the stone wall that had been hastily erected before the fall of the city, I nodded to the sentry, exchanging a short greeting about the pleasant night. Below, and not far, I could see the faint outline of my old household, now shorn of the burned roof but with the walls still erect. Beyond that was the Tiber, a faint glint in the starlight.

Gauls seldom patrolled this side of the hill, as there was little left between the Capitoline and the river. Any foray by the defenders of the hill here would find them in a narrow corridor, bound by the steep slope on one side and the water on the other with the northern and southern as choke points where a few of the Senones could hold a Maniple at bay.

Conversely, as the hill was the steepest at this point, it was unlikely for any assault to begin here by the Gauls. A man would have to support his mate for that man to wield a weapon. Unfortunately, that thinking, while correct, was for a frontal assault.

I walked along the top of the stones that barred the western via to the hill, coming to the much taller wall that encircled the Temple of Juno. A ladder had been placed against it, to allow the watch to climb to the top to make his sentry-go. Still, I was enjoying the cool breeze and was deep in thought about our method of leaving the city. I could see no defect in it, except for the slight possibility of our running into a group of Gauls in the darkness, but...

I was not sure that I wished to leave now, on the cusp of great happenings.

I climbed to the top of the Temple wall, the greater height giving me an unneeded and much farther view of the river. A night and day of bobbing in the river would bring us to the port of Ostia, and without much effort, even for a person of no ability in the water, such as Korax. From there, a skiff would be hired to our make our ship, anchored in the harbor. Shortly, the vision of Rome and its ashes would be only a memory.

Still, even a man as rootless as myself has an underlying need to call a place his home. Rome certainly was my birthplace, but that boy on the deck of the fishing boat was as another person... Suddenly, I wondered about the fate of those boats and my family. From my heights, I could see no vessels on the shore, which made much sense. A man with a home that could be moved at will would certainly have taken domicile, family and all away at the threat of the onrushing invaders. Possibly, they were even now anchored in the port of Ostia, giving no...

The sudden honking of the sacred geese, below in the courtyard of the Temple of Juno, brought me out of my reverie. Remembering my young distaste for the unfriendly fowls in the flock of my sister, I wondered at the reason for the deity to consider them as...

Now the birds began to cry in earnest, as if... I stared into the blackness of the courtyard, trying to see anything - and without success. But... There, on the bare edge of visibility was movement of a sort. And far too much and too quickly for the single ancient priest and his pair of boy acolytes.

Instantly, I turned to the ladder and dropped to the top of the street blocking stones, barely using one rung in three as I almost fell in my descent. I did not bother with the guard on the wall - too much time would pass during his incredulous questions that would ensue if I told the tale. Without running the length of the stones to the other ladder, I just sat on the stone, swung around and allowed myself to drop the distance into the street. Now, at a dead run, I made for the bed-mat of the Centurion.

"Sos! Sos!" I shouted as I ran into the stone building past the surprised officer on the duty watch. The Centurion was of considerable age, but he came from his mat as a young man stung in his blanket by a scorpion. Without preamble, I said, desperately, "Sos! The Senones are in the grounds of the Temple of Juno!"

He made no question to my incredulous statement, only grabbing his scabbard and rushing for the door. To the men who were even now waking from my shouts, he yelled, "Sound the alarm! All men not on the wall to the Temple of Juno!"

Battles are seldom conducted at night. The problems of identification of friend and foe and of trying to carry a torch, along with a weapon and shield are almost insurmountable. Knowing thus, I ran to one of the piles of torches, kept ready on the unlikely chance of a foray of the enemy at night. With an armload, I ran back to the wall, even ahead of the assembling men. Climbing the ladder to the top of the piled stones with as many as I could clasp between my off hand and my breast, I said to the guard, "Bring your torch, and quickly." He was just looking at me, not understanding my urgency, nor the sudden stirring in the camp. "The Gauls are in the temple!"

Now he strode to take the burning lamp from its holder, and we hurried to the ladder leading to the top of the temple compound wall. We could see the first of the soldiers running along the via - at least the men carrying torches were evident. At the base of the wall, I said, "Hold here until our men reach the gates." My worry was that a man holding a light would be an easy target for any bowmen below in the compound. Probably, that is what happened to the two guards that were detailed to walk the wall and roofs of the temple.

Measuring the pace of the Romans running up the street, I made my move. Telling the guard to follow, I climbed the ladder and set the pile of torches on top of the stones. Then, stooping to touch the cone to the flame of the one carried by the soldier, I held it upside down until it was well aflame, then stood and tossed it far into the compound. The arcing flight of the torch gave dim light to my eyes and verification to my fears. Indeed, the enemy was in the temple, but not in the numbers that I had feared.

The torch hit the ground, but still gave the vision of shadows for the Romans now entering the temple gate. Quickly, I lit one after another and threw them here and there into the grounds. The honking of the geese was now submerged in the clamor of battle as half visible shadows hacked and thrust. The men of the Centurion quickly overwhelmed the infiltrators, following the path of their entrance back to the far wall, behind the acolyte quarters. The light of day showed that a few Senones had quietly climbed the steep hill, then quietly feathered the two guards on the top of the buildings. With the long trunk of a needle tree laying against the building exterior, the branches shorn to make short rungs, some vigorous Gaul managed to reach the top of the roof of the quarters of the acolytes, carrying a knotted rope to allow his fellows to follow. Fortunately, that method of infiltration was slow and tedious, with only one man reaching the top at each time. But, had the geese not sounded their call, and the Gauls allowed to accumulate in the temple throughout the night - as the Romans had done in the siege of Veii - the ending of the tale could have been much different.

The reaction of the Centurion was immediate. The torches on the walls were placed to illuminate the outside wall and view of the slopes, as usual, but the guards were placed back in the shadows, rather than beside the flames as if they were standing at a nighttime campfire.

For myself, I received some unneeded accolades for my action. "You have some strange abilities for a scribe, Lucius," was the comment of the Centurion. I merely nodded and repressed my smile on hearing, once again, that old comment. "And much wit at the top of your chine. Had you not discovered the incursion, we would now be comrades in Hades."

I was still not a soldier but was given the status of staff member to the Centurion. I had little else to advise, but the unofficial rank allowed me much greater freedom on the hill. I could now come and go without the requirement of giving my cause and waiting for approval.

It would make our flight much easier, should I decide to depart the city.

Pestilentia (Plague)

Little else happened for a quarter month, although the news circulated around the camp that the youngest male of the Fabii family had been found in his quarters, slain. That it was not a natural death was indicated by the bodies of his two hangers-on, discovered lifeless of wounds in the atrium. It was a topic to alleviate the boredom of camp life and welcome to all that the last of that despicable line was ended.

Then a call came from the guards at the eastern side of the Capitoline. Hurrying there, and climbing to heights, we could see a single Gaul, standing in the middle of the Via Longus. He was holding a long sword but by the end of the blade, rather than the hilt.

"It would appear that the barbarians want to discuss our little confrontation," commented one of the officers.

"Aye. Mayhap they wish to surrender and find their way home," japed another.

The Centurion just looked for a moment, then said to a man, "Give the signal to agree." The officer pointed to a soldier who stepped forward with his blade and held it up by the point in mirror to the man below. Now the Gaul stepped forward until he was about halfway up the slope of the hill, still in the middle of the road. In accented, but understandable Latium, he called, "The Chief of the Senones, Brennus, wishes to treat with the leader of the Romans. He gives oath that the delegation will emerge escorted and unharmed without any course of the discussions."

The second of the Centurion, stood forth and called, "Mayhap your chief would come to meet with us, as it is his move to talk!"

"Nay. We are fully familiar with the method of discussion by Romans when the talk is not to their desire!" Once again, even though in Hades with his siblings, the despicable Caeso was defiling the reputation of all Romans.

"I will go."

All turned to look at me, in surprise. The second said, "Nay, man. We would like as get you back as skinned meat, and salted for measure."

I shook my head. "I have spoken with this Brennus, at Clusium, and know him to be an honorable man, given to keeping his oaths."

The Centurion looked at the man in the street for a moment, then turned and said, "I would dislike seeing you spitted on a pole, but we will find what it is they wish to discuss. If you wish, then go."

I was let down on a knotted rope, and walked down the hill to meet the Gaul, he patiently waiting with his sword still clasped by the end. I recognized him as one of the advisors to Brennus but did not know his name. He just nodded and we began the walk to the encampment of the Senones, in the vast expanse of the forum.

Here, in the streets, the smell of corpses had greatly decreased over the months, but was still evident as we passed the ravaged bones of the dead, laying where they fell. I assumed that the dogs of the city had feasted on the banquet, although my wonder was that any had escaped the fires. Of course, the scavenger birds had feasted mightily - that we had seen from the fortress of the Capitoline. Then... I saw the rodents moving in the shadows, a rare site in the daylight hours in the days of the populated city, even in the poorer quarters. But these were innumerable and large - fat, even. They, no doubt, were responsible for the cleanliness of the bones in the streets.

The further we walked, the more prevalent were the animals - rats, as they were called by Korax - even to the point of darting across the street in the sunlight. There was little now to make my gorge rise, after a lifetime of seeing death and destruction of guilty and innocent alike, but these... flesh gnawers made my skin prickle at the sight of their numbers and the assumption by the animals that it was they, not men, who now possessed the city.

The camp of the Senones was neat and laid out as I had seen before, although their ropes were held by heavy stones, rather than stakes that could not be driven into the pave-stone covered ground. The forum was almost unrecognizable, with most of the buildings now ash, and the stone walls of those remaining little more than empty compounds open to the sky.

We threaded our way between tents, moving to the center of the Forum area. Apparently, their looting of the surrounding countryside had not been without loss, as I saw many a man laying on his mat and being cared for by the women. Without doubt, they were recovering from wounds.

Suddenly, ahead and in front of a gaudy tent was the man I remembered from the discussions at Clusium. The massive form of the Chief was grinning as I strode up, stopping a spear's length in front. "We are met again, Junius the scribe. And I must say, of all the men to come striding from that hill top, you are the last that I expected. I would have thought that a man of your travels would be away and reading his scrolls in some far city by now."

I bowed to the Chief, then replied, "Aye, the thought has entered my mind more than once. As has the regret not to have done so."

"Come. Sit within and let us become acquainted with each others travels since last we met."

Wine was brought, and bread and cheese, and we talked as old acquaintances, rather than two enemies sitting in the ruins of a destroyed city. He gave me the story of his battles, of which I knew the tales of most - at least the results, and he gave credence to the generalship of Camillus, and admiring words for his utter destruction of the looters of Albalonga. For myself, I gave the tale of my moves and the decisions behind them and my slaying of Caeso, to which he gave hearty praise. "You have robbed me of the revenge that I had planned for that spawn of Aericura and his hell-demons. But, a favor by a friend is still welcome. One hopes that his death was not immediate."

"He watched it approach even as his lifeblood emptied to the floor. But... A thousand deaths are not enough for the man who began this strife, and in which many Romans and Gauls have seen the end of their days."

"Aye, and that is the purpose of my askance to treat." He called for more wine, then leaned forward to speak. "We are people of the open land, and a city is of no use to us. We will depart, moving back to the lands to the north, should your commander see to assuage our grief with sufficient gelt. A treaty will be signed, and both peoples left to grow and prosper on their own."

I kept my surprise within myself. This was news of a magnificent flavor, and I had no doubt of the truth coming from the chief of the Senones. But, what was the fee that he would demand?

The discussion over, he called for a meal in the interests of peace, and we discussed other than the wars and discords of the two lands. It was almost as if we were back on the banks of the upper Tiber, speaking as men wishing for the enlightenment of knowledge, rather than two ambassadors of warring lands. Finally, that I might return to the fortress on the hill before the fall of darkness, he bade me farewell and wish for a good life whatever the outcome of the strife.

As he called for an escort, I just stood, as orders were given in the Gaulish tongue, then bowed once again to take my leave. But, the eyes of the Chief were not on me, but looking to the side. Sharply, he barked a question, or order - replied to with a stuttering voice. I turned to see a man - young and accoutered for battle - standing as he replied, but swaying as the mast of a ship in a heavy swell. Suddenly, he bent at the midriff, coughing in spasms, then heaving a quantity of red wine to the stones. The hair stood on my neck as I realized that his discomfort was not from an overusage of his cup, but from his belly itself. The redness was his own lifeblood.

Two men carried him away by his arms, and the Chief turned back to me. "My apologies, Junius, my friend. Several of my men have eaten tainted meat, it appears. But, I give you my farewell and wish for a long life."

I returned the complement and turned to follow the men - now only three - detailed for my escort. As we passed through the encampment, I looked more closely at the distressed men in the tents - men who seem not to have wounds. Many were naked, the better for their womenfolk to apply wet cloths to their bodies, but the lack of garments also allowed me to see that some of the men had ugly bubos on their thighs and upper arms. And more than once, I saw the redness in a wad of cloth that indicated that the man had eaten of the same tainted meat as the one at the tent of the Chief.

I climbed the slope of the via to the knotted rope, now waiting for my return, and shortly was standing with the Centurion and his officers - even a few of the aged Senators that had managed to bestir themselves from their soft mats.

"...And his fee will be a weight of gold equal to the heaviest man in his camp. For that payment, he will leave the city and the region, and put his name to a treaty that will give lasting peace between our lands."

The discussion started immediately, with every man trying to give his opinion and all different than the last. Finally, the Centurion called for silence, saying, "The gold is nothing. Even that amount is trivial in exchange for all of Rome, but..." He looked at me. "What is the trust that can be put into his words?" A pause, then, "Lucius! Do you answer?"

I had been furiously thinking of the sights that I had passed in the encampment below, and only listening to the debate with half an ear. I started, then said, "Nay, Sos. There is another... happening that is of great importance, but of which I cannot put a reason to." I gave my description of the coughing man, and the vision of the men being nursed along my path of walk. When I described the ugly raised bumps of their thighs and arms, an old Senator suddenly burst out with a curse to the gods. As all looked in surprise, he began to explain.

"It is the pestis! The plaga! We are all doomed should we remain within a day's walk of Rome!"

The Centurion had no need for a panicked doomcryer, even one so august as a Senator. "Nay, gather yourself, noble one, and explain your meaning."

The old man nodded and spent a moment to arrange his thoughts. "As a young man, I once traveled to the city of Circeum with my patér, long ago. There we resided as some negotiations were made between Rome and the men of that city, but as a boy I would wander the waterfront, watching the boats come and go, and with strange cargos from every part of the world. One morning, a ship moved into the port, ignoring the shouts and cries of the harbor master as it drove ashore under tattered sails and only one or two sailors on board that could be seen. To my young eyes, it was excitement indeed, to see the point of the hull imbed itself in the wooden piers, and far enough to reach the mast, even."

What this long winded explanation had to do with the Senone's encampment was a mystery, but all listened with interest. "The boat was shattered, sinking to the depth of the water in only a few heartbeats, with a multitude of rats jumping for their own safety - hordes of them." He looked at me, then continued, "The men on board were as this man has described, throwing their life-blood with every cough and with upper limbs overlaid with the blue and black sores - and those running the festering suppuration of an evil smell."

Now, he definitely had the attention of the men standing around him. All had heard of the plagues that devastated this city or that, but those happenings were long ago or far away. None - other than the Senator, apparently - had ever experienced such a calamity.

"It was little thought of, other than as a point of lively conversation for a day or so, and the living sailors were taken to the medicus for healing. But, within a half month, or less, the people of Circeum were themselves falling ill, and in great numbers - festering with the boils and blood spasms that our scribe has described as happening just below us."

"What was the cause?" asked an officer.

The Senator spread his hands. "Nay. I only know that the evil malady came on that boat from a far land, but as to what was the propagator... This man has told of innumerable rats in the city, and the boat of that plague in my youth was filled with them. Perhaps it is the rodents that carry the disease."

"The disease that is being described below did not arrive on a boat," countered another. "The barbarians have no concept of either ships nor shipping."

The Senator replied, impatiently, "Nonetheless, if we remain in the vicinity, then we too will die, one after the other, as will the Senones, to the number of four in five."

"The news needs to be carried to the Dictatorius Camillus at Veii," said the Centurion. "He must not enter the city, and by waiting, he may find his foe to be handed into his hands without strife."

A sudden thought hit me like a bolt of lighting. So as to not allow another to mar my sudden plan, I said to the Centurion, "Sos, if this plague is indeed spread from man to man, and in only days, then I should leave at once so as not to pollute your garrison. I will take the message to the Dictatorius, should you agree, and the time in the travel will give notice as to whether I carry this pestilence."

There was some discussion, but the plan was agreed on with haste, much of it from the fear that I had engendered with my speaking of being a carrier of this new foe. It was agreed that I would take my man and my women, who could not be left here alone without a male of responsibility. That agreed to, I hurried to inform both Korax and Ravana of our departure, even this night.

"The river!" shouted Korax. "Why do you not ask me to swim to Memphis, as that would have the same chance of success?"

I smiled. "Nay. The Tiber is calm in this season, barely deeper than you are tall. And you will be in the water for only a few heartbeats. You have my oath on it." Ravana just nodded. She would travel where I said.

The balance of the day was spent in preparing. I needed a number of items - three ropes sufficient to span the river, two waterbags and a leather sack with hard rations. Long before the sun had set, I was ready and resting for the night's labor.

The moon was in half light, but the night was cloudy and dark. Unless we carelessly stumbled into a group of wandering Senones, there was little chance of our being seen. The Centurion was on the wall with us, and several men, all accoutered for battle. "These men will escort you to the river, in the case of the odd barbarian who is unable to sleep." He put his hand on my shoulder, then finished with, "May the gods go with you, Lucius the scribe. Tell the Dictatorius that the barbarians will usurp the Capitoline only after every man is dead, and that we wait his appearance with bated breath."

I had long told Korax and Ravana of my new name - actually now being Lucius Junius - so as they would not mar my tale by wondering aloud at the change. "Aye, Sos. I will be in Veii in a quarter month at the latest, unless we appear to have been touched by the plague. If indeed that becomes true, we will move to the north, away from any danger to the army until we are either dead or recovered."

With another clasp of my shoulder, he ordered the knotted ropes dropped and the escorts began to descend. For Ravana, she was circled with a smoother line, and I carefully lowered her to the street below the stacked blocks. Then in heartbeats, both Korax and I were down. Following the men, we slowly threaded our way along the short road - a via that used to lead to the Pons Sublicius - the bridge leading over the Tiber to the Via Aurelia - the road to Ostia.

Of course, the bridge had been burned that night with the rest of the city, but it was no matter. At the bank, I prepared the three ropes that I had brought, tying one around Korax, another around Ravana and the last to our leather sack holding our rations and purses, and to the waterbags. I had lashed the spear of Korax to his back knowing that otherwise, he would drop it in the Tiber at his first thrashings.

Swimming the river easily, I felt of the knots that I had put in the end of each rope that would tell me of what - or whom - it was attached to. Firstly, I quickly pulled on the one that was attached to our supplies and it was soon on the bank beside me. Next, I gave a double tug on the rope of Ravana, receiving the same reply in return, then began to pull it to me with haste. She arrived in mere moments without even her hair being wet, obviously paddling with success to keep her head free of the water. Now, I did the same to the rope of Korax, but he arrived with much less aplomb than the woman, sputtering and choking the water from his nose and mouth.

"By the gods, my Greek friend. You would drown in a wetted sponge if your woman did not give watch for you." He was not in the mood for jesting and returned the jape with a long series of quiet curses. "Silence," I said quietly. "Come, we have to be far away before the light of dawn."

Once again, the bone-throws of the gods had freed their puppet, far below, from certain death.

The Wanderer

Triumphus

As Veii is only about one hundred stadia from Rome, the journey is easily made in one day on horseback and less than two at a leisurely pace. Ours was considerably longer as we did not wish to travel the road that was direct. That route would take us far too close to the extended encampment of the peoples of the Senones, so we made a long sweeping curve to the west and north. And there was another reason for not arriving too soon.

I had given the reason for my departure as protection against my having the precursor to the plague now infesting the foe, even without any real belief that I was carrying it. I had touched no ill person in the camp, nor come within range of their breath, and my sojourn was brief. Still, on the slight chance that I was indeed the walking curse of the plague, I would wait a quarter month before my arrival in Veii. The army of Camillus was the last hope of Rome, and its decimation would place my city in the dusty scrolls as a lost city of yore.

Our path took us around any hamlets and villages that had been ravaged by the Gauls, and the few dwellings we passed were occupied by men - and women - who had no knowledge of the outside world nor any happenings between warring powers. Neither did they have any need for silver and gold, and as we had nothing else to trade for food, our intercourse with them was brief and usually only consisted of our being watched by suspicious eyes as we passed this crude hut or that. Still, our small store of jerked meat was sufficient for life, if not sumptuous eating and our wine was used sparingly for cleansing the water that we obtained from the streams that we crossed.

In a few days, no sores had broken out on my body, and we made the last few stadia to the ruins of Veii. Our first touch on that city was as we were accosted by a small detail - a patrol that was scouting the wilderness for precaution. Seeing us, the men strode to intercept and soon were standing in our path, their officer demanding our cause.

"Salve," I called. "We are from Rome with a missive for the Dictatorius Camillus."

Their leader, a Decanus with eight men, looked in askance at our party. "You do not look like a representative of importance - with a Greek in company, and a barbarian woman."

"Even so, I have a message from the Centurion of the unit in the city, even now holding out against the Gauls." A pause, and then with more emphasis. "And it is of importance and has the need of haste."

"Tell me the message and I will determine your need."

This was not the first overbearing young officer that I had played at words with, so I strode forward, hands clear of my weapon until I was within hand reach of him. "As I say, my missive is of importance, even as the Roman soldiers and citizens are dying to hold the city until relief. I will see my friend Camillus and now, else I prophesy that you and your men will watch the coming battle from your vantage point of a crosstree!"

The key word here was friend. Despite any doubts of the officer to the trueness of my declarations, no young soldier can chance offense to a friend of the supreme commander of the army. After a pause, he said, "Come. And if it be not what you say, that crosstree of which you spoke will be yours."

"By Jupiter and his Triad distaff. It is Junius the scribe or I'll never believe my eyes again." The greeting was from the Dominus of the House of Camillus as I was called into his tent. "I was told that you had been destroyed by the spawn of Fabii."

I smiled as I shook my head. "Not I, Sos, as you can see. The tale is false, or concerns some other unfortunate with my name."

"Come. Come. Take a cup and tell me of your story. The Decanus says you have a missive from Rome itself."

"Aye, Sos, and of importance to my thinking. And that of the Centurion of the forces in the Capitoline." For hours by the nonexistent waterclock, I gave he and his staff the tale, answering the innumerable questions that my story brought to the fore. Finally, he sat back thinking, as I rested my tired voice with good wine.

"This Centurion of which you speak. Is he named Veranius?"

"Alas, Sos," I replied. "I have never once heard his name - either from himself or his officers."

"But he is competent, in your opinion, to hold out until relief can arrive?"

"My opinion, Sos, is that he is the finest Centurion in the Roman army. He has held a few hundred men against thousands, and all with their spirits high enough to spit in the face of any Gaul in range."

He had called for medicuae and sages for information about the strange plague that was infesting the camp of the Senones. Some were familiar with it directly, having seen such during their lifetimes, and others in readings of past pestilence outbreaks. The consensus was that the malady was brought by the rats, as those repulsive rodents had accompanied all outbreaks in their knowledge. All agreed that for the Romans to enter the city now, for any reason, would probably mean death for most.

The senior medico gave the common opinion. "We should wait. It is entirely possible, if the information that this man has brought is correct, that the gods may do our work for us and we merely need to collect the benefit."

With my assurance that the Capitoline fortress was in good stead with the defenders, and that they were not in danger of starvation or thirst, the decision was to wait. And to send out scouts, to test the extent of this malady of the Senones. For we three, the Dictatorius ordered a tent made available to us, alone, and orders given that we were to have full access of the camp, even to the headquarters of the leader.

Camillus had ruthlessly weeded out the political officers and noble Tribunes whose ability was of use in parades and little else. Competent men, even of lowly Plebeian origin were raised to the ranks of lesser Centurions and Optios. The ranks were now being transformed from a mob of hopeful glory-seekers, and with sweaty work, into a hardened army. Daily, we watched the spearmen and velites turned and formed and advanced across this field or that, and the calvary - few as it was - wheeled around the outsides of the formations in support.

The citizens of Rome - those who had wisely fled before the Senones, had taken over the ruins of the city of Veii, waiting for the chance to return to their homes. Of course, the knowledge that the dwellings that the people hoped to return to were now just piles of ash was not known to the citizens as yet. The fact of the massive burning was not hidden from the people, but most assumed that this quarter or that had sustained some damage from fire, but in the main the city was waiting for their return. A major surprise was in store for them.

Using my directions as a guide - and my advice that the men be chosen from those that could swim - a few messengers slipped into the fortress of the Capitoline, bearing orders and returning with news. I knew that just the touch of friends on the horizon would be a great elation to the defenders. We learned that the disease was ravaging the men in the camp of the foe and no further attempts at attack were made on the fortress.

One set of orders, made imperative to the Centurion, was that any rat was to be ruthlessly speared and disposed of immediately over the wall and without any touching of its body by a man. Even the spear tip was to be immediately cleansed by immersion in boiling water, or lacking that, by plunging it deeply into the sand several times. And any man showing a symptom detailed in a delivered scroll, was to be expunged from the fortress, to wait on the far side of the river to die or recover as he would.

Finally, a horseman from the hidden camp at the side of the Tiber, by the Via Aurelia, arrived with news from the Capitoline that the Senones were abandoning the city, striking their tents with some difficulty. Immediately, riders were sent out to the army that was fortified at Ardea, now under the command of the son of Camillus, Lucius.

The martial skills of Marcus Camillus, as compared to those of Quintus Fabius, were as a trireme to the leaky skiff of a river thief. He had long contrived his moves and had planned well. Very well, indeed. With his few cavalry used for messenger service, he coordinated his marches, he coming from the north across the Tiber, with those of his son, Lucius, approaching from the south. The Senones, many sickly and weak, and strung out in a line of march stretching from the burned ruins of our city almost to the looted village of Finenae in the northeast, were caught within the grasp of the Roman army from the north and the Latium forces from the south. The men of the Gaulish tribe - those who were not suffering from the pestis - fought with bravery and fury, but the men of Rome were in no temper to give either quarter nor mercy. Long after the battle had been decided, the Maniples of men strode north at pace, their wide and disciplined lines of spearmen trampling any into the ground that could not move at a similar or greater gait. This included, of course, the oldsters, women and children of the Senones.

By order, no prisoners were taken, to become slaves of their enemies. This was a logical decision by Camillus, rather than a need for vengeance. He well knew that the coming winter would be thin of food for even the reduced populace of Rome, with nothing left to feed other mouths.

Korax and I watched a portion of the battle from the low hill used by the headquarters of Camillus. I had no desire to enter into the slaughter of men now scattered and without the support of their fellows. The entire series of events, from the first coming of the Senones to their destruction on the south bank of the Tiber, was as a folly played out on the acting boards of the forum - at least to my thoughts. Thousands - nay, men and women and children in the tens of thousands had perished, along with their cities and hamlets and villages - and tribes - because of the acts of men, each imbued with a bloated sense of self-worth and vanity.

Still, unbidden came the feeling of pride in my people in overcoming a travail that would have deleted the names of many cities from the scroll of history.

As the night fell, the men of the headquarters staff were walking around the low hill in a state of euphoria, each relating to the other deeds seen that had already been enumerated at length by their fellows. A thought struck me, looking across the fields to the road, filled with innumerable corpses of both Senones and Romans, although the former were greatly in excess as to numbers. Walking up to the Dictatorius, I asked, "Sos. Might I give an observation?"

He nodded. "Aye, Junius. Any words from you will be welcome."

I pointed to the road. "The via beside the Tiber is as a mirror of the streets of Rome in the past months - the very condition that caused the invasion of rats and their plague..."

He gazed across the fields for a moment, then replied. "Your worth is as that of a Century, Junius - and not as a scribe, but as a man who can look beyond the present. Aye, you are correct. We will need to make our winter encampment far from the reach of the winds blowing across this area."

And thus it was. On the southern bank of the Tiber, between Rome and the port of Ostia, the encampment of the army was laid out, and at a distance to preclude either the plague or the stink of the city from reaching the men. Most of the citizens made their stay for the winter in the hovels and shanties that had already been found or built in the ruins of the city of Veii. This would cause a problem in the next year, but for now, it was food that was the concern.

Korax made the journey to Ostia, to meet with Ahirom and the women - still waiting at anchor in the harbor - then to dispatch the ship to ports further down the coast for cargos of food, and nothing else. When our other ship touched at Terracina, it too was dispatched north with a full hull of hard rations.

The Greek returned to our tent at the encampment with both Vera, the cosmeta, and his woman, to set up a domicile for the winter. Ravana and her servant were overjoyed to see each other, still alive and healthy. There was little of the mistress and servant relationship between the two women. Rather, they were as girlhood friends that could enjoy each others presence without strife. Of course, the tales of Korax, now with time to spin his stories, were listened to, wide-eyed by all three women and with awe of both his prowess in his many heroic actions and equally in my escape from certain death again.

Guards around the city during the winter prevented any from entering - neither citizens on their legitimate desires to recover what was theirs, nor looters, as prevalent as ever in the aftermath of misfortune. The numbers of the opportunistic thieves had been reduced somewhat by the number of bodies hanging by their heals from the structure of the viaduct. Camillus wanted no person to enter the city and return with the plague in his body, to infect the closely stationed soldiers in the camp - or the citizens waiting out the time in Veii. In the spring, after the cold and rain and snow of winter cleansed the streets, then the return would begin.

During the long winter nights, our tent had many conversations on our futures, and even the two additional women were allowed their say and questions. Rome would recover its majesty - all that was needed was time, but its future glory would be long in coming. Even now, as Camillus had attempted to resign his post as Dictatorius, the remnants of the Senate refused his renouncement and declared his position to be in effect until the city was well along in its restoration.

As the warm season began to dawn, it became apparent that many of the citizens that had fled to Veii had made the decision to remain and make that their place of home. Knowing that Rome needed every man, woman and child of the greatly reduced number of citizens if it was to be restored, he decreed that Veii would be emptied by the summer solstice, and sent details of the army to carry out his order.

Thus began the rebuilding of Rome.

I was offered the position of Archivest Primus Novus - the same as before but with greatly increased duties - and power. And I would report only to the Dictatorius himself. There was even a hint that a cognomen might be added to my name and the beginning of an entry into the minor nobility of the city. It was greatly satisfying, but...

I was in my middle age, still firm of body but neither with the unbounded vigor nor the erotic appetites of youth. I had no desire for progeny nor a great household with all the social aspects of such, and coupled with the fact that the rise of the city from ashes would be long and hard, I gave my effusive appreciation to the noble but declined the position. Even as the peoples were entering the gates to examine what would become their lifework, I was making plans to depart.

And Rome did survive and even waxed in power and stature among the cities of Latium. In part, it was because of the demise of the weaklings and fools, the slackers and indolents in both the war and the hard times that followed. But in the ashes of the city, a stronger people grew and began to prosper. In time, it was thought that Rome might become mighty indeed, ruling from the northern mountains to the border of the Greek settled domains in the south of Latium.

I have visited the city a handful of times since that time of strife, more for interest in seeing the recovery and the satisfying my wandering feet, than any real reason for the journeys.

With the long thoughts, hashed out and argued during that winter, we left the port of Ostia with our two ships, striving across the Great Sea for the city of Carthago. As the relations between Rome and Greece with the huge city on the southern coast of the Great Sea had been less than cordial over the years, I came as citizen of lower Latium, as did Korax. There, men from the Latium lands to the north and the Grecian lands from the east had mixed for years, which would explain the beard of Korax and the lack of facial hair for myself. Besides, a city will welcome even a demon with open arms if he arrives with sufficient gold.

Our last entry into the ashes of Rome before our departure was to visit my roofless domicile at the foot of the Capitoline and gather up the various stashes of coin and metal that had remained hidden all through the travails of our sojourn in the city. With such wealth, we had no difficulty in establishing a prosperous and respected household in the merchant quarter of the city.

Carthago, like Rome and Athens and Memphis, was endowed with a great librarium, available to any upon payment of a small coin and there I could resume my quest for knowledge. As to Korax and his woman, Mira, they welcomed once again the warmness of the southern shores that drove the aches from their old bones. Ravana settled in as my mate, apparently satisfied with her lot as the woman of a wealthy household. Again, I hired a servant to escort her around the city at need, so as not have the active woman confined to a single domicile.

The time now passed without the violent adventures of our pasts. Apparently the gods had tired of the game they had been having with myself or else had carved another figure with which to play. I wished that person good fortune in his life, now destined for excitement and danger.

I opened a small scribery, where I taught the art of the three languages with which I was familiar. I cared not for the antecedents of the young men who applied - only that they be swift of mind and willing to learn. We would roam the city as I lectured and pointed to this sign and that script, waiting for the students to tell me of its meaning.

Korax, of course, had long ended his voyaging, preferring to frequent the local taburnae and jaw with other Greeks long from home. We sold one of the ships, then the other a few years later when Ahirom had begun to feel the effects of age. For a while, we became shippers, contracting for cargo to be taken to this place or brought from that, but eventually, even that went by the wayside - mainly for the lack of any enthusiasm on my part. We had wealth in plenty to live out our lives without labor, and any excess seemed foolish if it required effort with no interest.

Coda

My life, as I dictate these scrolls, is approaching its inevitable end, as will happen to all men. My eyes have long since lost the ability to read or write on a scroll and my wind is short. My water has to be made frequently and I tire easily even before the afternoon rest. My interactions with the written word is only through my young scribe-students.

But, thusly do I close out this over-long tale of a young man from a fisher-boat on the Tiber...

Ahirom has taken a last voyage back to his native land of Phoenicia to live out his life and to allow his body to be prepared in the way of his people, after that day on which he would depart for the far lands of the dead. Much sadness did I have to see him depart. He had been a faithful friend, even without the consideration of his courageous act of pulling the spikes from my limbs - an act that could easily have caused nails to be driven into his own.

My lifetime mate, Ravana no longer has the golden hair of the north, but rather a gleaming white coif that is even as lovely. Her skills on the mat have never waned, even as my needs became ever further separated by days. Even her cosmeta, Vera, is a woman far on the other side of middle age, but the pair are still inseparable. Indeed, many citizens of the city of Carthago think of them as sisters, without knowledge of their error.

I have made friendship with the high priest of the Temple of Astarte, just as with the priest of Amun, Senemut, in Memphis. Many a pleasant evening have we sat in the temple veranda, discussing matters ranging from one side of the known world to the other and even beyond. I have made a pact with him, backed with the gold in my vaults, for Ravana and Vera to receive protection and independence upon my death, should it come before theirs.

Korax, my friend from first arrival in Greece as an escaped castaway, has long since departed to his reward on the slopes of Olympus, as has his mate, the widow whom he called Mira. He will be waiting there for me, a cup in his hand and a ready curse on his lips at my tardy arrival. His was a gruff friendship, long on the mocking of ideas and curses for any setback, but as steadfast a comrade as could be found on this side of the river Styx. I long to see him again after many years of his absence.

In my tally of my years, my numbering comes to seven and eighty, far in excess of the usual span of a man. As I complete my story, this scroll and its copy will be sent to the archives of Rome, and to those of Carthago, someday maybe to be perused by another who has the interest in gathering knowledge as I have had, over most of the years of my life. That putative reader of future times will know all that was my life and my actions and hopes and dreams.

And finally, when I step off the ferry boat onto the far shore of the river Styx, I will learn at long last, of the existence, or nay, of that gameboard somewhere on the slopes of Olympus and of the little carved figurine that once represented the essence of Junius the Scribe.

End of Scrivener of Rome

Adnotatiae

Adnotatiae (Notes)

What and who is real in this story?

Marcus Furius Camillus. (446 - 365 BC) He was indeed a high-born and important leader in that era of the Republic.

The House of Fabius and the brothers, Quintus, Numerius, and Caeso. But... The facts of the family and their actions are few indeed. Even the names of the two lesser brothers are uncertain.

Lysander - a real Spartan admiral with considerable skill.

The Battle of Aegospotami. (405 BC) That battle ended with Sparta in control of the Greek mainland. The fact that it actually happened is accepted, but the actual stories of the battle(s) are highly suspect.

Amyrtaeus. King of Egypt in 404 - ???BC. The date of his overthrow is given as a range (401 to 398 BC.) by the few records that exist. He supposedly threw the Persians out of lower Egypt and his time of rule was known as the Twenty-eighth Dynasty. There is no record of his battles nor of how he defeated the Persians although it is fairly certain that he actually existed.

Nepherites of Per-Banebdjedet, or of Mendes, depending on the source. Usurper of the throne of Amyrtaeus and the founder of the Twenty-ninth Dynasty, ruling from 398 BC to 393 BC. Little is known of the man except his name and the fact that he killed his predecessor.

The Battle of Allia. (388 or 387 BC.) The collision between the Senones and the Romans at this small stream probably happened, but historians differ greatly on the facts and the results. Some write that no battle was fought at all - that the Romans looked at the numbers of Gauls and fled to Veii. Others give the tale that the fighting was desperate and bloody, with the stream red with blood for days. Between those two extremes are various other historical writings. You can pick the one you choose with equal chance of its being the correct history.

The first burning of Rome. (387 BC) This is a most unfortunate and (probably) true fact. The Gauls did supposedly destroy the records and documents of Rome, along with the city entire, leaving little for the historian before that date but myths and histories written many hundreds of years later. Note, however, that some historians consider the story of this burning of Rome - by anybody - to be a tale and nothing else. Once again, you may pick and choose the history that suits.

The burning, the plague, the demand for a man's weight of gold, and the warning of the geese in the Temple of Juno, even the perfidy of the family of Fabius are all part of the myths of the early Republic. It would be wonderful to know if such are made up of whole cloth or if they had some basis for the tales. We are unlikely to ever find the truth of that history.

Printed in Poland
by Amazon Fulfillment
Poland Sp. z o.o., Wrocław